Flyboys, Round Engines and Spooks

A Historical Novel

Lee Croissant

Flyboys, Round Engines and Spooks

Printed in the United States of America by Lightning Source Inc..

ISBN 978-1-937862-17-6

Library of Congress Control Number 2012910552

Published 2012 by BookCrafters, Parker, Colorado.
SAN-859-6352, BookCrafters@comcast.net
http://self-publish-your-book.com

Author's website: www.leecroissant.com

I would like to dedicate this novel to my wonderful wife Barbara. It takes a special kind of woman to be a pilot's wife. She anchored our marriage and family all those years when I was gone, more than I was home, flying to all corners of the globe. It takes a rock solid woman to stay married to a military man who is gone for years at a time and in harm's way. After I left the military, retired from the airlines, and finally stayed home every night, she tolerated my passion for writing and the long hours I sat pecking at my computer. I cannot thank her or love her enough.

I would also like to dedicate this book to those who flew in EC-47s: low, slow, alone, unarmed, and over enemy territory . . . especially those who came home in body bags . . . and those who didn't come home at all . . .

Wes: I hope you enjoy the story

Lee Crassat

303 841 7729

The author (bottom row far left) with his select EC-47 crew at Nakhon Phanom, Thailand.

ABOUT THE NOVEL

Everything in this novel is accurately depicted, the airbases, runway headings, missions, even the radio frequencies. The culture, times, and places are correctly presented and essential to the story. Many of the flying events, as depicted, were real. Out of respect to those who were traumatized, injured, or lost their lives, no representations of real aircraft losses are depicted; fiction is employed in this area. The story line and characters are fiction. Through the eyes of the fictional characters this novel presents an exciting, authentic, and never before revealed perspective of the Vietnamese enigma.

* * * * * * * * * * * * * * * * * * *

Flyboys, Round Engines and Spooks involves a lot of exciting airplane flying as it's a revealing story about flyboys, their airplanes, and their escapades during the Vietnam War era. The novel is not about fighter pilots flying upside down, and not about blood, guts, glory and fearless heroes. Certainly we have to pay homage and honor those veterans that were involved with the carnage and horrors of that fiasco, both on the ground and in the air, but this book is not about that. Not all pilots were involved in that part of the war.

Young Eddie Werner, the primary character, was unable to get his cherished fighter pilot assignment out of pilot training. Instead he was sent to Southeast Asia to fly old World War II era airplanes: piston powered propeller driven transport aircraft. For him it opened the door to unique times and places, an intriguing and nostalgic experience living and flying with the last of the "old prop job" crews. Ignored by the media and scorned by the jet jocks, these renegades lived in their own convoluted world of radial piston engines, propellers, dripping oil, spark plugs, irregular meals, and brushes with danger. All were mixed with Asian splendor, endless jungle, and an abundance of Asian women. The air crews hopped from country to country as frequently as modern day commuters hop to and from their homes and work. It tells of the end of the nostalgic propeller era and the end of one pilot's youth and innocence.

The narrative places the reader inside the cockpit and inside the mind of the young pilot. It captures the senses, awe, and adventures of flying. It involves the CIA's clandestine operations in Laos and the Plain of Jars that for so many years was classified and hidden from the American public. Flying a World War II C-47, Eddie takes the reader on CIA missions, flying low, slow, unarmed, and alone—deep into enemy held territory and over endless jungle covered landscapes. He witnesses and is involved in things that will shock most Americans. The story is a time warp to the World War II era of propellers and slow lumbering airplanes, a warp that occurred in the midst of jet fighters, Viet Cong, and rock and roll music.

The story takes place during the late sixties and early seventies. Jane Fonda was calling American soldiers and aviators war criminals. Mass war protests were attended as social events by America's youth, hippies roamed the streets high on drugs, free love flourished, and American puritan values were being challenged by an upside down world. The media bombarded the average American with the horrors of war with movies, books, and biased news articles about the Vietnam War. *Flyboys, Round Engines and Spooks* reveals an authentic inside view of America's most controversial war and exposes the media's misrepresentations and omissions

i

inflicted on both the American airmen of the era and the American public. It is a must read for those who are too young to remember the Vietnam fiasco and a must read for those that still don't understand what happened.

Those who know Lee Croissant will recognize similarities between him and his fictional character, Eddie. Lee was told to write about what he knows best, so similarities do exist. Large differences also exist. When Lee Croissant first reported for duty in Southeast Asia, he was a twenty-eight year old air force captain, an experienced B-52 bomber crewmember, and happily married with a child on the way. Eddie, the main fictional character, was a new second lieutenant, in his early twenties, unmarried, unworldly, and eagerly seeking adventure and romance.

This adventure story was also written with non-pilots in mind. Buried within the text are descriptions and explanations so non-pilots can follow and experience the cockpit dramas and awe of that lost era without being buried with confusing and technical terms. Photos are provided in the rear of the book to assist in aircraft identification and locations.

Previously classified information revealed in this novel is currently available on the internet. Some things are still classified—they are not mentioned in this book.

* *

ACKNOWLEDGMENTS

I would like to take this time to thank Bob Dydo, John Sweet, and Col. Steve Mac Isaac for their technical contributions on the AC-119K Stinger gunship. Until recently we never knew each other but we served in Southeast Asia at the same time and flew over the same enemy positions. I flew during the day and they flew at night. Certainly we passed each other many times as we commuted back and forth from our workplace. I also need to thank Diane Woods. She spent countless weeks correcting my poor grammar, undisciplined punctuation, and a multitude of typos.

PHOTO GALLERY and GLOSSARY

The photos located in the end of the book are included so as to serve as references to help the readers visualize the various aircraft. Indeed, few people know what a C-124 was and very few ever heard of the highly classified EC-47. These photos are also included for establishing an air of authenticity to the times and the places that are depicted. To view these same photos in color, as well as many other photos, visit website: leecroissant.com.

A Glossary of military terms and acronyms is available in the back of this book.

* *

The photos of the airborne C-124, C-141, and C-133 are stock photos from the aircraft manufacturers. The remaining photos are from the author's personal photo album.

CHAPTER ONE: THE CALLING
DECEMBER 1969

The two North Vietnamese MIG 21 fighter aircraft slipped over the ridge of mountains that separated North Vietnam from Laos and headed west into Laos. Their destination and intended target was a solitary American aircraft. It was circling aimlessly over the vast expanse of mountains and roadless jungle that stretched hundreds of miles north from the Laotian Plain of Jars. The sun reflected brightly off the polished aluminum of their MIG supersonic fighter planes. The bright red star on their tails displayed the pride and dedication of the two Russian trained North Vietnamese pilots. Their call sign, Test Flight Two, was designed to confuse anyone eavesdropping on their radio frequency.

The operators in the People's Army of Vietnam (North Vietnamese) ground control intercept radar facility had been waiting for this opportunity. They had been operational for a week and it was their first opportunity to get a clean kill on an American aircraft, without risking the loss of their own fighter planes. Tucked away in a limestone niche, carved just below the peak of a mountain eight miles inside the North Vietnamese border, they could see with their new radar well into the northern section of their Laotian neighbors to the west. Their new ground control intercept (GCI) site made it possible for them to monitor American aircraft support operations in the highly contested Laotian Plain of Jars, where the People's Army of Vietnam was battling America's allies, the fierce Hmong tribesmen. They could also see far north where Towhead Three Three had been lazily flying an oblong fifty mile orbit. For this shoot down, the American aircraft with a call sign of Towhead Three Three would be just right. It would make the headlines in the American newspapers and would add a new dimension to the war in Laos.

"Test Flight Two, I have radar lock on, climb to twenty-two thousand feet and fly heading two seven zero degrees. I have your traffic one hundred four miles . . . negative hostiles in the area. Do not answer." The North Vietnamese radar controller was keeping their radio usage to a minimum and as ambiguous as possible.

Unfortunately for Towhead Three Three, this North Vietnamese foray into Laos was taking place during one of many unproductive and ineffective "bombing halts" dictated by the American President. The bombing halt was structured so no American aircraft could fly anywhere in North Vietnam, even if in hot pursuit. The North Vietnamese fighters' plan was to shoot down Towhead Three Three in Laos and scoot back across their border before the American Air Force could react. The Americans' own self decreed rules would prevent them from pursuing the MIGs into North Vietnam.

* * * * * * * * * * * * * * * * * * *

In the cockpit of Towhead Three Three, their radio came to life, "Towhead Three Three, this is Invert on guard emergency frequency. I have two bandits exiting the fishmouth, position channel ninety-eight bearing zero eight zero at one zero five miles DME, tracking a two seven zero degree course. Towhead Three Three, if you read me, it looks like they're fast movers coming hell bent to get you. You're the only aircraft we know about in that area. I'd suggest you get the hell out of there."

Eddie sat stunned . . . in disbelief. "Bandits" was the code word for unknown aircraft of suspected enemy origin, probably enemy MIG fighters. The fishmouth was a portion of the North Vietnamese border that had a fish mouth shape on the map. It couldn't be happening to him! With all the antennas his highly modified World War II C-47 cargo aircraft had, the wind drag was significant. The fastest they could fly in level flight was 120 knots, which would convert to 138 miles per hour. The MIGs, as they probably were, would be coming somewhere around 500 knots. To get the hell out of there was not an available option. They were on a top secret mission, far from any military operations, thus had no American fighter planes flying cover for them. Probably the nearest American fighter planes were several hundred miles south, along the Ho Chi Minh Trail.

Eddie had checked in with Invert, the American ground radar controller, after taking off from Nakhon Phanom Royal Thai Air Force Base in Thailand. Eddie and his crew were flying out of the remote air base, located just across the Mekong River in Thailand, in support of American covert operations in northern Laos. They had maintained radio silence thereafter. Eddie knew that while they were crossing over the ancient Plain of Jars and the high mountains surrounding it, the American "Invert" radar had silently monitored their flight path.

Unfortunately, Eddie's reconnaissance mission required him to fly way north, all the way to the Chinese border. Up there, they could only be tracked by Invert if they flew above 18,000 feet. Without cabin pressurization and without supplemental oxygen on board, flying that high was not an option. Twelve thousand feet was their sustainable limit. Invert could not see the Towhead C-47 on their radar but had locked on to the much higher MIG fighters as they crossed over the dividing mountain ridge from North Vietnam. The Invert operator knew Towhead Three Three was somewhere up there and he was broadcasting the Towhead aircraft a warning, in the blind. A warning just in case the Towhead could hear him. In fact, if Eddie's aircraft had been any less than their current 12,000 foot altitude, he and his seven crew members wouldn't have been able to hear the radio warning.

"Towhead Three Three, this is Invert broadcasting in the blind. If you hear me, I estimate eight minutes until the bandits are in your area. We scrambled F-4 fighters out of Udorn; they're coming pedal to the metal. Their estimated time of arrival to your area is sixteen minutes. Do you copy?"

"I copy," Eddie broke radio silence, not knowing if Invert could hear him or not. That meant the bandits, if they really were MIGs, would have six minutes to shoot him down and a two minute head start back across their border and safety. That would be easy pickings for the highly maneuverable MIG fighter planes. They only needed a minute or two to maneuver into position and use their cannons to rip his unarmed, slow C-47 transport aircraft into shreds.

Eddie was shocked and upset with their exposed position. Without fighter air cover and as transport pilots, neither Eddie nor his co-pilot had any air to air combat tactics training. Even if they had been trained in air combat maneuvers, it wouldn't have improved their situation. Their slow and low C-47, with its World War II heritage, and Eddie, were both way out of their league.

"What the hell am I doing here?" Eddie thought to himself. "It wasn't supposed to be like this!" He looked at the thick jungle below. "Would he, his aircraft, and his crew spend eternity together down there, scattered among the endless jungle?" The pilot's cliché was "bend over and kiss your ass goodbye." There wasn't any room to bend over in the tiny cockpit so Eddie closed his eyes and tilted his head back . . .

* *

It all started for Eddie, back in Colorado, a long time ago. Eddie's thoughts wandered all the way back to his family's Colorado farm, July 1950. Back to when he was a sun-browned five-year old boy. He was curious to a fault about everything except farming. On that fateful morning he was still in bed. It was a cloudless July morning, shortly after the sun was up, and the world outside his open, unscreened window was just coming to life. He was awake and listening to two birds in the plains cottonwood tree, just outside his window. They were having an argument over the caterpillars that were eating the tree's leaves. Each wanted the tree's gourmet worms for himself. He was quite familiar with the two birds. Every summer their kind would nest in the cottonwood trees that surrounded their farm house. He easily recognized their calls but he didn't know their real names. Eddie called the birds Yellow Belly and Gorgeous and didn't have the faintest idea they were a Western Kingbird and a Bullocks Oriole. The only printed material in their home was the *Bible* and the *Farm Journal* magazine and Eddie didn't know there was such a thing as a bird identification book. There also was no such thing as kindergarten at their rural school, and as he hadn't started first grade yet, Eddie couldn't read anyway! There was no one in their rural farm community who could tell him what kind of birds they were and there was no one in the community who even cared.

As Eddie lay in bed enjoying a pause in the ongoing bird disagreement, he heard a distant sound that intrigued him. It was unlike any farm sound he had ever heard and as it grew louder he rolled out of bed and looked out his window. At the far end of their sugar beet field he saw an airplane, a yellow, bi-winged, single engine airplane as it flew just a few feet above their sugar beets. It was flying straight toward him! It was spewing a fog trail and Eddie instantly knew what was happening. He had heard of farmers spraying their sugar beet fields for webworm and he had overheard the neighbors talking about how much more effective it was to do it with an airplane. The propeller blew the spray around and the chemicals were blown up under the beet leaves where the bugs were. Eddie never imagined that his father could afford such an expensive treatment, but there it was.

Eddie launched himself out the window. The haystacks provided the best view in their farmyard and he scurried up the closest stack. He had on only his shorts and the dry alfalfa hay was hard on his bare feet, but he couldn't have cared less. By the time he topped out the haystack, the yellow Stearman crop sprayer had reached the close end of the field, next to their yard. At the last instant the Stearman stopped spraying and pulled up smartly. It passed directly over Eddie at a distance of less than fifty feet. Its engine noise was deafening. Eddie dived for cover in the hay as the gorgeous yellow bird climbed steeply into the sky behind him. Eddie rolled over to watch it make a half right turn, then reverse its direction with a slow and perfect left chandelle turn. It was absolutely beautiful and Eddie was paralyzed with awe. The reversed airplane lowered its nose and passed back low over Eddie as it dived back onto the sugar beet field and continued its spraying work.

Eddie lay back on the hay stack and it felt as if his heart was racing a hundred miles per hour. The engine's sound consumed him and at that instant the little farm boy bonded with the airplane. He had found himself and his calling and his method of escape from the farm. From that day forward, Eddie was different from all the other farm boys in his community. He was imprinted with the sound and thrill of flight and would nurture the condition for the rest of his life. He knew that someday he would become a pilot, then fly away, far away to exotic places and have mystic experiences beyond imagination. In his day dreams he would also marry a beautiful woman in the faraway place—an exotic woman unlike anyone his community had ever seen.

He built his first model airplane with money he earned by hoeing weeds in the neighbor's garden. It was a World War II Stearman trainer and he painted it yellow, just like the crop-duster he had imprinted with. His family drove the thirteen miles into Greeley every other week for groceries and other supplies. The trip to town provided his vital link to the hobby shop and their delicious stacks of balsa aircraft replications. His room soon was filled with model airplanes hanging from the ceiling. His parents knew there was something wrong with Eddie but German parents didn't discuss those kinds of things with their children. They knew that kids "got crazy ideas" and with time Eddie would grow out of it. After all, their farm was almost paid for and someday Eddie would be inheriting it and would be carrying on their family tradition of farming.

But Eddie never had any intentions of staying on the farm. His dreams and fantasies of flying away thrived despite the absence of support.

The family never visited the library in Greeley and Eddie didn't even know that Greeley had a library. Their rural school was visited twice each year by a bookmobile and each school child was allowed to choose two books from the closely censored selection. Books about aviation were absent. Books on bird identification were also absent. Eddie's passion bubbled slowly, yet persisted. During his years at Greeley High School, he was too busy trying to find his own identity among the mass of sophisticated town kids and too busy trying to figure out how to get laid. He succeeded at neither. At Colorado State University his fortune turned and he gorged on the books he discovered in the library system. He became a self taught aviator, having never set foot in an airplane. His favorite book was called *Stick and Rudder* by Wolfgang Langewiesche. His father, however, forbade him to ride in an airplane as they were "inherently dangerous." Asking for money to join the local flying club was out of the question and only increased Eddie's yearning.

It was the military draft that rescued him from his dilemma. He was ripe for the draft on the day he graduated from college and it was easy for him to convince his parents that joining the air force was better than letting the army draft him. He sold them on the futility of spending two years digging foxholes and marching around. He lied when he told them he had no choice when the air force sent him to officer's school for a second lieutenant's commission and then off to pilot training.

CHAPTER TWO: TACHIKAWA

Eighteen years after the yellow Stearman sprayed Eddie's father's sugar beet field, a blue staff car picked Eddie up at the Bachelor Officers' Quarters at Tachikawa Air Force Base in Japan and dropped him off at the Tachikawa Air Terminal. It was Fall of 1967 and America was deeply involved in the Vietnamese War. He had passed the air force entry tests to become a pilot, received his commission as a second lieutenant, and endured the long, challenging, one year of basic pilot training. He and his class of newly trained pilots were the same patriotic stock that the military establishment had been producing for the past 191 years and their nation had never lost a war. His classmates were eager for a piece of the action, for glory and excitement before the war was over. They all lusted and contested for the limited number of fighter plane assignments that were handed out at their graduation.

Eddie accepted a C-124 assignment without protest: much to the amazement of his classmates. He wanted to witness the exotic Orient, the people, the places and the mystic. He was certain that the C-124 freight hauling aircraft was his track to experience his ambitions. He had just finished six weeks of C-124 training before his long flight to Japan.

The Tachikawa morning was overcast and hazy, the temperature in the sixties, and there was very little traffic or other signs of activity on the base. Six in the morning was too early for the administration types to be out and about. Eddie had arrived from the States only two days earlier and the previous day he had been processed in and given a quickie review flight and "new guy" check ride in a C-124—a four engine piston powered freight hauling aircraft. The introduction flight and check ride were required by regulations and performed quickly so the squadron could use Eddie the next day. They needed him to fill an empty co-pilot seat as they were short of pilots. It was September 1967 and the Vietnamese War was in full bloom. Back in the States, the anti-war factions were active, but confined to college campuses and Washington DC. They were the politicians' problems, not Eddie's. He was about to report for his first operational flight in an air force C-124 aircraft and fulfill his persistent dreams of adventure.

Only after Eddie had arrived at Tachikawa and met his sponsor, Captain Jim Beckle, did he find out that the 22nd Military Airlift Command (MAC) was not just another global freight hauling outfit. They were assigned the specific task of hauling everything too large to fit into the smaller C-130 workhorse freighter aircraft, and hauling the oversized cargo into Vietnam! It was a little closer to Vietnam than Eddie had expected but Jim Beckle assured him they never spent their nights in Vietnam. Instead they spent their nights at great places like the Philippines, Thailand, and Okinawa. Also, every two weeks they would fly north to Tachikawa, Japan, for four or five days off while their aircraft received maintenance.

At the terminal, Eddie threw his duffel bag over his right shoulder and steadied it while he carried his newly issued flight bag in his left hand. A mixture of adrenalin and testosterone flowed in his blood. The terminal was a huge open arena, the size of several basketball courts. There were less than thirty chairs in the huge arena, all in a small cluster on the far side. To his surprise, the only human activity was two airmen sleeping on the floor in one corner, using clothing pulled from their duffel bags as pillows. The terminal building was an old wooden structure, probably built not too long after the American occupation of Japan in the late forties. In those days, all aircraft had propellers and Tachikawa's 6550 foot runway accommodated anything that the military flew. In its heyday it was a thriving aerial port. When jet aircraft took over the passenger and long distance freight role, Tachi, as it was usually referred to, was abandoned to the C-130 and C-124 propeller "birds" that could handle the short runway. The newer jets were all shifted to the longer runways at nearby Yakota Air Base. There had been an attempt to negotiate additional land to lengthen the runway at Tachikawa but the local Japanese Communist party had purchased the land at both ends of the runway. They blocked the Americans' expansion efforts. At most, half a dozen passengers per day were using the Tachi terminal for transportation. They were couriers or possibly someone in the military wanting to catch a free hop on board one of the C-130 and C-124 freighters.

A small wooden sign with the word restaurant and an arrow pointed up a set of heavily worn metal stairs. Eddie packed up the stairs and through the open doorway. To his immediate left was the typical GI food production set-up: stainless steel cabinets filled with yesterday's fruit cocktail, tapioca pudding that had turned hard on the top, and an opened two quart can of tomato juice. The grill was a massive, black, cast iron affair that was common to every military establishment in the world. The only restaurant patrons were a crusty looking major, sitting with a couple sergeants at a table, to Eddie's far right. Eddie checked his watch to see if he was late. He wasn't, so he lugged his bags over to their table and asked, "I'm looking for Captain Jim Beckle. Anyone here know him?" The sergeants remained seated as they were in the presence of a senior officer, the crusty looking major. Captain Beckle had been scheduled to fly with Eddie on his first flight south to the war zone.

"Throw your bags in the pile, son," the old major directed with a bored flick of his thumb. "There's been a crew change and I'm supposed to give you your cherry ride." He took a long draw from his coffee cup and looked back up. "You ready to earn your keep?" The major's flight suit looked like it was older than the Tachi terminal and it had been washed so many times you could almost see through it. Eddie wondered how he kept it from tearing.

"Why not?" Eddie answered the major's question. "I gotta skin this skunk sometime."

The older sergeant looked like he'd been in every bar in the hemisphere and his flight suit was unable to hide his thick muscular frame. He had huge rough hands that weren't particularly clean. His ruddy complexion indicated he was not a sun lover. His closely cropped crew cut sported a lot less hair than the clean cut, younger sergeant sitting on his right side. The younger sergeant was medium built, and also light complexioned, with light blond hair. Both sergeants' flight suits, probably clean and crisp several hours earlier, were spotted with dirt and a liberal dose of oil smears. That meant their extensive pre-flight, crawling all over the aircraft, its engines, and into the wing tunnels, was complete. Eddie looked away and tossed his bags on the bag pile.

"I'm Major Baxter, Chief of Standboard," the major, in a more civil tongue, informed Eddie as he pointed with his thumb at the old sergeant and continued. "This here's Sergeant Maxwell. Everyone calls him Max." Standboard was a military term that referred to the Standardization Board, a senior staff of instructors charged with the training and the maintenance of crewmembers flying proficiency. The major used his right thumb again to indicate the younger sergeant, who was working on a skinned knuckle with a napkin. "This is Morey . . . hell! I don't even know what your last name is?" The major leaned forward and read the sergeant's last name on his nametag. "Morey," he read out loud. "Well, I'll be damned."

All the crew members wore a squadron patch on the right shoulder of their flight suits. It was circular and contained a burro with a heavy pack on its back, climbing up hill. The background was red and an outside white ring contained the words "22nd MAS." This was the 22nd Military Airlift Transport Squadron.

Eddie felt exposed with this group and hoped they would break him in gently. There was no telling the number of initiation tricks a group of older veterans could have up their sleeves. Another crewmember entered the door, scanned the room, hefted his bags across the floor and tossed them into the pile. He set his flight case by an empty chair. He was a young black American with silver first lieutenant bars, slender build, a bouncy step, and a friendly smile. His afro hairstyle had been cropped short so as to comply with military regulations. He had cloth navigator's wings over the cloth name tag on the left side of his flight suit and a 22nd patch on his right sleeve. "Spaulding's my name," he introduced himself with a friendly smile and extended his hand to Eddie. "You've probably played with my balls." The table erupted with laughter. Satisfied, he changed his tune. "My name's Quincy Washington. I guess I'll be your navigator for the next couple of weeks." He looked around the table and gave each of the other crew members a nod of recognition. "I guess this motley crew has a quorum. Let's eat."

"No loadmaster?" Eddie asked. Each C-124 crew was made up of six crewmembers: two pilots, two flight engineers, a navigator, and a loadmaster.

"Hampton's his name. Loadmasters live a separate life," Major Baxter offered. "He's out at the airplane strapping down our load and computing our weight and balance. He probably ate breakfast at 3:30 this morning and spent the rest of the time rounding up our freight and loading it. He'll sleep once we get airborne and work again off-loading once we get to the PI." Then he added, "While we go to the bar for a cool one." Eddie had already learned that PI meant the Philippine Islands.

The crew filed through the cafeteria line and the two grinning Japanese cooks took their orders and repeated them in broken English. The menu was limited to eggs, bacon, pancakes, more coffee, and toast. It was tough to screw up an order but it happened a lot. They produced the same foul tasting bacon and grease cooked eggs served at military chow lines back in the States. Eddie smiled to himself as he stared at his eggs and marveled at the military's standardization.

"Cover em with Tabasco sauce, it cuts the grease," the oldest flight engineer, Max, told Eddie. "I got some in my bag if you want some. Gets worse the further south ya go. We all carry an extra bag with canned food from the commissary. Eating on these trips gets erratic and lots of time it's only canned beans, crackers and canned peaches."

"We'll get you outfitted with a bag and groceries at the commissary at Clark Air Base in the PI," Quincy offered. "Just about everybody carries three bags on these trips: a flight bag for flying stuff, a duffel bag for clothes and stuff, and a food bag."

"Isn't there a galley on the airplane?" Eddie was sorry he asked as soon as it came out. There had been no galley in the previous C-124s he had trained in. The crew laughed harder than they did over the Spaulding's ball joke.

"We got a rack full of vacuum tubes for the radios and such," Quincy offered. "It creates a lot of heat and it works great to warm up any leftover pizza from the night before. Other than that all we got is a coffee maker and our food bags. You want a galley you gotta fly in C-141 jets. Trouble is jets stink like jet fuel and you never get laid." Everyone nodded their agreements.

The group settled down at their table and devoured their greasy eggs and not too bad pancakes. Eddie felt an awkward silence . . . "You married?" he asked Major Baxter.

"I don't know," was the major's reply. Everyone else at the table broke eye contact and concentrated on their eggs and bacon. "Used to be. When we first got here we lived in the guest housing on base for a couple of weeks. It takes about a year to get base housing, so we rented a little paddy house off base for sixty-five dollars a month." He continued shoveling in his breakfast as he talked. "That was almost two years ago. At Tachi it gets colder than hell in the winter, not much snow but penetrating, moist cold, and no sun. My wife about froze to death in the paddy house and the base exchange ran out of electric blankets the day before we arrived. She put up with it for about three months and I went about my flying in the sunshine down south; like the dumb shit that I am. Then one day I got back from a sixteen day trip down south and when she saw my sunburn and stack of dirty clothes—something snapped. She flew back to the States to visit her mother and I haven't seen her since." The major looked at Eddie nonchalantly and pondered out loud with a flat face, "We don't write much but I get a letter from her lawyer about every two weeks. I don't read em, just throw em in the trash. I'm glad you asked, though. Maybe I should read one of her lawyer's letters? Or maybe I should write her and ask if we're still married?"

"Guess it's pretty rough living off base then," Eddie commented, wondering why he couldn't keep his mouth shut.

The major shrugged. "Actually, we had it easy, we were within walking distance from the side gate and my wife, when she was here, spent every day playing bridge at the officers club. Some women just aren't cut out to be military wives. She was my second one like that."

"You gotta see Green Hall," Quince interrupted. "It's an old aircraft factory, three stories tall, with wide corridors and tall ceilings. It was built by the Japanese during the war and it has thick concrete walls and a thick roof so the American bombs couldn't destroy it. After the war the American Air Force converted the concrete fortress into a giant apartment building. It has its own officers club, a non-commissioned club, a theatre, commissary, and small base exchange. They even got a beauty shop and a liquor store. It's like a small town inside one huge building. It's about three miles off base, like an American island sitting in the middle of medieval Japan."

"Sounds nice!" Eddie tried to sound congenial.

"God-damned Peyton Place," Max threw his hands up. "It's a wife and children dump."

"From what I hear, everybody's fuckin everybody," Quincy added. Both flight engineers nodded their heads yes.

"There's wives in there that haven't been outside in two years. No shit," the younger sergeant with the name Morey leaned back in his chair as he spoke and grinned. "They hate Japan and stay in their American shelter. It's a huge storage shed for families. There's lots of screaming kids riding tricycles up and down the halls, toys all over the place, and horrible half dressed wives with hair unkept. You gotta see Green Hall, God-damnedest zoo you'll ever see.

"On the other side," Morey held his right index finger up, smiled, and continued, "Some of em get out and enjoy living in a foreign country, the wives, that is. Lord knows the prices are cheap over here yet some of em still manage to spend every nickel their husbands make. But some just hibernate and stew in their own juices. Lot of em end up going back to the States."

Eddie kept quiet and didn't ask the group anymore questions. It was more information than he needed.

After they finished eating, without being asked, Quincy dug into his flight bag and tossed a small stack of papers on the table and offered, "I checked the weather and its CAFB all the way." Eddie smiled to himself. CAFB meant clear as a fucking bell. He had heard it used during pilot training but this was real world stuff. Quincy continued, "I spun all the winds into the flight plan and left the required copies at the command post. We got a 40,000 pound fuel load, three pallets of freight totaling six thousand pounds, two passengers, and I figure nine hours plus ten minutes enroute. I told the loadmaster we'd take the two passengers, if that's okay with you?"

Major Baxter looked the flight plan over in detail, nodded his approval, then flipped it to Sergeant Maxwell. He in turn looked it over in detail while his partner, with a nickname and last name of Morey, looked on. When they were satisfied Sergeant Maxwell flipped it back to Quincy and replied, "Looks good to me." While the flight plan was being examined no one spoke.

"We'll go over it after we get set up at cruise," Major Baxter assured Eddie who was relieved. He wouldn't have known what to look for if they had flipped it to him.

Everyone struggled with their baggage, down the stairs and out to the flight line. The bird was waiting for them. It was the same one Eddie had flown around the air patch the day before, during his refresher flight and check ride. He still wasn't used to its size.

When Eddie was receiving his air force pilot training in Arizona, a C-124 had landed and spent the night there. The C-124 had made a precautionary landing with one of its engines shut down. To Eddie, it looked like an aluminum cloud on final approach, as he was accustomed to the tiny sleek T-38s and the toy-like Cessna T-37 trainers. The awkward, slow aircraft touched down beautifully and Eddie remembered it making all kinds of moans and groans as it taxied to the ramp. It sounded as if the brakes needed new linings, or maybe the airplane was just old and had arthritis. Three of its four propellers were turning and one stood still. The propellers alone looked larger than an entire T-38 trainer and the aircraft had an ambience that suggested a bygone era. Eddie had never seen anything so huge. It parked at the end of the flight line then the three live props slowed to a stop.

In a few minutes a metal ladder extended down from its belly and the crew climbed down to the ramp. Their baggy, dull green flight suits had big sweat patches from their armpits to their waists. Their boots were not shined and only one of them wore a hat. The C-124s were neither air-conditioned nor pressurized. The crew's appearance was definitely not a good example for the spit and polish students and Eddie's peers were appalled at the crew's slovenliness. The crew ambled over to the engine with the dead propeller and with their fingers sampled the fluid that dripped from the engine onto the concrete ramp. They sniffed it and two of them tasted it then quickly spit on the ramp. It reminded Eddie of a group of male dogs examining a bitch in heat. They held a brief emotionless discussion among themselves, then repeated their conclusions to the Williams Air Base maintenance man. Satisfied, they returned to the belly hatch and extracted their bags. They dumped themselves into the back of a waiting line maintenance pickup and headed in the general direction of the transient quarters. Eddie was intrigued, as he sensed there was adventure lurking in that big beast. Adventure like he'd imagined after reading the Steve Canyon comic series in the Greeley Tribune. It definitely appealed to an ethnic German farm boy from Colorado.

When graduation from pilot training approached and it was Eddie's turn to select an assignment, he picked a C-124 to Tachikawa, Japan—the 22nd Military Airlift Squadron. His choice was easy. All of the fighter pilot assignments went to his classmates with the highest grades, so he picked the C-124 from what was remaining. The C-124 assignment was to a foreign base in Japan, and close to South East Asia, where he was sure to taste the flavor of the war going on. He would taste the flavor without all the danger as the C-124 was not designated a combat aircraft. Certainly he would experience the Orient and all its mysteries. He definitely would be getting as far away as possible from the routine and eternal farm life in Colorado.

During the remaining two weeks of basic pilot training, none of the instructors wanted to talk to him about the C-124; it was as if he had chosen an unthinkable horror. He could have had several different stateside based assignments, flying jet freighters or jet aerial refueling tankers. But he chose the old, slow aircraft nicknamed the Shaky Bird. All the instructors could do was to express their sympathy that the class didn't get more fighter assignments. But it was the C-124 itself that chose Eddie. Eddie just couldn't get that big heap, sitting on the ramp, out of his mind. If he couldn't be a fighter pilot, then he would be one of "those" guys.

The aircraft was basically a warehouse on retractable wheels, plus wings, a tail, and on each wing two giant piston engines. Because of its fat fuselage, its size was deceiving from a distance. Its wing span was 174 feet, only 11 feet less than a B-52 bomber. It stood 48 feet tall and when sitting on the ground the pilot's cockpit windows were eye to eye with the windows in a three story building. Each of the four engines, Pratt and Whitney 4360-63As, had 28 pistons (cylinders) and developed 3800 shaft horsepower each. They were huge radial engines with four rows of seven cylinders mounted in circles around the central power shaft. The old pilots called them "round engines." They had two stage single speed internal superchargers. The round engine design was as old as aviation and certainly antiquated for the modern jet age. The 4360 engines were the largest piston engines ever used operationally on an airplane, and they were a nightmare of moving parts. Each engine's lubricating oil tank capacity was 82 gallons. Each propeller was 17 feet in diameter and weighed 950 pounds. The aircraft weighed 111,000 pounds empty and could fly as heavy as 194,500 pounds. That means it could carry a combination of 83,500 pounds of fuel, freight and crew. The bad part was that it was noisy, unpressurized, and it flew slowly and at low altitudes.

* * * * * * * * * * * * * * * * * * * *

Eddie's engineers opened the belly hatch and pulled the ladder down. The aircraft's massive nose clamshell doors, used for loading and unloading freight, were closed and ready for flight. With the clamshell doors closed, the belly hatch and the extendable ladder were the crew's only access to and from the ground.

Eddie cautiously climbed the ladder and emerged into the cavernous cargo area. The floor space was 73 feet long. There had been provisions to install a middle floor so 200 troops could be hauled on the two floor levels. But he had been informed that all troop hauling had been assigned to the faster turboprop C-130s and the all jet C-141 aircraft. The older C-124s were just used to haul freight. With the mid deck removed they could haul oversized freight, such as a forty foot semi truck trailer, helicopters with their rotors removed, or any combination of up to 60,000 pounds of freight.

The crewmembers took positions from the ground, up the ladder, and into the cargo hold. They formed a fire bucket line and handed all the baggage up through the hatch. The duffel bags were secured with a tie down strap to the cargo floor while the flight bags and food bags continued up the next ladder into the cockpit. Out of curiosity, Eddie examined the three pallets of freight; they took up only a small portion of the otherwise empty cargo floor space. They were basically repositioning the aircraft to the Philippines so the small amount of freight was just miscellaneous items. The loadmaster had tied the pallets down securely to the aircraft's floor and they were stamped:

REPOSITIONED TO THE PROPER DESTINATION BY THE 22nd MAS.

There were two airmen sitting on the canvas fold-down seats located alongside the outside edges of the cargo area; the same two airmen that Eddie had seen sleeping in the terminal. In the rear of the cargo compartment there were brown army blankets and fresh pillows on two bunk beds. Also there was a small desk functioning as the loadmaster's "office."

Once up the second ladder, Eddie felt at ease in the cockpit. It had been only about ten hours after he had flown his check ride in that same aircraft. The cockpit was located in a separate compartment, in the ceiling above the front portion of the cargo compartment. Access was via a ladder from the cargo floor and up through a hatch in the cargo compartment ceiling. Once inside the cockpit and with the access hatch closed, the compartment had more the atmosphere of a ship's wheelhouse than an aircraft. With three bunks in the rear, one top bunk and a double-wide lower bunk, a tiny latrine on the right side, it was a living quarters and flight deck all combined. In flight, the flight deck compartment was much quieter and far more comfortable than the freight deck below—where Old Shaky derived its nickname from the unfortunate passengers who had to ride down there.

The two pilots sat forward in two comfortable seats and numerous windows provided a magnificent view of the world. They had adequate but basic flying instruments, post World War II styles that had become archaic by Eddie's time. Behind the left pilot's seat was a navigator station that also had archaic instruments, with exception of a modern LORAN set that was used to determine the aircraft's position. LORAN receivers measured, with great accuracy, signals from a handful of land based long range transmitters throughout the Pacific. Navigators could read the squiggly lines on their LORAN'S oscilloscope and quickly and easily plot their aircraft's exact position on their maps. The bunks in the rear were full length and had thick comfortable foam pads. The biggest item in the cockpit was the flight engineer's panel, located on the right wall. It was both arms spread wide and just as tall, a wall filled with dials, gauges and levers, plus a small desk top to do paperwork. It was there that the internal operations of the aircraft took place: electrical systems, hydraulics, fuel, and it was the control zone for the four cantankerous Pratt and Whitney engines. The second flight engineer had no permanent seat. His duties called for him to wander about the aircraft's nooks and crannies, many in compartments accessed with hatches through the cargo floor below, and to relieve the other flight engineer at the panel.

The crew took their seats and built their own little nests of manuals, paperwork, headsets, seatbelts, etc, then performed their cockpit flow patterns to position all their switches properly for engine start. Eddie was in his proper seat, the right side, and for the first few legs of flight he wouldn't actually fly the airplane. The aircraft commander sat in the left seat and was the civilian equivalent to the captain in an airliner. Eddie computed the take-off speeds based on their aircraft's weight, outside temperature, and altitude above sea level. He cross-checked his computations with the flight engineer's computations to ensure their numbers agreed. Eddie called clearance delivery on the aircraft radio and both Major Baxter and Eddie copied their flight clearance. The clearance included their destination, the radio frequency to use after airborne, the transponder code so that air traffic control radar could identify their individual aircraft, their route of flight, and their assigned cruise altitude. The names of the navigational points were all strange with Japanese names. His tasks would include the co-pilot duties of reading the checklists, raising and lowering the gear, and the continuing tasks of monitoring and assisting the pilot flying in the left seat. Headsets were on, bags opened, airport and departure charts (maps) were selected and clipped in place, pencils were positioned—it was time to go to work.

"Before start checklist," Major Baxter called.

"Radio," Eddie called as he read from the checklist.

"On," the major replied as he double checked that all the required radio switches were on and the proper frequencies were selected.

"Forms 781 and 365F," Eddie read.

"Checked and signed," the major replied. These were the maintenance forms and aircraft log book forms. The major had checked that all were signed off by maintenance and the aircraft was both ready and legal to be flown.

"TOLD card."

"Completed," the major replied. TOLD stood for take-off and landing data, the information Eddie had computed and cross checked with the engineer. It was written with a grease pencil on a plastic card and placed in front of the throttles, so both pilots could read it.

"Parking brakes," Eddie continued.

"Set, pressure's up." The major checked that the brakes were set and that hydraulic pressure was within the 2650 to 3100 PSI range for the 3000 pound per square inch hydraulic system.

When the checklist was complete, the major turned to Sergeant Maxwell and commanded, "Start em up, Max."

The flight engineers start the engines in a C-124. Eddie's job as co-pilot was to guard the brakes and insure that the aircraft didn't roll forward, as well as monitoring the engine gauges and oil pressures as the engines were started. They went through the procedures and the first engine stuttered, flop flopped, and finally roared to life . . .

He closed his eyes for a second to totally absorb the sound. Eddie had the same thrill run up his spine that he had experienced at Tinker Air Force Base in Oklahoma, when they first started the C-124 engines during training. The sound of the reciprocating radial engines had taken Eddie back to the yellow Stearman and all the World War II movies he'd seen during his youth. There was no sweeter sound. When that first twenty-eight cylinder radial engine had coughed, sputtered, and came to life, Eddie knew he was going to be friends with Old Shaky.

When he opened his eyes he was a little embarrassed. Major Baxter was looking at him, smiled and said, "How can any man not be in love with an engine that has twenty-eight jugs?"

Eddie smiled and nodded yes. The exposed cylinder heads on aircraft radial engines were called jugs.

"Gotta love it," Major Baxter continued. "You'll fit right into this outfit."

By that time the number one engine had settled down and was running smoothly—the ground scanner was counting the turning propeller blades as they turned on number two. As number two barked to life and settled down, the blades were turning on number three, just outside and to the rear of Eddie's window. After all four engines were started and rumbling their idle song, the before taxi checklist was performed and Eddie called for taxi clearance. Major Baxter released the brakes and advanced the four throttles slightly—they were taxiing away from the front of the giant maintenance hangar. Too much power and their propeller's wind blast (prop wash) could damage the hangar doors. Eddie was impressed at how deftly Major Baxter handled the brakes on the big monster. He never jerked the airplane and was so smooth the brakes barely howled. It was something Eddie had problems with during training at Oklahoma. The engineers went about their complex duties as if casually riding a bicycle. Eddie was struggling to keep up.

On the run-up pad, adjacent to the end of the runway, the major carefully positioned the aircraft and set the brakes. As they swung around, Eddie noticed several tall bamboo poles outside the fence that were flying the

Viet Cong flag. About half a dozen Japanese were furiously snapping away through the fence with cameras and telephoto lenses. Eddie wondered what kind of intelligence they could gather from a photo of a twenty year old freight plane. Then Major Baxter smiled and called, "Run em up Max, and let's make that a manifold five zero run-up, all four at one time." Power settings in piston powered aircraft are set using two levers for each engine. The throttle sets the power, measured in inches of pressure in the fuel/air manifold. The function is very similar to the throttle in a car. The second lever sets the desired RPM, the propeller's revolutions per minute.

Eddie scowled at the major, "I don't remember setting the engines at such a high a power setting during our run-up when I was at C-124 School at Tinker. We also did them one at a time."

"Want the new guy to see this?" Max asked Major Baxter.

"Ah . . . yeah," Major Baxter hollered over the interphone, back to Max at his panel. He used his thumb again to send Eddie back. "Hurry, unhook and get your ass back there, up in that hatch with Morey."

As Eddie wiggled his way out the top hatch, just big enough for two medium-sized guys to share, he saw what was going on. The top hatch gave them access to see out the top of the aircraft fuselage, a grand 360 degree view. From there the scanner could watch to make sure the wing tips cleared obstacles and didn't hit anything when they taxied. The scanner also used the top hatch to observe the engines during run-up.

In addition to a deafening roar from the high power settings, the four huge propellers stirred up a gale force wind. The Japanese protesters, outside the fence, were lying flat on the ground and shielding the tops of their heads with their hands. The protesters were being peppered with flying rocks from a conveniently placed pile of gravel. That day, two camera lenses were broken and three tents went flying.

Max slowly pulled the throttles back and the C-124 stopped straining and bucking against its locked brakes.

"Little cruel, isn't it?" Eddie asked, as he settled back into his seat and re-buckled his shoulder straps.

"Communists own the land just outside the fence," the major grinned. "Base maintenance dumps an occasional load of gravel just inside the fence, prop wash does the rest." Then he snickered and admitted, "I know the guy in charge of runway maintenance.

"My father was a prisoner of war not ten miles from here," Major Baxter continued with a straight face. "They tortured the hell out of him because he was a B-29 pilot. He never recovered his health after the war. The way I figure, they got three strikes against um: what they did to my old man, they belong to the Japanese Communist Party, and they're flying Viet Cong flags.

"Besides," the major waggled his head in disgust. "I've been stoning em like this for two years now and the stupid little bastards still set up their tents, waive their Viet Cong flags, and wait for the rocks. You would think that they would have enough brains to at least get out of the way or dig some foxholes."

Eddie nodded his head in agreement. Then Max performed the run-up according to the book; checking each engine, one at a time, at a moderate power setting.

Eddie set the tower frequency into his UHF radio, 289.6, and was thrilled as he heard his voice over the radio, "Tachikawa Tower, MAC Two Eighty Nine is ready for take-off."

"Roger, MAC Two Eighty Nine, you're cleared take-off runway one nine, maintain runway heading, climb to and maintain two thousand feet. Contact Yakota departure after take-off."

In order to avoid misunderstanding each other, and the tragic results which could occur from misunderstanding the numbers that pilots and air traffic controllers communicate with, they pronounce each singular number: runway 17 would be one seven, heading 280° is pronounced two eight zero, and manifold pressure 28 would be manifold pressure two eight.

Eddie pressed his radio transmit key again and read back the instructions.

The major taxied the aircraft onto the runway, lined it up on the centerline, and once again set the brakes. "You got the throttles, Max," he called. "Take-off power when you're ready."

"Engines are still a little warm from that manifold five zero check, but everything looks okay," Max responded as he slowly advanced the power on all four engines. Both Eddie and Max continuously scanned the gauges for the correct responses as the engines spooled up. The giant engines were so complicated and fickle that, other than when taxiing the aircraft on the ground, aborting a take-off roll, or when the pilot pulled the power off when landing, the pilots called out their desired power setting. The flight engineer would set the power with a second set of throttles at the flight engineer's panel.

Major Baxter released the brakes and Eddie announced to the tower, "MAC Two Eight Nine on the roll." With the major's right hand loosely guarding the four throttles and his left hand steering with the tiller (ground steering wheel), the aircraft accelerated, rumbling and groaning, toward the far end of the concrete strip.

Eddie scanned the engine instruments on the center panel and with the stop watch timed the acceleration. He was looking for thirty to eighty knots in fourteen seconds. It was right on the dot and he announced "GO" in a loud strong voice, just as he had been taught. If the acceleration to eighty knots had been more than fourteen seconds he would have announced "REJECT" and the major would have aborted the take-off. The slower than calculated acceleration would be an indication that something was wrong and continuing the take-off was not advised.

Although not taught to do so, both pilots instinctively watched the end of the runway move closer and the airspeed indicator advance. Each judging if the airspeed would reach lift off speed before they arrived at the end of the runway. There wasn't a pilot in the world that didn't do that, regardless of how many checks, timings, or other gimmicks were used to insure that the plane would fly in time. As they approached the end of the runway Eddie announced, "Hundred four knots, rotate." The major eased back on the yoke and the silver behemoth broke free from the earth's surface and gracefully sailed over the perimeter fence, sailed over the flag waving communist protesters that occupied the departure end of the runway, then over closely built paddy houses, shops, and crooked streets below. Eddie was fascinated at the scenery—his arrival had been so busy he hadn't a chance to go off base and see the foreign country he was stationed in. The deep penetrating rumble and drone from the four Pratt and Whitney engines shook and vibrated every being and thing below. The old Japanese women, scrubbing their wooden sidewalks, as they did every morning, barely looked up as the conquerors from their great war passed low overhead. They had learned to tolerate the intruders.

"Gear up," the major called out and gave thumbs up signal (the traditional thumbs up is the universal cockpit signal to raise the gear and is a backup for the verbal order). Eddie's gazing was interrupted as he pulled the gear lever from its down slot and slammed it up against the top position. On the end of the handle was a clear plastic wheel about two and a half inches in diameter. It was common for manufacturers to place a tiny wheel on the gear levers so as to make sure the pilot knew which lever was for the landing gear. It was more of a tradition than a necessity. At Tinker Air Base, the instructor told Eddie's class that in a C-124, they were physically moving a hydraulic valve with the handle and they should raise it as forcefully as possible. He told them that each time they raised the gear lever they should slam it up as if to break it off. Then, the force would be sufficient to insure that the valve had moved fully open. The lever did not break and Eddie watched the hydraulic pressure drop off, felt a slight thump as the gear seated itself against the mechanical up-locks, then the hydraulic pressure came back up to its normal pressure.

"Gears up, pressure's up," Eddie announced to the crew—then he placed the gear handle to the center neutral position. It was procedure in a C-124 to fly with the gear handle in the neutral position, which released hydraulic pressure from the gear lines. Relaxing the hydraulic pressure in the landing gear hydraulic lines during cruise prevented maintenance problems from developing. Mechanical over center up-locks did what one would guess, they held the gear up in flight.

Eddie switched to frequency 257.8. "Departure, this is MAC Two Eight Nine through seven hundred feet for two thousand, squawking zero six zero zero."

"Roger MAC Two Eight Nine, this is Yakota Departure . . . radar contact seven hundred fifty feet. You're cleared on course and climb to seven thousand." As Yakota Air Base was only fifteen miles from Tachikawa, Yakota's approach and departure control, with a thirty mile radar control area, managed the traffic for both airports.

The lumbering Shaky Bird climbed at a modest six hundred feet per minute and ninety seconds after take-off the world below faded away. There was nothing outside but white, the world below could have been but a fantasy. They were IFR, instrument flying conditions in the clouds. Eddie felt comfortable and at peace in the airship as Max adjusted the engines to a cruise climb power setting.

Everyone on the crew had his housekeeping jobs to perform. The navigator logged the departure times, weights, and passenger information. Then he went about laying out his JN navigational charts (maps) and drew their filed route. He turned on his LORAN set and gave it an operational check. He would take over navigating the aircraft, dictating to the pilots the headings they should fly, as soon as they departed land and headed over the Pacific Ocean. He would also provide information to the pilots when they called the oceanic air traffic controllers and made their required position and progress reports. Sergeant Morey was in an accessory compartment below the cargo hold, performing an after take-off checklist as he looked for fuel, hydraulic, and oil leaks. Sergeant Hampton, the loadmaster, came up to the cockpit and made a pot of coffee. Then, balancing three cups of coffee on a tray, he backed down the stairs to the main cargo hold. He carefully made his way back, past the cargo, and served the surprised airmen with the first act of kindness they had received in weeks. The fold out canvas seats were not comfortable to sit in so he invited them to use the two loadmaster's bunk beds that were installed in the rear of the cargo hold.

The cargo hold was noisy and drafty; Old Shaky was living up to its reputation. Upstairs, except for the heavy deep drone of the four engines, the crew compartment was comfortable. The crewmembers still needed to use their headsets and crew interphone for conversation. Max had all his manuals lined up and ready in case he needed them and he split his time watching the myriad of gauges for fluctuations and deviations from the norm, and reading a thirty-five cent paperback novel. The engineer's knowledge and understanding of complex engines and systems rivaled that of the gods, at least from Eddie's viewpoint. Major Baxter placed the aircraft on the autopilot, watched it for a few minutes to be sure it was functioning properly, and then he sat back and relaxed. He lit up a foul smelling cigar and proceeded to use the cockpit floor as an ashtray. Eddie was disgusted with the major's filth, foul smoke, and Eddie thought to himself that the cigar looked more like a big turd than a smoking device. The major was the senior officer in the cockpit and the aircraft commander, so no one said a word.

There was a minimum of talk; everyone went about their jobs in an expressionless manner, as if they were bored with the routine. Yet watching closely, Eddie realized that everything was being performed with accuracy, procedure, and order. Eddie needed to also look busy so he got out his charts and inspected their route of flight. There were lots of new things that had not been on his stateside charts, things like FIR boundaries, the boundaries each nation claimed as their airspace, and there were open water areas where the airspace was international.

Suddenly they popped into the bright sunlight and were lifting away from the cloud cover under them. The white floor of clouds stretched out in all directions and just ahead and to their right was Mount Fuji San. It was breathtaking as its volcano cone plunged up through the clouds and stood unchallenged and alone. It was a snow capped spectacle reserved for those fortunate to be flying. The rest of the crew was occupied with their duties; they had observed the scene countless times in their years flying out of Tachikawa. Eddie pulled his camera from his flight case and snapped off a series of ten photos, each seemed better than the last. The mountain was framed on the right side by the leading edge of the aircraft's long graceful wing and its two purring engines and propellers. The bright silver wing and engines contrasted with the brown slopes and snow rimed volcano top.

Eddie thought to himself, "Someday I'll have to explain to my grandchildren that those blurry things were propellers and explain why my airplane didn't have jet engines."

They leveled off at 7000 feet and after thirty minutes the cloud undercast dissipated and revealed an endless dark blue ocean. Eddie called in the position report that Quincy handed him and then forfeited his maps for the view outside. He had the sensation he was watching a travelogue. They were low enough that he could see the larger waves and the patterns of the ocean swells. The ocean background sported occasional patches of young cumulus clouds backed by crystal blue sky. The clouds would grow with the day's heat and by the afternoon they would display their splendor to the ever ending waters. They passed over a small boat; Eddie couldn't make out any people on it but it looked like some sort of fishing boat. Ocean and more ocean passed below him as he sat staring out from his own little world.

Major Baxter reverted to reading his tattered paperback as he sucked on his cigar and exhaled the foul, carcinogenic smoke into the cockpit. The air force regulations specified when smoking in a cockpit, for safety reasons, the smoker was not allowed to lay the cigarette, pipe, or cigar down. Turbulence could dislodge it and a fire danger could exist. So Major Baxter kept the cigar in his mouth, except when flicking ashes on the floor. Sometimes he was busy and he just let the ever-growing tip of ashes fall onto his flight suit. It was a filthy habit and the cigar would get soggy from his saliva and unsightly to look at. Eddie would wince whenever the major swallowed. But, the major was the senior man on the crew and it was a military cockpit.

As Quincy plotted the airplane's progress on his chart, a sort of miniature depiction of what was going on outside, he occasionally gave the pilots a heading change of several degrees. The major would steer the autopilot to the new heading, but in general they just droned on. The navigator was the master of such mysteries as determining their position by taking readings from the sun or stars with his sextant, just like the ancient mariners. There was a special hole, with a ceiling door, cut into the roof of the aircraft for the sextants periscopic tube to fit into. By combining the celestial position with precision track plotting (dead reckoning) on his map, the navigators seemed to always know exactly where their position was. The C-124 navigators with the 22nd MAS were fortunate as their aircraft had each been equipped with the latest state of the art LORAN. As the LORAN'S position data was quick, easier, and far more accurate, celestial sky navigation was relegated to a back-up procedure and only practiced enough to maintain proficiency.

Eddie was deeply satisfied with his situation. Not only was he at the threshold of realizing his boyhood dreams, but he was on a secret mission, a quest he had devoted himself to less than a year ago. It was an obsession he had never told anyone about for fear they would question his sanity, or worse his uncaring, bravado pilot image. This obsession had it roots tied to the Willy Officers Club stag bar. Willy was the nickname for Williams Air Force Base in Arizona, where he had attended basic pilot training.

The officers club at Williams Air Force Base, usually called the "O'club," was dear to the student pilots' hearts. It was a sprawling single story building that was immaculately maintained. The landscaping was Arizonan, with a gravel base displaying cactus and desert trees and very little lawn. The main interior consisted of a large formal bar and an elegant dining room. Student pilots did not frequent that part of the club; it was a quiet haven for base permanent staff and their wives and the coat and tie requirement served as an effective deterrent. That was not the part of the club that was dear to the student pilots. Student pilots entered by the side door and that was just fine with them. When on base the guys virtually lived in their flight suits and seldom dressed up. The side door opened to a hallway that led to an informal, blasé cafe where everyone fed on hamburgers and fries.

A second opening led to the Stag Bar. Only men were allowed in the Stag Bar. It was a place to let one's hair down, use colorful language, and bond with your band of brothers. The air force encouraged this as many of the school's graduates would depend on each other in combat, not too far in their futures. It was a sanctuary from wives and girl friends, not only for the student pilots but instructors and staff officers alike. If anyone received a phone call from a woman while in the Stag Bar, the bell would be rung and it would automatically cost the guy a round of drinks for everyone in the bar. It had been a second home for the bachelors like Eddie; their unscheduled time had been split between studying or hanging out at the Stag Bar and practicing their newly acquired images. Friday afternoons, after all the flying was over, the Stag Bar was the place to be. Instructors and students alike washed away their differences and everyone talked flying in flamboyant terms as they maneuvered their hands as if airplanes. It was here that the students were introduced to the terminology and the "true poop" about operational airplanes, bombs, bullets, and heroics. The students never stopped learning and sucked up the bravado, like a roomful of young gladiators. Eddie was in heaven; at last he had found a home.

The stag bar was made of heavily polished dark wood, similar to the formal bar in the front of the club. But years of spilled beer, arm wrestling, and horseplay in general had altered it into a masterpiece of nostalgia.

The backdrop was not as elaborate and massive as the main bar in the front of the club but the backdrop in the stag bar was far more inspiring. Without trimmings and ornaments, a massive five foot wide set of air force wings hung on the wall. It was carved out of a single piece of monkey pod wood and spoke a single and powerful message to all patrons. On the rear wall, opposite the bar and where a scattering of tables took up the bar overflow, hung a large velvet painting. It was of a partially nude, exceptionally beautiful Asian woman. It was said that an instructor pilot had brought the painting back from the war in Vietnam. The woman in the painting was highlighted with overhead lights and she beckoned with her smile. She suggested foreign intrigue, adventure, and possible immortality. She was affectionately called the "Lady" and was included, with a tip of the glass, in all toasts. Many a downhearted student pilot had found his inspiration through her beckoning smile and after numerous beers, the determination to continue his struggle for graduation and his wings. Was she secretly beckoning the young student pilots to Southeast Asia and the war? Female black widows kill and eat their mates after sex. Was she one in disguise? Eddie was secretly infatuated with her, as were half of the other student pilots on the base.

It was one of those silly things people sometimes have running around in their minds and they can't get it to go away. Did such an exotic woman, or women like her actually exist? If so where? The other side of the world was such a vast place! She represented everything Eddie had ever wanted, not just in a lover but adventure, intrigue, probably danger, and chance. In high school Eddie had studied about Aphrodite, the Greek mythology goddess of love. She had been represented as a modest and lovely goddess, the sweetness of love. But her adventures and actions had caused widespread misery and bloodshed. Men craved her, went to war for her, and her lovers were willing to die for her. Could it be possible that this was a painting of a modern day version of Aphrodite, Asian in form, whose charm and likeness had captured his soul? Eddie was obsessed with his fantasy of seeking her out, who she was, and why the hypnotizing lures of that painting? There, sitting in his first operational C-124 flight and on his way to the Philippines, Eddie just knew he was on his way to finding the woman of his dreams.

* *

After almost two hours of uneventfulness and deep thoughts, Major Baxter slipped his paperback back into his briefcase and looked at Eddie as if he had just noticed him for the first time. "You ready to go to school?" the major asked, out of the blue.

"Uh . . . yeah," Eddie reacted in shock as he wondered what the old major had up his sleeve. Dream time was over.

"Pull out your charts and manuals again," the major instructed. "I saw you staring at em a while ago. Let's go over em and see what we can learn about flying around in this old shithouse."

The next three hours were filled with a wealth of interesting information and facts. Eddie was surprised at how much the crusty old major knew about flying and that he would actually spend hours passing his wealth on to a green young lieutenant. They discussed foreign airways, radio procedures, cockpit duties and responsibilities. The flight engineers participated in the class and Max gave Eddie an advanced course on the care and feeding of Pratt and Whitney 4360 engines. The major made the learning a challenge and interesting by describing an emergency situation to Eddie. He then let Eddie talk his way through the problem, followed by a critique. He called it playing "what if." It was like grad school after the basic C-124 ground school he had received at Tinker Air Base in Oklahoma.

Eddie sucked up the information; it was all useful stuff he needed to know. Compared to what he was being exposed to, flying the T-38 trainers back at Willy had been quite simple. Eddie suspected Major Baxter wasn't unfriendly after all. He just wasn't friendly! He lived in his own unkempt world, minded his own business, and was an accomplished pilot with a remarkable knowledge about the world of the C-124. He was congenial with everyone but friendly with no one. After several hours and just when Eddie thought his head was going to explode with information, they called it quits and everyone broke out their food duffel bags and shared their

16

commissary wonders. Eddie, without a bag of his own, was their guest for lunch. The two flight engineers shared a bottle of hot peppers while they scarfed down crackers dipped in chili con carne that had been warmed on the vacuum tube radio rack. Combined with several cups of hot coffee, Eddie understood why old sergeants seem to have the constitution of cast iron. You are what you eat!

Quincy ate more civilized chow. He shared his tuna on crackers, peanut butter on crackers, canned peaches, and a candy bar. Major Baxter dug around in his bag, which seemed to contain mostly cigars and paperback books, and produced a can of fruitcake, canned pears, and a bag of white discs for his upset stomach. Eddie wondered about the white discs mixed with cigar tar and the Tabasco he had dumped on his eggs that morning. "What if it all set up like concrete in his stomach?"

They all shared a little of their fare with Eddie, everything except the white pills that the major kept for himself.

As they ate the endless ocean slipped by underneath. At 230 miles per hour and at 7000 feet, the never-ending ocean and its never-ending waves and swells seemed boundless as eternity. It was soothing to Eddie's soul. All of his life he had wanted to get away and be that "other" person inside him. He wanted to find that "other" side of the world. He was now in that other land, the land where somewhere the Lady on the painting surely must live. Everyone to some extent has certain hidden feelings and dreams, and Eddie's feelings and his insatiable appetite was a monster that needed to be dealt with. He felt it was about to be fed. The endless slow flight and endless ocean brought all these feelings to the surface and he was able to slowly explore them and savor their possibilities of reality. His mind wandered and his head bobbed as his thoughts consumed him.

"Why don't you go in the back for a while?" the major's voice broke Eddie's trance. Eddie snapped alert and saw the major jerking his thumb towards the bunks in the rear of the cockpit. "Regs only require one pilot in the seat over water. I'll wake you in a couple hours."

Eddie found the bunk thick and comfortable. It was a pleasure to get some distance between himself and the major's endless cigars. But he couldn't go to sleep. He tossed and turned. Without the mesmerizing ocean to watch below, the magic was gone. Also, he felt like he needed to sneeze but couldn't.

"It's the vibrations from the inboard engines," Mac shouted from the engineer's panel, his voice just carried over the noise from the four thundering engines. "The bunks are directly in line with the inboard propellers and your nose hairs pick up the vibrations and resonate. Try sleeping with your arm draped over your nose and it'll dampen the vibrations in your nose hair."

"That's really dumb," Eddie thought to himself. "Is this one of those practical jokes he had been warned to watch for from the engineers?" Eddie draped his arm over his face to satisfy Mac and within a few minutes he was in a deep sleep, this time serenaded by the engines' deep comforting moan.

As Eddie slept, life went on in the cockpit. Quincy took readings from his LORAN every half-hour and plotted their position on his chart. He then measured the angle in degrees they needed to turn in order to adjust for wind changes and maintain their plotted track. He instructed Major Baxter to turn the determined number of degrees. At the reporting points shown on his chart, he gave the pilot the name of the point, time over the point, altitude, and the name and expected time over the next point. The pilot in turn reported the data to the oceanic and air traffic controller via the high frequency radio. The oceanic controller plotted the information on a giant ocean chart and checked to make sure there was no other plotted traffic that would conflict with their flight path. Over the South Pacific and at their altitude, there was rarely any other traffic to contend with. Mac traded places with Morey and flopped into the top bunk, his arm draped across his face. Morey performed his engineer's duties, scanned the gauges for irregularities, monitored fuel burn against the flight plan, and as they burned off fuel and the plane became lighter, he checked his graphs and re-adjusted the power settings. Below in the cargo compartment, the loadmaster checked the straps to insure the load was secure; then took a turn in one of the rear bunks. The two passengers agonized over the endless flight in the loud vibrating cargo hold as they played endless games of cards.

Eddie awoke with a start and looked at his watch. He had been asleep for an hour and a half. He rolled out of his bunk and slipped back into his pilot's seat on the right side of the cockpit. The major looked up, smiled, and then said, "You got it." He unbuckled and worked his way back to the urinal. He told Eddie he "needed to empty his sump tank."

Eddie checked all the gauges and couldn't find anything out of order so he returned to gazing out the window panorama before him. They had been airborne over six hours and the ocean's appearance had changed. The dark blue of the deep ocean was being slowly replaced with blotches of lighter blue tones. Under the intense tropical sunlight, and as the ocean water became shallower, the color slowly morphed from a dark blackish blue to lighter blue tones as the bottom reflected light. They were approaching the Baton Islands that were strung out for over 200 miles north of the main Filipino island of Luzon. An island appeared, then another, then they were scattered all across the ocean. The light blue waters accented the white beaches and the palm trees covering each inviting island. Underwater reefs protected some of the islands and could be easily seen from their low altitude. Eddie fantasized about the fish and turtles that called the reefs home. The water inside the reefs was very shallow and a brilliant turquoise color as the sand reflected sunlight. Scattered cumulonimbus clouds completed the splendid scene.

The larger islands had huts on the beaches, set back against the tropical palms, and at 7000 feet Eddie could just see what he assumed were children who were playing in the water. Small boats were resting on the beaches. Occasionally the water would change to a darker blue as they passed over a deeper ocean channel between the islands. A rusty colored freighter passed under them and Eddie wondered what cargo they were carrying, what kind of men operated such a boat, and if anything illegal was going on. Certainly they all carried knives. The concept of Milton Caniff's character, Steve Canyon, was alive and well in Eddie's mind. His thoughts raced forward to the main island, thoughts of slowly rotating fans in open air bars, men dressed in tropical white suits, and barefoot dark skinned women dressed in light dresses and danger written all over them.

Eddie's gauge scan revealed he was picking up an ADF navigational radio signal from Luzon—the main and the largest island in the Philippines. It was where Clark Air Force Base was located. It was a left over US facility from World War II and the main feeder air base for the Vietnamese "conflict." He informed Quincy of the ADF reception and turned the aircraft slightly to track the signal inbound. Quincy closed out the navigation portion of his navigation log and poured another cup of coffee to wash down the last of his peanut butter on crackers. Eddie noticed rice fields on one of the ever-larger islands and small sail powered fishing boats. In the distance, large billowing cumulus clouds marked the location of the main island of Luzon.

Major Baxter returned to his seat, strapped in, burped loudly, and said, "I got it." They coasted in over the large landmass, the island of Luzon. Eddie called the Clark Air Base Approach Control frequency listed on his Clark airport chart and as if by magic, they answered. They gave Eddie the weather, which was clear and hot, and a transponder code to squawk. Eddie dialed the code into his transponder box and Clark responded, "MAC Two Eight Nine, radar contact forty miles north, cleared direct Clark and descend to two thousand feet."

The major called for engine manifold pressure reduced to two five inches and Max slowly pulled the throttles back from cruise power to twenty-five inches of power. The major dialed a small amount of nose down trim into the autopilot pitch wheel and they slowly descended, still maintaining a healthy speed as they traded altitude for airspeed. Healthy speed, at least for a C-124. Eddie's heart rate was above normal. Their flight path led them down a huge wide valley between two mountain ranges. The mountains were covered with thick, dark green tropical jungle. The valley floor's features were rice paddies, corn fields, and nipa huts. Nipa Huts were made from cane, thatch, and bamboo, and were the huts the rural people lived in. Flimsy in nature, they were ideal for the tropical hot climate and frequent rainstorms. The building materials were all local and free for the taking. Between the fields of rice, tiny fields according to Colorado standards, and along the narrow dirt roads and paths were banana trees. There were also carts being pulled by water buffalo. From their lower altitude Eddie spotted a farmer in a rice paddy—his hands guiding a walking plow pulled by a water buffalo. Then in the next field were several water buffalo feeding on plants in knee deep water and one was wallowing in the nearby mud.

"Carabao," the major informed Eddie. "Car-a-bau. Caw, roll an "r" with your tongue like the Spanish, ah, bau, it's the Spanish influence. It's pronounced and spelled differently from the caribou we got in Alaska. They're not the same animals. We took the Philippines away from the Spanish in 1898 and we gave the Filipinos their independence after World War II. They use carabao as tractors in the fields, to pull their carts on the road, they milk em, and they're really good to eat. They're Asia's answer to Little Abner's Shmoos."

From his performance handbook, Eddie extracted the approach and landing speeds for the aircraft's projected landing weight. He wrote the numbers on the plastic speed card and placed it on the center console. Then he read the descent checklist and the major and Morey responded with the proper terminology.

When the checklist was complete the major called, "Flaps ten." Eddie checked that their airspeed was below the flaps ten maximum operating speed, then moved the flaps lever to ten. "Sure is pretty, props twenty-one hundred," the major continued.

"It's a paradise," Eddie answered in awe.

"RPM twenty-one hundred," Max replied, as he advanced the prop levers a small measured amount. The propellers outside responded with a higher pitch. Crewmembers were required to call for and repeat back all power settings with precise terminology so there was no possibility of misunderstanding.

"Don't get your heart broke when we get on the ground," the major advised. "Those people down there live in a tropical paradise but most are poor as church mice. And their government is corrupt as hell. Around the base there's lots of prostitution and crime. The younger guys love the prostitution; you can get an absolutely beautiful girl to stay all night for a carton of Salem cigarettes. But ya gotta watch your backside or she'll leave with your wallet or have her boy friend and his buddies waiting in the alley for you."

"I set the ILS frequency in number one nav radio," Eddie informed the major. Instrument Landing System (ILS) is a type of precision electronic guidance system for flying approaches into airports. It's used primarily during weather approaches.

"Don't ever change someone's radio or nav frequencies without them calling for it," the major sternly rebuked Eddie. "My half of the center radio console belongs to me when I'm flying and your half is mine also. Put the wrong frequency in a guy's navigational receiver without telling him and you could both end up under a pile of bent up aluminum—because you followed the wrong bearing. The pilot flying is the boss and the pilot not flying is his assistant. It makes no difference if the pilot flying is in the left seat or the right seat. He makes the calls. You got that?"

"Yes Sir!" Eddie replied as he remembered he was in the military and the junior man.

"MAC Two Eight Nine, you got the runway?" Clark approach asked over the radio.

Eddie looked into the distance, down the valley. On the left side and isolated in the center of the ever widening valley floor was a solitary, small volcano, symmetrical in shape. His chart called it Mount Pinatube and the top was 478 feet above sea level. Its slopes were covered with undisturbed tropical forest. On the right side of the volcano, just as his chart indicated, was a long runway. Eddie snapped a quick shot with his camera then looked over at the major and their eyes made contact. The major nodded his head affirmative.

"MAC Two Eight Nine has the runway in sight," Eddie replied over his radio.

"MAC Two Eight Nine is cleared visual runway two zero, contact Clark tower on two eighty nine three."

"Manifold two one, gear down," the major continued as if their little altercation had never occurred. "Wait till you sink your teeth into their fresh pineapple. It's not bitter like that stuff in Hawaii. Its sweet and it'll melt in your mouth. It's sweet like that in Thailand too."

Eddie placed the gear handle to the up position to reactivate the dormant landing gear hydraulic system, and then slammed it into the down position. At the same time the engine's manifold pressure crept back to twenty-one inches of pressure as Morey eased the four throttles back a small amount.

"Manifold two one," Morey confirmed.

"Three green," Eddie announced that all three landing gear were down and locked and their green down indicator lights were illuminated.

Major Baxter responded with, "Flaps twenty."

Eddie checked to see if they were below the flaps twenty maximum speed, moved the flap handle to the flaps twenty detent, then monitored the flap position indicator as it moved to the twenty degree indication.

"Flaps thirty . . . flaps forty . . .," the major called as he placed his right hand on the cluster of four throttles.

The approach was a thing of beauty. With the checklist all done, landing flaps confirmed, landing gear down and clearance to land from the tower, the major eased back on the throttles, eased back on the yoke and added just a pinch of rudder and aileron to perfectly align the aircraft fuselage with the painted runway centerline. Their airspeed had been deteriorating and was decreasing through the landing speed on the landing card as the flying aluminum warehouse squeaked onto the runway. On the long runway they didn't need any reverse thrust, but the major put the propellers into idle reverse to insure the mechanisms were working. Their next stop would be Vietnam!

Eddie was all eyes out the window. "What did you expect?" the major asked with a chuckle. "Water buffalo for tow trucks?" Eddie answer was an excited grin.

The main parking ramp was crowded with lots and many types of aircraft. Some Eddie had never seen or heard of before. There were civilian passenger and freight jet planes from the States, old B-47 bombers that had been converted into reconnaissance and weather aircraft, a B-66 with modified extra long wings, C-130s and C-141 freighters, and lots of fighter planes. There were lots of camouflage paint jobs. The air was heavy with the stink of jet fuel. Off in the distance was another ramp with an assemblage of fighter planes, most of them F-4 Phantoms. All had camouflage paint. Behind the metal fence were buildings, some single story and others several stories tall and no different than in the States. What was different were the palm trees everywhere and huge spreading deciduous trees, some covered with vines that sported a myriad of colorful flowers.

The reciprocating propeller engine transient aircraft ramp was a little different. There were more C-124s than Eddie ever expected, several C-123 freighters, and one funny looking light plane with Air America written on its side. Also there was a camouflage painted World War II C-47 Gooney Bird and an all black World War II B-26 bomber. Eddie grabbed his camera and clicked off a few rounds. He had to remind himself it was 1967 and not 1944.

"Don't let the guards catch you taking pictures," Morey instructed from the flight engineer's position. "Lot of this shit is classified and they'll ream you a new asshole." Eddie lowered his camera. The ground marshaller guided them into their parking place, which was between two other C-124s. Both had 22nd squadron markings. The ramp was covered with oil stains from the leaky radial engines. Stains on the ground were a bad habit that C-124s had in common with real birds. At least the ramp didn't stink of jet fuel; instead it had the sweet smell of high octane aviation gas.

"I can't believe all the Shaky Birds," Eddie wondered out loud as the ramp guide man crossed his arms to signal stop and drew his finger along his throat, the aviation signal to "cut" the engines. They finished the parking checklist and did a reverse drill unloading their personal items from the aircraft. This time Sergeant Hampton had the nose doors opened and the twin ramps extended, so they could walk down the front ramp instead of using the belly hatch. Hampton was in the back unbuckling the freight and the rest of the crew loaded their bags into the waiting blue van. As he walked down the ramp, Eddie stretched and it felt good to walk after sitting most of nine hours. Then he was greeted with a blast of air that was intensely hot and humid. Despite the diversion from the intense tropical heat, Eddie couldn't take his eyes off the World War II C-47 that sat in the next row, facing their aircraft. Morey joined him in his admiration.

"C-47s are called Gooney Birds. This one is a spy bird and it's renamed an 'EC-47,'" he said. "Camouflage paint like a gunship model but look at all the strange antennas. It's a forty thousand dollar airplane with a million dollars worth of top secret equipment in its belly. They use it for reconnaissance." It was then that Eddie noticed an American in fatigues, armed with an M-16 rifle, guarding the door to the strange looking EC-47. "It's probably a replacement aircraft being ferried in from the States," Morey speculated.

"I wonder what it's like to fly that?" Eddie wondered out loud. Then he silently wondered why they needed a replacement. He felt they were getting closer to the action.

"It's tricky to taxi, a dream to fly." Major Baxter joined them in their admiration of the modified C-47. "It's kinda like being in love with a whore. Soo good and soo bad. I got about a thousand hours in em."

"Whores or C-47s," Max joked. Major Baxter didn't answer.

"I heard that for pilots, flying a Gooney Bird is like screwing an Asian whore," Morey continued. "You're not really a man until you've done it."

"Someday I'd like to," Eddie answered.

"In love with a whore, screw an Asian woman, or fly a C-47?" Morey asked with a smile.

"All three," Eddie concluded. "I'm here for the full nine innings." He meant every word.

CHAPTER THREE: LA LA LAND and PLACE OF FRIVILOUS ACTIVITY

Their blue air force crew van pulled up to the front of a wooden one story building which was located adjacent the Clark Air Base ramp with all of the C-141 cargo jet aircraft. A large sign on the building read, "Aerial Port," and underneath was a smaller sign that read, "Authorized Personnel only." Above the single door was a third sign that read, "Military Airlift Command." Major Baxter crawled down from his jump seat next to the driver, stepped outside of the van, and saluted an older lieutenant colonel who was ambling towards the van. The lieutenant colonel was wearing the standard well worn tan flight suit. In addition to a 22nd patch on his right sleeve, he wore embroidered silver oak leaves on his shoulders, the rank of lieutenant colonel, and on his left breast a cloth name tag that spelled Duncan. Black embroidered cloth command pilot wings were centered above his name tag. The lieutenant colonel was well groomed with shortly cut, thinning hair, and about twenty pounds overweight. He carried himself with conviction.

"Colonel Duncan, Squadron Commander," Quincy whispered to Eddie. "He's a good guy . . . he flies his share of our missions."

"Baxter," the lieutenant colonel returned a quick and limp salute, then shook Major Baxter's hand. "I got a deal for you." The lieutenant colonel ignored the rest of the crew in the van but spoke loud enough so they could hear without straining themselves. It was a nice courtesy as he knew they were all listening. "We got a turn for you tomorrow; they want us to take a runway paint striper over to Binh Thuy, Vietnam, and bring back a forty foot truck trailer. It's a TACAN unit that got laced with mortar shrapnel and the civilian tech reps refuse to spend the night in-country. So, we gotta bring it back here to get it repaired." TACAN is a military ground based aviation navigational transmitter. American military aircraft, with TACAN receiver sets installed, can determine their exact bearing and distance from the TACAN's ground position. The military TACAN is more accurate than VOR stations that provide the same information to civilian aviation. The military TACAN ground installation is mobile and can be installed and transported in a semi truck trailer and airlifted in large freighter aircraft such as a C-124.

The colonel paused while the assignment was absorbed by everyone, then continued, "The next day they want us to pick up two helicopters at Danang and spend the night at Taipei. On the third day you can drop the choppers off at the repair facility at Osaka, Japan, then hop over to Tachikawa. That'll have you back home three days from now. We got two new pilots coming in and I need you back at Tachi to get em checked in and signed off. We're still short of pilots."

The lieutenant colonel finally looked into the van and his eyes met Eddie's. "This the new guy?" he addressed no one in particular. "I see you didn't have time to get your name tags sewn on your new flight suits back at Tachi. Sorry about hustling you into the cockpit, but you heard what I told Baxter. We'll get you back to Tachikawa in three days so you can have a few days to get settled in. Least you'll make it in-country in time to get your ticket punched for the month." The lieutenant colonel stuck his hand into the open window and shook Eddie's hand. This surprised Eddie, as it was quite informal for military protocol.

Eddie managed a pleasant look and smiled as if he understood everything that was going on. The lieutenant colonel and Major Baxter turned and strolled over to the Military Airlift Command (MAC) building and through the command post door. In the van, Max pulled out a bottle of Old Turkey bourbon, opened it, and passed the bottle around. Everyone took a swig out of it and passed it on. Eddie tried not to wince too much, as he wasn't an accomplished bourbon drinker. Eddie didn't say anything but was surprised. They were drinking bourbon, straight out of the bottle, in an air force van on the flight ramp. The squadron commander was only a few hundred feet away.

"We're done flying for the day," Mac answered the look on Eddie's face. "Down here everyone kinda loosens up after a day of flying. Gets rid of the vibrations from the aircraft and helps you sleep."

"Sleep—my ass!" Quincy popped in. "You enlisted guys screw such ugly whores you gotta be drunk just to stand um."

"Better than those stewardesses you officers pick up at your O'club," Mac returned. "All you ever get for a shopping trip and dinner is a hand job." Eddie was raised on the farm so all the coarse talk was familiar to him—typical macho men talk. But he was taken back at how loose these guys were and how easily the officers and enlisted mixed. It was contrary to what he had been taught at Officer's Training School. In the Pacific, on an airplane crew, under the shadow of a war, it seemed quite okay.

Eddie was sweating profusely. The intense humid heat and the second passing of the bottle were having their effect on him. He looked around and everyone had a deep sweat patch under their arms, but he seemed the only one to be uncomfortable.

"You'll get use to it . . . kinda," Quincy smiled and gave Eddie a friendly fist on his shoulder. "Welcome to La La Land."

* * * * * * * * * * * * * * * * * * *

At the transient quarters office the enlisted received non-availability vouchers, which was exactly what they wanted. The enlisted temporary living quarters on base were all full so they could stay off base and collect per diem. They hired a taxi and seemed in a hurry to get off base and on with their extra curricular affairs. Off base they would rent motel rooms and have a little money left over, a perfect set up for merriment and mischief. Eddie and Quincy checked in at the transient officer's counter, where they still had space available. Major Baxter would be on his own to find housing once he finished his business with the squadron commander at the MAC Command Post.

The transient officer's quarters were a grouping of trailers in a large parking lot, next to an old baseball field. On base and within walking distance to the officers club, they were conveniently located to accommodate the mass of MAC C-141 jet crews as they staged their freighters, pony express style, back and forth across the Pacific. The trailers had no landscaping and stood in straight bleak rows on the asphalt parking lot. They were obviously a recent addition because of the war just across the pond. The trailers were adequate, similar to what one would expect to see in small towns next to large construction and mining sites in the Colorado Mountains. They were the result of the competitive bid system in the Department of Defense and Eddie's mattress was obviously the lowest bid. It made Eddie wonder about the rest of the war machine. Eddie's room was tiny, maybe five feet by seven, and just enough room to undress and sit on the single narrow bed. The important thing was that the trailers were air-conditioned and Eddie and Quincy had a trailer all to themselves. Eddie was glad the major wasn't social and would hopefully be assigned to a different trailer. The break from the cigar smoke was a welcome relief for both of them.

Eddie and Quincy each took a long refreshing shower and their informal civilian clothes felt good after the twelve hour day, nine of them airborne. The bourbon kick-start put Eddie into a good mood. Quincy suggested they walk over to the O'club, catch the end of happy hour, and check out the action. Eddie felt dehydrated and welcomed the suggestion; a cold beer would be paradise. The fifteen minute walk, which took them through the permanent officer's quarters, was like a walk back through time. Clark Air Force Base was built after the

Americans and Filipinos took back the Philippines from the Japs in World War II. The base was a memorial to the American presence. Elegant housing and facilities were added shortly after the end of the war and not much had changed since.

The wide streets and the sidewalks were lined with beautiful trees, tropical deciduous hardwoods with spreading branches and covered with various mosses, vines, and epiphytes. The houses were wooden, single story, and spread generously on their oversized lots. Large shingled roofs, with patches of moss on them, extended over covered and screened porches that accented the entire fronts of most homes. Originally the windows contained wooden louvers to accommodate the tropical climate and occasional light breeze. By 1967, window louvers were replaced with glass and window mounted air conditioners were installed.

As they walked the sun was low and the warm light accented the colors of the abundant bougainvillea, hibiscus and vines. The tranquil scene was punctuated with occasional children's laughter, calls from brightly colored birds, and smells as the Filipino servants cooked the evening meal. Eddie felt General McArthur's presence. What a magnificent walk it was and Eddie was enthralled.

The officers club at Clark was located on the edge of a large grass covered oval, commonly called the parade ground. The parade ground's open interior was ringed with more large tropical trees and there was an impressive set of tennis courts. The oval had been witness to many grand parades and ceremonies. The officers club was a strategic social focus; it was a vital crossroads in Southeast Asia. It accommodated a constant tide of air force personnel going to and from the Vietnam conflict—a short flight across the China Sea. Almost all air force aviators passed through its wooden front door sooner or later. The air war in Vietnam was a main event; there hadn't been any serious combat since the Korean War. The entire corps of air force career officers, from old salty veterans to anxious young lieutenants, was pressing to exercise their chosen profession in the combat zone. The valuable experience plus the generous distribution of medals made participation in the air show a must for career ambitious officers. The club provided traffic in war stories, other stories, and outright lies, as well as inside information on the goings on across the pond to the west. Old friendships were re-established and new ones were formed. Civilian contract aircrews, flying cargo, human and otherwise, were granted club privileges during their layovers. Their pilots, navigators, flight engineers and stewardesses added to the pool of American schoolteachers, officers' wives, civilian technicians, and nurses from the large Clark Air Base Hospital.

The clubhouse had a wide accommodating set of steps that narrowed toward the top and led to a large double door. The air inside was conditioned and cool. The main club lobby featured a huge wooden Filipino landscape carving on its wall. It depicted a scene with palm trees, a Filipino dressed in a loincloth, and his carabao. The foyer led to a formal dining room that was half filled with patrons dining in luxury. An eight piece Filipino band played Glen Miller on the stage and the sounds drifted throughout the halls. To the left was a wide portal that opened to their objective—the main bar and the daily happy hour. The spacious saloon had the typical heavy wooden bar that extended along the right side of the room. There were numerous tables and most were filled with revelers, mostly men, but a scattering of attractive women. All of them were Caucasian. The humid tropical air of their walk and the cool air in the lobby was replaced with cigarette smoke and noisy conversation.

The bar was crowded with men, a montage of cigarette smoke, military uniforms, flight suits with strange unit patches, some with no patches, various colored unit scarves and civilian clothing with lots of shirts displaying colorful tropical colors. Almost all had dark suntans and short haircuts. The uniform insignias depicted everything from pilots, navigators, administrators, doctors, nurses, and special forces. The bar was cluttered with drink glasses, beer steins, and ashtrays. Everyone at the bar seemed to be talking, bragging, or boasting louder than the next guy. Eddie spotted numerous hands zooming about doing air maneuvers and he knew they belonged to the pilots, who commanded the most respect, and therefore attention from the handful of non-talkers. The pilots had a swaggering, flamboyant, fighter pilot look. The only thing missing was a large painting of the Lady. But Eddie felt he was getting close to her origin. Behind the bar was a huge wooden carving of another rural Filipino scene, this one included a Nipa hut, a beautiful Filipino girl in a sarong, and a volcano in the background. Eddie recognized the volcano as the same one he saw during their approach into the Clark runway. Eddie recognized no one in the crowd but he had the impression that everyone was there! Chivas Regal on the rocks was the special—two for fifty cents.

"Over here!" A young captain in a flight suit stood up and waived at Eddie and Quincy. He was standing by a large table filled with guys, half still wearing flight suits and each flight suit had a 22nd patch on the right sleeve. Eddie followed Quincy to the table of jubilant aviators and Quincy wasted no time introducing Eddie to the collection. "Guys, this is Eddie, he's the new co-pilot that arrived three days ago. Say hello to Eddie." The group raised their glasses and simultaneously said, "Hello Eddie." They were loud enough that half the bar looked their way. A Latino looking pilot sitting on the far side of the table offered, "Sit down and buy us all a round of drinks."

"See you met the group," a familiar voice came from behind Eddie. He turned and was face to face with Jim Beckle, the pilot who had greeted him at the Tachikawa Officers Club on the first day he had arrived. Jim had briefed him about their mission and had given him his introduction flight and check ride. Eddie was surprised to see him again—1800 miles from Japan. Jim was wearing the traditional 22nd tan flight suit, a ten inch sweat line under each armpit, and flight boots that looked like they had been used in the Bataan death march. "They can buy their own drinks," Jim rescued Eddie from the challenge.

Jim had departed Tachikawa after Eddie that morning and had only recently landed. They had proceeded directly to the O'club, sweaty flight suits and all, in order to get in on the last of the happy hour. They would check in at the transient officers' housing desk later that evening, hoping all the base transient quarters were taken. Thus they could get their coveted non availability slips for per diem. All the off base motels had swimming pools to spend free time socializing and drinking with friends. Also, women were not allowed in the base transient quarters and off base there were no rules. Extra chairs were carried from the corner of the room and Eddie gingerly joined the bedraggled group of fliers. They would become some of his closest friends in the coming years. He noticed a velvet lined leather cup and a pair of dice sitting on the middle of the table.

The Latino guy that had generously offered Eddie an opportunity to buy the group a round of drinks was called "Conejo." He was a Puerto Rican math major from New York City. He was a first officer, a senior co-pilot that was next in line to upgrade as aircraft commander. He had been waiting for the advancement for two months. However, the flying schedule kept the instructor pilots and aircraft so busy there wasn't time for his upgrade training and check ride.

Every overseas outfit had its whore monger. Conejo was the twenty-second's. Conejo, Spanish for rabbit, earned his nickname for his attraction to whores, specifically quickies; those that banged their clients anywhere and anyplace they could find shelter from the general public. Two American dollars was usually the price for a quick wam, bam, thank you ma'am. He earned his reputation one day while shopping with a group of 22nd lieutenants in Angeles City. It was a decrepit village outside the Clark main gate where everyone shopped for woodcarvings, wicker furniture, oil paintings and cold beer. The group had been sorting through a collection of monkey pod carvings, looking for bargains, when Conejo excused himself and slipped through a side door into the alley. He was back in ten minutes and when asked where he went he informed the group that he knew a girl who lived in a hut out back. Every time he was in the area he would stop by for a quickie. He explained it was his duty because she was the only source of income for her family. It was as if he had an obligation to fulfill and he seldom visited off base without sharing his pay with at least one or two deserving street venders.

That evening, during Eddie's first night in La La Land, others at the table included Jake Olivetti, otherwise known as "Slick." His specialty was the stewardesses who crewed the chartered airliners loaded with soldiers (GIs) going to and from the States. The empty airliners frequently spent the night at Clark and the stewardesses relished the horny, sun tanned, young air force aviators that flowed through Clark Air Base. They relished the aviator's willingness to spend money freely and the aviators anticipated and hoped they would, in return, get a little round-eyed (Caucasian) sex. It was safe for the stewardesses—their boy friends and husbands back in the States would never learn of their wild Philippine indiscretions.

There was Andrew Blackwell, "Andy." He was a well-groomed and well-mannered Air Force Academy graduate who had ambitions of becoming a general. Andy was very private about his personal life but everyone knew his preference was two prostitutes in the same bed. It was rumored that his wife, from a very wealthy stateside family, liked two men in the same bed whenever Andy was away on a trip. Then there was "Ching," a brilliant young scholar from M. I. T. and of Chinese descent. He kept an extensive, detailed diary of each day's events. He was a navigator and had plans to continue his education after his military obligation. He wanted to teach. His diary was to be his notebook from which to write a best selling book. Everyone took him lightly about the book but respected his intellect. Ching wasn't his real name but no one could pronounce it, so they all called him Ching. It had a nice oriental sound to it and he liked it as it sounded like a cash register. He never had sex with anyone.

The group of fighter pilots at the bar occasionally swiveled slowly on their chairs and scanned the crowd at the tables behind them. Fighter pilots were at the top of the pilot pecking order and thus controlled the center section of the main bar. They could talk and look at the same time; it was as if they were scanning for enemy aircraft. Their scan would stop briefly at the rag tag group of 22nd aviators. They would scowl lightly and with disdain: then continue their visual sweep of the room. The 22nd group was not well kept, wore no neck scarves displaying their unit colors, and drank beer, the beverage of peasants. Fighter pilots sipped hard liquor.

There was a handful of wannabes at the bar and several majors and colonels who had enough rank to bypass the pecking order. It made no difference what or if they flew. On the far left was a small group in flight suits, without patches and no scarves. They kept to themselves and spoke quietly—never to someone that they didn't know. These were the spooky guys and they flew secret missions. Some dropped and retrieved special forces teams behind enemy lines with unmarked aircraft and helicopters. Some flew U-2s and took photos over mainland China. Three of them weren't even in the military. They flew various small transport aircraft, many which were designed specifically for landing on short unpaved runways. These guys' organizations had names like Air America and Ravens. Everyone knew the government civilian agency behind their operations was secret, but everyone knew the secret. The spooky guys were always serious and never talked about their jobs. They "couldn't give a damn" about the pecking order at the bar. Loud boasting fighter pilots and the spooky guys were attracted to each other about as much as gasoline and water.

Eddie reveled in the ambience. As he sat silently sipping the cold beer he realized why C-124 crews drank beer most of the time. Long hours in un-pressurized aircraft left them fatigued and dehydrated. Hour after hour of low frequency propellers and reciprocating engines, pounding and penetrating their bodies with sound, turned them into putty. The bottle in the crew van was a good jump-start for their dead bodies but they needed beer to ease them back down to mother earth. They needed the beer to re-hydrate, relax and regain their normality. Then maybe drink some hard liquor. Eddie observed the fine details involving the social structure at the bar, and like the fighter pilots, he slowly scanned the crowd. Eddie also stayed out of the conversation at the table; their conversation was like listening to a foreign language. He needed to learn the walk before he could do the talk. Eddie's college ways and his Willy student pilot days were history. He was in La La Land. Another round of beer was ordered and the dice were sent around the table. Each aviator rolled to see who would get stuck with the tab. Eddie lost and everyone laughed as Eddie faked a look of disgust at losing. There were ten guys at the table and he secretly wondered if he had enough money on him to keep up with the crowd. When the beer arrived the tab was only three dollars and forty cents. Eddie was instantly relieved; at those prices maybe this place really was Shangri-La. He tipped the waitress a dollar and after she left they informed him that he tipped her a full day's wages. Eddie was humiliated but learning.

Famished, with the next round he ordered two hamburgers and was pleased to see they were accompanied by a generous serving of French fries. He wolfed everything down and finished his beer. The day had been a long one and the beer had done its job. He was back on the ground but some engine noise was still in his head. This was Eddie's first day in his new life and he couldn't stay up with this crowd. He needed training and conditioning, which would come with time. What he needed most was a good night's sleep.

Eddie informed the group he was calling it a night and eased out of his chair to leave. "I'll go with you," Quincy joined him out the door into the foyer. "We best check in with Major Baxter to see what's going down in the morning."

"He's probably at his trailer house," Eddie agreed.

Quincy smiled and motioned with his head. "Follow me. You gotta see this. It's where old man Baxter spends every evening when he's at Clark." Quincy led them down the foyer and past the main dining room. The band was on break and stood clustered in the hallway, smoking cigarettes and sharing a common ashtray. With their shiny black hair, dark skin, and beautiful white embroidered shirts, they looked very sharp. Quincy opened a normal sized door, the first door Eddie had seen in the club that wasn't carved into a Filipino landscape. The small room was filled with dense smoke. Several tables and lots of chairs were provided for the room's occupants, but most were standing and crowded around one table where a serious poker game was being held. The players were four older men in civilian clothing, probably in their early forties, and Major Baxter was one of them. He had a cigar in his mouth and a glass of beer next to his pile of green American money. Eddie saw several twenties in the center of the table. There was a lot of loose cash lying on the table and the look in the spectator's faces, standing around the table watching the game, indicated the seriousness of the engagement. Eddie held back while Quincy approached the major, squatted next to him, and they quietly held a brief conversation. Major Baxter never looked away from his hand of cards as he talked. Quincy then retreated and motioned with his head for Eddie to follow him out the door.

"Five o' clock at the housing desk," he informed Eddie as they exited the massive front door and headed back toward their trailer. "Just like Colonel Duncan said, we got a Binh Thuy turn-around tomorrow, a Danang pick up the next day, and with luck in three days we'll be back to Tachikawa in time for happy hour."

The insects were singing in the trees; the moist evening air smelled sweet from a fusion of papayas, mangos, and lemon grass. There was a roar in the distance . . . then it came closer. The two aviators knew it was a jet on its take-off roll. The sound came closer then faded. In the distance he saw a cluster of lights moving rapidly into the night sky. Flashing white and steady red and green, the cluster of lights was standard but the rest of the aircraft was invisible in the night sky. Who was he, what was he, and where was he going? Was it a spook on some clandestine mission or a fighter being ferried to Vietnam? Then the sound was gone and the tranquil evening regained its dominance. What a wonderful evening it was. Tomorrow it would be Vietnam and Binh Thuy, wherever that was. Eddie was exhausted and the air conditioning and clean sheets felt wonderful. He slept well.

* *

The windows in his room were taped over with black fabric so the MAC day sleepers would be rested for their next stage of the big freight shuttle into Vietnam. They kept their C-141s flying twenty-four hours per day. Eddie was startled when his alarm went off. Quincy was up and ready in a flash, then Eddie shaved and grabbed a quick shower. As he slipped into a clean flight suit it dawned on him that this would be his first day in Vietnam. They stuffed yesterday's smelly flight suits into their duffle bags, brushed their teeth, and walked through the front door to the transient quarter's desk—all within twenty-five minutes. Major Baxter was waiting; he was wearing what looked like a new flight suit.

"Mornin," he greeted them and grinned as he checked out Eddie who was also wearing a new flight suit. Eddie's was without a name tag, rank, or squadron patch. It was one of the few times Eddie had seen the major smile. "We both got these damn new overalls," the major complained. "They're really hot until you wash em a dozen or so times. Then the fabric will open up and breathe."

The flight engineers collected their non-availability slips and together the crew walked across the tarmac to the single story, white, cinder block building that housed a diner style restaurant. It was just getting light and Eddie could hear the sounds of aircraft engines as the day fliers prepared to go to work. On the other side of the trees and buildings, the hum of a turboprop C-130 Hercules freighter could be heard as it commenced its take-off roll. Clark was busy twenty-four hours each day. The aircraft lifted clear of the trees and turned slowly to the right as it headed west, the direction of Vietnam. It was painted in camouflage colors, appropriate for its probable destination, its four synchronized propellers humming a pleasing sound.

"Three fifteenth trash haulers like us. C-130 Hercules, everyone calls them Herky Birds," Max answered Eddie's unasked question. "All of us freight delivery guys are called trash haulers—we don't consider it a derogatory term. We take pride in keeping our grunts on the ground supplied with everything they need. The 315th C-130s fly with camouflage colors. Most of the spooks C-130s are painted dull black and Air America's C-130s are polished silver aluminum." Then another hum could be heard and another identically camouflaged C-130 took off and banked due west. The Herky Bird drivers were already at work. The breakfast was the usual eggs, bacon, and pancakes. The crew ate their fill as it would be a long day until the next real meal back at Clark. In between there was only their food bag and Eddie hadn't time to make up one of his own.

At the command post the three officers disappeared behind the restricted door while the flight engineers made a bee line to the aircraft and started their extensive pre-flight. The major disappeared into a back room for his own private consultations with the staff. Quincy showed Eddie the flight planning room, how to get the weather for their day's flying. He gave Eddie a short course on how he filled out the flight plan and came up with a suggested fuel load for Major Baxter. The flight planning room was about what Eddie expected, weather charts and airways charts all over the walls. There were three large very old metal tables with hard rubber tops to lay out one's paperwork. Safety bulletins were tacked to everything. There was one other crew in the room, all wearing new looking flight suits and polished boots. They were all majors and wore blue neck scarves. After they left Quincy looked at Eddie in disgust and explained, "C-141 pukes from the States. This morning I saw em leave from the trailer next to us. They fly in pressurized jets, have hot meals from their oven, and only fly into the large safe airfields in-country. I would guess they were from a reserve squadron, as pretty as they looked. It's near the end of the month so they all come out of the woodwork and fly their one trip a month in-country to get their tickets punched." In-country was slang for inside South Vietnam.

"What's this tickets punched thing?" Eddie asked. He was glad to be alone with Quincy as he could ask questions without feeling intimidated.

"Combat pay," Quincy explained. "Two hundred dollars per month extra pay and five hundred dollars per month tax exemption for everyone that flies inside the combat zone. You'll get paid this month cause of today's mission. It's kind of a rip in a way because it's for guys like the Thud pilots and F-4 jocks that tangle with the MIGs, and the forward air controllers and so forth. They deserve every cent of it and more. But to qualify all you gotta do is to fly inside the Vietnam airspace; you don't even have to fly as far as the shoreline. Us 22nd guys all get combat pay every month and in a way we work for it, even though our mission is transport and is relatively risk free. The rip is that whenever the end of the month comes around, guys from the States and senior staff members from all over the globe show up and wanna fly or at least ride with us. They want an easy Nam turn, like we got today. They all want their tickets punched for the month so they can get their two hundred dollars extra. I wouldn't be surprised if Major Baxter shows up with a couple of slick and pretty colonels to ride with us on today's Nam turn."

"What's with this Major Baxter anyway?" Eddie wondered out loud as he digested the ticket punching information. "Is he as cold to everyone as he is to me?"

"He's his own man." Quincy watched the doorway to make sure the major didn't become privy to their conversation. "This guy's old and all worn out, but he's a legend in some circles. This is his third war, A-26 bombers in World War II and Korea, and to keep him safer they put him in C-124s to finish his career. He's got over thirteen thousand hours, but he's only a major cause when he was young, he screwed up. During World War II he was flying an A-26 someplace over here, up high, when he spotted a lone American B-24 flying along down low. The story, as I heard it, was that he dived down on the bomber from behind and picked up a lot of excess speed. He shut down both engines just before he passed the bomber. With both props dead still he went by and gave the pilots the finger. Then he did a split S and when out of their sight, below and behind them, he restarted his engines. It was a great stunt, except the bomber had been converted into a three star general's personal aircraft and the general was in the cockpit flying that day. They were the only two aircraft flying at that place at that time and they nailed him. He got a month off without pay and a letter in his file. So he's turned into a bitter old bastard who will never hold a staff position. But he does know how to fly. Listen to him because he's a damn good no bull shit instructor pilot."

"World War II," Eddie wondered out loud. "He must be really old."

"I heard that he got out of the military after World War II and was recalled during the Korean War," Quincy continued. "That would be about a six year gap as a civilian. Apparently he had a hard time as a civilian after World War II and that was when his first marriage went bad and he got a divorce. No one knows how many marriages he's had since then but at least three that I know of. Anyway, when the Korean War was over he stayed in the air force and made it his home. I'd guess he's about forty-five or forty-six years old now. He probably only has about twenty years in the air force. There's a lotta older guys around that were recalled during the Korean War then stayed in the service. We got a number of flight engineers over forty years old, with similar stories."

* *

It was getting hot by the time the officers got to the airplane, did their baggage drill, and built their nest in their front seats. The flight engineers finished their pre-flight and downed a large supply of water from the jerry can under the coffee maker. Eddie had time to inspect the yellow runway paint striper that Sergeant Hampton had spent two hours winching on board and strapping down. It showed recent patches where it had been welded and someone had painted the name "Elsie" on its cowl. It struck Eddie as a strange weapon for fighting a war.

Eddie sat in his seat waiting while the engineers finished their tasks. The sky had lost all of its morning redness and the humid heat had set in for the day. Eddie resolved to wash his flight suits several times the first chance he had. A strange colorful bird flew overhead, intent and in a straight line for some personal task unknown to Eddie's world. A four ship of camouflaged F-4s took off, followed by another C-130, then a C-141. The EC-47 was missing from the ramp as well as the weird looking Air America Pilatus Porter. All of the birds had work to do.

The flight engineers, at last, were finished with their pre-flight and they read the before start checklists. When they were finished the major barked, "Start em up, Mac."

The big radial engines roared as they erupted to life, one at a time, and they announced to the world that propellers and round engines weren't dead—yet!

After their run up and magneto checks, they had to wait their turn for take-off behind a United DC-8 charter and an all black C-130 with no markings. Eddie listened to the radio on tower frequency while they waited. An old four engine, C-54 passenger plane landed and took its time clearing the runway. It slowly taxied to a turn-off adjacent the recip ramp. According to regulations, the spacing was too tight for the Flying Tiger Stretched DC-8 freighter that was following it in.

"Tiger go around," the tower ordered. Although the C-54 was near the far end of the runway, the rule for civilian aircraft was that no aircraft was allowed to touchdown unless all other aircraft were totally clear of the runway.

"We can fit in just fine," the Flying Tiger responded. "He's almost clear and it will cost us five hundred dollars in fuel to do a go around."

"Tiger, make a five hundred dollars go around," the tower commanded. Black exhaust erupted from the DC-8 on short final as the pilot advanced his throttles and raised his nose, some flaps, and gear.

"Tiger's on the go," one of the Tiger pilots called.

"United Two Eighty Nine is cleared takeoff, expedite your take-off. Break. Break. Tiger's cleared for a short visual final," the tower instructed. "There's no one on final behind you and you're clear to land."

"Roger that, Tiger's cleared to land," the civilian freighter confirmed. His voice sounded terse.

"United Two Eighty Nine is on the roll." United would be gone before the DC-8 completed his visual traffic pattern.

Eddie watched in amazement as the heavily loaded Flying Tiger DC-8 slowly climbed and turned a tight right circle onto a visual downwind pattern. He then rolled out level for less than one minute, dropped its gear, and continued the circle in a descent. He rolled out to wings level just before touchdown.

"That was one tight pattern for one big son of a bitch," Quincy remarked from his position, leaning forward over the pedestal between the two pilots.

"I think he just shaved a couple hundred bucks off the cost of that go around," Mac remarked as he grinned in amazement.

"It was pretty," Major Baxter added, "pretty because he knew what he was doing, at least it looked like he knew what he was doing. Let an inexperienced pilot try that and they could have bent aluminum and freight strung out in the rice fields. Heavy, slow, tight turns are touchy business when climbing in a big overloaded aircraft. It all has to do with the backpressure on the control yoke. It's the backpressure that causes the stalls, don't overload your wings on a tight turn. That's gospel to C-124 drivers." The major looked Eddie right in the eyes to emphasize his words of wisdom. "This guy was either good or lucky. Hotdogs sometimes not only kill themselves but they kill all the other people in their aircraft."

Then it was Eddie's crew's turn. Their take-off roll was by the book and they lifted off, passed low over Angeles City, slowly climbing over fields, huts, and then jungle. With their heavy runway striper and enough fuel to return to Clark, the old bird climbed slowly and rattled a lot of pots and pans in the nipa huts below. The view was fantastic and Eddie followed the major's orders as they accelerated; he retracted their flaps in increments as their speed slowly increased. Then he performed the after take-off checklist while keeping one eye out the window. As fuel in Vietnam was at a premium, if possible, they always carried extra fuel with them so they could make the round trip without needing to refuel in-country. As they clawed their way upward, below they transitioned from the jungle patches and farms to Manila Bay. The fishermen had packed their nets and their lanterns from their night fishing and were on their way back to port and the fish markets. The fishermen fished at night in the huge bay with lanterns to attract the fish. Inexperienced aviators often confused all their lights for another small city. It was almost time for the fishermen to have a meal of fish and rice and to get some sleep in their nipa huts.

The airway made a slight turn to the right and they passed over Corregidor Island, its rugged beaches and forbidding hillsides unchanged from the raging battles it witnessed during World War II. The water was crystal clear and the coral formations beckoned from beneath the shallow blue waters. They were the final resting place for many Americans and Japanese combatants. Bataan Peninsula lay quietly covered with jungle, as if ashamed of the horrors the Japanese committed on American and Filipino prisoners during the Bataan death march. Eddie looked down and thought of all the suffering the prisoners endured. Major Baxter had a stoic expression and looked off into the distance; those men had been his generation and it had been his war. Wars and women were the same; your first serious involvement was the hardest to shake. Except for the engines' drone, the cockpit was silent as they flew over the sacred ground.

They leveled off at 6000 feet, the cruising altitude with their heavy load. Max set cruise power according to the tables in his performance book. He then slowly scanned with his overhead oscilloscope and checked the firing pattern of each engine's spark plugs, a total of 224 plugs. Aircraft reciprocating engines all have two spark plugs in each cylinder for both redundancy and to get a cleaner fuel burn. He made a short list of several spark plugs that would need to be replaced when they returned to Clark Air Base.

Major Baxter told Eddie "you got it" and climbed out of his seat and put on a fresh pot of coffee. Then he opened the hatch and climbed down to the cargo hold and discussed something with Sergeant Hampton. Eddie babysat the autopilot, scanned his gauges, and then resumed his watch out the windshield. Sergeant Maxwell finished his cruise check and dug into his bag, pulling out several porno magazines. He offered one to Eddie but Eddie declined. He preferred looking out the windshield at his new home in the sky. Quincy was finished with his first LORAN position fix and accepted one of the magazines. Eddie would learn that full colonels

30

wore brim hats. Younger pilots insisted on wearing cloth folding flight hats, which when folded were easily transported in the pockets of their flight suits. Flight engineers liked to wear baseball hats even if they were not approved uniform, navigators had big wrist watches and only enlisted chewed tobacco. Flight engineers loved porno magazines.

Eddie so loved being alone and watching the China Sea roll by as the four reciprocating engines hummed their deep rumbling song. There was no other traffic near their low altitude. Occasionally he would notice an aircraft way up high but down on the deck it was just Eddie, the ocean, and the ever-changing display of fair weather cumulus clouds. Occasionally one would lie in their path and Eddie would gently turn with the autopilot to miss the cloud's solid bump; but close enough to just slip the tip of their wing into the fluffy cloud as they passed. The aircraft would nod gently from the light bump, as if it understood their sally from course. With time, the sky, the ocean, the clouds, the aircraft, and Eddie all became one.

Eddie called in their position reports on the high frequency (HF) radio as Quincy produced them every 200 miles. Then Eddie scanned his gauges for the umpteenth time and fell back into his trance. Later, Major Baxter crawled back into his seat and broke Eddie's fantasy with the ocean. Eddie looked at his watch and was surprised they had been airborne for three hours; the major had taken a nice nap in one of the bunks. Eddie wondered how late the major had stayed up with the poker game and if he won any money; discretion kept him from asking such a personal question.

"We at the Vietnamese FIR yet?" the major asked Quincy as he finished his yawn. He then took out another cigar and lit it up with a diamond kitchen match. Eddie was sorry the old goat had not slept longer as the foul stink continued its daily contamination of Eddie's clothing, skin, and lungs.

"Just coming up on it," Quincy replied. "Time three four, six thousand, call Paris on 278.4 and request direct Binh Thuy, if you'd like."

"Ya just got your ticket punched," Major Baxter looked at Eddie and smiled. "You're two hundred dollars richer. The Vietnamese FIR is the oceanic edge of Vietnamese airspace. Inside the Vietnamese FIR we don't have air traffic control like everywhere else in the world. It's a combat zone, no flight plans, no air traffic controllers; you can fly anywhere you want and at any altitude you want.

"The US Air Force, however, maintains GCI sites, ground control intercept radar sites," the major continued. "GCI sites' primary purposes are to watch for enemy fighters and to guide our fighters for an intercept. But they're radar sites and monitor all air traffic. They just monitor air traffic and everybody does what they want. But everyone is expected to check in so the GCI operator knows who they are." The major then dug into his flight bag and gave Eddie a slip of paper; it was just the size to fit into one of the extra plastic pages in Eddie's new flight booklets. Then he explained the paper's contents, "Here's a copy of a list we made, it's got all the GCI sites in Vietnam and Thailand and their frequencies. That's where Quincy got the frequency for Paris GCI. Don't lose it. Right now we gotta call the GCI for the Saigon area, Paris GCI, and let them know who we are, our altitude and position, and where we're going. And tell them we're climbing to eight thousand feet. Best get a little higher in case there's any unfriendly activity we need to clear. We burned enough fuel so we're light enough to climb to eight thousand feet."

Eddie made the call and requested direct Binh Thuy and told them they were out of 6000 feet altitude and climbing to 8000. Paris gave Eddie a different transponder code to squawk, which he dialed into their transponder. The new identity code showed up on Paris's radar screen and the Paris controller returned the call. "MAC Three Three, radar contact. A heading of two six zero degrees will point you toward Binh Thuy."

Eddie felt his heart beat increase just a little as Major Baxter said, "I have it," and turned the knob on the autopilot. Their aircraft turned slowly to the left and as they approached 260 degrees he rolled out level on course and they climbed to 8000 feet above sea level. They were in Vietnamese airspace and Eddie tried to contain his curiosity and excitement. At last he was about to see the mysterious place that demanded so much of the world's attention.

As the water passing under them changed from an almost black to lighter and lighter shades of blue, the coastline came into view. They continued their cruise, 8000 feet and 195 knots true airspeed. There were several small islands, ringed with crystalline turquoise waters only a few feet deep. Jungle growth covered the island's interiors. Smoke could be seen coming from one of the huts on one island.

The shoreline on another island was a mix of sandy beaches with turquoise shallow waters and rugged cliffs dropping off into deeper darker blue water. Other than the beaches, jungle grew everywhere. Other than a few fishing boats with beautiful dark red sails, there was little sign of life. The mainland ahead of them was relatively flat with little to speak of in the way of hills.

"Do I make my position reports to Paris?" Eddie turned and looked at Quincy, who was leaning over the pilot's center pedestal and enjoying the view out the pilot's windshields.

"Just like we said, no more position reports and no air traffic controllers in combat airspace, we just fly where we wanna go," the major repeated. "Once Paris knows who we are they'll track us on their radar and if it looks like anyone's gonna run into us, and if they notice it, and have time, they'll give us a warning. But they aren't required to. It's nice to know the GCI site is available. If you ever get hit or in trouble you can call them and they'll give you a heading to fly to the nearest suitable airport and they would initiate a rescue effort in case you go down. Other than that don't bother them and clog up the radios."

Quincy added, "In ten or fifteen minutes we'll be in radar range of Paddy, the GCI site at Binh Thuy and you can call them and give them our estimated time of arrival. At this altitude, their radar can see us about sixty miles out and they share the same radio frequency with Paris GCI. At sixty miles we'll also be able to pick up their TACAN distance and bearing and we can track in on it. That is, if they have a working TACAN. We're supposed to haul a damaged one back to Clark."

They were passing about thirty miles south of Saigon, just inland and parallel with the South Vietnamese shoreline. As the shoreline curved away from them they drifted further and further inland and the jungle gave way to more and more rice fields—flat land with hundreds of irregular shaped, tiny fields that were separated by narrow dikes. An occasional roadway threaded its way through the paddies and numerous canals provided the abundance of water the rice fields thrived upon. Tiny villages were randomly dispersed and the scene looked tranquil, like an ideal place to visit. Eddie pulled the Binh Thuy TACAN frequency off the runway chart and, after telling the major what he was doing, dialed it into the TACAN receiver. The TACAN navigational receiver locked onto Binh Thuy and the display read fifty-seven nautical miles at zero eight zero bearing *from* the TACAN. Eddie called the tower on 278.4 and told them they would be landing in about fifteen to twenty minutes.

"They either got two TACAN vans down there or got their damaged unit to work again," the major observed.

The scene below transitioned into thousands of rice paddies—flat terrain, and numerous canals as far as Eddie could see. Roads became rare. Tree lines followed some of the dikes and canals and occasionally there was a small island of trees with a cluster of huts, similar to Filipino nipa huts. Small boats were the primary means of transportation and they could be seen plying the canal waterways as everyone went about their business. Eddie could see why the North Vietnamese wanted to take over the delta; its rice production had to be phenomenal. The scene was so peaceful.

Spread out below them was the legendary Mekong River Delta. They were flying over a huge fan-shaped flat plain with a lace like pattern of water channels. The Mekong River had its origins in western China, drained waters from China and Burma, formed the border between Thailand and Laos, drained central Cambodia, then slowed and spread out into thousands of fingers as it crossed the massive delta region of Vietnam. There it dropped its heavy, rich load of silt which nourished the rice paddies of the delta. Eventually the spider web of tributaries drained into the South China Sea. Binh Thuy was located between two tributaries of the Mekong, basically an island in the middle of the delta region.

The North Vietnamese and Viet Cong in the Delta region received the vast majority of their war supplies through a back door that was ignored by the American media. The American public had no knowledge of this supply route. The NVA supplies were offloaded from ships from many nations in the Cambodian western seaport of Sihanoukville. Then transported by contracted Cambodian civilian trucks over Cambodian roads, nicknamed the "Sihanouk Trail," to Phnom Penh, the capital of Cambodia which was located on the main stem of the Mekong River. There the NVA war supplies were divided among willing boat operators and smaller trucking operators. The trucks would transport their half of the supplies due east, just short of the Cambodian/Vietnamese border, where they would be distributed to NVA soldiers operating out of the Cambodian sanctuary and into South Vietnam. The other half of the war supplies, those delegated to the Delta region, would be loaded into small boats and infiltrated through the thousands of river fingers into the South Vietnam delta area.

The extensive canal network and dense jungle foliage that lined the rivers and streams made it very difficult and dangerous for the Americans to stop the North Vietnamese supplies. American military personnel, dying by the thousands, begged for an opportunity to shut down this flow of materials upstream; at the source, the seaport near Sihanoukville. But to no avail. Supplies, therefore, just kept flowing out of Cambodia and the Americans continued losing their lives in one of the world's largest swamps. Binh Thuy was a vital air force base located in the middle of this quagmire called the Delta.

"Where was the war?" Eddie wondered as he sat looking out the window. From 8000 feet the subtleties of river boat traffic, alleged ambushes from the river banks, coercion and torture of the native population by North Vietnamese infiltrators, and alleged rampaging American soldiers were invisible episodes.

As if by cue, there was a significant puff of white smoke in one of the tree lines, in Eddie's two o'clock position and several miles out. "What was that?" Eddie lit up like a light bulb and then there was another puff along the same tree line.

"Artillery, maybe mortar," Major Baxter nonchalantly announced. "We'll be far enough to the left of it we'll probably be okay."

"Probably?" Eddie asked as two more smoke bursts worked their way down the tree line.

"Probably," Major Baxter replied. "Nothing is a hundred percent."

The tree line under fire passed on the right and the TACAN distance (DME) was decreasing through thirty miles. Eddie pulled the tower frequency out of his approach flip chart and called the airfield tower, giving them their location, altitude, and intent to land. At the major's command, he read the descent checklist. The major still hadn't started his descent yet. Eddie was getting a bit nervous—they wouldn't be able to get down fast enough for a stabilized straight in approach.

"How far out do you usually start down?" Eddie asked, trying to sound ignorant and not rile the major.

"Ain't the same over here," was the major's reply. "Let down too early and you'll draw fire from some of those tree lines and islands. There's gomers down there that would love to put an AK-47 slug through our ass, we're so big and slow. A low-and-slow straight in final approach, like we make everywhere else in the world, would make us sitting ducks." Soon the DME was reading only twenty miles and the airfield was about to disappear under their nose. The major pickled off the autopilot, called for an engine manifold reduction to fifteen inches, maintained 8000 feet altitude and bled off the airspeed. He called for the gear down, then flaps ten as the speed decreased through 170 knots, flaps twenty under 164 knots and flaps thirty when they were under 148 knots. At 140 knots and with the gear down and full flaps, he pushed the nose over. They dropped well over a thousand feet per minute at their 140 knot airspeed. The Binh Thuy runway was just in front of them.

"Got ya in sight, MAC Three Three, you're cleared for an overhead to runway two four, left pitch. There's traffic on short final, winds calm," the tower announced for all to hear.

"MAC Three Three," Eddie responded. "Left pitch runway two four."

"With a tight, downward, three hundred sixty degree spiral onto the runway, like we're gonna do," the major spoke as he flew, "we stay as close as possible to the airfield boundary. If it's night time we keep our exterior lights all off and only flash them on for a second or two if the tower needs to see our position." As they descended steeply, directly over the airfield fifteen hundred feet above the ground, the major rolled left into a steep fifty degree bank angle with minimal back pressure on the yoke. The nose fell and they dropped from the sky, in a steep left hand spiral.

Their pitch out reminded Eddie of his favorite World War II movies. Morey was at the engineer's panel and at the major's command he advanced the propellers to 2700 RPM. The four 4360s, quiet during the descent, came alive as the propellers speeded up, in position for either a go-around or stopping on the 6000 runway. As they rounded their base turn onto final they were dropping through eight hundred feet above sea level. The runway was eight feet above sea level so they had about 792 feet to go.

"Manifold one seven," the major called and Morey adjusted the throttles and replied. The giant engines had cooled considerably during their steep descent, despite the fact that Morey had kept the engine cowl flaps (air flow vents) closed to retain as much heat as possible. The major wanted to give the engines a little more power on final to warm them for use in reversing or if they needed to go around. Adding a bunch of power to a cold engine was a sure way to crack the extensive array of exhaust manifolds, if not the engine cylinders themselves.

"The brass back in the States would shit if they saw us drop this big beast and roll it over like this," Eddie thought to himself. "Shit hot!"

Major Baxter advanced the throttles just a little more to shallow their descent rate, then as they approached the runway he slowly pulled the giant engines back to idle power as he smoothly rolled onto the asphalt runway. He pulled the four propeller reverse levers up and waited for Eddie to call four green propeller lights, which indicated that all four propellers had functioned properly and all their blades had rotated into reverse position. He then applied just enough reverse power to stop easily, but no more than necessary. In this country, no one wanted to stay the night because of abused engines. No one at the airfield wanted them to stay either. Everyone knew that C-124s had a reputation of dripping fresh oil all over their ramps and their size made them "mortar magnets" (easy targets). Max climbed up the ladder from below, where he had served as an observer watching the engines out the side windows during the final phases of the flight. He opened the overhead hatch and pulled himself halfway out, so that he could see the wing tips and assist Major Baxter as they taxied onto the parking ramp.

As they taxied slowly to the ramp, the brakes howled several times, getting everyone's attention. Eddie had his camera out—he couldn't resist banging away at the scene outside. It was pretty much what he expected. The base was hewn from filled-in rice paddies and was made up of single story wooden structures, a few painted unattractive browns, some natural and without paint. A lot of plywood had been used, probably brought up the Mekong on barges as were most of the other supplies and items found at the isolated air base. The perimeter fence had numerous bunkers and gun positions, manned by a combination of South Vietnamese and American combatants. In front of one of the nicer looking and larger buildings was a pair of flags, the South Vietnamese and the Stars and Stripes hung side by side. A montage of smaller utility aircraft was parked on the ramp. There were five Canadian built C-7 Caribou mini-freighters, a cluster of O-2 forward air controller aircraft, two C-123 freighters, numerous Huey helicopters, an army OV-1 Mohawk reconnaissance aircraft, and several small single engine O-1 Birddog reconnaissance aircraft. Absent were jet fighters, C-141 transports, and chartered civilian aircraft. This was a forward base. A Vietnamese enlisted man marshaled them into their parking spot, next to the C-123, crossed his arms to signal stop and pulled his index finger across his throat. The flight engineers had the aircraft's auxiliary electric power unit started and running and Morey cut the engines at Major Baxter's command.

Within seconds a rumbling sound occurred and Eddie realized it was the nose doors opening and the ramps being lowered. The huge clamshell nose doors hydraulically opened to expose the entire front end of the cargo compartment. The two sturdy fold up ramps were hydraulically adjusted to fit the width of the paint striper's wheel tracks and the loadmaster hydraulically extended and lowered them to the ramp. Elsie the paint striper could be driven out the front of the aircraft and onto the concrete parking area.

Through the nose opening and the associated ramps, the loadmaster could load and unload any type of self propelled vehicles, tanks, trucks, and even paint stripers. A powerful, electrical cable winch was attached to the rear of the freight bay so non-motorized freight, pallets, helicopters with their rotors removed, trailers, etc, could be pulled up the ramps and into the freight compartment. At destinations the same non-motorized freight would be dragged out the nose of the aircraft and down the ramps with whatever tractor or tug was provided by the destination airport. It was crude 1955 technology, but with a lot of ingenuity and hard work by the loadmaster and the airfield's ramp helpers, the job always got done.

Sergeant Hampton was wasting no time. About a dozen Vietnamese emerged on the scene and Sergeant Hampton was ordering and pointing the small crowd into an efficient work detail. It all made Eddie quite nervous.

"You'll get used to them," Major Baxter grinned. "Ramp helpers, we call em Rampies. The Vietnamese aren't lazy people and are great in assisting the loadmaster with his manual labor chores. But, you gotta watch em! We never leave the airplane without one crew member to watch over them; otherwise they might seed it for us."

"What's seeding mean?" Eddie looked at the major.

"There have been instances," the major explained, "fortunately never with our squadron, where they pull the pin on a grenade, stick it into a glass container to hold the arming handle down, and hide it balanced in some overhead place in our aircraft. Ya never know when ya got a Vietcong mixed in with the crowd. After take-off, it'll shake loose, fall to the floor and the glass will break. Then the grenade will go off. Other than the aircraft commander, who has lots of other things to do, everyone takes turns guarding our aircraft. Max is already down there watching Hampton's backside. Quincy and I'll slip into base ops and do the paperwork for our return flight. You can hang out and watch the unloading operations. I'll teach you the paperwork in due time."

Eddie let himself down the side ladder—an awkward alternate affair along the side of the fuselage. The main cockpit ladder had been raised out of the way as Elsie the paint striper was about to be driven out the front doors. The Vietnamese were everywhere and he quickly found his way down the ramps and out of the way. He took several good photos. The air was sultry hot and he was sweating profusely. The tiny Vietnamese were scurrying about and looked comfortable in the humid heat. Eddie's stomach was growling but he didn't want to beg food from the other crewmembers. So he strolled down the flight line and into the operations building (base ops). Major Baxter was swearing and Quincy had his eyes rolled back. Their return freight wasn't the forty foot TACAN trailer they had expected; it had been changed to a damaged D-8 Caterpillar, complete with armor plating. It was 15,000 pounds heavier than the trailer was supposed to be. Major Baxter sent Eddie to get Max and his performance charts. The performance chart indicated they could just make it off, a maximum weight take-off from a 6000-foot runway with 98 degree heat at sea level.

Eddie's stomach kept growling, so Max suggested Eddie visit a little restaurant he'd seen behind base operatioins. Major Baxter nodded toward the back door and Eddie needed no encouragement. He expected a military kitchen, but it was a bare bones civilian restaurant. It was a wooden unpainted shack, with five wooden tables, rusty metal chairs, and a crude counter manned by a grinning Vietnamese. He was slender, about five feet four and one hundred pounds, dressed in an off white, loose, long sleeved shirt, black pajama looking pants, and rubber thongs. Maybe thirty years old, he had short chopped hair and a tiny mustache. Two American Air Force airmen, in sweaty camouflage tee shirts and fatigues, sat at one of the tables. They were drinking some sort of strange looking beer and were obviously not in the habit of standing when an officer entered the room. Eddie couldn't remember his protocol training from officer's training school, but decided that restaurants would be a stupid place for such tomfoolery, especially at a remote base in a war zone. A sign on the counter said Chicken Fried steak, $1.75.

Eddie strolled over to the counter, "I'll have the chicken fried steak and a Coke with lots of ice." The Vietnamese looked at him and smiled, then said something in Vietnamese. Eddie repeated his order but the Vietnamese only stood and smiled. Eddie then pointed to the sign and the Vietnamese nodded and scurried back into the kitchen. Eddie took a chair at a table by himself as he pretended he wasn't sweating. An overhead fan churned the thick humid heat but it did no good. Time hung for a few minutes and the bored airmen said nothing.

The Vietnamese reappeared from behind the counter and placed a can of slightly cool Coke in front of him and a plate with a sandwich on it. Eddie examined the sandwich, pulled it apart, and saw it was a peanut butter and jelly sandwich. He motioned the waiter back and pointed at his sandwich and pointed at the sign.

"I ordered a chicken fried steak!" The Vietnamese smiled back and pointed at the sign, nodded his head yes, and smiled again before he disappeared behind the counter. Eddie looked at the airmen as they were trying to contain their laughter.

"Might as well eat it . . . Sir!" one of them said and then snickered. "The only food they ever sell here is peanut butter and jelly sandwiches. Stolen beer and stolen pop is what they specialize in. They got no ice."

"What about the sign?" Eddie asked and pointed to the chicken fried steak advertisement.

"Probably stole if from the officers club." Both airmen laughed. "He can't speak or read English. All he knows is the words for beer, Coke, and 7-Up. Welcome to Vietnam." Eddie ate his sandwich and drank his Coke in silence and felt like a dumb shit under the watchful eyes of his enlisted observers. When he was finished the little Vietnamese man suddenly reappeared and held out his hand, obviously for money. Eddie dug into his pocket and handed the man two one dollar bills. He looked at the airmen and asked, "Think that's enough?" The Vietnamese took one look at the money, then quickly disappeared with the money and the empty dish.

"Don't you have any MPC?" the older of the two airmen asked. "It's against the law for us to use American money with the Vietnamese. On the black market he'll trade that American money for Vietnamese money and make out like the bandit on the exchange rate. He'll get three to one in value."

"Nobody told me anything about needing MPC," Eddie lied a little bit. "I never heard of it being against the law to use American money."

"Where you from, Sir? Mars?"

"I came in on that C-124 parked on the ramp. We came in from the Philippines." Both of the enlisted men laughed again.

"That's as far away as Mars, I mean, as far as we're concerned. MPC is military script, we call it funny money. That's all we ever use over here. Best get yourself some MPC before you come back to this place or the military police will arrest ya. They don't give a shit about those bars on your shoulders . . . Sir."

"Thanks for the advice." Eddie was totally uncomfortable and made as quick an exit as he could without breaking into a full run.

When out of sight from the airmen he slowed his pace. The hot humid air was just too much to hurry. Back at the aircraft it was amazing how fast and efficient Sergeant Hampton was managing the eager Vietnamese ramp help. The paint striper was gone and there was a GI slowly backing a khaki-colored monster of a caterpillar up the ramp and into their airplane. They had been right. Armor plating was crudely welded over its engine and cockpit areas and a large earth-moving blade was attached to its front. As it inched up the ramp Sergeant Hampton was all over the scene, making sure the monster's tracks centered on the adjustable aircraft ramps and that its progress into the airplane was safe and did not endanger either the dozen spectators or the aircraft. Eddie wondered what the caterpillar's story would be if it could talk.

The take-off was as the performance chart advertised. They rolled to the end of the runway and lifted off just in time to clear the row of shabby buildings inside the base perimeter fence. It was amazing how accurate and reliable the performance charts were. Then they rumbled over the rice paddies and turned eastward over a wide finger of the Mekong River. With their heavy load and slow climb they were sitting ducks for anyone waiting in the tree lines with a rifle. Major Baxter called for climb power on the engines and climbed at the recommended climb speed, plus twenty knots. The heat was intense and the engine's cylinder head temperatures stabilized at five degrees below the red line limitation. Eddie turned and noticed that Max had the cowl flaps almost closed. As they climbed at barely 500 feet per minute, the entire crew sat as if on pins and needles, afraid to imagine how vulnerable they were. Eddie watched every tree pass by and hoped every farmer was friendly. On the ground, everyone looked up at the giant aircraft clawing for altitude over their rice fields. Major Baxter rolled the lumbering warehouse over to the left for about a fifteen degree turn, stayed on the new heading for a few seconds, and then rolled right for about forty degrees, then back again.

"If the gomers are trying to set up to shoot at us, at least we don't wanna climb out in a straight line and make it easy for em," the major explained out loud to no one in particular.

Eddie imagined that any of the guys he had grown up with could hit their slow moving fat target with one shot, regardless of any bank angle. When they were kids, they used to shoot running jack rabbits with their rim fire twenty-two rifles and this fat bird would be a piece of cake.

"They told us at Tinker that when we were flying in a combat area we should climb at the highest power possible, maximum continuous power, and at the book climbing speed for the steepest climb angle. Am I missing something?" Eddie knew he was the greenest member of the crew but he just had to ask; he wanted to get out of there and climb as fast as possible.

"Our regulations," Major Baxter looked at Eddie, "are written by senior administrators back in the States. Few of them have ever flown in a hostile environment like this and in this heat and humidity. It sounds good on paper to fly at the highest possible power setting and the steepest angle, but it just doesn't work well over here. In this severe heat, it's way too hard on the engines, they work too hard and overheat. If we were flying at maximum continuous power and at the slower, recommended climb speed, our engines would overheat right through the red lines. We would have to keep our engine cowl flaps wide open and that would keep the engine cylinder heads only a few degrees under the red line. But the drag from the open cowl flaps would negate any climbing advantage from the higher power setting.

"We find that by setting a more conservative power setting, climb power, and climbing twenty knots faster than recommended, our engine cylinder temperatures stay comfortably below the red line, the engines aren't strained by the higher power setting, we can climb with our engine cowl flaps three quarters closed, and climb just as fast. That way there's a lot less strain on our engines. Taking care of our engines in this environment is vital.

"Unfortunately, whenever there's a high ranking officer on board or some standards inspector from some other outfit, we gotta follow the regulations and abuse our engines with the higher power and slower climb speed. We have lots of colonels and stateside weenies that ride with us once a month. Our engines get abused enough that they usually fail before they reach their scheduled overhaul time. It's because of them that our engine failure rate is so high. Whenever we're alone, we pull em back to climb power and faster airspeed."

Eddie listened and learned. This was the true life stuff that he could never learn in a classroom or a book. His eyes, however, never stopped searching the tree lines and watching for gun flashes from the villages. He took brief interludes to monitor his panel gauges and engine gauges.

Baxter smiled and thought to himself, "This Eddie's got a lot to learn in the next year or so. Someday us old farts are going to retire and guys like Eddie are gonna be running their own crew. It's good that he's asking questions."

They continued their climb to a cruise altitude of 7000 feet and retraced their route over the delta. Occasionally, white explosions still popped up along the same large tree line they had witnessed on their way in. Something serious was going on down there. Eddie felt secure and remote in his seat, watching the action below through his window. Paddy GCI warned Eddie's flight that there were fast movers (jet fighters) in that same area, so they took a wide detour south from the activity. Eddie strained his eyes but couldn't spot the fighters that he knew were out there.

"Aircraft putting in air strikes are a bitch to spot," Quincy informed Eddie. "Even if the GCI guys warn you of the target area, ya can't see em. They're hard to spot cause they're small, fast, and have camouflaged paint.

"They work with small forward air controller aircraft that finds their targets and marks em with smoke rockets. While the fighters are bombing the marked ground targets, they have to monitor two radios full of chatter. In addition they're circling the target and trying to keep each other in sight, spot the target smoke marker on the ground, and calculate bomb drop information in their head, in addition to watching their fuel gauges and flying the aircraft. They do all this while the gomers on the ground are trying to shoot em down."

"That's comforting," Eddie smiled and made eye contact with Quincy. "Have we lost any aircraft to artillery shells or mid air collisions with fighters putting in bomb strikes?"

"Haven't lost a single Shaky Bird in Vietnam yet," Quincy remarked proudly and knocked on his wooden desk top. Eddie looked down at the dissipating smoke in the distance and wondered what those guys' lives were like.

Soon they were "feet wet," a navy term for flying over the ocean that had been incorporated into air force jargon. Everyone settled down into their usual routines. With the autopilot engaged, Major Baxter lit a cigar and opened a paperback novel. Max returned to his porno magazine and a bag of stale cookies. He was actually reading the text! Quincy alternated between short naps, taking LORAN fixes, and passing forward the position reports. Eddie monitored the HF radio, as required by regulation whenever they were over water; while he gazed out the window in awe. The HF radio was a long distance radio that allowed higher authorities to stay in contact with them. It was loaded with static and the reception was sporadic. Eddie paid little attention to the actual time.

They had been airborne about two hours when Max tapped Eddie on the shoulder and pointed to an oil pressure gauge on the pilots' center panel. Eddie had scanned his gauges only five minutes prior and all had been fine. The needle on the oil quantity gauge, marked #2, was lower than the others and it was slowly working its way toward zero. The oil temperature gauge was working its way higher towards the red line and the correlation of the two was confirmation there was an oil problem occurring. Major Baxter watched the scenario play out and casually asked Max to record the numbers. These numbers would be given to the mechanics at Clark to be used in their troubleshooting.

"Oil quantity has gone from seventy-five gallons down to twenty gallons in three minutes and the oils heating up." Max had his hand on the number two throttle and was feeling for vibrations through the throttle linkage. The throttles were physically connected to the engine and would vibrate if the engine was vibrating.

"We better feather it before we ruin the engine or it catches fire," Major Baxter commanded.

Sergeant Maxwell announced, "Feathering number two," and pulled his number two fire control lever aft. It was a four in one lever and consolidated the essential actions of shutting down an engine into a single procedure: (1) shut off the engine's fuel mixture control which caused the engine to stop running, (2) armed the electrical circuitry for the fire extinguisher, (3) closed all of the engine's firewall valves (the firewall was a fireproof partition that separated the engine from the wings), and (4) commanded the electrical propeller motors to rotate (twist) the propeller blades into the wind (feather position), so as to create minimum air stream drag.

The engine went silent as engine number two's propeller blades feathered into the windstream and coasted to a stop. As the engine wound down the major disconnected the autopilot and added a little rudder trim so the aircraft would fly straight with the asymmetrical thrust. With an engine inoperative, the aircraft twisted sideways from the unbalanced power on the wings. The side twisting torque was called "yaw." Pilots countered the yaw by applying an opposite force with their foot pedals that moved their tail rudder. During the initial phase of the engine shut down procedure, the C-124 required a great amount of leg strength to hold enough rudder pressure to keep the aircraft flying straight. Thankfully, there was a crank, actually a small wheel device about eight inches in diameter, called the rudder trim. By adjusting the rudder trim for the tail rudder, the required leg pressure could be decreased until the aircraft flew straight without any rudder (pedal) pressure from the pilots. Then the aircraft flew as easily and straight as if all four engines were working.

When trimmed for straight flight, Major Baxter re-engaged the autopilot, looked out his left side window, and confirmed the propeller had stopped turning. The second engineer, downstairs, looked out the left window and confirmed the propeller had stopped turning, and there was no fire, smoke, or fluid leakage.

Max looked up the three-engine cruise power setting for their altitude, weight, and outside temperature. Then he advanced the remaining three engine throttles to the new power setting. Eddie opened his checklist to page E-2 and read out loud the portion marked ENGINE FAILURE/FIRE IN FLIGHT. Each crewmember responded to the checklist as if they were sitting in a classroom. Eddie was almost disappointed. It was a non-event.

"Shit," Major Baxter voiced his opinion when the checklist was finished. It pretty well spoke for the entire crew. "Could be that we're gonna miss the trip tomorrow to Taipei . . . I got a new gun cabinet that's ready to be picked up." He wasn't at all concerned about losing an engine but upset because he might not be able to pick up his custom made furniture from the Ricardo Linn Furniture shop in Taipei.

He looked at Eddie and instructed, "Call the MAC Command Post at Clark and alert them that we got a sick engine. Don't tell them that we shut it down or they'll all get into an uproar. I've shut down more engines than everyone combined in that command post." He motioned with his thumb toward Max, "And Max has probably shut down more than I have. What I don't need is for them to be sending me advice on how to fly this blimp. These old 4360s won't run without oil to lubricate their hundreds of moving parts, so anytime you're sure you're losing oil or oil pressure, ya gotta shut it down. Without oil the engine will overheat, then seize. When an engine this size seizes it's a sudden stop and the spinning propellers, with all their weight and inertia, can twist off from the engine shaft and go spinning away. The props are in line with our cockpit and if a spinning prop ever comes through the cockpit, we're all hamburger. Notice we didn't get in a hurry," he instructed Eddie. "Ya get in a hurry and ya make mistakes. The only time ya gotta get in a hurry is when you're on fire. I mean ya see flames, not just smoke, or when a propeller runs away out of control." Major Baxter was obviously in a preaching mode and Eddie sucked up the advice.

Eddie, only half serious and primarily to stimulate more conversation while the major was in the preaching mode, asked, "At Tinker they told us that in-flight the engineer could go down into the "P" compartment under the cargo floor, open the access door, and crawl out through the tunnel space into the wings—to the back side of the engines' firewalls. I inspected and crawled in the tunnel at Tinker cause I wanted to know for my own curiosity that the wing was that thick and it really had a crawlspace, a tunnel in it. Of course I did it on the ground without the engines running. Couldn't one of the flight engineers crawl out there and add more oil to the engine oil tank? I know we carry extra oil in the space under the cargo floor."

"Don't know of an engineer dumb enough to do that," was Baxter's answer. "First off, when you get a major oil leak, those engines can throw away oil a hell of a lot faster than you can drag it out there and pour it in the reservoir. Second, a sick engine covered with oil can catch fire and the engineer would be charcoal in a few seconds. Third, it's miserable out there, those engines put out an amazing amount of heat and noise."

Eddie digested the advice, then called the Clark MAC Command Post on the HF radio. He advised them they had a rough running engine and were flying at reduced speed. They would probably be ten minutes behind their previously estimated arrival time. The major nodded his head in approval. Eddie grinned to himself but was not sure why. So much for training in the States, this crew was the real world and had their own set of rules and procedures.

The aircraft flew quite well on three engines. They cruised about ten knots slower than normal and the three remaining engines ran a bit hotter at their higher power settings, but well within the perimeters of safe operation. Everyone went back about their tasks as if nothing unusual had happened. Eddie settled back down and out of curiosity got out his performance manual. He looked up another chart they had studied back at Tinker. It was labeled two-engine cruise. Major Baxter watched Eddie out of the corner of his eyes and chuckled, "What's the matter, son? We got ya worried now?"

"Just curious," Eddie answered as blasé as possible, but he was concerned at what he was seeing. According to the chart, at their weight and outside temperature, the aircraft couldn't maintain level flight at sea level with only two engines. "Chart shows here if we lose another engine we can't stay airborne," he announced to no one in particular.

Max pulled out his book and checked the same chart, then studied it for a while. "You're right . . . somewhat. If we lose another engine we can't maintain level flight, but with the remaining two engines at maximum continuous power, and from this altitude, we would drift down at a very slow rate and could possibly make it to land before we ran out of altitude."

Eddie continued his inquisition, "In the movies they throw out everything they can in order to lighten the airplane."

"Lots of luck throwing that forty-five thousand pound caterpillar out our five foot paratrooper side door!" Max countered.

Eddie bit his lip and was sorry he'd made such a naive remark.

"Throwing that caterpillar out the side door is the load master's job," Morey quipped and laughed. "Don't worry about it."

"Bullshit aside," Eddie was serious. "Could we probably make it to land if we feathered another engine?" Eddie made eye contact with the half-grinning flight engineer who threw his hands up and shrugged his shoulders. Eddie wasn't happy with everyone's unconcern, but he let the issue drop.

"Probably," Major Baxter remarked after a three-minute silence. "If ya wanted to be comfortable ya shoulda picked C-141 jets. Besides, don't worry about it. Chances of losing two on the same flight are so small, I'd bet my whole pot against it if it was a poker game." Eddie shrugged to demonstrate his unconcern, but he kept a sharp eye out for the coast of Luzon with its suitable landing fields. Eddie also wondered if Major Baxter was a very good poker player.

"I'm gonna call the Oasis Hotel on the HF," Max announced. "You officers wanna go off base tonight? Chances are we're gonna have a day off while they fix our number two engine."

"I've got a poker game lined up at the club for tonight," the major turned and made eye contact with Eddie. "I'll stay at the trailer houses." He shrugged his head at Eddie. "If you and Quincy wanna go off base go ahead, just call the command post and let em know where you're at."

Eddie looked at Quincy and received a thumbs up. Max caught the gesture, called the Oasis Hotel on the HF radio, and made arrangements for a pick up at the command post in two hours. Eddie was fascinated that they could use their military HF radio to call civilians and make personal arrangements. Probably the military didn't know, or just didn't feel it was a big deal. Whatever, there was a war going on. Rumor had it that the Oasis Hotel was affiliated with the Filipino HUK guerilla insurgents and the hotel used their radio for HF communication with other parts of the Philippines. The 22nd crewmembers never asked questions—no reason to screw up a handy way for making reservations and passing personal messages.

It was quiet for a while, then Quincy passed up another position report and Eddie passed it on over the HF radio. Later, the MAC Command Post called to check on their sick engine and Eddie lied and told them it was still usable at reduced power. They slipped in over the Lubang navigational station, started a slow let down abeam Corregidor Island, over Manila Bay, and Eddie obtained the weather and active runway from the Clark Approach Control. Checklists were performed and they made a visual straight-in approach to runway zero two. The major brought it in low over the base perimeter fence and greased on another landing. As they taxied in, with two fire engines following them, the major turned to Max and instructed, "Write number two engine up as feathered on short final with no time to notify the command post." As they slowly taxied to their spot on the recip ramp, their number two engine stood at frozen attention for all to see and wonder. In the 22nd's own little world, it was their own badge of courage.

The baggage drill was routine. Sergeant Hampton stayed with the plane while the rest of the crew rode the blue crew bus to the aerial port and Major Baxter went inside. The crew transferred their bags, except for the major's, into the adjacent waiting minivan. The van's door was labeled "Oasis Hotel." It seemed to Eddie that everyone except him knew Jose, the Filipino driver. Morey pulled a fresh bottle of Jim Beam from his bag, broke the seal, and passed it around. Everyone drew deeply from its golden throat. Eddie was exhausted, it had been a short day but the heat and humidity was a drain on his rooky body. After the constant beating of the engines and propellers, the stress from his first engine failure, very little to eat, Eddie took a second draw on the bottle and asked, "Can I help pay for this?"

"Compliments of the enlisted, Sir," was Morey's reply. "You scratch our back, we scratch yours." Eddie could feel the strength seeping back into his body and took another draw on the bottle.

For a while everyone just sat and enjoyed the air conditioning in the van. Eddie wondered out loud, "Nothing seems to rile Major Baxter; that old fart is a tough one to figure out."

"Don't underestimate him," Max commented. "I got a look at his form five one time and he had over 13,000 hours flying time, jumped once, and walked away from two total smash ups. He knows his way around. I guess the two totals are why he's only a major, but I'd fly with him anywhere." Eddie was amazed at how many stories were floating around explaining why Major Baxter was only a major.

"We ready to go, Sir?" Sergeant Maxwell asked Lieutenant Quincy.

Quincy finished his drag from the bottle and looked at Sergeant Maxwell, "Let's wait till the major releases us. He'll be out soon. And you can keep that Sir shit for the brass. We're alone now." Quincy handed the bottle to Max. "You're old enough to be my father."

"Yeah, who knows?" Max reflected. "I just might be. What did you say your mother's name was?"

The restricted door swung open and the major emerged, sauntered over to the van, and opened the door. The major looked around to make sure they were alone, took a long drag on the bottle, and handed it back to Morey.

"Gosh, Major Baxter! You're back so soon. I thought you might have a lot of paper work to fill out over that engine shut down." Morey was joking with a big smile.

"Don't underestimate me, Sergeant," the major tried to look tough but it was obvious he enjoyed the comment. "I found a staff sergeant that wants me to bring him two Papa San chairs from Okinawa. He agreed to do all my paper work for me in exchange for the chair's transportation. You guys be sure to check in with the command post so they know where you're staying. Right now it looks like we got tomorrow off. I'll check back at the transient desk later this evening and get non-availability slips for you guys staying off base. You don't need to stop at the transient quarters' office." The major crawled into the waiting blue air force van and headed for the trailers.

"Let's go, Jose," Max ordered the patient Oasis driver. It was obvious that Max was the undesignated leader of their motley troupe. "You got any girls that you could send to our rooms, some that aren't all wore out? We're thinking about having a little party."

"Yessir, Sergeant," Jose responded without hesitation. The brown skinned driver looked back at Sergeant Maxwell and grinned. His perfect white teeth and shiny black hair illuminated his enthusiasm. "I know some girls that just came in from Pao Lang, a little village from Mindanao. They're very nice . . . clean too. How many you need?"

"You bring two to my room an hour from now," Max replied. "I'll pay four dollars each if they're as good as you say. But none of those old street hags you tried to pawn off on me last week." Max leaned forward and slipped two packs of Salem cigarettes into the driver's glove compartment; the door was missing and it was full of miscellaneous junk. The cigarettes were payment for the transportation, plus tip.

"Five dollars!" the driver protested.

"Four dollars . . . and, if they're as good as you say, we'll take two more. But only after we see the first two."

"Okay," the driver closed the deal and slipped one of the cigarette packs into his shirt pocket.

Eddie was surprised at the simplicity of the transaction, as if they were bartering for a taxi ride. The dilapidated mini bus scurried down the boulevard and provided Eddie with his first good look at the rest of the base. There were large very old looking Acacia trees lining the roads, spreading their limbs and offering shade from the hot tropical sun. Everywhere there were little clumps of vegetation, banana trees, palms, and climbing vines of bougainvillea. Their brilliant pink and red blossoms accented the dark green vegetation. The ground cover was freshly trimmed native grass, naturally watered by the tropical rains. The buildings were spread out, leaving room for future growth.

Their van skidded to a halt at the side gate, allowing the American air policeman to inspect their interior. He noticed the almost empty bottle on the floor, eyed each crew member in their sweaty flight suits, and then locked onto the 22nd patch on Quincy's right shoulder. "You the guys that passed overhead here a while ago, had an engine shut down?" he asked.

"Ya, that was us," Max admitted with pride.

"You looked a little low; next time let me know you're coming," he smiled. "I'll open the gate for you." He laughed at his own joke then snapped to attention and gave them a sharp salute. Quincy returned the salute. The American air policeman stepped back from the van and the driver proceeded out the legendary side gate.

The outside road paralleled the base fence on the left and along the right side of the road was a long row of shabby looking storefronts and shacks. A cluster of colorful jeeps and their drivers waited in a group. The shop wares for sale were hung out in front to tempt the passersby. Eddie could see velvet paintings for sale, mostly of nudes copied from *Playboy* magazines, and stacks and stacks of woodcarvings. The woodcarvings were carved out of what they called monkey pod in Hawaii. There were wooden bowels and large spoon and fork sets designed to be displayed as wall hangings. One shop displayed religious carvings and several had wicker furniture. Other than the merchandise, everything was shabby and dirty looking. The hawkers were all out in front trying to flag down passing vehicles. Their children, dressed in rags, played on the ground. Vines, trees, and a mix of native weeds filled every space not taken up by a building. Banana trees, chickens, and dogs set the pace; the entire scene was covered with dust from some previous dry spell. There had been no rain in several days and the dirt road was filled with pot holes, freshly dried in the sun. The bus bounced continuously as Eddie hung on to his seat.

"You'll have plenty of time to buy stuff," Quincy noticed Eddie's interest. "Ya gotta barter and everything is really cheap. Their economy is a wreck. Tomorrow I'll take you to some of the better shops where they know us 22nd guys. You'll get better prices and they won't steal your watch and wallet."

Eddie gambled and let go of the seat railing with one hand as he took another drag from the almost empty bottle. He was happy and not necessarily from the whisky—at last he had a part in the movie.

They turned right and entered a housing area where Americans lived off base. The cinderblock houses had louvered windows, some with glass, some without, and large sweeping low pitched roofs. All the houses were painted white. All had white wooden picket fences and a sign with the occupants name on it. The houses were modern ranch style, well kept, and had the usual cropped grass, tropical trees, and bougainvillea with brilliant pink flowers.

"Off base housing," Quincy continued his tour guide duties. "You rent em from the local Filipino owners for around one hundred twenty-five dollars a month. Not so bad if you buy an air conditioner from the base exchange, chain it down good in the window, and cover all your other windows with plastic or glass to keep the cool in. The base has no authority or regulation over these houses and they're much nicer than the off base paddy houses back at Tachi. The only thing is that here you have to pay twenty-five dollars per month extra to the local Huks; else they'll steal you blind. Pay em off and they'll watch out for your house. They even have their own guards walking the streets at night, with automatic rifles, to keep the other thieves out. It's a cheap price for protection."

They made another hard right turn and pulled up in front of a large sprawling single story motel. A large wooden sign read The Oasis. A half dozen young bus boys, dressed in long black pants and crisp clean flowery sport shirts, scrambled to help the crew with their bags.

"Hello, hello," they all greeted the crew by flashing big smiles. Eddie felt like some sort of dignitary.

"Watch your bags," Quincy coolly warned Eddie. "Never let em out of your sight. They'll go through em and steal your goodies so fast you won't believe it."

Eddie looked the bag boys over again. "They sure seem friendly to me," he innocently answered.

"They're hustling us for tips like at any hotel. But be careful, they want your trust so they can get your luggage alone for a few minutes and go through your bags," Quincy cautioned Eddie. "They'll also try to sell you everything from women to clothing. Don't trust them or ever give em money until you've gotten to know your way around here. Stick close to your crew and never go out at night alone. There's always 22nd guys around so you'll be able to have a great time and still be safe."

The open air tropical lobby was without walls, simply a large wide roof on supports, with free standing reception desk and office partitions. Eddie had lived his entire life in Colorado and the concept of rooms without walls had never occurred to him. He was a four-season guy in an always warm one-season country. The tile floor, with its native water buffalo scene, continued uninterrupted from the curb, through the lobby, and down the covered walkways to the rooms.

They signed in at the desk; Quincy and Eddie shared a room. Eddie was struck by the beauty of the girl behind the desk. She was the first Filipino girl he had ever seen up close and she was beautiful, to the finest detail. She didn't have the Oriental look he had seen during his short stay on the base in Japan. The Japanese girls had slanted eyes, short bowed legs, unfamiliar gestures, and a false act of helplessness. This girl was a picture of confidence, a brown skinned beauty with dark flashing eyes. She was small in stature, about ninety-five pounds, and stood erect and proud. She had long, shiny black hair, small delicate lips, and a set of perfect white teeth. Her teeth fascinated Eddie; it seemed that all Filipinos had perfect teeth. She wore a multicolored mini dress that revealed a slender yet attractively proportioned frame. Eddie soared into a world of fantasies as she moved about her business behind the counter.

Quincy pulled Eddie from the counter and his dream world and pointed him down the walkway. "We gotta keep moving to keep our bags in sight," he lectured Eddie. "There's more where she came from." Eddie noticed that the enlisted men were following a different group of bus boys to a different wing of the motel. The officers and enlisted were more comfortable living apart from each other. As they walked, Quincy explained how many of the 22nd enlisted operated. "Some of the enlisted like to stay on base in the transient barracks where their safety is guaranteed. Others prefer staying in the various off base motels of their choice. Then there's a handful of flight engineers that own bars and whore houses downtown Angeles City. They usually stay in one of the upstairs rooms; the whores use the remaining rooms for work. Most all of the enlisted buy cigarettes, they run about twenty cents a pack in Tachikawa. They sell em on the black market down here for fifty cents a pack. They also use em as barter—one pack will get you a ride in a jeepney, two are worth a meal, and a carton will get you a girl for all night. There's also a big market for air conditioners, TVs, and stuff like that. Doesn't have to be new; used stuff from Tachikawa fetches a good price down here. The enlisted stuff em into the under-floor compartments of our airplanes at Tachikawa. Then, here at Clark they go back out to the airplane after the officers are gone, pull the booty out, and sell it to both local GIs and local Filipinos. Everyone knows about it but no one really gives a damn. The enlisted aren't paid nearly as much as the officers, so the money they make on the side kinda evens things out."

"Can I get you some girls, or anything to eat or drink?" the lead bus boy offered as his two assistants placed their bags in their room.

"Lumpia for two and four San Miguel beer," Quincy ordered. He slipped each of the Filipinos a quarter and the young men's eyes lit up at the generous tip. "There's more if nothing gets stolen from our room." He established solid eye contact with the young Filipino leader— eye contact was something difficult to establish with the Japanese back at Tachi.

The room was what Eddie expected: twin beds, a single bathroom in the rear, and the traditional poor oil painting hanging on the wall. The only things Filipino were the rattan furniture and the painting of another scene of a water buffalo, nipa hut, and palm tree.

"Five fifty apiece for the room," was Quincy's answer to Eddie's thoughts. "Ten if you want a single. Air force will reimburse us each eleven dollars per night for staying off base, so it's not a bad deal." Eddie crawled out of his flight suit and threw it into the corner. It was already starting to stink as the day's sweat began to ripen. "Bus boy will wash our flight suits from today and yesterday for a quarter. We'll give em to him when he delivers our lumpia. They'll have em on our door sill at five tomorrow morning. Nobody will steal em; they see laundry service as a source of income so nobody steals laundry, least from us 22nd guys." Eddie had no idea what lumpia was but the cheap cleaning bill and the San Miguel beer sounded great. He added his yesterday's flight suit to the pile by the door.

The shower was wonderful. The bourbon had dampened Eddie's weariness and he was looking forward to a few beers and something, whatever lumpia was, to eat. He stood under the cool water and maneuvered so it struck his face directly, then down his naked body and into the rusted drain in the stained concrete floor. Through the water he heard a knock on the front door and assumed it was the chow. Then he heard a lot of laughter and realized they had visitors. Quincy had mentioned there were other 22nd guys around, so Eddie assumed it was more new guys to meet. He continued his shower and tried to place the day's events into perspective. Back at

Tachi, Jim had told Eddie that most of the flying out of Clark was pretty boring and tiresome. It consisted of a series of shuttles back and forth into Vietnam with occasional over nights in Bangkok or Okinawa. So far, Eddie was pleased with everything. He could do this for a living. He certainly never expected to fly with an old fart like Major Baxter but it was turning out to be a real learning experience.

Outside the bathroom door someone was called a son of a bitch and there was laughter. It sounded like five or six guys laughing, and a woman's voice. Eddie recognized Jim's voice, his instructor pilot from Tachikawa. All of a sudden the shower curtain parted and a Filipino girl slipped into the shower with Eddie, wearing only a smile and saying nothing. Her mischievous grin, naked body, and blatant boldness stunned Eddie. She was not the same girl he had seen at the reception desk but she could have been one of her sisters. She looked no more than twenty years old, had beautiful brown skin, the same beautiful features, and the same long shiny black hair. Her delicate breasts were perfectly formed and her nipples were erect. Eddie could hear all the guys in the other room laughing as she offered her open hand and he realized the bathroom door was wide open. Eddie was dumbstruck! He didn't know what to do, so he handed her the soap. The guys outside the open door laughed and one of them hollered, "That's not what she wants."

She closed the shower curtain, widened her smile, and slowly soaped him down, with special attention to his personal areas. As he rinsed off the soap, he couldn't resist the temptation—she allowed him the pleasure of exploring her curves with his hands. His arousal was obvious.

"Enough, you horny bastard! Welcome to the 22nd." It was Jim Beckle, he had a beer in one hand and with the other he reached through the shower curtain and shut off the water. Other guys were crowded in the doorway and saluting with their beers. Eddie recognized several from the previous evening at the Clark O'Club and he assumed the others were 22nd. None looked exactly sober.

"I see you've meet Vicky and like her," the tallest one teased as he offered Eddie a beer and starred at Eddie's personals. "Ya like her a lot!" Eddie was wrapping a towel around his waist and trying to conceal his boner. "She sorta belongs to the 22nd," the tall one continued. "We figured we would get you off to a good start. If you want anything else from her you'll have to pay for it like everyone else around here." Vicki grabbed a towel and dried off while she led the troop of voyeuristic drunks out of the bathroom and into the bedroom. While everyone introduced themselves to Eddie, she showed not the least bit of modesty—smiling at Eddie and the others. She toweled her provocative frame and pretended not to care as she afforded private exposures to everyone's view and delight. She then slipped into her brief panties, pulled her stylish mini-dress down over her head, then continued towel drying her long black hair.

The tall guy was introduced as Tally Wacker; his real name was Jerry Whacker but everyone just called him Tally. He was a tall slim individual, rugged in appearance, with wide shoulders that were out of proportion with the rest of his body. He spoke with a twinkle in his eye and a heavy hillbilly twang. There was Smokey, a nondescript Caucasian who never offered his real name and had a propensity for practical jokes. The name on his flight suit said Robins— he was too far gone to say much. Conejo and Slick, from the officers club happy hour the night before, completed the group.

Eddie dried with his towel while the group watched Vicki. He slipped into a pair of Bermuda shorts and a light-weight short sleeved shirt. Everyone else wore similar loose tropical clothes. Vicki manipulated her long, black, damp hair into a knot on the top of her head. It revealed her delicate neck and made her look quite sophisticated.

Eddie was half way around the world, had his ticket punched in Vietnam, had to shut down an engine in-flight, was half a sheet to the wind on bourbon, and was fantasizing about the naked squadron whore he had just publicly showered with. So far it had been a good day.

* * * * * * * * * * * * * * * * * * * *

The lumpia was wonderful, a Filipino dish made of anything on hand—fish, shrimp, beef, or whatever, mixed with vegetables and placed in dough blankets. Then deep fried and served hot. Served with seasoned

44

dip, it was basically a Filipino copy of Chinese egg rolls. There were as many variations as one could imagine and Eddie was instantly hooked on the new food.

The group flowed outside and down the sidewalk to the pool. They carried their extra beers and the remains of the lumpia to a large table next to the pool. Then they dragged in enough chairs to seat everyone. The pool was quite large and kidney shaped. The water was crystal clear and clean, something not common with the lower priced hotels in the Angeles City area. An expansive tile deck surrounded the pool, featuring an elevated wooden deck for sunbathing during the day. American big band music came out of speakers somewhere in an area edged with banana trees, bushes, and tall grass. The setting was nostalgic, a perfect way for the warm, humid Filipino day to end. Eddie was surprised at the tile, a modern design and no water buffalo or nipa hut. A large outdoor bar adorned the far edge of the pool, featuring a base of vertical rattan and a solid piece of dark rich wood for the top. The top was formed from one solid piece of tropical Nara wood, three feet wide, three inches thick and over fifteen feet long.

A young Filipino man, in a bright red sport shirt, stood behind the bar. Jim flagged him over and ordered another round of beer for everyone and two more plates of lumpia. Vicki declined the beer but helped herself to the lumpia. Talk was casual, about flying. It was true, pilots really do talk about women whenever they are flying and about flying whenever they are on the ground around women. As Eddie finished the lumpia from the generously filled tray, he pondered the difference a day had made. The night before he felt awkward with that crowd, but one night later, he was just another guy.

Vicki was not included in the conversation. She sat modestly and patiently, occasionally exchanging glances with Eddie as he half participated in the camaraderie. Others noticed but pretended not to notice. He felt as if he was being worked over by a pro, but the whiskey was working, the beer was great, and the evening was warm. Her beautiful brown skin and shiny black hair glistened in the pool's reflected light. Eddie decided the movie that he was living in was a Bogart movie, an Asian variety.

He returned to reality as a two ship formation of F-4 fighters broke free from the nearby runway and rocketed overhead into the late afternoon sky. The thunder from their afterburners broke the pool's quiescence and abruptly ended their conversations. As peace returned, everyone continued as if the disturbance had never occurred and Eddie resumed his live fantasy.

It was like that in a cockpit. A conversation could be taking place and if they received a call on the radio, or something involved with flying the airplane demanded attention, the conversation would cease in mid-sentence. The required task would be completed and the conversation would continue as if never interrupted. This idiosyncrasy sometimes spooked non-flyers but Vicki was used to it.

Eddie was mesmerized with Vicki; he felt very vulnerable.

* * * * * * * * * * * * * * * * * * * *

Eddie had never been exactly a Casanova with the girls. When he was twelve years old, one of the neighborhood farm boys, a nineteen year old, got one of their neighborhood girls pregnant. The girl's father had confronted the boy when he was changing the irrigation set in a field of sugar beets and the two of them had gone at each other with their irrigation shovels. It was just like the knights of old with their swords. The old man won, beat the hell out of the young boy, and put him in the hospital. The next day, Eddie's father had taken him and his mother to see the boy at the hospital. He was all bruised and bandaged, with cuts across his scalp from the shovel blade. When they left the hospital, his father told Eddie's mother, in front of Eddie, "The son of a bitch knocked her up and he got what he deserved." He then turned to Eddie and shook his finger at him, "Just let this be a lesson for you!" It took Eddie a few minutes to comprehend what "knocked her up" meant, but he managed because every twelve year old farm boy knew all about breeding, be it their cattle, chickens, women, or a neighborhood girl. It left a permanent scar on Eddie's romantic ventures.

In high school and college he was never very popular with the girls. He was acceptable looking, had a trim muscular build seasoned by working on a farm, and maintained a closely cropped crew cut. His family was ethnic German and very strict. Eddie had manners drummed into him, but around strangers and especially girls, he was very reserved. Social graces around girls were not taught on the farm. At Greeley High School the "town" girls were not interested in a farm dorkus as a boy friend.

Eddie never forgot the "knocked up" lesson and as a teenager he seriously avoided the farm girls from his community. He would never take a chance on knocking one of them up, least his father would hit him in the head with a shovel. He convinced himself that the farm girls all wanted to get pregnant, get married, and live on a farm. Even without his father's pregnancy threat, Eddie couldn't imagine farming and raising a bunch of rebellious children—especially on the same family farm with his father. His father was an old school German, ruled with a clenched fist, and thought of nothing but farming.

Eddie carried the baggage from his rural culture and high school days to college. At Colorado State University he felt uncomfortable whenever on one of the occasional dates that he had. He did date several girls, several times, and had some interesting petting sessions. He had even gone skinny dipping one time. But his lack of technique, lack of self-confidence, and inherited shyness resulted in his never making it all the way into any of their hearts, or their panties.

His virginity problem was never solved and Eddie lived as an independent youth, with private frustrations. Eddie never dated during his year at pilot training; he concentrated on perfecting his profession and his only diversion was the mystique surrounding the painting of the Lady.

* * * * * * * * * * * * * * * * * * * *

Eddie was totally unprepared for Vicky at the swimming pool. For most of his short life he had planned on running away to a land of mystique and adventure and beautiful women. But at last he had arrived in La La Land and he was overwhelmed with fear of failure.

Two rounds of beer and a lot of fretting later, Smoky, Quincy, and Jim decided to go to the Casino. They only half-heartedly asked Eddie to join them. He declined, taking their hint. The Casino was located downstairs from the main lobby of the motel and was supposed to be a secret, but everyone knew about it. Eddie didn't understand the secret bit; they needed customers to justify its existence. The others decided to call it a night as they had to fly early in the morning. That left Eddie and Vicki sitting at the table, a very obvious and courteous thing for them to do.

"Sure you wouldn't like a beer or something?" he asked Vicki after the crowd had gone. He had consumed all he needed and was new at this. Without the background of the other guys and their standard macho conversation, he was searching for words alone with Vicki.

"Something would be nice," she replied as she put him at ease with her dark shiny eyes. "Maybe we go to your room and relax together? Quincy maybe spend half the night in the casino; he like to gamble."

"Sounds good to me," Eddie replied, then quickly added, "Going to my room, I mean . . ." He was trying to be cool as he stood up but he clumsily stumbled over the chair next to him. Vicky tried to hide her smile.

They walked, holding hands like teenage sweethearts, back to his room and into the air-conditioned blast of cold air. The room was a mess. The guys had only been there a short time but there were empty beer cans strewn about and a cigarette was squished dead on the bed stand, next to a clean ashtray. Four stinking flight suits, two days worth of flying for the two occupants, greeted them inside the door. Quincy had forgotten to give them to the bellboy. Once inside, Eddie closed the door slowly as he wondered how to approach Vicki.

"You give me ten dollars," she broke the silence and the sensuous mood with her brazenness. She stood there with a serious look on her face, her tiny hand outstretched. Eddie was startled.

"I'll pay you five dollars, like everyone else does." Eddie couldn't believe himself. He was bartering for pussy just like the enlisted did in the crew van. He was put off by it then and was disgusted with himself.

Vicki sensed his problem and used her skills to salvage the deteriorating negotiation. "I need make living just like everyone else. I have family in Baguio, my mother, three sisters, brother, my grandmother. I only income they have." Then she lowered her eyes and continued her well-practiced routine. "Besides, all guys in the 22nd pay me ten dollars; they tell everyone they pay five dollars so they can be like big shots." She held out her arms and continued, "Look at me, I'm clean, I only go with guys that I know and I get checked for VD every month. I no steal from you because everyone in the 22nd know me, and besides, you make lots of money and you just get your ticket punched and you need to be a real pilot and make love after your engine quit today."

Her show was worth ten dollars but Eddie swung his head no and grumbled, "Eight dollars," for effect.

"Eight dollars, this time a special introduction!" she answered quickly and Eddie realized he had been a push over. He started to undress, feeling cold, like whenever he was undressing in a doctor's examination room.

"Pay me now, please," she demanded. "You always pay before you do fuckie me."

Eddie was thoroughly disgusted with the events but his German stubbornness carried him forward. He wanted this woman and eight dollars seemed like a real bargain. Vicky looked beautiful and luscious. He was standing with his shirt off and his pants down around his knees. He knew he looked like a fool as he bent over and fished through the pocket of his crumbled pants. He pulled out his billfold, and gave her a five and three ones. He tried to not let her see how much money he had left in his wallet.

"I'll be right out." She grabbed the money and made a beeline for the bathroom, as if she needed to hide her dignity. Eddie looked after her, needing to use the bathroom himself. The beer needed one last round of attention. He thought about pulling up his pants and running out the door, but the room was his and his actions would get back to the other guys in the squadron. He pulled his pants back up and moved a few things around, trying to clean up the room. Why, he didn't know. She was just a prostitute and already had his money. Things were going a little fast for him. "Was he getting in over his head?"

The bathroom door opened and Vicki re-emerged. She was wearing only a bath towel and her long black hair was loose and beautiful. She looked very provocative and Eddie changed his mind for the fifth time that evening. Despite the shabby room and the distaste of their recent bartering session, Eddie was enthralled with the beautiful young woman.

"I'll be right out." He caught himself repeating Vicki's line and he made a beeline for the head. He had to pee like a race horse. Vicki's dress was neatly folded on the bathroom shelf and he imagined his eight dollars neatly folded away somewhere in the creases. "I guess we'll just have to trust each other," he thought. "Besides, it's only eight dollars and it was a life time experience." Then he realized he was in the bathroom with the door closed and his pants were on the floor in the bedroom—with his wallet in the pocket! "What a dope he was." He would have to sharpen up on his street skills.

He turned out the bathroom light as he opened the door. Vicki had turned off the overhead room lights. She was standing by the dresser, across the room from the bed, and had just turned on the forty watt dresser lamp. She turned and looked at him, then let the towel drop to the floor. Stark naked, she walked across the room and gracefully slipped in between the sheets. She had the grace of a cat. A thrill ran through his body as he had never imagined being alone with such a beautiful creature. He finished disrobing on the move and followed her between the sheets. After a short pause, he gently ran his hands all over her responsive body. She felt different from the several college girls he had experimented with. Her dark skin was taut, and she was lean and strong. Her nipples were rigid and sensitive. His right hand followed the curves of what his eyes had lusted. He explored every dip and bend. She responded to his crude foreplay and actively moved the process along. Eddie had been told that American girls preferred preliminaries to actual intercourse. Perhaps Vicki hurried things along because she was a professional and interested in getting "it" done. She seemed impatient while he wanted things to drag on forever. She let him drive but she was directing the traffic. It was her job and she was good at it. He was amazed when she seemed to produce a condom from nowhere and at how deft she was at quickly rolling it onto his penis.

He succumbed to his desires and consummated their business arrangement. It was the ride he had always fantasized, maybe better. Half way through she rolled over on top and sat straddling him. They finished with all the open violence and passion of two wild animals.

Eddie eased her off and realized he was sweating profusely, as was she. The sweat just added to the lust of the affair. Vicki rolled out of bed and headed for the bathroom and left Eddie lying on his back—decompressing. With her it was obviously a business and she could turn it on and off like a machine. He quickly checked his wallet. It was still in his pants pocket and all of his money was still there.

He lay back on the bed and contemplated his accomplishment. "Why did she have to be a whore? He could love a woman like this." But he knew, sub-consciously, he had to keep things under control. LBFMs, he was disgusted when he first heard the guys use the acronym for Little Brown Fucking Machines—their description of Asian prostitutes. Now he understood. You can rent them by the job, hour, or the night, anywhere in Southeast Asia.

Vicki returned, comfortably nude, and sat on the edge of the bed as they talked. "You married?" she asked in an innocent manner. Eddie couldn't keep his eyes off her.

"No, I've never had that experience," he answered. But he wondered, "Do prostitutes get married?"

"I'm not married, yet," Vicki confided, nonchalantly and answering his thoughts. "But I do support my family at my village. My father was killed in government raid when they looking for Huks four years ago. . . I know what you thinking. I know it wrong for me to be call girl, but my family is good Catholics. Our village very poor and my family need food. There no jobs for my brothers and this way we have money, everyone to eat, and my brothers and sisters can go to school."

"Your father was a Huk!" Eddie exclaimed.

"Not all Huks Communists!" she answered defensively. "Huks want to get rid of the bad Marcos government and want to fix all the bad things the government does to people," she lectured. "Many Huks pretend with the Communist Huks because they give guns and ammunition and radios, like that. Our people remember Japanese very much and will never let outside people to take over our country again." She lay on the bed next to him on top of the sheets. Eddie noticed her pubic hair was sparse. "You need to know there are two kinds of Huks, most like my father. They only use the Communists. The other Huks that want Communism for Philippines are need to be controlled. Sometimes the two kinds of Huks fight each other. The Chinese and Russian Huks make all the trouble for Americans. My father's Huks know that the Americans are important. The Americans pay much money to President Marcos for air bases here, but people also make money from business around the bases and from jobs working on base. I pay one dollar each week to the Huks so I can work here Oasis Hotel. If I get into trouble Huks will help me. They know who my father was. They have guns and are everywhere, you just no see them." Eddie didn't know if he should believe her or not, maybe some of it was true. But regardless of the truth, it was one hell of a story.

"You pay four dollars each month to the Huks?" Eddie prodded her for more information. This stuff couldn't be found in text books.

"All working girls do, and jeepney drivers, store owners, maids on base, everyone pays to the Huks and the Huks keep things okay for the people. Lots of the leaders are business men in Angeles City and most Huk guards are volunteers and work for little money. The government men stay away from here unless they come with lots of soldiers."

"I guess four dollars isn't that much," Eddie reflected.

"Lot for the maids and base workers. Normal wage one dollar each day. When I work on base a maid for colonel, he pay thirty dollars each month, big money for woman. When maid I pay one dollar and fifty cents each month to Huks."

"Is that where you learned to speak English so well?" Eddie asked.

"I take care his children and help cook and clean house. He have two Filipinos work his house. I work three years, then he move back to America."

"When did you become a prostitute?"

"Colonel have go away party and lots of people come. It was end my job. I drink too much colonel whiskey and went to bed with three Americans of Twenty-Two Squadron. They think me call girl and give me fifteen dollars. In morning I saw I make two weeks pay on one night and I like it, they nice to me. So, I kept stay

48

with Twenty-Two Squadron and here tonight. I not need pimp, I can say no when I not like man or he look dirty, maybe have clap. I lots of time here at Oasis and Twenty-Two Squadron men nice to me and Oasis nice to me cause I good for business and make no problems. Oasis also pay Huks. I have best arrangement. I have bed other side street I can sleep for twenty cents each night, if I not sleep here with customer. I go home my village ten days each month." The conversation ended as she slipped back into the bed and gave Eddie a repeat performance. After the second time, he was whipped and fell into a deep sleep. The long day of flying, the booze, heat and humidity, then unleashed first time sex were more than his strong young body could handle.

When Quincy came in and closed the door, Eddie woke with a start. The lights were on and Vicky was standing next to his bed, slipping her dress on. Eddie looked at his watch and was surprised he had been asleep three hours. Quincy and Vicky both laughed at his dumbfounded expression.

"You stay with me as customer!" Vicky lectured with her index finger. "If you sleep like that with girls from street or maybe bar, you wake up in empty room. You wallet, you wrist watch, electric shaver, maybe you clothes, all gone. Too much to pay for some pussy." She giggled at herself.

CHAPTER FOUR: CITY OF ANGELS

The next morning Eddie had a bitch of a hangover. Quincy came out of the bathroom drying his nude frame with a plain white bath towel. He grinned at Eddie and remarked, "Looked like you had a good time. Vicky winked at me and gave me a thumbs up when I came in last night."

Eddie sat up and held his head in his hands. "Fuck me, who are you guys? I came over here to fly airplanes and to see the war from a safe distance and you guys corrupt me beyond all decency."

"Isn't it great?" Quincy laughed. His white teeth glistened next to his black skin. Eddie wondered if Caucasians were the only people that had crooked, off white teeth. "You'll get your share of the flying, believe me. After six months you'll start to think that you live in our old birds." After a pause he continued, "I checked in with the command post last night and they released us for the day. They're still working on our number two engine. I was thinking that after we shower, we can get some breakfast here at the motel restaurant; then we'll grab a jeepney downtown. I'll show you around the shops and point out a couple of restaurants that I like."

The eggs and pancakes were wonderful, and for his first time ever, Eddie had fried bananas. Eddie had coffee. Quincy had a Miguel beer as a jump-start. As they ate Quincy smiled and with his mouth half full of eggs, casually asked Eddie, "Did she give you the story about her grandmother and her family? Ya know! How she's putting her brothers and sisters through school because her Huk father was killed by the soldiers? I've heard that story at least a half dozen times from a half dozen different guys." Quincy was married to a beautiful woman who worked for an advertising agency in Tokyo. He had the reputation of always being faithful to her.

Eddie choked on his load of pancakes and when he finally got them all down he laughed, "Yeah, I'm afraid I might have bought that one. When she stripped naked my brains all slipped down into the head of my dick."

"She's sweet talking, good looking, and I hear she's heaven in bed, but she's still a whore. Don't forget that!" Quincy reminded Eddie.

They flagged down a jeepney and Eddie had another first time ever ride. Jeepneys evolved after World War II, when lots of American Jeeps, some abandoned, many stolen from the American Army, were pressed into service for civilian transportation. The Filipino propensity for colorful artwork prevailed and their jeeps became brightly decorated and ordained with excessive trim. The art work that covered them was a mixture of both Catholic religion and Pagan heritage. Colorful and garish, jeepneys were used to provide unregulated taxi service. More jeeps were imported and a national tradition was born. One had their choice of flagging down a "regular" jeepney, paying a very low fare that was set in each driver's mind, and squeezing in between a usually full load of sweaty Filipinos. Or, one could flag down a "special," pay a little more fare and ride in privacy. Quincy and Eddie rode a special south along the perimeter road just outside the Clark Air Base fence, across the railroad tracks, and down the main street and into Angeles City. As they bounced along from pot hole to pot hole, Quincy leaned over and explained to Eddie, "If you ever take one of these by yourself and they turn off into a side street or alley, jump out and run to beat hell. Get the number if you can, there's one on the side of each jeepney. Chances are he's trying to take you somewhere he's got friends waiting, and rob you.

When you get back to the Oasis tell the manager the jeepney number and he'll take care of things for you. The Huks love to beat the hell out of jeepney drivers that try to rob Americans under their protection."

Angeles City was booming. Rag tag shops were everywhere. Children and prostitutes mixed with GIs and locals on the sidewalks; dogs and skinny, dirty chickens were abundant. Whores, soldiers, con artists, and thieves all co-existed in this unsightly haven of crime and unsavory business. It was a blight that had grown from unregulated contact between a people who were poor and American servicemen separated from their own culture—with pockets full of cash. This was a thief's den that neither the Americans occupying the air base nor the Filipino people could take any pride in. There were jeepneys everywhere as people were transported to and from their daily business. The buildings were wooden and mostly in disrepair. Downtown, a good number of the buildings were two stories, with shops, bars, and restaurants below and living quarters above. The term "living" was a stretch; maybe existence quarters was a better description. Even the birds reflected the neighborhood. Those in the tough neighborhoods, such as they were riding through, had birds that were dirty brown and black. They were rough ugly birds that were always squawking and fighting. The vegetation they sat in was scrubby and unattractive. The nicer neighborhoods, such as back at their motel, had fuller and greener foliage and the birds were colored purples, reds, and vibrant greens.

Quincy hustled Eddie through a downstairs bar and up a set of loosely assembled wooden stairs. At the downstairs bar several GIs were hanging out. A handful of slutty looking girls were working them over, rubbing their barely covered breasts against them and reaching inside the GI's trousers. Eddie was surprised to see drunken GIs that early in the day; however they did appear to be enjoying the attention. Upstairs, on the street end of the building, was a decent sized room. It had a half dozen tables, worn wooden floors, stucco walls painted bright blue, and no pictures on the wall. A smattering of worn, mismatched chairs completed the décor. Extending rearward was a single hallway. It had doors that opened to the various bed equipped rooms where the bar girls both lived and took their clients for sex. Eddie and Quincy opted for one of two tables located on the store front balcony—through a set of dilapidated French doors. It was shady and afforded a good view of the street scene below. By 10:00 p.m. that night there would be a dozen drunken GIs hanging over that same balcony's rail, shouting at the rowdy crowd in the street below and making an occasional trip down the hallway to the rear bedrooms for a quickie. That morning, Eddie and Quincy were the only occupants. As they settled into their chairs, an older woman with a bad left eye hobbled up the stairs and asked if they wanted anything to drink and if they wanted any girls. They both ordered a San Miguel and were very specific in saying no girls. Eddie certainly didn't want a shark frenzy like they had just witnessed downstairs.

They relaxed in the shade as they watched the hectic street scene unfold below. Two young Filipino men, wearing makeshift uniforms, casually worked their way down the street—checking things out and occasionally asking questions as they went. They both were wearing small submachine guns that hung from slings over their shoulders. Quincy had no idea if they were soldiers or Huks or bandits looking for someone. "I just leave them alone and they leave me alone," was Quincy's advice. "You don't even wanna know who they are!" Quincy hesitated and with a straight face he continued, "Angeles City turns into South East Asia's most notorious sin city whenever the sun sets. It was reported, however, that drunken 22nd trash hauler pilots and navigators, under trance from oversized erections of undersized penises, would go places after dark in Angeles City that a squad of sober marines, armed with M-16 machine guns, would be afraid to enter." Eddie rolled his eyes and smiled at Quincy's humor.

The bar's speakers were blasting the air with the worst of American culture, at least in Eddie's viewpoint— Country Western Music. It was okay for others but it reminded him of growing up in Colorado. The farm community he grew up in was surrounded by cattle ranches and endless miles of prairie. Eddie loved the prairie and grew up around the cowboys. Guys with cow shit on their cowboy boots, huge silver belt buckles, a wad of tobacco stuffed into their cheek, and hats they never took off. He was good friends with a number of them. In Eddie's immediate community most of them were real cowboys. However, in Northern Colorado there was also a significant number that were "all hat and no cows." Their cowboy boots were always clean and expensive looking. They had never branded or castrated a calf and had never "fixed" a fence. In Eddie's opinion, these phony wannabes were just cross dressers from reality. Why, he had no idea. Eddie's mother frequently reinforced his opinion when she told him that wearing a hat indoors was bad manners, she called it costume dressing. But the thing that bothered Eddie the most were the cowgirls and the cowgirl wannabes. They also wore the boots, big belt buckles, and pearl buttoned shirts. They spoke with phony West Texas drawls and used their tits as a weapon to tease poor farm boys like Eddie. Maybe Eddie's prejudice had something to do with when he was a freshman home from college for the summer. He had put some moves on the wrong cowgirl at Nick's Place—a bar in a one horse prairie town called Snyder, Colorado. Her cowboy friend beat Eddie's face into a pulp and cracked two of his ribs. He looked like one of the phony cowboys and Eddie had no way of knowing he was also a sophomore football player for the University of Colorado. The country music they were playing in that Filipino bar was the last song he had heard in Snyder, Colorado, before he barfed and then passed out on the bar room floor.

Two slutty, unkept Filipino girls came up the stairs and zeroed in on Eddie and Quincy. Boldly sauntering over, each chose a victim, and without a word proceeded to rub their hands all over them—in places that Eddie didn't want them to touch. Eddie's tried to reach inside his pants and he grabbed her hand and held her off. Quincy suffered the same humiliation. Both Eddie and Quincy countered the girl's movements while trying to protect their pockets that contained their wallets. The whore's objective, crude as it was, was to arouse their prospective clients. All Eddie could think of was the phrase "Clap Trap."

"You want fuckie fuckie?" Eddie's attacker whispered in his ear. He got a heavy whiff of an odor, a combination tobacco smoke, perspiration, and something that was possibly fish. She needed a bath and especially to wash her hair.

"No fuckie fuckie, go away!" Eddie threw her groping hand away and returned his hand into his pocket to insure his wallet was still there.

"We no fuckie fuckie cause we have clap!" Quincy explained with a straight face. "You go wash your hands or you get clap too."

The girls got the message and both gave Quincy the finger. "You number ten GI!" the uglier one exclaimed. She turned to Eddie and wrinkled her nose and upper lip, "You too, fuck head!" Then they tramped down the stairs. Their scale in Asia was just the opposite of the American scale. For the Asian prostitutes, number ten was the worst and number one was the best.

Eddie and Quincy both laughed and Quincy added, "Now you know why we stay at the Oasis and not downtown. I would never come to Angeles City if the best buys on wood carvings, oil paintings, and wicker furniture weren't down here. I just felt you needed to see this place to believe it."

Their beers finished, Quincy stood up and announced, "Let's go do it." They felt their way down the stairs and out through the bar. Eddie noticed several new GIs had joined the bar, while the previous two were nowhere to be seen. The same sleazy whores, minus two, were hanging onto the new guys, giving them the treatment. "Whores," Quince quietly explained. "They try to get you to buy em drinks—then they serve the girls watered down Coke and charge high drink prices. After you leave the bar girls get a cut on the tab. If they get you to rent their room, by the hour, to screw, they get a cut of the room rent as well as half the price of the trick they turn. Most of em are no better than common thieves. Give em money up front then let em out of sight and it's the last you'll ever see of them. They're required to get a venereal disease check-up once a month. But if you're stupid enough to screw one and she's on the last week before her check, lord knows what you're exposing yourself to. Conejo, the 22nd's Latin lover, is the only officer in our squadron that screws these street whores down here and no one knows how he keeps from getting all clapped up. He claims he goes bare back but I really think he uses rubbers."

They ambled down the wooden sidewalk the bandits had previously searched. "There're lots of beautiful, really nice women in the Philippines," Quince conceded. "Some of the most beautiful women I've ever seen are in the Philippines and in Thailand. But you'll never see the nice families and the decent women in this rat hole. Today we just happen to be walking downtown in the asshole of the Philippines. The rest of the Philippines are something the average GI never gets a glimpse of. If you ever get away from the American military bases you'll find that the majority of the Filipino people are wonderful and the women are decent and honorable; mostly poor but nice."

Eddie wondered if maybe the painting of the Lady had been from Thailand. It certainly couldn't have originated in the Angeles City quagmire.

They ducked through a doorway filled with hanging beads and into a small shop filled with woodcarvings. A little boy, maybe two years old, naked and dirty, scurried from them and through another bead-filled doorway in the back of the shop. He peered back through the beads with his big brown eyes to see what he ran from— then disappeared again. He needed to blow his nose. An old woman dressed in a baggy cotton print emerged. The dress was red with large white and yellow tropical flowers printed all over it. Gaudy, but people with dark skin can get away with wearing bright clothing. This poor old woman probably wore it because it was the only half way decent dress she had. The floor was dirt and she wore no shoes. Her feet were dirty and uncared for, her long black hair a tangled mess, and she was very wrinkled. For some reason Eddie instantly felt a kindness for her. She smiled and showed several missing teeth, the rest were black as coal. This frightened Eddie.

"Nice to see you again," she greeted Quincy. "Is this your friend?" She turned to Eddie and again displayed her black teeth with her grin. "You buy wood today? I give you very good price."

"My friend's first time in the Philippines," Quincy replied. "I'm showing him Angeles City. I brought him to your number one shop to look around. Maybe someday he buy and you give him number one price . . . okay?"

"Number one price," she nodded her head yes then cackled and coughed. She smelled like tobacco of some sort. They slowly worked their way around the shop and the old woman with shiny black teeth followed at a comfortable distance. It was hot and very humid and there was no breeze in the shop. Eddie broke into a deep sweat as they strolled around. The sweat got in his eyes and they burned fiercely, so he repeatedly wiped his forehead and eyes with his short sleeves and his loose shirt tail. His pits were wet down to his pants and he was very uncomfortable. Quincy pretended not to notice and the old woman wondered if Eddie had some sort of disease.

There were monkey pod bowls filled with wooden fruit for US $1.25 each. Eddie thought it was $1.25 for each piece of fruit and was surprised the $1.25 was for the bowl and all the beautifully carved fruit. There were wooden Carabao of all sizes, beautiful large serving bowls of all shapes, and ugly face masks for one's wall. There were lots of porno carvings; Quincy's favorite was a wooden man wearing a wooden barrel. When the barrel was slipped off, an oversized penis mounted on a spring, would pop straight out. As a result of years of bartering, Quincy knew what price to offer for each item.

"It's nice and it's cheap, but what do I want with any of this stuff?" Eddie asked. "My quarters will be at the BOQ back at Tachi, and the way it looks I won't be spending much time there."

"Back in the States this stuff costs ten times what it costs here," Quincy explained. "Buy it and when you get a bunch of it in Tachi, wrap it all up in a box and send it back home. Military mail rates are cheap. The bigger stuff you pack and store in your room, then ship it back to the States as household goods when your tour is up. Your family and relatives back in the States will go nuts over it. For us married guys, it's easy cause we got more room in our houses to store stuff. Makes great Christmas presents too. Buy your wood, wicker, and rattan in the Philippines, shoji screens in Okinawa, stereo equipment in Japan, ceramic elephants in Vietnam, jewelry and bronze ware in Thailand, and custom made furniture in Taiwan. Korea's got beautiful wooden chests. It's a once in a life time opportunity to stock up on this stuff for next to nothing."

Eddie still wondered if he needed any of it.

They thanked the old woman and moved back into the sun. Quincy continued, "The ground pounders can't shop all over Asia like we can, and us trash haulers are the only ones that have extra room in our airplanes to transport stuff. Especially stuff like furniture from Taipei. When I buy things, I buy several and then sell the extras for my cost to the non-flyers back at Tachi. Sometimes I take orders from them when I go out on trips. In exchange they have my wife and me over for dinner, invite us to parties, buy us drinks at the Tachi bars and treat us like kings. I do them favors and they do us favors. The 22nd's like one big family."

"Did you see that old woman's teeth?" Eddie tilted his head toward the shop. "They were shiny black. Is that some sort of disease down here?"

Quincy laughed. "Betel nut, it's a nut from a plant that the old people chew on. It's a mild narcotic and stains their teeth black. Sometimes they get a little numb when they chew it and the juice drools out their mouth and down their front. The juice is a dark red. You'll see a lot of old people with black teeth here and in Vietnam. It's the drug of choice for old depressed poor people. It's free for the picking."

"You chew that shit and we'd never find you in the dark," Eddie joked with Quincy. "Black teeth and a black dick, those girls would really have the stories to tell their friends!"

Quince grinned and remarked, "Maybe I could get the white girls to pay me. I'll have to talk to my wife about that."

They visited rattan stores and priced portable rattan bars with thick, solid wooden tops and six rattan bar stools—all for US$125. They would sell for a thousand back in the States but were so big you needed a C-124 to haul them. "I just happened to have one of each," Quincy bragged to Eddie. "C-124 and a bar." They toured wicker shops and visited art galleries and looked at hundreds of oil paintings. Most of the paintings were trash but there was an occasional jewel in the bunch. Eddie saw one he almost bought. Framed, it was $12.00 but Quincy told him the price was too high.

Lunch consisted of more San Miguel and they each had a plate full of lumpia. Eddie always thought that only women went shopping. But there they were, shopping and having lunch on the other side of the world. And he was enjoying it. Finding the better made items and bartering a decent price was more of a sport than Eddie first expected. As the day progressed, they stopped at a restaurant called Poppaguyo's and had a water buffalo steak and a big order of French fries. The water buffalo meat was lean and dark and had a light and delicious flavor. Then they visited more shops as Eddie tried to remember which ones catered to the 22nd and which ones to watch out for.

Later they caught another special back to their motel, wolfed down two hamburgers and an order of fries from the restaurant, then took cold showers. They put on fresh, dry clothes and caught the motel bus on base to the officers club. They arrived at 6:00 p.m., later than they wanted but in time for the tail end of happy hour. Quincy called operations on the club's hallway phone and when he hung up, he announced that the next morning they had a 7:00 a.m. departure for a round robin to Danang, Vietnam. "If we can do it right, we'll be back here in time for happy hour tomorrow night. We still have time this evening for a few brews and a good night's sleep. Eight hours from bottle to throttle." He winked at Eddie as they crossed the hallway into the main bar with its smoky happy hour crowd. Eddie already felt at home with the crowd. They were the same people, some with different names and different bodies, but the same people as the previous evening.

Eddie and Quincy scanned the crowd for a 22nd table but none was to be seen. Tally Whacker was at the bar talking to a shorter guy wearing flashy tropical civilian clothes and a crew cut. The guy had his left arm raised, hand extended, flattened, and upside down. He seemed intense as he explained something to Tally. He was either a fighter pilot or a wanna be. Tally looked reserved, as if he really didn't believe the guy, or at least give a hoot. Tally spotted Quincy and Eddie in the doorway and capitalized on the opportunity to excuse himself. He left the fighter pilot up side down, in mid air, and mid story.

"Guy's nothin but bull shit," Tally announced with a thick drawl as he approached Quincy and Eddie. "There's a bunch of 22nd guys downstairs—they're having a board meeting. What say we amble down and join em?"

Eddie studied Tally as they followed the sound of rock and roll music down the wide flight of stairs, located through a doorway on the right side of the main upstairs hallway. Tally was thin and bony but sinewy and strong. Eddie suspected he could handle himself quite well in a bar room brawl. Eddie smelled pizza. At the bottom of the stairs, on their left, was a small shop that displayed Filipino handicrafts in its window. The door was open and two well-dressed, older Caucasian women were tending the store. "Officers wives club," Tally answered Eddie's curiosity. "They sell street merchandise, mostly to transient aircrews that don't have the time to go off base. You know, like the C-141 crews and the visiting dignitaries. They close at seven in the evening. because the night crowd gets a bit rowdy in the Rathskeller."

The next door on their left was a walk up pizza counter, the answer to Eddie's curiosity. At the end of the short downstairs hallway was an open double door that led to the Rathskeller. The wide door presented a bar scene not dissimilar from a stateside Friday afternoon college bar. The large room was overfilled with tables, smoke, and people. A five piece Filipino band was doing a credible job imitating The Doors and bringing down the rafters. On a raised dance floor in front of the band, young men were dancing with very attractive and obviously American girls. The girls wore mini skirts, big hairdos, showed lots of skin, and displayed no inhibitions. They flashed their eyes, obviously enjoying the hustle they were evoking from the GIs. Everyone was going one hundred miles per hour.

The noise from the band and the crowd made it difficult to talk. "The guys came down here at five so they could get a good table for our board meeting," Tally shouted to Eddie as they spotted a table full of 22nd guys and a mix of girls—strategically located in front of the dance floor. The guys were all in civilian clothes, some clothes more wrinkled than others. Most of the girls were dressed less scantily than the dancers and most were attractive, but a quick scan didn't reveal any that were standouts. There were a few chairs left around the combination of two tables. The tables were full of beer glasses, dirty ash trays, pitchers of beer, and a set of leather dice cups. Quince and Eddie helped themselves to empty chairs and one of the young Caucasian girls at the table stood and offered her chair to Tally. This seemed a bit odd to Eddie but his inquisitiveness was short lived when she piled into Tally's lap as soon as he sat down. She put her arm around him and gave him a long swig from her glass. Eddie sat and sucked in the scene as the girl next to him poured him a beer then sat quietly.

The first thing he noticed was, except for the couple of Filipino girls hauling pitchers of beer to the thirsty crowd, there were no Filipino girls in the crowd. It was Americana! The girls at the 22nd table, as well as some of the other tables, were more conservatively dressed, had practical hairdos, and seemed at ease with the scene. One table was packed with flashy chicks with daring exposure and Dallas style coiffures.

The girl seated next to Eddie followed his scan across the room, then leaned over and shouted into his ear, "flight attendants! The ones with their tits flopping all around and their mini skirts trimmed up to their asses are all flight attendants with the airlines. They bring a load of soldiers over to Vietnam, spend a couple nights here at Clark, then fly a load of survivors from Vietnam back to the States. They come here to pick up horny officers like you. The rest of us are school teachers and nurses here at Clark. We teach dependant children and the nurses work in the Clark Air Base Hospital. The nurses are officers in the air force, we school teachers are civilians." Eddie believed she was a schoolteacher, she had that look. The nurses' quarters was called the White Palace, a tall multi-story stucco building with its own bar and snack shop. As most of the nurses were older, mature, and hardened, they didn't mix that well with the Laurel and Hardy party boys at the Rathskeller.

Eddie struggled to think of something clever to say to the schoolteacher and was pleased the noise made it appropriate for him to just nod and smile. She was attractive, short cut brown hair, tiny nose slightly turned up, a smattering of freckles, a catchy smile, and a modest red dress. She was a low maintenance kind of girl that some guy would marry someday and they would raise a family. She looked like she had the nesting instinct. Eddie never expected he would encounter American women so far from home, especially decent looking ones. Everyone introduced themselves to Eddie the new guy, but with the noise of the bar, Eddie couldn't really hear their names yet remember them. He just smiled and nodded his head as they spoke. It didn't take but a few minutes before the table full of people ignored him and continued their conversation. That was just fine with Eddie, although he really couldn't understand how they could hear each other with the noise.

The cute girl on his left was named Tweedy; he had picked that up during the introductions. Eddie assumed Tweedy wasn't her real name as it seemed everyone in Southeast Asia had a nickname. She sat quietly with a rather forced pleasant look on her face. Her real name was Becky Craven. Next to Becky sat Slick the Italian lover, then Conejo, and Jim Beckle. The three guys were having a discussion that had something to do with brewing beer, but Eddie only caught bits and pieces through the crowd noise. They were all three smoking, which was common for the 1960s. Next to Jim, at the end of the table, was another girl. This one had a round full face, no makeup, and long brown hair done into a single massive pigtail that hung straight behind her head. With all the effort to remain unattractive, Eddie felt she still had a pleasant look. He eventually would discover that her name was Bethany Swartz. Everyone called her Beth to her face and "Stinky" to her back. She had a problem with body odor, feminine hygiene to be exact, and it was worse sometimes than others. No one had the nerve to mention it to her so they all just called her Stinky to her back and when it got really heavy, they would light up cigarettes, watch the smoke for drift, and give preference for chairs upwind from her. Apparently she never caught on. Other than that, she was a wonderful person, friendly, caring, and intelligent. There was just one more thing, her legs were funny shaped, thick on the bottom and skinny on the top, like they were installed upside down. Eddie noticed that when she left the table and walked toward the bathroom. Of course, no one ever mentioned that to her face either as she was well liked and an accepted member of the 22nd Board of Directors.

The Board of Directors was just a handle for any gathering of four or more 22nd crewmembers and their followers at the Clark Air Base Rathskeller. Continuing clockwise around the table was Andy Blackwell, the straight laced academy graduate that liked kinky sex, then another girl. Her name was Katherine and everyone called her Katy. She was a no holds barred kind of person who called her own shots and lived life to its fullest. She was a flight attendant, but not like the flashy kind that kept distracting the men at the 22nd table. Katy was attractive without need for all the flashy accessories. She looked as if she might be part oriental; her shiny black hair was trimmed short enough that it required minimum maintenance. Pleasantly endowed on the top, a slim waist and lively rear end, she only had to stand and walk to draw the necessary attention she so enjoyed. She worked for a small government owned airline that was called Southern Air Transport. They flew old surplus military DC-4 and DC-6 aircraft on scheduled routes between Yakota in Japan, Kadena Air Base in Okinawa, Clark Air Base, and sometimes showed up on the ramp in Tan Son Nut Air Base, near Saigon. Recently they started flying 727s. Everyone knew Southern Air Transport was a subsidiary of Air America, but there was no way to prove it. Air America, in addition to all its clandestine CIA funded operations, also flew legitimate operations under separate, legitimate names. In this case, they shuttled military associated civilians between bases in Southeast Asia.

Air America had its origin after World War II as a legitimate Chinese freighter airline called Civil Air Transport. Later they were bought out by bogus people and bogus investors, received a new name, and became a member of America's clandestine arm.

Katy lived near Tachikawa in Japan, as did most of the Southern Air Transport crewmembers. They were eligible for on-base military privileges including the officers clubs, commissaries, and medical care. Lord knows some of them needed the medical care; they lived and worked in a man's world and most were dedicated and hard working aircrew members. Off duty, they were at liberty to screw as many guys as they had the urge to, and some had a very healthy urge—as if a patriotic duty. They frequently needed treatment for VD. In those days, the pill was a relatively new method for preventing pregnancy and they took full advantage of the freedom it gave them. The other good thing was that in the sixties, there were no venereal diseases that couldn't be cured with a big dose of tetracycline.

Next to Katy was her girlfriend, a new flight attendant with the same Airline. Like Eddie, she was fresh in from the States. She didn't speak the entire evening as her two years in a local junior college left her totally unprepared for what she was witnessing. She probably didn't know her employer was the cover for a secret government owned operation. The rest of the group consisted of Smokey, Quincy, and immediately on Eddie's right sat Tally with his lap full of wiggling woman. Tally and his lap dancer, Trish, were busy finding a comfortable way to fit together and kept whispering things in each other's ears and giggling. Eddie ignored them, as well as everyone else did. He could almost feel the heat they were radiating. The entire place was hot anyway; it certainly couldn't have been designed for a crowd of such magnitude.

The rock and roll music reminded Eddie of Friday afternoons at Colorado State University. He had always been shy about dancing in high school, for good reason. He had never learned to dance. There had been the German weddings and a few wild nights at a German bar with an Omp Pah Pah Band—located across the highway from Johnson's Corner. All German kids knew how to Dutch Hop, a crude form of the Polka where everyone drank volumes first, then tried to stomp as hard as they could without braking their dance partner's foot. Eddie had never learned how to do any other kind of dancing.

Then during Eddie's junior year in college, one Friday afternoon, Eddie had gone bar hopping in Fort Collins with a friend named Leonard. From La Salle, Colorado, a farm boy just like Eddie, Leonard seemed to always be operating a little farther toward the edge of the envelope. He was famous for turning over outhouses on Halloween night. Leonard had talked Eddie into going out on a blind date that afternoon with his girlfriend's room-mate. Eddie was surprised at how attractive the room-mate was. He'd expected the worst from a blind date but maybe Leonard, with his loose and risky manner, had what was needed to know and surround himself with the better looking girls. Eddie's date must have felt sorry for him as he was a little socially challenged. So she poured a few extra beers down him as a primer. It worked and within an hour she had Eddie in a back corner of Clancy's and they were putting on some serious dance moves. She had all the right moves, the right looks, and he had the right number of beers. Everything all came together that night and Eddie made a brief excursion outside his farm boy limitations. Not that he got laid, but he learned how to dance to rock and roll music. He didn't dance very well, but he thought he was doing it well and couldn't care less what anyone else thought. That's what dancing to rock and roll music is all about. It was from that night on that Eddie loved rock and roll music, the harder and louder the better. To him it represented an escape from reality and the real world. He fell in love with rock and roll music but never danced to it again; it seemed he was always too sober or too soused.

Eddie never dated his dance instructor again. He grew from the experience and exposure but despite the fact that she had the looks, the moves, made cute conversation, and almost sucked the tongue out of his head— she had no depth of character. She was all looks and no brains. He couldn't invest his emotional assets in someone like her when he knew that sooner or later she would get bored with him and move on to some other mesmerized college-boy. So Eddie and his date, her name was Sally something, made out for the last time on the way back to the girl's dormitory. Eddie got a little too friendly with her when they were parked and making out and he was rewarded with an elbow in his ribs. It was just as well.

Back at Clark Air Base, the Rathskeller band finished playing their set and the noise level lowered to that of a moderate freight train. One could converse without shouting too loud. At the same time, two more guys threaded their way through the maze to the 22nd table. They still had on their flight suits and the standard sweat stains revealed they had just returned from who knows where. Eddie took advantage of the situation. He wasn't acclimated to the tropical heat, smoke, noise, too much beer, and he felt a bit queasy. He leaned over to Tweedy and asked, "What say we go for a walk outside and let these dudes have our chairs?"

"Why not!" she responded reflexively. "This board meeting is getting bogged down; I could use some fresh air." She slid her chair back and followed Eddie through the crowd. They climbed the stairs and exited the wooden main club doors. Outside it was a typical Clark evening: humid with the evening temperatures in the eighties, no breeze, with night insects singing their songs of love and lure. Eddie took a deep breath of the tropical air. Some flower, unknown to him, was blooming its heart out and filling the night air with its fragrant scent. He liked that. There was no hint of cattle and manure smell, like on Colorado farms.

Eddie and Tweedy instinctively held hands as they slowly strolled along the sidewalk and into the adjacent Officer's residential area. Neither had spoken since they departed from the board meeting, their silence a perfect expression. The tropical night said it all.

As the mood played itself out, Eddie was the first to speak. "I got the feeling you weren't really enjoying yourself down there. Are you okay?"

"I've been over here too long," she lamented. "This is my second year teaching over here and I'm thinking about making it my last. I'm getting to be one of 'them.' We drink too much, I've developed a filthy mouth, I'm stuck in a never changing world, it's always summer, and every day is the same. All anybody ever talks about is sex and I'm just as guilty as the rest. When I ever return to the States, I'll have to really work on cleaning up my English. For Christ's sake, I'm a school teacher.

"I'm tired of paradise," she continued. "I miss the snow and getting my car stuck." She paused a few seconds as if contemplating, then decided to continue. "I miss the possibility of having a real boy friend and going out on real, traditional dates, you know . . . being picked up in an automobile, dinner, a movie, stuff like that. There's really no place to go around here on a date except the bars. There's the O'club here, the O'club annex on the hill, the bar in the nurses' quarters. Nurses and teachers almost never go to the bars off base because they're crawling with prostitutes and drunken GIs. It's bad enough at the bars on base. At first it was a blast but I'm worn out. It's really an intellectual vacuum over here cause we're cut off from the rest of the world—the real world."

She mumbled on, "I came from a dull, unhappy home and I thought this teaching tour over here was paradise. I guess it is, or was? I have plenty of guys hit on me. At first it was exciting and I've had a couple of really good flings. But over here it's all about transient and nobody ever gets the thought of the war out of their minds. All the guys are away from home and horny and lonesome as all get out. Here at Clark we get guys going through snake school, jungle survival school the air force calls it, before they continue to their assignments in-country. They think they might die so they're trying for their last piece of tail. They're in such a hurry they lose their cool . . . then in a week or so they're gone and you never see em again. Maybe Katy likes these one night frenzy fucks but it's not my bag. What a bunch of shit most of them are! Occasionally there's a decent guy, but it's the same old story. A hot steamy couple of nights and they're gone. I'm just tired of the whole rat race."

"Wow!" Eddie reflected out loud. "I wonder what I got myself into. I just wanted to come over here and fly airplanes—hopefully into interesting places. And I never expected to find American civilian girls over here."

Tweedy smirked, smiled, and replied, "You'll get plenty of that."

Eddie burst out laughing. "American girls or flying?"

"Actually both . . . you idiot!" Tweedy giggled. "Flying for sure. There's plenty loose round eye girls around here if you wanna play their games . . . and lots of cheap whores off base. It just depends on how bad off you are and how low ya wanna stoop."

"I hate making decisions." Eddie faked a serious look. "You seem nice."

"Don't get your hopes up," Tweedy blurted out, and then was embarrassed. "You know, I don't mean you guys in the 22nd," she shifted the conversation. "You guy aren't as bad as the rest of em. Sure, you all wanna get into every girl's pants, but you're decent about it and can take no for an answer. Maybe it's because you guys have been around here for so long and you have your whores in every country, it takes the edge off your aggressiveness. You don't have just a year to do it all in like the other guys. You have three year tours. You guys are around long enough to be old timers; you're not here today and gone forever. There're always some of you around.

"Most of the 22nd guys are honest with who they are," she kept babbling. "Well, mostly, but better than most. You'll come through Clark fifteen or twenty nights every month and you guys accept us girls for what we are. Hell, sometimes your Board Meetings look like a freak show—between all the weird guys in your outfit and all the imperfect women that you guys let sit at your table. We all seem to need each other." There was a silence as they both reflected. Then Tweedy curiously asked, "Where in the hell do they get you guys in the 22nd anyway? You live like animals year after year and you seem to thrive on flying, booze, and women—yet most of you seem to be pretty decent guys. Are you pre-selected for this or do you guys change after you get in the 22nd? Maybe it's some chemical they spray in your airplanes so you just keep on flying—tell me seriously, are you married? Do you guys retain your sanity by going back to Japan to be with your normal families one week each month?"

Eddie took his time before he answered. He really wasn't representative of the image she just painted, but he could see himself being just like that sometime down the road. He really needed time to comprehend what she was asking. "No, I'm not married. I've never really had a serious relationship with a woman." He hesitated for a few minutes as they rounded a corner in the officer's housing and were on track back to the club. He thought of the heavy petting he'd done a few times in college, but touches and feelies really wouldn't count in La La Land. The only time he ever had intercourse with a woman was with Vicki, the night before, and she was a prostitute! One whore and that's it.

It wasn't much of a track record in the crowd he was currently running with. He decided to keep his closely guarded secret just that, private and secret. "I'm just a new guy down here, this is my first trip. It's kind of a gee whiz ride like the first time I ever flew supersonic. I really know less about the 22nd than you do." He hesitated for a few seconds. "You really paint the 22nd guys out as a group of womanizing bad asses—I can't imagine an entire squadron of pilots and navigators fitting the single stereotype you just painted. A lot of those guys are married."

Tweedy hesitated and smiled. "Not all the guys, I was just talking about the group of guys you're mixed up with down in the Rathskeller. They like to stay off base in the motels and raise hell, never miss happy hour at the club, party hard downstairs in the Rathskeller and are constantly in the hunt for a little pussy. Guess that's about half of all the 22nd guys. The rest are a few bachelors and most of the married guys." She giggled, "We teachers refer to them as the 'shadows.' We know they're around and we can see them sometimes if we look, but we don't pay any attention to them. They're not interested in womanizing and wild partying. They stay in the trailers on base, eat upstairs in the club dining room, rarely attend happy hour or join the group in the Rathskeller cause it's too smoky and loud. They spend their days off playing golf on the base golf course and playing tennis across the street from the officers club. Hell, I don't know. Maybe they read books in their rooms? It's like they're afraid of the Filipinos off base and only once a month they get together in a sizeable group, for protection, and go off base to shop for themselves and friends back at Tachikawa."

Then they were silent as they walked. Eddie suddenly realized he may have just made a friend, not a sex thing but just a friend, the type you could talk about things and feel at ease. He'd never had a friend like that who was a girl, unless you counted the farm girls in his farm community back in Colorado. But he never really counted them. They held hands again and took their time walking back to the club. Neither of them spoke. They didn't have to. Eddie didn't miss the snow and didn't miss getting his car stuck in the snow. The weather, the company, and the evening were just fine for him.

As they approached the club, Tweedy looked over at Eddie and asked," Ya wanna sit on my favorite spot?"

Eddie stopped, looked at her and put his hands on his hips. "You're a strange girl, Tweedy, whatever your name is. First you tell me you're tired of all the stuff going on over here, then you ask me a kinky question like that! I'm really getting quite confused."

She laughed and pointed at the steps leading to the officers club front door. "You idiot, on my favorite spot on the steps over there."

"That's even stranger, but if you wanna do it over there, I'm game if you are." He smiled at her and they both laughed at their joke.

She led him to the far side of the steps at the club's main entrance and they sat down side by side on the tiled surface. They were out of the main flow of foot traffic but afforded a great view of the people as they came and went from the club. They sat there for over an hour, watching the people, each in their own thoughts. What kind of story had led each passer-by to Clark, what were the people thinking, and what would be their future? There were men in their thirties and early forties, dressed in nicer clothes and the conservatively well dressed women with them were probably their wives. They probably lived in the base housing where Eddie and Tweedy had just strolled. They were probably having dinner with other senior officers and having discussions about promotions, staff positions, and manning requirements. The women would be comparing their maids and their shopping trips to other countries. There was a mix of younger guys, the late happy hour bar crowd, all sporting their short haircuts and military issue watches. Their faces reflected a hint of awe. They were probably also new to La La Land and just passing through, attending snake school at Clark, then onto the conflict just across the China Sea. Girls came and went from the Rathskeller, both the miniskirt and the school teacher/nurse type, some of them left with guys. Giggling, they exchanged whispers and waited for one of the various shuttle buses for the off base motels. Meat markets they called that kind of bar back in the States. At Clark that's all there was. At Clark everything was more intense, more serious, and almost desperate. As if in a hurry before it was all over.

"So what's the deal with being a school teacher over here?" Eddie broke their silence with his curiosity.

"Wow! You really are new," Tweedy responded. "There's a large population of military here at Clark that are permanent party. At least they call em permanent. They don't come and go in days or in weeks as the temporary duty transients do. Most are on three-year assignments and most of them are married. They have their families over here and either live in base housing or in rented houses off base. We have schools on base where we teach their children as if they were in stateside schools. I teach third grade. It's a government contract, pays okay, and gives me a chance to travel and see the world until I figure out what I'm gonna do with my life."

"Where ya from?" Eddie asked.

"My turn," Tweedy countered. "Where are you from?"

"Colorado. I grew up on a sugar beet farm in eastern Colorado, along the South Platte River—this is a pretty big step for me, ya know. All the goings on and stuff." Eddie realized he was painting himself as a hick so he looked away and told himself to shut up.

"Got any brothers or sisters?" She asked.

"Only child," Eddie replied. He felt a bit uneasy; he wasn't very practiced at having personal conversations with girls.

"That's probably why you're so quiet and shy," Tweedy giggled. "That's okay! It's kind of nice to talk to a guy without being hustled." Eddie was embarrassed because she saw right through him.

Quincy came out the door and took a seat next to Eddie. "I was wondering where you guys went. I saw Major Baxter in the card room and he said he had our flight moved up to a six o'clock departure. We're gonna do a round trip to Danang and back to Clark. We probably should get some sleep cause we gotta get up at four in the morning, we're gonna meet at four-thirty for breakfast. You seen the hotel bus anywhere?" He looked at Tweedy and winked, "We'll be back tomorrow afternoon if things go well with our load."

* * * * * * * * * * * * * * * * * * *

The alarm shattered Eddie's sleep. Painfully awake he stared at 4:00 a.m. on his watch. "Let's get rolling," Quincy ordered as he pounded on Eddie's door. He had already popped out of his bed, grabbed his B-4 kit, and was headed for the bathroom. Eddie was somewhat less enthusiastic. The hour of the day reminded him of having to milk the cows at o'dark thirty in the morning. For a few seconds he wondered if he had improved his lot with this new life. They managed to get their duties finished and met the flight engineers at the Oasis main desk. The hotel clerk was more than happy to accept American money rather than Filipino Pesos. The flight engineers looked like death warmed over, but after a quick bus ride back to the base, and lots of hot coffee, pancakes, and sausage at the diner, they were up to speed.

While the major talked to someone in the back room at operations, Quincy and Eddie filled out the flight papers. The information sheet listed their freight as 20,600 pounds. At the aircraft, the cargo hold was full. Their load was a mix of items, mostly boxes, everything packed on pallets which were already loaded and carefully tied to the floor. Eddie asked Sgt. Hampton what was in all the boxes and crates.

Sergeant Hampton shrugged and answered, "All kinds of stuff, I guess. I never pay attention except for the weight. That's unless it's ammo or bombs or stuff like that, then I'm supposed to tell the rest of the crew." He smiled, "I guess so we can all worry."

The scene was the same as it was two mornings prior. The bright, orange sun rose over the low tropical hills with the promise of another hot, humid day. The strange colorful birds mixed their calls with the various aircraft noises and the smell of fuel and exhaust filled the air. The flight engineers completed their aircraft pre-flight check in thirty-five minutes and returned to the cockpit sweating and grimy. Eddie compared his take-off data with the flight engineer's for accuracy. They cranked their engines up, the exhaust stacks coughed and sputtered to life, one by one, and they dampened out the distant pierce of jet engines. They took their place in line with the other morning departures and soon were rolling down runway two zero. Eddie cross-checked his stopwatch and called rotate after their speed matched their take-off calculations. He raised the gear on command and they passed over the base perimeter and soon left Angeles City behind them. As they reduced to climb power and started a slow cruise climb toward Lubang VOR, Eddie looked down at the countryside passing under them; they were still less than a thousand feet high. Smoke was curling from the morning fire in each nipa hut as they passed overhead. Once again it all still seemed more like a dream to Eddie. He wondered what kind of a day the people below had yesterday and what they had planned for their current day. They were separated by less than a thousand feet and yet their lives were so totally different.

The gauges all looked good, Major Baxter engaged the autopilot, scanned the gauges one more time, and then eased himself out of his left seat. "You got it," he told Eddie. "I had a late night playing bingo." He winked at Eddie and continued, "You fly the next leg back to Clark, then we'll alternate legs the rest of the trip." Eddie was thrilled—that meant that he would actually get to fly the airplane, although from the co-pilot's seat. He would take it off, land, and call for all the checklists, gear, flaps, and call the power settings. They would alternate legs so he would get fifty percent of all the take-offs and landings. The major would always be in command, regardless, and he would still correct and instruct Eddie as he flew. There was so much to learn but things were going well for the farm boy. Eddie was also pleased that the major elected to take his turn in the bunk rather than light up a morning cigar.

At 8000 feet altitude, Eddie leveled the aircraft with the autopilot pitch dial, clicked on the altitude hold switch, and called for cruise power. He noticed the throttles come back a little and heard a significant drop in the RPM. The props slowed and took larger bites, a fuel saving technique first taught to military aviators by Charles Lindbergh during World War II. The major's snores filled the rear of the cockpit as he slept off the night's indiscretions; his arm was over his face in the classic C-124 sleep pose. They passed over Lubang VOR and Quincy gave Eddie a heading to fly over the open ocean ahead. Eddie called in their position report and reported the weather as clear.

He scanned the gauges again and assumed his over water trance and daydreams. There wasn't a cloud in the early morning sky and Eddie wondered what Danang was like. He had been told it was called Rocket Alley because the Viet Cong gave them almost daily doses of 122mm rocket attacks, five to ten rockets per day. It was a harassment that got everyone's attention. They rarely hit anything important, except early in the war they hit the ammo dump and blew-up a good sized chunk of real estate. Eddie wondered if that was why Major Baxter moved their flight up one hour; the attacks usually came later in the afternoon. It was also, on some days, the world's busiest airport and handled more aircraft than Chicago's O'Hare Field. At Danang, however, they had only two runways and O'Hare had many. He also heard that the instrument glide slope was over four degrees, when normal glide slopes were three. This resulted in a very steep instrument approach and was intended to keep the aircraft higher and out of small arms fire until they were over the secure airport boundary. He dug out his Danang airport charts and studied every detail on every page.

With time Quincy had Eddie alter the heading four degrees to the left and Eddie called in a current position. As the day heated up, small cumulus clouds formed and beckoned for Eddie to come over and play, as he did when flying solo training flights back at Willy. This time he stayed on course and grinned to himself at the memories. Eventually they passed over a series of small, uninhabited atolls; some just barely broke above the water line and most just showed their presence with the light blue shallow water. His map indicated they were at the south end of the Parcel Islands, administered by China and claimed by Vietnam. Major Baxter snored on in his bunk while the flight engineers changed seats at the panel. Eddie's body wanted to sleep but he fought it off as the next leg would be his turn in the bunk while they cruised.

He continued his thoughts. His mind wandered and he marveled at the thought that he was a grown man and a pilot flying in the Vietnam Theater. He wondered how he'd met a decent girl the night before, Tweedy, just like he'd met some nice girls in college. But nothing really happened, just like in college. Tweedy was a nice girl, he felt at ease around her and enjoyed conversations with her, but she didn't ring any bells for him. She was a nice American Caucasian girl that represented everything good, like a Norman Rockwell painting, apple pie and reality. But he wasn't looking for reality; he was trying to escape from it and wanted adventure and passion.

Besides, he just might be in love with the squadron Filipino whore. He realized he had a passion for bronze skin and long shiny black hair. Maybe that painting of the Lady, back at Willy, had put some kind of a curse on him, like the Mona Lisa smile or something. At least none of the guys were aware of his shortfalls. The only thing any of them knew was that he'd had a session in bed with Vicki two days prior. Was there something wrong with him? Why had he never had a serious relationship with a woman? Was he really on the path of screwing his life up or was he just visiting a brief sideshow? At least he had burst through the shell and was escaping his youth and the family farm.

* *

When they were a hundred miles out, Quincy woke the major up so he could tend to his personal needs, get a cup of coffee, and clear his head before they entered the heavy air traffic into Danang. Eddie canceled their IFR flight plan with the overseas controller and then changed to 278.4 on his UHF radio, the frequency for Panama GCI site in the Danang area. He listened to traffic. "Hot dog flight is pop eye!" someone announced. Someone else was talking about a daisy chain and to tighten it up. Then Hot Dog signed off for tactical and Nail came up announcing out of smoke, bingo, and RTB Danang. From his bar room gleanings, Eddie knew that Popeye meant going in and out of the clouds. A daisy chain was formed when a formation of tactical aircraft or gunship helicopters flew in a circle. When working a ground target in an area that had potential for anti-aircraft fire, each aircraft would protect the vulnerable rear end of the aircraft in front. This way everyone in the daisy chain had their rear end covered. Theoretically the gunners on the ground were hesitant to disclose their positions with gun fire. Out of smoke meant a spotter aircraft was out of target marking smoke rockets, bingo meant he had just enough fuel remaining to return to his base, make a normal traffic pattern and land. RTB meant returning to base. Going tactical meant that the aircraft using Hot Dog as a call sign was changing his radio frequency to work with a spotter aircraft—to work on a ground target. Eddie checked in with Panama so they knew who and where he was.

When fifty miles out, Eddie switched his radio to the Danang ATIS (airport information) and copied a recording of the weather, active runway, type of approaches in use, and the barometric altimeter setting. Danang was one of the few airports in Asia that had a separate radio frequency for listening to the recorded weather and current landing procedures. The separate ATIS frequency reduced the vocal traffic on the tower frequencies. As expected, it was hot and humid with wind less than five knots. They were using visual approaches into runways one seven left and right. A runway's name, such as one seven (17), was the magnetic direction of the runway (170°). With the good weather, Eddie's crew would not need to use the steep instrument approach. However, in the clear daylight, they needed to keep their visual approach close and tight. Even in good weather, the steep four degree instrument approach was used by the large, heavy, stateside freighters—those unfamiliar with the airfield and in need of a little more guidance and assurance. Assurance they were at the correct airfield and lined up on the correct runway. Vietnam was no place for mistakes!

Major Baxter climbed into the left seat, fastened his seat belt, placed his headset on his ruffled crown, and adjusted it. He stunk like cigars although he hadn't recently smoked one. He scanned the engine gauges, set his TACAN to the same frequency as Eddie's, channel 77 for Danang, then cross-checked the bearings and distance from the station with Eddie's indications. Good pilots are always cross checking instrument indications. Thirty-five miles out the major called for a small power reduction and with the autopilot pitch wheel he dialed in a shallow descent. The nose lowered and the airspeed slowly increased as he traded altitude for airspeed on their way down. Like a car speeding up when it went downhill. Eddie performed his checklist duties and set the plastic card, listing the proper landing speeds for their weight, on the throttle console. The plastic card, with grease pencil writing, also displayed the weather and the various approaches in use.

An island came into view; the map called it Cu Lao Cham. A mile wide and five miles long, tropical rainforest covered the island and deep water was dark blue along the eastern edge of the shoreline. On the west side, in the middle of the elongated island, a coral reef created a small shallow lagoon. Inside, a calm bay of crystal clear, turquoise, shallow water led to a splendid white beach. Several small boats adorned the water's edge and a dozen huts were strung out on the narrow beach. From their altitude, the island looked no different than those he had seen north of the Philippines. Quincy remarked, "I know some guys that stayed low when departing Danang, so they could get some good pictures of that place. They picked up six bullet holes from that village. Things ain't always what they seem."

Their headsets revealed plenty of activity just ahead, about to come into sight. The main coastline emerged from the distant haze, the same tranquil scene: beautiful tones of water, beaches, fishing boats with large, single sails. When a break occurred on the radio, Eddie blurted out, "MAC Four Four, C-124 twelve southeast, three thousand feet, landing Danang." As busy as the tower was there was a need to keep radio traffic as brief, clear, and precise as possible.

There was way too much traffic for an overhead 360 degree pitchout like they used at Binh Thuy. The runway was only a few miles inland from the beach and the town of Danang was under their visual traffic pattern, so theoretically, exposure to ground gunfire was minimal.

"MAC Four Four, enter a left downwind for runway one seven left, call when abeam tower, break, break. Zorro flight keep your speed up, cleared to land, roll to the end, break, break. Trail Two Eight, start your base and land behind the F-4 following the A-1s on short final, then exit immediately, break, break. MAC Five Three slow fifteen knots and continue your straight in. There'll be an O-2 making a left base and landing short in front of you. Let me know if you have him in sight."

"MAC Five Three has the traffic," was the reply. The C-141 slowed its straight-in final approach behind the F-4 fighter, knowing there would be a light, twin engine Cessna O-2 turning just in front of him. Forward air controllers, usually called FACs, flew small, slow aircraft low to the ground, hunting for enemy targets. Once a target was located, they fired a smoke rocket at the target to mark it, so the fast moving, bomb dropping aircraft would have an easy reference for his target. MAC Five Three hoped the slower O-2 could get its butt off the runway quickly, so they could land their heavy freighter without having to abort the approach and go around.

"Trail Two Eight copies short behind the Phantom." The chatter continued nonstop and Eddie finished the before-landing checklist. Major Baxter entered the downwind for a left pattern at 1200 feet altitude, the reciprocal engine traffic pattern altitude.

Then the proverbial monkey wrench in the gearbox occurred, "Attention, all aircraft! Attention, all aircraft!" the tower blurted out. "There's an A-1 entering the one seven left downwind about midfield, I have no radio contact with him, everyone be alert, I think he's gonna land. You got him MAC Four Four? He's coming at you from your right."

Eddie spotted the A-1 fighter cutting into their flight path, diagonally from their right side and dangerously close. "Tally Ho, two o'clock and he's close!" Eddie shouted over the radio and pointed with his finger so the major could quickly spot the piston driven fighter.

"Got him," Major Baxter shouted as he honked back on the yoke and passed over the A-1. He then rolled into a hard steep right 360 degree turn to get separation space. The major advanced the throttles himself, then called for RPM twenty-seven hundred, manifold four zero. The flight engineer then properly set the power. They were so close, as they rolled into a forty degree right bank, Eddie could look down inside the fighter's cockpit and see the look of surprise in the pilot's eyes. Then the A-1 disappeared under them and out from their left side. The ancient, 1950 vintage propeller-driven single engine fighter had South Vietnamese markings.

"Tell the tower we're breaking out of the pattern and request a wide three sixty to re-enter," Major Baxter barked.

"Tower, MAC Four Four is breaking right out of left downwind for one seven left, we missed the A-1 and we're clear. Request a right three sixty to re-enter," Eddie announced on the radio while he leaned forward and looked out his side window for additional aircraft. There might have been a formation of them. "Clear right," he assured the major that he was looking and could see no other aircraft. Major Baxter shallowed the steep turn he had initiated, called for a reduced power setting and continued his turn for a wide re-entry circle. The tower told them to tighten up their circle and follow the Caribou that had just entered on a downwind behind the renegade A-1. The major called for flaps twenty and manifold one eight to slow down and tightened their circle. Then he smoothly lowered the silver C-124 aircraft back down to traffic pattern altitude, continued the circle, and rolled out again in the Danang traffic pattern downwind. "Manifold Two Two," he called and they settled back onto pattern altitude and the speed indicated 140 knots. They were two miles behind the slower Caribou. Eddie was impressed at how the major handled their big bird.

"Damn rat race," the major mumbled. "Every time I come in here there's some sort of crisis going on."

"They otta pull that guy's wings!" Eddie snapped. He was a little shaken up and was trying not to show his adrenaline rush to the rest of the crew.

"He's a South Vietnamese pilot," the major observed. "Probably can't speak English, or maybe he has a radio failure and doesn't know the American radio out procedures." While talking, Eddie and the major were both clearing outside the aircraft and listening with one ear to the tower frequency. They both heard the tower clear the O-2 to land, cleared Sandy Four Flight to enter left downwind for runway one seven left behind their C-124. MAC 55, another C-141, checked in at the outer marker for a straight-in instrument approach to the same runway.

"MAC Five Three, go around, maintain runway heading and expedite to and maintain three thousand," the tower called as the errant A-1 fighter started his base turn. "Expect a visual as soon as I can clear out some traffic."

"MAC Five Three on the go to three thousand," the C-141 replied. "Don't wait too long with the visual, we're a little low on fuel."

"Copy that," tower replied. "Amend your altitude to two thousand, and upon reaching the far end of the runway turn left to heading zero eight zero. We'll fit you in for a visual behind the American A-1s entering downwind. Break, Break, Vietnamese A-1 on base turn, if you can read me you're cleared to land runway one seven left, Danang."

"Tower MAC Four Four is abeam," Eddie called.

"MAC Four Four, follow the Caribou starting base. He's landing behind the errant A-1 turning short final and you're clear to land behind the Caribou. Give him room cause he's slow," the tower responded. And so it went. The major slipped their ungainly freighter onto the runway behind the light weight and slower Caribou, dropped all four 4360's into reverse and took the mid field turnoff to the freight ramp. The caribou landed long and followed the A-1 off the end of the runway. It was a group of well-trained and versatile military pilots working together in an operation that would have broken a dozen rules for civilian flying back in the States. Eddie's adrenaline was flowing.

As they taxied to the freight ramp, Eddie got his second look at Vietnam—his first look at Danang. What a contrast it was from Binh Thuy! Binh Thuy was a low-key airfield situated among the rice paddies, its infrequent traffic mostly local and in direct support of local skirmishes with Viet Cong. In contrast, Danang was "Battle International Airport." The extensive concrete parking ramps were covered with every type aircraft imaginable. There were rows of F-4 fighters in their camouflage paint jobs and rows of bombs under their wings. The bombs left no doubt as to their purpose. Maintenance trucks and mechanics were everywhere. There was a mix of navy and marine A-6, A-7 and A-4 fighters. It was more efficient to operate navy aircraft from airfields than from carriers. The navy was using both. Numerous C-130s, C141s, C-123s, and civilian DC-8 freighters covered the large freight ramp and the adjacent ramp held a mixture of Air America aircraft and helicopters. The miscellaneous ramp held a mixture of what looked like a combat air museum, there were also Jolly Green Giant CH-53 rescue helicopters and there was a grouping of A-1 Skyraiders. The low, slow but very maneuverable A-1 Skyraiders were famous for their bombing and gunnery accuracy and their long loitering abilities. They were perfect for rescue work and supporting American troops on the ground. A Vietnamese ramp marshaller was guiding the errant, radio silent A-1 fighter into a parking spot on the miscellany ramp. Eddie had his camera out. In a frenzy he banged away the rest of his roll of film.

"Ya know what tally ho means in English?" Quincy asked.

"No, but I bet you're gonna tell me," Eddie replied as he focused and snapped a shot.

"In England it means there goes the little fucker!" No one laughed so Quincy went about folding his charts. Quincy had a reputation for dry jokes.

"It's against regulations to take pictures, Sir," Sgt. Morey reminded him. "No one's gonna say anything when you sneak them from your co-pilot seat but I would strongly recommend you don't go walking around the ramp taking photos. The MPs will be all over your butt."

"Thanks for the advice," Eddie looked back at the sincere flight engineer. "I'll be more careful." It was the second time Eddie had been warned.

They had to hold for a taxi route to open—then they were marshaled into position next to another C-124. The major set the brakes. They shut down their engines and performed the mandatory checklists. Below, Eddie could hear clangs and clunks as the loadmaster opened the nose doors, lowered the ramps, and prepared the freight for unloading. A half dozen Vietnamese, riding a large forklift, arrived and disappeared under the aircraft's nose. "Rampies!" Major Baxter remarked in disgust.

The markings on the C-124 next to them indicated it was from a national guard unit. The crew was standing outside watching the ramp workers load two small pallets of freight into their aircraft. In addition to dark green new flight suits, they wore bright red neck scarves. All had their hats on and had shiny boots. They were sharp looking and Eddie suddenly realized that his squadron didn't even have unit scarves and most rarely, if ever, shined their boots. Few ever wore flight hats when loitering on the ramp. The 22nd guys looked like bums when measured against the stateside reserve crew.

"Don't let their good looks bother you," Quincy remarked. "They come over here one trip each month to get their tickets punched and they go home after one in-country landing at a large, secure airfield. I guess they don't like to sweat all the time and fly with their undersides exposed to Charley and his guns. I call them wannabes. I think they envy us, secretly. The 22nd is the most decorated unit in the Military Airlift Transport Command and everyone knows that we get all the tough assignments: the oversized, awkward loads, the shitty backcountry airstrips, and we do it right." Eddie thought of the rag tag C-124 crew he first saw at Willy and he knew he was in the right outfit. He no longer was a wannabe.

"You wanna walk over to ops with me, motor mouth?" Major Baxter asked Quincy. He nodded toward Eddie, "You can stay here and sneak a few more photos, maybe watch the rampies to keep em honest while Hampton is busy working." The two of them left the cockpit. The normal ladder that allowed cockpit access with the cargo deck had again been raised out of the way to make room for the forklifts. So the major and Quincy again had to use the backup side ladder. The two flight engineers also scrambled down the side ladder and as one watched the rampies the other started their pre-flight. The fuel truck was waiting for a radio call from base operations as they were anxious to turn the planes around and get rid of them as soon as possible. Others were waiting to use the valuable ramp space. The 22nd bird wouldn't need fuel as they brought enough from Clark for the round trip.

Eddie was alone in the cockpit. He installed a new roll of film in his camera, opened the overhead hatch, and stuck his head out just far enough to take several more photos. Chances were good that at least some, if not many, of the rampies regularly debriefed the North Vietnamese about the daily ramp activity. They probably already had access to any information that he could photograph from his lofty perch. There were two camouflaged C-130s parked in the corner of the ramp and they were loading pallets of freight using their rear ramps. There were parachute rigs attached to each pallet. These were destined for low altitude extraction onto remote runways that were too dangerous to land on. They simply lowered the rear ramp in flight and flew a few feet above the runway. The parachutes, when deployed, would pull the pallets out the back—they would skid to a stop on the runway as the C-130 flew away. On a third aircraft they were off loading, by hand, rubber bags full of something. Then it dawned on Eddie—he realized they were body bags and they weren't empty. It gave him a hollow feeling in his guts. Eddie put on his telephoto lens and shot an entire roll of the ramp activity, avoiding the body bags. Then he let himself down the side ladder and down one of the open nose door's ramps, being very careful not to get in the way or ran over.

There was an American staff sergeant accompanying the Vietnamese rampies so Eddie's watching services were not needed. The crew on the other C-124 was still loitering, waiting for something or someone. Eddie took his wrinkled flight hat out of his flight suit pocket and placed it on his head, then sauntered over and introduced himself. He was sweating profusely, as were the other C-124 crewmembers. They were waiting for their aircraft commander, Colonel something or other. He was at the aerial port, trying to get their load reduced so they could carry enough fuel to fly non stop to Yakota. That annoyed Eddie as he felt they should be more cooperative about the war effort and carry as heavy a load as was needed. Their personal wishes should come secondary. They were friendly and invited Eddie up to their cockpit for a cup of coffee so he followed them up the two stories to their cockpit. What a shock it was for Eddie. The 22nd cockpits had the paint worn off the aluminum floors and all the knobs, dials, and table tops. The upholstery was badly worn from continuous use. The guard aircraft looked like it just came from the factory. Everything was new looking, clean and neat. On the one side panel was a poster that showed a clean cut captain sitting in a clean C-124 cockpit and under the photo the poster said:

A COUPLE DAYS EACH MONTH AND YOU CAN SEE THE WORLD AND GET PAID
JOIN THE MISSISSIPPI AIR NATIONAL GUARD
183rd Air Transport Squadron

From the national guard's aircraft cockpit, Eddie could see his own aircraft. As quickly as the pallets were off-loaded, the rampies began loading the cargo for the next leg. It wasn't what Eddie expected; it was a beat up H-34 helicopter with the blades removed. Eddie excused himself and hurried back to his own bird. As he boarded the aircraft, he could see bullet holes and chunks missing from the chopper and there was a large dark stain on the chopper's floor. It was dried blood and Eddie had a funny feeling. It was the first real evidence of the war he had seen close up. He was glad he was in the C-124, but the dried blood made him feel guilty. Sergeant Hampton pulled the chopper up the ramp and into position with the electrical winch. Everyone seemed in a hurry. The fueler was pumping fuel into their aircraft.

Eddie crawled up the side ladder into their cockpit and found Quincy. He was looking at a computerized flight plan and referring to various charts he had scattered about the cockpit floor. Quincy looked up as Eddie climbed through the floor hatch and explained, "We got a change of plans. Now they want us to go back to Tachikawa like we were supposed to do before we lost that engine. They're loading the helicopter right now. From here we fly to Taipei and spend the night. Then in the morning go on to Japan, off load the helicopter at the IRAN heavy maintenance facility in Osaka; then we'll fly on to Tachikawa."

Eddie had never heard of an IRAN before but it really didn't matter. He was shocked to see a computerized flight plan. The war had gone high tech, at least at the MAC Aerial Port at Danang. "I got other news also, not something you want to hear," Quincy continued. "I overheard a couple of conversations around the command post, that's why I came out here to flight plan. Colonel Atkins is riding with us, all the way back to Tachikawa. He's a full colonel and has a very nasty way about him. He's some kind of Deputy something at the 315th Air Division headquarters and we're under his command, way under him. And is he pissed! He has the Danang Aerial Port in a complete turmoil and everyone is stumbling over each other to stay out of his way. We were supposed to be passing through here yesterday to pick up two choppers and deliver them to Osaka, Japan. He flew in yesterday morning on the jump seat of a C-141, direct from Yakota. He had this thing all set up so he could get his ticket punched then get the hell out of Danang with us after spending only a couple of hours on the ground. His plan was to load his furniture in Taipei on our aircraft, and be home at Tachikawa the next day.

"But . . . ! No one told him we lost a day yesterday repairing our failed engine and he's really pissed about that. It meant that he got down here a day early. I mean really pissed! He arrived at Danang and nooo ride. So he had to spend the night in Rocket City." Quincy smiled and Eddie could tell from the pleasurable look on his face, the story was not over yet. It was easy to guess what was next.

"They got enemy rockets yesterday afternoon and he had to hideout forty-five minutes in a damp, uncomfortable bomb shelter, while fifteen Viet Cong rockets proceeded to blow up a bunch of dirt and some unlucky, but empty jeep. To listen to him, the rockets were aimed directly at him. And that pissed him off. Can you imagine the balls on those Viet Cong; they tried to kill him!" Quincy joked. "They missed the flight ramp by a country mile. Then when we were in the pattern to land today, he discovered we were scheduled to take a light load of timed out F-4 engines back to Clark Field in the Philippines. That pissed him off more. So he called back to headquarters, and after chewing on some poor sergeant's ass for five minutes, he ordered them to change our orders back to the original helicopter load, spend the night in Taipei, dump the cargo in Osaka the next day, and on to Tachikawa. Then he discovered that we were taking two large choppers and there would be no room left over for all of his furniture in Taipei. He's planning to haul a big load of furniture back to Tachikawa. And that pissed him off. So he had them reduce our load to one chopper—and that's why I'm doing my flight plan out here and not in the command post. Take my advice. Don't do anything to piss him off; he's looking for a head to rip off."

"So we're not going back to Clark tonight?" Eddie remarked with his dumbest look, then with a smile.

Quincy smiled and showed his white teeth, "God, I wish I were just a dumb farm boy from Colorado. Life would be so simple!" They both had a good laugh.

"What the hell! Welcome to the 22nd," Quincy commented as he folded one of the charts so as to display only the new route they would be flying. Eddie thought of what Tweedy said about 22nd guys coming and going all the time. He understood why she was looking for something different and more stable; he would be a no show at Clark tonight. Major Baxter was pissed because he had planned a revenge poker game with the guy he'd lost $180 to the previous evening. The engineers were pissed because they had purchased a wicker table set for one of the maintenance guys back at Tachi and, believing they would return to Clark that evening, they hadn't loaded it on board the aircraft. Quincy never got pissed, ever, and had plans to live over one hundred years and still be sexually active. Eddie really had no plans, he was just a tourist.

The flight to Taipei went surprisingly well. Major Baxter returned to the aircraft with a sack full of hamburgers and Colonel Atkins. The crew was happy to see the hamburgers. When the colonel came on board, wearing a clean pressed flight suit with patches from the three types of aircraft the 315th commanded, he shook everyone's hand then proceeded to get undressed. Eddie noticed the colonel had an ugly stomach paunch and was wearing boxer shorts that had been ironed. The colonel commandeered several blankets and proceeded to immediately fall asleep in the lower bunk. He snored, snorted, and gurgled like a pride of lions eating a zebra. Apparently being pissed off for a long time and having strangers trying to kill you with explosive rockets wears one out. The upper bunk, therefore, for the rest of the flight was not used because there wasn't a man on board with balls big enough to risk crawling over the top of the colonel.

The departure from Danang was almost as hectic as the arrival. The air force tower controller was like a maestro conducting a symphony. He mixed slow planes with fast ones, mixed landings with take-offs, and seemed to always have several aircraft using the runway simultaneously, always without a glitch. He knew where each aircraft was supposed to park. He knew the performance and capabilities of every aircraft, and the skilled military pilots responded to his directions with confidence. It had to be the greatest air show in the world. A decrepit C-47 Gooney Bird taxied by them, its nose art an old man in a wheel chair. The chair had wings, the old man was wearing a leather flying cap, and the lettering said "Antique Airlines." Eddie ran out of film. The major was annoyed about Eddie taking all the pictures but he said nothing. He felt assured that the buzz would wear off with time, as everything became usual and mundane.

The major taxied the airplane onto the runway and aligned it down the centerline. As they slowly rolled he said, "You have it."

"I have the airplane," Eddie gleefully responded and called for takeoff power. The major started his stopwatch for the timing check. When the major called rotate, Eddie lifted the airplane off and called for the gear up, then flaps up as they climbed and increased their speed. He was thrilled as their aluminum warehouse slowly climbed out and they skimmed over the Vietnamese countryside. As soon as they were clear of the airport traffic the major had him make a hard turn to the east and they slipped over China Beach and moved their shadow onto the blue green waters of the South China Sea. After they were feet wet, Eddie called for the after take-off checklist.

"No sense giving ourselves any more exposure to Charlie than we need to, the pay's the same," Major Baxter explained the reason for his call for the quick turn toward the beach.

When they leveled off at their 9000 foot cruising altitude, with an invitation from Major Baxter, Sergeant Hampton joined them from below. They broke out the stale hamburgers and shared a pot of coffee. Sergeant Hampton remarked how glad he was that he had joined the air force, flying in C-124s, and not in the army flying in H-34 choppers. None of their other crewmembers had anything to add, they had all seen the dried blood. The colonel's snoring confirmed he was asleep, so they could carry on their conversation over the interphone. With the heavy drone and rumble of the four engines, the Colonel in the bunk, without a headset, couldn't hear a word that they said.

Major Baxter was in a rare talkative mood, as if the pissed off colonel had somehow stimulated him. "I learned something new about those reserve C-124 jet jocks from the States. It seems the reservists and all the staff pilots in the States now try to get their flights scheduled so they land late in the evening on the last day of the month. They drag their feet so their take-off is after midnight, then they get their tickets punched for two months. That way they only have to come over here six times each year."

"Son of a bitch!" Morey ranted. "How do you think those guys that are getting shot at for their salary and have to live the whole year inside Vietnam must feel about that? Like those A-1 pilots back there at Danang and the mechanics that work twelve hours a day keeping those airplanes all running."

After several minutes of silence, Quincy conceded, "At least with them coming over here only six times a year, we'll have fewer of em riding with us and abusing our engines. Maybe our engines will last longer."

Eddie was proud to be a pilot in the air force and to be doing his part in Vietnam. The 22nd crewmembers worked for their combat pay even if they flew low risk missions. He was, however, doing a slow inside burn about the colonel bumping the second chopper so he could transport his personal furniture. Did patriotism count? What about responsibility?

After the coffee and hamburgers, everyone settled down. Eddie got in his two hours sleep; he slept in his co-pilot seat. Major Baxter sat his turn in his seat and read a beat up thirty-five cent paperback novel. He frequently scanned the instruments and tracked the engineer's activities at their panel. He was a pro. He could usually tell when something was wrong with an engine just by its sound. He claimed that the engines talked to him. On this flight, he was outranked by the sleeping colonel, so the major refrained from smoking a cigar—no sense in annoying a sleeping lion.

Taiwan was another nation for Eddie to add to his rapidly growing list of countries. Their capital city, Taipei, was particularly interesting. In addition to being Taiwan's largest city, it had a unique approach to its airport. The city and its airport sat in a valley in the northern end of the island; the approach was from the sea and up a wide, gently sloped valley.

Several hours later, Eddie was flying the ILS (instrument landing system) precision approach into Taipei; the major was watching Eddie closely and checking everything twice. The weather was reported to be 400 feet overcast ceiling above the ground and was definitely instrument weather. Down to 200 feet above the ground was as low as they were allowed to fly on the ILS approach. If they didn't see the runway when they were 200 feet above the ground, they were required to call a missed approach and go around. The major briefed Eddie that they would both have their hands on the controls while Eddie flew. The major winked and said, "I don't wanna go around, so if I feel uncomfortable about anything, I'll say I have it, you let go, and I'll land it." The colonel, also an experienced pilot, was standing in the middle, behind the pilot's center console, drinking a cup of coffee and watching everything closely. He had changed from his flight suit to a clean set of 1505s, the tan, air force, short sleeved summer uniform. The whole scene made Eddie more than a little nervous. Major Baxter was playing with the rules, a little, in front of a very influential full colonel. Technically, Eddie had too little experience to be flying with such low weather ceilings. But with the major's hands loosely on the yoke they were legal, technically. Maybe Major Baxter didn't care, but Eddie didn't enjoy being out on a limb.

The Taipei ILS had an electronic glideslope and Eddie kept his two instrument needles, the left/right localizer and the high/low glideslope indicators both centered as they let down the electronic glide path into the valley. It was solid clouds outside; the gear and flaps were down and the checklist was completed. As they descended below a thousand feet, they couldn't see the valley walls on each side but everyone in the aircraft was keenly aware they were there. To maintain the proper approach airspeed, Eddie called out small changes of manifold pressure (power) to Morey, at the flight engineer's panel.

The C-124's climb rate was too slow to fly the normal missed approach procedure; the valley's edges were too high. So the major requested and received permission for a course reversal from the air traffic controller, in the case of a missed approach. If the weather was below two hundred feet and they had to go-around, their amended missed approach procedure was to reverse course, a tight 180 degree turn, and fly back out the same way they came in. The controller advised them he would hold any subsequent aircraft until they were safely on the ground.

Approaching four hundred feet, everything was still white outside and the major instructed him to continue. "Your needles are centered and stable; take her on down to two hundred feet." At three hundred feet the clouds became ragged and they caught glimpses of the ground below. The runway suddenly appeared directly in front of them and the major called, "Runway in sight, flaps going to full, you have the airplane, it's your landing," as he moved the flap handle to its lowest notch, full flaps.

The major then called out, "Flaps are at full."

"I've got it. My landing," Eddie reassured everyone out loud and he eased the throttles aft and applied medium back pressure on the yoke. The airspeed bled downwards and the airplane came to almost level flight with a nose high attitude. They settled onto the runway and there was a squeak, squeak, from below. The two greatest sounds to an aviator were squeaking tires on landing and the sounds a round engine makes when it is being started. They were on the runway, rolling on their main wheels on the concrete, their nose wheel still a few feet off the runway, and traveling one hundred miles per hour. The landing wasn't as pretty as the major could do, but Eddie would have plenty chances to practice. Eddie gently lowered the nose to the runway and pulled the four reverse levers up. The electrical motors located in the hub of each propeller whined and the propeller blades twisted so they would throw the air forward instead of backward.

The major called, "Four green lights, all propellers are in reverse," and Eddie moved the throttles forward to forty inches of manifold pressure. The reversed propellers pulled the aircraft to a slow taxi speed with minimum usage of the clumsy brakes. Eddie then eased the throttles back to their idle power setting and moved the propeller reverser levers back to the forward position. The propellers swiveled out of the reverse position and the four green reverse lights went out.

"I've got it," Major Baxter called.

"You have the airplane." Eddie turned control of the aircraft over to the major and tucked his hands under his legs so the colonel couldn't see that they were shaking. The major steered the aircraft's nose wheel with the steering tiller. There was no way that any of them could know that someday the old downtown airport would be replaced and a new and much safer airport would be built along the sea coast.

Eddie called the ground controller as they cleared the runway and they received taxi instructions to the transient ramp, which he easily located on his airport diagram. Eddie pulled out his camera and the major reached over and swung his head no. "Not here! Don't even let em see your camera on this ramp!" the major spoke with a stern voice. "With China just across the strait, the Taiwanese Nationalists and the Chinese military are staring across a very small stretch of water and right into each other's eyes. There's a continuous no shit serious military security alert here. They'll shoot your ass if they see you taking pictures."

Eddie put his camera down and for the first time noticed there were soldiers with rifles and radios guarding every aspect of the airport. There were, however, few military aircraft on the civilian airfield. A Fairchild C-123 with Nationalist military markings and six ancient C-46 freighters were all the military aircraft Eddie could see. The soldiers everywhere made it obvious they were on a high level of alert. The civilian terminal ramp sported over a dozen commercial airliners flying several different foreign markings. There was one American airliner, a Boeing 707 with Pan American logos.

"Technically this is a civilian airport, but everything here is overseen by the military," Major Baxter explained as he set the brakes, turned to Morey, and drew his finger across his throat. "We maintain a military account here as we support the Military Assistance Advisory Group, called MAAG, and our Embassy is here in Taipei. The Chinese like the 22nd C-124s to spend the night here because we're good for business. We haul a lot of furniture and chicken feathers out of here." Eddie let the chicken feathers thing drop as it was time for the before leaving aircraft checklist. It was beginning to seem to Eddie that all they ever did was read checklists.

By the time they got their bags unloaded through the belly hatch, there was a Nationalist soldier standing guard next to their nose wheel. A Mercedes van took the crew to the passenger terminal and an English speaking manager greeted them. He assured them there would be a fuel truck available the next morning and he would be available to help them with their paperwork and flight plan. He mentioned a 9:00 a.m. departure to Osaka the next morning. Eddie wondered if Colonel Atkins's staff had called ahead to cover all of their bases. How else would the Chinese know all about their next day's flying? Did the 22nd always receive such fine service? Major Baxter used the telephone in the manager's office and reconfirmed what the Chinese manager already knew. Colonel Atkins, accompanying the crew, had very little to say.

The minibus, waiting for them outside the terminal, had Grand Hotel printed on its doors. The driver grinned wildly as he helped the crew with their bags. "The Grand Hotel sends a mini bus every time a C-124 lands," Quincy told Eddie. "Final approach is about five hundred feet over their street and we're the only people that fly C-124s in here. Ya can't miss our distinctive low bleating sound signature. There're lots of hotels that are nicer here in Taipei, for the same price, but you can't beat the Grand's service. In the past, the guys had been having a lot of problems with theft in their rooms when they were out shopping or eating. Also some of the merchants were screwing the guys over with high prices and poor quality merchandise. The guy that owns the Grand is some kind of local bad ass and we've had no problems since we assured him we would use his hotel exclusively."

Taipei, from his view through the window in the mini-bus, was an exciting sight for Eddie. The people were smiling and busy with their daily tasks. There was no sense of the thievery that he had heard of, as if one could see or feel such things. But Eddie was a naive new guy on his cherry trip to La La Land. The downtown area had some impressive looking office buildings and hotels, while the rest of the city was sprawled out with shabbier looking single and two story buildings. People were everywhere. The poor working class people wore loose, dark colored trousers, both the men and the women, and loose unkept shirts and blouses. Some wore shoes, but as in most tropical environs, most wore either sandals or what Americans call shower "flip flops." There were a lot of open markets; most were simple clusters of kiosks, where everything from food, lots of fruit, clothing to brooms, and furniture were being hawked. The humid air was heavy with the same pungent, rotten smell that Eddie would encounter throughout most cities in South East Asia. Every unused edge of the crooked and narrow streets was lined with bicycles and fly-loaded garbage. The streets were filled with thousands of tiny Japanese cars and hundreds of thousands of rusty bicycles.

The three story Grand Hotel's masonry exterior had a coarse look, but inside the tile and woodwork reflected improved workmanship. The lobby was large and open; the existing furniture was sparse but well crafted. The crew agreed to meet in the lobby in twenty minutes and made arrangements with the mini bus driver to take them to Ricardo Linn, the furniture manufacturer that was preferred by the 22nd crewmembers. The elevator gave Eddie a flashback to the United States. Its brass plate read Otis of Chicago but it was ancient and its wire cage moaned as it slowly cranked them to the third floor. As Eddie followed the bus boy down the hallway, they passed several giggling and very sleazy looking young girls who were going the other way. They looked Eddie over, head to toe, and giggled some more. When they had checked in downstairs, Eddie noticed several tainted ladies sitting at a small bar at the far end of the lobby, but he was too busy to take a good look at them. There was laughter and giggling in two of the rooms as Eddie passed by and he realized the Grand Hotel was, among other things, functioning as a whorehouse. The bell boy accepted his American quarter as a tip and asked Eddie if he wanted a girl for his room. Eddie politely declined the offer and the bellboy politely exited. The room was tiny, clean, and also quite sparse.

From his window he had a view of the rear of the hotel where an addition was being added. The addition was crawling with Chinese workers, as if an anthill. Some were barefoot and some wore rubber shower shoes. They all wore either black rolled up work pants or flimsy Bermuda style shorts. All were bare from the waist up, working as if in a hurry and elated with their labors. Everything was being done by hand and they worked on flimsy bamboo scaffolding that was tied together with cord. The bamboo ranged from three to five inches in diameter and had to be exceptionally strong and resilient to hold up the weight of all the workers, plus their building supplies. On the ground cement was being mixed by hand in wooden troughs, shoveled into buckets, and pulled up hand over hand with ropes to the level of construction. It had been several years since Eddie had worked that hard.

Across the street he could see what was serving as a fire station, a dilapidated garage. It was a wooden building with Chinese signage. It was recognizable as a fire station as there was an old fire truck in the open lot next to the building. A half dozen Chinese men were running around wearing rubber rain coats and uncoiling a fire hose. Eddie was thrilled! How many Americans get to actually see an authentic Chinese fire drill? Americans use the expression all the time, and Eddie was witness to the fact that a Chinese fire drill did appear quite unorganized. Then he closed his curtain and turned the noisy air conditioner to full cold.

After a quick shower, Eddie jumped into some light weight civilian clothing and hustled downstairs. The guys, minus the colonel, were all assembled in the lobby and waiting for him. "The colonel said we're to go to Ricardo Linn's without him and to meet him in his room at eight this evening for dinner. We should dress civilian casual," Major Baxter announced. "I'd strongly suggest everyone attends."

"I assume that means officers only?" Max confirmed.

"No, he said he wanted the whole crew to be there. I've done this before and he puts out a really good spread for everyone."

The minivan ride could best be described as hectic. They almost ran over two different bicycle riders, several children, and an old lady that at the last second exhibited an exciting jump out of the way. If it had been the Olympics, she would have scored a perfect ten for timing. But the minivan driver seemed unfazed. He drove by constantly honking his horn—never slowing for anything or anyone. He was exceptionally skilled at doing double swerves.

Once they were out of the downtown area, Eddie was amazed at all the slums and poverty. The driver dropped them off at the Ricardo Linn factory and waited for them to conduct their business. The building was quite large, a run down building that, except for the furniture manufacturing that went on inside, would have passed for a very old warehouse. There were twenty or thirty carpenters, all busy cutting and shaping all forms of custom furniture from beautiful chunks of teak and mahogany wood. Other than an occasional electric drill and a single electric wood plane, all the workers were using hand tools. Some of them were ancient looking and came in various shapes and functions that Eddie had never seen before. They were making furniture from scratch! Huge logs were laboriously cut into slabs by hand, then cut, planed, chiseled, and carved into perfect imitations of American style furniture. They also employed a large number of small boys that did nothing but sandpaper work. Eddie assumed they were apprentices but the truth is their impoverished fathers had sold them into servitude. From such primitive methods, the resultant furniture in the show room was splendid. The show room's primary purpose was to display samples and to suggest ideas for the mostly foreign clientele that ordered custom furniture. Everything cost probably one fourth of what it would be valued back in the States. They could, the English speaking showroom manager told Eddie, duplicate any piece of furniture in ten weeks. All they needed was a photo, magazine cutout, or a sketch with dimensions.

Ricardo Linn was one of several furniture builders that catered almost exclusively to American military personnel. Eddie was told the American Navy ships, when arriving in the Asian theater, commonly spent a few days in port at Taiwan. They made Taiwan their last port of call prior to returning to the States. The ship's personnel, mostly the officers, would order furniture during the first calling. They would take delivery on their last calling and store the booty in the ship's holds for the return trip to the States. For the 22nd, it was a bonanza. They had capacity, in their numerous under deck compartments as well as unused space on the freight deck, to transport large and bulky furniture back to Japan.

Colonel Atkins had proceeded directly to Ricardo Linn from the hotel, by taxi, and had beaten the crew to the furniture factory. He was in the back, looking debonair and important in his crisp air force uniform as he inspected completed furniture. As he approved each piece from his list, a swarm of boys would attack it with cardboard and twine and place the wrapped item on one of two large trucks that were waiting.

He saw the rest of the crew arrive and asked the major if anyone else had anything they needed to take back to Tachikawa. The colonel didn't speak directly to any of the other crewmembers but he seemed in a good mood. The major had a large mahogany dining room table and a gun rack ready for pick up and Morey had a large teak gun cabinet ready. The major's table and gun rack were for one of the military doctors back at Tachi. "Have em marked clearly so we don't get em mixed up back at Tachikawa, then have em put on one of my trucks," the colonel instructed the Chinese manager that followed him around the storage area.

Then the colonel addressed the major again, "I've made arrangements with Ricardo and the airport manager to have everything delivered to the flight line in the morning."

Quincy had explained to Eddie that the furniture could be shipped back to the States at the end of his tour, duty free, as a part of his household goods. The only problem was that it wasn't kiln dried like American furniture. So once it was back in the States it would need copious amounts of lemon oil applied, until it had a chance to acclimate to the lower humidity. Without the oil, the furniture would crack and warp when it dried.

The ride back was much improved; they almost hit only one bicycle rider but did scare the hell out of one raggedy looking dog. Everyone was surprised to see the dog and Morey remarked, "I'm surprised no one had eaten it!" There were lots of chickens running around with most of their feathers missing. When Eddie mentioned this everyone had a good laugh and told him to be patient, he would soon find out why. They had the driver drop them off in a small shopping district that catered mostly to tourists.

Eddie had never seen or heard of Batik before. Batiks were a popular Asian method of creating decorative wall hangings. Similar to paintings, Batiks were cloth colored with dye instead of paint. The fabric was covered with wax, all except the parts they wished to dye with water soluble stain, then immersed in the liquid dye. The waxed areas would repel the dye and the unwaxed areas would stain from the dye. The wax was then melted and removed and the procedure repeated, with different wax patterns and different colored dyes, until the multicolored artwork piece was complete. They were displayed in large books, like rug samples. They made excellent gifts as the fabric artwork could be rolled up and mailed and took very little room to store. When mounted in picture frames, they were very popular with the American military personnel.

The talented Chinese produced wonderful artwork. They also had beautiful flower arrangements for purchase, made from dyed chicken feathers. Eddie finally realized why the chickens had their feathers missing! As hot and humid as it was in Taipei, Eddie imagined that the chickens were probably glad to have their feathers plucked. There were oil paintings, bamboo serving trays, lots of jade jewelry, and other decor. Major Baxter bought several miniature jade trees, about fourteen inches tall, that had been ordered by the customs inspectors back at Tachi. For thirty-five cents each, two flight engineers bought seventy-two bamboo serving trays. Also to fill purchase orders from their friends back at Tachi. It was common for ground pounders at Tachi to give a standing order for some particular item—then wait for however long it took the airman to spend the night in the appropriate country where the item was available for sale. Eddie wondered about getting all the stuff into the mini van but Quincy told him everything would be delivered to the hotel lobby by the storekeepers. "Just tell them you're staying at the Grand Hotel and your stuff will be delivered. Everyone knows the owner and no one wants to cross him." There really was an advantage to staying at a whorehouse with a bad ass owner!

They caught a taxi back to the hotel. The hotel's van driver hadn't been able to wait for them as he had to meet a 727 from the Philippines at the airport. The ride was again a thrill a minute. They shared the streets with women carrying super large bundles on their heads, men walking bicycles loaded with merchandise, and a number of three wheeled vehicles powered by noisy two cycle lawn mower engines. There were children

72

playing in the streets and the same dog they had seen earlier. The dog kept looking around like he was nervous, maybe afraid of being eaten, and the carload of aviators had another good laugh.

They arrived back at the hotel at 7:30 and had just enough time for a beer or two before their mandatory meeting in Colonel Atkin's room. Quincy, Max, the load master and Eddie headed for the bar located next to the hotel. Major Baxter said he wanted to go upstairs to see if the colonel was back— he wanted to talk to him privately about something. Morey went back to his room for a couple of aspirin.

It was a shabby local bar, with a bare, well worn wooden floor, and dirty stucco walls decorated with various booze posters. It was no different from thousands that had sprung up all over Southeast Asia. American GIs in Vietnam were provided one week's rest and relaxation (R&R) for each year of combat duty. The U S government provided the GIs free transportation to and from their choice of a dozen or more locations, Taipei being one.

The lights were dim but the air conditioning was on full blast and was a welcome relief from the humid heat on the streets. The unmatched tables and chairs offered little hope for comfort, so they chose to sit at the bar. The four of them were the only clients.

The bartender was some piece of work; a young Chinese girl, her dress and bearing suggested a multi-function profession. She had on, what Eddie began to realize, the standard uniform for young women who catered to American GI's favors; a one piece flowered mini dress with no bra. Most of the dim light was coming from various beer signs over the bar—enough light that Eddie could see her long black hair was a mess. Her shapely legs were entombed in black high leather boots. The remaining exposed skin suffered from badly snagged, black net panty hose. Her cute butt looked like it was chewing gum when she walked. She was a claptrap, a little brown fucking machine, a true LBFM.

Eddie studied the large velvet painting that hung on the wall behind the bar. Surrounded by shelves of the usual bar trivia, it was a painting of a nude Caucasian woman sitting in a provocative pose on a bed. A desk lamp with a flexible shaft was focused on the painting, presumably to highlight the painting's features— oversized pointing breasts. Eddie studied the painting for a minute and came to the conclusion that the velvet painting and the bartender had something very much in common. They were both very sloppy, a failed attempt at beauty. It was interesting to Eddie that in Asia the bar displayed a painting of a round eye (Caucasian) woman, and back at Willy they displayed a painting of an Asian.

"Evening," she addressed the group as she looked the three aviators over as thoroughly as they were looking at her. She stood her ground and waited for the GIs to make a commitment first. There was an ugly wad of mascara hanging from the lower left false eyelash.

"We been shopping and need a beer," Quincy broke the silence. "Ya got any cold San Miguel?"

"Yeah," she answered without a smile. "All you GIs think it's made in the Philippines, but it's made in Hong Kong by Chinese refugees."

"Whatever," Quincy smiled. "As long as it's cold." Her face would have been beautiful, had she not abused herself with excessive makeup. Eddie wondered how old she was. The beer was cool, not cold, but the air conditioning made up for the temperature deficiency.

"I'll get this one." Eddie bought the first round. Fifty cents apiece was the most he'd paid for a bottle of beer since college. He slipped the bartender a quarter tip and the four of them tipped their bottles in unison, Eddie, Quincy, Max, and Sergeant Hampton.

"War is hell!" Quincy toasted. They clicked their bottles, gulped them down with big swallows, then settled down to sip and enjoy the next round.

At 8:00 p.m. they used the stairs rather than risk injury, or worse, on the ancient Otis elevator. The colonel's room was on the second floor, at the end of the dimly lit hallway. The floor manager, a young Chinese boy who looked about fifteen, gave them a grin of approval as they passed him at his tiny second floor desk. He was dressed in a clean uniform of white pants and shirt, his jet black hair shining even in the dimly lit hallway. Eddie wondered what was going on as Quincy hesitantly knocked on the door.

"Come on in guys," Colonel Atkins greeted them as he opened his door and motioned the way with his hand. He was wearing the same clothes he had on at Ricardo Linn. The colonel had rented a suite with a large living room. It was furnished with two gaudy sofas, coffee tables, and a wooden bar with stools. Several large batiks were hung on two of the walls and a large wooden four season teakwood screen filled the far right corner. The screen was carved relief about an inch deep and the detail was intense, a montage of mythical Chinese figures in hand to hand combat. On the left side of the room was a table covered with large bowls filled with sliced fruit, sweet and sour pork, shrimp in some sort of a red sauce, and a gooey looking bowl of something that Eddie had no idea what it was! A large bowl of fluffy white rice dominated one end of the table and a large container, full of unopened beer bottles, was on the other end. Plates and chopsticks as well as western forks were waiting for them. "Help yourselves," a much friendlier colonel encouraged the self conscious crew as he took a plate, built a base of rice, and piled on the gooey looking stuff. Eddie could see the concoction was probably chicken and some green pieces that were probably local vegetables, all mixed into some sort of sticky paste.

The crew looked at each other, then cautiously filled their plates and opened themselves a beer. They were all famished and it was no time to ask questions. Major Baxter emerged from the bathroom, buttoning his pants, and rejoined his plate and half-empty beer at the bar. The dominating and feared Colonel Atkins had transformed himself into an actual human—he opened a beer for Eddie as he came to the end of the table. The colonel joined the major at the bar and they resumed a conversation on manpower requirements. Both the 22nd and the numerous C-130 squadrons fell under the 315th jurisdiction. It seemed that every unit was short of pilots. Eddie and the remaining crewmembers sat on the sofas and ate their meals in awkward silence. The beer was not very cold but provided them with something to hold in their hands, to look pleasant.

There was a knock on the door and Morey, who was late, looked terrorized as Colonel Atkins opened it and invited him in. The colonel tried to put him at ease, to no avail. When his plate was filled and his right hand was holding a freshly opened beer, Morey joined Max and Sergeant Hampton at their sofa. Eddie had to smile; the enlisted were keeping to themselves on one sofa and he and Quincy sat at another. Thirty minutes earlier, without the colonel and major's presence, junior officers and enlisted sat at ease together and drank at the next door bar.

There was another knock on the door and Eddie wondered what's next, the entire crew was already present. The colonel opened the door and invited in seven giggling Chinese girls, plus the beaming young floor manager. The colonel handed an envelope to the floor manager and slipped him a loose American one-dollar bill. The manager's eyes lit up and he disappeared down the hallway. The colonel motioned for the bubbling young girls to help themselves with the food. None of them had spoken a word of English, just Chinese and nonstop giggles. So he motioned with his hands and fed himself with imaginary chopsticks. They all giggled again, and then pitched into the rice. They had few manners but gargantuan appetites. Most ate with their mouths open, but when they giggled they covered their open mouths with their hands.

When Colonel Atkins had the gaggle of girls occupied he turned to the crew in their sofas and grinned. "Thought you guys would like some lap dogs to go with your supper. Food and girls are all paid for, so have yourselves a nice evening. Some of the furniture we're hauling tomorrow belongs to some of the staff at our embassy in Tokyo. They wanted me to do some kind of a thank you for your help in transporting it. Take any of the girls you want to your rooms, but remember we have a nine o'clock departure in the morning." Then he looked at Sergeant Hampton and strongly suggested, "I'd like you to be at the aircraft at seven in the morning. I'll be at the gate with an escort for the trucks and we should be able to load the furniture in an hour. Ricardo Linn is sending a crew along with the trucks to help you load."

Sergeant Hampton responded in his best military voice, "Yessir! I'll be there."

Eddie thought, "So that's how a colonel gets his first general star. The furniture is for the embassy staff."

As the girls wolfed food from their plates, they scattered among the crew and sat on the floor and on the coffee tables. They were all young, so young that it made Eddie feel really unconformable. In addition to speaking no English, they appeared to feel awkward—more so than the crewmembers. They would look at each other, at the guys, and then back at each other. Then they would giggle nervously again. They all wore the usual lightweight mini dress but they were simpler than the norm. On their feet they wore unattractive shower shoes.

Their feet were rough and showed signs of growing up barefoot. Their hair was clean and well combed. They were fairly attractive and didn't have the slutty look of most whores. Obviously they were new at their craft. These girls looked like green recruits, fresh from the countryside, and Eddie got a sick feeling in his stomach. He remembered one of the instructors at the bar back at Willy telling how the Chinese wanted only boy children. The girl children were frequently sold in servitude to dealers for work in factories or as prostitutes.

The evening progressed awkwardly; the guys hurried their beers in hopes of feeling more relaxed. The girls ate, what seemed to Eddie, enormous amounts of rice and Eddie wondered when they had last had a big meal. After eating their fill, the girls went to work, caressing and rubbing their selected crewmembers in awkward attempts to sexually arouse them. It was obvious they had been coached to do so but they weren't very practiced at it. In a lighted room and in front of crewmembers he'd only met a few days previously, Eddie was terrorized. He was being exposed to traffic in human flesh. As before, he wanted to get up and run. As before, if he had bolted for the door it would have been a disaster. He did suddenly stand up, almost knocking his clinging teenager to the floor, as he decided to take a long whiz in the bathroom. That would at least buy him some time. When he returned Colonel Atkins and one of the girls were gone.

Major Baxter was still leaning against the bar, a really pathetic looking old man. His half unbuttoned shirt revealed an ugly paunch for a stomach and he was, as usual, half smoking, half chewing another one of his smelly cigars. Back in the States a man of his bearing would have qualified for, at best, a job as a bulldozer driver or a welder. Major Baxter had chosen a different course for himself. In the air force, during World War II, he had excelled as a young pilot in the overseas combat theater. At least until he pulled his now famous diving stunt with both engines shut down. If that was true? For such a non-dynamic individual he had successfully thrived well into his forties and ended up spending his remaining air force days in an old cantankerous freighter aircraft. He had salvaged a life from this safe haven of repeated adventures which included women (mostly prostitutes), several wives if that could be called an adventure, foreign travel, a slight element of risk, a twenty-four hour each day poker game at the Clark Club to augment his retirement fund, and a place to sleep. Who could ask for more! Yet the overriding fact was, besides probably being the most skilled pilot in the squadron, the guy was still a slob. What would be in store for such a person when he was forced to retire from the air force? Would he be an unwanted bore and no one would believe his stories. Or would he somehow find a niche where he could continue his chosen existence? Maybe he was the answer to the question, "Where do those old, Forest Service, fire fighting, slurry bomber pilots come from?"

His teenage "date" was rubbing her slender body against him, her hand inside his pants. Eddie was relieved when the major decided to leave for his quarters and his date followed three steps behind him.

With the brass gone everyone began speaking at once, but not so loud that the colonel in the next room, with the door closed, could hear them. Colonel Atkins was obviously busy but it was still prudent to speak at a near whisper.

"What the hell's going on here?" Eddie whispered as he took his seat and his lap dog resumed her crude rubbing and feeling of his unresponsive private areas.

"He's just setting us up," Morey whispered. "All this crap we haul around for the people at the Embassy would make for a juicy story for some newspaper reporter. The deal is, if we've all been compromised with whores, none of us could say anything without ruining our air force careers. Us married guys could really be fucked in more ways than one. The word is that whenever he's planning a big haul back to Tachikawa for the Embassy, he 'influences' who his crew members will be so things will go smoothly.

"What the colonel's doing for the Embassy people, besides making sure that he makes general, is only one step away from what we do for ourselves," he continued. "We all transport a hell of a lot of Jade out of here to Japan in addition to the custom made furniture. Sooner or later all of us crew members will drag back some Jade and furniture, if not for ourselves then for our friends back at Tachi. Think about all the stuff we drag home from Bangkok, Okinawa, and the Philippines. It's just too cheap not to. So technically we're all just as guilty as the colonel."

"But we don't bump freight to make room for our stuff!" Eddie thought to himself.

The rooky Chinese prostitutes couldn't understand a word they were saying as Morey continued his lecture on ethics; "I'll bet one hundred dollars that the colonel has at least several boxes of expensive jade items for Sergeant Hampton to stow under our cargo floor. I know the owner of this hotel deals in jade, and he also operates this place as a whore house. I wouldn't be surprised if this food and these girls are all a part of the same negotiated package to smuggle his jade into Japan.

"Same thing in Bangkok," he looked at Eddie. "James Jewelers in Bangkok sells all of us 22nd guys jewelry and bronze tableware really cheap, for less than half the price that he barters down to with the other GIs. In turn, whenever we spend the night in Bangkok, we usually smuggle several trays of jewelry into Japan for him. James has a store in Tokyo and his Tokyo guy picks up the stuff from us when we land. Without Japanese import taxes he makes a mint out of it. The inspectors at Tachi know never to look in the under floor compartments. Sometimes we actually bring stuff back for them. In fact, I think I remember someone mentioning that there was some stuff on this load for an inspector. We're all in cahoots together."

"I don't wanna violate any of these little girls," Eddie stated as he looked at Morey and changed the subject. "This one rubbing my crotch probably isn't more than fourteen or fifteen years old. I'm not a pedophile and I don't believe in this stuff. It's forced servitude."

"Then don't fuck her," Morey was serious. "None of us can do anything about what goes on here in Asia. It's not our culture. If you feel uncomfortable with it, don't do her. Put your wallet and loose money in your pillow case, and sleep on it. Not that anyone would ever have the nerve to steal anything from you in this hotel. In the morning she'll leave. If you don't take her to your room with you, the floor manager probably won't collect his share of the revenue and her pimp won't make any money from her. He would probably beat her. Just take her to your room and let her sleep in the bed with you, ya know, like your dog slept with you in your bed when you were a kid. You didn't screw your dog either—did you? . . . I hope!" Everyone in the room had a little laugh, a quiet laugh so as to not disturb Colonel Atkins.

Eddie grinned and attempted to keep the mood a little lighter. "Be careful what you say about my dog, Sergeant . . . I loved that bitch . . . besides, we only did it a couple of times."

After a pause, Mac had his say, "When you come down here without the brass, if ya don't let the hotel send a girl to your room, they'll call you about every hour and ask you if you changed your mind. It'll drive you nuts and you won't get any sleep. If ya don't wanna screw one then you just tell them to send one up to your room anyway. It's only four dollars extra and then you can get some peace and quiet and sleep. Make her sleep on the other side of the bed if ya feel guilty or on the floor if you're a bad ass. An extra four dollars is a bargain for a good night's sleep."

Eddie still didn't sleep well that night. With the naked teenager next to him, it was impossible to relax. He lay awake thinking, "This must be the weirdest event in my life! No one would ever believe me." It took over an hour before he was able to convince her that he didn't want "Fuckie Fuckie." Fuckie Fuckie was the only word in English that she spoke. He knew she was afraid if she didn't perform with him, she would get in trouble in the morning. But she couldn't speak English so he couldn't tell her no one would ever know she didn't have sex. Her pimp, the hotel, all involved would be paid and no one would know. She was probably purchased by her pimp and he was probably only interested in making his purchase price back and then pure profit.

In the end they both fell asleep from exhaustion. When he did dream, Eddie dreamt he was a little boy back on the farm, helping his mother butcher chickens. It was his job to pluck the feathers. When the teenager slept, she dreamt of being a little girl back on their rural farm, helping her mother pluck their chickens' feathers for sale in the city. In all of his fantasies about the mystical orient, it was never supposed to be like that.

CHAPTER FIVE: COMING OF AGE

Eddie had been flying the C-124 out of Tachikawa for a little over six months and things had settled down considerably after his first hectic trip south. Flying eight to nine hours in an average day, even with his days off for crew rest and a couple of free days back at Tachikawa, he was averaging better than 110 hours of flight time per month. Commercial airline pilots were restricted to a maximum of 100 hours each month and 1,000 per year but the military was more lenient. In Southeast Asia, if necessary, flight time regulations were sometimes ignored.

As far as flying freight into South Vietnam was concerned, things were starting to get routine for Eddie. But it was still interesting and exciting. Each trip south from Tachikawa Eddie flew with a new combination of crewmembers. Once his crew had been scheduled for a routine round trip to drop off another load into Binh Thuy, in the delta region where he had flown his first trip south in the C-124. The flight was on the last day of November and a full colonel from some state side organization had bumped Eddie from his seat, for the day's round trip flight. The colonel said he wanted to "re-familiarize himself" with the 22nd's mission. Everyone knew he really just wanted a milk run to get his ticket punched. That was okay with Eddie, as if he had anything to say about it. Eddie spent the day in Angeles City, shopping for Christmas presents to send home to his friends and relatives in the States. The crew caught up with him that evening at the Clark Air Base O'Club. Eddie was at the bar taking advantage of the twofers they were offering—two of any bar drink for forty cents. The guys were laughing when they approached Eddie. "Man, that colonel is more than a little pissed that he bumped you."

"Now what did I do wrong this time?" Eddie wondered out loud to the group. The pilot and navigator laughed again.

"Nothin, he's just pissed in general. On our approach into Binh Thuy we picked up a single hit; we think it was from a twelve point seven or fourteen point four millimeter machine gun. As luck would have it, the slug hit the main hydraulic tree in our P compartment and knocked out all of our hydraulics. We didn't even know we took a hit. Hell, we didn't even know anyone was shooting at us. Our hydraulic pressure didn't get down to zero until we were on the landing roll and realized we had no brakes—thank God for reversible propellers to stop us. It took three hours for the Binh Thuy mechanics and our flight engineers to patch us up enough to get back to Clark. The flight engineers did wonders with what little was available for them to work with. Now the Clark mechanics have to replace the hydraulic manifold and purge all the hydraulic lines. Anyway, it scared the shit out of the colonel and made him late for an evening staff briefing." Eddie wondered if it would have also scared the shit out of him, but he said nothing. He often felt guilty when sitting at the bar and listening to all the self-proclaimed "heroes" as they talked about getting all shot up and saving the day for the troops.

* * * * * * * * * * * * * * * * * *

Tech Sergeant Leon Devereux, the number two flight engineer, stood facing the front of C-124 number 3-30034. He pointed at the number one engine (numbered from the aircraft's left to the right) with his extended left hand and his index finger extended while he held his right hand in the air with his index finger sticking straight up. As usual it was hot and humid at Clark Air Base and he was sweaty and oil stained from the lengthy pre-flight. After making a last visual sweep of the entire aircraft to ensure all ground personnel were clear and all the ground support equipment was clear, he twirled his right hand and called over the hot-wired microphone he was wearing, "Clear on number one."

"Turning number one," came back the voice of the first flight engineer, Master Sergeant Swifty Romano, who was sitting at the engineer's panel. Also sweaty and dirty from his portion of the pre-flight aircraft inspection routine, he engaged the number one start switch. The electrical starter motor slowly turned the engine crankshaft and simultaneously put into motion the myriad of parts connected to it—including the propeller. The electrical power generator cart, plugged into the forward right side of the aircraft, lowered its pitch and strained as the number one aircraft engine's starter pulled heavy electrical amperage through the black connecting cord.

"Turning . . . Two blades . . . Four blades . . . Six . . . Eight . . . Ten . . . Twelve. . . Fourteen . . . Fifteen, we're good," the Cajun sergeant from Louisiana called from the ground. Radial aircraft engines sometimes leak a little oil into their lower cylinders whenever they sit overnight or longer. Prior to starting engines, the flight engineers hand pulled (turned) the propellers through several full revolutions to insure none of the cylinders had oil in them. Air is compressible but fluids, including oil, are not. An attempt to start a radial engine with oil in a cylinder will rupture the cylinder. If the propeller will not rotate by hand, the cylinder containing oil must be drained before the start is continued. In addition to pulling each engine through by hand, the first task when engaging the electrical starter is to turn the engine several more revolutions with the starter motor, with the fuel and ignition cut off. This insures the cylinders are clear of any oil or residual fuel and ready to fire up. On the C-124, the engineers turned the engine until fifteen propeller blades were counted.

With the assurance that all four rows, totaling twenty-eight cylinders, were clear of all fluids and sucking only pure tropical air, the second generation American from Mexico, Master Sergeant Romano, continued holding the starter switch in the engaged position. With his free hand he switched on the ignition. He then lowered the same free hand and brought the fuel mixture lever out of the shutoff position to the "sweet" position, a position he had learned ten years prior from his instructor. Then he slightly advanced the throttle a smidgen. The Pratt and Whitney R-4360-63A radial engine coughed as the fuel and air mixture entered the first cylinder and was ignited by the dual spark plugs. Then in a series of coughs, fits, bellows, and hacks, the remaining cylinders responded to the high octane gasoline mist entering their intake ports and ignited.

The tricky part—a combination of experience, skill, and feel—was next. Sergeant Romano played the fuel mixture control and throttle back and forth with the skill of a concert pianist as he nursed the hacking, coughing engine to life. Not too much fuel, not too little fuel, but the correct delicate balance of fuel mist and air according to what his ears and his gauges told him were needed. The finicky and particular 4360 was pleased and came to life. Hundreds of individual parts within the engine settled down into a symphony of motion and the hacking and coughing smoothed out to a gentle bubbling as its 950 pound propeller turned a little less than one thousand revolutions per minute. The 4360 was the largest and most powerful reciprocating radial aircraft engine ever to fly on a production aircraft, and he was its master. Each engine seemed to need its own combination of medicine to start and Romano was an expert at instantaneous analysis and cure. Sgt. Romano released the starter switch, checked the oil pressure gauge, saw it was settled in the green band, and called, "Ready for two."

On the ground, Sgt. Devereux looked number one over for smoke, leaks, and was assured by the familiar bubbling sound that number one was settled and happy. He then pointed his left hand at the number two engine with two fingers extended and again raised his right hand with his index finger extended in the air. He again twirled his right hand, "Clear on number two." The dance continued until all four engines were soon bubbling contently at idle power.

In the right seat, Eddie glanced at his number one oil pressure gauge, then the hydraulic pressure gauge. He then resumed his watch outside to make sure the aircraft stayed in one spot. The hydraulic brakes were set and wooden chocks blocked the wheels. But it was his job to make sure, as his instructor back at Tinker had emphasized, "damn sure," the aircraft didn't roll as the engines were being started.

* * * * * * * * * * * * * * * * * * * *

All four engines were running and Sergeant Devereux was on board. He had buttoned up the belly access hatch, crawled up the ladder into the cockpit, closed the cockpit hatch, was half way out of the top crew hatch, and ready to watch the wingtips during taxi.

Eddie's aircraft commander on this trip, Jim Beckle, looked at Eddie and nodded his head. They worked well together and there wasn't much need for talk. Eddie had learned a lot of technique from Jim. It seemed that every pilot he worked with had a different bag full of techniques and tricks.

"Clark ground, MAC Two Three on the recip ramp is ready to taxi," Eddie called as the crew chief on the ground pulled all the wheel chocks and was standing off the left side with a salute.

"MAC Two Three, taxi to and hold short of runway two zero, use taxiway Charley. Follow the two F-4s that will be coming up on your right."

"MAC Two Three, taxi two zero on Charlie, tally ho two Phantoms," Eddie replied.

They taxied behind the two fighter aircraft to the end of the runway and pulled off onto the reciprocal engine run-up pad. After their run-up, they rejoined the line of aircraft waiting to take-off. They were number five. The line was moving slowly as a number of aircraft needed to land and landing aircraft had priority. There was an unusually large amount of traffic for the middle of the day. It was not unusual to see F-4s landing and taking off from Clark Air Base, as it was a fuel stop for aircraft in transient from the States and for major maintenance. It was a bit unusual to see them with a full rack of bombs hanging from their wings. They would be meeting up with a tanker over the ocean and would be ready to put in air strikes when they made landfall.

* * * * * * * * * * * * * * * * * * * *

It had been an unusual morning. They had flown the previous three days in a row, hauling shuttles into Vietnam, unloading their freight, then racing back to Clark so as to make happy hour and hangout with the rest of the trash haulers. After three eight hour days, Military Airlift Command (MAC) regulations required the crew be given a full day free from duty to avoid "accumulated fatigue." Eddie and his navigator, Ching the Chinese MIT graduate, slept in at the Oasis hotel after a heavy and late night at the Oasis Hotel bar. The Oasis kept close tabs on the girls that worked the crowd there so the two of them were only disturbed twice while having a serious, although somewhat drunken, conversation. It seems that Ching was quite well informed on Asian history and he felt like filling Eddie in on the history of Vietnam—with emphasis on the events that led to the war. That lasted until one in the morning, before they stumbled off to their room.

About eight the next morning, a Filipino boy knocked on their door and told them they were supposed to call their "boss man." Eddie couldn't get a hold of his boss. Jim Beckle was staying in the trailers so he called the command post and was told they were being placed on alert. There was no flight for them yet, but their day off was cancelled. They couldn't drink anything alcoholic and were required to stay close by the Oasis, where they could be reached by phone. Eddie hesitated a few seconds and decided it would be futile to argue with the caller. No use beating up on the messenger!

"What's going on? Did we lose a C-124?" Eddie queried the airman on the other end of the telephone line. His mind was trying to build a picture that made sense.

"I don't know for sure myself," the airman sounded sincere. "It sounds like things are heating up over in Vietnam. We're setting up a lotta airlift for support, just in case they need us. I gotta go, lieutenant—Sir. Bye."

Eddie and Ching sat down at the Oasis restaurant table with Slick Olivetti and a new guy Eddie hadn't met before. Fred McMullen was tall, light complexion, sandy hair that wouldn't lay down, few words, a big watch, and eyeglasses. He wore the usual faded tan flight suit with a 22nd patch, black cloth name patch, captain's rank and scruffy boots. Eddie knew right off that this was no new guy to the 22nd, new only to Eddie. He was wearing navigator wings and a pair of glasses. Like so many young men with ambitions to be pilots, Fred hadn't scored 20/20 on his recruitment eye test. Instead of being a pilot, he had to settle for being a navigator. It was all there for Eddie to see.

"What's going on?" Ching wondered out loud as he extended his hand to Slick.

Slick shook his hand and they grinned at each other. It was obvious the two of them had shared some adventure together. "I was going to ask you the same thing," Slick answered. "Seems everyone's getting phone calls and no one knows what's happening." Slick wrestled with a mouthful of chewed eggs and pancake.

"Sounds normal for the military," Fred spoke for the first time. "Bout time you guys got used to it. They'll probably call us all in a couple of hours and tell us it's just some kind of a drill."

* *

Five hours later, Jim Beckle called for take-off power and Eddie hacked his stopwatch. They had a load of class A munitions on board (ammunition and artillery shells) and were on their way to Bien Hoa Air Base, about fifteen miles north east of Saigon. The South Vietnamese wouldn't let the Americans fly aircraft loaded with bombs in and out of Saigon's civilian airport, Tan Son Nhut. Therefore the Americans had occupied, upgraded, and used Bien Hoa Airfield a little farther away from the city. Bien Hoa was previously a South Vietnamese Air Force airfield but with the American build up, the South Vietnamese Air Force was essentially a tenant.

The trip across the South China Sea was always pleasant for Eddie, that is if one of the engines didn't act up and need to be shut down. The trip gave him time to reflect and work on the puzzled world. What was it that had brought him to this strange new environment? Was there really such a thing as fate? He never believed in fate, but he was open to new ideas. Who would he turn out to be like? Did his uncles have any of these feelings during World War II, or were their feelings only of the horrors of war? Were they denied these feelings of contemplation and wonder? He could have joined the national guard or the reserves and served his military duties on weekends, plus two weeks each summer at some god forsaken camp in Texas. He had, instead, been driven to wander and explore.

Eddie had the lustful wanderings of a young male reaching for maturity, something not unique to the human species, but common throughout the animal kingdom. Every spring, year old prairie dog males have those same lusts, and wonder away when the new year's crop of pups is crowding the den. The older adults are nippy and the young male's presence is no longer welcome. The young males wander off across the countryside, looking for that something their former home and environment lacked. Without the security of their family's holes in the ground, and a barking community to warn them of danger, most perish. Coyotes, hawks, badgers, owls, even automobiles as they cross roads all take a heavy toll of life. But for a few, the newfound pastures offer endless opportunities for life, places ideal to dig holes and re-establish. With luck, sooner but usually later, a female will be lured as she wanders too far from her colony and the cycle will start all over again. If not, the male will live out his life and grow into a crusty, feisty old rouge.

It was the same lust for wandering that drove Eddie to fly, to fly away and seek out a new life. Would he become a crusty, feisty old rogue—like Major Baxter? Or would he establish a new home?

Eddie had re-structured and became one of "them." One of the sweat soaked crew he had envied as they crawled down the ladder of a C-124 at Williams Air Force Base in Arizona. He became indistinguishable from the other members of their close knit group of trash haulers who hung out at the Clark O'Club—often seen drinking in bars in Bangkok, Okinawa, Taiwan, Japan, and even Korea.

He had dreamt about this place as a child. With his childhood's limited store of knowledge, the details were never clear and the location was fleeting. It was always the same dream, the same scenario. He was Steve Canyon, right out of his childhood newspaper funnies. Now the details had assumed structure. There were deviations in the imagined scenario, life was not as comfortable, and the reality more harsh, but other aspects were as tantalizing and exciting as in his youthful dreams. He welcomed them all. The good accompanied the bad, as he grew and matured into the image he had crafted.

He wasted no time searching for opportunities to achieve heroism or fame. His quest was just a longing and curiosity to participate in his imagined world of La La Land and he felt an immense comfort in the knowledge that he had at last arrived. He would walk down the main street in Angeles City, surrounded by thieves, Huks, GIs, military police, con-men, shopkeepers, bars, shabby restaurants, shabby whores, and ordinary Filipinos, and he felt comfortable. He had become "of this place." Eddie had found the imaginary land of intrigue and mystery, beautiful women, easy sex, flying airplanes, and the romance and charm of faraway places.

The officers club bar at Tachikawa was his safe haven whenever he was not "down south" flying. The entrance from the lobby was through a doorway with strings of beads guarding its contents. Passing through the beads and into the bar was like stepping out of reality and into a foreign movie. Centrally located in the large room was a massive oval bar that dominated the scene. Booths lined the room's outside walls and cocktail tables with large comfortable chairs were scattered about. The walls were covered with exquisite, dark, wooden paneling and the seat covers in the booths, chairs, and along the well polished bar were made from real black leather. On the left wall and covering almost the entire span of the wall, the rich wood paneling was replaced with a huge illuminated fresco. It depicted a C-124 on final approach to an unseen runway behind the viewer. The aircraft was passing low over a Japanese temple and in the lower right corner two Japanese field workers were poised as they watched the graceful behemoth approach from the heavens. Mount Fuji San dominated the fresco's background.

A small stage was tucked into the far right corner. On it a grand piano and a set of unattended drums. Eddie never did see anyone play the drums but the piano player was mesmerizing. She was an attractive, tiny, young Japanese girl and played six nights each week. She was a master of modern jazz, playing Dave Brubeck, Ramsey Lewis, and Amhad Jamal, with all of the passion and soul as the masters themselves. She played with no printed music in front of her, no accompaniment, her eyes closed, her head bowed, and she gently swayed with the music as she played in the dim light. Dimly lit, it was the perfect place to get lost. Eddie would sit and listen to the piano for hours at a time—the ambiance was intoxicating. On the bar, as a reminder of reality, the ashtrays were fashioned from the butt ends of brass artillery shells.

Yet, he was still restless. Three months after he arrived in Japan, Eddie had moved out of his bachelor living quarters (BOQ) room on base and into a small, rented apartment just outside the main gate at Tachikawa Air Base. Through a Japanese car broker that the other guys in the squadron had put him in touch with, he purchased a used Cedric for $800.00. He'd never heard of a Cedric before, they didn't sell them in the States and he was pleased with the design and workmanship of the nimble little car. The price was a steal. No longer living in government quarters, he received $85.00 per month housing allowance. His apartment only cost him $45.00 per month. His apartment became his base camp, half of the living space was living space and the other side was storage.

It was as if Eddie packed his thoughts and desires into a suitcase every time he departed Tachikawa, then set off to seek fulfillment and closure on all his ambitions. There were new items to consider buying, new women at the bars, new airfields to land at, new things to be seen, an exceptional buy on rattan bar stools in Bangkok, the perfect restaurant for French onion soup, water buffalo steak, a great commissary to refill his food bag. There were ideas on what to do when his military commitment was up, they were all out there waiting to be searched out and explored.

Fly all day, eat, drink, sleep . . . fly all day, eat, drink, shop for oil paintings, sleep five hours . . . fly all day, eat, drink, shop, drink some more, eat, sleep . . . spend the day at the pool waiting for orders to deliver a sensitive load of freight into a special airfield. Eat, sleep . . . fly, spend four hours on a ramp while they unloaded the freight and hoping you didn't get mortared. Fly, eat, get drunk at the club, sleep, spend the day off shopping for bargains . . . spend a night with Vicky . . . and on and on it went. They occasionally flew oversize cargo but commonly they flew standard cargo, a mix of a little of everything from food, clothing, mail, spare parts, engines, and toilet paper. You can't fight a war without toilet paper. They were accomplished trash haulers. Once he flew over 130 hours in one month.

Then, two weeks later he would arrive back at Tachikawa with a load of stuff to sort through. He would mail the smaller stuff back to the States for his folks to store in the barn. He would pack the larger stuff into his apartment and go on a sleeping binge to rebuild his body and mind. During the first six months, Eddie flew with about half of all the crewmembers in the 22nd at some time or another and they had shut down six more engines. Most of the shutdowns were related to oil pressure and oil quantity problems, but all of the shutdowns had been routine. Eddie no longer considered it a big deal.

At Tachikawa, twenty-second crews for outbound aircraft were randomly assembled from who was available, then sent south with an aircraft to fill the flying assignments. As a result of this randomness, he flew with different crewmembers almost every trip south. As a bachelor, the squadron had no qualms about sending him south before his turn came up. It gave some married guy a few more days with his family. He was eager to fly and had no real ties at Tachi; it was just fine with him. He would volunteer for another trip south as soon as he'd finished his laundry, caught up on his sleep, and spent an evening at the O'club listening to the little Japanese girl play the grand piano. If it was more than a couple days until he was sent back south he would haunt the bar at the club, as if some lost animal searching for a lost mate, or maybe looking for something to kill and to eat. His comfort and solace came when he was airborne and cruising, the other pilot asleep in the bunk, and the endless ocean and billowy cotton clouds slipping by with the peacefulness of a religion. There was always something new and exciting beyond the horizon, waiting for him to finish his meditation and reflections in his chapel in the sky.

Eddie saw Tweedy a few times at the Clark Club but the spark just wasn't there. For Eddie she was a domestic link to the States and she was just too domestic to get excited about. She had a bad habit of complaining and was too negative about things in general. He spent an evening or so every month with Vicki, in his motel room, but she was still a prostitute and her exotic appeal moderated with each session. As for the bar whores and the street prostitutes, he stayed clear of them. They were walking clap traps and their very presence was degrading. Most all of them were tacky and disheveled. One had to be really bad off to feel any appeal toward their merchandise. Conejo, the rabbit, was the exception. The guys in the squadron said he was so horny that he would fuck mud.

Then there was the war in Vietnam. His discussion with Ching the night before was really an eye opener for him. He had known nothing about the Asian venture he was participating in. In Officer Training School and during pilot training, it was all "rah rah rah, kick the enemy's ass." Everything had the atmosphere of a high school pep rally. Politics was not discussed and absolute loyalty to the president was required of all good officers. Each student pilot tried to out "patriotic" each other. Patriotism had become like religion to his peers. From Ching, Eddie was shocked to hear what a bucket of bumbling bureaucrats they'd had for presidents, and still had in Washington. He learned how they had gotten the United States involved in the war.

What Eddie had never known was that the Chinese had occupied Vietnam for over a thousand years, before the Vietnamese were able to drive the Chinese occupiers out. Then the French conquered all of Vietnam, Cambodia and Laos during the last half of the 1800s and had titled the confiscated land to French Barons and Vietnamese collaborators. The southern delta, with its vast rice harvests, produced huge profits for the privileged owners and administrators. Elsewhere, mines and rubber plantations were developed along those same lines. The administrators, the privileged land owners, and French occupiers treated all the rest of the Vietnamese brutally. The hatred for the French occupiers and the horrible treatment of the working class Vietnamese festered and grew for decades and decades.

A man named Ho Chi Minh was born in French occupied Vietnam in 1890 and raised with an intense hatred of the French occupiers. He excelled academically and was educated in a French school, became a sailor, and ended up living in France in the 1920s. He studied Karl Marx and converted to communism, idolized the Russian revolution, and dreamt of a similar revolution to expel the French in Vietnam. After studying and traveling in Russia, he returned to a remote area of China—just north of the Vietnamese border. When the Japanese gained control of Vietnam during World War II, he met with American operatives. They supplied him arms and supplies to conduct guerrilla warfare against the Japanese occupying all of Vietnam. It was during this action he discovered the brilliant guerrilla warfare tactician named Vo Nguyen Giap. He and General Giap became lifelong friends.

After World War II, Ho Chi Minh, expecting a free and independent Vietnam, declared independence on September 2, 1945. The Declaration of Independence that he read to his supporters in Hanoi was almost an identical copy of the American Declaration of Independence. Instead the European and American victors placed the northern half of Vietnam under Nationalist Chinese control (Formosa) and the southern half was under British protectorate. That didn't work. Neither country wanted the responsibility and problems administering their resistant protectorates. Under pressure and diplomacy by the French, backed by the Americans, the French then regained control of all Vietnam. This brought back all the old hatred of the French that was harbored by the Vietnamese. All of the Vietnamese, except the privileged landowners, were outraged. Ho Chi Minh, with his guerrilla force still in place, seized the opportunity and waged his famous guerrilla war against the French occupiers. The United States played a part in this debacle by backing the French with massive amounts of military supplies, including cargo aircraft flown by American mercenaries. It was to have serious consequences years later.

After Ho Chi Minh's Viet Minh Guerrillas defeated the French at Dien Bien Phu in 1954, the Geneva conference of July 1954 split Vietnam at the 17th parallel. The division of Vietnam into North and South Vietnam was supposed to be a temporary division; elections for a unified Vietnam were scheduled to be held in July 1956. Ho Chi Minh accepted temporary administration of the northern half and the French sympathetic Ngo Dinh Diem was placed as administrator in the southern half of Vietnam. Ho Chi Minh had a reputation for ruthlessness and practiced genocide toward opponents to his communist form of government, a ruthlessness he had learned from studying communism under the Stalin regime in Russia. When the separation into two Vietnams occurred, approximately 800,000 refugees fled North Vietnam. Most fled into South Vietnam, others fled into Laos, Thailand, and Cambodia. Ho Chi Minh resisted this exodus and thousands of refugees were killed during their escape efforts. The result, however, was a solidified Ho Chi Minh communist government in the north and a corrupt, French-backed government in the south.

General Giap and Ho Chi Minh never, not for one second, gave up their intentions of controlling all of Vietnam. During the exodus they sent thousands of loyal Viet Minh communists to South Vietnam and Laos, imbedded within the throngs of refugees. These Viet Minh, loyal to Ho Chi Minh, were to live in South Vietnam and Laos and serve in the event a nonviolent political coup couldn't be achieved. They were hidden reserves in place to serve as the core of his plan B: an insurgency and armed revolution to gain control of all Vietnam and Laos.

In the south, Ngo Dinh Diem never intended to participate in the scheduled 1956 national unification elections. All indications were that he would lose to Ho Chi Minh in an all Vietnam election. Ngo Dinh Diem conducted rigged and fraudulent elections within South Vietnam and declared the Republic of Vietnam as an independent country—with him as leader. Thus the two separate Vietnams, the northern half under firm control of a devout, ruthless communist and the southern half under control of a corrupt, insensitive president who was sympathetic to the hated French.

The South Vietnamese people faced a lose, lose, situation. They could side with the Viet Minh insurgents, support the communist insurgency, and forfeit their hopes for a free, fair and democratic government. Or they could side with the same old suppressive corrupt government, and continue living under a dictatorial regime.

There had been a valid underground movement to replace the dictatorial Diem government in the south with a populist democratic administration. But the insurgency had been infiltrated by Ho Chi Minh's refugee loyalists and it was soon controlled by the communist infiltrates from the north. The communist controlled underground movement was named the Viet Cong by the American press. With intent to prevent all of Vietnam from falling under communist control, the United States entered the fray supporting South Vietnamese efforts to establish a democratic government. The presence of the United States only complicated and worsened the turmoil. The Americans bumbled around in South Vietnam, displaying a massive amount of ineptness and total misunderstanding of the Asian situation.

If what Ching had to say was true, after spending a thousand years getting rid of the Chinese and seventy years getting rid of the French, expunging the Americans from South Vietnam and taking over control looked like an easy task. In the eyes of Ho Chi Minh, President Johnson must have seemed like a simple lackey. Yielding or any negotiated peace was not in the cards for the North Vietnamese. They wanted it all and were willing to risk everything for absolute victory. The Americans weren't strongly committed and Ho Chi Minh knew this. Ching set into motion some questions Eddie had never considered before.

President Johnson hadn't the faintest idea how to handle Ho Chi Minh and General Giap. Ching said you must always place yourself in the mind and the thoughts of your enemy. President Johnson was overheard referring to the North Vietnamese as little jungle bunnies. He had no idea or respect for the enemy and certainly didn't care what they were thinking. As it turned out, Ho and General Giap were making fools out of the politicians in Washington. The American people, including Eddie's pilot training class, had been kept in the dark. Lessons on Asian history and culture didn't sell well in America's commercial media. They wanted body counts and photos of atrocities. These ideas from Ching upset Eddie, causing him a sleepless night.

* *

As they started their descent and coasted in over South Vietnam, the radio traffic was hectic. It was obvious that something big was up. The sun was low in the west and everything looked surreal and ghostly. There were helicopters and aircraft all over the place. There were areas on the ground where explosions were going off and smoke was rising. The smoke varied from white to brown, depending on the type munitions that were being used and the composition of what was being blown up. Eddie felt sorry for the grunts on the ground, and then it struck him; on the ground was where they would shortly end up.

"Bien Hoa approach, this is MAC Two Three, descending through five thousand, twenty miles east for landing," Eddie announced when he could find an opening between all the chatter.

"Covey Three Zero, I copy an air strike one five miles, one two zero degrees, you're clear to proceed, I'll keep traffic north of you, break break. Attention all aircraft, air strike one five miles on one two zero radial off Bien Hoa TACAN. Be advised there is also scattered artillery and a firefight due east at eight miles. Break break. MAC Two Three you're clear to continue on a straight in for runway two seven. You heard the firefight on the ground eight miles east. I suggest you keep it high and a little to the right. Contact the tower five miles out. Be advised the pattern has heavy traffic."

"MAC Two Three copy." Eddie answered the approach control on his UHF radio. He looked at Jim Beckle and asked over the crew interphone, "I was told that we're not supposed to go into a field that's hot?"

Jim hesitated for a few seconds, and then formed a determined look on his face. "Approach control didn't say anything about the airfield itself being under fire and those poor bustards on the ground are gonna need what we got in the backend. Let's continue." Then he looked back at Sergeant Romano, the flight engineer at the panel, and called, "Manifold two five. We'll flatten out and stay at four thousand feet until we pass over that area where all the crap is going on. I can see most of it from here. I think it's that cluster of smoke and explosions down there." He pointed forward and over the nose of the C-124. "We won't go in unless the airfield itself looks safe." That was as close as Eddie wanted to get to that "stuff." Four thousand feet high would keep them out of practical small arms range of the gomers and above the army helicopters. Army helicopters seemed to be everywhere down low. Both Eddie and Jim were swiveling their heads, watching for other aircraft, and the air strike fighters just to their south. It didn't do any good to look for artillery shells being fired; they couldn't be seen in the air and were too fast to be dodged anyway.

As they passed over the area of activity, Eddie changed the UHF radio's frequency and called the tower, "Bien Hoa tower, MAC Two Three, four thousand feet, six miles east for landing."

"Hawk Two Four flight of two, I see you're in the pitch, cleared to land, follow the pair of A-37s turning final break break. Misty Three Three, you're cleared to pitch your discretion, follow the pair of F-100s in front of you, cleared to land, break break. MAC Two Three follow the single F-100 about to pitch left in front of

84

you. You look a little high, are you going to be able to get down for a straight in?" Eddie looked over to Jim, who swung his head no and made a pitchout motion with his left hand.

"We're too high for the straight in. Requesting a left pitchout," Eddie responded.

"Keep it tight, MAC Two Three, I'm busy. Plan on a fifteen hundred foot left pitch out. Call me when you're in the pitch," the tower replied, then continued with other traffic.

Jim was in his best form. He called for reduced power and set up a slow, steep descent so they passed over the center of the field at 1500 feet, flaps forty, 140 knots and gear down. As he rolled into a steep left fifty degree bank angle he called for manifold one five inches.

Eddie called the tower, "Bien Hoa tower, MAC Two Three in the left pitch."

"MAC in the left pitch, keep it in tight. I've got some fireworks a little way outside the south perimeter. Follow the F-100 on short final and clear to land." Jim kept the fat freighter in a tight steep left turn as they spiraled down into the melee below. They were coming around on the downwind, still a thousand feet high, and Jim rolled out temporary before making his turn into final. They were abeam the spot where they wanted to land. "Ya gonna make it Shaky?" The tower was worried.

"Got it made," Eddie responded to the tower's inquiry as he caught Jim's eye and received an affirmative nod. "Gears down three green," he reassured Jim they were configured to land. It's during times of heavy stress that a pilot could forget to lower his landing gear.

"Open the cowl flaps, we need more drag. We're not going around, too much shit going on," Jim announced. With gear down, low power, wing flaps forty, and the engine cowl flaps open, the bottom dropped out on the Globemaster C-124 and they dropped from the sky. As they passed through 500 feet, Jim made a steep turn to final. With the low power setting, he carried an extra fifteen knots of airspeed to break the steep descent and flare for landing. There was no going around and back up into that mess. Jim was a pro and the flight engineer had flown with him before. Otherwise he would have protested the call for open cowl flaps. Open engine cowl flaps would create more drag and faster descent, but also force additional air to flow over the engines. It would cool their cylinders and possibly damage them if too much reverse thrust was used after landing.

Smutch smunch, the main gear kissed the concrete and Jim lowered the nose wheel, then brought the prop levers into idle reverse. "Three green," Eddie called. "Four's not going into reverse." Jim added only a smidgen of power to engines number two and three so as to maintain symmetrical reverse thrust. With the small power application he created only a small amount of reverse drag. The smidgen of power wouldn't damage the cooled engines. "Tower, MAC Two Three, we need to roll out a little longer than normal, we got an engine that's not going into reverse," Eddie called.

"Approved Two Three," the tower responded. "Flapjack Three Three, make your landing short, the fat bird is going to take a little bit longer to clear the runway."

"Flapjack wilco."

Bien Hoa had a 10,000 foot runway; it was twice as long as a C-124 needed so they were able to slow to taxi speed with a minimum of reverse props and a moderate dose of brakes. They still had 4000 feet to spare. As they taxied to the ramp the flight engineer wrote himself a note to write up the inoperative reverse on number four engine on their way back to Clark. He Scotch taped the reminder note to his panel. Bien Hoa Air Base, as busy as it was, wasn't the place to request maintenance.

The base was a mess. They taxied by the A-37 and F-100 ramps. Over a dozen aircraft were damaged from mortar and rocket shelling. Several buildings were burnt, still smoking, and the sounds of gunfire came from the base perimeter. The base was definitely hot (under enemy fire). Vehicles were moving about frantically and it seemed that everyone was wearing a flack jacket and carried a firearm. Eddie was stunned by the battle damage. The base was still functioning, but it was unsettling to see such destruction inside a supposedly secure air base perimeter. The aerial port building was intact. After engine shut down, Eddie, Jim, and Ching hurried to the aerial port as Sergeants Devereux and Romano did their post and pre-flights, checking the airplane for holes, and guarding their aircraft. The loadmaster, Staff Sergeant O' Riley, expedited the unloading of their cargo, which was all on pallets. Everyone, from the crew through the Bien Hoa ramp workers, wanted the Shaky Bird unloaded and out of there—ASAP.

The excited airman first class behind the counter was full of chatter: "There're rumors that the Viet Cong had breached the outside wall of the American Embassy in Saigon and nineteen of them had made it through the hole in the wall. Five marines had stopped them in their tracks, on the perimeter grounds, and a relief group of soldiers had arrived a few hours later and killed all the Viet Cong in a gunfight." The pupils in the airman's eyes were enlarged—as if he were on drugs. But it was just the adrenaline flowing.

"They said that in Saigon the Viet Cong came out of the woodwork like a bunch of rats, they were everywhere. We got attacked here at the first light this morning by what they claim was at least two battalions of Viet Cong and a smattering of North Vietnamese regular soldiers. The fighting outside the perimeter has gone on all day and is still in progress," the airman explained. He was a young black man, probably not over twenty years old, and the whites of his eyes, the fright in his eyes, stayed with Eddie for the rest of the week. "I think we got sappers on the base, who knows what'll blow up next." Eddie knew that sappers were enemy Viet Cong who would cut through the perimeter fence, then run around throwing bags containing explosives into buildings and under aircraft and other vehicles.

Jim turned to Eddie, "Maybe you'd better go back to the airplane and help guard it. We'll hurry things along here."

On his way back to the aircraft, Eddie wondered, "We crewmembers haven't any guns. How are we going to defend the airplane if we see some little black pajama guy with a satchel bomb and an AK-47 rifle?" The sun was setting—under different circumstances he would have enjoyed the colorful tropical sunset, but he suspected that most of the color was from fires and explosions reflecting off the scattered layer of clouds. "Or were there no clouds, and the fires and explosions were reflecting off a layer of smoke?" In the distance, the rumbling and thumps were continuous.

There was a C-133 from Travis Air Force Base, California, parked next to Eddie's C-124. They had landed behind Eddie's aircraft, just shut down their engines, and the crew had exited their monstrous aircraft. Eddie saluted the full colonel with pilot wings and a major with navigator wings as they headed toward the aerial port. Both had the spit polish image of a stateside based crew. The C-133 was a huge four engine cargo aircraft. It had a wing span five feet wider than a C-124 and the fuselage was twenty-seven feet longer. Also built by Douglas, it was placed into operation six years after the C-124. It was intended to take advantage of the newest technology; powerful turboprop engines that allowed faster cruise speed, pressurization, and heavier loads. Turboprop engines are a jet engine that turns the shaft for a conventional propeller. Although they use more fuel per hour than the reciprocal engines on aircraft, such as the C-124, the turboprops require far less maintenance and developed more power with less engine weight. Back in the States, the C-133's additional length allowed it to carry a fully assembled Atlas ICBM missile. The longer fuselage and high mounted wings gave it beautiful looks. The C-124 and the C-133 both carried outsized cargo, but the C-133 carried twice the weight and cruised over one hundred knots faster. The aviation industry felt it would be a natural replacement and spell early retirement for the C-124. But that was not to be.

The C-133 had not been an altogether successful aircraft and only fifty were built. The grapevine claimed the aircraft was plagued with vibrations and harmonics; problems from their four synchronized propellers resulted in structural fatigue. A number of C-133s did disappear over the open ocean and it was rumored that many of the crewmembers were secretly afraid of the airplane. With its reputation as a widow maker and as it was unusable on short runways and dirt fields, production was halted. In 1968, the remaining fleet was still supplementing long-range freight operations but it played a minor role in the overall air force cargo moving fleet. The newer pure jet C-141 was stealing the long haul freight show and the remaining C-133s were being used as back-ups. The trash hauling C-124 was still around and doing the oversize work in-country, flying into shorter runways, unpaved runways, and supplementing the mainstay combat theater freight mission of the C-130 turboprop. Not many people outside the great Asian air show even knew the C-133 existed.

That day on the Bien Hoa ramp, the C-133 crew members were milling around the outside, inspecting their aircraft. Eddie sauntered over and looked under the fuselage where they were all pointing. There was a nice row of nickel sized holes stitched along the fuselage belly.

"I heard a ching ching ching when we were on final," the technical sergeant with a short crew cut informed the master sergeant.

"Yeah, I heard it too . . . now I know what it sounds like to get hit by gunfire," the older master sergeant commented and seemed a little amazed. "Boy, is the colonel gonna be pissed when he sees this!

The hole looks a little bigger than from an AK-47 rifle. I hear they have a twelve point seven millimeter machine gun that's fifty-one caliber and very similar to our fifty caliber gun. I bet that's what hit us," the master sergeant continued. "Anybody see any tracers?" Everyone waggled their heads no.

The technical sergeant added, "Can't see out the belly of an airplane, I bet a fifty-one caliber would have tracers."

"Not down this far into South Vietnam," the master sergeant was still speculating. "Maybe they don't use tracers this far south, so they don't give their ground position away."

"Son of a bitch," the first lieutenant wearing pilot wings added. "We're gonna be grounded here and probably get the mush pounded out of us with rockets and mortars tonight. I'd just as soon have turned around at Clark and not had my ticket punched." He noticed Eddie standing slightly behind him. His eyes went to Eddie's 22nd patch and for a few seconds he seemed a bit hesitant.

"You with that C-124?" he nodded his head in the direction of Eddie's bird as his confidence returned. "We were on long final when you pulled that show off pitchout. You guys must be frustrated fighter pilots."

"Yeah, you're probably right." Eddie maintained a non-committed tone of voice. "Just for the hell of it, how high were you guys flying when you picked up these holes?"

"On final approach," the cocky first lieutenant bragged. "About twelve hundred feet, maybe four miles out, we were right on the glideslope when they opened up on us. The colonel was cool as a cucumber and never varied an inch from the glideslope. He used to be a bomber pilot and he's got nerves of steel."

Eddie spotted a few drops of liquid on the belly of the aircraft, cautiously touched one of them with his finger, then touched it carefully to his tongue. "Water, it's condensation on your cold metal and the tropical humidity—we C-124s don't fly high enough to ever get condensation."

"Yeah, and you're not pressurized either. You must be embarrassed, ya know, to have a nice airplane like us parked next to your collection of old scrap parts. I see you dress the part also."

It was the opening Eddie was waiting for. "Least we aren't so dumb that we descend down and fly right through the middle of a firefight on the ground. If you guys would have come in high and pitched out like us frustrated fighter pilots, you wouldn't have picked up all these holes. By the way, when you depart from here, you're not gonna be pressurized either. Those holes will whistle like a shithouse in a windstorm when you try to pressurize."

"Least we followed the regulations!" the lieutenant countered. "MAC rules state we're to use the glideslope whenever electronic glideslope guidance is available. You guys violated the regulations."

"What's the regulations say about letting the enemy shoot holes in your airplane?" Eddie countered and pointed his finger at the lieutenant. "You'll have plenty time to look that one up, while you fly back to the States. That is, if you ever get out of here." Eddie lowered his head and walked back to his bird. He stood off to the side and watched the unloading progress from his pile of "old scrap parts." The C-133 crew had to wait until Eddie's C-124 was unloaded as there was only one freight crew working that portion of the ramp. All the rest of the Vietnamese ramp workers failed to show up for work. "Ching," he contemplated. "Sounds like a cash register, is a nice Chinese name, and the sound of a bullet hitting metal."

At Bien Hoa, air strikes were being launched in a frenzy. They were hauling and dropping bombs like they were popcorn, some pilots flying four or five missions per day. After years of skirmishes and guerrilla conflict, at last the war had blown up into an open battle. This type of action gave the American's fire power the advantage. Eddie wondered if things would develop and come to an end soon and he would be sent back to the States and its boring reality.

It was dark before Eddie's crew finished offloading their freight and the necessary pre-flights and checklists were completed for engine start. There had been no rocket or mortar rounds inbound to the base during their short visit and they were eager to be on the move. Next door, the C-133 crew was holding a conference in front of their aircraft and scratching their heads. Meanwhile an unwatched Vietnamese crew was off loading their cargo, utilizing their rear freight ramp.

During their taxi to the runway, Eddie asked Jim if he wanted to depart with their exterior running lights on or off. This had been the subject of many 22nd crew discussions and normally came up after three or more beers loosened their tongues and opinions. The 22nd official stand was that for all night approaches and departures in Vietnam, exterior lights would be off, so as to not attract unnecessary small arms fire from unfriendlies. If the tower needed to know where the aircraft was, the crew was to flash their lights on and off until the tower acknowledged their position, then the lights were to remain off again. Some crewmembers felt, however, that there was more danger from midair collision with other aircraft around the busier bases and it made more sense to leave the lights on. Everywhere else in the world exterior lights were always illuminated so other aircraft could see each other.

"There's a lot of shit happening on the ground tonight, so let's go with our lights out," was Jim's conclusion. Eddie was relieved, he also felt that way but it was not the co-pilot's call.

The take-off roll and liftoff was normal, the tower was still using runway two seven. Eddie turned off their exterior lights immediately after raising the gear handle. The tower instructed them, "At five hundred feet turn left to zero eight zero degrees and climb to nine thousand feet."

Jim called for Eddie to raise the flaps. Then he called "climb power" to Sergeant Devereux. At 500 feet indicated (above sea level), Jim rolled the aircraft into a thirty degree left turn to reverse course, and head back east towards the Philippines, heading 080 degrees as instructed. It was dark outside and the firefights on the ground resembled a lot of fireworks, some much larger than others. Some of the stuff looked like roman candles.

About half way through the turn something very big passed over them, very closely! "ZoopPPP" and it was gone. It was so close they could hear it over the heavy, deep bellow of their own engines. So close they could see the red exhaust from its engines and they felt a bump from its air disturbance. "Shit!" Jim hollered. "Did you see that?"

"We were so close that I felt it," Eddie heard himself bellow. "We god-damned near bought that one!"

"Lights on!" Jim called. "There's aircraft all over here, the Viet Cong can go to hell."

Eddie reached up and turned on all the exterior lights as Jim rolled out on a 080 heading and they climbed through 1000 feet altitude. Because they were empty they were climbing at a healthy 800 feet per minute; good for a C-124. Just as Eddie looked over the nose at all the lights flashing and tracers crisscrossing on the ground, a solid string of tracers rose up straight at what seemed to be their cockpit. Half the way up, and before the tracers reached their cockpit, they exploded in a huge ball of flame. In the center of the ball, Eddie could clearly see the silhouette of a disintegrating American Huey helicopter.

"Whoa!" Eddie exclaimed, instinctually throwing his arm up to shield himself. Then just as quickly they passed over the ball of flame and were in the darkness again.

"Turn the god-damned lights off again!" Jim hollered and Eddie immediately complied. Eddie's hand was shaking and it took two tries to get all the switches. Nobody said a word as they climbed out in the dark, the chatter on the radio continued, the engines bellowed, the propellers clawed for altitude, the war below them went on, but in the cockpit there was silence. Passing 4000 feet Eddie contacted Paris GCI and was told they were too busy to talk to him. They leveled at 9000 feet and Jim had the flight engineer set up cruise power. Over water, as they approached the Vietnamese FIR, they contacted the enroute oceanic controller on the HF radio and opened an over water flight plan. Eddie read back their clearance and radioed in the navigator's estimated time to their first check point.

Eddie was the first one to speak about what they had just witnessed, "Ya think they were shooting at us and those poor bastards just got in the way? They had their lights off, so no one should have been shooting at them."

"God knows," Jim replied. "It's hard telling what happened back there. It sure looked like an American Huey helicopter though."

"I feel like shit," Eddie moaned. "If we caused those chopper guys to get killed, I can't tell you how bad I feel."

"It's not our fault," Romano joined in. "This war is not the fault of anybody on this crew. Our job is to do our job and that's what we're doing. We're hauling trash and what happened, happened."

When they arrived back at Clark, everyone was in a somber mood. The enlisted sat in the crew van waiting for the officers to finish with the aerial port. When the officers had finished their paperwork and rejoined the rest of the crew, they opened a bottle of Jim Beam and passed it around in silence. As there was no cargo to offload, Sergeant O'Riley didn't have to stay with the aircraft. He was riding with the rest of the crew. In the aerial port operations room, Jim and Eddie were faced with a dilemma. The command post had planned them for a six o'clock departure the next morning. It was eleven p.m, and a six o'clock departure wouldn't give them the required eight hours sleep. In addition, they had already flown four long days in a row and were overdue for a regulation twenty-four hour crew rest period. Jim explained the MAC regulations to the sergeant behind the desk and the sergeant explained the 315th PACAF duty regulations, or the lack of 315th regulations, during an operational emergency. By then the whole world was aware of the intense Tet Offensive that was being fought in Vietnam. It certainly met the definition of an operational emergency.

Jim thought about asking to see the colonel in charge of the port—then he thought of the poor grunts back in Vietnam and how silly his insistence on eight hours of sleep would sound to them. He and Eddie returned to the crew bus and explained the catch twenty-two. Everyone was dead tired but allowed their two cents' worth. Even the enlisted were asked their opinions. Military protocol called for the officers to make the decisions and the enlisted to follow orders but on a close-knit aircrew, and especially when the officers were young and lower in rank, camaraderie and crew loyalty often overrode military protocol. It was the synergy that mattered. After seeing the helicopter blown up, the conclusion was to go. The bottle of Jim Beam was stowed for a later day. Jim returned to the dispatcher and told him, "We'll be here in the morning in time for a seven a.m. departure. One more hour won't make any difference. My loadmaster will be here at four a.m., he can sleep both ways in-flight. If MAC wants to hang me for breaking the rules, they'll have to wait till I get back from Vietnam. At this point I really don't give a damn."

That night Eddie didn't sleep well, again. The sight of that scared airman's eyes at the aerial port, a midair miss by inches, those tracers coming up, and that explosion with a Huey in the center; they forced a reality check. So went MAC 23's first day of the TET Offensive!

* *

The next morning the Clark Air Base drill was the same, except everyone was quiet. They ate a larger than normal breakfast and the enlisted scrounged a dozen boxes of field rations from a source they kept secret from the officers. According to Sergeant Devereux, "At least we'll eat if the day turns to shit." The enlisted always seemed to have their priorities in order. Everyone's food bags were getting a bit low as there hadn't been any time to drop by the base commissary. The cockpit bunks were occupied for the trip across the pond. Jim and Eddie traded turns and each got an hour and a half sleep in a lower bunk, while the flight engineers took turns in the top bunk. The loadmaster slept in a bunk in the rear of the cargo compartment. They had a load of Class A explosives. This time they were carrying 40,000 pounds of large bombs for Danang Air Base where the fighters, flying around the clock, were depleting the normal munitions reserves.

It was Eddie's turn to fly and upon arrival at Danang, per instructions from the tower, he slipped into the busy pattern and followed a two ship formation of A-1s around base and onto the left runway. Just before they touched down, a "Mayday" F-4 came out of nowhere, over the radio, and said he was behind a C-124 "just flaring, over runway one seven left." Both of Danang's runways were operating at full capacity. Eddie used a considerable amount of reverse thrust to slow and quickly cleared the runway. As they cleared the runway and reversed course on the taxiway, the F-4 rolled past them, its drag chute deployed, and dense black smoke bellowing from its left engine tailpipe. As the F-4 passed out of sight behind them, the fire trucks took the runway and followed the battle-damaged jet to the ramp. Eddie, taxiing away from the scene, assumed the F-4 cleared the runway because in less than a minute the tower cleared a C-130 for a take-off. There wasn't time for the ground crews to check the runway for debris from the crippled F-4. The greatest air show on the earth just went on and on and on.

Danang was even busier than Bien Hoa had been the day before. The large freight ramp was so congested with aircraft they had to wait thirty minutes on the taxiway before a parking spot opened up. Eddie had plenty time to take a roll and a half of 35mm slides and drink a cup of coffee before they were ready to shut down their engines. With his telephoto he got some good photos of freight being offloaded from C-141s and being transported to one corner of the ramp. There it was being sorted into smaller piles and rapidly loaded into smaller "Bookie" C-123s and C-130s. Final delivery would be into the countless short jungle strips located in the haze to the west. Then it was Sergeant O'Riley's turn to go to work.

The munitions they were carrying, big bombs, had been loaded and O'Riley was off loading them with the C-124's second method of handling freight. There was an electric powered overhead winch mounted on a rail that spanned the entire length of the cargo compartment's ceiling. Cargo on pallets could be picked up with the electric overhead winch and motored back and forth in the cargo compartment. There was also a set of bomb-bay type doors, belly doors underneath the bottom of the aircraft, near the rear of the cargo compartment. Over the belly doors was a removable section of the cargo compartment floor. The floor section could be lifted with the overhead winch and placed out of the way in the rear. With the belly-bay doors opened and the floor section removed, the winch could be used to raise freight from the ramp below, through the open floor, motored to its designated tie down spot and set on the floor of the C-124 cargo compartment. O'Riley was reversing the process, picking up the bomb pallets with the winch, motoring them until they were over the open hole in the floor, and lowering them down onto a waiting trailer on the ramp.

The bombs, mounted on small special pallets, one bomb per pallet, were time consuming to unload. Considering the nature of the cargo, the unloading had to be done very carefully. It was crude and slow work, but the C-124 was early 1950s technology in a late 1960s war. While O'Riley was unloading the bombs, the rest of the crew took what was left of their food bags, a couple boxes of the sergeants' field rations, and sat on the concrete ramp and had a meal. It was way too hot and humid to stay in the cockpit. The ramp was a very busy place, with tractors pulling trailers full of freight to and from a multitude of aircraft. The only safe place to sit and relax was between the two main landing gear.

"I can't get yesterday out of my mind," Eddie worried out loud as he finished the last of his canned fruit and was picking through the field rations: crackers, canned mystery meat and canned fruit and fruitcake. He noticed the normal oil drips coming from the number two engine and had moved a little further under the wing. Eddie was referring to the helicopter that was blown out of the air the day before, under them after take-off. The rest of the crew still wanted to digest their feelings about the incident and weren't ready to talk about it.

"I wonder if that C-133 crew ever got out of there?" Jim changed the subject. "If there wasn't anything vital dripping out of their belly and if the cockpit stuff was working, I would have preferred flying it out of there like it was, unpressurized. Sitting there on that ramp, scratching my head, and waiting for another rocket attack was dumb." Jim was sitting just inside the left main tire and was using it for a backrest. "They could patch those holes at Clark. They were right in the belly area and probably just went through the skin and into the freight. Good thing they weren't carrying bombs, like we are today."

"Boom!" Sergeant Romano grinned and answered for the whole crew. "I don't think they could have gotten a mechanic at Bien Hoa even if they wanted one, with all the damage from the mortar attack and all those fighter launches. I'll bet a MAC cargo plane would have been last priority for maintenance, one level below impossible."

Sergeant Devereux added," They would have pulled their C-133 out of the way and let it sit."

It dawned on Eddie that they were having a picnic, but instead of enjoying it in the city park in Greeley,

Colorado, they were sitting in the middle of a war and chatting like a couple of women. He grinned to himself at the novelty. He then covered his ears with his hands as an aircraft, a C-141 four engine jet freighter, was starting up his engines in front of their C-124. The conversation terminated as everyone gathered everything that was loose, and everyone hunkered down knowing what was next. Covering their ears, they sat like a band of Arabs in a sandstorm. They leaned into the jet exhaust as all the engines were started and the pilot advanced his throttles to slowly roll out of his parking spot. It was the start of the C-141's long journey back to the States.

The C-141 was empty, lightweight, and probably had only enough fuel to get back to Clark in the Philippines. The pilot still needed just a little more than normal thrust to initiate the C-141's movement to taxi. The additional thrust and the subsequent burst of intense jet blast came just as O'Riley was lowering one of the bombs down through the rear belly-doors. The heavy jet blast swung the 1000 pound bomb around, sidewise on its extended winch cable. The chain sling slipped and the bomb slid clear of its pallet. The unarmed bomb fell tail first onto the waiting trolley, flipped its nose onto the ramp, and then settled down to a few small quivers as it settled onto the hot concrete. "Clang, chunk blob blob bup!" It happened so fast that no one had a chance to react or duck. Then it was over.

Eddie felt his heart skip a beat and was so terrorized he was speechless. Devereux's eyes opened to twice their normal size and he muttered something that sounded like "Sacre' bleu" in Cajun French.

Jim swung his head back and forth slowly, as he muttered pure American English: "Fuck me . . . fuck me . . . fuck me." Everyone stared at each other and was surprised, then totally thankful to be alive. While the bombs had no fuses attached, they still were delicate Class A explosives. To an aircrew with no explosive training, an unbelievable miracle had occurred. They were alive, it hadn't blown up! Had it blown up, the entire load of bombs would have followed suit. The Vietnamese trolley tenders, on the ground, ran for a hundred yards. It took ten minutes for them to settle down before they would return to the undersides of the silver Shaky Bird. After four minutes, O'Riley climbed down the crew hatch's extended ladder. He was white faced and still shaking from the adrenalin.

It was late in the afternoon when they finally got the bombs unloaded, aircraft buttoned up, and were taxiing out for take-off. Everyone was still in a somber mood. The dropped bomb made their second day of the Tet Offensive another thrill they really didn't need. Jim was having a running conversation with Sergeant Devereux about the peripheral aircrew concept in South East Asia. President Johnson was under heavy pressure from his constituents to limit the American manpower in Vietnam. He was responding to the pressure from the media and youth demonstrations. But there was no visible pressure for him to limit the numbers of American servicemen stationed "outside" the Vietnamese War zone. The flying organizations stationed outside the borders, which the 22nd was a part, flew daily missions into Vietnam but were not counted in the Vietnam manpower tally. They were also not credited with having served a tour in Vietnam, something which Eddie was later to find out.

There was a long line of aircraft waiting for take-off clearance. Eddie checked in with the tower and they were number eight in line for the left runway. They had worked their way up to number four when there was a loud kahwoomp, an explosion occurred somewhere behind them. Sergeant Devereux was still looking out the top hatch and hollered over the crew interphone, "Shit, now we're getting mortared, or rocketed, whatever the hell the difference is. Something just buzzed in and exploded about three hundred yards east of the MAC ramp."

"Kahwoomp . . . Kahwoomp . . . Kahwoomp." Then the tower came back on the air.

"Attention all aircraft, Danang is under attack. All aircraft stand down and stay clear of the traffic pattern until we get some artillery assistance. One seven left landing traffic, orbit right hand patterns over China Beach until I can get back to you. Is there anyone out there with less than fifteen minutes of fuel and absolutely has to land immediately? These things usually don't last very long."

"Tower, this is Covey Zero Six," a drawn out southern voice called. "I'm an OV-10, a little west of y'all returning to land at Danang. I was just about ready to call y'all for landing when that first rocket hit. I saw where it came from. The smoke trail came from a walled courtyard with a small grouping of white buildings with red tile roofs, about two miles off the departure end of runway one seven left. If you can get some artillery, I can direct it in and get those guys. Every time they pop a smoke trail toward the air base, it's followed by an explosion inside the base perimeter. I know it's them."

"Covey Zero Six, I appreciate the help, but we already called the Monkey Mountain artillery guys and they said all their guns are working on helping troops in contact. It'll be ten to fifteen minutes before they can get to our problem." There was a pause as the tower frequency was strangely silent. Everyone was mulling over the idea of sitting there, enduring an ongoing rocket barrage. "Kahwoomp . . . kahwoomp," the barrage continued.

"Tower, this is Bookie Two Two, the C-123 number one for take-off. I'd rather take my chances taking-off and getting the hell out of here than being a sitting duck here at Rocket Alley."

"Bookie Two Two, cleared take-off your discretion, turn left immediately after take-off to avoid the source of the rockets. Stay below five hundred feet until over water. I have numerous aircraft at traffic pattern altitude in orbit to the east. You'll need to go under them." The C-123 wasted no time and was rolling down the runway on his getaway.

"Tower, this is Spad One, flight of two A-1s that are now number two for take-off, behind the C-141. That Covey got any smoke left?"

"Yeah," the Covey answered without using the tower operator as the middle man. "I got one stick left."

"Tower," the Spad replied. "If you can give me and my wingman permission to taxi across the grass and around this C-141 in front of me and if that covey can put smoke to mark the target; I got just the right thing hanging under my wing for those gomers. It weighs five hundred pounds."

"Permission granted," the tower replied. "You guys work it out and let me know when I can get back to my business."

There was about a fifteen second silence over the radio as two more incoming rockets impacted and a small storage shack next to the MAC ramp was blown into pieces. They were getting close and in the next few minutes the crowded MAC freight ramp could be taking direct hits.

The two A-1 Spads taxied across the grass and into position on the runway.

Jim turned to Eddie and remarked, "This is better than television. We're right in the middle of everything."

"I'd rather watch it on television. I want out of here," Eddie faked a snarl and grinned back. The truth is he had just been thinking the same thing. Everything outside the windshield seemed unreal; he couldn't believe he was witness to such an event.

"Smokes on target," the radio beamed from the Covey forward air controller. "Put your bomb or rockets or whatever you got into the walled compound about twenty meters to the south of my smoke."

Instantly the A-1s revved up their single Wright 3350 radial engines and the pair roared down the runway, lifted off, and pulled up their gear. The Spads crawled up to about 700 feet—then the lead aircraft rolled sideways and dropped out of sight. There was a large explosion and the lead Spad climbed back up into position for his wingman to rejoin their formation of two.

"Tower, you're back in business," the Covey called.

"Spad pilots get free drinks at the bar tonight, break break," the tower announced. "Danang tower is open for business. Which of you guys orbiting out there is about to run out of gas? Don't all you guys speak at once."

They sat for another ten minutes as the tower worked on the backlog of aircraft waiting to land. At last their turn came and the four radial engines pulled their silver C-124 down the runway and up into the Vietnamese air for their return trip to Clark. The tower still had a large number of aircraft to land and he was organizing them into an extended line on the east, downwind side of one seven left. He requested Eddie's aircraft to maintain runway heading until passing 4000 feet so as to avoid the orbiting aircraft. As they were passing 600 feet they flew over the cluster of building scraps that had been the source of the mortar attack. It was still smoldering from the Spad's 500 pound bomb. There was a noticeable secondary explosion as they passed over the burning compound and the airplane bumped a little from the concussion. Jim looked over at Eddie and smiled, "Their ammo is still cooking off." At 4,000 feet they made their turn and headed for Clark.

The word at the Danang Command Post was that the gomers had been pretty well beaten back around the major air bases and army facilities, and the insurgents had suffered massive casualties for their holiday efforts. For the Americans, fear of being overrun had changed to reserved optimism.

Back at Clark they were too late for happy hour but they were holding a board meeting in the Rathskeller. There were twelve guys from the 22nd at the large table and six groupies, consisting of five schoolteachers and Katy from Tachikawa. The group was quieter than normal. The girls could sense that the guys' work was draining them of their usual energy. The others in the Rathskeller were also subdued. Eddie and Ching each had a pizza, a couple of beers, watched some flight attendants shake their tits and butts on the dance stage, then retired to the trailers as they had another seven a.m. departure—this time for Hue. So went MAC 23's second day of the Tet Offensive!

* *

The next morning there was a patch on the right stabilizer (horizontal tail) of their aircraft, about fourteen inches in diameter. No one knew exactly what it had been, probably a rock or a piece of metal, or even roof tile. The secondary explosion of munitions from the A-1's bomb had apparently thrown something into the air and Eddie and crew had unknowingly picked up a "hole."

Day three of the Tet Offensive started out just like all of Eddie's other "fly" days had for the last six months. Everyone had breakfast at the Cinder Block Cafe, and the officers did flight plans at the MAC Command Post. Their day's assignment was to fly a load of cargo to the Hue airfield, just south of the demilitarized zone—the border between North and South Vietnam. Then they would return to Clark. They loaded enough fuel so they could get there and back without refueling in-country. This time they were hauling a forty foot truck van with something classified inside it. Whatever it was, their total cargo weight was 25,000 pounds. An armed courier/guard would accompany the van and would stay downstairs guarding his van.

Jim had been called in the middle of the night and informed that his wife was injured in a car accident back at Tachikawa. They had a seat for him on an empty C-141 that was flying to Yakota Air Base near Tachikawa. The squadron performed a midnight search for a new aircraft commander and they found Major Baxter at his usual poker game at the Clark Officers Club. He had finished giving an annual check ride the day before and was set to ride the same C-141 back to Yakota Air Base in Japan that they were putting Jim on. Eddie hadn't flown with Major Baxter in almost six months.

Eddie was no longer the new guy and felt comfortable flying with anyone in the 22nd, but he didn't look forward to flying with Major Baxter's cigar smoke. He hoped it would be for only one day and they could find a different replacement for the remainder of their crew's trip south. Eddie and his crew had been out seven days, so they probably had a week to go before their aircraft would need to return to Tachikawa for its scheduled routine maintenance. However, with the Tet Offensive, everything was up for grabs.

As they taxied out, did their run up, then sat in line for take-off, Eddie hoped this would be a dull routine day. The previous two days had given him enough thrill and adventure. He yearned for the routine flights and good layovers his assignment had afforded him. During the two previous days he had discovered that he didn't like having the crap scared out of him. He'd seen enough "combat" and was ready to just haul trash.

The major was the same as the last time Eddie flew with him, his usual isolated self, who kept his opinions to himself. He lit a grossly bad smelling cigar during the climb out. It seems that almost every pilot in the 22nd had a quirk when flying. One guy hummed, Major Baxter chain smoked cigars, one rocked his head continuously while in-flight, one tapped constantly with his pencil. It was only to be expected when you spend most of your time, for months, then years, in a seat just looking around.

As soon as they leveled off and set cruise power, the major excused himself, took a leak, put out his cigar, and crawled into the top bunk. As the major had his arm across his nose and was facing the rear of the bunk, he didn't see Eddie turn in his co-pilot's seat, hold his nose with one hand, and give the thumbs down to the flight engineer. Sgt. Devereux smiled and returned the thumbs down rating of the major's cigar smoking habit—

then was joined by Ching with the same gesture. The major was tired, he only had three hours of sleep and his snores soon joined the drone of the four 4360s and the crackle of the HF radio over Eddie's headset. It was a nice concert and Eddie slid his seat back, put his feet up on the lower instrument panel edge, and defaulted into his usual trance. It was his thinking time again and with the scattered clouds sliding by and the dark blue ocean below, he felt whole again. This would be an easy flight, a cake walk out and back. The van they were carrying wouldn't take very long to pull out through their nose door and they would get back to Clark in time for happy hour. Eddie was looking forward to hanging out at the big bar upstairs and listening to the stories. With all the recent action taking place in Vietnam, the stories would be flowing fast and furious.

Just as Eddie finished calling in their halfway reporting point it happened. Sgt. Devereux asked Eddie to look at the oil pressure and quantity on the number two engine. Eddie had caught a little motion on the gauges out of the corner of his eye and was trying to decide if it was serious enough to disturb the rest of the crew. "Wake the major up," Eddie directed Ching—then he noticed the major was already crawling out of his bunk. The guy had a sixth sense.

"Whata we got?" the major stood behind the flight engineer's position and the two of them carefully analyzed each fluctuation in oil pressure and the slow decrease of oil quantity. Then all of a sudden the oil quantity dial began a rapid drop towards zero and the major called "feather number two" as he crawled into his left pilot seat. The flight engineer pulled the lever and as ordered, the engine quit from fuel starvation, the propeller blades twisted into the wind and stopped as if at attention, and all of the fluid valves in the engine's firewall closed. Eddie switched off the autopilot and added enough rudder trim to offset the aircraft's asymmetrical power.

Major Baxter looked out his side window and saw that the propeller was stopped and feathered, then slipped on his headset and called "scanner report" over the crew interphone. Eddie hand flew the autopilot disengaged airplane while the major oversaw the engine shutdown routine.

"Looks good down here," came a voice over the interphone. It was Sgt. Romano who had scurried downstairs into the cargo hold as he performed his scanner duty. The pilots only had a partial view of their engines from the cockpit, but the scanner downstairs could see everything through the side windows. The scanners view was particularly helpful in the case of an engine fire. "There's oil all over the nacelle and it's smeared down the side of the airplane, the aft windows are useless."

"I got the airplane," the major informed Eddie as he finished adjusting his seat, and was ready to fly.

"You have the aircraft," Eddie replied and released his grip on the yoke.

Eddie and Sgt. Deveruex performed the Engine Failure checklist: cowl flaps closed, oil cooler closed, prop selector fixed pitch, boost pump off. When he was finished Eddie informed the crew, "Engine Failure checklist complete."

Sgt. Devereux proceeded to look up and set the three engine cruise power settings for their weight, altitude, and outside air temperature. The charts called for a 6000 foot cruise on three engines, so the Major let the aircraft slowly drift down from 8000 toward the recommended altitude of 6000. It was a drill everyone on the crew had performed many times.

"We're going back to Clark," Major Baxter announced. He started a thirty degree angle left turn. "I'll turn it around and from here it's closest to head for Poro Point, then down the valley into Clark. You got a heading for me, Ching?"

Ching spent about sixty seconds with his chart, his plastic plotter, and his trusty E6-B analog computer as he plotted a new course to Poro Point. Then he gave the major a heading to fly and estimated times for the next reporting point and estimated time of arrival (ETA) to Clark Air Base. With Major Baxter's permission Eddie called the over-water controller on the HF radio. He informed them they had to shut down their number two engine and were returning to Clark. He gave them the estimated times and informed them they needed no assistance. With the highly classified truck trailer on board, the major didn't want to fib about the engine and claim it was running at reduced power to minimize paperwork. People in high positions would want to know why they had turned around and the armed escort in the cargo hold downstairs wasn't stupid. The controller replied with a new clearance via Poro Point at 6000 feet. The major re-trimmed the aircraft, switched on the autopilot, and fumbled in his bag for his used cigar and a sex novel. "You got it."

"I got the airplane," Eddie replied as he took over responsibility for flight control of the airplane and braced for the cigar smoke. Within minutes everyone was settled down into their own world again.

"Care if I use the HF radio?" Swifty Romano asked Major Baxter. The flight engineers had just swapped duties and Swifty was in the flight engineer's seat. "I got a ham radio operator's license and I'll only be off the MAC frequency for ten or fifteen minutes."

"Help yourself," the major let out a puff of dark foul smoke as he continued reading his paperback. It was titled *The Last Door On Your Left* and had a picture of a provocative woman walking down a hallway.

Swifty changed the HF radio channel and started searching for someone to talk to. Eddie switched off his HF monitoring and welcomed the relief from the ever present static. Over the roar of the engines and with his HF switch turned off, Eddie lost track of what Swifty was doing behind him. After about five minutes, Swifty tapped Eddie on his shoulder and asked, "What's your folk's telephone number?"

"Wadda you mean my folk's phone number?" Eddie twisted around in his seat and looked at Swifty who was sporting a grin.

"I got Senator Goldwater's ham radio station on the air in Phoenix, Arizona. The guys back at the NCO club said he has ham operators, twenty-four hours a day, operating his amateur radio. If you give em a phone number they'll call your relatives and phone patch you through. The Senator will pick up the tab for the phone call."

"You gotta be shitting me!" Eddie cocked his head. "It's Greeley, Colorado, number 048J3. We still have party lines out in the country." Eddie switched on his monitor switch and within a minute could hear the phone ringing.

"Hello?" it was Eddie's mother's voice. He could recognize it anywhere.

"Mom, this is Eddie calling. It's good to hear your voice."

"Eddie, where are you! Do you need us to pick you up at the airport? Your dad needs you to help with the irrigating. It's been so dry this summer."

"I'm over the ocean," Eddie tried to sound calm for his confused mother. "I'm in an airplane and we're about two hours from the Philippines."

"I must be dreaming. They don't have telephones in airplanes. I asked your cousin about that. He said there were no telephones where you are. Are you sure you're not in Denver?"

"No, Mom, I'm on the other side of the world. We're talking over the radio and Senator Goldwater is paying for the telephone bill."

"I don't know Senator Goldwater and I don't know what's going on. Come home, your dad needs you."

Eddie's mother had an eighth grade education and was raised on a remote homestead farm on the prairies of eastern Colorado. She was a loving, caring woman, a wonderful mother but was not tuned into the ways of the world. Having a son away in the military was hard on her and it was not kind to confuse her, so he altered his approach. "I just wanted to call you and tell you everything was okay and that I'm okay and I'll write you a letter explaining everything. You can have my cousin John help you with the letter."

"When you coming home?"

"I don't know, Mom. I just want you to know that I love you and I'm okay and I'll write you . . . Goodbye."

"Goodbye!" Eddie heard the telephone click.

Eddie sat enveloped with emotion and despair for a few minutes while Max placed another call for the loadmaster to talk to his parents. World War II had been so hard on his family and he knew his mother was still living in that era. It was a wonderful thing that Senator Goldwater was doing, but it was just too much for a simple farm woman to grasp.

After everyone else had a go on the HF connection, Swifty signed off and everyone resumed their thoughts. Major Baxter didn't have anyone to call; he claimed he didn't have any folks or friends left in the States. The three engines pulled their craft back towards Clark Field.

An hour later, just as a line of billowy clouds on the horizon indicated where the Island of Luzon would be, Eddie heard what he really didn't want to hear. "Sir, we got problems," Swifty announced over the interphone. His voice was serious and Eddie felt a surge flow through his body. "Our number four has been acting up a little, oil pressure and temps are all okay, but I'm having a hard time keeping it leaned properly. I think I've seen a few minor fluctuations on the fuel pressure, but they're really subtle. I don't know if I'm imagining them or not . . . Oops, there we go again, it was real. Sir, I think we have a fuel leak somewhere on number four."

Major Baxter turned in his seat, motioned toward Devereux sitting on the lower bunk, and announced over the interphone, "Get Devereux downstairs to look for vapors trailing from number four. Don't change a thing on your number four engine settings. If we got a leak and we're not on fire, I don't wanna change power or anything that will change the flow of fuel or air out there and maybe cause a fire to ignite. We need that engine for another hour and a half so we'll just let it run as long as it ain't on fire."

The crew didn't need to be told that a fuel leak in the vicinity of very hot exhaust manifolds was an invitation to a fire. Baxter continued his instruction, "If we see a flame, we'll shut it down immediately. If we gotta shut it down, our drift down should get us close to Clark. I think on two engines we could at least make it to land. If we don't catch fire, we'll let down into Clark by reducing power on engines one and three only, we won't alter our airspeed, and number four's fuel flow and air flow won't change. When we cross the threshold at Clark, you shut down engine number four with the fuel tank valve. We'll starve the entire nacelle of fuel and eliminate the chances of fire. It won't burn if there's no fuel to the engine. You can feather the prop with the fire handle during the rollout—after the engine is fuel starved."

The major was a take-charge man and had all the answers, but he still kept his cool as he sat there gumming his unlit cigar. Eddie was impressed. The previously interesting China Sea below took on a hostile, dark, forbidding look. The Philippine island of Luzon, somewhere beyond the horizon, was a welcome chunk of solid land but so far far away. Eddie no longer had an appetite for its rich history. Its beaches were only a place to belly land their aluminum cripple.

"We got lots of heavy vapor coming out of number four. It's a big leak," Devereux announced over the interphone from his observation position on the right side of the aircraft cargo hold. As if on cue the affected engine coughed lightly. "If that son of a bitch ever gets ignited they'll see our smoke all the way from Clark. It'll burn our wing clean off."

Eddie switched the UHF radio transmitter selector to 243.0, the military UHF emergency frequency. He was going to alert anyone listening of their situation and get a rescue escort airplane on its way from Clark.

"I'll decide if our wings gonna burn off or not," Major Baxter reprimanded Devereux over the interphone for everyone to hear. "Sergeant Devereux, you just scared the shit right out of our co-pilot." He nodded towards Eddie, "Eddie, stay off the damn radios. All you would do is shake up the command post and clutter up the air with all kinds of radio calls and questions. Besides that, we're too far out for the UHF radio; ya gotta still use the HF. There ain't a god-damn thing they can do to help us at this time and you have no idea how much paperwork it would generate for me. We'll just slip in there and everything will be just fine. We'll tell em we feathered number four on short final and didn't have the time to call em."

"My God!" Eddie thought. "We got one engine shut down and a second ready to catch fire and all he is worried about is the paperwork. What are these old MAC pilots made of?" Old Shaky just plowed on, maintaining 6000 feet on three engines. "This plane is as stubborn and dumb as its crew. It still thinks everything is all right!"

Major Baxter opened his sex book and pretended to be reading. Eddie noticed he was holding the book upside down but didn't say anything to the senior officer. Eddie hoped the major was just deep in thought and not withdrawing from reality. Swifty actually opened a can of cold chili and ate it while he closely watched his panel full of gauges. Some people need to eat when they're nervous or upset. Things were so switched around. Now the world outside his window was reality and inside was a television scene.

"I got flame coming out of number four's cowl, Sir," Devereux announced over the interphone. And indeed they did. The vapor trail had been replaced by a dense white billowing smoke and flames were licking out of the gaps around the closed cowl flaps. The smoke trail was a perfect imitation of the sketch of a burning engine example in their flight manual. Next to the picture the caption read, "Dense white smoke from cowl flap area—feather and prepare to abandon aircraft." It dawned on Eddie that MAC didn't carry parachutes in their airplanes.

Major Baxter disengaged the autopilot, turned to Swifty, and in a tone of voice one would expect from someone ordering a drink from the bar, reviewed the procedure: "Close all fuel tank valves outside number three, fuel starve number four first. I want all the fuel lines out there to be empty." He hesitated for a second then finished, "When the engine snorts from fuel starvation feather number four." Eddie was numb as he transformed from a young college graduate into a mature air force pilot. Eddie's adrenal glands, orange colored endocrine glands located on the top of both his kidneys, simultaneously contracted and pumped out an unusually large burst of adrenalin.

Swifty performed the procedure as directed. The engine sputtered, spit, then wound to a stop from fuel starvation. After the engine sputtered, Swifty pulled the fire handle and number four propeller obediently rotated its blades into the wind stream. The plume of smoke thinned and in less than a minute disappeared. The fire had been starved to death. The crew and old Shaky were bonded soul mates and shared the same destiny. They were carrying a load of freight and their aircraft couldn't hang on to its altitude with two engines shut down. Eddie had studied the two engine chart enough to know that with their non-jettisonable load, the best they could do was a shallow descent down to sea level. The big forty foot truck trailer in the cargo hold below couldn't be thrown overboard. They were screwed.

"Maximum continuous power on, let's see, what have we got left? Number one and number three," Major Baxter ordered. No one smiled at his attempt at humor. Swifty advanced the throttles to get all they could out of the remaining two engines, without overstressing them and causing further failures. In order to maintain their most aerodynamically efficient airspeed of one hundred forty knots indicated, they had to descend at 200 feet per minute. They were at 140 knots indicated, a little faster than climbing speeds, in cooler air, so Swifty only had to crack the cowls a smidgen to keep their last two operating engines' temperatures below the red line. The major turned to Eddie and reluctantly said, "If you can raise Clark on the HF radio, tell them we're down to two engines. Request equipment standing by and tell them we may land a little short. Request a rescue chopper out our way just in case."

Eddie realized that the major was no longer concerned about generating paperwork, which only reinforced Eddie's feelings that they really were in deep kimchi. Calling for help was something Eddie wanted to do more than anything in the world. He selected the HF radio and blurted, "Mayday! Mayday! Mayday! This is MAC Two Three declaring emergency, hundred sixty miles west of Poro Point. Two engines failed, two engines remaining. Mayday! Mayday!"

"Roger MAC Two Three, copy mayday. What are your intentions?" The enroute controller didn't sound as interested as Eddie would have liked him to be.

"Our intention is to abort the mission, return to Clark, and stay airborne as long as we can!" Eddie confessed over the radio. All of a sudden everyone listening in on the aviation frequency knew that he was a little uptight. "Our ETA to Clark is one hour ten minutes, fifty-five minutes to Poro Point. We'll be requesting runway two zero and equipment standing by. Also request helicopter escort! "

"Easy kid, you gotta have a little faith in old Shaky," the major reached over and placed his hand on Eddie's shoulder. "We'll do a lot better once we settle down into thicker air and maybe we can hold her off when we get into ground effect."

Eddie looked out his side window and tried to settle down. "It's almost gone now, Sir." He hesitated and added, "The fire and smoke, Sir, not the wing!" It was then Eddie decided to keep quiet as he was not in full control of the words coming out from his mouth. He tried to remember all he had been taught about ground effect at Willy:

Ground effect is an additional lift that results when the wing of an aircraft is approximately two thirds of its span above the ground or water. The additional lift is gained from the redirection of the wing's induced drag (downdraft). As the aircraft continues to descent, ground effect increases and when ten percent of the length of the wing span above the ground, induced drag is reduced forty-eight percent.

Eddie also remembered that the instructor told him ground effect "is a useless phenomenon in today's high performance aircraft. It could cause an aircraft to float a little when landing." Eddie's check ride at Willy, in a T-38 trainer, was at 600 miles per hour and he landed at 170 miles per hour, with a wing span of twenty-five feet. Two thirds of twenty-five feet was insignificant. Now, he was in a low speed and low performance aircraft with a wing span of 174 feet and they were going to be pressed to make it to Clark before they settled into the jungle, or worse yet, an ocean full of sharks. Two thirds of 174 feet could be their salvation.

As they drifted lower into thicker air, what the major said was true. The lower they drifted the less descent rate was necessary to maintain 140 knots. The cockpit was silent as everyone's eyes were on the descent rate, the altitude remaining, and on the Poro Point TACAN reading that was displaying their distance from the TACAN station—located on the seacoast. They drifted off course a little to cut short the corner at Poro Point. It saved them maybe three minutes. As they passed over the beach and made a shallow right turn, directly toward Clark Air Base, their two remaining engines roared out their best. From their position, Clark was down a wide flat valley. The higher hills along the sea coast were the reason they had not been able to fly, earlier, directly towards Clark. Eddie could see the people on the ground as they worked their rice paddies. The ones in front of them looked up nervously and several water buffalo snorted and ran. What a spectacle they must have been to those innocent farmers—a huge aluminum cloud, 500 feet in the air, and slowly descending. Time dragged on and in the thicker air it was only necessary to descend at thirty feet per minute in order to maintain the most efficient airspeed. Re-starting engine number two was not an option, the oil quantity gauge indicated empty.

Everything had become very personal and Eddie was deadened with fright. A cold numbness crept upward from his stomach and caused a partial paralysis of his throat and neck muscles. He had a fixation on the ground in front of them as his mind kept updating his mental calculations. Where would their descent rate result in an impact with the hard stuff below? Would it be into jungle or some poor farmer's rice paddy? The expression to "buy the farm" was no longer an idle remark. He didn't want this to happen; it wasn't part of the deal. He was disappointed in the airplane for failing in its duty. They had told him back at the squadron that the 22nd, the Double Deuce the sergeant had referred to the squadron, "hadn't had an accident in over five years and they were damn proud of their record—considering the places they flew into." Little good that did for Eddie. They were about to bust up one bird, real good.

"Bellied a B-26 into a rice paddy in Korea one time," the major started babbling. "What a damn mess that was. I god-damn near drowned in that muck they farm in. You know what they use for fertilizer? Human shit! Damn I hated that place! It was cold and miserable and the girls all had crabs and lice." Eddie couldn't believe how calm the major was. They were almost down and he was telling stories about the Korean War. "If this crate goes in, it'll be a different story." Major Baxter was flying down a wide and shallow river bed that led to where Clark was located. Eddie could see Mount Pinatube a little to their left. That was good, at least they weren't lost. The river bed was free of trees and would provide a clear place to belly land. The water level was very low and the river consisted of small shallow channels of water but mostly sand bars. "This time I'm gonna put her right in on her belly, and we can climb out the top hatch onto the roof of the fuselage. That way the chopper can pick us up with his cable and winch and we won't even get our feet wet. Now that's what I call class."

"I can't wait!" Eddie gave the major his opinion with a side glance.

The rest of the crew were quiet, their two feathered propellers stood still as death itself and there was nothing they could do to change their fate. Everything they could do had been done and all they could do was wait out the crap shoot to see what the results would be. Time seemed to stand still as they each contemplated their probable demise. After an eternity of agony, their DME indicated twenty miles from Clark TACAN, but by then they were down to one hundred feet above the ground. Eddie could see the base helicopter racing out to intercept them but they were too low to see the base. He called the tower with their fifteen mile position and the tower cleared them to land. It seemed a little ridiculous to Eddie. What was the tower going to tell them, "Fly around a while? We're not ready for you to land yet?"

"You god-damn right we're cleared to land," he blurted over the radio to no one in particular. Pilots weren't supposed to swear over the radio but Eddie didn't care. He had a great excuse.

While Eddie was having his hissy fit, Old Shaky slowly leveled off at seventy feet above the river bed. They had settled into ground effect and the additional lift was just enough to hold them off the ground.

"That ground effect is good stuff if you got long wings like this crate," Major Baxter continued his idle talk. "Them stubby winged high performance airplanes could never do this. Call the tower again and tell them to keep the runway clear cause we're planning to be on their concrete in a few minutes." Then he turned to Eddie and remarked, "We're too low for them to see us and I sure as hell don't want some admin puke waiting on the runway in his staff car."

"Tower, this is MAC Two Three, we're a few feet over the northeast rice paddy and with any kind of luck we'll be on your runway before you can see us. The aircraft commander wants you to keep everyone off the runway." Eddie was feeling hopeful as he spoke . . .

* * * * * * * * * * * * * * * * * * * *

The major nursed the ground hugging bird over a small group of huts and some trees that came within feet of their belly. It bled off a little of their airspeed. Then there it was in front of them, 10,500 feet of solid concrete, 150 feet wide, six fire trucks, and half the base personnel waiting to watch them crash.

The major carefully timed his call and ordered, "Gear down—now!"

Eddie responded quickly—then an eternity later called, "Three green, the gear is down." The gear and its associated open gear doors caused more drag than the aircraft could uphold. It settled down onto the wide runway with its two remaining engines still running at maximum continuous power and wing flaps still up. It was a smooth soft touchdown that was the trademark of Major Baxter's landings.

Eddie felt relief like he'd never felt before. He was soaking wet and felt very weak. He hoped he wouldn't throw up. Major Baxter pulled the throttles back to idle and gently braked the sick bird to a slow taxi. The runway was long enough that they didn't need any reverse thrust, especially with asymmetrical engines operating.

The major turned to Eddie, hesitated, glanced back at the flight engineer and declared, "I've had enough practice for one day." He had an uncharacteristically friendly and upbeat tone of voice. "What say we park this thing and go get a beer?"

There were fire engines everywhere and Eddie thought, "How sad if a crew made it this far, then climbed out of their aircraft and one of them was run over by a fire truck." Then something else struck Eddie as odd. When they feathered number four, the major was chewing on a wet unlit cigar. Eddie remembered specifically that when he made his ten mile call to the tower, the major was still gumming the wet sop and there was about one and a half inches left. He was really working it over. Now that they were safely on the ground, the major was no longer gumming anything and his ashtray was empty. He usually flicked his ashes on the floor or inadvertently allowed them to fall off onto his flight suit, the human pig that he was. There was no soppy butt anywhere and Eddie wondered, "Was it possible that this steady and calm old fart had emotions after all and that sometime during the last few seconds of the flight he had accidentally swallowed his cigar?"

They turned onto the taxiway and were welcomed home by the ground controller. Apparently everyone had gotten the word that there was an aircraft in serious trouble. There hadn't been a serious accident in several months so a sizable crowd had gathered and was anticipating a real "weenie roast." A pickup truck with a large "follow me" sign led their way. Follow me trucks were usually utilized when dignitaries or unfamiliar crews landed, so they could be led to the parking spot that had been planned for them.

Eddie looked down at his hands and they were shaking uncontrollably. He looked over at the major and saw he was holding out his right hand—it also was shaking. Their eyes met as they both laughed out loud. "It's the adrenalin!" the major explained. "It'll take about five minutes to burn off—then we'll stop shaking." It was the first time Eddie had ever seen the major smile, yet alone laugh. Eddie twisted around in his seat and looked at Swifty. He too was holding out his hands and looking at them in amazement as they trembled in a quick palsy.

Swifty looked up at Eddie and muttered, "Thank god it's only adrenalin, I thought maybe I was having a heart attack!" They all three laughed. Ching, not laughing or moving, sat in his navigator's seat with his hands flat on his desk top. His eyes, looking straight ahead at nothing, were very round for an Oriental.

"Happens to me every time I crash an airplane," Major Baxter sat looking at his hands.

The "follow me" truck led them on what spontaneously developed into one of the finest parades in Clark's recent history. Behind the slowly moving follow me truck crept the star of the show. The crowd of people had gathered to watch them crash, but when they made it down safely the crowd switched allegiance and cheered the returning heroes. The size of the crowd at an emergency landing is usually proportional to the size of the airplane and the C-124 would have made a very big splash. The C-124 limped along, two of its engines shut down, oil dripping from its inboard left engine and smeared and dripping all the way along its fat fuselage. Number four was a dull white from the smoke and fire that no longer came from the engine. Sergeant Devereux was sticking out of the top hatch, waving furiously at the crowd and keeping the crew inside informed of the activities. As he gradually regained control over the adrenalin, Eddie opened his side window and alternately took photos and waved at the crowd. Behind the crippled bird were four fire engines, two ambulances, three maintenance vans and four staff cars. What a grand parade it was!

The follow me truck led them directly to the wash rack. As it turned out, they weren't getting guest treatment. The commander at Clark didn't want that "dirty oil can" dripping all over his ramp and ordered it washed before anything else. Eddie looked at his watch and it was only eleven in the morning. "Damn!" He was ready for the four o'clock happy hour. For once he had a real story of his own to tell at the bar. Who knows, maybe even a fighter pilot or two would take the time to eavesdrop on his story.

Sergeant O'Riley would have to stay with the aircraft. After the wash job he would need to unload the classified van and assist loading it into another C-124—so it could be flown out ASAP by a replacement bird and crew. The airman courier that had stayed with his precious cargo in their ill fated bird was an inoperative mess of jangled nerves. He would need to be replaced.

They shut down, abandoned their sick bird, and the crew van dropped the major off at the command post. Major Baxter was in a foul mood again because they would have about five pounds of paperwork for him to fill out. He told the crew not to wait for him. After checking for messages from Tachikawa on Jim's wife's condition—there were none—the crew cracked open their bottle of booze and left. They were looking at a day or probably more off, and hopefully a replacement aircraft commander. Major Baxter's Chief of Standardization position kept him too busy checking and training crewmembers.

The oil leak could probably be fixed fairly fast. They shut down the engine before it ran out of oil, so the engine itself would be okay and not need changing, just repair. Number four, however, had burned and it would take an engine change and some structural repair in the vicinity of the engine nacelle. Waiting until number four caught on fire had given them just enough extra mileage to make it to Clark. The price of a new engine and some structural work was a small price to pay for the extra mileage they had eked out of the fuel-leaking engine.

Eddie had the rest of his day all planned. After some swigs from the crew bottle to relax a little, he and Ching could check back into the Oasis Hotel, load up on beer at the pool, stagger to happy hour at the O'club, finish getting stinking drunk, talk half the night, then sleep until they woke up sometime tomorrow. His plan was similar to everyone else's on the bus.

So went MAC 23's third day of the TET Offensive!

CHAPTER SIX:
PIGS, CHICKENS AND COCA COLA

Because of the Tet Offensive, the Clark Air Base aircraft mechanics were swamped with work. Eddie's crew was informed it would be a minimum of four days before their aircraft would be ready to fly again. Number four engine's cowling needed a lot of extra metal work to replace heat warped sections from the fire.

Eddie talked with Colonel Duncan and got a two day release from duty. There were several spare pilots available at Clark, the Tet Offensive had the entire squadron roster down south, but things were slowing back to normal.

The next morning Eddie wasted no time. He threw a few overnight items in a "Saki" bag and caught a jeepney ride to the Angeles train station. He wanted to see first hand the countryside he had recently flown over, with two engines out, and be among the real Filipino people he had seen staring up at them. He bought a train ticket to San Fernando, the town near Poro Point where the TACAN navigational station was located. Where they first made landfall with two engines shut down. It was a little over a half days trip via the local railroad and he felt the higher priced private room would isolate him from the very experience he was seeking. So he bought a second class ticket. The train followed the same valley north that they had followed southbound to Clark in their crippled aircraft. He planned to spend the night somewhere at San Fernando, then the next morning either hop a bus or return by train back to Angeles City. Normally the Americans that traveled that far north on the Luzon train, always in first class, were on their way to a different destination. At San Fernando they would board a bus that climbed a steep unpaved road and wound its way high into the mountains. Their destination was the mountain top Filipino resort town of Baugio and the American military recreation facility called Fort John Hay. This mountaintop facility had been established in 1903 by President Roosevelt. Camp John Hay was noted for its cooler climate, golf course, swank officers club, and attractive enlisted facilities. Eddie didn't have the time to indulge in such luxuries. He didn't play golf and had no clothing to dress for dinner.

The second class train ticket to San Fernando came with wooden bench style seats and the requirement to handle your own baggage. At the Angeles City train terminal, a single wooden ticket office, he stood in line with all the locals waiting for the train to arrive. It was a mix of people. He guessed a lot of them were heading away from the sin city atmosphere of Angles City and traveling to their more peaceful and sane villages. There were also a half dozen crates of chickens, several cardboard boxes full of fresh fish, and two live pigs making the journey. It was a mad house when the train pulled in; it already had a load of humanity from its originating station in Manila. Eddie squeezed onboard with all the rest, pausing to help several individuals who were struggling with crates of merchandise and heavy bags of unknown booty. He guarded his wallet carefully and was the only white guy in the crowd, but he went largely unnoticed. The Filipinos from the Angeles area were accustomed to American service men.

He found a seat between two Filipinos. The one sitting against the half open dirty window was a young man who gave Eddie a quick uncaring glance and had nothing to say. The woman on the aisle side held a naked baby girl about a year old. He squeezed in between them, slid his Sake bag under the seat, and sat down. He looked around the crowded rail car and wondered if he had made a mistake buying a second class ticket. The woman he was sitting by looked in her late twenties and was dressed in a loose gingham dress, was barefoot, and her long, black, shiny hair had been combed for the train trip. She looked tired. As the train rolled out and clanked and shook its way into the country side, another small girl, this one about five or six years old, came strolling casually down the aisle and joined the woman next to him. He realized that he had probably taken the girl's seat and her mother was too polite to say anything, if she even spoke English. The older girl stood in the aisle by her mother and looked prepared to continue standing for the duration.

The mother struggled to pull a handkerchief from her bag, while holding on to her baby, and gave it to the older girl to clean her dirty nose. Eddie offered his hands to help stabilize the baby. The mother looked at him, smiled showing her perfect white teeth, and handed the baby to him. It was a normal thing to do for the domestic trusting Filipino villager but it took Eddie by surprise. He took the naked child and sat it in his lap. The baby looked up at him and gave him a judgmental look, then snuggled up and made herself at home. The older girl wasted no time in climbing onto her mother's vacant lap. Eddie noticed that several of the others in the packed train car were watching the white skinned GI and his Filipino experience.

He got what he asked for and actually enjoyed the innocent trust that had been thrust upon him. It was hot, humid, and uncomfortable, yet he was having a good time. He bounced along on the hard wooden bench, holding the naked brown child, watching the rice patties, water buffalo, and bamboo stands as they passed by. The fertile valley floor had been cleared of its jungle cover for hundreds, probably thousands of years, and every available piece was growing something of value. The train must have been going at least fifteen miles per hour.

Within twenty minutes the train slowed and stopped in a small village. It had about fifty bamboo and wicker nipa style huts and half a dozen rickety wooden buildings. There were a few beat up vehicles in the potholed, dirt street but far more two wheeled carts being pulled by water buffalo. There was movement among the masses as some struggled to the doors and down loaded their baggage from the train. Others stuffed their baskets of bananas and pineapples and personal items onboard, and then squeezed into the few empty seat spaces. Food and drink venders boarded, worked their way through the crowd, then departed as the last riders boarded. The last riders to board had to stand, holding onto the adjacent seat backs for their balance. The odor of perspiration was getting heavy. Slowly the train chugged out and they were back in the countryside. A group of children playing in the water, a small boy washing his water buffalo, a stand of banana trees, an old couple walking along the pathway between rice patties—it was a continuous scene passing by.

Suddenly he felt something warm in his lap so he held the baby girl out with his arms. Water was flowing from between her legs and all the onlookers in the immediate area started laughing. Eddie looked around and couldn't help but laugh out loud at himself. The baby finished her chore on the floor—then Eddie sat her back on his lap. He felt wet and a little cooler, his old grungy pants ideal for such occasions. The mother was embarrassed and gestured to take back her child, but he nodded his head no; it was okay. The whole incident, without his presence, wouldn't have turned even a head. Babies were kept naked; it was the easiest and most practical way to handle this frequent event. He didn't even want to think of a worse scenario happening. They continued down the track and repeated the off load and on loading drill at every village they came to. It occurred daily in the lives of these people. Too poor to own a vehicle, their vital link to and from civilization was the train.

The young man next to Eddie, the one that wouldn't smile or speak, finally got up at one of the train stops and took his cloth sack of personal items with him. The woman and the older child slid into the aisle to let him out and Eddie, still holding the sleeping baby, followed them. There was very little leg room and he needed to stand and stretch anyway. As soon as the young man cleared their bench, the woman and child pounced back into the vacancy, occupying the middle and window positions. Eddie immediately took the aisle seat. A place to sit was not something to risk. After they were settled, the mother, with her older daughter now with her own seat, held out her hands for her baby. This time Eddie gladly handed the baby back to her. After all, who knew when it would be pee pee time again?

After several more hours of sweat, rocking with the train's motion, stops and starts, lingering urine smell, and absolutely stunning landscape, another little girl made her way through the people standing in the aisle and stopped next to Eddie's bench. She was wearing a plain home sewn dress, maybe six years old, barefoot, with big beautiful brown eyes to match her dark brown skin. A child that beautiful should be on a poster somewhere. She looked Eddie over until he was almost embarrassed, then she handed him an opened full bottle of Coca Cola.

"Here," she smiled, then stood waiting, holding the drink out to him. "It's for you."

Eddie was confused. "How come you're giving me this Coke?" He knew that these poor people rarely had the money for such a luxury item.

"It's from my grandmother," the girl was having trouble hiding her pride. "She doesn't speak English and she bought this for you."

Eddie was taken by the generosity but still in a quandary. "Why does she want you to give this to me?"

"Because we live in a small village way back in the mountains and you are the first GI she has seen since you drove the Japs out during the war. She wanted to do something nice for you."

Eddie did a quick calculation. It was about twenty-five years since the Americans, with the help of Filipino guerillas, drove the Japanese invaders from the Philippines. He accepted the Coke but was overwhelmed with emotion. He had done nothing to deserve the gift.

"You speak good English," Eddie searched for something to say. "Where did you learn it?"

"We have a Christian missionary in my village and they have a school for all the children. My older sister went there for three years and I go there too, when I can. The white ladies only allow us to speak English and they tell me I'm a quick learner."

"You're a nice girl. You must like the Christian ladies a lot."

The little girl stood for a while, then asked Eddie, "Are you going to Hell?"

"No, I'm going to San Fernando," Eddie's heart skipped a beat. "Why do you ask?"

"The white lady says we're all going to hell unless we get born again. But I don't want to get dead so I can be born again. My mother told me that my grandfather got dead from a Jap soldier and he never came back." She stood for a minute . . . then continued grilling the white stranger that her grandmother respected so much, "Do you believe in heaven?"

Eddie was in a tough spot. This conversation was far too complicated for a small village girl to understand. "I believe that heaven and hell are both on this earth and they are both all around us. Most people have a problem telling the difference and they live in heaven or hell because of their own doings."

"Will I go to hell if I don't get dead and washed in the river? The white ladies told me I would."

"No, sometimes people say things to you that you will only understand when you grow up." The little girl liked Eddie's simpler answer and said, "Bye," then she disappeared back through the crowd.

Eddie had found what he was looking for, a reality check. The next morning he bought a return trip, first class, and took four rolls of photos from his open private window. The Filipino country side was indeed every bit as beautiful from the ground as it had been from 300 feet in the air. The little girl's big brown eyes, the innocent girl with the Coca Cola, it was what he needed to heal. He hoped his photo of her turned out. Her image stayed in his mind for a long time. With children that beautiful, they must grow up into beautiful women. Certainly his love had to be out there somewhere. So went Mac 23's fourth and fifth day of the Tet Offensive!

CHAPTER SEVEN: KAY FROM PLANET NIBIRU

The next morning Eddie felt like death warmed over. All of the second hand cigarette smoke and an uncountable number of drinks at the bar had taken their toll. His mouth felt as if a squad of barefoot Viet Cong had marched through it and his head rang like a bell. Ching woke him up at 8:30 a.m. and while Ching took his shower, Eddie lay in bed trying to get his thoughts and orientation organized. After determining that he was in a room at the Oasis in the Philippines, the previous evening slowly all came back to him. After returning from his train excursion up the valley to San Fernando and back, he had linked up with Ching and they wasted more of their youth with another drinking session at the Oasis bar. They dug deeper into Ching's historical analysis of the Vietnamese conflict and the opposing viewpoints between the North Vietnamese and Western politicians. For Eddie from the farm, it was another history lesson and the equivalent of a college course 101 into opposing philosophies. The numerous gin and tonics only made things more confusing. Some day—make that some year, he would have to knock off the booze.

Ching had been on the phone with one of his aerial port buddies and he reported that Jim's wife wasn't hurt badly. It was just 22nd policy to remove a crew member from flying whenever a family member had a crisis. He also discovered there were two 22nd birds on their way south, manned with fresh crews, and a spare aircraft commander for MAC 23. As their contribution to the Tet Offensive, the 22nd maintenance crews at Tachi had worked overtime and had done a great job. They got the extra two birds through their scheduled maintenance and ready a day early. At Clark Air Base in the Philippines, the maintenance crews were swamped with work and their damaged C-124 had a low priority. Thus another several days before their aircraft would be ready to fly.

After showers and shaves and mucking their mouths out with toothbrushes, they caught the hotel bus to the officers club. Eggs and pancakes were topped off with a body restoring chocolate malt. The chocolate malt was a hangover recovery trick that Eddie brought with him from his college days. That morning, before they left the motel, Ching had ordered a roast pig with trimmings for the swimming pool at six that evening. Ching had previously spoken with the head cook at the Oasis. The cook had told him that for US$35 and a day's notice, he could butcher and roast one of the pigs that were kept in the fence behind the swimming pool landscaping. They lived off the waste from the motel's kitchen. The cook promised a Hawaiian style luau with a Filipino touch. With the two crews coming south and due in that afternoon and the 22nd crews already flying out of Clark and returning from their daily shuttles, there would be plenty warm bodies to split the tab. It was a good deal for everybody except the pig.

After breakfast at the officers club, Ching and Eddie spent the best part of the day dozing in chaise lounges in the shade at the officers club swimming pool. There were plenty base wives and a collection of nurses and flight attendants to watch between dozes.

After four hours, several hamburgers, and a half dozen Cokes to complete their re-hydration, Eddie and Ching called the command post and got another twenty-four hour release from duty. They pronounced themselves well and caught the bus back to the Oasis Hotel.

As Ching wrote a message for the arriving crews and gave it to the hotel clerk, Eddie checked out a small group of disheveled looking American flight attendants who were signing in at the other end of the desk. They were a good looking bunch of young women, but looked very tired in their wrinkled uniforms. Eddie's guess was that they had just finished a long military charter across the Pacific Ocean. They were chatting about their time off and the activities available in the Clark area. One in particular caught Eddie's eye and the flash of her smile and bright blue eyes invited Eddie's interests.

"Coming or going?" Eddie asked the obvious.

"Just landed," she flashed Eddie a larger grin. With a raised eyebrow she suggested, "Maybe I can come later on. What room are you in?"

"One fifteen," Eddie blurted out without thinking.

"I'll take room one fourteen," she instructed the clerk without any reservations and handed her key back for the room exchange. "I'll see you at the pool," she encouraged Eddie. With that she picked up her new key and headed down the outside walkway, trying to catch the Filipino boy carrying her luggage. She never looked back. It took a couple minutes for Eddie to digest what had just happened. He hadn't even had a chance to invite them to the pig roast. Should he be delighted, or just let it pass? Ching witnessed the event and was in as much of a puzzlement.

Eddie and Ching decided to blow off the girl, got their keys, and sauntered down the sidewalk to their shared room. "I left a note about the luau for the clerk to show to all the 22nd guys as they check in," Ching informed Eddie. "I told them we were all chipping in and buying a pig for dinner this evening. They should be at the pool at six."

"Knowing our crowd," Eddie joked, "you should have told them that it wasn't going to be a gang bang but a real roasted pig—luau style—to eat—you know—like in food." Eddie dug out a five dollar bill and handed it to Ching for more than his share of the feast.

Ching laughed in his light Asian manner, "You been over here too long."

* *

Eddie was floating on his back in the pool, one of the few athletic things that he could do very well. She arrived out of nowhere. Her name was Kay and she was wearing one of those knit bikini swim suits made of coarse, thick knit with thousands of tiny peak holes in it. She pulled up a chaise lounge and proceeded to lay herself out for viewing. Eddie almost drowned as he forgot he was in the deep end of the pool. She was really something to look at, slightly built, graceful as a ballerina. She could have qualified ten in style for the chaise lounge mount at the Olympics. Short black hair, petite flat stomach, her piercing blue eyes complemented her dark rich tan. She smiled again at Eddie and her white teeth flashed in the tropical sun. She kicked off her multicolor flip flops and with sophistication pulled a bottle of cocoa butter oil out of her bag.

"Wanna rub some oil on my back?" she offered Eddie the bottle, then laughed at him as he struggled clumsily from the pool. She rolled over onto her stomach and untied her top, taking care to allow Eddie a too brief glimpse of her delicate small breasts.

"She's so frigging beautiful, she doesn't need any tits," Eddie thought.

He opened the bottle of cocoa butter and slowly messaged some into her enchanting back—she was a goddess! Her skin was soft but her tiny muscles were hard. She was a tough, physically active person.

When he finished, at least as far as he dared to go, he felt like he wanted a cigarette—and he didn't even smoke!

Eddie ordered them each a gin and tonic from the bar boy, a good tropical drink. Rumors claimed there was quinine in tonic. One needed to keep their quinine level up to prevent malaria; it was the perfect excuse. He needed it badly, a drink that is. He pulled up a chaise next to her, stretched out in the hot sun, and casually asked her what airline she worked for.

"United," she sounded rather bored. "Stretched DC-8s. Been doing these Vietnam shuttles for two years and I've heard it all. I could probably guess your story. You fly fighters, you're not married but ya really are and you're horny. Your wife's back in the States just like my boyfriend, so it's okay. So why don't we just skip the rest of the usual shit and be honest with each other?"

"Wrong guy," Eddie looked over at her. "I fly ugly slow transports, I have no women in my life, and I'm not hurting for sex." He was on a roll so he continued just for fun, "I have three testicles but only one of them works, and I'm a special agent for the CIA."

"Well, at least you're honest." She smiled without hesitating and showed no emotion. "I'd like to see your testicles sometime but right now I wanna get some sun." Their drinks arrived. Eddie showed his room key and had the drinks put on his room tab. They drank their coolers and lay in the sun in silence.

Eddie was lost in amazement over the prize he had on the line.

Ching appeared out of nowhere. "Eddie my man, the cook said our roast pig was looking real good. Six o'clock we eat. The other guys should be in at any time." Ching bowed and gave a modest oriental wai to Kay then pulled up another chaise, next to Eddie. "Mind if I join you?"

Three more flight attendants from Kay's crew showed up and went through their arrival routine. None said anything, which was unusual. They smiled at everyone, each pulled up a chaise lounge and placed their towels carefully on their chaise; then proceeded to remove their robes, slowly, as if doing a strip tease. Eddie knew it wasn't for Ching and him. He wondered if maybe it was some sort of an ancient ritual to the sun god. They gracefully settled into their chases and proceeded to rub themselves down with cocoa butter.

It was a great show and Eddie and Ching pretended not to watch. All three sported Texas bouffant hairdos, bikini swim suits, lots of makeup, two of them sporting large breasts. The same two had slightly flabby stomachs, evidence of their good life and lack of proper exercise. They reminded Eddie of the Holstein milk cows back on the farm—big mammaries and grooming themselves in the sun. Petite little Kay was far more attractive.

The one named Missy leaned over to pick up a dropped bottle of sun oil and her exaggerated stretch placed a heavy strain on her already challenged bikini top. For a moment Eddie and Chink held their breaths, waiting for the dam to burst.

"Son of a bitch!" Ching murmured under his breath and slowly sat up. But the straining container held.

She glanced a low key acknowledgement their way—then with her mission accomplished she rolled over in her chaise lounge and displayed her bronzed buttocks. Eddie wondered if there was something symbolic about the way she ended her routine, by displaying her buttocks.

Ching whispered to Eddie, "If I had tits I'd be beautiful."

"Not really," Eddie whispered back. "You're stuck with ugly."

It wasn't but a few minutes before the three stews couldn't remain silent any more and they ignored Eddie, Ching, and Kay. The topic was the opportunity that their overnight stay at Clark Air Base afforded them. They could hustle all the horny military guys—those who longed for attention from a round-eyed woman. It seemed the current game was to make bets before landing at Clark on who could tally the highest monetary gain during their layover. Included in their tally were free meals and free drinks. The big trick was to be taken on a shopping trip off base and have everything paid for by their date. Providing free sex was considered an optional technique but of no value unless they snagged a real stud. If the stud's performance was explicitly described and the other contestants approved, the hard working flight attendant was rewarded twenty dollars worth of bonus points. They made no effort to conceal their blatant scams from Eddie and Ching; it was obvious the two flyboys didn't measure up to their standards.

"What pros," Eddie thought, "not that much different than Vicky. Only Vicky delivers with a lot less effort and a lot less cost. Possibly a lot more value also."

Kay looked over at Eddie and rolled her eyes. He wasn't quite sure what that meant.

In the distance came the low frequency moan of radial engines as they spooled up to take-off power. The moan and vibrations first affected those who were most familiar with its sound, those who had spent thousands of hours surrounded by the bleating engines. As it grew louder and closer, Kay's empty glass on the metal

106

serving tray picked up the song and began resonating with the vibrations. She moved the glass and set it on the tiled deck to stop the rattling.

"What the hell is that?" one of the new stews sat up, looked around, and asked no one in particular. The 22nd guys knew. A C-124 was on the roll, runway two zero. It rose from behind the jungle foliage like a giant Phoenix Bird . . . like a thousand tubas bleating a single deep chord. As it passed low over them it folded its gear into the wheel wells and the tone assumed an even deeper chord. The buildings and the tables and the very earth shook to its deafening song and the entire populace was spellbound with its slow-motion passage. There wasn't a single adult, child, or dog that didn't fail to look up and stare in awe at the giant aluminum aircraft. From below, Eddie was awed at how its fat fuselage didn't appear as dominant and its long slender wings were a picture of aerodynamic grace. Aspect ratio the fliers called it. It represented a more nostalgic era of flying and reminded the older Filipinos of the grief their innocent land had suffered during those horrible years of Japanese occupation. Then it was gone and the pool area returned to its norm as if nothing had happened. Nothing, except Eddie's heartbeat was faster and for a few seconds Eddie tried to hold the image. That was his true love, not these hustling playgirls at the pool.

"Told you it was slow and ugly," Eddie smiled and looked at the half alarmed Kay.

"You fly that piece of shit!" she exclaimed. "I guess you weren't lying, I'll bet you really do have three testicles."

The other stews laughed and one asked, "What's this about three testicles?"

"Never mind, he's mine," Kay responded indignantly.

"This chick comes on too strong!" Eddie thought to himself.

By 5:00 p.m. the pool party was booming. Word of the 22nd's pig roast had circulated quickly. Three more 22nd crews arrived and joined in the melee along with several F-4 pilots, one United Airlines pilot, four guys that no one knew, three schoolteachers that Ching had invited, two nurses, and several enlisted from the 22nd. Vicky showed up and settled in with the enlisted group. She knew better than to compete with the stewardesses who were the center of attention. Eddie thought Vicky looked great and the other stewardesses ignored her as if she had the plague. The three Stews and Vicky all had the same thing on their minds, hustling. They were no different than the guys. The sun was hot, the noise grew louder, the gin and San Miguel flowed, the bartender made a month's wages in tips, and people started slurring their speech. The pool became a tumult of grab ass and dunking and the two schoolteachers and one stew returned grope for grope with the guys. One schoolteacher lost her top momentarily and she struggled to get it back on and to cover herself, but not before everyone else got a good look. She received a round of applause.

It was too loud for Eddie and when he returned from his room from going "potty," as the Stews called it, he settled into a single unused chaise lounge that was positioned a short way from the crowd—in the shade. He needed a pause in the imbibition and wanted, instead, to observe the action from a distance.

Kay was still in her aggressive mode, pitting fighter pilots against trash haulers and mocking their machismo. Eddie could just overhear their jousting for her benefit and attention.

"I heard that smelling all that jet fuel could give you cancer and cause erectile dysfunction," a C-124 pilot taunted the jet jocks.

"I don't know about that. How come us fighter jocks always end up with all of the girls?" was the retaliation.

"That's because you take them on shopping trips downtown Angeles City."

"I hear that some fighter pilot in your outfit got it backward and he broke wind and flew into the ground."

"Is that right? I was told that you C-124 guys don't need navigators on those old rumbling crates. I heard that they use so much oil and fly so low that if ya ever got lost over water, all ya have to do is turn around and follow your oil slick back to land."

"I just couldn't fly in an airplane where ya can't stand up and piss, like a man. Someone told me that you guys in those aerial stovepipes whiz in a bottle while sitting down. That's gross. I thought only girls peed sitting down."

"You know, I hear you C-124 guys have little dicks. That's okay, around home—but when you're out on the road, it just doesn't get the job done."

"You know, it's easy to spot you trash haulers at the bar. Your socks are down around your shoes, your pants are on backward, and your tongues hang out of the side of your mouths. I'll bet it's from flying around in those un-pressurized airplanes."

"How come they make you F-4 Pilots fly around with a navigator in the back seat? Is that because they're afraid you'll get lost?"

"Not really, that's so if we get shot down, we'll have fresh meat to eat."

"Why is it that the C-124 pilots, with propellers, screw themselves from place to place and you guys in the jet stovepipes suck and blow yourselves from place to place.

"What a strange culture?" Kay thought to herself. "Hanging out means flying upside down and buying a farm means crashing."

A four ship of F-4s flew over in a tight and perfectly spaced echelon formation. The tower had switched runways and they were landing runway two. When over the center of the airfield, they pitched out crisply, exactly four seconds apart, and circled tightly spaced spirals for landing. The noise drowned out any conversation and their audience looked on in admiration and silence. There was even a little envy in the hearts of the transport pilots watching. Then a guy everyone called Goofy said, "Fuckin G forces," and pulled back with his right hand as he imitated a tight turn with the control stick used to fly fighters. He then fell over backwards into the pool.

The mood softened and the pilots continued with less cutting zingers:

"You know, one of the reasons why I like flying in a C-124 is because I can look out my left window and see a row full of engines and I can look to my right and see lots of co-pilots, flight engineers, navigators, and even more engines. It's just sort of comforting and I like to have coffee brought to me, a standup head to take a pee in, and four inch thick mattress in case I wanna take a nap. I haven't wanted to fly upside-down in years."

Another C-124 pilot said, "You know, I had a dream last night. I dreamt I was flying a C-124. Then I woke up and sure as hell I was."

"I had a dream when I went to bed last night; it was a wet dream . . . then I went to sleep." A guy no one knew confessed.

"A little C-124 wisdom for you fighter jocks from us transport pilots. Never piss on an electrical fire."

"Sometimes we trash haulers forget where we parked our airplane and we hafta layover, emphasis lay, an extra day," Eddie hollered for the group to hear. "That is, those of us that have enough balls to do it." Eddie looked at Kay and held up three fingers. She rolled her eyes again but kinda liked this hick.

A little later the same guy that fell in the pool came wandering and weaving back from the restrooms. He was worked up, very drunk, and had another story to tell:

"I asked some guy where the men's room was. He just pointed down the hallway. I went through the door and it was full of some very hostile women. I told them they were in the wrong toilet and had to threaten some of them to get em to leave. My next problem was that I couldn't find any urinals . . . the stupid Filipinos forgot to install them so I looked for an empty booth. There was a faggot in one of em. I could tell he was a faggot cause I could see under the door and he was wearing ladies' shoes and had shaved his skinny legs. I told him if he came out of there I would break his god-damn neck. The faggot assured me he wouldn't come out if I took my piss and left the bathroom in peace, which is what I did." He looked over at Eddie and warned, "If I were you I wouldn't go in there . . . unless ya really gotta go. Then take someone with you to guard the toilet door."

Eddie looked over at Kay and smiled. She smiled back, pointed her finger at herself and nodded her head yes. She would watch for him. No one had the heart to tell the drunk that he had been in the Ladies' restroom.

Eddie stretched out on his chaise lounge, sweated in the shade, and wondered where he fit into this crowd. In La La Land, individuals experienced the freedom to conduct themselves, not as their previous environment had dictated, but as they had always wanted. For the first time in their lives they were without their native cultural restrictions and they reassembled themselves. A lot of experimentation was going on. Relocated to a remote, unstable, transient, and sometimes fatal corner of the globe, individuals had the option to shed their family roots and re-juggle their social standards. Social mores and the opinionated judgments of relatives and friends were subject to re-evaluation and restructure. Some of the deviations and alterations were temporary experiments. Some fit so well they would be permanently adapted and would be carried back to America. These transported values and personalities could shock friends and relatives and would sometimes lead to frustration, conflict and divorces.

Schoolteachers at the various military facilities in the Philippines, Okinawa and Japan, were exposed to this same enlightenment as the GIs. Some of them seized the opportunity to participate sexually with the abundance of desperate young men. No one back home would ever find out. Others got fat as butterballs using food as a therapy. Some slept as much as possible, as if sleep would make the time go by faster. Others blossomed as they took advantage of the wonderful scuba diving, inexpensive travel to other exciting Asian destinations, and the wonderful friendships that were available. They took correspondence courses, improved their golf games and worked out at the gym.

It was open season for personalities and conduct. Eddie was sitting alone and watching the pig roast party develop. What he was witnessing was a spontaneous group personality clinic. Some were trying to figure out who they were and some were trying to forget. Maybe Eddie was really not alone.

Kay climbed out of the pool after a cooling dip, her slim cat-like grace commanding attention from all the men present. She looked up, her eyes met Eddie's, and she gracefully strolled over to his haven in the shade. He was lying on his back with his hands clasped behind his head. Eddie wondered what this unpredictable vixen was up to next. He didn't have long to wonder. Without a pause she crawled on top of Eddie's supine torso, dripping water and all, and lay down on him. Her spontaneity caught him off guard but he was delighted with how comfortably she fit. He lowered his arms and placed them around her slender waist and pulled her in close.

"Gotcha," she whispered into his ear. "Let's get married, I want you to beat me, fuck me, and make me write bad checks . . . I wanna have your babies."

"I could never beat you, but the rest sounds like a great life," Eddie whispered back. "But I heard that female black widow spiders eat their males after they tire of having sex."

"Damn, you called my bluff. Yes, I wanna absorb you into my blood stream and have you in me for the rest of my life. Let's get started right now, right here in this chair, and fuck till we pass out. I gotta fuck first before I suck your blood." She squirmed and ground her pelvic mound into Eddie's personals.

Eddie felt a cringe of panic and wild thoughts raced through his mind, "There are no limits to this woman! She's gotta be crazy or at least mentally unbalanced. Yet, she's the most exciting woman I've ever met in my life."

"Who the hell are you?" he whispered into her ear.

"I'm your best dream and your biggest fear, all wrapped up into one," she whispered softly. "I know that you want me and I know that now that I'm here, you're scared shitless. Relax, I'm from another planet, I'm not here to hurt you. I'm only taking blood samples and I'll be gone tomorrow." Then she kissed Eddie long and deep and wet and sloppily. "All I want is to be sensuous and pleasurable for once," she changed her tack, "with a nice guy that I'm attracted to. Without all that crap and nonsense. I really don't need intercourse. Lord knows I've had enough of that. I just want you to be sensuous and to kiss me and hold me. Just be nice to the real me. Can you do that?"

Then after a pause she again changed her tack. "I've spent so much time over here that I'm approaching the borderline. I just act like I'm nuts so I can protect my sanity. Can you understand that?"

Eddie was thunderstruck and he whispered, "You're probably the only person out here, besides me, that's not nuts." He knew it wasn't true, but he also wasn't ready to blow away a chance of getting into her knickers.

"I can do that," he continued playing the game. "Not getting any sex is the story of my life, but not necessarily my choice." They both laughed quietly and without malaise.

They lay together and held each other in silence. She felt so good on him. "Was she really just a lost soul, fighting for her sanity, seeking her own destiny, and hiding behind a brazen, outspoken alter ego?" Eddie hoped so much that it was true. He also felt the need for a friend. "Or was she nutty as a fruit cake?"

As promised, the pig arrived at 6:00 p.m. A small group of young Filipino men, in long black pants and white Filipino Barangs (white lace shirts worn outside the pants), paraded back and forth from the kitchen. The table was covered with a plastic colorful tablecloth, large bowls of rice, mixed fresh fruit, and a roasted pig complete with his head, tail, and hooves. The pig's skin was crisp and dark brown. When a young Filipino waiter cut into it, steam rose and juice dripped from the sweet light meat.

"A war should not be wasted," was the group toast and the feast began. The food was a common denominator. The trash haulers ate with their new fighter pilot friends, the school teachers discovered a moment of sanity among the chaos, strangers sat with strangers and the group of three Stews ate without offering to help pay. The stews worked the crowd of men, still looking for the perfect mark. Kay sat silently next to Eddie. Kay had slipped Ching three dollars for her share and both she and Eddie were well aware that her companion stews had not. Despite the drop in the noise level and the occasional pause to suck down the delightful pork slices, everyone was still soused with booze. They ate with gusto, licking their fingers as if starved, and laughed at each other's jokes. After their meal, Kay's three flight attendant friends slipped away with their pick-ups and caught a Jeepney off to somewhere. They didn't leave unnoticed.

Then the heavens opened up. As the first heavy drops of warm rain started to fall, everyone stood up as if statues, knowing what was to come and calculating where to find shelter.

"Let's go to my room," Eddie hollered at Kay, who was returning from the bar with a pair of Gin and Tonics. The two of them headed off as the rain increased with intensity. They were getting soaked.

"Ya, let's go to Eddie's room," someone else shouted and others pitched in. Eddie had made a tactical mistake when hollering at Kay.

"Eddie's room, Eddie's room, Eddie's room," they all chanted. Eddie and Kay quickened their pace but there was no way they could lose the horde of wet, drunken party-goers. There was no way Eddie wanted that group of wet, dripping drunks in his room.

As Kay and Eddie scurried down the sidewalk they passed a door that was slightly ajar.

Kay dropped Eddie's arm and explained, "Just a minute, that's Missy and Shannon's room, two of those other stews I'm here with. I'd better close it."

"You mean two of those bitches that didn't pay for their pig meal?"

"Yeah! Are you thinking what I'm thinking?" Kay replied with a wide smile.

"In here, everybody!" Eddie shouted and Kay opened and waved the way through the door for the horde. More drinks were ordered and the horde had a wonderful time partying, dancing to the radio, playing grab ass, telling lies, and sitting wet on the twin beds. Late that evening the two snooty stews returned to find their room trashed and their beds wet from the rain soaked butts of unknown guests. What goes around comes around!

Eddie and Kay quickly slipped away from the evolving disaster, scurried down the sidewalk, and into Eddie's room. Giggling and flashing each other, they slipped out of their wet swimming suits. Naked and wet, they slipped between the sheets. They first enjoyed childish horseplay then progressed into passionate foreplay. As Eddie made a subtle gesture toward intercourse, Kay withdrew and placed her finger on his lips as if to silence him. "Let's not do it," she whispered into his ear. "Let's not just bring this to a conclusion and end it. This is too good for just a wham, bam, thank you ma'am. I want more, let's see how far we can go with our emotions and desires, let's see how high we can get with our passion, and use our restraint from intercourse as an intoxicant." And they did. She taught him that it was the journey that counted, the beauty of a woman's body, her passions and where and how she liked to be touched. How sensuous the human ear can be when daintily manipulated with the tongue. How sensitive the underside of a woman's breasts can be and to massage the lower portion of a woman's back. Together they achieved a level of sensual intensity he had never imagined possible. When they reached a level they could no longer tolerate, they both exploded with orgasms, without intercourse. They collapsed and decompressed holding each other tightly in their arms.

110

After a long period of silence and caressing, they slipped into tender, careful intercourse that lasted an eternity and ended by rocking the heavens with passion. Kay was on the pill, so they didn't have to make the usual awkward pause to place a condom into play. They decompressed slowly again, lay there for several more minutes, then both burst out laughing with joy.

Eddie realized that Kay had just ruined all fuckie fuckie prostitutes for him, from that time forward. There was another whole world of love making he had just been introduced into.

They talked until two in the morning when Ching dragged in. "Whoops, excuse me," he apologized for the intrusion as he came through the door. "I'll come back later."

"No, you stay," Kay instructed. She was unfazed by the intrusion on their interlude on the bed. She crawled out of bed naked, unashamed, and casually slipped on her swim suit. "I've got to get back to my room and get a few hours of sleep. I have a flight back to the States this morning." With a quick kiss on the cheek she bid goodnight to Eddie and disappeared from his life. Eddie was totally spooked!

She left him confused, frustrated, fascinated, and enlightened, all in the same package. She was a fantastic woman but unpredictable as hell. Was she for real? Was she a borderline schizophrenic? Was she a full blown schizophrenic? Could she be a flight attendant and completely nuts at the same time? Did one need a woman that unstable and that close to the edge of reality in order to break through their own personal bounds?

He never saw Kay again, but for a long time she occupied one of the most exciting yet apprehensive spots in his mind. It was as if she had been a spirit passing through his vision, a sexual mentor sent from another planet. She replaced Vicky as the object of his sexual fantasies, but he always knew she couldn't have been the one to satisfy his quest. Goddesses from the planet Nibiru never had lasting relationships with farm boys from Colorado. He had to be careful.

PERSPECTIVE

On the morning of January 31, 1968, the Viet Cong launched a surprise nationwide attack in South Vietnam. It was on the Tet holiday, an annual holiday when Vietnamese warriors on both sides of the strife traditionally returned home to be with their families. The Viet Cong offensive, dubbed the "Tet Offensive" by the American news media, had hoped to achieve an overwhelming victory and successful seizure of South Vietnam. A general uprising of the civilian population was expected to support their communist backed offensive. It was supposed to be a humiliating defeat of the South Vietnamese Army and the occupying American Forces. Instead, the uprising of the civilian population never developed and the Viet Cong suffered a humiliating and major setback in their plans to assimilate South Vietnam. The Tet losses were 45,000 Viet Cong along with a smattering of North Vietnamese soldiers, versus losses of 1536 US, Korean, and Australians and 2788 South Vietnamese Army. It was an overwhelming victory for the Americans and their allies. Unfortunately, 14,000 South Vietnamese civilians were killed as collateral damage during the country wide intense fighting.

The commercial American news media, in their quest for Nobel prizes and highly profitable anti-war headlines, re-wrote the events with their own spin on the facts concerning the Tet Offensive. The American public was bombarded with the misrepresentation that the uprising had been a major military victory for the communists. The American media effectively turned the Tet Offensive into a major publicity victory for the Viet Cong and North Vietnam. Perception is everything!

The inept political leaders in Washington would not allow the American military to take advantage of the badly defeated and depleted enemy forces. Instead of allowing the American military to administer the coup de grace, they continued authorizing only the usual limited and heavily regulated defensive positions in the field. They restricted offensive maneuvers and continued restricting air strikes in North Vietnam. The continuous restraints placed on the American military subsequently allowed the North Vietnamese several years to restructure and re-supply their decimated remaining Viet Cong forces. To replace their staggering losses of Viet Cong, Ho Chi Minh infiltrated South Vietnam with large numbers of North Vietnamese soldiers.

From that time forward, the Americans would battle the highly trained North Vietnamese soldiers in South Vietnam. For the Americans it was clearly a military opportunity missed. For the North Vietnamese, it was the start of a highly successful media campaign, using the American media as their instrument, to convince the United States to withdraw from South Vietnam. It gave the North Vietnamese license to over-run South Vietnam.

CHAPTER EIGHT: POT-POURRI

A general mixture of loosely related ingredients; in this case, a mixture of loosely related episodes.

TRANSFORMATION

Eddie's second year as a Shaky Bird pilot in Southeast Asia became a blend of events, some enlightening, some disgusting, some surprising, and some routine. Each landmark experience was sprinkled amongst weeks and sometimes months of uneventful flying. The total, the endless flying and the blend of memorable events, all combined to form the ingredients that morphed Eddie into a seasoned Asian veteran. The people, their cultures, the jungle and the ocean were his seasoning. He blended them into his soul, opened his imagination and allowed his unique surroundings to have their way. Where it would take him was up to the winds and imaginary gods.

Caucasian long timers in Asia, something that all 22nd crew members gradually became, each gradually followed their own calling. Without their awareness, some became booze heads. Some became poker addicts and gambled endlessly like Major Baxter. Some became whore hounds like Conejo and some became stern and rigid military figures. Some were walking zombies, waiting for that final trip back to the States. Others, the "shadows" as the school teachers called them, the straight arrow married guys appeared quite normal. They seemed unaffected by and not noticing the dynamics of the events that unfolded daily around them. They shielded themselves with their stateside upbringings and teachings and acted normal out of respect for their marriage vows. Because they were military and restricted to their narrow political opinions, discussions about politics were limited and heavily seasoned with patriotism. They pretended to be unfazed by their environment and pretended normal lives; they were clones of their western, puritan culture. But they too were internally affected, unknowingly altered by their surreal environment. There was no perfect defense as all were touched by their strange world. Some sustained subtle personality changes and some developed more obvious effects. None would ever be the same again.

Eddie had noticed this transformation of other crewmembers and he kept expecting to wake up some morning with an epiphany; the realization of who he was and what he was doing among this cornucopia of options. But it didn't happen that way. He remained a drifter among the souls as he wallowed through various phases. In some ways he had become more like a native. He had become of "this place." Steamed white rice had replaced his ethnic German preference for potatoes, fish replaced beef, and his desire to eat fruit matched that of the Asians. He had developed the preference for knee length loose fitting pants and sandals made of black rubber tires with braided colorful cord. He had money and he spent it on loose silk shirts with large, sometimes gaudy multicolored patterns. He only expended energy when necessary and no longer sweat profusely in the heavy humid tropical heat, or at least he was unaffected and not annoyed by it. With the intense heat and humidity, he took noon naps whenever possible. He felt no regrets. He was filling his void and his lust for wandering with abundant material, however material far different than he had imagined. Had he discovered a perfect world, it would have indeed been a boring disappointment.

Whenever he had a free day at Clark or Bangkok, he ventured more and more away from the areas where Americans could be found. Sleazy bars, venders hawking their wares, hustle, and theft—he avoided those places more and more in exchange for the rural countryside. He had the money to hire a car and driver for the day, at a price less than a taxi for a ten mile ride in Denver. He used the opportunity to explore and absorb what he had previously overlooked, the real people that lived and worked and thrived in the exotic lands of the Philippines and Thailand. Fresh cut pineapple was indeed the sweetest and tastiest thing he ever imagined. The Asians rarely ate candy or chocolate and the wonderful sweet pineapple was probably the reason why. Chewing on a slip of sugar cane was rural candy. Walking along the dikes, between rice patties and accompanied by a bevy of smiling, partially clad brown skinned children, was a great way to wash away yesterday's disappointments. The rural people of both countries, surrounded by their plight of rural poverty, always seemed relaxed, smiled at each other, and openly loved their families. They all took care of each other's children and were nice to strangers. The prostitutes and hustlers surrounding the air bases were only an anomaly created by the poison of American presence and the American dollar. Eddie felt comfortable with locals, and sometimes he forgot that he was indeed and undeniably different from them.

Eddie's flying skills continued to evolve. Their daily shuttles from Clark Air Base, into and out of Vietnam, were described by one navigator as "days and days of sheer boredom interrupted by moments of sheer panic." Eddie, however, was never bored. He was stashing most of his salary into his savings and he was stashing flying time and experience into his log book. When flying, he listened to the sounds of his engines and developed a feel for every subtle change of their rhythm. He was where he wanted to be. All he had left was to realize what he wanted to be. He was building up reserves for those future opportunities. There were rumors that Singapore Airlines was hiring American ex-military pilots and there were Boeing 727 pilot jobs available in Japan with JAL. The Singapore thing sounded exciting, but Eddie was leery about the Japanese contract flying. It really didn't offer much of an escape from the mosh pit outside the Tachikawa gate he currently called his residence.

Flying over the water was Eddie's solace, the time of his meditation. Eddie sat alone by the hours in his lofty perch with the seat next to him empty and the rest of the airplane behind him. It was as if an imaginary force was thrusting him through the air over an unlimited plain of water. He had the world to himself. It re-established his perspective. "How many millions of years had these eternal bodies of ocean and air shared their undisturbed existence? Had there ever been an airplane before, that low, over that part of the vast horizon? Or a passing ship? Certainly over thousands of years there had been some interesting voyagers!" And he wondered if the voyaging crews shared his same thoughts, or were they consumed with the events of their vehicles and where they had been and where they were going? Americans frequently tend to preoccupy their minds with immaterial junk and fail to notice the very sum and substance of their existence.

The passing of his aircraft would be brief; then the vastness, the waves and the clouds, would have their peace returned. He sat for hours at a time, absorbing the clouds, air, and prairie of ocean—the grand wonder of geology and physics that formed them. He wondered and marveled at the randomness of the puffy clouds, why were they at their exact spots in the vastness, not a mile to the left or two thousand yards to the east? Why their shapes and the ever moving swells and the deepness of the water? What wonderful creatures must live in that boundless ocean? Did they know who they were and would anyone care when they died? Then he would snap back to reality and realize that he had instead lost conciseness with time, the distinction between dreams and reality had been compromised. He then pitied those spit shined jet airmen crossing the ocean at incredible heights and blinding speeds. Their jets were so impersonal. They could not possibly feel the waves and the currents and spend hours as he just had. How much they were missing.

Sometimes the fluffy, light, alto cumulus clouds would become numerous and his aluminum airship would require guidance to weave its way through the open channels and canyons. It was fun to stick a wing tip into the fluffy light clouds when it got a bit tight, or to get caught in a blind canyon and burst through the clouds at the closed end. There would be some light turbulence—then they would burst back into the bright sunlight. He used his weather radar to see through and examine the cloud's sensitive interiors, and to seek out the soft spots through the bumpy white cotton.

Then there were the stars at night, millions of heavenly bodies reflecting their tiny white messages off the empty sea below. Which direction was up and which direction was down was sometimes impossible to tell without reference to their gyroscopic stabilized flight instruments. No wonder the ancient ones believed in gods and heavenly messengers. It was wonderment that he never grew weary of, his presence in their venue was an honor. Eddie bought himself a book and learned the stars' names and developed a special fondness for the constellation Orion. This familiar piece of the sky would follow him, provide solace, and look after him for the rest of his life.

Their loads were always different. It was a sideshow watching the loadmaster conduct the loading and off loading. Without sophisticated floors with built in rollers for pushing pallets back and forth, as were found in the newer C-141s and C5-As, loading and off-loading was a crude but intriguing art form. If small enough and light enough, the cargo could be lifted up through the opened floor toward the rear of the aircraft, and traversed into position with the overhead moving winch. Everything else, with or without its own wheels, had to be skidded and dragged on and dragged off through the airplane's open nose doors. Shoring with wood was often required, crude but effective. Yankee ingenuity was the ace in the hole.

Elsie the paint striper would show up every so often, waiting on the freight ramp, tolerating the heat, rain and humidity; waiting for a ride to her next destination. Too big to fit inside a C-130, she waited, sometimes days and occasionally weeks, for the 22nd fat birds to show up and tend to her transportation needs. She serviced all the paved runways in Vietnam and the US/Thai air bases in Thailand, where she would dutifully lay down her yellow and white guide lines.

There were good times, "picnic lunches" on the ramp while they were waiting for freight to show up or maintenance to be completed. Each would pull out his latest find of canned or dried food from his food bag and it would be a shared grandiose meal. The fellowship, joking, and good times made an otherwise miserable existence a study in camaraderie. Sometimes Eddie or some other crew member would pick up a couple of pizzas at Clark and keep them cool over night in the refrigerator. The trailer houses all had refrigerators and the off base motels were always happy, for a quarter tip, to store pizzas over night in the kitchen's coolers. Then the next day, enroute and while cruising over the dark blue China Sea, the crew would all gather in the cockpit and share pizza re-warmed on top of the hot radio vacuum tube rack.

In addition to Clark there were layovers in Bangkok. The air force operated out of six Royal Thai Air Bases in Thailand and frequently the services of a C-124 were needed. The C-124 layover airport at Bangkok was not a military base, but Don Muang Airport, the international civilian airport that served Bangkok. The American military had contacts for fuel and Thai civilian maintenance. The tiny little Thai mechanics were, in many cases, wonderful at solving problems in their old C-124s. The crews stayed downtown where all the shopping and bar activity was concentrated. The thirty minute ride from the airport into downtown Bangkok provided some of the most hazardous experiences the 22nd crews were subjected to. Everyone called it kamikaze driving and all wanted the back seat. The "shotgun" position up front and next to the driver was too stressful and dangerous. The officers stayed at the Chaophya Hotel in Bangkok as the entire hotel was leased by the US military. The downstairs facilities were turned into an officers club. A quick taxi ride to James Jewelers offered preferred shopping at discount prices. James, the owner, usually had several cases of merchandise waiting to be delivered to his agent at Tachikawa. The buffalo steaks and French onion soup in Bangkok, provided by James, were the favorite of the crews as well as the private and special massages given by the tiny Thai girls.

Then it would be back to work, flying long hours over water, at home in the sky.

HELLO DOLLY

Larry Adams and Eddie flagged down a base taxi in front of the Clark Officers Club. It was just getting dark and Larry and Eddie felt good after they each had a shower at the Oasis Motel and a couple of twofers at the Clark Officers Club happy hour bar. It was the first time Eddie had flown with Larry Adams and the two of them hit it off instantly, they worked well together in the cockpit. The taxi driver opened the door for his fare to get out. A very attractive woman emerged, early twenties, with a short pixy hair cut, soft silk mini dress and the greatest set of legs Eddie had ever set his eyes on. She emerged from the taxi and right into Larry's arms and gave him a kiss as if he was a long lost lover. Eddie was amazed and shocked, as was the taxi driver, the group of flyers waiting for their hotel bus, and the older colonel and his wife in their formal wear just approaching the steps to the club. The taxi cab siren finished her showy kiss and pulled back to look up and down Larry's handsome frame. Then she continued her play with the crowd's minds, "Were you guys on your way to my motel room? You know I work by appointment only."

"I haven't seen you in three weeks," Larry addressed her, ignoring her last statement, "when we all had dinner at the Tachikawa Officers Club. My wife never shuts up from talking about you . . . I won't ask you what you've been doing with your time."

She smiled in a very personal way and Larry continued, "Have you met Eddie? Dolly meet Eddie." Larry smiled and performed an abbreviated curtsy for Eddie. Eddie was still reeling but managed a pleasant, but slightly frozen face. "Dolly's a Southern Air Transport Stew and lives a couple of doors down from our paddy house, outside the side gate at Tachi. Dolly is a really good friend of mine." The good friend part was obvious to Eddie. He was in the middle of a lust surge and was unaware he was staring.

"Can you speak?" she addressed Eddie. After blatantly eyeing him from head to toe, she commented, "Everything looks just fine to me. Does the cat have your tongue?"

"I was just trying to figure out how to get rid of Larry," Eddie heard himself speak. "So we could split a bottle of wine and some cheese or something." It was a dumb thing to say but it was the best he could muster under the pressure.

"You must be new over here?" Dolly smiled and lied. "We haven't had any decent cheese in the commissary in over two years." Then with a sparkle in her eyes she teased Eddie, "But the wine and something could be kinda fun sometime. Right now I'm with Larry." She gave Eddie a big smile and latched onto Larry's arm. She obviously loved playing to a crowd.

"Why don't you guys continue your sparring in the taxi?" Larry broke in. "We're gonna go off base and have a nice meal at Poppaguyo's. Ya wanna join us, I'm buying?"

"Why not?" Dolly was quick to answer as she crawled back into the taxi, still talking. "Damn it's good to see you."

"Side gate," Larry instructed the driver and piled in behind Dolly, as if a dog in heat. Eddie settled on the right front seat anticipating, but not knowing what. He was a little spellbound and once when he turned to speak, he saw Larry and Dolly smooching up a storm. At the side gate they spilled out of the base taxi, paid the driver a generous dollar bill, and walked the short distance past the guard and out the gate. They merged into the melee of brilliantly painted and decorated Jeepneys with their waving drivers. Behind them the row of shacks, shops, and bars were in full blossom. With barefoot and scantily clothed children, old women hawking their wares, guys competing for taxi fares, and young Filipino girls hawking their wares, it was a National Geographic special. The darkened scene between the shacks teemed with hidden life and sinister goings on and there was the smell of wood smoke and water buffalo dung in the tropical humid air.

"Watch your wallet," Larry needlessly warned Eddie. Eddie had both hands in his pockets protecting all of his valuables.

"Poppaguyo's," Larry addressed a driver randomly selected from the selection of Jeepneys. "One Peso."

"Three pesos," the driver bartered in return. Larry pulled an unopened pack of Salem cigarettes out of his pocket and gave the driver a brief glimpse of what he had in his hand.

"Let's go," was the response.

The three of them piled into the rear seat of the open sided jeep and Larry leaned over and spoke into the driver's ear, "Straight to Poppaguyo's, I know the way. If you take a side street I'll slit your throat before you get stopped." The driver, unoffended by the threat and as a player in the off base scene, nodded acknowledgement. He understood he was doing business with street savvy GIs. He honked his horn and waved at a friend, swerved

116

to miss two dogs, one pig, and three pot holes full of muddy rainwater as they picked their way downtown. One of the pot holes had a water buffalo standing in it.

"You're one mean son of a bitch," Dolly smiled and praised Larry, softly so the driver couldn't hear her. "Remind me never to cross you."

"Filipinos are poor," Larry defended the driver. "They have to be aggressive just to make a living."

"If ya think cutting someone's throat in the bathroom and stealing their clothes, watch, and money is a living," Dolly rebutted. "I've even heard of them hiding under the beds at a whore house and removing the money from a GI's wallet, from his pants on the floor, while the girl is getting it on topside. Most guys check to make sure their wallet is in their pants when they're done but almost none of them check to see if their money is in it."

"Sounds like a gang bang is the safest way to go. It never hurts to have a couple of friends watching you get it on and looking out for your wallet on the floor," Eddie remarked. He had been listening in on their conversation as they weren't as quiet as they thought.

"Or do it on the floor next to your pants," Dolly added.

"Or do it with your pants still on, just down around your ankles," Larry speculated.

"Or do it yourself, alone. That works and is free and safe," Eddie concluded with a grin. Dolly decided Eddie was okay.

They bounced over a set of railroad tracks and Eddie saw a sign that said:

MEDICAL CLINIC AND LABORATORY
Dr. Ben M. Dizon
VD Check-up — Smear — Pregnancy Tests
Newest Contraception — painless, economical
Nothing to take — no anesthesia required
Fits in ten minutes

The sign was obviously advertising diaphragms but it was behind the times. The recent revolution in birth control was the pill.

A Jeepney full of drunken GIs passed them going the other direction, waving beer cans and shouting obscenities. They had several wild eyed local whores mixed in with their lot and they were gone as fast as they came. Eddie's carriage came to a short section of sidewalk and a sign that read Poppaguyo's. Larry slipped the driver the pack of Salems and they bailed out. The driver asked Eddie, "You want another girl? I can get you a very nice clean one very cheap."

"They're gonna do me tonight," Dolly answered for Eddie. "I've already got their money."

"We're gonna do it on the floor," Larry chipped in.

"With our pants on," Eddie couldn't resist.

"I'm gonna do fuckie fuckie and suckie suckie at the same time," Dolly announced.

Neither Eddie nor Larry could top that and the driver shrugged his head and drove off. Dolly always had to have the last line.

During the few steps from the street to the restaurant Eddie received three more offers. A little barefoot boy, about five years old and wearing only a pair of shorts, offered for sale a nice looking sail boat made from a water buffalo horn. Another offered to shine Eddie's shoes, unfazed when Eddie pointed out he was wearing sandals. A teenaged girl, with about two pounds of makeup, asked Eddie if he wanted to, "go short time," before he had dinner with his friends.

The owner operated an authentic restaurant with a conspicuous absence of sleazy bar girls inside his establishment. He charged a bit more but prices in the Philippines were so reasonable that none of the Americans really cared. It was one of the few places, off base, where married officers, nurses, and schoolteachers could dine without feeling like they were in a whore house. A Trader Vic's, however, it was not. It was a restaurant in one of the most degenerate towns in the Philippines and previous attempts at painting and decorating had improved the décor of the thirty year old building; but it still needed a lot of work. After they took their seats Eddie, for the first time, got a really good look at Dolly. She lit her own cigarette with a tiny bronze lighter and inhaled so deeply it almost made him dizzy. Then she blew her smoke on a large fly that was gobbling a tiny drop of gook on the table. In addition to her traffic stopping form, she had sparkling light blue eyes, the color of aquamarine. Her occasional glance, as she babbled with Larry, pierced Eddie as if to read his very thoughts and soul. Her personality was light and bubbly and filled with laughter and humorous expressions. She was obviously well educated.

These were all qualities most men only dream of but Dolly was much more. Her light bubbly conversation was laced with the foulest of profanity. The vulgarest of words flowed lightly from her tongue as if she were saying lace, lovely, and kindness. The content of her conversation was filled with command of sex, men, Taipei, jade, and most surprisingly, a working knowledge of airplanes and the piloting of them. She was a woman like none Eddie had ever met before. She fit naturally into the world of water buffalo steaks, gaily decorated Jeepneys, and the fast moving boom town of Angeles City. Back in the States she would be a foul mouthed noisy bar fly. Instead, in Southeast Asia and under the shadow of the war, she had become a star player everywhere she went. She played to her endless audience of horny, lonely GIs. A prostitute she was not, she was a flight attendant with Southern Air Transport, the CIA front for Air America.

They ate buffalo steaks (carabao) and consumed numerous bottles of San Miguel. Eddie stayed out of Larry and Dolly's busy conversation and enjoyed the ambience, the scene, the people, and their place in the world. He overheard Larry and Dolly speak of relationships; they were obviously very close and Dolly was accepted by Larry's wife and their small, special group of friends. He heard her tell Larry that she was just like the 22nd guys, a bastard spin off from the real war and real world. He heard her tell Larry she was not interested in breaking up any marriages as there was more than enough single cock to go around. She said she didn't enjoy other women, they bored her. All of her friends, except Larry's wife and Jan somebody, were men. "This is really a terrible thing to say, what with the war and all, but I don't ever want it to end," she said.

She also spoke of babysitting for a couple at Tachikawa and "was doing all right until the little beggar shit in his diapers. Believe me there are limits to what I'll do for a hot meal, clean sheets, and a diamond on my finger. Marriage and raising a family isn't one of them." Dessert was fresh custard (flan) that melted in their mouths, followed by another beer and Dolly smoked another cigarette. The way she handled her cigarette reminded Eddie of Lauren Bacall.

"I know who you are now!" she pointed her finger at Eddie. "You're the co-pilot that was with old man Baxter when you feathered two engines on one leg, what was that, six or seven months ago? . . . Hello! . . . the world calling."

Eddie was startled when he realized that Dolly was talking to him again. He had been staring. "Yeah," he bought some time to recover from his trance and the effects of countless beers. "It was actually over a year ago. It gave me a wonderful opportunity to see some of the Filipino country side." Eddie decided that he'd had enough to drink for the evening. He was elated; Eddie had at last met the legendary Dolly from Japan.

She was a rare woman, one that could only exist in the special atmosphere that existed in the periphery of a war zone. Certainly not one of a kind; there had been Dollies during World War II, during the almost forgotten Korean War, and certainly Dollies would exist in future wars as certainly as future wars themselves would exist. The sparkle in her eyes, her straightforward non-condemning attitude, her legendary loving and bedroom antics, her aptitude with shop talk, all reserved her a special place in the hearts of many a warrior. To young men, so far from home during times of sacrifice, so vulnerable and uncertain, she was the living, breathing Varga girl. As Illustrated by Alberto Vargas in his famous World War II series of pin-up posters. Guys like Eddie held her up with the same esteem as images of B-17s, P-51 Mustangs, and names like Iwo Jima and General Patton. She commanded a permanent place in their hearts and souls.

This particular Dolly was an occasional member of the 22nd Board Meetings, a lover to more than one 22nd trash hauler, and a good companion and friend to all. It was rumored that Dolly was as entertaining to have a conversation with as she was to sleep with. She was a trophy on display. Oddly enough, as 22nd favorites, she and Vicky never knew each other.

Dolly and Kay, the United flight attendant from Planet Nibiru, were a special breed of woman. There were probably only twenty or thirty of them in that category that were scattered around Southeast Asia. Some guys called them high end camp followers, some called them less classy names, but there was no denying they played their roles with all the class, glamour, and character imaginable. Imagination was not in short supply to the young warriors participating in the world's greatest live movie, called "The War." These select women stimulated bravado, flaunted their beauty and charm, and made many a young man's tour a little less burdensome. Most guys served a one year tour, had their gee whiz and oh my gosh experiences, then they went home and proceeded with their normal lives. Eddie had passed the twelve month standard and was on his way to his two year anniversary. He was doing the long haul in La La Land and he was no longer blown away by surprises and anomalies like Dolly. He also suspected that each of them, Dolly and Kay, had a cold spot hidden somewhere in their souls that made them like they were. And he suspected it would never melt in a thousand years. He remained at arm's length, learned from the experience, and enjoyed watching the show.

ABORT

The sun was just coming up when they took the active, runway two zero at Clark Field. Eddie had accumulated enough time in the aircraft that whenever it was his leg to fly, he was allowed to fly from the left seat. Eddie had passed his second check ride and was officially titled a First Officer. On the legs that Eddie flew, the aircraft commander would sit in the right seat and play the role of co-pilot, referred to in the manuals as the pilot not flying (PNF). When it was Eddie's leg to fly he was the pilot flying (PF).

Both pilots checked their compasses during the turn onto the runway and Eddie called for "take-off power." A two ship formation of A-1s was pitching out overhead for their landing as Eddie's craft accelerated underneath them and passed the seventy knot acceleration mark. "Boom pop, pop, pow," Eddie's number one engine let loose and both pilots and the flight engineer simultaneously shouted "ABORT."

Eddie, as the pilot flying, pulled the four throttles to idle position. There was plenty runway to roll to a stop without using reverse thrust and possibly compounding the situation. He applied light braking and let the crippled bird roll out and stop.

"I think we blew a cylinder on number one engine," the flight engineer announced. He was the pilots' eyes and could examine all the gauges and make a quick determination of the problem The two pilots didn't even glance at their gauges as they were charged with keeping the aircraft heading down the runway and slowing to a stop. "Okay if I shut it down, Sir?"

"Feather number one," Eddie called and as he glanced to his left out the side window. He noticed that his highly experienced engineer was already feathering the engine. Asking for permission had only been a formality. The propeller was still slowly spinning and was just finishing its task of twisting its blades into the headwind.

Eddie was amazed as he thought, "These 22nd flight engineers take better care of their engines than their wives."

"Tower, MAC Two Four's aborting runway two zero, we need to go back to the ramp," Eddie's aircraft commander called from his co-pilot's seat. "Negative assistance required."

"Rain Dance flight, go around . . . aircraft on the runway aborting," the tower instructed the A-1s that were turning short final.

"We're awful low on gas. Can the Shaky roll to the end and we'll be able to fit in behind him just fine."

"Shaky aborting, roll to the end, break break . . . Rain Dance flight you're cleared to land short behind the fat bird." The two ship formation of old propeller driven fighters landed and slowed easily, then turned off for the transient ramp. The C-124 crew finished the engine failure checklist, the after landing checklist, and made plans for their day off. No adrenalin flowed; it was just another day at work.

COLONEL DUNCAN

All squadron commanders carried a heavy responsibility. Colonel Duncan carried an extra heavy responsibility due to the eclectic nature of the 22nd's outsized freight mission. Operating out of the peripheral areas around Vietnam, into a combat zone, his squadron's home base was located in Japan. Via a C-124, his home base and his work assignments were a day apart. With all the merriment that took place at their layover stations, the separation of married crew members from their families for weeks at a time, he needed to be a master at juggling personalities and situations.

Eddie's crew was in a jovial mood as they rode the crew bus onto Clark Air Base and piled out for a breakfast at the cinderblock diner. They were scheduled for one more Vietnam turn, then the long flight back to Tachikawa for aircraft maintenance and some days off. They had the previous day off and the prior evening they had loaded three massive wooden bars into the rear of their aircraft's cargo bin. Two were for personal use, for shipment back to the States with their household goods. One was to be auctioned off at the Tachikawa Officers Club. It would be a silent auction, where participants bid for the item on a posted piece of paper. The profit was for donation to the Tachikawa Base Charity Fund for distressed enlisted families.

Max was Eddie's senior flight engineer and Jim Beckle was his aircraft commander, an ideal crew setup. Jim was teasing Max, giving him a friendly bad time while they wolfed down enough chow to last them for their shuttle to and back from Danang. "Bet you been flying in C-124s so long you could start the engines in your sleep."

"Don't know, I'll have to try it sometime . . . but I do know that I could start all four engines simultaneously," Max replied nonchalantly.

"Not true!" Eddie jumped in. "As much electrical power that starting one engine draws from the ground power cart, there's no way a cart could turn all four at once. It's just too much. I know the aircraft's APU couldn't do it either. Besides, you don't have enough hands and fingers to work all the switches at once. I think you over extended yourself on that one."

APU was an acronym for auxiliary power unit. C-124s had DC electrical batteries, just like automobiles, and in flight received their electricity from generators, one on each engine, similar to an automobile. Except a car has only one engine and one generator. On the ground, with the engines shut down, the power from the two storage batteries was very limited. So whenever available, a ground power unit (GPU), usually called a power cart, was hooked to the aircraft and it provided electricity for lighting, maintenance, operation of electrically powered hydraulic systems, and the large electrical draw necessary to start the engines.

For use, whenever an external electrical power (GPU) was not available, a gas turbine auxiliary power unit (APU) was built into O compartment, located underneath the cargo floor. The aircraft's APU used battery power to start, burned aviation gas from an engine fuel tank (#10), was very noisy, and used only when necessary. Its electrical output was slightly less than the ground power units but sufficient.

"Bet ya a case of beer I can do it," Max bragged.

"You're talking to the wrong man," Eddie corrected. "Jim's in charge of this show, remember? I'm only the errand boy with a fancy name of co-pilot."

"I'll call you on that," Jim smiled at Max. "Make it a case for Eddie, a case for me, and a case for the navigator. I'd take that bet."

So the bet was on. Everyone, smiling confidently, completed their pre-flight chores. Eddie and Jim planned a party for that evening with the beer they were going to win from their smart-ass flight engineer. At last, the anticipated moment had arrived. They were connected to an external power unit, a sizable gasoline engine that turned an electrical generator. The aircraft's engine starters would each draw their power through the single connecting cord from the one lonely cart.

The second flight engineer, on the ground and in front of their aircraft, cleared the area visually, smiled, and raised both hands in the air and gave a nonstandard start signal. He raised four fingers on each hand and twirled both hands in a circle.

"Start em up, all four at once," Jim called over the interphone. The remaining crew members giggled as Jim gave his order.

Max carefully and deliberately bent over and removed his shoes and socks. He then doubled up and lifted both bare feet onto his table top and he proceeded to carefully place his toes against his required switches. With his free hands he depressed the remaining necessary switches and buttons. As needed he flexed his toes.

All four propellers started turning, the power cart moaned and strained to keep a usable current flowing. Max held all four starter switches down with one hand while his other hand moved about quickly and performed his necessary tasks. His toes held the remaining switches in place. All four engines coughed, sputtered, and sprang to life.

It was brilliant and the crew erupted into a cheer as Mac smiled and finished his after-start tasks.

"Shit!" Eddie grinned and rocked his head. "This has to go down in history as one of the 22nd's greatest accomplishments. It was worth three cases of beer just to see that."

"I saw that!" a voice came in over their head sets. It came from no one on the interphone. It came in over the radio.

"Who could that have been?" Jim asked.

"Sir," the loadmaster spoke up in a sheepish voice. "I forgot until now. Last night I heard that Colonel Duncan is down here and is scheduled to depart fifteen minutes after we are."

"We're dead," Jim moaned. "Looks like I'll get it in the rear tonight . . . let's get the hell out of here." So they flew to Vietnam and back, everyone silent and somber.

* *

That night the three commissioned officers on their crew, Jim, Eddie, and their navigator, were sitting in a row at the Clark Officers Club happy hour bar. Their sweaty, smelly flight suits weren't that popular with the other bar customers but the three of them couldn't care less. If things couldn't have been worse, Colonel Duncan also had just landed and he strolled into the bar and took an open seat next to Eddie. He ordered a beer, turned to the guys, and smiled.

"Have a good flight today?"

The three of them nodded together. "Yeah," Jim spoke for the group. "Everything went okay."

"Yeah," the colonel smiled. "Me to." There was no mention of the four engine quick start they had inadvertently demonstrated to the squadron commander. But from the way he was smiling, they knew that he knew.

Jim bought the next round of drinks.

The three of them, along with the rest of the squadron, would have followed their leader into hell and back. He knew when to bet and when to fold. Colonel Duncan was one of the last of the good guys.

CHAPTER NINE: DUC TAO

Someone had turned on the lights and was tugging on his shoulder. Eddie sat up for a moment wondering where he was, then realized he was in a transient trailer bedroom. He looked at his watch. It was 4:30 a.m. Then he looked up into Larry's grinning face. Larry, wearing only his shorts, looked like he had also just been awakened. "What the hell's going on?" Eddie asked.

"I just got a call from the command post and they want us to go to a place called Duc Tao and to leave ASAP," Larry explained. "You go wake up the navigator in the next trailer and I'll get back on the phone and contact our enlisted. They confiscated a loadmaster from a crew that arrived inbound and he's already loading our cargo." Then Larry left.

Eddie was laced with misery. He only had five hours sleep, they had been on a twenty-four hour release and he had attended a board meeting at the club. He quickly calculated that it had only been six hours since they left the officers club, but with breakfast, flight planning and everything, it would be about eight hours when they would take-off. That would just make him legal. He wondered if the rest of the crewmembers were legal.

It was a busy time. Eddie, Larry, and their navigator gulped down breakfast at the cinder block café, attended a mission briefing at operations from an intelligence officer, flight planned, and hurried out to the aircraft. Eddie was operating on remote control. When they arrived at the plane the fueler was gassing their bird and their crew's loadmaster had just reported for duty. He was inspecting the tied down load, swearing like a trooper, and maintaining a running argument with the two army staff sergeants that accompanied their freight. Their freight was a large D-8 Caterpillar, with an earth moving blade mounted in front, and large sheets of steel armor bolted and welded over the engines and around the operator's position. The name Greta was stenciled on both sides of the armored engine. Loadmasters were very fussy about their loads and he wasn't happy with the way the rampies had secured several tie downs. He redid them, but he was also upset that there was a full load of fuel in the Caterpillar. That was against the rules and the aerial port had obtained a waiver for that deviation. But neither he nor the earlier loadmaster had been briefed. The two army sergeants were dressed in fatigues and carried field packs and rifles. They were the caterpillar's drivers. At Duc Tao they would stay with their charge.

Too soon Eddie found himself listening to the familiar roar of the engines and as Larry gave him the thumbs up, he raised the gear. Eddie was flying as co-pilot, pilot not flying, because of the complicated nature of their destination and the short unpaved runway. He was existing minute from minute. As they slowly climbed out over the mud flats north west of Manila, he agonized at the thought of spending another day in such pain.

Then Larry spoke some of the sweetest words Eddie ever heard, "You look like hell. Why don't you go grab a couple of hours sleep in the bunk? I'll take the bunk on our way back." Eddie made it to the bunk and fell asleep in less than three minutes.

Such sweet relief! It was interesting how when flying an aircraft, after a while, it became a part of each crewmember—to the depths of their very soul. He slept like a baby, yet was aware of every propeller RPM change. He sat up wide awake at the smell of fumes when the flight engineer's cigarette lighter failed to light, then immediately fell back to sleep when he realized where the fuel smell came from. The navigator had brewed a fresh pot-full of coffee and the army sergeants had been invited up to the cockpit. It was the first time in their careers that an officer had ever made coffee for them. Eddie heard their voices in his sleep, but unlike the strange fumes, their voices hadn't disturbed him. He heard the power reduction when they started down and was up and into his seat without needing to be awakened. He felt a little guilty for sleeping the entire leg, but noticed the other bunk had been slept in. It had been used by the flight engineers.

The jungle below them looked as if it was a giant shag rug and someone had taken a rake and swept it back and forth, laying the carpet in different directions. Each width was, however, several hundred feet wide and been caused by American C-123 defoliant spray planes called "Ranch Hands." The Ranch Hands applied their "2 4 5-T" chemical spray, dubbed "Agent Orange" by the media, where the enemy was suspected to be hiding in the jungle. The powerful spray would kill the foliage and deny the enemy a place to hide. The sprayed swaths were in various stages of re-growth and formed the colorful patterns. Eddie, from his experiences growing up on a farm and his university studies, suspected the spraying would have a degrading and long lasting effect on the ecology. What he didn't suspect was that the 2 4 5-T used in the jungles of Vietnam, unlike the harmless 2 4-D his father used on their farm, would poison the systems of both the American military and Vietnamese people.

The crews of these C-123 Ranch Hands needed nerves of steel to fly low over the jungle as they sprayed their defoliant. They exposed themselves to frequent small arms fire and insisted their bullet holes be patched with shiny aluminum, not painted. These shiny patches, contrasting with the dark green camouflage paint of their aircraft, were considered their personal badges of courage. Some of their aircraft had so many shiny aluminum patches on them they looked like a Dalmatian. Eddie wondered why they were fighting an enemy in the jungle, man to man, when the real foe was up north in Hanoi—off loading cargo ships full of weapons and ammunition and under complete immunity from American warplanes.

Intelligence had briefed Eddie's flight crew on the unpaved landing field. It was a 4000 foot strip carved out of the jungle. It was a dirt runway and they had been waiting for the rain to let up and the soil to dry enough to support the C-124's heavy footprint. The aircraft performance table showed that a C-124, with their planned cargo and fuel load, field elevation and forecast temperature, could land in 3500 feet. With the cargo removed, they could take-off in 3700 feet. Eddie was glad Larry was flying. After three and a half years flying the Shaky Bird, Larry was at his peak and he possessed solid judgment. He was a skilled pilot and capable of flying right on the numbers. Larry and Eddie had practiced short field landings several times while landing at Clark and Eddie was grateful they had the foresight to do so. Normally the squadron assigned the highest ranking and most experienced officers to fly into the "dicey" strips. But it hadn't rained in several days so the mission had to go immediately. No 22nd major or colonel pilots were available.

MAC flying rules required the pilot to cross the runway threshold no less than fifty feet high, to prevent anyone from ever landing short. Eddie mentioned this, jokingly, to Larry and received his expected response, "Those desk jockeys back in the States don't have anything else to do but write rules for us to fly by over here. It's probably a good rule for them, cause they don't fly that much and aren't that proficient. But if we cross the threshold fifty feet high, we'll land too long and end up in jungle on the far end of the runway. I'm gonna bring us in right over the trees and put us down on the first two hundred feet of the dirt strip."

The extra sleep was enough to revive Eddie's young body and he was eager to do "this thing." Larry gave a detailed pre-landing briefing to the crew so everything would flow smoothly, quickly, and without anyone getting hurt. Approach and landing speeds were carefully and precisely computed and Larry briefed that, instead of the faster MAC recommended flare speed, he was planning to touch down at only five knots above stall speed. That was a very slim margin for such a large aircraft. Immediately after touchdown and as soon as Larry lowered the nose wheel down on the ground, Eddie was to push and hold the yoke all the way forward to stick the airplane onto the runway—a normal C-124 procedure for all landings. Larry would steer with his left hand on the tiller and come in with the brakes quickly but not so quickly as to blow any tires. If needed, he would utilize differential braking to steer. His right hand would drop the propellers into reverse. While holding the yoke forward Eddie would call the green reverse lights, which indicated the propellers had moved into reverse position, then read and call out, at frequent intervals, the engines' manifold pressures. Larry would add reverse thrust power with his right hand and advance it to fifty-five inches of manifold pressure (power) according to Eddie's call outs. Larry would be too busy looking outside and keeping the aircraft centered on the barely wide enough runway to read the gauges for himself. The flight engineer would watch the landing from an overall perspective and alert the pilots of any deviations or signs of trouble.

As soon as the aircraft stopped, the loadmaster would open the clamshell nose doors and lower the extendable ramps. The first flight engineer would stay at his panel and the engines would not be shut down. The second flight engineer would also be down stairs and would work both sides of the caterpillar, popping loose the tie down chains. The driver and his assistant, with the "all clear" from both the loadmaster and the second flight engineer, would start the tractor's engines and drive out and down the twin ramps and clear of the runway. Then the two downstairs crewmembers would use the hydraulic system to pull the ramps up and close the clamshell doors. When the doors were closed, the loadmaster would notify Larry over the interphone. The upstairs crew would then be clear to taxi and take-off, or as Larry phrased it, "Haul ass out of there." The engines would never be shut down and the intelligence officer told them the troops on the ground had been briefed to "stay the hell out of the way of the propellers." They planned to spend less than five or six minutes on the ground. When finished off-loading downstairs, the second flight engineer would hustle upstairs to his usual top scanner position out the top hatch. He was to only pop his head out the top hatch as needed; to remain exposed up there would be an inviting target for a sniper.

Larry also reviewed the dust storm phenomena that could occur when landing on non-paved runways. Just after landing on dirt runways, the higher forward speed would keep all the dust and dirt that was stirred up by the reverse thrust on the propellers—behind the aircraft. As the aircraft slowed, however, the reversed propellers would draw the dirt storm farther and farther forward. At some point, if the engines were pulling the reversed propellers at a high enough power setting, the dirt storm would be sucked forward of the slowing aircraft and the pilots would lose sight of the runway. They wouldn't be able to see and steer the aircraft. At that point there were two available options. First, as they rolled out, Eddie would need to note the exact aircraft compass heading needed to steer in order to stay pointed directly down the center of the runway. He would, if the dirt storm caught up with them, every three or four seconds and in addition to his other duties, watch the compass heading and call out steer left, steer right, or steer neutral. Larry would be steering in the blind. Second option, the pilot flying could reduce the amount of power on his engines, which would reduce the forward thrust and the dirt storm leading edge would move back behind them. The pilots would then regain their outside vision. Reducing thrust would, however, lengthen the distance it would take for the aircraft to stop. The pilot's skills at balancing the two options with split second decisions was why they got paid the "big bucks," as Larry referred to his modest military pay.

It almost worked as briefed. They started off with a pass, 1000 feet high, over the field to check things out. The radio operator on the ground informed them with his hand held radio, "the runway is dry, wind calm, and stop screwing around and advertising your intentions."

Eddie responded by reminding the guy on the ground to keep his men away from their aircraft because their spinning propellers would whop their heads off, even with their shoulders. That was all Larry needed, he decided all was good and wanted to get on the ground as soon as possible. He rolled over into a steep left turn and called, "Manifold one five, RPM twenty-seven hundred." With the G forces they were pulling the caterpillar remained pinned to the floor. With the low power setting, the airspeed bled off rapidly and Eddie followed with the gear and flaps as speed allowed. Down they fell, then a little roll out to extend the downwind to set up the needed final approach.

Larry called, "Manifold two zero." He was purposely lower than normal on the turn to final and had to shallow the descent rate to get to the runway. He did this on purpose so he could use a higher power setting to keep the engines warm, yet maintain his calculated approach speed. During the turn to final he kept just enough back pressure to keep the caterpillar hugging the floor but not too much to induce a stall or degrade

124

their descent angle. Larry was good. On final Larry said, "I have the throttles." He moved them slightly back and forth to maintain the exact airspeed he wanted. With the engine cowl flaps closed, the engines stayed warm. As they approached the edge of the tree line, Larry pulled off a little more power and increased their descent rate to maintain their airspeed. Their increased rate of descent dropped them down over the end of the jungle and onto the runway. His round out for landing bled off the rest of his airspeed above stall and they were solidly on the runway. One hundred feet from the approach end of the runway, with the nose wheel coming down, he pulled the throttles to idle power. Eddie wanted to savor the moment but there just wasn't time.

"You got the yoke," Larry shouted.

"I got the yoke," Eddie shouted and pushed forward, holding the nose wheel onto the dirt runway.

"RRRRrrrrooooo————ooooorrrrrRRRRRR," the propellers came down through flat pitch and went into reverse position.

"Four green," Eddie hollered and Larry re-applied power.

"Forty, forty-seven, fifty-five, hold her there," Eddie called out the manifold pressure.

It was a massive amount of power turning the four reversed propellers and with Larry heavy on the brakes and the soft runway surface, they decelerated rapidly. Then Eddie became concerned. Just as Larry had cautioned, as they decelerated through fifty knots, the massive dirt storm their aerodynamic behemoth had stirred up was sucked forward and past their windshield. They were blinded. As briefed in training at Tinker and by Larry, Eddie immediately called out the compass heading then in quick intervals gave Larry steering directions. "A little left, hold it, little more left, slightly right." Larry steered blindly through the dust and dirt straight down the runway. As the airspeed slowed through twenty knots Larry came off with the engine power to thirty-five inches and the cloud moved back. They could see again. As the airspeed approached zero Larry came out of reverse and they were stopped—fat dumb and happy—about 300 feet from the end of the runway. Intelligence didn't have to worry about the runway, it was plenty dry.

They taxied to and stopped short of three waiting soldiers. "Open the doors!" Eddie shouted over the interphone. The aircraft was vibrating slightly as the loadmaster was already operating the hydraulic powered nose doors.

Eddie looked around and saw nothing except jungle surrounding a dirt runway. Then soldiers started to stand up and he noticed bunkers and gun positions that blended with the scene. He heard the caterpillar roar to life and in another thirty seconds the aircraft shifted from the caterpillar's movement as it moved forward and down the ramp. It emerged from under their nose and lumbered off the runway and into the jungle. Several soldiers waved at the cockpit, then followed the armored bulldozer. The soldiers were dirty and unshaven, wore camouflaged trousers and boots, and flak jackets with no shirts underneath. They all carried M-16 rifles and had bulky ammo belts. Eddie had no idea why they were grinning in that hell hole. Eddie stared around at the jungle and wondered who was hidden and staring back. He tried to maintain a pleasant and harmless look, just in case they were Viet Cong. He was shaking quite badly from the adrenaline.

"Check list," Larry commanded and Eddie responded, being very careful to get everything right.

The clamshell doors closed with a shudder and over the interphone the flight engineer shouted, "Doors are closed! Let's get the hell out of here."

Larry released the brakes and advanced a little power. Eddie looked over and could see through a cut swath of jungle where several soldiers were shouting orders at the caterpillar driver—each pointing in a different direction. The second flight engineer raced up through the floor hatch and opened the top hatch. He peaked out just enough for his eyes to clear the edges of the hatch. The remaining GIs along the edge of the strip dove for cover as the four Pratt and Whitney's kicked up another dust and dirt storm. They slowly eased up to the end of the runway.

"We'll never make it," Eddie volunteered his opinion. The checklist was done but there was not enough room to swing their large aircraft around and point it back down the runway. All along, their wingtips had been passing over low bushes, soldier's bunkers, and empty fifty gallon fuel barrels, but there was not enough room to turn around. A grove of young palm trees and tall bushes were blocking their turn space.

"Eddie's right, Sir," the top scanner spoke over the interphone. "There's just not enough room to turn around."

"God-damn it," Larry swore as he stopped the aircraft. "Those guys back at Clark said this place had been inspected and it could accommodate a C-124."

"Get that caterpillar back down here," the flight engineer suggested. "He can push those trees over in a few minutes. The longer we sit here the sooner we're gonna get our asses blown up."

They had started their left swing around and had stopped with about fifteen feet of their right wingtip just short of the cluster of young palm trees.

Sergeant Clark lowered himself from the top hatch and came forward to the pilots' stations. He pulled Larry's headset back and hollered into Larry's right ear. "I think if we go slow we can push our wing over those trees, there's no hardwood out there, just palms and bushes. The outboard prop is far enough in that it'll clear without hitting anything."

"You sure the wing can take it?" Larry looked the sergeant straight in the eyes.

"If we go real slow," the sergeant again spoke three inches from Larry's ear. "The palm trees should bend over without much force. We don't wanna knock em over. We wanna slowly bend em over."

The two professionals locked eyes for a few seconds and Larry made his decision. "What the hell! If we stay here very long, Charlie's gonna have a nice fat bird on his prize list. Get back to that top hatch and watch us real close as I push up against em. If it looks like we're gonna break anything, if those palm trees don't look like they're gonna bend easy, stop me."

Larry looked over his shoulder and as the sergeant stuck his head out the hatch, he slowly advanced the two right throttles and rode the left brake. The right wing slowly came about, slowly pushing over the obstacles; each palm tree gave way like a giant blade of grass. The top engineer talked them around. "Keep coming, lookin good, lookin good, keep coming, lookin good, we're clear." They finished their turn and were facing back down the runway. The dirt and dust were still settling from their arrival.

"Get that hatch closed!" Larry hollered needlessly. The second flight engineer had already closed it and was looking over the first engineer's shoulder. Four eyes are better than two at the flight engineer's panel. It would be a "water" take-off. Most take-offs were "dry." The engineers would purposely keep the engines' fuel air mixture rich, so the extra fuel vapor would serve as a coolant to prevent the cylinders from overheating at the high take-off power setting. This technique almost always provided enough engine power for the take-off, 3250 brake horsepower (BPH) per engine. To get the last ounce of power, the full 3500 BPH for each engine, the C-124 had a thirty gallon tank of water/alcohol mixture for each wing. A water injection system sprayed water into the fuel air mixture for each engine. The water provided the cooling to prevent overheating the engines. With the water replacing the extra fuel requirement, the engineers could lean the combustible fuel air mixture to its most productive ratio. Voila, more power was produced. The water tank would run dry after five minutes, but that was enough to get airborne and underway safely.

"Max power," Larry called, then as an after thought and reminder, "Make it wet."

Larry and Eddie both rode the brakes as the flight engineer advanced the power, turned on the water, and both flight engineers leaned out the engines, two apiece. Both engineers checked the gauges. Eddie held the yoke forward as the beast bucked and strained on its leash.

As the engines approached the full sixty-two inches of manifold pressure and the flight engineer was satisfied with the lean fuel air mixture, he hollered, "Looks good back here. GO!" Larry nodded his head and both pilots simultaneously released the brakes. The aircraft leapt forward and they were off.

Eddie never even tried to get an acceleration check on the short runway. He looked out the side and watched his wing-tip pass over the trash, debris, and jungle grass along the side of the runway. He tried to ignore the end of the runway quickly coming up on them. He then stared at the engine gauges and was surprised the engines didn't overtemp. The water was working!

"Whoom . . . Whoom," everyone felt two concussions midway down the runway. The engines all looked good and it was too late to stop anyway. Eddie called out the airspeed every ten knots so Larry could concentrate his vision outside. At the last second Larry honked back on the yoke, the fat bird broke free, and they gracefully rose over the trees. Without the weight of the caterpillar and with only two hours worth of gas left, they were very light weight.

"Gear up," Larry hollered, this time not wanting to release his grip on the yoke to give a thumbs up signal.

The hydraulic pressure cycled up to normal and the gear door lights went out. "Gear up, standing by flaps," Eddie hollered.

"Milk the flaps up slowly," Larry commanded. "So we can accelerate and not lose lift."

Every knot of airspeed they gained made Eddie feel better. "FAC drivers at the bar told me to stay on the deck until you're fast enough to zoom up," Larry explained as they zipped along fifty feet over the tree tops. "The lower you are the harder it is for them to get a shot off at you." As they approached the 238 knot red line, their maximum allowable airspeed, the old bird was starting to shake. Larry again honked back and they zoomed toward the sky. Again they had fudged on MAC regulations because MAC had an additional restriction of maximum 180 knots indicated airspeed. It had something to do with a cracked wing spar on one of the stateside C-124s. Their speed bled off quickly and Larry rolled into a quick left turn, then into a hard right turn to make it more difficult for any gunner to track them.

In their right turn, Eddie could see back at the tiny clearing they had just departed from and he could see two plumes of smoke rising from the far half of the runway. It made him feel sick. They were either mortar or rocket impacts. The gomers had the runway zeroed in, just waiting for a prize. If they had hit in front of them, the craters could have torn a landing gear off. If they had hit them, they would either be dead or about to be dead. Their presence had been indeed noticed by strangers and they had gotten out about ten seconds ahead of the enemy. When the army guys referred to C-124s as mortar bait, they knew their business.

Larry saw the smoke also and grinned from ear to ear, "Beers on me tonight." Eddie felt good as he belonged to something—with his aircraft and this crew. They could have their fancy paint jobs, jet engines, and neck scarves—this crew and old airplane were his kind of people.

"Pyramid, Pyramid, this is MAC Three Three, off Duc Tao, direct Ben Hoa," Eddie called their position out to anyone listening. He wanted the world to know that they had just done a nifty piece of flying.

They had planned their fuel load so as to be as light weight as possible in and out of Duc Tao, in order to make their landing and take-off distances as short as possible. Once their job was done, they had just enough fuel to get to Ben Hoa. They would gas up, and then try to make happy hour back at Clark. That was the stuff the 22nd crews were made of.

CHAPTER TEN: A WHOLE LOT OF SHAKING GOIN ON

The little community of Tachikawa was constantly in motion so it was easy to blend in and out of it. No one missed Eddie when he was out on trips and he was a welcome member whenever he was home between trips. The Tachikawa Officers Club was his center of social life but he stayed low key. He slept a lot and usually farmed out his laundry to the mama san that managed his apartment building; all three apartments. Just outside the Tachikawa Air Base east gate, where his apartment was located, Tachikawa City was not a large town but a rather small, sprawling, disorganized village. It had grown under the prosperity the American air base provided.

His last trip south had arrived at Tachikawa at 7:00 p.m. It was amazing how fast the word spread whenever a plane was coming in from down south. After they taxied to the ramp and were waiting for the customs inspector to finish inspecting their bags, a small group of onlookers gathered and waited. Like vultures around the kill. It took them no time to round up a truck and when the inspector was finished, everyone pitched in, spectators and crew alike. They down-loaded the booty of oriental treasure and distributed it to the various crewmembers' quarters. Then Eddie slept for twelve hours.

The next day he decided he needed to devote a little time to getting to know Japan better. He'd been all over a good portion of South East Asia but had not taken enough time to play tourist in his home neighborhood. He drove his Cedric out into the countryside and experienced the narrow roads with deep concrete "benjo" ditches for edges. Traffic was heavy on the inadequate roads and frequently blocked as Kamikaze style truck drivers and male automobile drivers would park their cars in the middle of the road while they urinated in the benjos. Some things about Japan were still medieval. That afternoon the fifteen mile drive to Atsugi Naval Air Base took an hour. It was worth the irritation as Atsugi had a navy exchange that sold guns at great prices. He bought a Remington model 1100 shotgun and a Browning 7mm magnum rifle for less than half what they would cost in the States. They were manufactured in Japan, something that Eddie hadn't known.

He spent the next day wandering the back streets of Tachikawa City, photographing the people and their unpainted buildings. Apparently there was an additional tax on buildings that were painted, a sort of tax on the rich, so everyone maintained the bare wood look. In the damp climate almost all of the buildings and houses were a natural dark brown. The brownness of the wooden sidewalks and the buildings contrasted beautifully with the colorful kimonos, the bathrobe-style beautifully embroidered robes that half the women still wore. The other half wore traditional western dress and Eddie was careful to avoid getting any of those wearing western garb into his photos.

It was a unique time for Japan. The people were in transition between their old traditions and the influence of the new western culture. The little girls, in their tiny kimonos, were cute as buttons and loved to pose for the American GI. He visited several Pachinko parlors, the Japanese favorite pastime. They looked like vertical pin ball machines. For the equivalent of thirty-five cents, which he paid in Yen, he could purchase a bowl of rice and curry sauce for lunch. Everything was clean and there was no risk from eating street vender food.

Considering that the average Japanese worked for about a dollar a day and Americans paid thirty dollars per month for house maids, the thirty-five cents was expensive for the food. But he didn't mind paying the GI price. He assumed the locals made the same purchase for the equivalent of ten or fifteen cents. It took him thirty minutes to eat his rice and curry as they gave him wooden chop sticks, there wasn't a fork or spoon in sight. The Japanese in the restaurant were polite not to laugh at him in his presence, but he could hear a lot of conversation and snickering in the restaurant's doorways. That evening he joined several couples from the squadron and they caught the train, thirty minutes into Tokyo. They had a wonderful meal at the Sanno Hotel and got loaded on the hot Sake. It was a pleasant day and evening.

At 5:00 a.m. the next morning he was awakened by the telephone ringing and ringing and ringing. It took him a moment to wake up; he had been in a deep sleep. He grabbed the ringing demon next to his bed and at the same time realized he was in his apartment outside the east Tachikawa gate. "Hello," he mumbled. "Eddie here."

"This is Sergeant Hayley," the voice on the phone answered. "I'm sorry to wake you up, Sir . . . I know you're not scheduled to go back out for two more days." As he listened, the last few weeks' events came back to him. It had been a short trip. He'd flown with a full colonel from FECAP headquarters at nearby Yakota Airbase. The squadron allowed certain flyers assigned to ground jobs in the Tachikawa/Yakota area to fly with them occasionally, so they could maintain flying proficiency and of course get their tickets punched for combat pay. This colonel had a lot of influence in structuring their overnight stays, where they would layover, and their departure times. It was essential for the squadron to yield to his every wish. Eddie, as a more senior co-pilot, was assigned to be his babysitter and to make sure he didn't bend any 22nd aluminum. They had only been out five days, but had been on shopping junkets in Bangkok, Clark, and Taipei, in addition to getting the colonel's combat pay authorization for two months.

"There's been a bad earthquake in Misawa. It's our fighter base up north on the island of Honshu," Sergeant Hayley explained. "Civilians and military both took it in the shorts. Our American air base up there is in bad shape and headquarters has ordered an all out airlift from Tachikawa. Colonel Duncan wants all available crewmembers at the squadron briefing room ASAP. I gotta go . . . ASAP, ya got that, Sir?"

"Yeah, I got it. I'll hustle right over." Eddie hung up and sat on the bed a few minutes longer to wake up.

* * * * * * * * * * * * * * * * * * *

"What the hell's going on?" Eddie asked Jack Mastronardi as he slipped into the seat next to him.

"Nobody knows much," Jack answered, in a lowered voice as if there were spies in their midst. "Guess the northern part of Honshu caught one hell of an earthquake last night and base communications has been going ape shit ever since. They lost all contact through normal communications with the Misawa Air Base and there's no Japanese civilian communications working either. All that expensive equipment they got and I hear the only way they can get through to Misawa is by an amateur HAM radio set. Some sergeant has one in his house at Misawa. It didn't get damaged and they're using a portable generator to power it. The sergeant is temporary duty at Clark and the air force has confiscated his house and is using his radio gear. I heard that his wife is the only one home and she's drunk as a skunk. Apparently they're having a hell of a time. She won't shut up and she's ordering everyone around like the Queen of Sheba."

"Ten-Hut!" the first sergeant cracked out, reflecting years of military discipline and practice.

"He must have gotten it in some other squadron," Eddie thought as he and all the other crew members snapped to attention.

Colonel Duncan entered stage left and approached the single podium. He had a manila folder in his hand, two enlisted office clerks following him, and they all had on their blue uniforms. As he stood there at attention, Eddie realized two things: it was the first time he had ever seen their squadron commander at Tachikawa, he'd only seen him at Clark AFB. It must have been a quirk of fate that he was home for this adventure. Second, it was the first time Eddie had stood at attention since he graduated from pilot training.

"At ease," the lieutenant colonel addressed them, "and be seated. I'll get right to the point." He continued without hesitation and read from a telegram: *At twenty-eighteen local last night the northern islands of Japan were struck by an earthquake measuring seven point five on the Richter scale. This event caused massive power outages, disrupted underground utilities including water, sewage, gas, and communications. No causality reports received although believed to be high.*

He then continued, looking at his charge, "We got our work cut out for us. We got through to Misawa using a HAM radio and we've received an urgent request for help from the base commander. They need drinking water and medical supplies first, then portable shelters, food, and a thousand other things. FECAP has delegated the 22nd and the 815th flying Jennies, with their C-130s, to be the primary airlift organizations until they can get an airlift organized and in from stateside. The 815th has almost all of their C-130s down south and they only have four C-130s here at Tachikawa. Two of them are shot full of holes and are grounded for repairs and the other two are all torn apart for scheduled maintenance. That leaves us. We got four C-124s here, two are ready to go, one will be out of scheduled maintenance in several hours, and the fourth is an engine change that the maintenance guys will work on non stop and have ready sometime this afternoon."

Lt. Colonel Duncan paused as if he really didn't want to continue. Then he spoke, "As you may know, the runway at Misawa is ten thousand feet long. The information we got is that only the east forty-five hundred feet are usable and it ends with a three foot wide crack. There are several other big cracks beyond the one at forty-five hundred feet. They can't send any jets up there cause there's no way they're going to send MAC's prize C-141s into a forty-five hundred foot, questionable airfield with bad weather. I don't even know if a C-141 could operate into a forty-five hundred foot runway.

"Our first bird in will have to confirm everything I'm saying. They claim the tower, with the help of their backup generator, is working The weather is stinko with rain and low ceilings; their new ILS landing system and approach control radar are out of service. They assured me they would have them back in service by the time our first bird arrives. We're gonna have to depend on you aircraft commanders and crews to really be heads up, be careful in deciding if it's safe to land or not. You'll have enough fuel for both ways and two hours holding. Whatever decisions you make up there, make damn sure you don't bust any birds. You know I'll back you up whatever your decisions are but let's not make the existing disaster worse by piling up an airplane. Loadmasters are out there now loading up. We got permission to truck emergency supplies from Fuchu Air Base, thirty minutes north of here. We want the first bird to launch an hour from now, or as soon as the loadmasters get their freight tied down. The emergency supplies at Fuchu were stored on pallets so that's really helping speed things up.

"My first sergeant has your flight orders. Pick em up on your way out. I've got Ivanoff and Eddie going out first, followed by Barkley and Pulaski, then Fausey and Mastronardi. Adams will act as my operations officer and I'll send my first sergeant over to the MARS room to coordinate the HF communications with the HAM radio at Misawa. You should be able to talk to him on your HF radios once airborne. Any questions?"

"What's the actual weather up there right now?" Nit Noy asked.

"Two hundred ceiling and a half mile visibility, light drizzle. It's at minimums." He looked around for more questions but everyone seemed a little dazed, so he nodded at his first sergeant.

"Ten-Hut!" They stood up and six bewildered pilots and three bewildered navigators followed their respected squadron commander from the room.

They picked up their orders as they left for the flight planning room. First Lieutenant Pulaski, everyone called him Nit Noy, began one of his usual spontaneous outbursts. "PACAF has a thousand birds in South Asia and our bastard squadron of C-124s gets to test the broken runway. MAC claims we belong to PACAF and PACAF claims we're MAC birds. Our orders are cut out of the 19th at Clark for the 315th that has jurisdiction over our aircraft. We're under emergency orders from the State Department to fly the army's emergency supplies stored at Fuchu Air Force Base to the Fighter Base at Misawa which is a Tactical Air Command Squadron assigned to the Occupational Forces under the coordination of the U S Embassy. As Fuchu Air Base

130

has no runway they're trucking the supplies the fifteen miles to Tachikawa air base in navy trucks and the reason that we have to fly the approach into a half of a runway with an ILS that has not been flight checked since the earthquake is that nobody can find anyone else that will do it . . . piece of cake."

He looked at Eddie, smiled and asked. "What is it that you guys don't understand?" He continued, "I guess it's the same old shit, it's up to the crews to pull it off. Did you notice the key words in Colonel Duncan's presentation? He said whatever decisions the crews make, he'll back us up. That's it in a nutshell. Get in your airplanes and make it work."

"What about runway lights?" Eddie wondered out loud to Major Ivanoff as they laid out their charts and weather printout on the large table used for flight planning. Because of the damage from the earthquakes, their flight had a lot of characteristics like flying in Vietnam. There was no air traffic control available in northern Japan; the earthquake had taken care of that. They did, however, file with the local Japanese—just for their departure procedures.

"Colonel told me they're sending flares up with the second bird. They won't need runway lights until tonight," Major Ivanoll reassured his crew.

"I gotta look at a map of that area." Eddie insisted. Major Ivanoff eyed Eddie with a look of approval. "We shoulda asked if their TACAN was working," Eddie continued.

"TACAN's out," the major replied. "Colonel told me while we were waiting for everyone to show up for the briefing. But we'll let Henry get us up there with his bag full of tricks. You've flown with Henry before, haven't you?" He nodded at the major who was their navigator and was silently looking over the sparsely written plans for the flight.

"Yeah," Eddie looked at Major Henry Meyer and smiled, "We had two trips south together." Major Meyer smiled back at Eddie and winked. On one of their trips, Eddie had stumbled onto Henry as he was in the process of sneaking a bar girl into his transient crew trailer on base. It was strictly forbidden and one could get into a lot of trouble if caught. Two military policemen on routine patrol were rounding the corner of the next trailer over. Eddie had immediately bent over and acted like he was sick and going to throw up—the momentary distraction saved Major Meyer from a letter in his permanent file. The next day he bought Eddie drinks and a steak dinner at the O'club. Henry was a fifteen year navigator with a good background in C-130s and B-52s and served as the squadron standards officer for navigators. He had an excellent reputation for his navigational skills. Colonel Duncan had been very careful about picking the first crew to go into Misawa. It made Eddie feel proud to be picked as the co-pilot on this crew.

They picked out two ONC maps, which displayed all of the ground features they would need to study. "We can paint all of the ocean shorelines with our weather radar on our way up there and get azimuth and distance from prominent points for our fixes. With this overcast weather, celestial fixes aren't gonna be available and without any traffic control I need to use the radar as a backup to my LORAN fixes," Henry briefed. "The weather radar will work fine and also allow us to line up on final approach. The base is not that far from the shore line so we can position ourselves with our radar over the water, for a straight in approach. This little bay right here," he pointed for his crew members to memorize. "If we fly right over the center of it we'll be lined up on final approach for runway two eight. All we'll need is the ILS electronic beams to follow to the runway. The weather sheet calls the wind calm so let's hope it doesn't switch and we get a wind from the east. The local weather for there is being forecasted from here, so we'll have to call on the radio for a weather update when we get into range. We can't take a tailwind into that short piece of runway. With the mountains west of the airfield, the only instrument approach is from the east.

"Eight hundred foot hills west and north of the field," Henry continued as he studied out loud. "I'll compute our timing to the runway, based on our approach speed, from the shoreline to the airfield. That'll be our backup to the approach you pilots will be flying." He pulled his issue stop watch from his pocket and clicked it on and off to make sure it was working. "When the times up and we don't have the runway in sight, we'll have to go around so we don't over fly and get into those hills west of the runway. A missed approach turn to the left will keep us over the low and flat shoreline." Eddie was all ears.

Navigators always caught the brunt of the jokes in addition to having to do most of the cockpit's paperwork on their missions. They were always hunched up over their tables with their E6-B hand-held analog computers, computing and shooting the sun and stars with their sextant, and playing with their LORAN receivers. Their world was a mystery to most pilots; over water their directions went unquestioned. They used their stopwatches to time distances during instrument approaches, somewhat annoying to the pilots when they knew they had the approach wired. Navigator's real value, in addition to cockpit secretary and their enroute directions, was that once or twice during a lifetime they would remind the pilots that they forgot to put their gear down just prior to landing, or that the pilots had read their approach plates wrong and the stopwatch timing indicates they need to pull up because there was a hill out there in the clouds. That day Henry received no cruel jokes and neither did the other navigator in the planning room.

The published military minimum altitude for the approach at Miaswa was two hundred feet above the ground. If they didn't see the runway at two hundred feet, they were required to "go around."

Major Ivanoff took his turn, "We'll fly the approach and go around at four hundred feet the first time, to have the guys on the ground listen and hopefully get a glimpse of us. We need to determine that the approach system is working okay and has us lined up with the runway . . . One thing we know for sure is they'll be able to hear us. Then we'll go down to minimums on the second approach. If we don't like it we'll call it off and come back to Tachi and wait for the weather to improve."

"When's the weather supposed to improve?" Eddie wondered out loud.

"Two or three days," the major assured him. "Not good but that's no excuse to play hero and destroy our airplanes." It was the strangest briefing Eddie had ever experienced in his short flying career. Just get in your birds, fly up there into bad weather and a questionable approach, and see if you can pull it off without getting killed.

They hashed over the fuel load and cargo weights and filed for an altitude of eight thousand feet. It was a formality as there were no other aircraft out there and the air traffic control facilities north of Tachikawa had been rendered inoperative by the earthquake. They could fly at any altitude they wanted.

It was drizzling liquid smog outside; the air pollution in Japan was always terrible. The Japanese employees were scurrying around like wet rats as they helped load the freight into their aircraft. They projected a sense of urgency in their tasks as they knew well the hardship and suffering of an earthquake.

"This has got to be the craziest thing I've ever done," Eddie complained. He was helping one of their flight engineers throw a net across a group of fifty-five gallon drums filled with drinking water.

The sergeant straightened up and looked into Eddie's eyes. "I got a twenty year old son stationed at Misawa and right now I don't know if he's dead or alive. Take a good look at what we're carrying." He swept his arm around at their cargo. There were boxes marked as tents, C-rations, and blankets. There were lots of big crates marked with red crosses—medical equipment and supplies. "We're getting this son of a bitch off the ground in another thirty minutes or I'm gonna get myself a new set of pilots. You going along or not?"

The sergeant wasn't finished with the young lieutenant, "The reason we're flying instead of playing all that rulebook shit is that Colonel Duncan cares more about people than a promotion. If you haven't got the stuff to fly in these conditions then you better just keep on walking and keep on walking right past the pay window." It was very improper for an enlisted man to talk to an officer like that, but it was obvious to Eddie that this sergeant was under a lot of pressure and deserved some space.

"I'm in," Eddie answered crisply and finished helping get the rope net over the drums. Eddie dug his flashlight out and did an exterior walk around in the drizzle. It allowed him to settle down and he was sorry he had opened his big mouth.

At cruise altitude, eight thousand feet, the drizzle turned to heavy rain. Eddie turned on the wing leading edge lights and looked out at the rain. Floodlights were mounted in each side of the fuselage, just forward of the wing, and were intended for observing ice buildup. The clouds were so thick he could just barely see the outboard wing tips. With the lights turned off, it was as if they weren't in an airplane at all. It was more like a room, a very noisy room, filled with dials, levers, seats, desks, and windows painted black. Aircraft simulators were like that and Eddie felt that at any time someone would freeze the dials and they would all take a break and have a cup of coffee. But there was no break, each of them labored at their assigned tasks as they bored through the rain. Eddie felt cold and unattached to his duties and had to keep reminding himself that this was not some dream. He tried to remind himself what it must be like at Misawa but all he had to work with was a mental image of an earth quake in a grade B movie. Scale model buildings fell over plastic model cars and huge cracks opened up in the earth. There were cutaways of people screaming and being crushed and swallowed up in the earth cracks. The movie was poorly done and Eddie wondered if he really should be back on the farm helping his father irrigate sugar beets. They hummed and vibrated through the rain toward a place they had never been to before and had compassion for people they had never seen before.

The leading edges of the aircraft's wings slowly assumed a mysterious glow and the windshield assumed the same eerie light. Eddie had never seen anything like that before. It was as if he was having some sort of a religious experience, or maybe some sort of a vision. Whatever, he was getting spooked. Were they passing through a time warp? Maybe there really was a god and he was blessing their airplane. Suddenly a ball of light, about two or three inches in diameter, flew off their number four propeller. It bounced inboard, across the number three engine and all the way up and into Eddie's side window.

"GGGGAAAA!" Eddie hollered as he shielded himself with his arm from the certain impact. But there was no crashing of glass! Instead the ball came right through the glass as if it weren't there. It then bounced off the pilot's throttle quadrant, off the navigator's LORAN set, and flew into the rear of the cockpit and disappeared.

Eddie was speechless and frozen with fright. Then another and then a third ball came off and bounced their way into and then out of the cockpit, all taking the same path. The windshield glowed brighter and then dimmed in eerie patterns. "OOOOhHHHHH!" Eddie moaned, and was relieved he was still alive and functioning, despite the supernatural.

Major Ivanoff broke out laughing as did both flight engineers and Henry.

"What's happening to me? What's happening?" Eddie asked the crew in desperation. "I think I'm hallucinating."

"Saint Elmo's fire, needs to be dark outside to see it well," the major answered Eddie, then looked around at the rest of the crew who were still chuckling. "I'll have to admit that was about the biggest and prettiest I've ever seen, but it was just static electricity. It has lots of volts but almost no amps. It won't hurt you. You usually only see it under certain conditions, like cold rain. You've probably never seen any of it in the tropics. We got static wicks on the trailing edges of our wings to bleed static electricity off but sometimes it builds up too fast and glows or occasionally forms dancing balls. It's harmless to the aircraft cause we're in the air and not grounded, but it can really scare the hell out of any passengers ya got on board; or new pilots like yourself. It probably bounced through your window cause you got electrical heating coils embedded in the glass, off our throttle quadrant cause we have electrical prop synchronizers, off the LORAN cause it's an electric cathode ray tube. It's impossible to tell what it's gonna do."

"I thought I was a goner!" Eddie admitted and he felt weak and embarrassed. He studied the glow on his windshield and realized it was made up of thousands of tiny sparks. As the raindrops impacted they discharged their static load. The glow got brighter and dimmer as they passed through different swaths of rain. Eddie had been told he had to feather fifteen engines before he could be a real shaky driver; there was no mention about St. Elmo's fire. He wondered, "What else do I have to endure before I become an old timer?"

"You're doing just fine, kid," Major Ivanoff informed Eddie. "First time I ever saw Saint Elmo's fire I was flying alone, single pilot, in a P-38. A ball of that stuff appeared on my instrument panel, bounced around several times, then bounced outside, ran along my tail boom and jumped off into nowhere. I was only nineteen when I first saw it and I was the equivalent of twenty-three when it jumped off my tail."

"Really scares the passengers," the flight engineer added. "Once in a C-54, I had an old flight nurse pee in her bloomers when a ball of that stuff bounced down the aisle, between her legs, and disappeared into the latrine. I mean to tell you that old girl was as hard as nails and that Saint Elmo's reduced her to a babbling idiot in short order."

133

"Another ball of that stuff and I would have marked my own laundry!" Eddie added. It took a good ten minutes for Eddie to settle down and they continued, sometimes glowing and sometimes not, in the rain.

It started to get light outside but their visibility was still stinko. As they plowed their way north the temperature continued to drop and soon they were flying in freezing rain. It was also the first time Eddie had ever seen ice form on his aircraft and it was forming rapidly on the leading edge of their wings. Back at Willy, they told Eddie's class that whenever ice accumulation was detected, the only solution was to get out of the icing—climb, descend, or turn around. "Deicing systems, if you have them, are for staying alive until you can get out of the ice and not for sustained flight in ice."

"Light the de-icers, climb power," Major Ivanoff ordered and they added power to climb above the freezing level of rain. There was no air traffic control as a result of the earthquake so they just climbed on their own. The flight engineer set climb power and lit the auxiliary burners. The burners used aviation gas from the engine's fuel tanks. The burners created hot air that was pumped through a maze of small pipes, located inside the leading edges of their wings and tail surfaces. The hot air was released outside through thousands of tiny holes and they heated the aluminum skin and melted the ice. Each wing had its own burner and the tail had its own burner. Within a few minutes the heated leading edge surfaces were glistening wet and free of ice. The propellers were electrically heated. Each propeller blade had rubberized strips along its leading edge and electrical heating elements were imbedded within the strips.

They leveled at 10,000 feet. In the colder air they were above the ice forming flight level. But they were still struggling. Normally, they would have been okay above the freezing level; the moisture was in the form of frozen droplets and wouldn't stick to their aluminum skin. However, when in the freezing zone, the ice had accumulated far more rapidly than normal and another problem had developed. The amount of melted ice and freezing rain had been larger than the de-icing design could handle. As it melted from the de-icing heat along their leading edge, it ran back across the tops of their wings and refroze before it was all blown off. This phenomenon was appropriately called "run back." Only the leading edge of the wings and tail were heated. In addition to its weight, the run back altered the wing's shape and altered the smooth flow of air over the wing, reducing the wing's ability to efficiently produce lift. The huge blunt, unheated nose of the C-124 had also accumulated ice as it pushed its gigantic doors through the air. The nose doors had no de-ice system.

The crew wasn't sure exactly how fast they needed to fly with their wings' shape altered by the run back, so they had to error on the fast side and increased their power to fly faster. This would compound into more problems during their approach and landing. A faster than normal airspeed would give them a higher touch down speed, thus their landing roll would be longer. They couldn't afford that on Misawa's shortened runway! They needed to consider returning to Tachikawa and the warmer air where they could melt all the ice and then make a normal landing back at their base of departure.

"Ya want us to go downstairs and stomp the ice off the nose door? It'll help lighten us up a little," the second flight engineer asked. "I'll get the loadmaster to help me. We gotta get rid of some of this ice pretty soon or it's gonna pull us right out of the sky."

"Take Eddie with you downstairs," Major Ivanoff nodded toward Eddie. "Show him how to get the ice off our nose. The cleaner and quicker we reduce our ice load the better off we'll be."

"Can't screw around and wait too long when you start picking up ice," the flight engineer added for Eddie's benefit as they climbed down the ladder into the cargo compartment. "I've been in a couple of races to see if the ice melted off before we crashed. It's no fun."

While Eddie followed the flight engineer downstairs, Major Ivanoff plowed along at 10,000 feet and called Tachikawa on the HF radio. He told them to give the information about the ice to the crews behind them. The three of them, downstairs, worked their way forward and onto the closed and locked nose doors. Aluminum ribs formed the frame, similar to the wooden ribs in ancient sail boats. The door's frames were covered from the outside with a single skin of aluminum. The three of them started stomping on the skin, between the ribs, and every time it flexed they would hear a crack outside as a sheet of ice would break off into the air stream.

It was eerie, stomping and jumping onto something that thin, knowing that it was the only thing between them and 10,000 feet of air and a very cold ocean.

"I called Tachikawa and the birds behind us are going to come up low, hopefully under the freezing level," the major reported as Eddie strapped back into his seat.

The major looked at Eddie seriously, "The temperature was reported to be forty degrees Fahrenheit at Misawa, so they're eight degrees above freezing level and they're basically at sea level. The normal lapse rate, the normal rate temperature cools as you rise through the atmosphere, is three and a half degrees per thousand feet. Divide the eight degrees above freezing by three and a half degrees per thousand feet and you get the thirty-two degree freezing altitude at a little over two thousand feet. So if we make a quick descent down to fifteen hundred feet we will be flying in warmer air below the freezing level." The major paused to let Eddie catch up on what he said. Then he continued, "We were at eight thousand feet when we first started picking up ice so that means the freezing level has dropped a lot in a pretty short distance. That means we just flew through a cold front, from the warm side into the cold side.

"When we're ready to descend, I'll do a rapid descent down to pick up as little additional ice as possible. Once we're under the freezing level and in the warmer air we'll level off. At our flying speed it's windy out there and with the temperature a little above freezing the remainder of the ice should melt off quickly. "We're over the ocean so we won't run into any hills and we'll stay over the water until the ice is all melted off."

Eddie looked at their weather radar, which was focused downward. The land mass to their left was reflecting back their beam and showed various degrees of orange on the scope, an exact match to the shoreline shape depicted on their ONC maps. The flat ocean below them bounced their beam away and nothing came back so the radar scope painted the water as black.

"Bout forty-five minutes from Misawa and we're paralleling the coast fifteen miles over water," Henry announced to confirm the pilot's observations and deductions.

The major looked at Eddie, smiled and explained, "Here's something else to put on your aircraft commander book of knowledge. We're lucky, as long as the freezing level doesn't go all the way to the water, we can get under it and melt the remaining ice off before we land. The runway won't be frozen and slick so we can stop in time. These are all things I considered before we left Tachikawa.

"Whenever you're gonna fly anywhere that it's freezing on the ground and there's precipitation," the major lectured, "you gotta check the forecast, enroute freezing levels, and precipitation real good. You gotta know if you're gonna collect any heavy ice before you land. Ya might not wanna go if there's icing higher than you can fly, heavier than your de-icing system can handle, or all the way to the ground. Pick up too much ice at altitude or get run back like we got now, if the freezing temperatures go all the way down to the ground you could be in deep shit. You wouldn't be able to melt it off before you land. If ya got a long runway you could land with lots of airspeed and power. On a short runway, ice on your aircraft and a slick stopping surface are the main ingredients of the recipe for disaster. The new jets can punch up and down through this stuff real fast and have high volume de-icing systems so the danger of runback is a lot less. They cruise so high that ice is not a problem on top. Down here and flying an old recip engine aircraft, you gotta be smart like fox."

* * * * * * * * * * * * * * * * * * * *

"Misawa, Misawa, this is MAC Rescue Two Five," Eddie called several times on the tower frequency, but there was no answer. They had rapidly descended to 1500 feet, the air outside was thirty-five degrees Fahrenheit and the ice was melting. They were a little low for radio contact, but there was only a flat ocean and shoreline between them and Misawa. He was a little alarmed when there was no answer, so he switched over to 243.0, the UHF emergency guard frequency. The radar clearly showed the distinctive bay ahead of them that led straight into runway two eight. The ten mile rings on the radar showed they were a little over fourteen miles from the shore line. The major was slowing their melting ice carrier from 180 Knots to 140 knots in preparation for their approach and landing. Occasionally there would be a ripping sound as additional ice melted and defoliated. They were having no problems holding their altitude and airspeed with normal power settings. The icing problem was over and behind them.

"Misawa, Misawa, this is MAC Rescue Two Five. Do you read me on guard?"

"Mac Rescue Two Five, this is Misawa on guard, you are five by five. Boy, are we glad to hear your voice! Our tower radios are out of commission and we're operating with survival radios removed from our base aircraft. The only frequency we have is guard. Do you have doctors and nurses on board? What's your ETA?"

"Misawa, MAC Two Five, what's your wind, temperature, barometric setting and active runway? We're circling over water at fifteen hundred feet, outside the outer marker for runway two eight." As Eddie was speaking, Major Ivanoff rolled right into a wide three sixty degree circle to buy some time. "We don't have any doctors or nurses on board. Suggest you call Tachikawa on the HAM radio and repeat that request."

"Wind's calm, light rain, estimated ceiling two hundred feet and a half mile visibility, temperature is forty degrees Fahrenheit. Barometric setting is from a T-33 on our ramp, it shows 29.80. Our weather station is broke also. The weather is an estimate but the temperature is from a good thermometer. We strongly recommend using runway two eight, well, actually that's all we got. Have they told you we got a big crack in the runway, forty-five hundred feet from the threshold of runway two eight? There are several more cracks beyond that so the first part of two eight is the longest usable section."

"Roger that, Misawa, runway two eight, two hundred ceiling and a half mile. 29.80. We can stop short of the first crack. Is your ILS up and ready for us? We're not receiving anything."

"Uhh, there's another problem. Our ILS shack is destroyed, didn't they tell you that! All we got is the backup GCA radar, the van survived the earthquake. We're running it with a portable generator. We got a sergeant down here that's talked pilots down GCAs five hundred times in the past ten years and he's confident that he can talk you down. He's done what he called "bore sighted" the radar alignment and wants you to do a test approach down to around four hundred feet above ground level. He says our elevation is a hundred nineteen feet, so your go around altitude is five hundred nineteen feet above sea level. We have guys standing on both sides of the runway to listen when you go around. Hopefully they can tell by the sound if you're lined up over the runway or not. He says he's not concerned about the glideslope because he's measured the distance from the runway threshold to his van and his glideslope angle checks out. I can't believe they didn't tell you guys that we need doctors and nurses."

The major looked at Eddie and smiled. The radar guy was thinking exactly the same thing they had briefed back at Tachi. A test run with a built in altitude cushion for safety.

"We're just crew members, Misawa. Apparently someone dropped the ball about the nurses. We'll make sure they get your request." Eddie was working the radios. Major Ivanoff made a descending gesture with his hand to Eddie and Eddie relayed the message, "We're ready for the test approach if you're GCA controller is."

"I'm here on 243.0, listening," a different voice answered. "I got you on radar and have you rolling out from your three sixty turn. Fly heading two eight five, maintain fifteen hundred feet, this will be your final controller, start of descent will be in four miles." The controller assumed the calm monotone GCA controller voice that was so familiar to aviators. GCA stood for Ground Controlled Approach and basically was just as the name implied. A highly trained and certified radar controller on the ground would look at his radar screens and talk the aircraft down. He used two specialty radar sets, one designed for azimuth (left/right) guidance and the other one was a narrow beam that displayed a 2.8 degree descending glideslope. Eddie and the rest of the crew had not needed such sophistication down south at Clark and in Vietnam, but the stinko weather at Tachikawa had required they use GCA approaches many times to get home. Flying a demonstration GCA was a requirement on all initial and annual flight checks for every pilot.

Eddie didn't feel good about the Misawa approach, especially after getting the BJs scared out of him by Saint Almo's fire and the close call with the ice. He cross-checked their compasses with the backup "whisky" compass, crosschecked that both altimeters were set at 29.80 and their readings were within the allowed error tolerance of thirty-five feet of each other. He checked that both altimeter bugs (markers) were set to 519 feet and that both pilot's airspeed indicators were indicting the same airspeed.

"Heading two eight five, manifold two five, and RPM two seven hundred . . . flaps twenty," The major called. He turned off the autopilot and was hand flying.

"Manifold two five, RPM two seven hundred," the flight engineer repeated after setting the power. Eddie lowered the flap handle to the twenty degree detent. The major was relaxed but serious, both hands on the yoke. Eddie cross checked that the power settings were correct then scanned the engine gauges, airspeed, heading, altitude, then read out loud the flap setting.

"Two miles to descent point," the controller called. "Turn left three degrees, heading two eight two."

"Heading two eight two," Eddie called over guard frequency and the major complied.

"Approaching glide path. Do not acknowledge further instructions," the controller advised. During the final portion of a GCA, spoken words are reduced to a minimum. Eddie clicked his mike twice to acknowledge then ceased to verbally acknowledge further controller instructions. He did check carefully that the major complied with every directive. The weather radar showed them passing over the coast line, inbound. Their airspeed still had a few more knots to lose.

"Flaps thirty, gear down." Major Ivanoff ordered.

Eddie complied and repeated the major's instructions, "Flaps thirty—set—gear down three green, pressure's up." With the additional drag from the flaps and gear, the airspeed bled down toward the computed approach speed displayed on the plastic card.

"Start descent, turn two degrees left to two eight zero." Eddie watched the major slide the heading over to indicated two eighty degrees and lower the nose just enough to indicate a descent rate of 600 feet per minute.

"Manifold two one," the major called, the flight engineer complied and replied, Eddie cross checked.

"You're slightly right of course and twenty feet high on the glide slope, correcting nicely." After a few seconds the controller continued, "On course, turn right two degrees, on glide path."

Major Ivanoff called manifold Two Two. They flew down the invisible slot. It was pure white outside.

Eddie called, "Five hundred above minimums," as they passed through 1019 feet above sea level. The controller continued his coaching and kept the lonely aircraft's radar return on the course and on the glide path depicted on his radar screens. Inside the aircraft everyone was alert, constantly crosschecking and knowing that any one thing overlooked could spell their final flight. Their weather radar was set to its minimum range, antenna angled slightly down, and the gain (power) was turned high. The majority of the screen showed various shades of orange, the radar beam reflecting from buildings, parked aircraft, and other terrain and man-made features. A black line on the screen depicted the runway as the flat concrete did not reflect back the radar beam. It was reassuring to the MAC freighter crew. The navigator watched the radar, the pilot's instruments, and held his stop watch in his left hand. They had less than thirty seconds to go.

"Hundred above," Eddie called out at 619 feet altitude. It was still pure white outside.

"On course, on glide path, Sir," the controller's smooth voice finally cracked a little from the tension.

Outside it looked innocent, pure white, but everyone knew they were close to the ground, very very hard ground.

"Coming up minimums," Eddie called with a little more emphasis.

"Go around power five zero inches, flaps twenty . . . positive rate climbing, gear up," the major barked as they hit 519 feet altitude and he eased back on the yoke, into a stabilized climb and heading. The crew responded to the commands and the flight engineer slowly advanced the throttles to fifty inches of manifold pressure. No sense in overstraining the engines with maximum power, they were going to need them healthy for take-off if they got into Misawa. The four engines and propellers transformed over 10,000 horsepower into thrust and the aircraft was climbing 600 feet per minute.

Their navigator, Henry, didn't wait for any more instructions from the controller. He knew there were hills several miles off the end of the runway, and that translated into sixty seconds. He called, "Turn left to one one zero degrees."

As they completed the left turn and were heading back toward the ocean, and away from the hills, the major called for climb power, gave the controls to Eddie, and instructed him to level off at 1500 feet altitude. He then shook his hands and rolled his shoulders to loosen up and to relieve the tension. When loose, he called the GCA controller on guard frequency, "How'd it look down there? See anything?"

"Damn, Sir. You went right between our observers. Your sound was deafening and there was no mistaking where you were. They didn't see you but ya really stirred up the clouds. Your prop wash is swirling out of the bottom of the ceiling. You had it wired."

"How's the ceiling look down there, still at two hundred feet?" Major Ivanoff was concerned.

"Bout that, Sir, or real close if you know what I mean."

"I got ya, sergeant. We'll give it our best shot." They both knew the GCA controller couldn't say over the air that it might be just a scrunch less than two hundred feet. If he did it would have declared the weather below minimums and prohibited the major from doing another approach.

"Two Five, this is Two Six, we're thirty minutes south. How's the weather down there? Why are you working on guard?" It was the second C-124 from Tachikawa.

"We only went down to four hundred feet above ground level to check the GCA, their ILS is tits up. You probably heard that we passed right over the runway so next pass I'll go down to minimums. The ice is down to about twenty-two hundred feet feet. I'd suggest you hold at fifteen hundred feet and twenty miles east of the shoreline. That'll keep you out of our way. There's no traffic control here except the GCA controller on guard. The reason they're using guard frequency is that they got no tower radios, so they're using hand held survival radios from one of their aircraft. We're getting a real good shoreline paint on our weather radar. First forty-five hundred feet of runway two eight is all that's available, and we're using 29.80 on our altimeters."

"Gottcha, fly safe Buddy. Don't get carried away down there."

"Don't worry," Major Ivanoff replied. "I'm not turning it in till the mileage is all run out.

"Before landing checklist, I've got it." Major Ivanoff took control of the airplane and was ready for another trip down the slot. They flew east, over the water a few miles and turned back toward the small bay. As they turned back inbound Eddie pointed at the slim black void area on the radar and Henry reconfirmed it as the runway area. The big bright blob on the left was the small town outside the base side gate. The GCA controller picked them up again and after a repeat of their previous drill, they came down the slot. Eddie checked that both of their altimeter bugs were set at 319 feet above sea level, 200 feet above the ground. Again the major flew steadily and nursed the old bird to conform to the directions the controller called. They flew right down the lines painted on the controller's radar scope and directly toward the black runway line on the aircraft's weather scope.

"Hundred above minimums," Eddie called.

The major replied with, "Check RPM two seven hundred."

"On course on glide slope," the controller gave his final directions, and then added, "I can hear you, Sir, and you're right on target."

"Minimums," Eddie called, he could see nothing but white outside.

The major was purposely slow in initiating the go around. Eddie had heard stories about pilots going below minimums to find the runway, and bragging about doing it. Then killing themselves the next time they tried it. Eddie remembered that Major Baxter, back at Clark Air Base, told him to "Fly by the rules. If you wanna be different, you first have to be good. You aren't that good yet." It was comforting to Eddie that Major Ivanoff was good, very good, otherwise Eddie would have been screaming for a go around.

Eddie was unconsciously pulling slightly back on the yoke, ready to demand they go around. They were thirty feet below minimums when out of nowhere appeared, wet and very close, a long dark grey strip of concrete. The far end disappeared into the thick haze a little over a thousand feet in front of them and the illusion made the runway appear very short.

"Runway twelve o' clock, gear rechecks down," Eddie called as he had been trained to do as he reached for the flap handle.

"Flaps forty," the major called, slowly pulling the power off. The airspeed decayed as the flaps extended to forty degrees and the ground effect shallowed their descent. The major eased back on the yoke, the aircraft ran out of flying speed and plunked onto the runway. Not a grease job but a firm plant that indicated they were done flying and ready to get on with the business of stopping. Eddie took the yoke from the major and pushed it lightly forward. The aircraft nose wheel touched the concrete and Major Ivanoff selected reverse props. The propellers sang their reverse song, Eddie called four green reverse lights, and the major added more power. The major increased power to sixty inches at Eddie's coaching as the brakes simultaneously jerked, then took hold, and they slowed rapidly. Everyone wondered what was waiting for them just beyond the limits of their vision.

Eddie also wondered, "How did they determine it was forty-five hundred feet of good runway, everything else had been screwed up?"

Then a wide crack appeared in front of them. Their deceleration rate felt sufficient but Eddie noticed the major pressed a little heavier on the brakes. As they came to a halt and the major pulled the throttles back to idle, the terrain faded into white haze in all directions. The visibility was much less than had been reported to them. There was nothing in sight, not a building, a tree, not anything, just a short strip of concrete with a wide crack across it and white haze. It was as if they had landed on a foreign planet. The crack was jagged and nasty looking, two to three feet across and certainly would have taken out an aircraft's landing gear. The major had the props out of reverse and the engines were at idle and cooling. They just sat there, contemplating in silence about nature's little barrier out there. It would have ruined their day if they hadn't landed right on the button and pulled lots of reverse power.

"Jesus Christ," the engineer looked over the pilot's shoulders and finally broke the silence. He was staring at the crack with his mouth open. He returned to his panel: pulling levers and moving switches to care for his faithful engines and to get them properly cooled off. "I've only got a year and a half until retirement," the engineer swallowed and finished his sentence.

"You okay Two Five?" It was the GCA controller over the radio. "You're awful quiet out there."

"Ya hear anything at all?" It was Mac Two Six. He was also very concerned about his sister ship that was down somewhere.

Major Ivanoff answered their inquiries, "Twenty-Five is on the runway, time five four past the hour. There's a great big crack about three hundred feet in front of me that'll eat your lunch if you don't touch down on the end and use lots of reverse thrust."

"What's the ceiling?" MAC Two Six asked.

"A skinny two hundred," Ivanoff replied to his buddy. "The GCA had me right on the centerline. I used flaps forty degrees, no extra airspeed, and ya gotta put her right in on the end of the runway . . . Where's the ramp around here? You still on the radio GCA? If so, thanks. You did a hell of a job."

"Do a one eighty degree turn on the runway and watch for the first taxiway on your right. They're sending a jeep out to lead you," the GCA directed the lonely C-124. "You'll have to park on the taxi way cause the ramp is all busted up. Base engineers are already working on it and will start working on the runway crack as soon as you guys get a chance to bring us some more quick drying concrete. Park far enough down the taxiway so Two Six has room to park and off load behind you."

They turned around on the wet runway and slowly taxied back. Their current world faded behind them and as they crept along the new slowly opened up in front. They followed an endless strip of wet concrete, a runway in the fog lined on both sides with wet, green grass. Everything else was obscured.

"Weird," Eddie commented as they crawled along.

"After landing checklist," The major called, returning him to reality.

"There it is!" the top scanner called over the interphone from his viewpoint out the open top hatch. He had an umbrella with him and presented a rather peculiar sight. A concrete taxiway peeled off from the right side of the runway and they proceeded down its narrower way. A jeep came into view. It turned around and led them down the taxiway a little further, then stopped. The airman driver jumped out and raised and crossed his arms. Then he drew his finger across his throat. Out of his window, Eddie could just see the outline of a large metal hangar. Several dozen Japanese came out of nowhere. They had a frenzied look about them and the entire group headed straight for their airplane.

"What the hell's going on here?" The scanner called from his lofty perch out the open top hatch.

"You probably look like a Buddha up there. We did appear from the heavens," Eddie commented.

"Buddha never carried an umbrella," the flight engineer at the panel corrected, with his thick Brooklyn accent. "Now days deese Japs got television and watch America movies—they probably think he's Mary Poppins. Didn't that chick fly around with an umbrella?"

"Umbrella ain't big enough to lift this thing," the scanner played along.

"They don't know that," the engineer countered.

"Hope those propellers stop turning before they get here," the major reflected. "I'd hate to cut one of their heads off." The group of Japanese gathered in front of the airplane. The crew let the brakes set, had their auxiliary power unit running for electrical power and an auxiliary hydraulic pump running to maintain their brake pressure and operate their hydraulic nose doors and ramps. There were no wooden tire chocks to insure the aircraft wouldn't roll while being unloaded, so the brakes were essential. They climbed down the alternate ladder along the side of the fuselage, then out the open nose door and down one of the ramps as the loadmaster finished lowering it. The crew shook the Japanese crew's hands, western style, slapped them on their backs, western style, and exchanged grateful bows, Japanese style. Eddie knew they were pleased with the American flyers. The Japanese hiss to show displeasure and none of them were hissing. After a few minutes they all settled down into a single group, squatted in the rain, and waited. Eddie had no idea what they were waiting for. He really didn't understand the Japanese; they were so different from all the other Asians.

Finally three air force stake bed trucks and one fork lift emerged from the haze and wove their way around the squatting crowd. A full colonel let himself out of one of the trucks; he had on a wrinkled blue uniform and looked tired and haggard. On his left breast he wore command pilot wings and three rows of very respectable looking medals. Eddie's hatless crew saluted.

"Gentleman, I'm Colonel Williams, Base Commander." He returned the crews' salutes and extended a hand to Major Ivanoff. "You don't know how glad I am to see you. We'll get a crew started unloading your airplane right away. Sorry about the ILS mix up over the radio. We had some people that were confused about aviation terms. We got some walking wounded to send back with you." He was wasting no time.

"I'm Major Ivanoff, the aircraft commander. We're happy to do anything we can to help you out, but we gotta do something about all these civilians around our airplane. They gotta get out of the way before they get hurt."

"Fence is down in about five different places." Colonel Williams shook his head back and forth. Then he turned to his sergeant assistant, who was carrying a briefcase, field telephone and camera. "See if you can herd these civilians out of the way. They probably wanna help but they'll just get run over with our fork lifts."

"Sir, how bad are the American causalities?" Their flight engineer couldn't hold back any more, "I got a son stationed here."

"We got lots of bruises and broken limbs, only two American dead that we know of. None with the same name as your name tag. Give your son's name to my first sergeant and I'm sure he can help you out."

"Utilities are the biggest problem," he addressed the rest of the crew. "Everything underground is busted and broken and we got some buildings that are ready to fall over."

In the distance a faint rumble grew louder. It was unmistakably the sound of a C-124 with its propellers running at RPM two seven hundred. The sound grew louder. Then all of a sudden, out of the low clouds, loomed a huge shadow which assumed the silhouette of a fat Shaky Bird. It banked slightly then rolled out and changed sound as the power was pulled back to idle. Its nose raised a little then it settled and squeaked onto the runway. As the nose lowered to the runway the propellers came into reverse and it spewed water everywhere as the pilot brought in a generous amount of reverse thrust. The scene disappeared into the mist to their left as the four reversed Curtis electric propellers threw billowing clouds of rain forward. Everyone stood silently, hoping not to hear the sound of landing gear ripping from the wings. The unseen silver freighter fought to a stop, then called the GCA controller for taxi instructions.

"That'll be Two Six," Major Ivanoff informed the colonel, after it was clear there were no disquieting sounds to hear. "We'll have two more birds, one in a couple hours and, if they get it fixed, another on line this afternoon. The four aircraft should be able to make ten or eleven hour turns. Our squadron commander is sending up some flare pots for runway lighting so we can operate twenty-four hours per day. They should be in that second bird that just landed."

"I don't know how you guys can find the runway in this crud. I'm a fighter pilot and we don't fly in this kind of weather—unless it's an emergency," the colonel praised. "But I'm sure glad you guys got the balls to do it." For a colonel with command wings and being a fighter pilot, Eddie considered that the ultimate compliment.

The unloading went well. The Japanese civilians showed their usual respect for authority and quickly moved out of the way. The supplies were quickly fork lifted into waiting trucks and hauled off into the mist. With the help of the first sergeant and his field radio, Sergeant Carter found his son cleaning up broken dishes in the mess hall and just had time for a hug. It was a great hug, and because they were both grown men, they fought back their tears. Back on the ramp they loaded twelve walking wounded, four stretcher cases, and two nurses to care for them. The colonel told the major to bring back the nurses and lots more like them on his next trip.

They left their sister ship still off-loading on the taxiway and took off into the clouds without any clearance. They just announced their intentions over the guard frequency, revved their engines up in front of the crack, released their brakes, and took off toward the sea. They flew back at 1500 feet MSL until the outside temperature rose. Then they climbed to a higher cruising altitude. They didn't pick up any ice. Eddie flew the return leg and Major Ivanoff had a two hour nap while at cruise altitude. There was no guarantee a relief crew would be waiting for their aircraft when they returned to Tachi. When 300 miles out from Tachikawa, Eddie contacted the over water controller and received a clearance back into the Tokyo airspace and into Tachikawa Air Base.

As suspected, there was no relief crew waiting so the crew, minus their loadmaster, had a hot meal at the terminal restaurant. They were keeping it open twenty-four hours each day to accommodate the relief workers. They made a second trip that evening, taking turns in the bunks, and carrying a portable field hospital, a staff of sixteen medical personnel, plus lots of other supplies. They had six cases of typhoid vaccine. At landing minimums, the runway was easier to see at night as the illuminating flare pots pierced through the fog. They returned to Tachikawa dead tired from two round trips in weather, and turned their faithful bird over to a fresh crew. Major Ivanoff flew each leg into Misawa because of the dicey landing on the short runway and Eddie flew each leg back to Tachikawa. The second day the weather improved slightly to a 300 foot ceiling, and the 815th added three C-130 Herky Birds to the airlift effort. The 4500 foot runway was a piece of cake for the C-130 turboprop aircraft. The rain continued for three days and the C-124s and C-130s carried into Misawa, in addition to huge loads of everything else, 25,000 pounds of powdered fast drying concrete.

On the fourth day the weather broke. A cold wind came in from the west and blew all the moisture out to sea. The sun filtered through the scattering clouds and warmed the hearts, if not the homes, of the suffering. The cold wind made the tents and portable shelters a godsend. The base engineers at Misawa patched all the runway and ramp cracks with quick drying cement. With the clearing skies, a long runway, and suitable ramp, the pretty birds showed up. Eddie was standing on the patched ramp at Misawa when the first C-141 jet freighter landed and taxied up in front of the damaged base operations building. The first out were the photographers, some civilian, some military, then the crew. Three colonels and two master sergeants stepped off wearing freshly ironed flight suits, shiny boots, bright blue neck scarves, and of course they wore hats. The next evening American television sets and all that week the magazines and newspapers were filled with images of Japanese children drinking fresh milk, eating rice soup, and sitting in front of an American military field hospital. There was also an abundance of C-141 photos and their heroic crews that were flying supplies to the unfortunate people. True, the C-141s, in that favorable environment, hauled massive amounts of supplies during the next week. But there was no reference to the supplies hauled in during the first three days of need and the ugly aircraft that hauled it in. They were invisible. Eddie's crew and their sister 22nd crews had hauled in the milk, rice soup, tents, field hospital, and the doctor that tended the broken arm of the child that was photographed on that fourth day.

The 815th and the 22nd crews were too tired to give a damn. To them, the sun, clear skies, long runways, and C-141s meant just one thing. Sleep. They had traded naps enroute, and had four or five hours sleep before going back on duty to relieve an even more tired crew. They had wrinkled suits and reddened eyes that looked as if they had flown open cockpit through a sand storm. No wonder the photographers shied away from them. Each approach into Misawa had been a test of nerves; the weather insisted they prove themselves every time they came down the slot. Every crew member was up to the test. Every aircraft stopped short of the crack. The 22nd crews babied their engines and made power changes slowly, never overcooling them before applying heavy reverse, and they made low power cruise climbs. They treated their engines with all the love and respect a crew could ever show for four cantankerous old radial engines. The engines returned their love by performing flawlessly. Not a single engine failed during those four days of continuous service.

Eddie never felt closer to a group of men. They had a job to do and they did it, defeating the weather and countless other challenges. Tired and under stress, each man cranked out his job like a robot. Toward the end it was just too much effort to talk. As the first three days unfolded, Eddie thought about the C-141 crews waiting at Yakota for the weather to break, about transient fighter jocks drinking and maintaining their top of the pecking order at the club bar, and he wouldn't have traded places with any of them. The weariness, irregular meals, body odor, ice on their aircraft, the ever willing help from the Japanese civilians at both bases, all gave him the motivation and satisfaction that would carry him through months and months of uneventful flying.

CHAPTER ELEVEN: GOODBYE DOLLY

Eddie felt stagnated; he was down south on a two week trip with Larry, his favorite aircraft commander. Guys like Larry, respected by their peers, intense flying motivation, driven sense of duty, good looking and well groomed are sometimes too predictable and boring for their wives. The wives had to sit around and wait for their husbands to come home from two weeks of work, have several days together, then start the two week schedule all over again. Larry's wife had left him and gone back to the States and Larry had been drinking a little more than usual and not talking as much.

For the most part, aside from flying, Eddie was also suffering from doldrums. With time, the routine of eat, sleep, and fly wore away at one's soul and Eddie sensed it was converting him into one of the hollow zombies he was living among. The zombies had been there all the time but only recently had he started to fear he was becoming one. The gee whiz phase was definitely over for him.

He still used flying as an escape from reality and his stagnating existence. The brightest spot of each day was when the gear was raised into the wheel wells. When the gear was lowered and the aircraft slowed to a reasonable taxi speed, the doldrums set in again.

He was usually suffering from a lack of sleep and from dehydration, and he would take the easy way on everything. He grew to accept mediocre meals, malfunctioning showers, and dirty walls where he slept. The hassle at the Rathskeller required too much effort after a long day's flying and he had grown tired of the mental gymnastics one needed to exercise in order to be "cool." Despite his youth and bachelor status, experiences with women were no longer a big quest for him. He resorted to an occasional massage in Bangkok, but after Kay's lesson in sensuality, Vicky the whore was no longer very fulfilling. He cut her back to just once each month. His life was a crude form of existence: hauling impersonal freight from airport to airport in an old, non air-conditioned, oil dripping airplane. It was only natural that his unglamorous existence was reflected in his sex life.

He was making over $1,200 per month, which was pretty good for 1969. He made $888 base pay plus subsistence allowance (food), $86 for housing plus $200 flight pay, and $200 combat pay. Five hundred of that was tax exempt because he was flying in the war zone. Food and booze were dirt cheap and he was paid an additional per diem whenever he stayed off base while on a trip. As a bachelor, Eddie had lots of money and to him four or five dollars, one night each month, for Vicki was nothing. It was like a housewife at an eighty percent off sale at JC Penny. They really didn't need the merchandise but, hey, it was really cheap so it didn't make sense not to buy it. That was how he felt about Vicky.

This period in his life was like sleepwalking, half real, half dream. He had been with the 22nd for over two years and had a little less than a year to go before his Tachikawa assignment would be over. After Tachikawa and when he returned to the States, he would have less than a year's commitment to serve. Hopefully he could get an early discharge from the air force. Less than a year was not enough time for the air force to retrain a pilot in a different aircraft and recover their training expenses. So the air force was giving early outs to Vietnam and other overseas returnees, those with less than a year to go and wanted out. Once out, he could clean up his act and invest his saved up flying experience and money for a good life. Flying in Alaska or the Caribbean as a civilian charter pilot was still a viable dream in addition to dropping slurry on forest fires. The Forest Service contractors were always looking for pilots with lots of experience flying old round engine propeller aircraft. He could do that and have his winters free to spend in the Caribbean.

He still occasionally thought of the Lady. But in the morning, when he awoke, he knew it was just that—a dream. Expecting to find such a goddess was his nemesis. The ancient sailors had their mermaids and he had his Asian Lady.

The war was not going well, either. Washington seemed to have no idea how to handle the situation. Closer to home, the squadron's manpower allocations were all screwed up. Pilot replacements were hard to come by and eventually the 22nd squadron was "frozen." That meant no new pilots were being assigned. It was just another example of poor civilian oversight. Pilots in the 22nd were being asked to fly an additional ten hours each month to make up for the shortage from attrition. The stress was reflected in the increased number of wives who were fleeing back to the States.

Indeed, Eddie's bag of tricks and flying techniques grew larger and larger. He had logged over 2000 hours of flight time and had shut down nineteen engines. All the cowboy flying ideas were out of his system. So Major Baxter gave him another check ride and Eddie received his aircraft commander's certificate. He was ready to make the decisions and to live up to the responsibilities of managing a crew and the mission. However, with the supply of co-pilots shut off, he still frequently had to fly as the co-pilot on a crew and only occasionally did he get his own aircraft.

When out on trips and after a long day's flying, a couple of healthy drags out of the crew bottle followed by lots of beer was still his preferred drug. It induced relief and sound sleep. When rested and hanging out between trips at the Tachi Officers Club, he developed a taste for Chivas and water. Chivas Regal Scotch was only $4.25 a quart at the base liquor store so he bought a case and stashed it with the rest of his household goods for eventual shipment to the States.

****

It was a Wednesday afternoon and the upstairs bar at the Clark Officers Club was only half full. Eddie's crew had finished a quick early morning trip to Chu Lai and back, and the rest of his crew had gone downtown shopping. He paid for a beer at the bar and drained the bottle half empty with a single swig. The beer numbed his hot throat and washed away the dust and sand from the Chu Lai's freight ramp. It was dry season over there and the coastal winds constantly kicked up the dust and sand from the beach area. Built right by the ocean, Chu Lai served the American Navy and Marines as a Vietnam land base. Eddie's aircraft load was on pallets so it came off fast and they almost set a new record for a turn around from Clark to Vietnam and back. Eddie threw down a Chivas chaser and finished his beer. That would be enough to drive out the noise and vibrations from the flight, so he bought another beer just to enjoy. He was feeling a little better and spotted Conejo and a couple of 815th C-130 Herky Bird drivers from Tachikawa at a table. He sauntered over and joined them. He mounted his chair backwards and leaned it over slightly, resting his elbows on the chair's back. It was a macho thing to do.

Conejo, light weight, genetic suntan, and quick on his feet reminded Eddie of what a character from the Broadway play West Side Story should look like. The 815th Pilots looked disheveled and worn out also, they were still wearing their wrinkled and dirty flight suits. They had just returned from a weeks flying, all of it in-country including night lay-overs, and had experienced some fierce ground fire. During a low altitude parachute delivery of freight into an army air strip, they were stitched by a machine gunner—right up the belly of their aircraft. They were stitched from their nose and all the way back. It was a miracle that not a single crew member had gotten hit. They were really glad to be back at Clark and the Philippines.

"Where're all the people? Place's like a morgue?" Eddie wondered out loud as he looked out the window at the pool area. "No stews at the pool!"

"Shot down," an 815th captain with command pilot's wings commented. "The wives club got tired of the stews flopping their tits and their butts around the pool and the Rathskeller, so they came out with a dress code that drove the porno show off base. The guys followed like dogs in heat."

"Banned a big bevy of beautiful beauties by banning their butts from before our berry eyes," an 815th captain with navigators wings struggled to speak. The "B" words were half an attempt to be funny and half because he was drunk as a skunk. He was three sheets to the wind and Eddie was wondering if the guy would still be conscious at sunset.

"Some wife's husband got in trouble with some Pan American stew so now they're all up in arms about the short skirts, bikini panties, and the lack of brassieres," Conejo clarified the situation with a gloomier than usual face. "It won't last long. The club's gonna lose a lot of revenue from lost booze and food sales and the wives club won't have as many guys buying stuff from their store downstairs. Personally, I thought the reason we had wars was so the guys could get away from wives clubs.

"There's a couple of bachelors having a party at their house tonight. It's one block west of the Oasis Motel. They're charging three dollars to get in and it covers the cost of the drinks," Conejo suggested the alternate and shrugged his shoulders. "It's something to do. . ."

None of the other guys were motivated enough to speak, so Conejo continued, "Clark Air Base has a new colonel from stateside as a base commander. Apparently he doesn't have the balls to say no to the wives club. This same colonel also fired the little ninety pound Negrito natives that were used to patrol the perimeter fence at night. Said there was too much stuff being stolen. He replaced the Negrito perimeter guards with GIs. What an idiot! The Negrito guards were doing a good job protecting the perimeter. It's the new Filipino gate guards that are letting all their friends leave the base with stolen stuff in their trunks."

"I heard a rumor about a stolen fire engine," the command pilot said as he finished off his drunken navigator's beer. "Several Filipinos stole a fire engine from the wash rack, turned on all the flashing lights and sirens, and drove right out the side gate. The Filipino guard just waived them through and claimed he thought they were going to fight a fire. That's the last they ever saw of the fire engine."

"I heard that too," Conejo chuckled. "How in the world would you hide a fire engine? What would you do with it?"

"I heard that the Negrito guards who were fired crawled up behind some of the GIs while they were guarding the perimeter and marked an X on the back of their boots with chalk," the C-130 co-pilot added his two cents worth. "Those little bastards are like snakes in the grass, that's why they use em as instructors at the base survival school. Anyway, the next morning the Americans found the Xs and they were really spooked out. The colonel refused to believe the story and I do know they still have mostly Filipino guards manning the gates."

The drunken navigator tried to stand up, lost his balance, then fell over backwards into his chair and slid onto the floor. No one laughed. It had been less than eighteen hours since two bullets had punched up through his navigator's table and one had stopped in the steel plate he was sitting on. He had a right to get drunk. His two crewmembers helped him to his feet and steered him toward the front door. Conejos and Eddie's eyes met for an instant; then they both took a swig of cold beer.

"Thank god we don't do low altitude freight extractions in the C-124," Eddie commented as he watched the drunk flyboys exit.

"Yeah, those Herky Bird guys really hang their asses out," Conejo agreed.

Conejo then asked Eddie to join him in a ride to Angeles City to go shopping, but Eddie knew what Conejo was shopping for and he really didn't need any of that stuff. There was really no good time of the year to catch the clap. After the others left, Eddie returned to the bar and had a few more beers. He was finding that he liked to sit alone and enjoy the effects of his drinking without the bother of conversation and shop talk. He wondered whatever happened to all the fun and games on layovers. Chasing women, repeating stories for the tenth time—the Promised Land?

Eddie ate some pizza downstairs and realized it was six in the evening. It was time for an hour's nap back at the Oasis. Then he could wander over and check out the private party at the bachelor's house. He strolled outside and sat at his favorite place on the front steps and waited for the Oasis bus. There was a stewardess sitting on the concrete bench provided for the bus stop. She was probably waiting for the same bus. Eddie made it a point never to sit on that bench as it didn't provide the character the front steps had. She was an attractive woman, in her late twenties, and looked very used. Maybe it was the jet lag. She had all the moves and her act down pat. She knew Eddie was looking at her and she carefully avoided eye contact. With a nail file she worked on her fingernails.

"What a pity," Eddie thought. "She probably has no idea what a beautiful sunset we're having behind her back." Eddie didn't blame her for not looking at him. He also looked very used: short haired, rough mannered, dressed in wrinkled Bermuda shorts and a faded shirt that was not tucked in. Besides, he hadn't been home for over two years and he didn't know anything about the latest fashions, fads, and expressions. He could have been from Mars!

The hotel bus arrived on schedule and he slung his sake bag over his shoulder, hoisted his B-4 bag, and food satchel, and followed the stewardess onto the bus. She wore a fashionable short miniskirt. As he followed her up the steps he caught a glimpse of tastefully matching red bikini panties. Eddie assumed, with the new dress code, she had just been told to leave the officers club. She had good legs but her rear end was a little loose. She needed to exercise and tighten it up. The same could have been said about Eddie's rear. Eddie had always prided himself in keeping in good physical condition. As a C-124 crewmember, his lifestyle had changed drastically and he had allowed himself to slip into a non-exercise routine.

The bus stopped at the side gate and a Filipino guard entered the bus. He had a GI accomplice and Eddie assumed the Filipino was new and under training. It's hard to judge the age of Filipino men but Eddie guessed he wasn't over eighteen years old. The Filipino slowly walked down the aisle and eyed each occupant, as if he could spot a thief among the six Americans. He was brief and courteous with the stewardess but came up short with Eddie. This was an opportunity for the Filipino to show off his training. He motioned for Eddie to open his Sake bag for inspection. Sake bags were small, colored, canvas bags with a cord weaved around the top for closure and a hard round base so they would set straight on a table. Most of the 22nd crewmembers used them as oversized dop kits. Eddie could have cared less and out of orneriness he nonchalantly spilled the contents onto the open seat across the aisle. The guard, as well as the rest of the bus's occupants, was not impressed with the smell from Eddie's yesterday's shorts and socks. The rooky guard examined his Norelco shaver, old spice deodorant, and tooth paste. He shook the aspirin bottle and placed it back on the seat. At last his eyes lit up and the Filipino defender of base property seized two tiny blue plastic cases that contained four X (XXXX) brand ready wet condoms.

"Drogas!" He held them for his GI mentor to see. "Drogas bad boogie."

"They're not drugs. They're okay for GI," Eddie defended himself. What Eddie didn't know was that the Filipino's job as a replacement gate guard at Clark Air Base was a political appointment. It was a favor to the young man's influential father. He was the youngest son in a respectable Filipino family. During the young innocent man's upbringing, he had been shielded from the sin city atmosphere that existed in the Clark Air Base area and the young man had never seen a prophylactic before—especially a ready wet rubber in a pretty blue plastic case.

"Drogas, no can have. You come with me." The excited Filipino youth placed his empty hand over his service revolver. His mentor GI stood staring, not doing a thing. Eddie could see the flight attendant out of the corner of his eye and her eyes were getting bigger and bigger.

"They're rubbers, condoms from the BX," Eddie raised his voice but the Filipino was insistent. Eddie wondered, "Maybe he didn't know the base exchange was normally called the BX?" The stewardess looked like she was about to explode with laughter. Eddie wondered what she had in her own little purse.

"Look," Eddie tried a different tack. "No drugs, only rubber for fuckie fuckie. You know fuckie fuckie?" He still drew a determined negative stare. Eddie, in desperation, dug into the sake bag pile and pulled out a third blue plastic case. He cracked it against the seat rail, opened the case, and dangled the wet dripping rubber in front of the shocked Filipino's face.

The Filipino then realized what it was, his error, and turned pale as a ghost. He quickly retreated from the bus and waved them through. He wanted to end his mistake and humiliation as soon as possible. He then, in his confusion, gave a crisp military salute to the civilian Filipino driver. They passed through the gate. The Filipino's GI instructor was shaking his head and trying not to laugh at his charge.

"Fuckie fuckie," the stew exclaimed and finally burst out laughing. "Wait till I tell the girls about this."

Eddie let her have her laugh. He sat back down and was holding the wet dangling rubber out over the aisle so it wouldn't drip on him. "What should I do with this?" he spoke out of frustration, to no one in particular.

"That's an age old problem," the stewardess answered as she dug into her purse. She handed Eddie several Kleenexes.

"That's an age old solution," he answered, and wrapped the wet rubber for disposal after their remaining bus ride. "Thanks."

"You're one weird son of a bitch," she answered. She had a twinkle in her eyes.

* * * * * * * * * * * * * * * * * * * *

That evening, Eddie paid his three dollars at the door of the bachelors' house and took his chances on what was going on inside. The party was well underway. The house was a single floor ranch style; the windows were screened against insects, large wooden louver blinds, and no air conditioner. A comfortable light breeze flowed throughout the house, aided by several large electric fans. The large living room opened to a partially covered outdoor patio and the affair was lighted with strings of Oriental looking lanterns. Large outdoor tropical plants were in abundance. It was a beautiful setting. Several Filipino servants scurried about; their brown skin and black hair contrasted with their pure white barong shirts. The partial patio covering had an unusually large grouping of geckos. The tiny lizards clung upside down to the ceiling and seemed to be enjoying the party as much as the humans. They alternately caught mosquitoes, stared down at the people, and chattered with each other.

"Eddie! What a wonderful surprise!" It was Dolly, every GIs delight, the Vargas Girl. She was standing in the middle of the patio surrounded by a group of six men, basking in their attention. She was drunk as a skunk. The guys reminded Eddie of a pack of coyotes he had once seen; they were circling around a crippled antelope and readying for the kill. Dolly staggered over and planted a big wet kiss on Eddie, as if they were old friends. Eddie had to hold her up to keep her from falling. He had only met her once and it was Larry that she had fallen all over. She was probably too drunk to remember, or notice the difference. Eddie was a little embarrassed and a lot of annoyed. He had never seen or heard of that side of Dolly.

"Double scotch and water," Eddie ordered as he stretched his loose arm and snagged a passing waiter.

"Let me introduce you to my friends," Dolly continued loudly and dragged Eddie into the hovering group. It was as if she was collecting guys and Eddie was the latest. "Guys, meet Eddie. He flies old Shaky Birds. These guys are with World Airways, they fly MAC charter trips. Neat huh?"

"Evening," Eddie addressed the group without making eye contact. He hoped the waiter would hurry with his drink.

"Know what the definition of a successful airline trip is?" Dolly was thoroughly enjoying her role as the group leader and with a free arm pulled herself up against one of the World Airline pilots. She was so drunk she almost caused him to spill his drink. No one even noticed the threatened drink as she mashed her right breast against the amused pilot's arm. Her left breast acted as if it was trying to escape from its container and the World pilots were all in a trance. "It's when the flight engineer gets laid, the co-pilot gets to land the airplane, and the captain has a successful bowel movement."

No one even heard the joke or laughed but she continued boldly, "Know what the difference is between a hold up and a stick up—age."

"Have you known Dolly long?" one of the pilots asked Eddie. He was trying to determine if Eddie was going to spoil the group's intentions.

"Years," Dolly refused to shut up. "First time I met him he was stark naked and walking down the hallway at the Skyline Motel. I thought he was a navigator." There was a pause and no one offered Dolly the key question so she continued on her own. "Why did I think he was a navigator? Well, I'll tell you. He was wearing a great big wrist watch, had a little itsy-bitsy peter, and he was looking for someone to cash a check." Eddie didn't know whether to be offended or embarrassed, he had a hard shell but this was a bit much!

Dolly helped herself to one of the World pilot's drink, took a big gulp, and winced. "Wow," she exclaimed. "That's what I call a real panty dropper."

"Excuse me, I gotta go say hello to an old friend," Eddie injected, seeing the waiter with his drink. He snagged it from the tray and kept right on going. Dolly would forget him in about three seconds. He remembered when he had first met Dolly and the three of them had gone to Poppaguyo's restaurant in Angles City. Afterward Larry had gone on and on about how she was the perfect woman. Back then, Eddie was amazed at how she seemed to have her sexuality under complete control and was totally at home with men and the Southeast Asian scene. She was the perfect lady for every GI's dreams, always right on the edge.

But that was then. She currently looked as if she had fallen off the edge and crashed. Just as if she had been hit by an enemy bullet, Dolly had become a casualty of the war. He was so disappointed, not for himself as he never had any delusions about her. But he was sad for her, sad for her image and for what she had been. Now she was just another camp following drunk. In his mind she had fallen all the way from her precarious perch as Queen of the Orient to just another of the lost souls. He was seeing more and more of them.

The living room was filled with people. Eddie found himself a spot at a Nara wood bar, like the one they had transported to Tachikawa for the wives club auction. Everyone in the room was sorted out into the usual groups. The fighter pilots were dominant, projecting their image with words such as supersonic, on my back, flack, bandits, and bingo fuel. The next layer was airline pilots discussing layovers, bids, gross weights, and tax shelters. Then came the forward air controllers talking about marking targets with their white prosperous rockets, fox mike radios, taking rounds and bunkers. Next were the trash haulers, the C-130s, C-123s and Caribous. At the bottom were the outdated piston powered C-124s, C-47s and C-54s. Depending on the crowd and the mood, the C-124 guys often were not even allowed true trash hauler status. The women, from top to bottom, were stews from the major airlines, stews from the charter airlines, nurses, and then schoolteachers. There were several clean, respectable looking Filipino girls. Eddie wasn't sure of their status. The pecking order was brutal, unfair, and cruel, but human nature. There were always exceptions. Occasionally a strong personality would come along and its owner could jump categories at social events. But that was the exception. Dolly was a flight attendant with Southern Air Transport, the local CIA airline. She was an exception, had a strong personality and had jumped to the top. But, the top was too precarious and she was falling back, all the way to the bottom.

Eddie was tired of it all, the shop talk, Southeast Asian jargon, the entire scene. Maybe on his vacation he would go home for a couple of weeks, do some backpacking in the mountains, do a little trout fishing, or help his dad put up some hay. Helping his dad put up hay would be a healthy change from his current company! He felt lonely in this crowd, but he never felt lonely when he was by himself on the farm.

He finished his second double scotch and water, then strolled over to the self-help bar and mixed himself another. For something to do he wandered back into the living room. "Good evening," he positioned himself on the sofa next to a rather pleasant looking young woman.

"What's good about it?" she answered in a monotone voice and looked straight forward. It was then that he noticed her eyes were glazed and dilated.

Without another word Eddie detached himself from the sofa and made his way into a group of guys clustered in the corner. "Yeah, I got fifteen hundred hours in an F-84," one of them was explaining. "I think I spent about four hundred of them during take-off roll. If the air force would build a runway that goes all the way around the world, Republic Aircraft Corporation would build an aircraft that needs it. With a full load of bombs it would just roll and roll and roll. Talk about your life passing before your eyes."

148

"The take-off roll was so long, I used to be afraid I would fall asleep," another said.

"The take-off roll was so long I always needed to shave again when I finally got airborne," someone else added. Fighter pilots were always competitive!

Eddie moved to another group, mixed with guys and girls.

"I don't know where they get these young flight engineers now days." It was obviously an airline pilot speaking. His stateside haircut was carefully crafted and way too long for the military. "This kid asked me stupid questions all day long. But the real clincher came when he asked me if I slept in my shorts or pajamas."

"What did you tell him?" an attractive stew asked with an interested grin.

"I told him I usually slept in a flight attendant but I didn't have any clean ones with me tonight," he answered much to the delight of the crowd. "That kid was so stupid he thought prop wash was some special type of aviation soap."

Eddie moved on, this time through a door into a bedroom. There were about twelve people stuffed into the room, standing and sitting, all involved in their version of shop talk. Eddie plopped down on the bed, the only available place remaining in the room. The other side of the bed was full with four stews sitting up, all talking simultaneously. They looked over at him, his wrinkled civilian clothing, short haircut, air force issue watch, and then give him the same look one would expect if he were a muddy dog.

"Why don't you go take care of your friend with the big tickets?" one of them finally spoke to Eddie. The stewardess looked with disgust toward him. "She's in the john puking her guts out."

"Why?" Eddie asked her with a sly smile. "Did you offer her a job with your airline?"

"You're not funny," one of the other stews remarked as she got up and left the room.

"I never disturb a lady while she's confessing her sins into the great white toilet," Eddie informed the remaining three. Another one showed her disgust and left the room. Two were left sitting on the bed. One excused herself for the bathroom and promised the remaining stew she would be right back.

"Great," Eddie thought to himself. "If I had just a little more wit, I could have the bed all alone." Everyone in the room was ignoring Eddie and he reached over the edge of the bed to set his empty drink glass on the floor. There was an empty Coke bottle lying on the floor and Eddie picked it up. He was bored to death and to amuse himself he stuck it into the front of his pants and covered it with his faded loose shirt. He looked around and no one was watching so he rolled over on his back and looked down. It made a sizeable and erotic bulge. He suppressed a grin and felt satisfied with his presentation. He had just enough to drink to think it was funny.

Everyone continued to ignore him so he tried to draw attention. "Is my drink on the floor?" Eddie asked the remaining stew as he stretched and looked over her edge of the bed. In doing so he rubbed the Coke bottle against her. Her eyes lit up like a Christmas tree as she suddenly realized he might have more to offer than she had first concluded.

"You stationed here?" she was suddenly interested in him. She couldn't keep from glancing down at the firm masculine bulge in his pants.

"Temporary duty," he answered for lack of something better to say. "I get into Clark quite a bit of the time. You a stewardess?" He played along with the previously stuck up harlot.

"Yeah." She repositioned herself so as to more comfortably face Eddie. She felt lucky to have made her discovery while alone and she needed to work on it as quickly as possible—before her friends came back and tried to cut in on the deal. "I'm with Continental Airlines—been with em for five years. Did you find your drink?"

"No, I set it around here someplace."

"Sure you didn't set it on your side of the bed?" she asked and used the opportunity to look over Eddie's side. She rubbed her hip against Eddie as she looked and reconfirmed her find. Not the drink, but the bulge. For a moment, Eddie thought she was going to drag her hand across the hidden Coke bottle when she sat up, but at the last instant she chickened out. Several people in the room were watching out of the corner of their eyes, the bulge in his pants was turning into a scene stealer. He and his new found friend carried on a friendly conversation: who he was, what he did, did he miss the States and American girls, and she developed a surprising fascination with C-124s. He loved it, playing one of them along for a change. It was too bright in the room so when she poured herself more wine, out of the bottle sitting on the bed stand, she turned off the sixty watt lamp.

They became cozier buddies and she developed gun barrel vision. The combination of the huge gulps of wine she was taking and the bulge in Eddie's pants preempted anyone else in the room. It became a comedy for Eddie, as they invented excuses to rub against each other. Another person became too embarrassed and left the room and others turned sideways so as to peek and hide their smirks at the same time. The Stewardess was coming apart at the seams. She acted like a teenager in the back seat. She allowed Eddie good views down her blouse, like the good salesperson she was. She then stretched out alongside him, casually threw her leg over him, and slowly rubbed the Coke bottle with the inside of her knee. It even started to turn Eddie on. She was red hot and ready to find someplace more private. Eddie decided it was also time to move on, but he had a different direction in mind.

"Let's face it," he spoke just loud enough so all the remaining people in the room could hear. "You and I have got to get something straight between us." He waited for his statement to sink in and have full effect on his mesmerized audience. Then he faced the aroused flight attendant and finished his sentence, "You've wanted something all along and it's about time I gave it to you."

He sat up and slowly unzipped his pants. One of the women watching covered her mouth and whispered, "O, my God!"

He bent over to cover his secret and stuck both hands into his shorts. With both hands he grasped the Coke bottle and slowly pulled it out. Suddenly he felt a wave of panic. During all of his preparation and set up, he had been enjoying himself too much and forgot to think up a punch line. What the hell! He smiled and said, mischievously, "Things always go better with Coke."

There were a few seconds of silence after he unveiled the bottle and made his statement. Then the woman again said, "O, my God."

"You son of a bitch!" the stew slapped Eddie hard across the face, sprang off the bed, and stormed out of the room. The entire room erupted with laughter except for the other stew friend who had just returned from the bathroom. She stood spellbound, staring at the bottle. She had no idea what was going on. Eddie felt great as he stood for his audience, bowed, then zipped up his pants.

"I feel better now that I got that load out of my pants," he announced. "I think I'll get me another scotch and water and maybe go talk about airplanes with the fighter jocks at the bar."

CHAPTER TWELVE: THE WHITE MAN

It was April 1969 and Eddie was called into the squadron administrative office after he returned from a two week trip down south. He expected to be asked if he would mind a short turn around, for some whatever reason, and go out on another trip without his allocated days off. He expected to hear how much it would be appreciated. As usual, he was prepared to accept the proposition. That was what he did.

"I been reviewing everyone's records and I can't find any evidence that you took any leave since you've been here at Tachikawa." Master Sergeant Sweitzer looked up from a brown folder he was holding in his hands. The folder had Eddie's name stamped on the outside. "Ya know ya gotta take your leave or you'll lose it. Ya get thirty days each year, or didn't anyone ever tell you?" He looked at Eddie and grinned. "You're not allowed to accumulate any more than sixty days without losing the overage." He looked at Eddie and waited for a nod. "Shows here you went over your limit and ya already lost a month's leave. We shoulda caught it the first year you were in the 22nd but we only got so many people here to run the shop. The assumption is that each individual would oversee their own leave. I talked to Colonel Duncan and he says you gotta take a bunch of time off cause if ya don't you'll get burned out from flying."

"Guess it just slipped by me," Eddie muttered. He really hadn't seriously thought of taking leave, he had been so busy building flying time.

"I been looking over the crew schedule and we can spare you for the next two or three weeks—hell, four weeks if ya want to. Things have slowed up a little now; first we were short of pilots and now with the reduced flying we got plenty. The gomers are still whipped from the Tet offensive and are staying low. The demand for air freight has slowed and the colonel wants everyone to get caught up on their leave. Got any place ya wanna go? I can have your paperwork ready in an hour."

Eddie stood looking at the sergeant for a minute, then realized, "This is the opportunity of a lifetime, take it."

"Yeah, I guess I could come up with someplace to go," he nodded yes as he spoke. "Cut me some leave orders and I'll be back this afternoon to pick em up. Put me down for three or four weeks, whatever works for you."

Eddie's dreams and expectations of the Orient had not been fulfilled, at least not as he had planned. It was not that the flying and the places he had been to hadn't been exciting, but he had reached the point where everything was becoming too routine–occasionally mundane. Yes, he was burned out and getting a little stressed and agitated over nit noy things (nit noy, Thai for little). Also, it hadn't been the romantic emersion into the Asian culture he had hoped for. Everywhere he had gone he had been Eddie the pilot, Eddie the lieutenant, Eddie the GI. It would be nice to escape from his uniform and the American soldier stigma. He needed to lose himself in the civilian culture of places he still only dreamed about. He had plenty of money in the bank, maybe this was his time! It was the golden opportunity to seek out, once and for all, the promise or the disappointment of the Orient.

Eddie found a backpack at the BX, just the right size for his meager needs. He would travel light and live among the people. He had no need for the big Americanized hotels and the native Asian foods suited him just fine. He decided that in addition to his toothbrush, paste, and Gillette razor he would need several bars of soap, several sticks of deodorant, a roll of toilet paper, a handful of condoms just in case, and a couple of pairs of underwear shorts. He could buy extra pants and shirts or whatever else he needed from the natives—for next to nothing. There was no reason to carry them around. He also purchased a good supply of film for his trusty Pentax camera. By midmorning the next day he had grabbed a ride aboard a C-141 freighter that had stopped at Yakota for fuel. It was enroute to U-Tapao Royal Thai Air Force Base in Thailand. U-Tapao was a coastal air base one hundred miles south of Bangkok. The Americans operated B-52 bombers, KC-135 aerial re-fuelers, U-2 spy planes, and navy P-3 marine patrol aircraft. They also had Pattaya Beach, a world famous party town, just outside their main gate. He was in a hurry to get there and it was nice to ride in a fast, high altitude jet aircraft. It was not as nice as an airliner with soft seats and snacks enroute, but still a quick direct flight. The fast high altitude jets certainly had their place, just not for Eddie to fly as a pilot.

He spent the next evening in a seven dollar room next to the sea. Not pretty and clean, but a place to sleep. The room was located several miles north of the U-Tapao air base main gate. The beach was beautiful with white sand and a warm ocean. It had a surprising number of Scandinavian tourists. Unfortunately, it was adjacent the air base and visited by thousands of American GIs. They left the same imprint on the local economy as American presence did everywhere in South East Asia. Prostitutes, sleazy bars, and hustlers were everywhere. It totally ruined the nice beach. So Eddie paid a few dollars and rode for four hours in a bus on a hot bumpy ride to Bangkok. The bus was not dissimilar to a stateside school bus, except it had a large, uncovered, steel frame luggage rack on the top. The bus was painted in a wild gyration of colors that would rival the Jeepneys in the Philippines. It had non-functional shocks and possibly broken springs. In the searing tropical heat, dripping humidity, and the constant weaving to avoid, sometimes hit, massive potholes, it was the bumpiest and worst bus ride of Eddie's life.

Eddie was quite familiar with Bangkok but it was not his destination. The Oriental Express was a luxury train for tourists and wealthy Asians. It departed northwesterly from Bangkok, crossed the river Kwai, and then turned south along the western edge of the Gulf of Thailand. It followed the Malay Peninsula, crossed into Malaysia, and continued south all the way to Singapore. Singapore was located at the southern tip of the peninsula. The total trip covered 1250 miles. The Oriental Express trip to Singapore took three days, was fairly expensive, and was not what Eddie wanted. After convincing the ticket man that he wasn't crazy and really did want the local train, Eddie purchased second class fare on the local pigs and chickens special. This train followed the same tracks and route as the Oriental Express, but stopped at almost every village to load and unload passengers and freight. Utilizing the series of local trains that spanned the long route, the train trip would take six days from Bangkok to Singapore. Traveling on the local trains, getting off and on wherever he wished, Eddie's train trip took over three weeks.

Eddie spent several days each in various villages along the way. He chose which villages to get off by watching out the windows and choosing whichever place intrigued him as the train slowed to stop. Long walks in the country side, excursions riding an elephant, bicycle trips to neighboring villages and shrines, it was all good.

He also got off at a village called Surat Thani and caught another torturous bus, and then a ferry boat ride to a Thai Island called Ko Samui. Its beaches were beautiful beyond description. The Americans had not yet discovered this utopia. There was only a smattering of Caucasian tourists and he spent four days in a wicker and bamboo hut alongside the ocean. The cost was three dollars per night. Rice, fresh fried fish, and bread were an additional dollar fifteen per day. Cold local beer was a quarter per can. It was paradise. Away from the American influence, away from the tourist vacation spots, the military and the war, totally immersed in the local culture and cuisine, he discovered thousands of kind, friendly, and very poor people. It was nice being alone on the beach and not having to listen to shop talk all the time. He hadn't realized how much of a rut he had been living in. One day he rented a snorkel, mask and fins and explored the local reefs. Another day he walked around the entire island.

Five days later he was back on the train, looking for another interesting train stop. Not once did he ever feel threatened. He wore inexpensive clothes and was always patient and humble. He made a special effort to show respect for the older people. He knew that the Asians respected their elders far more than Americans did. He also exercised the same street smart habits he had developed while bouncing around Asia in the C-124. He learned to recognize the rougher parts of each town and village and avoided them whenever possible. He didn't go down back streets alone at night and was always aware of the people both in front and behind him. He was proactive and never let himself get positioned in a defenseless position.

Occasionally there were Caucasians in the larger cities, Penang, Kuala Lumpur, and the crown city of Singapore. But in the remote rural areas it was very rare to see anyone with white skin. Certainly there were more elephants than white men. As the trip progressed, he transitioned from the Buddhists of Thailand to a land of Moslems in Malaysia: then a total mix of religions and cultures in Singapore. Everywhere he wandered the people were always nice to him and treated him with respect. It was the basic nature of their religions and their cultures.

In the rural areas everyone was more curious and the little children all had to run up and touch him. He was a curiosity, an anomaly. Compared to their annual incomes, Eddie was quite wealthy, but he dressed simply and went out of his way to be kind and friendly in return. When he purchased fruit, fried fish, and cooked rice from the natives, he never displayed more than a few coins in local currency. In many rural areas no one could speak English. So Eddie became an expert at talking with his hands and had no problem finding food to eat and a sheltered place to lie down and sleep for the night. He sometimes would go for days without the need to mutter a single word. It was the tropics and it rained at least once each day, but the rain was warm and the sun always came out after each brief deluge. He followed the local's lead and never let the rain bother him; it took only a short time for his sparse clothing to dry out in the searing sun.

The women's dress and actions reflected their hard working lifestyle. They lacked the time and resources to tend to their beauty needs thus, they were not necessarily attractive. He did see an occasional younger woman that beat the odds and had striking features, but they were modest. After a quick glance they avoided eye contact. This was the custom of Moslems. The Lady was nowhere to be found.

Adventure, on the other hand, was everywhere. Without speaking a single word to each other, Eddie was able to convince a fisherman, for a small sum, to take him along on a day long fishing trip into the open ocean. It was a grueling day in the small boat, the sun was relentless and there was no shade available in the open wooden craft. Fortunately, Eddie already had a deep tan. But he still received a moderate sunburn. He frequently took off his shirt and rinsed it in the ocean, then put it back on. The drying shirt provided temporary relief from the heat. His baseball cap was a godsend. The fisherman watched Eddie out of fascination. The fisherman was barefoot, shirtless, wore only a pair of long tattered pants and seemed unbothered by the burning sun. His skin was almost black. It was impossible to tell what amount was from the constant sun and what was genetic.

Together they laughed at Eddie's plight and at mid day they shared the fisherman's fruit and a loaf of bread that Eddie had purchased for the equivalent of fifteen cents. He had it wrapped in a plastic bag to protect it from the ocean spray. They consumed all three jugs of water the fisherman provided. Eddie refused to think about the water's purity as the sun was just too hot and he had to drink it. The fisherman used a net which he strung out in a circle, then pulled it in by hand to a tight knot and pulled it on board. He shook the small trapped fish onto the bottom of the boat and placed them into buckets of water to keep them alive and from rotting in the sun. He kept a lid on the buckets to keep them from spilling in the rocking boat. Every hour he would dip the fish out with a strainer and place them in a fresh bucket of cooler water. By the end of the day they returned with two buckets full of small fish that Eddie assumed were used in soups or deep fried and eaten like potato chips. The fisherman lowered the single sail just prior to the harbor and they stripped nude and both had a cool dip in the ocean before they continued to the fisherman's dock. That evening he searched for and purchased a small meal of rice and fried tiny fish at the local marketplace.

That night Eddie had diarrhea and vomited several times. The next morning he approached an old woman working in the local pharmacy. Nether spoke each other's language and in desperation Eddie embarrassingly held his stomach, squatted and looked down between his legs and made a runny noise. He then touched his bottom and smelled what he acted was a stinky hand. She sold him several tiny white pills. One pill and within several hours he was feeling good enough to travel and he was back on the train. He never did know what the pills were but he saved the remaining white magic pills just in case.

After the first week of having people watch him out of curiosity, Eddie slowly realized that he really was different from them. In addition to his white skin he had been educated in a western university. In the larger cities there were lots of educated Asians but in the rural areas there seemed to be none. But his differences were far more than just education and white skin. He was culturally different, knew nothing about their ancient religions, was taller, and couldn't speak their language. As much as he tried to blend into their landscape, he was an alien Caucasian. Having grown up in eastern Colorado he had been accustomed to being white around white people. He never had seriously thought about how in the vast areas of the world, there were far more people that weren't like him than there were like him. With the 22nd, the military had temporally taken over and dominated the scene everywhere he had been. Once alone, however, and on his own in remote Thailand and in rural Malaysia, Eddie for the first time truly sensed his whiteness.

Considering the fact that Americans were making war and trying to shape the politics and conduct of Asians half way around the globe, Eddie began to question if he really liked being white. What about being an American? Who was this white man seeking an Asian lover, as if she would naturally come to him because he was white and an American? For all his efforts, his handicaps were too restrictive for him to get inside the Asian's minds. He had to be content with observations from the outside.

By the next day all would be well again and he captured photos of a people and a culture that was exalting: an old toothless woman doing her laundry in a stream on a rock, a naked baby staring with huge brown eyes, an elephant pulling a huge log with a sixty pound boy guiding the elephant while sitting atop the elephant's head. One photo was of three covered Moslem girls acting as if they weren't looking at him. There were wild flowering plants everywhere, flowering forbs, bushes, trees and vines. With the abundant rain and vegetation and an ocean teaming with fish, despite being dirt poor, the abundance of people had plenty to eat. They were dirt poor and yet lived rich lives surrounded by their families, religions, and cultures. Was there something Americans lacked? Eddie spent very little time speaking but every minute he was awake he was thinking and consuming his surroundings. Some nights he would have disjointed dreams, but every morning he would awake to a world as an alien in a remote village. With all the wonder, it still wasn't the place he had been seeking. He needed a place to dwell and to think and to observe and get his head straight.

He had also experienced some of the same feelings and thoughts when he first arrived in the Philippines. He knew he had a destiny but what was it? Was it his quirky fascination with a painting of an Asian lady, an airline pilot with Singapore Airlines, or an American airline? Maybe he would end up living in some Asian city as a representative of an American corporation!

After his railway trip terminated in Singapore, Eddie spent three days marveling in that international city. Its fantastic public facilities, the botanic gardens, zoos, the world's largest sea port and a modern international business downtown. He then flew commercial direct to Hong Kong and spent three days in what seemed like the world's largest merchandise market. It was overwhelming. Everyone seemed in a hurry and too busy making money. There was much to see but he had to get away from the frenzy. The people of Hong Kong lacked the slower pace and philosophy of the rural countryside. It was just too hectic and he moved his flight up one day so he could get back to Tachikawa. He was in a hurry to retreat back into his world of blue sky, aluminum wings, round engines, and headsets.

After he flew on an airline back to Japan and departed on his next trip down south, he finally had the time to reflect and absorb all that he had experienced on his leave. He had started his adventure with some definite questions he wanted to answer and returned with more questions than he left with. Maybe what was important was that he was asking the questions, and really not the answers.

CHAPTER THIRTEEN: COLLAPSE

June 1969, rumors had been flying for weeks. The Japanese Communists had been raising all kinds of hell off the ends of the runway at Tachikawa and there had been all kinds of high ranking officers and civilians touring the base and asking lots of questions.

The 22nd guys were going nuts asking each other what was going on. "Was the base going to be closed? Was the 22nd going to be moved to Yakota to utilize their larger facility and longer runways? Was the 22nd going to be moved to Clark, Bangkok, or even Hawaii? Were the 22nd crews all going to be sent to school and the 22nd converted into a squadron that flew the new and much larger all jet freighter of the future, the C-5A? If so, who would fly the oversized freight into the short dirt strips in Vietnam? Certainly they wouldn't risk the larger and very expensive C-5 into those god forsaken locations! Had the end come for the C-124?"

Secretary of Defense Robert McNamara had been overheard saying, "We're going to save money on our military operations, no matter how much it costs!" Would his money saving efforts result in the loss of an expensive, new C-5 on a short dirt strip in Vietnam?

In Thailand they lost a number of the new F-111 fighter/bombers during their baptism of fire. As a joke, the Thailand based F-111 pilots managed to get their stateside C-141 buddies to smuggle, from the States, an Edsel car bumper. The Edsel car had been a civilian business venture under McNamara's management and had been a massive failure. One night, they mounted the bumper above their base operations entry door and labeled it F-111, *McNamara's Flying Edsel*. The bumper didn't last long but the message was clear. Apparently none of McNamara's staff had the nerve to tell him about the joke and the man plowed on making stupid decisions. Would the C-5 be someday called the Flying Edsel II, as it burned at the end of the short dirt strip at Duc Tao? Eddie had been there and done that place. He knew!

* * * * * * * * * * * * * * * * * * *

Things finally came to a head. All of the 22nd birds had been ordered back to Tachikawa and were lined up on the ramp. The engines were still warm on the last ones to arrive. The flight line was impressive. All of the 22nd's C-124s at one place at one time. The Japanese civilians lined the perimeter fence and took countless photos of the spectacle, shook their heads, and did a lot of hissing.

The meeting was scheduled at ten in the morning and the crewmembers were instructed to wear their blue uniforms. Everyone looked and felt out of place as they awkwardly filled the room and selected a place to sit. As per military tradition, precisely at ten hundred hours the sergeant at arms called the room to attention. A group of high ranking officers, followed by three senior master sergeants and two staff sergeants, moved through the doorway and briskly to the front of the room. With the exception of the 22nd Squadron Commander, Lt. Colonel Duncan, none of them were from the 22nd MAS. Colonel Duncan was the first to speak.

"Gentleman . . ." It was so quiet Eddie was afraid to even breathe. "A brief history of the 22nd Military Airlift Squadron." He read from the squadron history records: "January 22, 1942, at Amberly Airdrome, Brisbane, Australia, twenty-five men from the Seventh Bomb Group were formed into the Troop Carrier Command. They had three transport aircraft and formed the nucleus of an idea, an idea that transport aircraft could efficiently move large amounts of men and equipment long distances in very short times. Thus, effectively multiplying the theater commander's instruments of warfare.

"In March of 1942, additional aircraft were contracted from what is now the KLM Dutch Airways. On April 3rd of that year the 22nd Squadron was formed within this group. Their first airfield of operation was at Essendon Airdrome, Melbourne, Australia. They were a rag tag group, flying a mix of L-4 Grasshoppers, C-56 Lodestars, DC-2s, and converted B-17s. The 22nd was not long to see action, supporting the Australian troops in combat in the Papua Campaign. Then they went on to establish a brilliant record of delivering combat cargo during the long and difficult battle against the Japanese in the Pacific. During this time they upgraded their aircraft to the larger C-46s and developed their own troop and cargo air dropping techniques." The room was silent; everyone knew this was not just a history lesson but the prelude to a bomb dropping.

"The post war era found the 22nd flying the new C-54 aircraft, operating a regular scheduled currier route in the Pacific. Their home field was Nichols Field in the Philippines. In 1947 they moved to Clark Field where they had better facilities. When the Berlin airlift was initiated, the 22nd provided ten C-54s and one hundred seventy men and officers to the cause. For their efforts they were awarded the United Nations Medal for Humane Action.

"After the airlift the returning men had another surprise for them. November 1948 their squadron had been moved to Tachikawa Air Base in Japan. They were," the colonel continued, "deeply involved in the Korean War. They received their first C-124 in 1952 and set new airlift records during the height of that conflict. Since that time the 22nd and their C-124s have established new standards in airlift usage and flexibility. They hauled the first captured MIG-15, hauled a solid gold Buddha for the Thai government, medicine for Doctor Dooley, typhoon relief supplies into Guam, and countless missions into Hanoi in support of the French at Dien Bien Phu.

"When the Vietnam conflict first erupted, it was only natural for them to be among the first to be involved. Their established routes and highly experienced crews paved the way for the combat re-supply system. As their older and more vulnerable C-124s were no match for the newer, high performance C-130 turboprops and other state of the art aircraft, they gradually took the back seat and developed into specialists—outsized cargo." Colonel Duncan placed his notes on the pedestal, looked over his audience, and spoke with a heavy heart. "Gentlemen, that brings us to today and I would like to turn this briefing over to General Dean from Headquarters Pacific Air Force in Hawaii." Eddie's stomach took a flip flop as the general briefly and coldly stated what they had all speculated and wondered about for so long.

"Gentleman, as some of you may be aware, or have suspected, as a part of the air force's modernization mandate to become a more efficient and an all jet air force, the C-124 is being phased out of operation. The expense of maintaining their large reciprocal engines and the resultant poor dispatch reliability has become unacceptable in today's modern jet air force. The C-124 will continue to be flown for several years by stateside guard and reserve units. What you may not be aware of is, as a result of numerous problems with local resistance from the Japanese Communist Party and increasing pressure from the Japanese government to repossess the Tachikawa Air Base property, Tachikawa Air Base will be decommissioned and the property returned to the Japanese government. During the next few months, the 815th C-130 Squadron and other current functions at Tachikawa will be relocated and incorporated into the functions of other air force properties in the region. As a result of the aforementioned actions, the 22nd Military Airlift Transport Squadron is being officially retired as of today."

The shock was devastating and rippled throughout the assembly. Eddie felt a chill run down his spine as he realized his well designed tour of the Orient was going to abruptly end. He looked around and it appeared that everyone had just seen a ghost. Metaphorically they had, they had seen the ghost of the 22nd rise from the living and it hung over the room in agony, no longer alive and not yet crossed over to the dead. Crossing over would take another month as the living crew members and its aircraft would be unwillingly removed from the scene of death.

The general continued with his butchering: "A number of your aircraft will be ferried to guard and reserve units in the States where they will augment their fleets. As crew members you will be dispatched to fly all but four of the remaining aircraft to Davis Monthan Air Force Base in Tucson, Arizona, where they will be delivered to the bone yard for scrapping. This reduction in C-124 numbers will drastically reduce air force maintenance costs. As the guard and reserve units phase out their C-124s over the next few years, they will eventually all receive replacement aircraft of more modern type. Your mission and tradition carrying outsized cargo in Southeast Asia will be carried on, in part, by the four remaining C-124s which will be reassigned to the 20th Operational Squadron at Clark. None of the crewmembers from this unit will go with these four birds. They will be flown by crews currently being sent from stateside units. As some of you may know, the 20th is not a Military Airlift Command Squadron and they will be flying a very limited number of oversized missions in-country. Whenever possible, MAC C-5s from stateside units will assume the bulk of the oversized cargo transportation."

Eddie realized what was going on. At the start of the Vietnam build up, operationally loaning the 22nd to the 315th in the Pacific had allowed the Military Airlift Command to rid themselves of another dirty renegade squadron of oil dripping, piston powered C-124 aircraft. To their surprise, under the 315th shadow, the renegade 22nd had been allowed to operate quite loosely and they had been very effective. When the results of the 22nd's performances were being rewarded with numerous unit and individual medals, MAC realized their error. MAC had lost not only their bragging rights for the awards, but also lost funding advantages associated with the 22nd's outstanding performance. Closing Tachikawa and dissolving the 22nd allowed MAC to regain, with their new C-5 jumbo jets, control over most of the outsize missions into the Vietnam Theater. They would rid themselves forever of a squadron of C-124s they still carried on their books, and gain additional justification for purchasing the new C-5A transports.

The general interrupted Eddie's thoughts as he proudly announced and beamed as if he was doing everyone a favor, "My staff is here with everyone's orders. We have orders for the crews designated to deliver aircraft to their stateside destinations and we have everyone's orders for their next assignment. We have everything all ready for you to pick up in room five of building thirty-four next door. But first Colonel Duncan wants to have a few more words alone with you."

The general nodded at the sergeant at arms and the sergeant stood to attention and loudly commanded, "Ten-Hut!" The room responded and the general and his staff filed out, leaving Colonel Duncan alone with his squadron of crewmembers.

"I still have furniture waiting to be picked up in Taipei," the navigator sitting on Eddie's left mumbled.

"Anybody wanna buy a bar in Angeles City?" the guy on Eddie's right whispered to him. "I know a couple of flight engineers that'll make you a good deal."

"I can't believe they're closing Tachikawa," the flight engineer behind Eddie exclaimed. "They just painted base housing, re-paved the streets, and built a new hobby center."

"Who the hell do you think they did that for?" the engineer next to him asked. "You don't think they spruced up the base for us, do you?"

"At ease," Colonel Duncan ordered and then stood lonely and forlorn in front of what was once his command. "I've known about this for several weeks." The pain was obvious in his face. "I was under strict orders not to talk to anyone but my staff about it. My staff here at Tachi also knew and we have been working long hours putting the details of this together. It hasn't been easy keeping this a secret but I have to credit my staff for keeping a secret when ordered to.

"I know how all of you feel. I'm losing my command, I feel like I've been disemboweled. I just wanted to tell you that you're the best group of can do fliers I have ever had the privilege to work with." He paused for a moment to choke down his emotions. "You can all walk away from this assignment carrying your heads high, knowing that you served the 22nd and your country with distinction. Thousands of guys on the ground in Vietnam had their jobs made easier, and hopefully we indirectly saved a few lives because of the cargo we delivered with your endless dedication."

He paused, then resumed his painful presentation, "I have one more bundle of bad news I need to tell you before you pick up your orders. As your commander I wanted to tell you myself, before you found out on your own . . . I don't know how to make it any easier than to be frank with you and tell you straight out. With the exception of a small number of loadmasters and flight engineers, the rest of you are all being reassigned to Vietnam for a one year tour." For the second time that day the 22nd crewmembers spirits cried out. Eddie felt like he had a spear driven through him, as did the rest of the pilots and navigators. The loadmasters and flight engineers all sat embroiled in turmoil.

Colonel Duncan continued, "When I heard of these assignments I called everyone in the States that I could and used up all my IOUs, but all I did was run into a brick wall. I tried to explain to the brass, where these assignments came from, that we've all served the equivalent of a tour in Vietnam, many of you for two, three or more years, but I kept running into the same brick wall. That brick wall is our 'overseas return dates!' "

Eddie was confused, everyone that was overseas had a scheduled overseas return date. It was the date when their overseas tour was to be over and they would be scheduled to return to the States. The colonel was about to explain the problem. "Overseas return dates have been used for some time now. It's supposed to provide a fair and impartial system of rotating assignments for personnel into and out of overseas assignments. Return from an overseas tour and your name goes to the bottom of the pile for another overseas tour. You can always volunteer to go back, but if there aren't enough volunteers then the air force assigns the individuals with the oldest return dates, or those new guys without return dates. It's usually a fair system.

"The air force is also using overseas return dates from Vietnam for Vietnam reassignments. You guys are assigned to Japan and all have expected return dates in your personnel files. Unfortunately, your return dates are not Vietnam assignment return dates because Tachikawa is not in Vietnam. Even your Tachikawa return dates have not been activated because you're still here! So with the closing of our squadron your names came up for a Vietnam assignment. For those of us that are stationed overseas, outside Vietnam, and haven't returned to the states, we don't have a recent overseas return date and therefore we fit the criteria as the most eligible.

"If you serve temporary duty in Vietnam and return to your home base in the States, the computer will reward you with a partial credit. With enough partial credits your return date will be updated. That's why the guys flying MAC aircraft out of the state side airbases are all sitting nice and pretty. They get these partial credits even if they are on the ground for only an hour or so in Vietnam. The data about our daily flights into the combat zone is not used because we never return to the States between flights. It's just a technical omission but the bureaucracy is not about to budge."

Lt. Colonel Duncan continued, "It stinks, but as much as I have been bitching and moaning to everyone back in the States, no one is listening. I even tried to get some of you reassigned to the 20th Operational Squadron at Clark to serve as instructors and crew members on the four aircraft they're keeping there. Nobody knows our mission better than we do. But the generals back in the States told me that all C-124 pilots, including guard and reserve pilots, were trained the same and could takeover their new oversize mission at Clark just fine." He paused, then spoke, "Gentlemen, to put it bluntly, we're screwed."

Eddie wondered about the C-130 guys. They were stationed outside Vietnam, just like the guys in the 22nd, and fly several weeks at a time temporary duty (TDY) shuttling cargo, just like the guys in the 22nd. But they normally spent their nights on the ground inside Vietnam, were exposed to frequent rocket attacks, and flew missions far more hazardous. If the C-130 guys didn't get an overseas return date from Vietnam, they were really getting the shaft.

* *

Eddie stood in line with the others as packets of orders were passed out to each fly boy, one at a time. He still felt a little dazed. It was so impersonal and cold but the military was like that. To them a small insignificant thing like a man's name on a set of orders was a minor administrative procedure. There had been no preliminary questioning as to who wished to go where or fly what, there was no choosing by seniority from a list of assignments to be filled. There was no swapping of assignments allowed, or consideration of marital status. There was just cold hard placement of names on sets of orders and an impersonal "here" by a staff member. As he stood in line Eddie remembered once being told, "If the military wanted you to have emotions, they would issue them to you along with everything else."

When he was handed a brown envelope with his name typed on it, he took it over to a corner so as to open it alone and in silence—like a dog goes off alone when it's handed a bone to chew. He could hear others sharing their news with such assignments as AC-119 gunships, Jolly Green Giant rescue helicopters, and C-123 freighters, all in Vietnam. His first set of orders was to ferry a C-124 and crew across the Pacific to the bone yard near Tucson, Arizona. His second set of orders was to report to England Air Force Base in Louisiana, to a unit called the 4412 CCTS, for flight training in C-47s. A third set of orders assigned him to report, after C-47 training, to Tan Son Nhut Air Base in Vietnam for assignment to EC-47s. Travel orders to Vietnam after C-47 training would be issued at England Air Base and Eddie stood in wonderment at his fate.

He had a flashback to his first trip south in a C-124. It was with Major Baxter and there was a camouflaged C-47 with lots of antennas parked on the Clark ramp. It had a GI guarding it and the flight engineer said it was an EC-47. Eddie had even joked about flying one someday. The flight engineer suspected, too casually for Eddie, that it was a replacement for one that had been lost in combat. The word ironic came to his mind. He had felt the same way toward that EC-47 as he had felt that day, so long ago, when he saw his first C-124. The one that had landed with an engine out at Willy Air Patch during pilot training.

He opened a bottle of scotch back at his apartment and, sitting in the middle of the purchases he had hoarded from half a dozen countries, he managed to finish most of it before his body and mind succumbed to the alcohol. He dreamt he was back on the farm in Colorado where life was simple and easy to understand.

* * * * * * * * * * * * * * * * * * * *

The out processing and departure from Tachikawa passed rapidly. Eddie immediately purchased a large amount of lemon oil and sopped his wooden treasures as wet as he could to prevent drying and cracking while in storage. He paid the four government contracted Japanese packers US$20 extra (a month's wage) to double wrap the wooden items, so as to hold in the fresh furniture oil. His apartment full of booty was then shipped to a storage facility in Colorado, as household goods, where it was placed in storage at government expense. He kept out one B-4 bag full of personal items and uniforms so he could travel light.

The trip across the Pacific, in the C-124 he was delivering to the bone yard, was long and boring. The exception was a two day interruption at Hickam Air Force Base in Honolulu. There the air force internal "ownership" papers on the aircraft were processed and delivery to the bone yard was formalized. The bone yard was air force slang for the storage and disposal yard at Davis-Monthan AFB near Tucson, Arizona. It was there that all decommissioned aircraft were destined to end up. It was officially designated Aerospace Maintenance and Regeneration Center (AMARC) a fancy name for an airplane graveyard. True, sometimes aircraft were recalled and put back into service, sometimes they were used as drones for aerial target practice, but most were methodically chopped up and melted down as scrap.

Eddie had first seen the bone yard during his first flight as a student pilot in the T-38. The first flight was an introductory flight, labeled the "gee whiz flight" by the students, because of the spectacular performance of the supersonic jet trainer. That was over three years earlier. In the speedy T-38, it took a little over ten minutes for him and his instructor to fly south to Tucson and Eddie's instructor requested a low altitude fly-by from the Davis Monthan tower. His instructor flew the aircraft low and instructed Eddie to get a good look at the bone yard. After they pulled up and headed back toward their assigned practice area he asked Eddie what he had seen.

Eddie mulled over the question and answered, "I saw over a thousand aircraft all parked in a big graveyard and a machine on one end that was chopping them up. What was I supposed to see?"

The instructor lectured, "I wanted you to see them chopping up our beloved aircraft when we're done flying them. My room-mate in pilot training went on to fly fighters and one day his single engine got sick and he tried to limp back to his base and save the aircraft. Despite the fact that his wing man begged him to bail out

159

and warned him that he wouldn't make it to the runway. He crashed on final and died while sitting in a perfectly good ejection seat. If he had saved his aircraft, I wanted you to see what would have become of the aircraft. My room-mate died for nothing. If you ever have to make the choice between jumping or nursing a cripple against the odds, I beg you to jump and live to fly another day. If you save the airplane, they'll just chop it up anyway." The lesson had been a valuable addition to Eddie's portfolio of flying lore.

After having their fill of hula music, rum with fruit juice, and fat tourists, Eddie and his crew collected their bone yard paperwork and continued their cross country flight to California. After a quick night's sleep, they flew to Tucson, Arizona. It was the crew's last landing in a C-124. It was a somber affair, landing an airplane they all loved so much and having no choice but to turn it over to the overweight master sergeant who greeted them with a "follow me" truck. As they taxied not a word was spoken in the cockpit, other than the required checklists and responses. The airplane was going to be trashed, so there was no need for the orderly after-landing checklist to get everything in order for the next flight. But the crew did it anyway, out of respect for the aircraft. Eddie felt like he was delivering a close friend to be executed. As they formed a daisy chain and handed their bags out the belly hatch of the faithful behemoth for the last time, Eddie noticed his grizzly forty year old flight engineer had tears in his eyes. Eddie looked away and choked back his own emotions. He felt sick to his stomach. This was without doubt a funeral. The scene would be re-enacted many times over the next few years. It was the end of a glorious era and the giant thundering fat bird would just be history. They finished their paperwork and the sergeant gave them a ride to the Tucson International Airport. There, old friends, brothers in arms, quietly scattered to the winds and their new assignments—never to see each other again.

CHAPTER FOURTEEN: MOLLY

July 1969, Eddie was riding in a commercial airliner on final approach into Denver Stapleton Airport. He hadn't called his parents so they didn't know he was back in the United States. He didn't call on purpose because he didn't want to argue with his dad over the telephone and he didn't want to confuse his mother with explanations she didn't understand. Once in Denver, he called his cousin and asked for someone to drive to Denver and pick him up and asked his cousin to drive over and explain to his parents that he would be home for ten days and then would have to leave again. Eddie retired to the bar to fortify himself for his return home. He didn't tell his cousin his next assignment would be Vietnam. There would be plenty time to tell everyone when he got home. He had visions of his mother scurrying about, butchering a chicken and peeling potatoes for supper. She so loved to cook and would be happy.

Eddie enjoyed the Coors beer and was pleased they had it on tap. He had grown up on it and he was glad to be back. He had the bartender run a tab and after a few refills he lost track of the time.

Deep in thought, he felt someone tapping him on his shoulder. He turned around and was shocked! His cousin had sent Molly, the girl from the farm next to his parents. He and Molly were the same age and had grown up together, attended Greeley High School together and had been best friends. But Molly had always wanted more from their friendship; she wanted to be his girlfriend. Eddie had always resisted her advances as he wanted to escape the complications and restrictions of a small tightly united farm community.

Molly had tears in her eyes and as he dismounted from his bar stool they hugged each other and held their embrace for a long time. She was soft and smelled wonderful, different from the Asian women. She looked so innocent compared to the round-eyes he'd encountered overseas. She was still about fifteen pounds overweight, at least according to Eddie's standards. For the first time in his life he gave her a kiss on the lips. Then he was embarrassed by her reception and aggressive response. He was in uniform and in a public place, but she felt wonderful!

Eddie managed to ease free from the bear hug and they found their way down to the baggage area and picked up his overstuffed B-4 bag. Eddie was surprised at how effortlessly Molly hefted his heavy bag into the car's trunk. He'd forgotten that farm girls were strong and accustomed to lifting heavy things. Then Molly drove Eddie home. She talked nonstop, a trait Eddie never liked in a woman but on that day he didn't mind. By the time they got back to the farm, he knew all that had taken place during the years he had been gone: the weather and its effect on the crops, crop prices, who got whom pregnant, marriages, who had babies, who won prizes at the County Fair with their livestock showings, and who died. All were things that would be important to a farm girl. It sounded to Eddie that there had been a few minor changes but everything was the same. It was as if time stood still in his farming community. Eddie just let her ramble on. Noticeably, she avoided any serious questions about Eddie's personal life and his assignment to Japan. Instead of the expected probing questions, she launched just a few light queries. "Did you like Japan and was it pretty?" She made an attempt at humor by asking if he could find any good Chinese food over there but Eddie waltzed away from the subject and returned to farm gossip. Japan and China were all the same to people from his remote farming community.

He had a strong feeling that Molly had been afforded access to the letters he had written to his mother and cousins. In them he had intentionally kept everything generic and free of details.

His mother was on the front steps waiting for him; she had her hair in a bun and was wearing the same checkerboard apron she was wearing when he left. His dad was still out in the field so he and his mother had a warm reunion. Molly followed them into the house. Eddie was uncomfortable about getting too familiar with Molly. She and his mother had been scheming together for many years and he wasn't surprised when Molly stayed for supper, then until ten that evening. The positive thing was that his dad was civil in front of Molly and he and Eddie didn't have an argument on his homecoming day. It was an awkward evening with lots of light talk, but at least it was civil. As he had guessed, the fried chicken was wonderful and it was nice to eat potatoes instead of rice. The home made cherry pie was to die for. The tart, sour cherries from Loveland, Colorado, had to be the best in the world.

The next morning Eddie awoke in the same bed and in the same bedroom he had grown up in as a boy. He was awakened by a familiar sound, a pair of Western Kingbirds quibbling in the cottonwood tree outside his window. It struck him that they were probably descendants of the very Western Kingbird that had argued with the Bullock's Oriole on that fateful day—so very long ago. That day, as a little boy, he had imprinted on the yellow bi-winged Stearman aircraft. He didn't believe in fate, but the memory of that event and its subsequent results was undeniable. Eddie smiled to himself, then rolled out of his bed and looked out his window. The scene brought him back to the present. His dad no longer stacked hay in that spot. A new metal machine shed now stood in the hay's place and the old wooden garage had been painted. That was a lot of change for a farm. Eddie could smell bacon frying in the kitchen and his old Levis, still hanging in his tiny closet, still fit him. Shirtless and barefoot, he wandered out to the kitchen and was surprised to see Molly helping his mother fix a big breakfast. They definitely had been scheming and Eddie was glad his stay in Colorado would be short.

"Morning," Eddie addressed his two busy cooks as he poured himself a cup of coffee and stood looking at the table, trying to select a place where to sit. He felt a little awkward, half undressed in front of the neighbor girl.

"Morning," they both replied in unison as they smiled. Molly strolled over to Eddie and gave him a big hug with a kiss on his lips. It was all he could do to keep from spilling his hot coffee. Eddie felt the blood rush and he was embarrassed at Molly's brash behavior, by her presence in their kitchen, and by her show of affection in front of his mother. German descendants didn't act like that, at least ethnic Germans living in Weld County, Colorado. Eddie realized he had instantly reverted to his conservative childhood upbringing. But as he looked up from the kiss he could see his mother looking at them and smiling. He couldn't help but smile back at his wonderful mother. It was good to be home but he felt more than a little set up and trapped. As he sat down he began planning his escape. He had planned numerous scenarios for his life and none of them could unfold with a woman as a companion. At least not a Caucasian farm girl.

The eggs were exactly like he remembered, fresh from the hen house, sunny side up, and served with crisp fried bacon, fried potatoes, and home made bread with home made jam. He was joined by the two cooks. They had coffee and toast with jam. They had eaten breakfast several hours earlier with his father, who was already hard at work in the fields.

Eddie was frightened at his mother's sly smile and Molly's slyer grin. They were both temporarily silent as they let the moment sink in.

"When you leaving again?" his mother assumed a somber face. Her bluntness was typical for the German farm culture they lived in. He could sense Molly tense up.

"Ten days." Eddie was thankful for the opportunity to discuss the thing on everyone's mind. It was an opportunity to put into effect his plan to shorten his exposure to Molly and to escape. "I'll spend four or five days around here, then I'm gonna go visit a couple of buddies from college and maybe get in a little fishing."

"Wish it could be longer," his mother wished out loud. "Your father could use some help on the farm and I miss talking with you. We'll have to get together and talk, I want to hear all about . . . where was it you were?" Eddie always worried about his mother's memory.

162

"Japan," Molly filled her in automatically.

"You going back to Japan?" his mother continued. It was the moment Eddie had dreaded but there was no way to hide it. Sooner or later someone was going to have to tell her and it was better if it was him.

"Vietnam," Eddie replied as nonchalantly as possible. "I'm going to Vietnam." Molly winced but his mother appeared unfazed. "Just for one year this time and I'll be flying transport airplanes hauling food and mail around. It's not dangerous." Actually he had no idea what he was going to do over there.

"Isn't there a war over there someplace? I saw it on the news," his mother calmly asked. "Just where is this place? I'm glad you're not gonna be in the war?" Eddie was relieved beyond his biggest hopes. His mother, in her isolated farm environment and her advanced years, was unable to grasp and comprehend what he had just said. Molly on the other hand was sitting stoically and tears were welling in her eyes.

"Why are you going back?" Molly asked as she tried to hide her tears and emotions from Eddie's mother.

"I'm not done yet."

"Done with what?"

"I don't know! That's why I have to go back. I need to find out," Eddie struggled. "Besides, I'm in the military and I have no choice."

Molly looked at her watch, slid her chair back, and carried her dirty plate to the sink. "Did I tell you that I work four days a week at Ranch Wholesale in Greeley? I have to be at work at ten." Molly walked out without saying another word. Eddie heard her pickup's engine start and he watched out the kitchen window as Molly drove away down the lane. She was crying profusely and Eddie felt a deep pain shoot through his body. It was 8:15 a.m. and only a twenty minute drive into town.

Eddie's mother washed the dishes and he dried.

* * * * * * * * * * * * * * * * * * *

Eddie decided it was time to face the music with his father. He could see him at the far end of the sugar beet field preparing to change the irrigation water set. Eddie slipped into his irrigation boots and rode his old Honda 90cc motorcycle out to join him. Together, without words, they worked together like they did when Eddie was growing up on the farm. They placed canvas irrigation dams in head ditches to backup the flowing water. Then, as the thirty inch deep ditch was just about full, they quickly worked the ditch bank along the crop side. They primed the pre-positioned, curved inch and a half aluminum tubes, so each tube would suction feed a small flow of water over the ditch bank and into a furrowed row of beets. When all the tubes were set, they made fine adjustments to the flowing tubes and were finished. It would take about six to eight hours for the water to reach the other end of the rows. Another section of beets would be irrigated and they would move the entire operation onto the next section. They ran water twenty-four hours per day during the hot summer growing season.

When everything was to Eddie's father's satisfaction, no small accomplishment as his father considered setting water to be an art form, they took a break. They drank from the canvas water bag that hung from every farmer's pickup, then squatted in the narrow strip of shade next to the pickup.

"You still gonna be in the army as long as you said you would?" his father quietly asked. There was no anger in his voice, only curiosity.

"Afraid so," Eddie answered cautiously, ignoring his father's calling the air force the army. Eddie knew that in his father's mind the air force was still just another branch of the army. No reason to correct him and ignite his father's anger. "I got almost two years to go and they'd throw me in jail if I didn't return . . . Looks like I'll be spending the next twelve months in Vietnam, flying cargo in a transport plane."

"Well, I don't think it's right to break the law and run from your duty," Eddie's father reflected his family's pride in being good citizens. "Least in a transport plane you won't get close to the front lines where the fighting takes place." His father was born in Russia, in an ethnic German colony, and his family came to America when he was a little boy. They took great pride in the freedoms they were afforded in their new country and they believed nothing was for free. Eddie's father lost two brothers in World War II.

"Hear some of the young kids your age are running to Canada to avoid the army." His father closed his eyes and took a draw on his cigarette. "Sure as hell don't want my boy to be like that."

Eddie was shocked. It was the first nice thing his father had said since his senior year in high school. Then, Eddie had volunteered to feed the cattle for one of their neighbors—until the neighbor recovered from a broken leg. Eddie's father thought that was a nice thing for him to do and had awkwardly told him so. Unknown to Eddie, the same neighbor had recently reminded his dad that Eddie had never been in trouble, was a hard worker, and that he needed to cut Eddie some slack when he returned from the army.

It wasn't that Eddie's father was mean or uncaring on purpose. Eddie always felt that deep inside, in an area that never showed, he loved Eddie. He just didn't know how to show it. His father came from a rugged "old country" family where the men served as roughshod patriarchs, ordered their wives and large families around and ruled their lives. His father had never been taught American parenting skills and still ruled and thought in the old school ways. Also, his father had always been unhappy with Eddie as Eddie's mother suffered complications during Eddie's birth. She couldn't bear any more children. It was as if it was Eddie's fault his father couldn't have a large family to help with the farm work.

"I just needed to know," Eddie's father resumed his curiosity about Eddie's military service. "Earl Johnson's got a slew of young teenage boys running around his place, more than he needs to work his farm. He asked me if I wanted to hire young Johnny to work for me a couple of years. I ain't getting any younger and it would be nice to have some young buck around here to help me out with some of the heavy stuff, with you being gone an all. Said Johnny graduated from high school this spring and wants a job to make some money so he can go to college. It seems like you maybe set the new standard around here." His father almost smiled, then continued, "Said Johnny could still live at home so he could work for me and save his money for school. I'm glad you came home so I could talk to ya. I don't want ya to think I'm replacing you; I got plans for when you're coming back. You know I ain't much of a letter writer."

"I think that's a good idea, Dad. Gives Johnny a chance to go to college someday and takes the pressure off me for not being around to help with the work." They both knew Eddie was twisting the thing a little, but after years of arguing and butting heads, it felt good for both of them to experience a small spark of conciliation.

"What's this about you having plans for when I'm coming back?" Eddie asked his father. Eddie was curious and suspicious.

"The Stroh place is gonna be for sale in a couple of years. The old man Stroh told me he was gonna give it all up and move to Greeley. It's got a pretty good house on it and I was kinda thinking if you and Molly got hitched, I could buy it and we could hire a third man and farm both farms. Kinda thought that we'd have enough land that we could start converting some of it over to irrigated pasture and start a small cow-calf operation. A lot less work that way. I'm getting too old to bust my ass growing sugar beets."

Eddie was upset again. "Dad, when you gonna stop telling me what to do and how to run my own life? Despite what everybody around here thinks, I don't have any plans to marry Molly. And while we're at it, I'm not planning on coming back here when I get out. I really wanna fly airplanes for a living."

His father let the bombshell sink in before he exploded.

"God-damn it! I told you to stay away from those airplanes! After all I did for you, helped you through college an all, now yer gonna go break your mother's heart and screw up my plans for retirement. God-damn it to hell!" He stood up and jumped across the ditch and re-adjusted a water tube he had been watching. It was not flowing just the way he liked and it needed adjustment.

"I'm sorry for your plans, Dad. But you gotta discuss things with me first. Ya can't just lay my life out according to your ideas and go arranging for who I marry." It was one of the few times he had ever talked back to his father; German sons raised under the old school just didn't do that.

"Get on your motorcycle and get the hell out of here. I don't wanna talk to you anymore," his father hollered and pointed down the road.

So went their discussion. It was somewhat longer than their usual conversations but the outcome was certainly the same. It was nothing very different from hundreds of times before.

When Eddie was a junior in high school his dad bought a new pickup. When the dealer wouldn't give him what he wanted for a trade in, he brought the old pickup back home. As it still ran okay, it could still be used for irrigating. Eddie adopted the old pickup, drove it during high school, college, and during air force pilot training. He received lots of kidding and was on the receiving end of many jokes but the reliable old junker had become his trademark. One summer, while home from college between his freshman and sophomore year, he borrowed a neighbor's compressor and paint sprayer and had repainted the pickup red. He left it at the farm when he was on his way to Japan and told his father he would be back to get it in three years.

That evening Eddie cleaned up after supper and drove his old pickup into town. There was a college bar not too far from the University of Northern Colorado campus in Greeley, so he slipped in for a beer and to check things out. That was a mistake. Although Eddie had only been out of college a little over three years, the world was not the same and the student body was not the same. Everyone had long hair and dressed like they were a part of a freak show, at least to Eddie's eyes. He was the only one in the bar with short hair, the only one dressed in trim neat clothing, and the moment he walked in he felt as if he was about twenty years older than this crowd of irresponsible youth. A slovenly young girl walked up to Eddie and stood for a moment looking him over. She was wearing a loosely fitted dress that looked like it had been fashioned from Purina feed sacks. She was braless and her tangled hair hung in formidable globs. She looked worse than the whores in the bars in Angeles City. She had to toss her head several times to keep her dirty mop of hair from blocking her vision. She stood uneasily. As she wobbled she shifted her weight from hip to hip. She was either high on booze or drugs, or both.

"Let me guess?" she pointed her finger at Eddie and he could see her eyes were dilated. "Either you're a narcotics agent, a football player, back from Vietnam, or just a dork."

Eddie hesitated for a minute then answered, "I'm gonna go with the dork option." He did a 180 degree turn and walked out of the bar.

The next place he stopped at was a bar located in a strip of cheap motels and dives that the locals called Garden City. It was a small municipality just south of the Greeley city limits. It had evolved from being the sinner's row when the city of Greeley had been dry and ruled by teetotalers. He stepped into the Lariat Bar and was greeted with a blast of cigarette smoke and country western music. He and the elderly bowlegged bartender, with a cigarette hanging out of his mouth and a worn, weather beaten face, were the only two men in the bar that weren't wearing cowboy hats. Eddie was the only one not wearing cowboy boots. The crowd was mostly men of all ages in their pearl buttoned shirts, but there were a few loose looking women working the crowd.

Eddie didn't wait for the cowboys to size him up. Under his breath he muttered, "I'm a dork." He pulled another 180 and left.

Just like Goldilocks, the third place was just right. It was a local bar in a little farm town of Lucerne, about four or five miles north of Greeley on highway 85. They had a pool table in the back and in addition to serving Coors beer on tap, served great hamburgers and fries. The drinking age in Colorado for 3.2 beer was eighteen, so the bar was filled with locals. They were mostly farm boys that didn't care for the hip scene in nearby Greeley. Eddie spotted a neighbor boy from across the Platte River that he had gone to high school with and started college with. His name was Carl Strup, another German farm boy. He had dropped out of college after his first year to help his dad work the family farm. Eddie knew that was a lie as Carl really dropped out of school because his partying interfered with his will to study. He was intelligent but had flunked out of school because of no discipline. Next to him was another farmer's son he knew from 4-H activities. His first name was Willy but Eddie couldn't remember his last name.

"Eddie!" They were both glad to see him and he was glad to see familiar faces. "I thought you escaped from the farm. You come slumming?" Carl held out his hand and slipped off his bar stool.

Eddie shook Carl's hand and patted his companion lightly on the back. "I came home for some fried chicken, Coors beer, and to see if there's any local honeys who are tired of humping your dead asses."

"How about your next door neighbor, Molly?" Carl's eyes twinkled as he shoved an empty beer pitcher towards the bartender. "Another full one and a glass for my friend."

"She wants more than riding, she wants a ring around her finger and I don't want a ring around my neck," Eddie joked. "I been dodging bullets ever since I been home."

"From what I been hearing on the news, you been dodging bullets in the army also."

"I'm not in the army; I'm in the air force. I only flew airplanes over there and I wasn't stationed in Vietnam."

"Army, air force, what the hell's the difference?" Carl threw his hands up in the air.

"When you're in the air force you don't have to sleep on the ground in the jungle and peel blood sucking leaches off your ass," Eddie explained.

"Whatever the hell you been doing overseas?" Carl continued, "I know you been in some sort of trouble?"

"Nothin I can't handle," Eddie answered and took a big swig from Carl's remaining glass of beer. Eddie hesitated while he looked at the mug of Coors, then he finished it off. Friends can get away with that. With a grin Eddie asked, "What makes you think I've been in some sort of trouble?"

"Feds, government people been asking around about you. They stopped by and talked to my Dad just a couple of days ago. They wanted to know if you ever got into any trouble when you were young and if you had a good character." Carl smiled and joked, "Good thing they didn't ask me cause I would've told them about the time we took the two college girls skinny dipping in Warren Lake."

"I remember that, mine looked like Popeye's girlfriend, Olive, and yours was even worse," Eddie laughed. "Once they took their clothes off, we couldn't get em to put their clothes back on fast enough." Eddie was more than curious, "Ya sure they were government men or are you just pulling one of your usual horseshit jokes?"

"Serious, man, they said they were investigators for some kind of clearance," Carl assured Eddie.

"Of course," Eddie palmed himself on the forehead. "Couple of weeks ago my squadron had me fill out an application for a top secret clearance. I bet that's what they were working on."

"What you doing that ya need a top secret clearance?" Carl looked concerned.

"I'm on my way to be stationed in Vietnam and the airplane I'm flying is some sort of spooky job," Eddie confessed. "I don't have any idea what kind of a mess I'm gonna be involved in. Besides, if I did know I couldn't tell ya anyway."

"Vietnam—Christ! I wish I could have talked to those guys. I could have made up some kind of a story that they would have discharged you." Carl was sincere.

"Thanks a lot, you bastard," Eddie smiled. "You could have gotten me kicked out of the air force. It would have ruined my career and I would have had to come back to Colorado, marry Molly, and farm with my dad. I'd rather go to Vietnam."

"You're gonna get yourself killed," Willy warned.

"If I was gonna get killed I'd been dead a long time ago," Eddie boasted, hoping he was telling the truth. Somehow he felt like a spectator in life and could never really bring himself to the reality that any of this was really happening. Or that he would ever get killed.

"Ok if I marry Molly then?" Carl asked and then laughed. "She's a lot of fine woman just going to waste."

"I'll take your old pickup," Willy put in his two cents worth, and then he smiled. "Least it's already broke in."

"If she'll have your ugly ass, go for it," Eddie addressed Carl and ignored Willy's insinuation. Trash talking girls was what his generation of farm boys did. It made them feel like studs. Eddie, however, felt uncomfortable about the direction their conversation was going. Molly really didn't deserve that kind of trash talk. The new pitcher of beer arrived and it diverted their attention.

After they filled their glasses and all three took a long drag on their beer, Eddie asked, "What's with these college kids now days? I went to the Blue Diamond over at the college campus and I've never seen such a crowd of weirdos in my life."

166

"Just be glad that you got out of there with your life," Willy spoke for the third time. "Now days they got those college kids all worked up over Vietnam and they been blaming it on the soldiers. They'd just as soon spit on someone like you as talk to ya. Most of them are on drugs anyway. They demonstrate and break things up then get pissed at the cops for making em stop. If they would have known you were going to Vietnam, they'd been all over your young ass."

"They just thought I was a dork," Eddie laughed to himself.

"Ya are. You shit head. Just like the rest of us," Carl reassured Eddie. They all laughed.

Eddie was pleased there were still some real people left in the world and had a wonderful evening with his friends. They drank way too much beer. The drive home that night was a little slower than usual. He stayed on the familiar rural back roads as there was no reason to screw up his plans with a DUI.

* *

Eddie worked for his father the next day and spent the evening changing an irrigation set. There was no sign of Molly. The third day he was unable to avoid the neighbors. His mother set up a potluck picnic in the back yard and everyone in the community was invited to see her son home from the army. It was set to start at 11:00 a.m. and it continued well into the day. The men were all busy with their farm work so they just dropped by to say hello and grab a quick bite for dinner. On the farm, dinner was the meal at noon and supper was eaten in the evening—after the cows were milked. The women stayed and gossiped until it was time to go home to milk the cows and do the evening chores. Eddie agonized over all the busy small talk and downplayed where he had been and where he was going—in the army! He was miserable with all the chatter but he was willing to do it for his mother. Molly was there but kept her distance. The whole community of gossips were watching them, like hawks on a telephone wire.

Molly's brothers could handle all the evening chores. So Molly stayed to help his mother clean up the picnic mess, milk the cows, and care for the chickens and hogs. Eddie helped where he could but the two women seemed to ignore him. Then Molly stayed for supper and stayed to help do the dishes. There was no place for Eddie to hide.

After everything was done for the evening, Eddie stood up from the table and volunteered to help his father change the water set. Better to argue with his father than get his foot caught in a trap!

"Nah, I can get it, been doing it myself for three years now. Why don't you kids take the car and go into town and see a movie or something?" He had never been so mellow; it obviously had everything to do with Molly's presence.

Eddie remembered nothing about the movie. Molly insisted they sit in the back row and almost squeezed the blood out of his hand, snuggled, but said nothing. He suspected she was still pissed off about his going to Vietnam, or maybe upset, uptight, or whatever at him because he wasn't responding to her charms. He was never any good at understanding girls. Once, someone had told him that guys thought with logic and women thought with emotion. She was obviously involved with her emotions. She did smell good and looked great. Eddie wondered how someone who milks cows, feeds pigs, and gathers chicken eggs could smell so good. It was one of life's great mysteries. She must be wearing some sort of subtle perfume! After the movie they made the customary stop at the A&W drive in and each had a root beer float. Then Eddie started for home.

Molly had other plans and she looked so good that Eddie gave in. They ended up parked by a gravel pit next to the South Platte River. He knew he shouldn't have agreed, but she smelled so good.

* *

When they were both fourteen years old and it was the annual last day of school picnic at their local Kuner School, Molly and Eddie had just finished their eighth year of school together. While the traditional afternoon baseball game was going on between the remaining adults, those that didn't have field work to accomplish,

Eddie and Molly slipped away from the activities and rode their bicycles a quarter mile to the Platte River Bridge. They followed the side road along the river that led to the weir for the Riverside Irrigation Reservoir. Alongside the road were a number of deep gravel ponds, remnants from the construction of Highway 34. These ponds were fascinating to Eddie and harbored bullhead, catfish, carp, and more excitingly crappie and bluegills for fishing excursions.

It had been a private and secret fantasy for each of them to go skinny dipping together in the remotest of the ponds, the one that was surrounded by dense trees and brush so privacy was guaranteed. Neither knew of the other's fantasy and neither led as they pedaled their bicycles as far as they could, then scrambled through the dense underbrush to emerge at the edge of the deep, cool, inviting waters.

They stood motionless for a minute, each afraid to reveal their deepest secret and urge. What to do next?

"Wanna go swimming?" Eddie cracked the silence with his adolescent voice. Even the birds in the trees and bushes were silent and waiting for what was next.

"I don't have a swimming suit," Molly offered. "But I guess I could go in my underwear."

"That wouldn't work," Eddie rationalized. "When we go back to the school they'll see your underwear is wet, it'll soak through your clothes and they'll know what we did. Maybe we otta go without any clothes on, ya know, skinny dipping." That was all that they needed. Without another word the two teenage best friends stripped naked in front of each other and stood facing each other, their eyes feasting. Eddie experienced an erection and Molly was tickled with delight.

He was delighted with the sight of her adolescent and forbidden fruit. She sported a cute patch of short curly black fuzz. Eddie was as traumatized as he was delighted and her parts were as cute as he had ever imagined. His body had recently been experiencing his first surges of adult testosterone and this was definitely one of those surges. He wanted so badly to touch her privates and ask a thousand questions.

"Come on, let's go swimming," Molly offered as she grabbed him by the hand. The two of them held hands and gingerly shuffled their feet along the sand in the cool deepening water. They giggled like three year olds.

Then the fantasy was over as quickly as it started. The cool water was just up to their personals when they heard laughter and voices in the distance. Some of the other school children were coming to go fishing. Eddie and Molly scrambled to get their clothes on and their composure regained before the others arrived, but it was all in vain. The others had decided to fish in a different pond. They never saw Eddie and Molly as they slipped back to their hidden bicycles and rode back to the school.

* * * * * * * * * * * * * * * * * * * *

That was then, now they were both grown up and both possessed the potential for grown up activities. The car had a bench style front seat and Molly wasted no time and made no effort to hide her intentions. She slid over next to Eddie and embraced him with a wet and hot kiss.

"So much for the possibility of her being pissed," Eddie thought as he returned the favor.

She tasted as good as she felt and before long they were wrapped up rubbing and enjoying each other's offerings, as much as two people with their clothes on could. He'd always wondered if she felt as good as she looked. She did. Without any coaching she deftly slipped open her blouse, undid her bra, and helped Eddie's hand onto one of her bare breasts. It was heaven and Eddie didn't resist. A full moon had recently risen over the plains to the east and its warm light illuminated her brazen display. Her breasts were wonderfully beautiful and her ample nipples were erect and beckoning. Then it was both his hands on her breasts and he felt her working on his pants. He then remembered he didn't have any condoms and if they continued he was about to expose her to pregnancy, the exact thing she probably had in mind. He didn't want to stop. But he had to.

She had his zipper open and was trying to pull his pants down. It's very tough to pull a guy's pants down when he's sitting on them, but she was determined and wasn't about to let such details get in her way. He grabbed her hand and lamented, "Molly, stop! This is the toughest thing I have ever done in my life but we have to stop. I don't have any rubbers and we can't take a chance on getting you pregnant. Unless you're on the pill?"

"Why would I be on the pill?" Molly gasped. "You're the only guy I ever wanted to have sex with and ever since I got puberty you been ignoring me like the plague. I've never screwed anybody before. All I ever wanted was you! Besides, I've wanted to have your baby ever since we were in grade school and I'm running out of time. I'm twenty-four years old and still a god-damned virgin. I love you and I've always loved you and if you don't come home from Vietnam . . . I want your baby to remember you. All I've ever wanted is to marry you, have your babies, and have our own farm."

Then she started crying, which was a big thing for a strong farm girl. All of her years of pent up emotion came out as she sobbed, wailed, and sobbed some more.

Then she realized the reality of what had just transpired. "Oh my God, I'm so embarrassed, will you ever forgive me? I ruined everything. I'm so stupid." She lay down on top of him and sobbed lightly on his shoulder. They embraced and lay together for a long long time. Neither said a word, she was too embarrassed and sorry, Eddie had no idea what to say. Two farm kids that had grown up on farms next door to each other, she was madly in love, he was frightened, and both were in lust. He certainly had feelings for her, but he had just seen her in a horny and out of control frenzy. That old instinct to flee from danger was welling up from deep inside him.

* * * * * * * * * * * * * * * * * * *

The next day Eddie cut hay. He hoped it would help mellow out his father, if that was possible. In addition to sugar beets, barley, pinto beans, and corn, they grew alfalfa for livestock feed. As a result of irrigation they were able to get three hay cuttings per year. They sold the excess as a cash crop. It didn't bring in any big bucks but they could sell a little at a time to people who lived on the outer fringes of Greeley and kept riding horses. They sold their hay for cash and thus avoided paying income taxes. It made nice grocery money. They still used the old fashioned method: Eddie cut the alfalfa with a tractor mounted ten foot sickle bar side cutter. After it was wilted and dried a half day, his father used another tractor and pulled a side-rake to roll the cut and partially dried hay into long narrow rows, called windrows. There it would cure and dry for several more days. Then, when "just right," they would pull a tire mounted baler up and down the rows and package the hay, tied with twine. The fresh cut hay smelled good. A flock of sea gulls followed him up and down the field, catching and eating insects that had been dislodged by his cutting bar. Eddie had no idea where the sea gulls came from or where they spent their winters. They showed up every spring, fed on crickets and grasshoppers in the irrigated fields, spent their nights on the many irrigation reservoirs that dotted the farmland, and disappeared again in the fall. Eddie enjoyed the setting and it gave him a chance to think and evaluate. The one downside was that the sea gulls pooped a lot as they hop skipped around the moving tractor. The drivers always had to use a tractor mounted umbrella when they cut and harvested their alfalfa.

That night Eddie informed his parents he was leaving in the morning to go visit college friends and he was taking his fishing and camping gear. He told them he needed to spend a little time in the mountains.

He raised the subject of hiring Johnnie as a field hand. His mother thought it was a good idea so his dad agreed to call Johnny that evening.

He planned to drive his old Ford pickup but his mother offered the car. She finally conceded because she understood that Eddie had grown up with that old pickup and was fond of it. His mother asked him if he was going to see Molly again and he told her maybe, when he got back from visiting his college buddies. If Molly wanted to see him?—he was just being nice. His father never said a word, except for something in German to his mother. Then he got up from the supper table to spend the rest of the evening in the field setting water. Because speaking German had been very unpopular during World War II, his parents only spoke English to Eddie and never taught him to speak their first language.

The next morning Eddie headed straight for the mountains. He had no intentions of looking up any old college friends. As far as he knew, most of them were probably dope smoking, lice haired beatniks who would hate his guts as a woman and baby killer. He was on the run now, and didn't want any more people experiences. He needed his freedom. He stopped off at Safeway and stocked up on groceries, then drove up the Poudre

169

Canyon, turned right at Chambers Lake, and parked at the trail head for the Rawah Wilderness Area. By noon he was having a sandwich at the 10,000 foot level and looking out over the eastern Colorado plains. The visibility was over hundred miles. He threw several crumbs into the clear bubbling stream, next to his perch, and watched several eight inch brook trout taste and then fight over their new found food. It was a beautiful day. The scattered cumulus clouds were accented by the clear deep blue sky. The sky at higher altitudes was always a deeper and clearer blue. He was sitting at an altitude as high as he ever cruised in the C-124. It was majestic and he was back at home in the sky.

He continued up the steep mountain until about the 10,500 foot altitude. He took the right split in the trail, over a much flatter stretch of tundra above the tree line, through a shallow saddle called Grassy Pass. He ended up in the company of numerous high mountain cirque lakes. They were deep glacial carvings and filled with clear water that was unfrozen for five or six months each year. He worked his way up the timber free hillside and found a magic open spot in the middle of several clumps of stunted willows. He could see to the east, halfway to Kansas, a beautiful fish filled lake below him, wide spread of alpine meadows, and not another human in miles. There were about twenty elk grazing on one of the open meadows and he could hear the tiny pikas in the rock talus slope behind him as they whistled to each other and cut and gathered grass for winter consumption. Two Golden eagles circled in an updraft from the west and everything was perfect for Eddie. He reveled in the pleasure of being a Colorado boy and knowing of such secret places.

It took no time until he was stretched out on top of his sleeping bag and sleeping soundly. The steep climb, the high altitude, and his heavy pack had exhausted him. He was at peace with the world and dreamt he was in a C-124, cruising at low altitude over blue green, turquoise, and dark blue ocean that was dotted with palm covered islands. He could feel the rumble of the 4360 engines, then a loud explosion off to his left. He felt something wet on his face and wondered if he had been hit. He felt the wet with his hand. Was it blood? Then he awoke with a start. He was surprised to be back in Colorado on a mountain side above timberline.

A late day thunderstorm was rolling in over the high peaks to the west and he realized that he was indeed awake . . . in the mountains! The cold wet rain on his face was refreshing and not the blood as he feared, the rumble of the engines had been distant thunder and the explosion had been a nearby lightning strike. It took no time to cover himself and his gear with the large sheet of plastic he brought for such occasions. As he hunkered under the sheet, he set up his fishing gear with a small gold colored mepps spinner. He knew that thunder and rain excited the fish and they would be feeding when the thunderstorm was over.

Eddie made his home at his spot in the high country. He spent his days climbing the rocks and watching the myriad of wildlife that inhabited the alpine during its short summer season. The high, steep mountain sides were home to big horn sheep and beautiful, white mountain goats, in addition to red fox, marmots, pikas, and weasels. Birds included golden eagle, raven, ptarmigan, and over fifty species of tiny summer birds. The tundra flowers were in full bloom, miniature versions of their lowland cousins, and the landscape was raw and pure. He was in photographer's heaven and he was glad he had brought his trusty 35mm camera plus his telephoto lens. "What would he ever do with all those photographs he had taken the past few years?"

The fresh trout, wrapped in aluminum foil and baked in hot coals, were excellent. He even had his daily dose of rice. He had purchased a box of the quick cooking variety because water boils at a much lower temperature at high altitudes. Regular rice took too long to cook. He also brought crackers, hard rolls and a big chunk of cheddar cheese which kept well in the shade and cool nights. And a big bag of trail mix.

He spent a lot of time lying on his sleeping bag and gathering his thoughts. A little weasel, in his reddish brown summer coat, discovered his camp and, having never seen a human before, came curiously close to Eddie. It would sit and watch him for hours. Eddie would have conversations with it and ask it for advice. In return, Eddie received the best advice of all: silence. They shared the cutthroat trout that he hauled from the lake each day. He was finally in the right venue for such thoughts about his pending tour in Vietnam. The possibilities of getting killed or worse like getting crippled or deformed! He wondered where his life and next adventure would take him. But his mission was secret so he had nothing to work with, thus no viable options to consider. He certainly didn't have the epiphany he had hoped for. All he could do was continue looking out the pilot's windshield as if watching television and enjoy the show. With only one channel he was obligated to watch it. It was what he did.

Molly was a tough problem. She was a wonderful, great person and quite attractive. Her brown eyes had a mischievous twinkle, and when not horny, she had a great sense of humor. But she just wasn't the girl for him. She had never even been out of the state of Colorado, only had one year of junior college, and would never be happy away from the farm. She just wouldn't fit into his life style. He had to be careful to walk a fine line between not being mean to an old friend yet not making any commitment. "You can take the farm girl away from the farm, but you can never take the farm out of the girl."

On the fourth day he had his Shangri La invaded by two backpackers as they hiked through the meadow below him. They spotted him by accident when a marmot whistled in the rocks above him and the hikers were searching for it with their binoculars. They studied him for a few minutes, saw he was watching them with his unshaven face from his hidden camp, and they decided he might be trouble. Who else but a weird recluse or a fugitive from the law would hole up like that? All the tourists, the very few that ever troubled themselves to climb the steep trail and venture that deep into the wilderness area, camped beside the lake with brightly colored tents. They were never alone and were noisy most of the time. Eddie was happy when they kept on moving and disappeared over the saddle in the next ridge. There was plenty paradise and seclusion for everyone. There was another set of cirque lakes over there and probably another curious weasel. But they would be noisy, maybe throw rocks at it, and scare it away.

On the evening of the seventh day Eddie drove the sun blistered old Ford pickup back into their family farm yard. He was unshaven and un-bathed. He smelled horrible, a combination of campfire, perspiration, fish, and mountain bog. But he was deliriously refreshed and his mother gave him a big hug. She was a farm woman and was used to bad smells, although she suggested he should shave and take a bath before supper. Eddie's escape plan was all falling into place. His father had hired Johnny, Eddie's mind was fresh, and he was ready to move on. That night at the supper table he informed his folks he had to leave the next day in order to catch his plane overseas. He didn't want them to know he had to first go through training in Louisiana for three weeks. They would have expected him to stop by again on his way westward, and he didn't want to handle another departure from the farm and Molly. His mother expressed sorrow that he couldn't stay any longer and suggested that Eddie should visit Molly that evening. Eddie conceded to his mother's wish. His dad was silent but didn't appear as upset like the previous time he had departed for the military.

* * * * * * * * * * * * * * * * * * * *

When he and his old ford pickup rattled into their farmyard, Molly greeted Eddie with open arms. They hugged in the middle of the farmyard and her parents and two of her brothers came out to say hello and to welcome him back from his visit with his college friends. They were very friendly, had always liked him, and were probably in on the conspiracy to get him and Molly together. After greetings, Molly and Eddie excused themselves from her family and walked back through the complex of corrals and barns where she claimed there were some newborn lambs. Eddie wondered if she had a condom with her and would be so bold as to propose sex in the barn. Then he wondered if she didn't have any condoms with her and would insist on having sex in the barn.

As they rounded the back side of their big barn, the sun was just setting over the mountains to the west and the sky was lit up with patterns of dark blue and pumpkin orange. Molly made her move just as Eddie expected. She pulled him in close, planted a wet kiss on his face and with one arm around his waist and one around his neck, she backed him up against the barn. For a nanosecond he wondered which one of them was the guy? It was a full body press. He didn't resist, there was no harm in sharing the pleasure and as his hands grasped her butt she squealed with approval. She reached down, and as she released her pressure against him and the barn, grabbed his butt with both of her hands.

They started grinding and he moved his right hand back up to cup her left breast. As she pulled back slightly and attempted to reach inside his pants he decided it was time to cool things off. He pulled his mouth free from her tongue attack and opened with his planned speech.

"Molly, we gotta talk. This can't go on any farther."

"I know," she responded apologetically and much to Eddie's relief. "I talked things over with my mother and she told me I was going about this the wrong way. I really do love you and I wanna have your babies and live on a farm and have a family and all that but she said that you gotta get back from Vietnam first." Eddie was pleased. Molly really was a remarkable woman and had just eliminated the need for a large part of his speech."

"I couldn't agree more," he screwed up and hoped he hadn't let his relief show a little too much. "We both got a little crazy . . ."

"Bet ya thought that tonight I was gonna throw you down in the barn and screw your brains out," she remarked and grinned at her proposal as she straightened her blouse out. Their eyes met and he resisted her charm.

"Thought I was a goner," he quipped back with a wide smile. "Ya gotta admit that it would have been good!"

Molly smiled and promised, "Someday I'm gonna screw you until you're too weak to stand up."

"Is that a threat?" Eddie asked with a grin.

"No you idiot." She slapped him crisply on his butt. "It's a promise."

They cuddled and kissed and talked and teased until the sun was gone and the day turned to dark. Then they walked, holding hands, back to Eddie's pickup and he drove home and packed.

CHAPTER FIFTEEN:
THIS HERE'S A GOONEY BIRD

August 18, 1969, Eddie sat in the classroom at England Air Force Base, just outside Alexander, Louisiana. He was wondering what destiny the air force had in mind for him during the next year in Vietnam. There was a scattering of captains wearing pilot's wings, but for the most part the group was made up of fresh young second lieutenants with shiny new wings. They just graduated from pilot training and looked apprehensive and lost. Eddie caught several of them staring at him in his 1505 uniform. Silver first lieutenant bars on his collars, Vietnam Service Medal, Air Medal with multiple clusters, and other miscellaneous "gimmie" medals complemented his deep suntan. The medals were those given to everyone who served instead of running to Canada, but the young lieutenants didn't know that. He stood out from all the others in the room as an obvious fresh returnee from Vietnam. He felt a little conspicuous and admittedly a little proud.

A rough looking master sergeant entered the air conditioned room and stood behind the pedestal. He was wearing a set of long sleeved camouflage fatigues with an air commando patch on his right sleeve. He wore cloth aircrew wings over his left breast pocket. His name tag said Crocket. His rank was displayed in stripes on his long sleeves. The sleeves covered what Eddie imagined was an ugly mass of thick hairy arms crawling with muscle. A special forces beret sat cocked on his head and his pants were bloused into a pair of camouflage jungle boots. Bulging with muscles and four rows of medals, he stood staring at the fresh meat and looked as if he had recently finished eating a bowl of freshly caught rats and iron nails. Eddie had seen his type on the other side of the globe and he wondered what the new lieutenants were thinking.

"Genamen, my names Sergeant Crocket and ah'm with the 4412 CCTS, under command of the 1st Commando Air Wing. I'm here to teach you how to fly the C-47, hereafter to be called the 'Gooney Bird.'" He spoke with a heavy, deep, southern accent and the new group, including Eddie, was ready to believe everything he had to say. To disagree would be to risk unthinkable physical violence. "Some of you are going to the AC-47 gunship and some of you are going to the EC-47. Don't you EC pilots sweat any bullets, we ain't gonna make air commandos out of you. Our job here is to just teach y'all how to fly the Gooney Bird. The AC-47 gunship guys will go on to attend a course at Hurlburt Field in Florida on how to shoot sidewise out of a moving aircraft. You EC types will go directly to Vietnam and receive on the job training on whatever the hell it is that EC-47s do. Don't ask me or anyone else on this base what EC-47s do because they either don't know or won't tell. It's secret. We haven't had to shoot anyone yet so don't go asking questions and be the first. You'll find out soon enough." Eddie looked around and noticed that everyone was looking around. Not a word was said.

The "no shit" sergeant distributed C-47 manuals and the class commenced with a nostalgic history lesson by the sergeant. Eddie had been waiting for him to tell them, "I could train monkeys to fly airplanes, but the air force insisted I use officers. I still got only a limited amount of bananas for training each pilot, and if you use up your quota of bananas and haven't passed the course, you're gonna be washed out." That had been Eddie's introduction during his first day in basic pilot training in Arizona—a long time ago.

"The C-47 Gooney Bird got its start as the civilian DC-3 passenger plane built by Douglas Aircraft, starting in nineteen thirty-eight," Sergeant Crocket started out. "When World War II came along the military had a huge demand for a reliable transport aircraft that could operate in and out of relatively short and rough airfields. The DC-3 had already established itself as a rugged and reliable airline transport and was a favorite of the civilian pilots, so it was selected for military utilization. The fuselage and floor were strengthened, a large two part door was added to accommodate paratroopers and larger cargo, and a rugged utility interior was created to replace the plush airline interior. The C-47 Dakota, as the military version was called, retained the same reliable and efficient Pratt and Whitney engines, fabric control surfaces, graceful lines, and angelic flight characteristics of the civilian DC-3. By the end of the war, 10,692 C-47s had been built in the United States.

"Just before World War II, the Russians imported twenty-one DC-3s from the United States and they copied the design, rivet for rivet, built their own engines, and from 1939 to 1952 they built a total of 6157 DC-3 copies. They were called the Lisunov Li-2. During World War II their Li-2s were used for the same military purposes as our C-47s. After the war the Russian production lines built them for use as domestic airliners. Douglas never collected a dime in license fees from the Russians.

"The Gooney Bird is named after a bird that lives on Pacific Ocean islands. The professors call it an Albatross and everyone else calls it a Gooney Bird. It's extremely awkward on the ground but a picture of grace and aerodynamics once airborne. After the war, surplus C-47s were snatched up and converted into airliners and freight haulers. Those retained by the American military served faithfully during peacetime military operations, the Korean War, and were still flying in reduced numbers when the Vietnam War heated up."

Sergeant Crocket strutted back and forth and pounded his right fist into his left hand as he spoke, "The military has used the aircraft for a multitude of modifications and missions. They even mounted pontoons on several aircraft so they could be operated off water. So when the call came out for an aircraft test bed to experiment with the radical new idea of shooting machine guns, bolted to the floor, firing out the side windows, controlled with a remote switch from the cockpit while flying a precise pylon circle around a ground target, the faithful Gooney Bird was used. The testing was very successful and the AC-47 gunship evolved and is in service in Vietnam still today. Everyone calls it Puff, the Magic Dragon, because Hollywood made a movie about it. Unknown to most, the C-47 was also developed into the very secret EC-47 many of you will be flying. All I can tell you is that EC stands for Electronic Countermeasures."

After the first day of class, Eddie and a young lieutenant he had just met walked out to the flight line and strolled along the row of sleek C-47s. The aircraft had all returned from the daily flight lessons they were used for. They were shiny, silver aluminum with white paint trim. They were clean and beautiful but so very small compared to the C-124. They were so very big for the second lieutenant that had joined Eddie in his walk. The lieutenant was used to the tiny T-38 at pilot training and was still in shock over getting assigned to a World War II transport. It was hot and humid in northern Louisiana and the sun was low in the sky. Grackles were fighting for the best insects on the concrete ramp and Eddie missed the tropics he had recently left. Neither flyer spoke. They had their hands in their pockets, something one wasn't supposed to do when in uniform. But it helped them to think and wonder what was in store for them on the other side of the world. The new lieutenant had a lot of questions for Eddie.

 Compared to what the C-124 had been, the classroom phase for the C-47 was a breeze for Eddie. The C-47 only had two engines and weighed roughly six times less than the C-124. All the systems, electrical, hydraulic, and fuel were extremely simple to learn and use. The new lieutenants, fresh out of jet training, complained about everything. They called the airplane an old clunker, a speed bump. Eddie just laughed at them and joked about the "Antique Airlines" nose patch he had seen on a C-47 at Danang.

The old master sergeant instructor took their remarks much more seriously. He told them, "Hold your tongues, the Gooney Bird is the best damn aircraft ever built. You need to show some respect, and once you've learned to taxi the tricky tail wheel with proficiency, learned to land in a thirty-five knot crosswind, and have one bring your young whiny ass home when it's full of bullet holes, then and only then can you bitch if you want to. I've never known a pilot that didn't love the old bird once he learned to fly it and know it."

The flying phase of their training started with several interesting twists: the normal crew was two pilots and a flight engineer sitting in the jump seat. The pilots had all the necessary switches and gauges in the front of the cockpit and they started the engines and made all the power changes. They did everything as if the flight engineer didn't exist. The flight engineer had no panel and almost nothing to do but to watch and assure the pilots didn't make any fatal mistakes. It was a good idea in a training bird but the instructor told Eddie that, "In Nam, some squadrons don't take flight engineers along because they need the weight allocation for extra fuel."

Also, the second lieutenants had problems starting the C-47's two radial engines. Much smaller than the giant twenty-eight cylinder 4360s on the C-124, the C-47 engines had only fourteen cylinders. Fewer cylinders meant far fewer moving parts and thus a vast increase in reliability. The C-47 engines, Pratt and Whitney 1830-90C Wasp engines, however, still maintained the cantankerous and sensitive starting characteristics of all radial aircraft engines. For pilots who had never flown a radial engine aircraft, this caused more than a little frustration. The hot shot, new jet trained pilots were humbled and frustrated.

Eddie's ears were tuned to the sounds of radial engines starting and he caught on to the C-47 engines' minor eccentricities quickly. Although they had fewer cylinders and were considerably smaller in size, Eddie was pleased when he started up his first C-47 engine. It had a similar deep throated, nostalgic cough, flub cough flub flub dub when coming alive that had mesmerized him in the C-124s.

The second twist was the taxiing. The C-47 was a tail wheel aircraft. Taxiing an airplane with a tail wheel, a free rotating tail wheel with no steering ability, is at first a very frustrating experience. To steer the aircraft on the ground, the pilot used combinations of differential braking, operated by depressing the tops of the left and right rudder pedals, and differential power from the aircraft's two wing mounted engines. C-47 propellers did not go into reverse. In a Gooney Bird, there was no such thing as a ground steering wheel, called a tiller in an aircraft. On the ground the tail wheel pivoted freely and was perfectly willing to go anywhere the front of the airplane wanted to go. Only the tail wheel, if the pilot wasn't careful, would frequently try to get there first. The pilot had to be alert at all times and anticipate the tail's actions. Their instructor told them to "just act as if there was a set of sensors in your seat cushion and every time the sensors detected that the muscles in your butt were relaxed, it sent a signal to the tail wheel to spin the aircraft around. Stay alert and tense."

The awkward method of steering led to some wild taxiing gyrations. The instructor pilots insisted that each new pilot have a minimum of two hours of taxi practice, straight lines, turns, and figure eights, before they would trust the new pilots to attempt the higher speed take-off runs and landing-rolls. The taxi practice was conducted on a very large and empty concrete ramp, so the fledgling Gooney Bird pilots weren't a threat to other aircraft or vehicles. After a day starting the engines and taxi practice, without achieving the proficiency required for actually flying the aircraft, Eddie shared beers that night with some very discouraged and humbled second lieutenants. He too had to learn the tricky taxi maneuvers.

The second day went well, and after another round of taxi practice all but three in the class were approved for flight. Eddie got his turn to fly the nostalgic grand old lady. The tail wheel was locked in the straight forward position after the aircraft was lined up on the runway for take-off. The tail wheel was unlocked after landing at the end of the landing roll and before exiting the runway. But the aircraft was still a challenge to "herd" down the runway. The steering practice came in handily as he followed the runway center line for 1500 feet then lifted gracefully into the air. There were no stopwatches or other callouts, it was just very simple: apply power, use rudder and a little differential brake if necessary to steer, accelerate, push the tail off with a little forward yoke, then ease back and the earth falls away. For Eddie it was like flying a little Piper Cub when compared to the C-124. The air work maneuvers and practice approaches were a snap; the aircraft had no bad characteristics and was steady as a rock. It didn't take him long to fall in love with his new little bird. Eddie still wondered what an EC-47 did for a living but knew not to ask.

CHAPTER SIXTEEN: NAKED FANNY

The United Airlines DC-8 made a long, low, slow, straight-in approach into Tan Son Nhut airport, located outside Saigon, Vietnam. As Eddie looked out the left passenger window, watching for gunfire from below, the thoughts of that C-133's belly stitched with bullet holes were still fresh in his mind. The smunch smunch of the main tires told him all was well and he held onto the armrest as the pilot threw the jet's engines into reverse thrust mode. With heavy braking they slowed to a walking pace, then made a left turn onto the taxiway. Eddie again looked out the window and saw they were passing a row of camouflaged UC-123K "Ranchhand" spray planes. They passed the freight ramp. It was less than half full of various freighters unloading pallets of cargo. Not a C-124 was in sight and they taxied up to the dilapidated ex-hangar they called the passenger terminal. He had a strange warm feeling about the familiar scene outside his window. He was glad to be home again and he smiled to himself.

He had been required to attend the Air Force Jungle Survival School at Clark Air Force Base before reporting for duty at Tan Son Nhut. Snake School, as the veterans called it, was a requirement for all air force crew members assigned to fly combat duty in the Vietnam War. Somehow, the C-124 crewmembers in the 22nd hadn't been included in that requirement, so this time around Eddie had to spend his turn in the barrel. The first half of the school was academic and they ended classes every day at 4:30. This allowed Eddie to re-visit his old haunts and he spent several evenings sitting on the front steps of the officers club. He even attended several sessions at the happy hour bar. But without the 22nd guys around, it just wasn't the same. He felt like a lost puppy, waiting for someone he knew to come along, but it never happened. He really didn't feel like visiting the Oasis Hotel to see if Vicky was surviving the 22nd's absence.

The second half of the school was a trip to the boondocks and four nights of camping and moving through the dense jungle with a Negrito guide and instructor. Their minimal gear consisted of a waterproof poncho, a small bag of rice, and a machete. The tiny black jungle inhabitant was a master of living off the land, eating native plants and fruit, and camouflaging himself. Eddie was fascinated by the instruction. The conclusion of the course was a mock escape and evasion exercise. The Americans were given a three hour head start. They had maps marked with a twelve square mile designated parcel of jungle they had to escape and hide in. Then the Negritos were turned loose to find them. Each American was to use his individual skills and recent classroom training to escape getting caught. If they weren't caught during a twelve hour period, they had theoretically escaped and were to walk back to the camp. If they were caught by a Negrito, they were considered captured and executed by the enemy. Each captured American had to give up a green chit that each of them was issued. The green chits were good for a fifty pound bag of rice so the Negritos were all very motivated.

Eddie took this exercise as a personal challenge. He spent his three free hours working his way deeply into the jungle, eventually finding the spot he was looking for: a tiny gully, washed out by some past deluge. It was about two feet wide and several feet deep and filled with tree leaves and other debris. It hadn't rained in a week and the duff was almost dry. He cleaned out a section of the gully, slightly longer than his body, and lined the damp bottom of the gully with his poncho. He then lay down on the poncho and folded it over himself. He pulled the dry debris over the top and settled down for a nice long sleep. He felt very confident.

After about three hours he was awakened by something small rustling in the leaves. It didn't sound like human footsteps but maybe some sort of an animal. Very slowly he raised his head and peaked through his covering. The biggest rat he had ever seen was sitting on his chest and was looking him right in the eyes. They had discussed jungle rats in the classroom. The instructor said they were easy to lure with food scraps and if killed with a stick made a nourishing meal. The instructor also had emphasized to them that it was vital that they kept themselves clean, especially their fingers, when sleeping. As long as they were clean the rats would normally not bite into human live flesh. The rats were scavengers just looking for scraps. Eddie had taken this to heart and he was, except for the usual sweat in the hot humid jungle, clean.

He slowly let his head down and remained motionless. He practiced the discipline that he had recently been lectured about in the survival classroom. The rat searched around for about another ten minutes, found nothing to eat, then moved on. Eddie was quite proud of himself and after making sure he was again completely covered, he went back to sleep.

More hours passed until he was again awakened. He heard human footsteps in the forest litter and he assumed it was a Negrito hunter. He was perfectly quiet and calm as he lay there. The Negrito would step over him. It was natural for a human to step over a very narrow gully. Eddie thought he was so clever!

The next thing he knew was that he was being poked by a stick and a Negrito kept repeating, "You give me chit, GI. I get rice and you get play dead."

The jig was up and Eddie sat up, emerging from his debris cover. He handed his green chit to the Negrito and while he was knocking the leaves from his clothing asked, "How did you find me? I was completely covered up."

"You stink, GI. Americans eat lots of meat and it makes them stink. I just smell you and follow my nose."

This had a very disturbing effect on Eddie as he trudged his way back to camp and joined the other "dead" airmen. They all exchanged similar notes. Eddie vowed he would shower before every mission, always wear a freshly washed flight suit, wear no cologne, use unscented deodorant, and above all eat less red meat.

Within six hours the local Negrito tribe caught all the American evaders with ease. The captured crewmembers were declared alive again and were plucked from the jungle with a mock rescue. A CH-3 rescue helicopter with a dangling rescue hook pulled them out of the jungle, one by one. As he was hoisted free of the trees, Eddie glanced at the thick jungle below him and up at the hovering whirlwind machine. He could see the open door and the burly crewmember waiting to pull him inside. To a downed crewmember, this would be better than winning the lottery. No wonder the fighter pilots would let rescue helicopter crewmembers sit with them at the bar and wouldn't allow the rescue guys to pay for their own drinks.

* * * * * * * * * * * * * * * * * * *

Most of the passengers on board the DC-8 had flown all night and everyone on the aircraft was dead tired. Eddie had been boarded after they refueled at Clark and therefore was rested and unwrinkled. After they deplaned at Saigon, there was no rest for anyone. They picked out their luggage from the baggage carts, loaded into buses, and were transported to another hangar for in-processing. Arrows split the mass into army, air force, navy, and other. Additional arrows split the air force group into enlisted and officers. Eddie dumped his bags into the appropriate pile and took his place in line. He was sweating. The un-air-conditioned building was stifling. He tried to remember why he had been so glad to see Vietnam again.

"Next," an airman second class motioned Eddie. It was the third line he had stood in and hopefully the last processing desk he had to endure before he was officially in Vietnam. Eddie handed his packet of personnel papers to the airman and looked around the depressing scene. Apparently they wanted to process and get the new arrivals on their way to their respective units as fast as possible. Large crowds every day in the same hangar would certainly be a good target for Viet Cong rockets, despite the fact that they seldom hit what they were aiming for.

"Sir," the airman broke Eddie's trance. "How many days leave do you have coming? It seems your last unit didn't fill it in on your form."

It was a gift from the master sergeant back at what had been the 22nd MAS. He had given Eddie his option. "I don't know," Eddie wondered out loud. "Very little. I used most of it up, I took four weeks several months ago and I took thirteen days while I was back in the States."

The sweaty airman looked up from his desk, eyed the Vietnam Service Medal on Eddie's uniform, and gave him a funny look. "Sir, this is Vietnam and we're all getting screwed here. I see that this is your second go around. Guys are dying. You're an Officer. Are you sure you aren't a little smarter than that?" Then he winked.

Eddie smiled back. "Let me think, I remember now. I have sixty days coming."

The airman faked a serious look and made the entry, folded the papers, slid them into Eddie's manila envelope and handed it back to him. "That's what I thought, Sir." They both grinned at the fact that they had just stuck it, although just a little thing, to the man. "That desk over there," he pointed to yet another line that Eddie hadn't visited, "Is where you gotta go next. Good luck, Sir, I see you're going to Naked Fanny. Kiss a Thai girl for me. It'll bring me good luck." Eddie had no idea what the airman was talking about!

* * * * * * * * * * * * * * * * * * * *

Again Eddie felt and heard the pilot pull the power off as he rounded out and the main wheels smunched onto the runway. This time he had no windows to look out. The air force C-130 freighter had been converted into a half passenger/half small freight affair and was called the Klong Courier. It flew clockwise from the Don Muong International Airport, Bangkok's civilian airport, to the six American Air Force operations in Thailand. They were located on American-built Royal Thai Air Force Bases (Takhli, Udorn, Nakhon Phanom, Upon, Karat, and U-Tapao). A second Klong Courier flew the route in reverse every afternoon. Klong was the Thai name for the filthy, stagnant canals of water that provided small boat transportation networks in Thai cities and villages. In early Bangkok, klongs were a substitute for streets and responsible for Bangkok's title as the Oriental Venice. In the sixties and seventies, klongs were slowly filled in and replaced with streets. In some areas where there was enough space, klongs and streets ran parallel and shared the same right of away. In addition to transportation, klongs provided a swimming area for young children, an open sewer system, and provided food with abundant catfish like critters and various edible water plants. The locals seemed immune to disease from the klongs but it promised instant diarrhea and worse for any GI who was exposed to the water. In the hot humid climate the klongs saturated the area with a heavy pungent smell that the locals never noticed and the Americans learned to tolerate.

Eddie had spent the previous night in Vietnam, in a sparsely furnished, open bay, non air-conditioned barracks. He tried not to complain, took a shower, and slept lightly. The next morning he was onboard an American C-118 transport flight from Saigon's Tan Son Nhut airport to Bangkok. There he connected with the Klong Courier. After an up and down uncomfortable series of short flights he was at his destination. The noisy C-130 didn't bother to shut down its engines on the ramp. The pilots just set the brakes, neutralized their spinning propellers thrust angle (flat beta) and the loadmaster lowered the rear ramp. Eddie and his bag were dumped onto the ramp, along with three bags of mail, an armed courier who was carrying a briefcase handcuffed to his wrist, and several hundred pounds of boxed freight.

The C-130's loading ramp was lifted and closed behind him and he leaned into the gust of wind as the pilot released his brakes, rotated his jet powered propeller blades into the forward thrust position and started rolling. As the prop wash increased, Eddie knelt and covered his head and hung on to his loose hat. The C-130 taxied away from the concrete ramp and towards the end of the runway. As quickly as it started the prop wash was gone. He looked up and saw a single engine Pilatus Porter parked in front of a tidy, small, wooden, brown base operations building. On the sides of the weird looking aircraft were the words "Air America." There was a civilian wearing khaki shorts, khaki tee shirt, and short clunky boots, carefully inspecting the Porter. The single engine Swiss built Pilatus Porter looked like a deformed abortion but was able to haul a heavy load and take-off or land on a 300 foot runway. Emphasis, 300 feet long, not wide!

The edges of the small airfield were ringed with tall jungle and as if on cue, a flight of three noisy squawking, multicolored birds flew across the ramp. It was as if those birds followed him around, everywhere he went. Maybe they were serving as vehicles for unknown gods or spirits? Why him? There were noisy birds present from the get go, that first morning when he was five years old and received his calling from the yellow bi-wing crop sprayer.

A van was waiting for the courier, the mail, and the freight, but as they loaded no one offered Eddie a ride. That was okay. He needed to get his bearings and he had no idea where to go anyway. The small base operations building was within easy walking distance. Eddie sat his bags down and his ears were still ringing from the four turboprop engines' heavy piercing whine. Then, as the van pulled away he was left standing alone on the ramp. He had his first look at what was to be his home for the next year.

Somehow, back in Vietnam, he had been requisitioned and re-routed to Nakon Phanom in Thailand. He wasn't going to live in Vietnam after all! Naked Fanny, as it was affectionately nicknamed by its American inhabitants, was officially named Nakhon Phanom Royal Thai Air Force Base. It was frequently referred to as the best kept secret of the war. On the Thailand side of the Mekong River that served as the Laotian-Thailand border, this hush hush American operation was off limits to the news media. It provided the Americans with a private back door to Laos. It was also the closest American base to Hanoi, the capital of North Vietnam—257 statute miles and thirty minutes by jet. It served as a primary recovery runway for shot up aircraft that were in trouble as they returned from their bombing forays into North Vietnam. The air force normally referred to it as NKP. Along with the other bases in Thailand that were constructed by the Americans, NKP had a Thai Base Commander with a small staff of Thai assistants. The rest, with the exception of the Thai soldiers that shared guard duty with American air policemen, were all Americans.

As Eddie looked across the concrete ramp he saw numerous protective revetments sheltering two squadrons of single engine A-1 fighters. They looked like something just out of World War II, but Eddie knew that the "Spads" hadn't gone into production until just after that war. They had been the workhorses of the Korean War, with their awesome bomb loads, eight hour endurance, and wing mounted machine guns. They were the first to score a kill against the Russian MIGs during the Vietnam War. With their slower speed and deadly accuracy they were the favorite support aircraft for the ground troops. With a single radial piston engine, four bladed propellers, wings loaded with a mixture of bombs, camouflage paint jobs, just sitting on the ground they just looked like death and destruction. Eddie had already seen them drop their bombs accurately. It was during the Tet Offensive when the Danang Air Base had been under a mortar attack.

Parked in one corner of the ramp were four of the ugliest airplanes Eddie had ever seen in his life. They were AC-119 gunships with a call sign of Stinger. They were old flying boxcar C-119 twin boomed, twin engine, cargo aircraft that had been given extra power with the addition of a J-85 jet engine under each wing. The jet engines augmented the thrust provided by an R-3350 radial engine on each wing. Holes had been cut on the left side of their fuselages and protruding out were four 7.62 mini-guns and 22mm cannons. The pilot circled his target and used high tech gun sights for aiming their massive firepower. It was similar to the AC-47 "Puff" gunship but more high tech and had more firepower. The planes were painted dull black as their missions were flown at night. The aircraft had a 1.5 million candlepower spotlight but it was seldom used. It pinpointed their position for the enemy and made them sitting ducks for gunfire from the ground. Eddie scanned the rest of the ramp and picked out a squadron of C-123 freighters and further down the ramp he saw a row of large dull black helicopters, without any markings. Everything had propellers. It was definitely Eddie's kind of airport.

At NKP there was no sickening smell of jet fuel, only fresh clean air. It was quiet. There was no aircraft activity, as if everyone was having a mid-day siesta. The setting was complete, Eddie was home again. He had been assigned to a small detachment of five EC-47 aircraft and in the far corner of the ramp sat three EC-47s. The other two were out working the morning shift across the Mekong River, somewhere in Laos. When it was time for the two morning birds to head back to NKP, two more would launch and cover the afternoon shift. These were not the slick winged silver and white beauties Eddie had flown at the training base in Louisiana, or the occasional DC-3 airliners he had seen during his college age ventures through flying magazines and books. These were stunning. These were special birds for a special mission.

Looking very much at home in the jungle setting, they had camouflage paint jobs, nose art painted below each cockpit window and covered with an array of different types and sizes of antennas. Their rear troop doors had been removed to save weight and to provide better ventilation for the backend crewmembers and their electronic equipment. The engines had been replaced with larger, more powerful versions. The aircraft looked like combat, mean and sinister, squatting there on the ramp in defiance to an unseen enemy. Armed guards were posted to assure no unauthorized personnel could approach as a handful of shirtless mechanics busily performed maintenance on the sister aircraft.

The EC-47 on the left had the number 304 painted on its tail. It was 1969 and she was in her third war, full battle dress, and twenty-eight years old. What a gorgeous aircraft she was! Below the cockpit's side window was a nose art painting of the same woman, in the same pose, that he had seen on the back wall of the stag bar at Willy. Eddie was frozen beyond belief for a moment; his eyes were wide open, mouth hanging open, and his arms dangling lifeless at his sides. Under the painting was her name: The Lady. He had the feeling he'd just met his soul mate. What a Grand Old Lady she was. Eddie's knees were getting weak and he felt faint. She was an airplane! His secret quest was an airplane! Or was there more to the story? Where did the inspiration for the nose art come from?

It was well over one hundred degrees Fahrenheit on the ramp and the humidity was well over ninety percent. Maybe the heat was playing tricks on his mind and he was just hallucinating all of this. As he stood on the white concrete in the glaring hot sun, a cold chill ran down his back and he shivered.

The place and the aircraft were for real and he was all by himself, alone at this place. He knew no one and had no clue about his assignment or even where to go. When standing on the North Pole there is nowhere to go but south, all directions lead south. For him the only way to go was into his future, but where?

* *

"You're gonna get run over, standing out here in the middle of the ramp." Eddie was jolted back to reality by a voice behind him. He turned and sized up a first lieutenant with wild red hair, riddled with freckles, light sunburned skin, and a mischievous smile. He was of average build and wore an air force issue watch and sunglasses. He had on a dark green nomex flight suit with the name O' Leary and wore his silver first lieutenant rank on his shoulders. There were no other markings and no unit patches. Hanging from an open side pocket was an officer's folding hat, wrinkled and dirty, which gave Eddie good vibes. The hat was wrinkled and dirty and the guy wasn't wearing it! Good also because he wasn't wearing a hot, brightly colored neck scarf.

"I got orders to report to Detachment 1 of the 360th Tactical Electronic Warfare Squadron," Eddie opened with a measured, nonchalant manner. He didn't want to show his heightened emotion over the recent and earthshaking discovery of his long sought for Lady. He needed time to think and absorb what was going on. "You know anything about them?"

"Not much," the redheaded lieutenant replied. "I'm a flight instructor for them . . . But I really don't know a whole hell of a lot."

"I'm not so smart myself," Eddie countered and held his ground. "Else I wouldn't be at this god forsaken place with you." The two lieutenants shook hands, smiled, and hit it off. Eddie picked up his single piece of luggage and asked the red haired spectacle, "Got any shade around here, and maybe a beer? I been traveling for two days and my ass is really dragging."

The redheaded lieutenant motioned with his head and the two of them set off across the ramp.

"How about we drop your bag off at my room?" He was a talker. "Then we can go to our Hooch and have a few brewskys with the guys. Later in the day we usually sit out on the patio and have a few beers and watch the air show as the guys come home from work across the river." He nodded his head in the direction of the Mekong River and Laos. "It's kind of a thing we do cause there isn't anything else to do on our days off. The OV-10s, their call sign is Nails, are the fanciest cause their airplanes are acrobatic. They fly OV-10 spotter aircraft. As they come back across the river, which is the border of Laos, each pilot shows off as he strives for the perfect pitchout, turn to final approach and a perfect landing. They know everyone is watching. Or maybe they do it cause they're elated that they didn't get their asses shot off. Hell, I don't know. That's just what everyone does. Our Gooney Birds are clumsier, but we also try for perfection. It's an okay air show, I guess. It's the only one we got." And Eddie thought that girls talked a lot.

"I really otta find my outfit first," Eddie resisted. "I gotta find a place to sleep tonight and I should report to my unit so they know that I'm here."

"Don't worry," the redheaded lieutenant continued as if Eddie hadn't spoken. "You're rooming with me. My old room-mate left for the States four days ago. My name's Dubhan O'Leary, everybody calls me Red. We're in the same unit. The colonel sent me over to see if you were on the Klong, but it's too late to do anything today." It was only 1:30 in the afternoon but Eddie didn't say anything.

"Tomorrow we'll find someone over at the hooch to show you our operations building and get you squared away." Red looked at Eddie and grinned, "Oh, by the way, welcome to the Towheads. That's our call sign. Our detachment's emblem is a cartoon Gooney Bird with a head full of billowing blond hair and an electrical cord trailing out its butt. Everyone on the base calls us the electric goons."

The quarters were surprisingly nice. The Towheads occupied a long, single story, wooden building that stood several feet off the ground on concrete pillars. It was a long row of rooms, motel style, with two officers to a room. Towhead Towers was painted in large attractive lettering at each end of the building and each door had a circular wooden plaque on it that displayed a silhouette of a Gooney Bird. Each door opened outside, onto an elevated sidewalk. In the center of the building was a commons room with showers, heads, urinals, and several washing machines for the maids. The Towhead Towers formed one side of a compound. On the other side of the compound was another building, another long row of rooms. The two buildings faced each other and in the center was an open commons, about 150 feet across. The other building was occupied by the Nails, the pilots that flew the OV-10 spotter planes. The brownish red stain on the wooden buildings blended beautifully with the lush vegetation found everywhere. There were clumps of banana trees and wide leaved jungle plants that would cost a fortune in a greenhouse in Colorado. For a military base, very close to a war zone, the setting was surprisingly tranquil and attractive.

A four ship formation of A-1s, their props in perfect harmony, passed overhead and pitched out in rapid, perfectly spaced, succession for their landing. They were the first aircraft movement since Eddie arrived. They were low enough that Eddie could see their bomb racks were empty.

Between the two rows of quarters, the flyboys had built an additional building from supplies scrounged from the base engineers. This wooden structure had two rooms and an outside wooden patio. It was called the Towhead Inn, sometimes called the Hooch, and was shared mutually by the Towheads and the Nails. One of the rooms was used as a lounge, with unmatched and worn sofas, coffee tables, and a great assortment of *Playboy*, *Time*, and *Outdoor Life* magazines. There was also a mix of twenty or thirty paperback books. It was a good place to hang out if you were tired of your room-mate. Considering the missions and being gone from home, sometimes having a place to be alone and have time to think was a nice thing.

The other room was the saloon. It had a roughly constructed wooden bar that spanned the entire east side of the room, and an assemblage of mismatched stools and chairs to accommodate its patrons. A noisy clanking air conditioner had been installed in a hole cut into the west wall. The west side, facing the Towhead Towers, also had a window, somewhat dirty, no curtains, but a window nevertheless. The walls supported a tacky set of shelves that contained a collection of wood carvings and other cheap local trinkets. There was also a huge life sized poster of Raquel Welsh entertaining the troops on a makeshift USO stage, a velvet painting of a nude Thai girl poised in an open C-47 door, a dart board, and a painted panel that contained the names of every pilot and navigator that had served in the year old Towhead EC-47 detachment. A heavy, twelve inch tall, wooden carving of a hand giving the finger served as a door stop between the saloon and the lounge. The dominant feature, however, was a beautifully carved wooden replica of an EC-47, with a five foot wingspan. It hung from the ceiling in the center of the saloon. It was perfect in every detail, including a vast array of antennas. It had camouflage paint and on each side of its nose was a painting of a multicolored butterfly, appropriately named the Iron Butterfly. Its heavy statement, along with the name of Towhead Inn, may have contributed to the Nails dislike of the Towheads. The Towheads dominated the saloon and the Nails were treated as second class citizens, which was an uncommon flip flop of the air force pecking order.

The Thai civilian bartender, Loat San, worked evenings and during the day the bar was self serve. There was a coffee can for money. Loat San was slightly built, about 120 pounds, which was average for Thai men. He was dark skinned and very clean. He always dressed in loose short sleeved shirts that hung out over his loose trousers and his thick black hair was cut short. His English was fair, he always smiled, and everyone liked him

The two groups, Towheads and Nails, mixed about as well as oil and water. Neither was allowed to discuss their classified missions in the presence of anyone outside their own unit. As far as the Nails knew, the Towheads just flew around and listened to the radio. The Nails flew their missions flying low and trying to seek out enemy movements. Needless to say they got shot at a lot and they wasted no time letting the Towheads know about it. The Nails laid it on thick whenever an opportunity arose, macho jibes and putdowns, degrading remarks about the Gooney Bird, anything to agitate the Towheads whose tongues were tied. Despite verbal onslaught, the Towheads stuck together and dominated the Towhead Inn. The Nails frequently visited the neighboring A-1 bar. As they shared common missions of guns and bombs, they could talk more openly with each other.

Eddie relaxed on the patio with the other Towheads who were off for the day but he was unable to prompt any conversation about their mission. Red explained the monsoon seasons to Eddie: sunny mornings and heavy rains almost every afternoon from April to October. From November through March it only rained occasionally. It was late September and they were in the second half of the wet season. They were having one of the rare monsoon season days that it wasn't raining.

As the sun lowered in the west, the airplanes came home to roost. The Towhead EC-47s, one at time, made their way back from Laos and their secret snooping. They turned forty-five degree bank angle turns into their downwind leg while their security service "radio operators" (ROs) in the back put the finishing touches to their day's intelligence reconnaissance reports. Radio Operators was the generic name for everyone in the 6994th Security Squadron who rode in the backend of the EC-47s. The more maneuverable A-1 Skyraiders and OV-ten Broncos flew crisp ninety degree bank turns and displayed expert airmanship as they returned from search and bombing missions along the Ho Chi Minh Trail.

As the day turned to dark they could hear other aircraft on the ramps, taxiing and running up in preparation for their departure into the night. These were the night fighters. There were all black A-1 Skyraider bombers, nick named Spads, departing on who knew what secret missions they would perform. A handful of C-123s cargo planes took off into the darkening night and Eddie wondered why freight aircraft would fly only at night. Next was the strained roar of the AC-119 gunships on their way to attack truck traffic on the Ho Chi Minh Trail. They could hear the approaching gunship's reciprocating engines. As the aircraft passed by the sounds of the two auxiliary jet engines became the dominating sound. It was impossible to hide the gunships' purpose and mission. They were big ugly mothers, painted black, with six nasty guns sticking out of their left sides. With their heavy loads of ammunition and fuel, they were ready to rain death and destruction on the tiny Vietnamese truck drivers from the north.

NKP had a daily routine. They flew two shifts, one set of workers flew during the day and the other set flew at night. Each group flew their assigned missions, exchanged wits and ordinance with highly skilled opponents, then returned to their oasis and enjoyed comfort and luxury at their base. The aircrews had air-conditioned rooms, maid service, officer and enlisted clubs, and two on base Thai restaurants. Off base, in town, were several bars and massage parlors that tended the aircrews' personal needs.

When it was dark and the night fighters were all launched, the group of Towhead spectators wandered over to the officers club for dinner. It was no big revelation for Eddie. They ate at tables and had Thai waiters, the food was mundane. Red informed Eddie that the best food was at the two on base civilian Thai restaurants. The entertainment was lousy; there was no other way to describe it. It was a group of local Thai musicians, peaceful and tranquil natives trying desperately to imitate American music and get paid for their efforts. They were dressed western style, including cowboy boots and hats. Apparently they thought all Americans dressed like that as they tried to imitate hard rock and roll on old instruments that would have been rejected by the Salvation Army. The Thais just didn't have the knack for music that the Filipinos had. A couple of scotches on top of the afternoon's beer helped mute their noise.

The usual pecking order of pilots existed at the officers club, not that anyone cared. Everyone preferred their own units' members. It seemed every unit had some level of classification on their mission and were more comfortable within their own circle of operatives. The C-123 candlestick pilots, those not flying that night, were childishly loud and most annoying.

That night Eddie threw a fresh sheet over his single cot, bid his room-mate Red goodnight, and fell into a deep sleep. Eddie would unpack his bag and get his base orientation in the morning. The Lady spent her night on the ramp with her sisters that all returned safely from the ancient land across the river. The Towheads didn't fly at night and their aircraft were nestled in a small group like a covey of quail. The two enlisted guards took turns catching naps, which was strictly against regulations.

* * * * * * * * * * * * * * * * * * * *

The next morning, Eddie strolled down the wooden sidewalk to the bathroom for a shave and a shower. As he entered the open door and walked up to the sink, he passed by four tiny Thai girls, probably in their late teens, sitting next to the washing machines. They were obviously maids as both washing machines were humming and bubbling. They were watching him, the new guy, and were covering their mouths as they quietly giggled and talked. He tried to ignore them as he shaved and went about his business. He needed to use the latrine but elected to finish his sink chores first. Another American strolled in, wearing only a towel and carrying a soap dish in his hand. He stopped to use the latrine, nodded his head hello to the girls as he peed, strolled over and dropped his towel in front of a shower stall. He turned on and adjusted the water temperature, and then took his shower. Eddie wasn't in Colorado anymore.

It was just what Eddie needed to get his nerve up and he also used the latrine, then he dropped off his clothes and took a shower. The little girls resumed giggling at him, covering their mouth which was their custom. He didn't care. He was more concerned with what the next twelve months had in store for him.

The operations building was a small one story wooden affair, about the size of an apartment and was surrounded by a tall chain link fence. The front door had a restricted entry sign and on both sides stood a clump of banana trees. The gap between the chain link fence and the building, on the left side, was occupied by a captured North Vietnamese 37mm anti-aircraft gun. Its barrel pointed menacingly towards the sky. Inside, Airman Second Class Hendrix was running the office and there were two rooms for the detachment's senior officers.

Lt. Colonel Bergstrom, the detachment commander, non-descriptive but courteous, was reviewing paper work in front of the airman's desk when Eddie entered the building. He introduced himself and asked Eddie to join him in his office, a warm friendly place. There was a nifty collection of war memorabilia scattered around and behind him were the traditional photos of the President, Joint Chief of Staff, and the Wing Commander. One of the side walls was dominated by a large photo of a B-52 bomber. Eddie assumed the colonel had been a bomber pilot before being shuffled off to run the detachment of Gooney Birds at NKP. The NKP job was a command job, which, with a little embellishment, could look good in his evaluation reports. Combined with some excuse for a Distinguished Flying Cross, which were getting easier and easier to get, he would qualify for promotion to full colonel when he returned to the States.

The scattered war memorabilia included a captured AK-47, a Viet Cong flag, and a fourteen by twenty inch photo enlargement of an airfield taken in Laos from the left seat of a Gooney Bird. The Gooney Bird's left wing was showing along the edge of the photo. The colonel asked a few generic questions to confirm Eddie's prior radial engine transport experience and then walked Eddie next door to the operations officer's office. The bald headed, stocky operations officer, Major Collins, had no words for Eddie and as soon as the colonel left the major turned Eddie back over to the Airman Hendrix. The two striper's desk was covered with paperwork and it was obvious who the "go to guy" was for operations. Major Collins returned to his office and closed his door with a solid slam, as if he didn't want to be bothered anymore. The airman processed Eddie's paperwork while Eddie sat in the chair next to the airman's desk. Nothing new was disclosed except when the paperwork was completed and filed, the airman looked nonchalantly at Eddie and informed him his Top Secret SSIR clearance hadn't come through yet, but it would be no problem.

"I requested a waiver yesterday and it just came in on the wire," the competent airman beamed. "So you're cleared to fly your missions."

Eddie wondered, "What good is a clearance requirement if an airman second class can request a waiver?" Then out of curiosity, he asked the airman, "What's the SSIR stand for?"

"Stands for Special Security Investigations Required," Airman Hendrix filled him in. "It's needed cause the guys in the back of your airplane gather raw, presidential level intelligence about the enemy. It's another layer above a regular Top Secret Clearance. Ya don't need it to fly the airplane but if ya gotta take a piss, the can is in the rear of the airplane and ya need the clearance to walk back there while the security service spooks are doing their thing."

"Higher than a Top Secret clearance to take a piss?" Eddie laughed.

"Yeah, sometimes it gets a little silly around here. Welcome to NKP! Guess there's some CIA spook somewhere without anything to do so he thinks up stuff like that for us to comply with . . . I really think the gomers know what we do. It's just that they wanna keep everything a secret from the American press. It's political stuff. The American press will print anything they can get their hands on, don't care if it's a military secret or not. They'll throw us in jail if we tell anyone about the electric goons but if the press gets a hold of it and plasters it all over the front pages, it's okay and they get a Nobel Prize. They're protected by the first amendment but us GIs aren't."

"Kind of a messed up way to do things!" Eddie commented. "The media getting away with treason, passing classified information to the enemy."

"Yeah, but it's the only war we got so we do it as best we can," the airman reflected. "Best act enthusiastic about the war around Major Collins." Airman Hendrix nodded his head toward the door belonging to the operations officer who Eddie had so briefly met. He quietly told Eddie, "The major's a Zoomie and he's kind of a cheer leader type. Thinks the Towheads are gonna win the war single-handed." Zoomie was a nick name for Air Force Academy graduates.

"Thanks for the tip," Eddie smiled. He knew the type. The friendly little airman walked with Eddie to base supply and Eddie was issued a pile of Nomex (fireproof) flight suits, combat boots, towels and stuff. The supply clerk also issued Eddie a Smith and Wesson 38 Special pistol, with a holster, box of standard issue shells, and a box of 38 caliber tracer rounds.

"What do we do with these?" Eddie held up the tracer rounds.

"Damned if I know," the supply clerk replied. "Everything's so god-damned secret around here I stopped asking questions six months ago. It says to give this stuff to Towhead pilots so that's what I do."

He also issued Eddie a pair of sunglasses, an air force standard aircrew survival kit and a pack of rescue flares. The supply clerk then disappeared for a few minutes and reappeared with cloth first lieutenant's bars, and cloth name tags with Werner stamped on them. There were enough for the four nomex flight suits. He pointed to the cloth name tags and cautioned Eddie to be careful with them because the ink was still a little wet. After Eddie signed for the lot, the clerk handed him a large paper bag to carry his stuff and wished him "good luck." Then he immediately went back to the paperback novel he had been reading.

Airman Hendrix helped Eddie carry his stuff and guided him to the intelligence building. It had a security fence and a guard at the door. He checked Hendrix's badge and Eddie's paperwork. He then called for

184

assistance. A sergeant showed up, he checked Hendrix's badge and Eddie's paperwork and escorted Eddie into the building. Airman Hendrix had to wait outside.

The sergeant led Eddie to what had to be a briefing room, six or seven rows of chairs and on the knee high stage were several items that were covered with cloth to avoid prying eyes. A briefing officer emerged from a door next to a large covered blackboard. The sergeant introduced Eddie then disappeared out the back door. The officer was a captain, ground pounder intelligence type, slightly overweight, balding, and friendly. He opened with a speech about security, probably one he knew by heart as everyone with a secret clearance or higher at NKP was required to receive the same briefing. He lectured on talking shop to anyone, or around anyone that was in hearing range, about anything that was classified. He warned about maids in the quarters, spies listening in at bars downtown, spies and news media listening in at bars in Bangkok, and to say nothing about the missions in letters home. It was blah, blah for ten minutes. Then he lectured about jail time for violating military secrets. It wore Eddie out. Eddie decided not to tell anybody any secrets.

He then issued Eddie a Top Secret SSIR security badge. Eddie had no idea where they got the photo from but it resembled the eight by ten photo in his personnel records. The intelligence officer mentioned nothing about the clearance not being finalized. Eddie assumed the security guy didn't know he had been given a waiver by an enlisted airman. Third, he issued to Eddie and had Eddie sign for a blood chit. Blood Chits, ten inches wide and nineteen and a half long, were made from fine white nylon cloth. They displayed an American flag and had printed text in English, repeated in translations in Burmese, Thai, Laotian, Cambodian, Vietnamese, Malayan, Indonesian, Chinese, Modern Chinese, Tagalog, French, and Dutch: *I am a citizen of the United States of America. I do not speak your language. Misfortune forces me to seek your assistance in obtaining food, shelter and water and protection. Please take me to someone who will provide for my safety and see that I am returned to my people. My government will reward you.* A control number was printed on the bottom to identify the downed flyer that the blood chit had been issued to. It made Eddie feel uneasy as he signed the paperwork and stuffed the elaborate handkerchief into his pocket.

"You know about sterile uniforms from survival school?" the captain continued.

"I was sick that day, tell me about sterile uniforms," Eddie lied. He felt the captain wanted an opportunity to expound on his vast knowledge.

The captain smiled arrogantly and expounded, "Anytime air crew members fly combat missions in Southeast Asia, they're required by regulation to have sterilized uniforms. Only your name and rank are allowed. No unit patches, no billfolds, no letters from home, no photographs, no nothing. In case you're shot down and captured, you're to have nothing on your person that will give your interrogator anything to use as a tool against you. Your best chance in resisting interrogation is to be a generic flyboy. Eddie didn't have the heart to tell the academic wonder that for over two years he had flown in and around Vietnam wearing a non-sterile flight suit.

Eddie had curried rice and water buffalo stew for lunch. The previous evening Red had pointed out where the two Thai restaurants were. Enlisted ate for free at air force chow halls but officers had to pay sixty-five cents for lunch in the same chow halls. The rice and curry was good for $1.05. It was an inflated price for Americans but Eddie could live with that. He bought a six pack of Olympia, found the swimming pool, and as he spread out in the shade next to the pool, the heavens open up. Eddie was caught in an afternoon monsoon deluge. He cowered under the eave of the pool house and endured the heaviest rain he had ever seen. In forty-five minutes the rain suddenly stopped and the sun was back out. This was a routine he would soon get used to. Tomorrow would be his first flight in an EC-47, but not a real mission. Red was going to fly Eddie around the air patch a few times so they could fill in some more squares on Eddie's paperwork. It would be a quickie flight around the pattern a few times, just like Eddie's C-124 check out at Tachikawa!

* *

Eddie and Red talked in their room that night. Red said the reason Eddie was probably sent to NKP was that his (Red's) tour was going to be up in two months. They needed a new instructor pilot to do training and give check rides. All they had been getting were new pilots right out of pilot training and they had been looking for someone with a little more flying experience for an instructor replacement, preferably with radial engine experience. Somehow the NKP EC-47 detachment commander heard through the grapevine about Eddie and his round engine experience. The colonel had either called in an IOU or fudged the back door paperwork that had been necessary to get Eddie away from his previously assigned EC-47 unit. Red was a little vague about the details. Eddie had been Shanghaied! It certainly was okay with Eddie.

"What's with the EC-47s anyway? I really haven't heard anything about their operation, here or in Vietnam," Eddie prodded.

"The reason you haven't heard anything about EC-47s is nobody talks. The air force acts as if they don't exist and never mention them to the media or anyone that doesn't have a need to know. Anyway, old C-47s are not something that grabs the attention of the news media. The media is just like the North Vietnamese Army gunners. The media wants news about jet fighters to make big headlines in America and the North Vietnamese wanna shoot down jet fighters to make big headlines in America."

"Sounds familiar," Eddie smiled. "Nobody ever heard of the 22nd MAS at Tachikawa, either."

"Yeah, I know what you mean. I flew C-124s also. But now that we're in EC-47s, it's a real blessing, ya know. We got round engine experience so we don't have to sit as a co-pilot for six months."

"You flew C-124s?" Eddie was curious.

"Yeah, out of Shaw Air Base in South Carolina," Red admitted.

"How'd you get here? Didn't you have an overseas return date?" Eddie pressed him.

"You know too much and ask too many questions," Red laughed. "Mostly we flew east, over the Atlantic Ocean to Europe. I did something that pissed our wing commander off and he had me shipped over here. He'd be pissed again if he knew I was at NKP and not Vietnam, dodging rockets and mortars every afternoon. I'll tell you about it someday, I don't like to talk about it much."

He hesitated a few seconds then decided it was okay to open up and let Eddie know just a little more about their mission. It was as if Red enjoyed making Eddie squirm for each bit of information. "This is real classified shit so keep it in the family. We don't want the media to get a sniff of this cause we got a couple things going for us with the EC-47s and we don't wanna spoil it. Did you know that the Russians built around two thousand C-47s during World War II? We gave them the engineering and plans and they built them for their air force."

"I knew that, similar story, different version," Eddie thought as he nodded his head.

Red continued, "They got some still around and they gave some of em to the North Vietnamese. Not very many people know this, and I remind you this is secret stuff. The North Vietnamese painted their airplanes to look just like the standard camouflage paint job that we use on our AC-47 gunships and our EC-47s. That way in broad daylight, they can fly around in Laos and South Vietnam and none of the Americans pay any attention to em. I guess they use em for flying generals and other important people around, or something like that, and they land on the back country air strips that the Americans have abandoned. There's abandoned airstrips all over the countryside." Eddie was speechless and Red continued, "That's one reason why the gomers are restricted from shooting at us guys cause they need positive identification and clearance before they can shoot at Gooney Birds. They don't wanna shoot down their own generals.

"That's also why you never wanna make an emergency landing on an abandoned dirt strip in the boonies if you're flying in Vietnam or along the trail. Ever since the Americans figured out the gomers were flying Russian Gooney Birds, whenever we abandon a runway the special forces plant land mines. They wanna discourage the gomers from using them with their Russian C-47 copies. We blew a few of their birds up but some are still out there."

Eddie wondered if this guy was for real or just really full of hooey.

"The second reason is the AC-47 gunships have the same paint jobs as we have. The Americans only fly their AC-47 gunships at night. Originally they flew some day missions in South Vietnam but they were sitting ducks for anti-aircraft guns. Without permission to return fire, which can take hours for the bureaucracy to process, they switched to flying at night. At night it's much harder for the gomers to see em and to shoot em down. Our

186

salvation is that the South Vietnamese and the Laotian Air Force also fly American built AC-47 gunships and they fly during the day time like us. They aren't under the same repressive restrictions the American crews are. When somebody shoots at them, the South Vietnamese and Laotians don't need to get permission from anybody to return fire. If the gomers on the ground shoot at em, they just roll over and hose the gomers down with a lead bath. So the gunners are reluctant to randomly shoot at camouflaged gooney birds."

"The third thing is that they don't wanna waste their ammunition and give their position away. Once the Americans have an accurate fix on a gun position, it's just a matter of time before the fast movers show up and bomb their communist asses back to the dark ages. They don't wanna risk getting blown up just to shoot down a miserable C-47. So they wait till they can shoot at a big prize, like a fast moving jet fighter, AC-130, or A-1, so they can make a big splash in the American newspapers." Then Red continued, "Don't think these guys aren't smart, the NVA that is, at least their leaders. They know what they're doing." Red shrugged, "Even if they did shoot down one of our EC-47s in Laos, I'd bet the air force would refer to it as an old World War II cargo aircraft that was in transit from Thailand to somewhere. For some unknown reason it strayed off course and over hostile territory.

"The gomer gunners get medals for shooting down American jets, same thing with us, medals for good deeds. Hell, medals are cheap for the governments to make, maybe a couple of bucks each, and guys go out and risk their lives to get them. It's a scam the governments have been doing for thousands of years. Bottom line is it's best for the EC-47s to keep a low profile and do their job and let the gomers on the ground eat their rice."

Eddie grinned and offered his two cents to the discussion, "I just thought if a fourth reason why they wouldn't bother shooting at us. Maybe it's because they think our airplanes are so old we're gonna crash sooner or later anyway—so there's no reason to waste their shells on us."

Red fired back with his counter jab and a laugh, "You really are full of shit. Maybe you and I'll get along just fine!"

* * * * * * * * * * * * * * * * * * * *

Eddie and Red walked out to the ramp the next morning and found an unused EC-47 that was free for the day. They wanted to get an early start to avoid the afternoon rain. The Lady was absent; she was across the border flying and Eddie didn't say anything about her to Red. He didn't want to be classified as being nuts during his first week at his new home.

They got permission from maintenance and the operations officer to take the airplane up for a local training flight and get Eddie's initial co-pilot check ride signed off. It was really just another formality. Red was the only instructor and would also be required to fly with Eddie and instruct him on his first electronics countermeasures mission. Red would then sign Eddie off, again, and Eddie would be placed on the schedule to fly as a co-pilot with any of the unit aircraft commanders. With Eddie's C-124 background, after he had a month in EC-47s, they would go through the drill again and sign him off as an aircraft commander. Two weeks later they would cut orders making Eddie a flight instructor. The air force thrived on paperwork, even in a war zone. After Red was gone, Eddie would be charged with training, check rides, and generally babysitting the pilots. He would fill out the endless amounts of paperwork. For new guys just out of pilot training and with no experience, the progression was a little simpler. They would fly as a co- pilot for six months and six months as an aircraft commander. Then they would have their tour complete and rotate back to the States and get on with their lives. It had been rare for new lieutenants to obtain instructor status during their one year tour.

As they walked across the ramp to their aircraft, Red filled Eddie in on the EC-47 fleet composition. "Up here and at Pleiku, in northern Vietnam, we got new Q model EC-47s with data processors to make the navigator's work a lot faster and more accurate. Also they have extra antennae, extra radio operator stations, and larger engines. The Vietnam P and N models have the standard gooney bird 1830 engines that develop 1100 brake horsepower. Like the C-47s you trained in at England Air Force Base in Louisiana. The Q models that we use and the Pleiku guys fly in southern Laos have larger R-2000 engines that develop

1350 horsepower each. With the R-2000s we can lift a bigger fuel load so we can fly seven hour missions, carry more radio operators in the back, and still meet the required takeoff performance. Our takeoff loads are limited by takeoff performance. We need a hundred foot per minute climb rate if we lose an engine on takeoff. The Q models fly the same way as the older models with the standard engines. Same power settings, airspeeds, and checklists. Also, if we lose an engine on a Q model, the remaining R-2000 engine will get us up and over the high mountains that ring the Plain of Jars. During the dry season the North Vietnamese Army usually owns the floor of the Plain of Jars and that's no place to go down if you don't have to. They usually don't take prisoners in Laos. I don't mean that they let them go; they just put a bullet in their heads and leave em for the vultures.

"The Q models are easy to spot, their propeller hub is longer and the oil cooler on the top of the engine is square and a little larger. It looks like it was home built. And they have shark fin antennae, a really big one on each side of the rear main door."

The inside of the airplane was about what Eddie had expected. When the aircraft was rebuilt for the electronic warfare configuration, the interior and all of the soundproofing had been stripped. There was a narrow aluminum walkway down the center of the cabin floor. Aviators call the walkway a cat walk, and the rest of the floor and walls and ceiling were bare structural ribs. The outside of the ribs was a single layer of outer skin. Everything had been stripped to the bare bones to save weight. There were five work stations installed; an operator's seat was attached to each work station. Four of the stations were for the 6994th Security Squadron Detachment's Radio operators (ROs), and the fifth was for the navigator who operated a strange looking navigation station.

Eddie had a good look at the navigation installations but knew he wasn't supposed to ask any questions about the various black boxes and their function. Red watched him with a grin then finally spoke, "I can't tell you anything about that stuff, but if you look on the back side of the black boxes the military placard tells you what it is, its serial number, and electrical requirements. You can see for yourself!"

Eddie looked and sure enough, he read Nortronics 1060 airborne data processor, Bendix APN-179 Doppler Navigation system, and the funny looking device bolted to the floor was a gyro stabilized drift meter. Eddie hadn't asked any questions and Red hadn't spoken any answers.

The cockpit had been rebuilt from the original C-47 configuration. The aircraft had been completely rewired to accommodate the electronic devices in the back end. At the same time they rebuilt the instrument panel and added a large, modern airline attitude indicator (gyro stabilized artificial horizon), to allow more precise flying. The altimeter was air force standard issue but the pilot's compass had been upgraded to a C-12, a state of the art and very accurate compass. The pilots had a modern Bendix AN/APS -113 weather radar set. It would be nice for penetrating weather during the monsoon season. There was no autopilot as it had been removed to save weight and maintenance. Eddie wondered about flying for the better part of the day without an autopilot!

The trips around the pattern were a breeze and they parked the airplane with an hour and fifteen minutes on the clock. It didn't take Red very long to determine that Eddie knew how to fly round engines and Airman Hendrix's effort to get him away from the Vietnam squadron was justified.

Red had the last landing for the day and as they rolled out, Eddie looked out his side window and commented, "Nice landing."

Red looked over at Eddie and faked a dumb look. "I thought you were flying, I had my hands in my lap when we landed." They both laughed at his joke.

As they walked back to their room, Eddie had a chance to pump Red for more answers, now that he was gaining Red's confidence. There was nothing that could bond two pilots faster than a half dozen trips around the traffic pattern, trading touch and go landings in an old World War II bird.

"What's with the tracer bullets thing?"

"It's something some staff weenie thought up about a year ago," Red smiled at Eddie's concern. "The idea is if we get shot down and have to make a crash landing, we're supposed to remove the gas caps and shoot our tracers into the fuel tanks to ignite the fuel. It would burn up the airplane and protect the secret stuff we carry in the back."

"How about that?" Eddie wondered out loud.

"No one's ever been able to tell me if it would work," Red continued to ramble on. "Recently they put foam in all our gas tanks so if we take a hit they wouldn't blow up or burn fast—theoretically! That kinda nullifies shooting tracers into the fuel tank. It's a perfect example how the right hand and left hand don't know what each other is doing. Anyway, it's really not necessary. The word on the street is that there's a standing order for the fighters to drop napalm on any downed EC-47, followed by high explosive bombs. That's overkill! I think they're a little paranoid about our equipment in the back. But ya never know what's true and what's not! Before one of our flights, I tried to find out more about these rumors. When I asked the intelligence briefer, all I got was a blank stare. Then he fed me the same old bullshit, 'You don't wanna know, so if you get shot down you can't tell them anything.' I get a little tired of the same old keep them in the dark and feed them just enough shit to keep them alive."

"Great story." Eddie looked down at his newly issued jungle boots. "Guess we know how concerned they are about our young disposable butts; it's the airplanes they wanna protect."

"Welcome to NKP," Red smiled.

Somewhere, Eddie had heard that before. Eddied asked, "I keep hearing reference to spooks. What in the hell is a spook?"

Red was quiet for a few seconds while he gathered his thoughts. "Spook was originally used to describe CIA intelligence guys; others called em cone heads. Some of the CIA guys are really spooky. We sometimes call our back end guys spooks. They're mostly the guys that were bookworms in high school and to avoid the draft into the army they joined the air force. They scored off the right side of the IQ and aptitude tests. Some of em have college educations but just didn't want to be an officer. Either way, they were really smart so the air force sent them to language school for nine months in California, sent them to spy school, at least the electric eavesdropping part of spy school, and they ended up in the back of our EC-47s. Technically they aren't a part of our detachment. They're in the 6994th Security Squadron and assigned duty in the back of the EC-47 fleet. They're a strange eclectic lot but highly skilled and respected. They listen to and copy everything the gomers send out over the radio waves . . . then they distribute the information to the military and civilian agency?"

"Hey, I'm a new guy," Eddie reacted. "I got no idea what we do up there. What civilian agency are you talking about?"

"It's classified, I can't tell you." Eddie couldn't tell if Red was joking again or serious. "But their initials are CIA."

Eddie had heard that before but decided to bite, "Not really. You say we're working for the CIA? Don't shit me, are you serious?"

"No shit." Red was dead serious. "According to what I've been able to figure out, basically the stuff we gather in the Plain of Jars goes to the CIA and the stuff we gather along the Ho Chi Minh Trail goes to the CIA and the military. But I really don't know that for sure. All combat missions over here, in Laos, Vietnam and surely in Cambodia, are dispatched with daily orders everyone calls "frags". The frags apparently describe the mission to be flown, which aircraft, the pilots and crew, ordinance type and how the mission is to be flown. Personally I've never seen a frag because I work for the EC-47s and they never show the frags to us. It's all secret stuff, only the back enders have a need to know and we just fly the airplanes where they tell us to go.

"I think the radio operators have some sort of radio in the back to call in the hot stuff they gather," Red continued his speculation. "But only hot stuff that can't wait. They transmit as few messages as possible. Their stuff goes out over a "scrambler' so if it's intercepted the gomers still can't figure out what the message is. Hell, I don't even know for sure who else has scramblers to decode the time sensitive stuff the back enders need to radio in. I assume the C-130 airborne command ships have de-scramblers and surely the CIA in Udorn has them. I don't know about the army! Maybe our intelligence needs to go through some sort of chain of command for the army? I suspect the vast majority of the intelligence we gather is turned in on the ground during the radio operator's debriefings. Guys tell me that our stuff is really good and useful. But you never know who to believe around here."

"Yeah, like you!" Eddie thought to himself. He assumed time would reveal what was true and what was a product of Red's overactive imagination.

Eddie was still trying to recover from finding out who and what the Lady was and now he was about to fly missions for the CIA. Well maybe, anyway . . . it was a big week for a farm boy.

"We're an extension of the EC-47 fleet that operates in Vietnam," Red babbled on and broke Eddie's thoughts. "Compared to being based inside Vietnam, NKP provides a way to patrol the northern portions of the Ho Chi Minh Trail with a greatly reduced travel time to and from our work area . . . We usually fly two flights each day along the trail, a morning flight and an afternoon flight. It's not very far from here to the trail. It's only about forty miles if you head due east from here. We copy the enemy's radio transmissions and record the positions of the North Vietnamese military units up and down the trail. The operations along the trail are called "Steel Tiger."

"Our second mission assignment is to provide primary information to the CIA in support of their secret war project. It's called Barrel Roll. We're providing support for General Vang Pao, the Hmong leader. He has a full division of mountain people waging a private war against the North Vietnamese Army in the Plain of Jars. Plain of Jars is further north from the trail. It's hush hush stuff. They don't even like us to use the term CIA, not even in our private conversations. We're supposed to use the term 'Civilian Agency,' or 'The Company' as used by the Ravens or the term the Air America guys use—'The Customer.'"

"I'm a bit confused so I guess it works," Eddie confessed. "What the hell is the Plain of Jars?"

"Most guys here just call it the PDJ. You'll find out soon enough. You and I are scheduled to fly a mission up there. We depart at six tomorrow morning." Eddie didn't like the way Red withheld information from him until he milked it out.

"Okay, whatever . . . by the way, how many EC-47s have we really lost over here? I have a Top Secret SSIR now, and I think I have a right to know," Eddie asked.

Red was taken back a little, his face showing a slight annoyance at Eddie's remark. "To start off, having a top secret clearance doesn't give you the right to know much of anything, least in this outfit. But I'll tell you what I know. We haven't lost any EC-47s here at NKP and we've been flying out of here for about a year. But we only been flying five or less aircraft. They moved three EC-47Q models up here, from Vietnam, April last year and now we're up to five aircraft. Our specific operation at NKP is called Commando Forge. There're three squadrons of EC-47s operating inside South Vietnam. In addition to all of South Vietnam, they cover the south half of the Ho Chi Minh Trail in Laos with Q models out of Pleiku and the birds stationed at Tan Son Nhut sneak into Cambodia on a regular basis. That's also hush hush shit, especially the part about flying in Cambodia. The squadron at Pleiku has had one shot down that I know about, a couple of em hit, and two destroyed on the ramp by enemy rockets. All in the past six months. The other two units have occasionally had losses but nothing alarming that I'm aware of. There's no way we can find out how many for sure, the whole EC-47 program is so wrapped in secrecy and their losses aren't publicized. Hearsay isn't that accurate. I'd guess since 1967 at least five or six, no more than six or eight from gunfire and about a dozen from non-combat accidents and rocket attacks on the ramp.

"The EC program used to get a lot of experienced field grade officers as pilots but lately all we been getting are green lieutenant pilots. So every once in a while we lose one on take-off or landing. They try to keep a total of fifty-seven EC-47s flying in Southeast Asia, but that's also classified. I assume that with combat losses, operational accidents, mortar and rocket losses on the ramps, and down time for maintenance, they would be lucky to have forty-five flyable aircraft at any given time. But that's just my guess." He looked at Eddie and asked, "Okay?" Eddie nodded okay.

* * * * * * * * * * * * * * * * * * *

The next morning Eddie and Red rolled out at 5:00 a.m. and had breakfast at the chow hall. Back at their room, they loaded their flight suits for the mission. With a small sewing kit, Eddie had attached his name patch and two first lieutenant silver bars on his nomex flight suit. The nomex flight suits were a heaver weight material than the tan washed ones he wore in the 22nd. They were a lot hotter to wear on the ramp but would be comfortable once airborne and in the higher and cooler air. The purpose in requiring the crewmembers to wear nomex flight suits was they were highly fire resistant. Eddie hoped he would never need to benefit from that feature.

Eddie loaded his flight suit with the personal survival kits he had built for himself. The instructors at the Philippines Snake School had stimulated him with lots of good advice. Eddie had purchased a half dozen plastic travel containers for soap bars and in these he had packed additional items not found in the air force standard issue survival vest; items that would come in handy in case he had to walk back home. He packed aspirin for pain killer, No Doze from the infirmary, fishing line and hooks, sewing needles, tweezers, single edge razor blades, extra 38 caliber ammunition for his pistol, a folding pocket knife with multiple blades, a tube of fungus cream, a small bottle of Mercurochrome, a roll of medical tape, a spare survival radio battery, three payday candy bars from the BX (chocolate melts in the tropics but payday bars remain edible), a small compass, and a waterproof container full of matches. If he did have to walk home, he was going to give those little buggers a run for their money. He had always wondered what all those extra zipper pockets were for on his military flight suit and for the first time he had filled them full. He slipped five tracer rounds in his Smith and Wesson, the unloaded chamber he left under the firing pin. If the hammer was hit by anything, the shock wouldn't go through and set off a live round. He strapped his gun belt on, flashing back to when he was a small boy and was given a toy western six shooter and holster for his birthday. This was for real. He was really going to war.

They each put on their air force issue survival vests made out of strong camouflaged fabric with large net breathing panels. These vests provided a multitude of additional pockets for each flyer's official survival stuff, a survival radio, signal mirror, pen gun signal flares, a water bottle, first aid kits, a commando knife, and water purification tablets.

A blue van picked them up at 6:00 a.m. and dropped them off at the briefing room. Red, Eddie, and Stu, their navigator, flashed their security badges at the guard at the door and settled in to the chairs on the front row of the briefing room. The rest of the crew chairs were empty. The briefer wandered through the door and pulled the cloth free from a large stand that held a map of Laos. There were red circles placed on the map, most in groups.

"I understand this is your first mission," the briefer spoke straight at Eddie. He handed Eddie a new plastic coated map that was a miniature version of the one on the stand. Red and Stu already had their maps out and were checking their hand drawn red circles against those on the stand. "These circles are six miles in diameter and represent known anti-aircraft enemy gun sites. This master chart is upgraded at least once each day, usually several times each day as new information comes in from aircrew debriefings. Most of our gun intelligence is from your neighbors, the Nails." He handed Eddie a grease pencil, "Keep the grease pencil. We got lots of em. Mark all the gun positions on your map and you can also use the grease pencil to write notes for the maintenance guys on your side windows.

Eddie thought of the captured 37mm gun just outside their detachment operations building and remembered that it was mounted on wheels. "They could move these guns out of the circles during the night and shoot down our asses the next morning. Are they allowed to do that?" he asked.

"Yeah, it's possible," Red answered Eddie's question. "They're allowed to cheat! But they haven't got us yet. I asked that same question when I was getting checked out and the intelligence guy gave me the government's viewpoint."

"What's that?" Eddie asked.

"In an operation this large, you have to expect losses."

The Intelligence officer didn't think Red's interruption of his briefing was funny. Eddie didn't know if Red was telling the truth or if it was just his usual bullshit. It was probably a mixture of both, Red was like that.

"Red here," the briefer flicked his head, "will show you how to keep track of your position in the Plain of Jars. Most people just call it the PDJ. Don't fly over any gun circles no matter what. It's not necessary to fly over known gun positions for the completion of your mission and we don't want to lose an aircraft. You'll coordinate where you fly with the navigator all the time. Everything else Red will show you on the job.

"There's nothing else that's different," the briefer looked at Red and Stu for the first time. "Channel ninety-eight's working, the North Vietnamese Army control all of the PDJ floor, and it's okay to over fly the mountain tops on the south, west and north edges, they're still ours. Stay away from the east end, there're guns, big guns, and NVA everywhere. If ya get hit and have to go down, land as far west on the PDJ as you can get. There's lots of Air America flights in and out of the mountain sites that are still held by the Hmong. Air America should be able to get to you within thirty minutes or less." He looked at Eddie and smiled, "The ROs get their own specialized briefing from their 6994th people. Fly safe. We don't want any dead heroes around here, just lots of good intel!"

Eddie assumed it would take several months to find his niche in this new organization and how to deal with the new challenges and apparently new dangers. It just happened that Red's way of coping was to portray himself as a nonchalant wise ass. Eddie never did figure out if it came natural to Red or if it was a nervous tick.

Red signed out an M-16 rifle and a container with 300 rounds of ammunition. In addition to the 38 special revolvers each crewmember carried, they were required to carry at least one M-16 and ammo—in case they got shot down. In reality that was enough firepower to shoot a monkey to eat but no chance of holding off a squad of North Vietnamese soldiers.

They crawled into the blue van waiting for them in front of the building. There were four sergeants sitting in the back, dressed identically like the pilots: sterile nomex flight suits, survival vests, and scruffy jungle boots. Eddie looked his radio operators (ROs) over. They didn't look like geeks or intelligence spooks, just regular guys.

$$* *$$

The van drove onto the flight line and stopped near the rear of an antenna laden Gooney Bird. As Eddie stepped out of the van his heart did a double flip and his stomach felt hollow. Not because this was his first mission into the mystery world of gathering intelligence, but because their assigned aircraft was the Lady. Red noticed that Eddie was a little tense during their walk around but he kept it to himself.

As they did their walk around, Red babbled on about the various models of EC-47s, "The older birds, with the standard engines down in Vietnam, have been flying operationally since somethin like 1966 or 1967. Everything's so classified it's hard to get an exact date. The older birds have smaller crews than we have, the navigators have to do a lot of manual computations and plotting on their maps. But I been told they get a lot of phrase from the GIs on the ground. Their aircraft are designated as P and N model EC-47s."

As they loaded their gear on board, Eddie was fascinated with the shark fin shaped antennas under the Lady's belly, especially the two, one on each side, just aft of the rear entrance door. He squatted down and had a good look at the unusual antennas. Red leaned over and in a low voice explained, "The shark fins have something to do with VHF or UHF radio direction finding ability. I'm not sure which. Most of the Vietnam fleet doesn't have the shark fins but apparently we need em up here in Laos. The Pleiku Q models also have em cause they fly the lower half of the Ho Chi Minh Trail in Laos."

Red showed Eddie the two ten gallon milk cans of water strapped to the rear of the cabin. "The RO's classified paperwork is printed on water soluble paper. If we get in a jam, they'll stuff all of their classified paper into these water cans and it'll instantly turn into mush. In case of a pending crash-landing, they have a whole destruct drill that they can go through that would deny the North Vietnamese any classified paperwork or equipment."

"Destruct drill, water soluble paper, tracer bullets into the fuel tanks, and napalm from the sky. That should about do it if we crash," Eddie summarized. "Are the milk cans classified?"

"Actually they are," Red grinned. "They verify that we use water soluble paper."

Red showed Eddie the urinal in the rear of the aircraft. It drained through a tube through the floor, so it was not to be used on the ground. "We don't shoot guns or drop bombs, but at least we have the satisfaction of pissing on the enemy," Red grinned.

The crapper was a metal chair with a metal hinged lid. It had a plastic bag inside. Out of courtesy to the guys sitting in the rear of the aircraft, it was to be used only in an emergency. There were enough parachutes for everyone, plus two extras. The parachutes were chest style and uncomfortable to wear on their long missions. So no one wore them. They did wear their body harness and kept their snap on chest chute within arm's length. The chest pack could be snapped on in several seconds if things suddenly turned nasty.

The radio operators and the navigator were busy sorting and arranging their paperwork and programming the tools of their trade. Eddie and Red made their way forward. Eddie built his nest in the right seat and Red took the left. Flight lunches, a box of miscellaneous sandwiches and snacks, had been delivered to their aircraft and the pilots positioned theirs so they would be accessible from their seats in-flight. Their checklist was short and in a few minutes they were ready to start engines. Red got the crew chief's attention in front of the aircraft, twirled a finger so he could see it, and nodded yes. The crew chief nodded yes, and then gave the standard start signal, pointing at the number one engine with his left hand and one finger, and twirling his index finger on his raised right hand. All was clear to start number one. The starting was quick and easy and the R-2000s coughed to life. After checking all the engine's gauges, Eddie closed his eyes and listened to the round engines run at idle. No disturbing sounds or vibrations so he felt they were healthy and ready for flight. Eddie noticed that Red, with his significant round engine experience, was also quietly listening to the engines. After both engines were lopping their sweet duet, the crew chief pulled the chocks, saluted, and Red advanced the throttles to clear the line of EC-47s. He then used a light tap on the left brake and advanced the right engine several inches of power. The tail dragger aircraft responded by turning to the left. There was no aircraft movement on the base as Eddie called the ground control and asked for taxi clearance for take-off.

"Towhead Two Two, taxi for take-off runway one five, hold short," the controller instructed. "Leave room on the run-up pad for a two ship of Spads about to taxi behind you."

"Taxi one five, hold short, copy the Spads," Eddie replied. They taxied to the run-up pad at the end of the runway and positioned themselves into the light breeze, then proceeded with their engine run-up check. Again Eddie and Red both listened carefully to their engines, this time at their higher power settings during run-up for their magneto check. The two ship formation of A-1s, call sign Hobo, called for taxi and joined the Towhead on the run-up ramp. The A-1 Skyraiders used the call sign "Hobo" whenever going out on a routine mission, as if there ever was such a mission that was routine for them. They also flew close air support for the CH-53 Jolly Green Giant helicopters that picked up downed airmen, sometimes under fierce enemy fire and very hostile conditions. When protecting the rescue choppers and downed airmen, the A-1s used the call sign Sandy.

The three aircraft sat wing tip to wing tip. As the three aircraft ran their engines up and checked their magnetos, Eddie was enamored with the two ancient fighters parked next to him. Their cockpit canopies were pulled back for cooling, their wings loaded with several different kinds of bombs, their 20mm cannon barrels protruding menacingly from the front of their wings. A blue van pulled up in front of the Hobos and two airmen, wearing ear protecting headsets for the noise, jumped out. The Hobo pilots, with their run-ups complete, shut their engines down and held their hands in the air. It was their signal and reassurance to the airmen on the ground that no switches in the cockpit would be accidentally activated. Therefore no bombs would be accidentally dropped on the ramp or rockets or guns fired. The airmen pulled the arming pins from the mixed load of bombs and the bombs were then ready to be dropped. Eddie was impressed. These guys were the real thing going out to do the real thing. He was also going out over the enemy, although he had been told they had a much safer mission. He still felt a surge of pride.

Eddie called the tower, "Towhead Two Two is ready for take-off."

"Towhead Two Two, cleared take-off, cleared on course. There's no other traffic in the area." After the Towhead took off, the Hobos restarted their engines and informed the tower that they were ready for take-off.

After they were airborne and the wheels were in the well, Red turned the aircraft left to 360 degrees. They were heading due north and into Laos. Eddie called Invert GCI on 278.4 and informed him he was off from NKP and crossing the Mekong. Invert was the ground based radar monitor, located at Nakhon Phanom, which monitored airborne activity in northern Thailand and Laos.

"I gotcha, Towhead, have a good mission," was all Invert had to say. That was their last radio transmission from their cockpit until they returned to NKP and were ready for landing. The rest of their business was classified and not for publication over the air. Red was flying and Eddie felt a chill as they crossed the Mekong. They were still quite low and could see the rice fields along the Mekong flood plain.

"Welcome to Laos," Red looked over at Eddie, "You just became a spook, or at least a spook chauffeur."

The Mekong flowed lazily a half mile wide below and to Eddie's left. To his right, the rugged karst mountains erupted from the flat Mekong flood plain and beyond that, and less than a half an hour away, was the famous Ho Chi Minh Trail. But they were on their way to another destination; the remote northern mountainous interior of the ancient Khmer Empire and the isolated Plain of Jars.

Laos was a landlocked, backward, poor mountainous nation. It was trapped in a strategic location between South Vietnam, then counterclockwise to North Vietnam, China, Burma (Myanmar), Thailand and Cambodia. It had a mixed and sparse population. The lowland Laotians controlled the few towns, the sparse low land rice growing areas, and the politics. The mountains were inhabited by dozens of archaic mountain tribes. The largest and most prominent were the Hmong tribesmen who lived in the highest mountains. The Hmong were animists that had lived their primitive mountain lifestyle, unchanged for centuries, and were known as fierce warriors.

Laos was mostly jungle covered mountains and contained a large amount of karst topography. Karst is a unique, rugged, and insanely beautiful type of jagged limestone. It formed beautiful spires, pinnacles, cliffs, and narrow valleys with a multitude of tiny flowing streams. The exotic limestone formations were covered with dense tropical vegetation, and limestone caves and caverns were common. The abundant rainfall created beautiful waterfalls and wisps of water vapor formed scattered low clouds. Morning mist hung between the peaks and gave the entire scene a mystical feeling.

With their steep, sometimes vertical, sides covered with wet slippery vegetation, the karst was all but impossible to climb and was uninhabitable. An occasional foot trail led the way through the narrow valleys formed by streams. The remaining Laotian mountains were gentler and habitable, similar to the Smoky Mountains in North Carolina. But covered with jungle. In some areas the mountains were much taller. These taller mountains were the home of the Hmong and in the center of the tall northern mountain maze was an opening, a 500 square mile flat valley floor. The French had named it the Plaine des Jarres. The plain's floor, varying between 3000 to 3500 feet above sea level, was surrounded by mountains as tall as 9,000 feet above sea level. As the name implies, there are lots of jars on the valley floor. The giant urns were carved out of solid sandstone, sometimes granite, weighing many tons and standing eight to ten feet high. This phenomenon had yet to be explained by the archeologists, their purpose and use a mystery. The jars had been dated over 2,000 years old. Everything was old in that ancient and wondrous relic of a country.

Stu gave them a new heading of 345 degrees to fly and they headed straight for the PDJ, 170 miles off their nose. They cruised, with all the drag from the multitude of external antennas, at 115 knots (132 miles per hour). They were much slower than a normal C-47 or DC-3. The Nails loved to tease the Towheads about receiving bird strikes from the rear. The Towhead's slow steady birds were, however, an ideal aerial platform for their work. With a seven hour fuel load this would give them over four hours loiter time in the PDJ and they would plan their return so they would land with fifteen to twenty minutes of fuel.

They were flying parallel to the Mekong, just inside Laos, and the radio operators were already busy in the back listening for transmissions. In addition to local radio transmissions along the way, the radio operators were able to copy long range HF Morse code transmissions from North and South Vietnam, Laos, and Cambodia. They were an airborne listening post.

While they were climbing through 2500 feet altitude, Eddie had the strange feeling that someone was watching him. He looked out his right side window and there, about fifteen feet from his wingtip, was one of the A-1s he had watched on the ramp. He looked left and the other Spad was on their left wingtip. They were also heading for the Plain of Jars. As fighter pilots had a reputation for being a little frisky, they were taking pictures of each other flying off the wingtips of the Gooney Bird. It was "slow" flight for them as they normally cruised at twice the speed of the EC-47. The one on Eddie's side grinned and gave a thumbs up. Eddie returned the gesture, not knowing that the Spad driver's thumbs up was for the Spad's wingman on the other side, the one with the raised camera.

The three of them flew along together, skimming the landscape below, while the radio operators and Eddie banged away with their own cameras—then sat back and enjoyed the moment and the view. There is no substitute for flying a large propeller airplane, low and slowly over the countryside, examining every detail of the world carrying on below. The Spads, one on each wingtip, and the Gooney Bird were relatives. The rolling green jungle below, with its occasional clearing filled with rice paddies and scattered thatch huts, was the essence of their world. Eddie looked around the cockpit and back down the cabin aisle. These people would be his family for the next year. Each was as enamored with the view as he was. Each was in his own world of thought. That was the stuff the old prop crews were made of. No screaming jet engines would ever replace the magic union between aircrews, propellers, round engines, and mother earth. Sadly, for the United States Air Force, they were the last of their kind.

Then their fixation on the moment was gone. The faster Spads peeled off and rejoined in a two ship formation, pulling away from the slower EC-47's nose. They had work to do. There were Hmong troops in contact with the enemy and they needed air support from the Americans.

* *

"I'm still curious about these gun circles we drew on our maps." Eddie was talking on the pilot's interphone, which wouldn't interfere with the radio operators' work in the back. "What size are these guns? How high can they shoot?"

"You probably don't want to know this," Red smiled at Eddie." But the intelligence guys claim that the largest guns we could face are thirty-seven millimeter, like the one parked outside our base operations. They have an effective range of up to seventy-five hundred feet above the ground and the ZPU-23 machine guns also can shoot almost that high."

"I thought we were supposed to stay at least 3000 feet above the ground. That means we're still in their range."

"Yeah," Red smirked. "The three thousand feet is to keep us out of range from the little guns, 'small arms' they call them—like the shoulder fired rifles the soldiers carry. But that's not much of a problem over the Plain of Jars. We fly at twelve thousand feet above sea level so we can have our three thousand foot clearance above the mountain tops that surround the PDJ. The Hmong control the mountain tops—usually, anyway. But ya never know! Also, in weather, at that altitude, we don't have to worry about running into any granite. When we wander over the PDJ, the floor drops to about three thousand feet so we have eight or nine thousand feet altitude above the valley guns. We don't descend down over the PDJ cause that would make us sitting ducks for the thirty-seven millimeter guns that are all over the floor. Anyway, it would waste fuel for us to climb and descend every time we cross in and out of the PDJ."

"What about shoulder fired missiles and surface to air SAM missiles?"

"Depends who you talk to. If you ask our intelligence briefers or any of the other desk jockeys they'll tell you there haven't been any reported in Laos. That's the policy; they don't want us to worry about such things."

"And . . ." Eddie looked over at Red. The guy was flying with one hand and with the other trying to peal an orange he was holding between his knees.

"I have the airplane," Eddie said.

"You got the airplane." Red now had two hands free and he attacked the orange with vigor. Red talked as he worked, "But the truth is there have been several reports of SAM sightings, some south along the trail, but for some reason the people that run our lives don't want us to know that." Red slid his side window open and tossed his orange peelings out the window. As was the C-124, the EC-47 was unpressurized. Their rear troop door had been removed and the open gap guarded with a single strap. Both pilot side windows could be opened at will. "Our fighter planes," Red continued, "have destroyed several Sam missiles that were still on their transport vehicles and there are some claims that a couple of them have been fired at the fast movers. I think those were the shoulder fired type but they're still SAMs. But the intelligence guys still refuse to admit their existence. The Nail forward air controllers are really disgusted and some of em are carrying their own cameras with them on their missions. They wanna prove they aren't making up the missiles.

"There're also a lot of really big guns, fifty-sevens and eight-fives, on the east end of the PDJ and the Mu Gia Pass area, so don't ever go over there. Flying at twelve thousand feet, the fifty-sevens and eight-fives will shoot you down in a nanosecond. They're towable and could show up anywhere on the PDJ floor. The NVA have controlled the floor long enough that there's no way to keep accurate locations on the guns. Best we got is the red circles that intelligence gives us."

"How come you know all this stuff we're not supposed to know?"

"I talk to drunk Nails at our Hooch and to buddies I know flying A-1s. They know all kinds of stuff that we're not supposed to know."

Eddie speculated, "We don't have any RHAW warning equipment on our EC-47s. If they ever fired a surface to air missile at us we wouldn't even know it before we were blown out of the sky." RHAW was an acronym for radar homing and warning. It detected enemy radar signals from surface to air missiles.

"Bad news, bad news," Red laughed. "Bad news is we wouldn't have any warning if they ever shot one at us and the bad news is even if we did know, as slow as the Gooney Bird is and as un-maneuverable as we are, there's no way we could dodge one. I suspect our radial engine heat signature is a lot smaller than a jet engine but I don't have any idea if that would make any difference. I can't do anything about it so I just don't think about it."

Soon the Mekong turned to the west and their straight north course carried them out over low hills, irregular karst formations, then over higher mountains. Eddie was flying. Without an autopilot, the Towhead pilots took turns hand flying. The mountains were coming up to meet them and Red told Eddie to climb up to 9,000 feet. There was very little sign of civilization, just an occasional cluster of huts and sometimes a glimpse of a trail winding across the face of a mountain. They were flying away from civilization.

There were two interphones in the aircraft, one for use by the radio operators and the navigator to coordinate and work their mission in the rear of the aircraft. The second was for the pilots and navigator. Every member of the crew had the switching option to listen to either or both interphones. Eddie switched them both on but there had been little back end conversation.

They had flown for forty-five minutes and the mountains were still rising. Red had Eddie climb to 12,000 feet MSL (mean sea level) to keep a safe distance from the ground.

"We'll call this number two," the radio operators' interphone spoke. "Let's get this guy's position."

"Pilot turn left to three three zero degrees and we'll get a line," Eddie heard over the pilot's interphone. He recognized their navigator Stu's voice. Eddie turned to 330 degrees and rolled out.

"Hold it perfectly steady," Red instructed. "He's gonna fix a line from us to the transmitting radio on the ground, the one that they just named number two. The oversized attitude indicator made it much easier to steady the aircraft when "fixing" a line.

"Got it. Turn right to Zero Three Zero," the navigator directed.

As Eddie started his turn Red checked his map to make sure there were no gun circles in their new direction. They held the new heading for ten seconds and again Stu instructed, "Got it, turn right to one five zero." Ten seconds after Eddie rolled out on 150 degrees Stu announced, "Got him. That's all we need, it's not real accurate but it'll do. Let's go upgrade our computer's position with a dop set, so we can plot our lines more accurately. Turn left to zero one zero."

Eddie complied and Red compared his red circle chart with the terrain feature out his side window. He looked up at Eddie and grinned, "Got any idea what's going on?"

"ARDF, Airborne Radio Direction Finding," Eddie guessed. "I think we just plotted three lines from our aircraft to a transmitting radio antenna. We positioned ourselves in three different places and where the three lines cross is the transmitter's location."

"You got it. We just plotted an enemy position."

"Actually we just plotted the location of one of our friendly positions," a radio operator's voice from the back came over the interphone. He had been listening in on the pilot's interphone. "But that's usable information also. Our customer also likes to assure themselves that the friendlies are where they're supposed to be."

"Whatever," Eddie shrugged. As if the radio operator could see him shrug over the interphone.

"What's so secret about using a direction finding antenna to locate a ground radio transmitter? They did that way back in World War II," Eddie asked.

"It's our speed of acquisition, ability to acquire weak signals from a distance, and we can do it all without spooking the enemy. The old systems required the aircraft to home in on the radio signal to establish a line across the transmitter. The enemy is not stupid, if they see an airplane over flying them back and forth, they would know what the airplane was doing and stop transmitting. We can fly out of sight from them or a straight line like a passing aircraft, and nail them without looking suspicious."

"We're gonna get a Dop set," Stu the navigator joined into the conversation. "Dop set is slang everybody uses for Doppler Set. My navigation set uses doppler technology and the magnetic heading from your pilot's C-12 compass to compute and follow the moving position of our aircraft. There are variables that, with time, cause our computed aircraft moving position to drift and our aircraft's position accuracy degrades. We have some spots on the ground, places that are easy to spot from the air, that the map makers have 'fixed' with great precision. At the start of each mission on the ground at the airfield and every thirty minutes during our mission, we'll fly directly over a dop point and get a precision update of our position. It works really well. Right now I'm looking through my drift meter that looks out the bottom of the airplane and guiding you to fly right over the dop point. When we're over the dop point, I'll record our position error and update our position."

Stu continued, "We have a radio transceiver back here and a KY-8 scrambler. We can transmit secure voice messages to the various appropriate agencies. They also have KY-8 units and they can unscramble our transmissions. If necessary they can act immediately on time sensitive intelligence. The NVA has no idea how fast we can locate the position of their radio transmissions and send them to the users. Sometimes, within ten or fifteen minutes, the B-52s drop bombs on the coordinates the EC-47s call in. B-52s fly very high and with the haze you can't even see them from the ground. The gomers have no idea where the bombs come from or how the bombers know where they are."

"I suppose while we're fixing one transmitter's position, the other RO's are copying their radio transmissions." Eddie was pleased he had figured out part of the operation.

"That's not anything you're supposed to know," the radio operator cut him off. "I probably already told you more than I was supposed to but us guys feel it's essential for you to be a part of the loop for us to be effective. Our total capabilities are not for advertisement."

"Turn three degrees right," Stu called. "Make that one more right . . . I got the dop set," he concluded. "Turn to three six zero, let's do some fishing."

"We EC-47s provide the bulk and most reliable intelligence to our customers. We track enemy movements and monitor their daily reports that list their unit's size and troop numbers." Red was taking his turn flying and talking.

Eddie was studying his map closely. He looked out in front and saw they were just coming up to a row of higher mountains and it looked like the tops had been trimmed off from many of them, leaving an exposed flat area a hundred or so yards in diameter. Beyond the mountains lay a huge flat prairie of tall grassland, spotted with clumps of trees and open spaces for a little farming. A series of small roads and trails connected widely scattered villages. It was the fabled Plaine de Jarres.

They were within radio receiving range of the Plain of Jars so Red reduced their power so as to burn less fuel. Their purpose was to serve as an airborne platform and stay on station for as long as they could. The lower power setting and resultant slower speed allowed them to stay on station over an hour and a half longer. The aviation term was "best endurance speed" and the book endurance speeds, which slowed a little as they burned off fuel and became lighter, were in the 95 to 100 knot range. Considering the fact that they did a lot of maneuvering and the flight controls became sloppy below 100 knots, the Towheads loitered at 105 knots indicated.

"Those tiny flat tops on some of the mountains are observation and artillery sites that have been cleared and leveled by the Hmong," Red spoke as he also looked out his windshield. "The tops of a mountain are the easiest real estate to defend. During the dry season the NVA usually take control of the PDJ floor, then the Hmong drive them back during the rainy season. It's a see saw, been that way for three or four years now. The Hmong have always kept control of the mountains. This is the wet season and the NVA have been a little more aggressive. They're still holding on to the valley floor and actually driving the Hmong further back into the mountains. It's a damn shame we can't bring some American tanks in here and just clean the NVA out of the PDJ. Our troops could easily wop their asses with our superior firepower and weapons and we'd have the Hmong to watch out for our backs . . . it's just the opposite of what we got going in Vietnam. Here the guerrillas, the Hmong, are on our side and the guys with the big guns, trucks, and tanks in the valley are the bad guys."

They spent four and a half hours working the Plain of Jars and made several excursions, at the request of the radio operators, into the mountains surrounding the open valley. They made dop sets about every twenty to thirty minutes and fixed the position of sixteen enemy radio transmitter locations. The other radio operators in the back had a count of twenty-three intercepted enemy messages. At 12,000 feet they were clear of small arms gunfire. The big guns that everyone knew were mobile and always a possible threat, stayed silent. The Towheads were just slightly out of the 37mm effective range from the valley floor but the mountain slopes surrounding the floor were higher and could place the guns well within range of their ancient aircraft.

The one big surprise for Eddie was that the pilots could open their side windows in-flight. It was something that pilots in higher speed aircraft and all pressurized aircraft could only dream about. Due to the shape of the nose pushing its way through the air, the airflow rushing past the pilot's open side windows passed by faster than the aircraft was going forward. The result of this accelerated air movement is described by engineers as the venturi effect. The venturi effect caused the cockpit air to be sucked out the window. With the rear troop door removed, air came in the open rear door, flowed forward through the cabin cooling the electrical equipment and the operators, into the cockpit, and out the open side windows. In the tropics it was comfortable and cool with the breeze flowing by. The open cockpit window also provided a handy place to toss orange and banana peelings.

Gooney Bird pilots needed to be careful with their paperwork and maps when the side window was open, as it could also be sucked out the window. If they leaned too close to the opening, the suction was so strong it could suck the sunglasses off their face.

The pilots always knew where they were by reference to their maps and using the TACAN. There was only one TACAN ground based electronic navigation aid for the Towhead pilots to use in the Plain of Jars. The single TACAN station, channel 98, was located in a small mountain ringed valley about ten miles south of the Plain of Jars. Red called the secure Hmong location the "Alternate." The Towhead pilots monitored the TACAN's signals closely on days when the weather prevented them from seeing the ground. The navigator in the back conducted his precision mission using the position displayed on his Doppler navigation set. The redundancy insured they stay out of the red circled gun emplacements.

On their way home they passed their afternoon replacement, another Towhead on its way north. Their replacement would probably encounter heavy rain clouds later in the afternoon and the pilots would have to rely exclusively on the TACAN for their navigation. Eddie felt good about their flight. It put to rest his fears that they flew a dangerous mission—this would be a cakewalk. He did feel their mission was important and valuable to the war effort.

The Lady flew like a dream. She trimmed out beautifully and required very little effort to hand fly. By taking turns with Red, at the end of the seven hour mission he was less fatigued than he would have been on a seven hour flight in the C-124 with an autopilot. The snacks were great. You could fly the unpressurized Gooney Bird with the side window slid open, and your elbow sticking out, just like a sports car. But it wasn't as fast as a sports car! With the window open the prop was spinning just behind you, only four feet away. It was about as close as Eddie would ever get to that old yellow Stearman with its open cockpit. Yes, his Lady, although not flesh and blood, was indeed easy to love.

CHAPTER SEVENTEEN:
THE ORIGINAL DON'T ASK,
DON'T TELL

Eddie woke the next morning feeling much better about his new job and his new digs. He stayed in bed and took a long look at the room he shared with Red. In reality it was Red's room. Eddie only had a small bed in one corner where he stashed his bags and slept. Red's room looked a little like Eddie's apartment had back at Tachikawa. Wooden carvings, bronze ware table sets, stuff was everywhere. He had the latest high tech stereo tape equipment, four Pioneer speakers, Akai double reel tape deck, stacks of tapes sent to him from his friends back in the Sates and a refrigerator full of beer. Apparently Red liked to drink in his room as well as the Hooch, which was located at least fifty steps from their front door. He had a homemade dart board and several darts with tattered feathers. It was questionable if the feathers would make it until the end of Red's tour.

The room had two chests of drawers, but Red had both of them filled. Although he lacked consideration for others, he was a hell of a pilot. Red had several suits, three sports jackets and numerous shirts folded in one corner. They were things that the local village tailor had made for him by copying clothing ads in *Playboy* magazine. When Eddie saw them he knew he would have to have some of that. The remaining drawer space was filled with wood carvings from Bangkok and other collectables. Under Red's bed were three more varnished wooden boxes that Eddie recognized as bronze table ware sets. Red was a hoarder! There was a porcelain elephant, bundles of batiks and more wood carvings. It appeared to Eddie that, although Red had flown C-124s based in the States, he hadn't experienced the Asian shopping opportunities the guys in the 22nd had. He was still in his shopping and hoarding mode. The walls were bare; Eddie would have to get some cheap local art work once Red left for the States and make the walls more interesting. Eddie decided he would have to ask Red for at least two drawers, for his flight suits, underwear, 1505 uniform and his small collection of civilian clothing. No reason to make a big deal of it. Red was just naturally rude and would be leaving in a few months anyway. Then Eddie would be the senior resident.

Eddie took a long shower and was still a little uneasy about the maids. He wondered if they ever cleaned the rooms or just always hung out in the johns watching the white guys' privates. Red was spending his day flying as an observer with a recently upgraded aircraft commander and Eddie had the day off. It was time for him to check out the base and get the lay of the land.

He took a long walk before the sun got too high and too hot, but the mild exercise still caused the sweat to flow freely. He poked his head into the gym and felt it was air-conditioned; it would be a good place to spend free time on his off days. There was a hobby wood shop next door. He walked over to the flight line and the first thing he saw was a sign that warned photography was prohibited, under penalty of the UCMJ. The Uniform Code of Military Justice was the manual for military law.

Sitting in the middle of the base operations section of the ramp were two unlike aircraft. The largest was a single lonely F-105 Thunderchief, one of the large fighter bombers that had been assigned the brutal mission of bombing the most difficult targets in North Vietnam. About sixteen inches of its left wing was missing, a ragged tear was curled up and the remaining portion of the wing was stained from an explosion. The rear of the fuselage, where its single jet engine was internally located, had dark fluid dripping out and it was forming a large stain on the new concrete ramp. Eddie walked closer to the Thunderchief and could see where the shrapnel had blown numerous gashes and holes into the oversized fighter's skin. Somewhere on the base was a thankful pilot who someday, as his grandchild sat on his lap, would praise his faithful steed for getting him across the Mekong River and onto Nakhon Phanom's solid concrete. The guys loved their F-105s and they affectionately called them "Thuds."

The other aircraft was an O-2 observer aircraft. Back in the States, Cessna was building the twin engine light weight aircraft, model 337 Skymaster, for civilian use. Its engines were mounted one in the front and one on the rear of its pod like fuselage, the front engine pulled and the rear engine pushed. It had two booms extended back, one from each wing that connected and formed the tail in the rear. It was not a very profitable aircraft for Cessna until the military ordered hundreds of them for use in Vietnam. This one had obviously been diverted from the normal military distribution system. It was painted dull solid black and had no identifying marks on it. The message couldn't have been clearer if they had painted VERY SECRET NIGHT OPERATIONS on its fuselage. Under each wing hung a pod of white phosphorus smoke marking rockets, nicknamed "Wiley Petes." It was definitely not your neighborhood, weekend, and private aircraft. Eddie guessed that its pilot, maybe military special forces, maybe a civilian CIA employee, had dropped in for the afternoon and a nice dinner before going to work in the black hostile night. Eddie imagined the guy who flew that unidentified aircraft was some kind of mean and spooky son of a bitch.

What Eddie didn't know was that the black O-2's pilot was call sign Squeaky. He had an unhappy childhood, was skinny, pimple faced, and the forerunner of modern day geeks. In high school the guys teased and picked on him constantly and the girls called him Squeaky to his face and Freaky to his back. After he graduated from college with a degree in physics, he joined the air force and became a highly skilled forward air controller in South Vietnam. He volunteered for a second tour and because of his reputed skills was invited to join a special forces unit. He became a specialist in flying nights and working with special forces units operating along the Ho Chi Minh Trail. He was currently a highly respected operative and hung out with a select group of bad ass mercenaries that invoked fear and nightmares among the North Vietnamese Army. He knew he was at the peak of his existence, known by few but held in reverence by the bravest. He was fearless and reckless, not wanting to go back to his previous life and held no fear of death. His once humiliating nickname of Squeaky was spoken with reverence among his peers. Neither Eddie nor Sqeaky knew that within the week, Squeaky would be finally shot down and killed by the NVA. He was just another unsung hero that blossomed under fire.

> *Yea though I fly through the valley of the shadow of death*
> *I will fear no evil*
> *For I am the meanest son-of-a bitch in the valley*
> … Goodbye Squeaky

* *

The silence on the flight line was unnerving, not an aircraft engine could be heard and no one was flying. Then in the distance he could see a little motion. There was maintenance going on in the A-1 revetments and one mechanic was working on the single EC-47 remaining on the ramp. Then he saw a blue maintenance van behind the row of C-123 freighters. Why weren't they out flying, hauling stuff? He strolled over to get a closer look at the freighters. He had never been up close to a C-123 and he was curious. Two armed GIs stepped out from under their shade and approached him before he was within a hundred feet.

"Excuse me Sir," the ranking airman placed himself directly in front of Eddie. "This area is restricted. May I see your ID?" Eddie fished his security badge out of his pocket and handed it to the airman first class.

After examining it the black skinned muscular airman looked at Eddie with a wince on his face. "You're not allowed access to the C-123 flight line. You'll have to move on down the way to your own unit." The airman nodded his head toward the single lonely EC-47 several hundred feet to the south.

Eddie was amazed and questioned the airman, "I got a top secret clearance. Certainly that allows me access to C-123 freighters?"

The airman looked at his badge again and handed it back to Eddie. "Sir, the date on this badge is two days old. You're new here. With all due respect, Sir, I suggest you restrict your movement and your curiosity to your own particular unit and its functions. This is not a base where you go around snooping and asking questions. You don't ask me any questions and I don't tell you any answers."

What Eddie didn't know was that the C-123 freighters, their call sign "Candlestick," weren't what they appeared to be. The Candlestick guys openly spoke of their mission to dispense flares from their open rear ramp to illuminate friendly units. They would deny the enemy the cover of darkness for sneak attacks. That was an effective cover story and they did that some of the time. The rest of the time their business was highly secret. They flew along the Ho Chi Minh Trail at night, at low altitudes, with a navigator looking through a hatch in the floor. The navigator used a night scope, the latest military technology that amplified the night light many hundreds of times. The user could literally see in the dark. Whenever the navigator spotted enemy trucks scurrying along the maze of roads under cover of the dark, they would call in a set of fighters and launch bright flares to illuminate the trucks. The fighters would take out the trucks with bombs and rockets. It was a hazardous mission as their aircraft was often silhouetted against a moonlit or star-lit sky and enemy gunners never hesitated shooting at them. Eddie thanked the airman, clipped his badge on his flowered shirt, and headed for the Gooney Bird.

"Excuse me, Sir. May I look at your ID?" a voice came from behind him. It was one of the guards that had been in the shade under the Gooney Bird's wing. Eddie removed and handed his ID badge to the guard who examined it.

"Looks like you're one of us. What are you doing out here?"

"I was just looking around," Eddie explained. "It's my day off and I'm out for a walk."

"Sir, if you have no business here you'll have to move on. We can't just have people hanging out around here for no good reason." So Eddie moved on. He wasn't even allowed near his own aircraft when off duty!

He moved down the flight line. The black unmarked CH-53 helicopters were obviously off limits to him and he crossed to the empty side of the ramp to stay clear. Their guards watched him closely as he passed by. In front of him was an aircraft hangar, the rounded roof and sliding front door more typical of hangars from earlier wars. In front of the hangar was a white Beechcraft A-36, a small single engine, four passenger, light aircraft that was popular with private pilots back in the States. At first he thought maybe they had an aero club on the base. They had aero clubs on some of the bases back in the States and non-pilot personnel could join and get their licenses if they wished. It would be fun to rent one, fly around the local area, and check it out. At closer examination there were numerous Beechcraft also parked in the hangar with a sign "Bat Cave" over the open hangar door. He noticed a strange looking metal protuberance mounted on top of the engine cowling and all the aircraft appeared to have longer wings than normal. As if on cue two guards emerged from the shade of the hangar and headed toward him. He turned and casually walked away.

"There's all kind of spooky stuff going on here," Eddie thought to himself as he sauntered back toward the housing area.

He passed through several rows of officer's quarters that were constructed similar to the Towhead's compound. He continued walking and arrived at the enlisted barracks. They were larger, single-story buildings, still built of wood. He had on civvies and he wouldn't attract any attention, so he stepped inside to check them out. They were open bay quarters but had tall dark green steel lockers arranged so as to provide smaller semi-private living spaces for four to six enlisted per space. There was a sloppy looking

Thai girl sitting on one of the beds in her panties and bra. She smiled and there were two teeth missing. Eddie wondered how she had lost them. Two more scantily dressed girls strolled by and ignored him as he stood in wonderment. Several enlisted men, in one of the enclosures, were engaged in a poker game. This base was loaded with classified aircraft and secret operations and there were women of questionable virtue wandering freely throughout the enlisted barracks. To the poor guys fighting inside Vietnam, this would qualify as enlisted heaven.

He continued his walk and confronted a huge concrete building surrounded with chain link fencing and an excessive number of guards. By now he understood. Don't ask, don't tell.

He wandered back to his room; he would save the base exchange for later. He needed to drag things out as he would be stuck there for a year. His assigned maid was in his room sweeping the floor. His and Red's freshly washed laundry was neatly stacked on each of their respective beds. She grinned at him as she covered her mouth, and then went about her tasks. He wandered over to the hooch. The bar was empty, except for one guy lying on one of the couches in the lounge. He was reading a paperback novel and didn't even bother to look up. Millhouse, the parrot, looked up and said hello to Eddie, then continued his attack on a large slice of orange next to a pathetic, plastic, miniature waterfall. The waterfall was not operational but had several inches of water in its pool. It gave Millhouse someplace to occasionally cool off by sitting in the water.

Millhouse was a green and blue parrot, the Towhead's mascot. He was named after Richard Nixon's middle name. Evenings he would limp around on the bar as he had a gimpy leg from a former injury. He loved to steal bites from the guy's dill pickles and his favorites were yellow hot peppers. He also loved to sip from the guys' drinks, and when soused take a dust bath in the popcorn bowl. It was a good life for a parrot. The Towheads loved him and tolerated his indiscretions. After all it was their mascot. None of them, the guys and the bird, had any choice about being there so they all made the best of it.

The Nails also had a pet. It was a pot bellied pig that lived in a space they arranged for him under their raised quarters. It was against base regulations for anyone to have a pet other than a bird or a dog, so the Nails named their pet pig Dog. The ruse seemed to work because no one seemed to care that Dog was a pig. It was a strange base. No wonder they didn't allow access to the media.

Millhouse just might have been another reason why the Nails didn't like the Towheads. In addition to the fact that Millhouse's poop had to be cleaned up from the bar, the Nail's pig mascot, Dog, wasn't allowed in the bar.

There was also Harold, but he wasn't really anyone's pet, He would never come down from the trees. The air base was built on a flat plain, a flood plain extending westward away from the Mekong. It was probably twenty or thirty feet above the normal high water mark of the river which was six or seven miles away. When clearing the jungle for the housing construction, they allowed occasional larger trees to remain, provide some shade, and assist the native landscaping. Harold was a very large lizard that lived in the tall trees in their compound. True, there was an abundance of small friendly geckos that inhabited everyone's quarters and patrolled the Towhead Inn's ceiling every night. In addition to being tiny and cute, they were decoratively acceptable as they always changed colors to match the ceiling. The ceiling was their upside down floor, and they ate mosquitoes and other small bugs. They were far superior to the sticky flypaper that was available free on the base.

No, Harold was big. Big, like in well over two feet long, stout build, and ugly as sin. Harold was in command of the tops of the tallest trees and everyone assumed that he ate the large tropical insects that sometimes came buzzing down, or maybe he ate flower blossoms and fruit. None could imagine that Harold would ever eat the friendly geckos but within the week, late one night while on a trip to the john, Eddie would actually see Harold catch and eat a gecko. Apparently Harold came down to feed in the lower branches late in the night when all the people had settled down in their rooms. What gave Harold his distinction was that he could howl like a banshee in pain, and then he would follow up with a series of deep, tuba like reverberating bleats. He didn't do this very often, maybe several times each night, but when he did everyone was reminded that he was the king lizard. He almost scared the water out of Eddie in the middle of his first night at NKP.

Eddie wandered out on the deck. In the shade was another guy reading another paperback novel. There was no wind and it was too hot to lie out in the sun.

"Where's all the guys?" Eddie asked the bored reader.

"Don't know. Think some of em went down to the pool to cool off."

From the Nail side, Aretha Franklin was wailing *Chain of Fools* and on the Towhead side an open door broadcasted Iron Butterfly's *In A-Gadda-Da-Vida*. The Iron Butterfly's endless song, seventeen minutes long, was exhausting as it went on and on, and it reminded Eddie that he was going to have to endure this confusing existence for a whole year. The Towhead's Q model aircraft on the ramp, the one that Eddie had earlier walked by, had a large brightly colored butterfly painted on the sides of its nose and it was appropriately named the Iron Butterfly. Eddie assumed it had been the inspiration for the five foot carving that hung from their saloon ceiling.

Eddie strolled over to their operations building and checked with Airman Hendrix to make sure he was scheduled to fly the next day.

"I wanna be scheduled to fly as often as possible," he half pleaded with the airman. "I need as much time as possible to get qualified as a flight instructor before Red goes home." He lied. He really wanted to fly as much as possible because he knew that too much time and nothing to do around this spook base would drive him nuts.

* *

The next day Red and Eddie were back in the air. They had the afternoon shift in the PDJ. The cockpit was the same but the antennas and their placement reflected subtle differences from the Lady. Red shrugged his shoulder when Eddie asked him about the differences. Red was a little odd, sometimes he was aloof and overplayed the secrecy thing. It was hard enough to get a straight answer from him with questions that related directly to their own pilot tasks. Then other times he was a motor mouth and would spew out everything he knew, which was much more than the intelligence briefers wanted him to know.

"Home in on channel ninety-eight," the nav called over the pilot's interphone as they were approaching the mountains and the PDJ area. "I'll get a dop set, then you can wander north into the plain at your own discretion. It's a little slow back here for now." Eddie was flying and he turned the aircraft so they were following the channel ninety-eight TACAN navigation beam straight to its source. Below them, in a small valley south of the Plain of Jars, a small scattered town unfolded. It was more like a village, with thousands of pock marks scattered randomly about. Each of the pock marks was where a North Vietnamese artillery shell, mortar round, or an explosive rocket had impacted. In the center of the valley was an east-west runway that ended abruptly at the west end. A few feet west of the runway end was a tall steep-sided spire of karst, maybe three to five hundred feet high. It was one of a half dozen karst spires in a small group.

"It's the Alternate. If anybody asks you never saw this place," Red informed Eddie. "Tell them it's just a rumor and doesn't really exist. I got the aircraft, take a good look outside. We okay back there Nav?"

"You got it." Eddie turned control of the spy bird over to Red and stretched to see all there was down there.

"Two degrees to the right," the navigator called from his drift meter as he directed the aircraft to pass directly over the Dop survey point on the ground.

"This place is Long Tieng," Red flew and talked. "It's the headquarters for General Vang Pao and his division of guerrilla fighters that the CIA supports. It's nothing to do with the Ho Chi Minh Trail. These Hmong guerrillas are fighting for their own home turf and we're supporting them because we also don't want the Hmong homeland, the mountains surrounding the Plain of Jars, to fall under North Vietnamese control."

Red finally decided to open up and explain what was going on down there. "According to the Geneva

Convention of 1962, Laos was declared neutral and all foreign nations were supposed to withdraw their military from this area. The Americans, like the dumb shits we are, pulled our troops out. The reason I said we're dumb shits is that there were prior treaties to neutralize Laos. The Communists, even though they signed the previous treaties, never paid any attention to any of em. So in 1962 nothing changed. The Americans pulled out and the North Vietnamese Army, their Viet Minh insurgents, and their Russian advisers never budged. They viewed it as an opportunity to gain advantage over us naive foreigners.

"When the war in South Vietnam heated up, we had to do something to stop the North Vietnamese aggression in Laos. The poorly trained and poorly equipped Laotian military was helpless against the well disciplined North Vietnam soldiers. In addition to controlling the Ho Chi Minh Trail transportation corridor, along the south eastern edge of Laos, the North Vietnamese Army was attempting to overrun and control northwestern Laos. They wanted its capital city of Vientiane, and to replace the Laotian political structure with their Communist model. The route the North Vietnam Army chose to Vientiane required that they control the area of mountains where the Plain of Jars is located.

"The North Vietnamese strongly deny that they have military on the ground despite the fact that evidence of their presence and aggression is obvious. The key to this thing is not fact but denial. They insist they have no military on the ground therefore they don't. That's how these people think. So, instead of openly placing American troops into Laos, our politicians decided to also use denial. Our denial is spelled Covert Operations! The military was instructed to operate secret special forces and SOG teams along the Ho Chi Minh Trail, inserting them and extracting them with helicopters. Both were task forces of kick ass teams of bad ass guys. They also recruited thousands of Thai 'mercenaries' to harass and cripple the North Vietnamese along their supply chain through Laos into South Vietnam.

"In the Plain of Jars, to stop the advancing North Vietnamese Army, the CIA recruited ex-American military combatants and had them secretly organize, train, and equip General Pao's Hmong warriors. This action is referred to as the CIA's Secret War and is separate and isolated from the war raging over South Vietnam. The Hmong tribesman, led by their leader General Vang Pao, are the only credible military force that stands between the North Vietnamese Army and their campaign to capture the Laotian capital city of Vientiane. The Hmong have stopped the advancing North Vietnam Army in the Plain of Jars. At this time there are over eighty thousand NVA soldiers operating in Laos and over half are spread out along the Ho Chi Minh Trail. The rest are stalled in the Plain of Jars by the Hmong warriors. In addition to gathering intelligence and tracking troop movements along the northern end of the Ho Chi Minh Trail, it's us Towhead's mission to gather intelligence about the North Vietnamese invaders in the Plain of Jars. The politics of the CIA supporting Hmong warriors is very sensitive and secret and we're right in the middle of it."

"I got the dop set; you're cleared to turn north," the nav interrupted. Eddie rolled left to 360 degrees as he listened to Red's revelations. Red had been at NKP long enough and snooped around asking questions long enough that he had figured things out.

"So Washington denies we have anyone on the ground." Red spilled it all out. "It's a stand-off of denial. But we got people down there working for us. It needs to be kept hush, hush and we gotta keep the media off balance and at arm's length. They try to discover and reveal our secret operations and that makes them our opponent. Personally I think it's treason when our media reveals our military secrets; it's as if they're working for the North Vietnamese. We executed the Rosenbergs for treason but now we turn our backs when the media does the same thing!

"There's an American agent, an ex-military civilian agent, with each unit of General Pao's guerrillas. They coordinate supply and bomb drops from the Americans, train the Hmong guerrillas on fighting techniques, and how to use modern weapons. Although they're not supposed to, I hear that they sometimes participate in actual combat. They each have a cover: relief workers, Red Cross, civilian adviser to the government. Hell, I don't know, but they all got covers. The treaty allows us to have civilian aid workers in Laos. We even have a civilian agency down there called AID, Agency for International Development. Half is legitimate and the other half is cover for CIA operatives."

As Red explained their mission, both pilots scanned the view outside their windows and reaffirmed their position. After scanning their engine's instruments and when satisfied, Red continued, "Then there're the covert American forward air controllers that fly spotter missions in the Plain of Jars for the Laotian and American Air Force bombers. They're called Ravens and they're stationed at scattered airfields throughout Laos. The rumor is that they're 'released' from the military and fly sheep dipped for one year. Sheep dipped is a term you'll hear a lot around this part of the world. It means they put all of their military clothing and IDs in storage and cross into Laos and operate as if mercenaries. That way if they get captured, our military and our government can claim they don't have anything to do with the captured American. I recently found out they really aren't released from military service, but technically and very secretly are assigned to the 56th Special Operations Wing at Udorn. They just disappear off record for a year. Either way, they dress in old civilian clothes, drink, raise hell and act like mercenaries. They do one hell of a job in their little spotter aircraft—directing bomb drops with their smoke rockets. The Ravens have been directing more and more American aircraft dropping bombs in the Plain of Jars. Our airpower kinda levels the playing field for the Hmong fighting against the North Vietnamese Army. The scuttlebutt I heard last week was that the North Vietnamese Army now has Soviet built 130mm long range artillery that is effective up to nineteen miles. It kinda makes things even. The Hmong have bombs, the NVA have artillery.

"The Ravens know this area lots better than the Nails. The Nails, OV-10 pilots that live across the commons from us at NKP, concentrate on trucks and supplies along the trail. But I hear they're flying more and more up here also. Then there's the civilian Air America pilots that haul the supplies for the villagers and soldiers that we're supporting. " Red laughed. "Over the radio they call rice, soft rice, and guns and ammo are called hard rice.

"Back to our discussion about Long Tieng," Red loved to instruct and teach. "Long Tieng is the town's name and the official airfield name is confusing, I've heard it was Lima Site twenty, Lima Site thirty, and Lima Site ninety-eight. I think twenty is the correct name. Lima sites are the tiny dirt runways all over Laos that Air America flies into to deliver stuff. They're the civilian counterpart to the trash haulers, only they use smaller airplanes and go into many smaller and more challenging dirt strips. Long Tieng is never called any of these names to keep the news media off balance. Everyone calls it the Alternate or channel ninety-eight. That's to help keep it a secret from the news media. Alternate is a generic aviation term that's used all the time because whenever pilots can't land on the airfield of their destination, they fly to an alternate airfield. Channel ninety-eight is the frequency of the TACAN located there. The media guys never know what airfield anyone is talking about. They monitor radio transmissions, you know. They're sneaky bastards. I guess there's good money for any media guy if they can sell an article that exposes our treaty violations."

"Bastards," Eddie swore.

"Traitors, is more like it. During World War II they would have strung em up for that," Red resolved.

"Anyway, what the hell. The North Vietnamese Army on the ground knows all about the Alternate. All ya gotta do is look down and see all of the artillery and mortar craters from the North Vietnamese Army. I really think Washington doesn't want the American public to know about the Alternate cause we're not supposed to be there. The Alternate is the home base for General Pao's Army, a busy Air America operation, and CIA operatives. They also got a bunch of Ravens there and a group of Laotian T-28s. It's probably the busiest non-existent airfield in the world. Laotians fly T-28s and drop bombs with em."

"Let me guess," Eddie smiled. "The Laotians got their T-28s from us and we trained them to fly em."

"Yeah, and we give them the airplanes, bombs, spare parts, and the CIA pays their pilots," Red agreed. "It's hard to find things out but I got a buddy at Udorn who told me they train the Laotians and Thai pilots at Detachment Six, First Air Commando Wing at Udorn Air Base in Thailand. They use American instructors under a program called *Waterpump*. The Laotians fly most of their missions out of the Alternate. I also hear the Laotians are flying some of our AC-47 gunships, but I haven't been able to confirm that. That's good if it's true, because they would be painted just like our aircraft."

Eddie had seen an American AC-47 gunship fire its guns one night when they were departing from Phan

Rang in Vietnam. Its three Gatling miniguns spewed a solid tube of fire from the aircraft to the ground, lit up the whole sky, and nothing on the ground could have survived. Eddie hoped all the North Vietnamese gunners on the Plain of Jars and along the trail had been warned of the danger from shooting at the "flying dragon," disguised like a Gooney Bird. They needed to be afraid of shooting at Gooney Birds.

"That's why we gotta keep everything so secret up here. According to the Geneva Convention we aren't allowed any military on the ground," Red replied.

"We legal to fly in Laos?" Eddie wondered.

"As long as we're based in Thailand and only fly over here we're not in violation of the treaty, so I'm told. But no, we're not on the ground but we're flying missions in support of Americans that are secretly on the ground so we gotta keep everything secret."

"What a dumb war," Eddie wondered out loud.

"It gets complicated," Red talked as they crossed a mountain ridge and onto the PDJ. Eddie had his chart out and was keeping track of the gun circles. The higher ground along that ridge would be the perfect place for a 37mm gun and well into range of their loitering Gooney Bird.

Red sat for a minute and let his anger simmer. Eddie pointed out a cluster of red circles on his map and Red altered their course thirty degrees left to avoid them.

"Fly three five zero," the nav instructed. Eddie and Red were not monitoring the radio operator's interphone so they didn't hear the activity going on in the back. They only heard the navigator when he switched over to the pilot's interphone and gave them instructions. Red turned to 350 degrees heading and held the aircraft steady while the navigator plotted a line. The data processor's computed line led straight toward the enemy radio transmitter. "Turn right to zero eight zero." They followed the navigator's drill and plotted three more bearings across the active transmitter. The processor computed the spot all four lines crossed, the estimated accuracy, and almost instantly the navigator had the exact coordinates of the enemy's position. The position, along with the recorded radio transmission, was important enough that it was scrambled and called into the CIA headquarters located at Udorn Air Base in Thailand.

"Right turn to one eight zero, let's troll back south again," the nav directed.

"One-eighty," Red responded and rolled the Q model into a left turn. The navigator didn't say anything about the turn in the wrong direction. They were just trolling anyway.

They flew back over the Alternate and Eddie began to appreciate the strategic importance of Long Tieng. He was looking down at the runway and the hodge-podge of aircraft parked along side. "That karst at the west end of the runway is frightening," Eddie remarked. It formed a vertical wall at the end of the runway.

"Yeah, it's definitely a one way in, other way out kind of place," Red remarked. As they flew past the Alternate, the sun reflected off the karst spires at the west end of the runway. "I hear they call that piece of karst the vertical speed brake."

"Ouch," Eddie winced.

As the afternoon progressed, a cloud deck had formed below them and cumulus clouds began billowing up from the carpet of white clouds. They were unable to take any dop sets the last hour on station but by carefully maneuvering around the billowing clouds and gun circles on their maps, they finished the mission.

They copied twenty-two pertinent messages and plotted the locations of thirteen radio transmitters, plus general locations of three more transmitters. Eddie realized that the radio operators weren't always just listening for random traffic. They often wanted to be at certain places at certain times. What Red and Eddie didn't know was that a large percentage of their missions were dispatched with objectives to work specific areas and look for specific unit's transmissions.

The North Vietnamese couldn't have had too good of an idea what those C-47s were doing, just flying around, or they would have been more careful with their radio transmissions. This was just another good reason to keep the EC-47's relatively simple mission a secret. No sense in letting *Time* magazine tell the enemy what the EC-47s were doing. Certainly the North Vietnamese intelligence community read the American newspapers and magazines. It made their job so easy.

Over the next month, Eddie flew two out of every three days, as he had requested. After his first two missions he was signed off to fly as co-pilot with any Towhead aircraft commander. He learned lessons in geography, lessons different than those drawn to scale and presented on maps by cartographers. Eddie learned that the pass between those two odd shaped peaks was usually open when the clouds were low. If daylight could be seen through the pass you could fly through there and it would open to a wider valley that led to the Alternate and a dop set location. Stay away from that big group of trees, or any group of trees on the flat portion of the PDJ because clumps of trees are good hiding places for enemy anti-aircraft guns. A hidden 57mm could reach up to their altitude and bring their mission to a blunt end. That chocolate brown river leads to a shallow valley that led east. Don't go there because where it makes a big bend, there was a big enemy encampment protected by numerous gun pits.

These were the things that Eddie, as an instructor pilot, would faithfully pass on to his students. If you have to put down, that strange fork in the river has a large flat meadow in the crotch and it would make a good place to belly in and take a defensive position until the choppers arrived. Once inside the Plain of Jars they were surrounded by a circle of mountains and a failed engine meant either a controlled crash landing or a marginal attempt to clear the high passes leading out of the tall rock ring. These elements all assumed more importance in proportion to the deterioration of the weather.

During those first few months of Eddie's flying, the enemy was silent with their anti-aircraft guns. It was not unusual, however, to see North Vietnamese anti-aircraft bursts and tracers as they fired at other aircraft down below them. It served as a constant reminder. Also, their enemy could just as well have been a failed engine or ground fog at Nakon Phanom. They returned home so as to arrive with fifteen to twenty minutes of fuel remaining—the nearest alternate was at Udorn—one hour away. They always asked for the Nakhon Phanom weather when forty minutes out and passing by only thirty minutes from Udorn Air Base in Thailand.

The cabin in the Gooney Bird was unpressurized and Eddie learned that long hours of flying at 12,000 feet, in an unpressurized aircraft, had its effects on the crews. Air force regulations called for crews to breathe supplemental oxygen whenever the cabin altitude was above 10,000 feet. Unfortunately, the supplemental oxygen bottles had been removed from the EC-47, both to save weight and to keep them from exploding if they were pierced by a bullet. The crews, therefore, were breaking the regulations every time they flew above 10,000 feet in the PDJ area. It was a war and everyone ignored the violation.

Nakon Phanom (NKP) was only 584 feet above sea level and the crew members' bodies were acclimated to that low altitude. At 12,000 feet, after several hours of intense concentration and without supplemental oxygen, the radio operators in the cabin sometimes would get cranky and start disagreeing and arguing with each other. This was a classic symptom of hypoxia, oxygen deficiency. It was something the pilots and navigators were trained to watch for and the busy operators in the rear of the aircraft didn't realize it was taking place. So, every time the radio operators got too feisty, the pilots would find an open and friendly held area off to the side and descend down to 8000 or 9000 feet. It would only take five or ten minutes in the thicker air and the operators would be the best of friends again. Then the pilots would climb back up and again fly over the higher mountains and enemy occupied real estate. The radio operators rarely realized why the pilots insisted on descending for a short time. It was one of those catch twenty-two things. If you told them they were hypoxic they would argue with you because they were hypoxic. So the pilots just told them it was an airplane thing and descended to lower altitude over a safe area for a while. This problem was peculiar to the Nakhon Phanom crews flying over the PDJ. The remaining EC-47 fleet, flying in southern Laos, Cambodia and South Vietnam, flew over much lower terrain and never had the need to fly above 10,000 feet.

Eddie eavesdropped on the radio operators, both over their interphone in the aircraft and when they were socializing before and after their missions. He picked up a piece here and a piece there and soon had a package of understanding. He started to understand where Red got all of his information. Yes, their mission was to monitor the radio wave spectrum for enemy transmissions (Morse, VHF, AM, CW, and SSB), copy or record them. Then they would transmit the scrambled, time sensitive intelligence over their radios to the appropriate agencies. The remaining intelligence was submitted at their de-briefings after each flight. He learned they had linguists in the rear. He never knew which radio operators were language trained but he suspected most spoke Vietnamese. It was no secret there were Russian advisers and technicians down there, and possibly Chinese. The EC-47 linguists were probably selected for the specific areas they were working or the specific radio operators they were hunting for. The various operator stations in the cabin were labeled: X station was the acquisition radio operator's position, Y worked with the navigator for transmitter location (ARDF), Q station had an MC-88 cryptic typewriter and Z station was message intercept with HF and VHF tape recorders. Positions and equipment varied slightly with each aircraft.

The Nails and other combat aircraft, as well as the ground friendlies, never knew where their briefers obtained their information about the enemy troop movements and where the bad guy troops were located. It was something for the Towheads to know and take pride in and for others to wonder about.

CHAPTER EIGHTEEN: A NEW ROOMATE AND A REAL SHOT IN THE REAR

Eddie checked out as an aircraft commander after only four weeks of flying. Then ten days later, when Red had an open day, Red started flying with Eddie again. They worked on Eddie's assumption of the detachment's duties as an instructor pilot. It was a formality but it gave Eddie and Red a chance to fly together a few more times. There was no substitute for Red's experience. Filling out all the paperwork was new but it presented no problems for Eddie.

In addition to the Plain of Jars, the detachment flew the other half of their missions alongside the northern section of the Ho Chi Minh Trail. Eddie wanted to fly these areas a few more times with Red to learn them better. The Towheads daily monitored the radio traffic along this spider web of roads and trails. Their steady flow of intercepted radio traffic and transmission locations was of significant importance to both the CIA and the clandestine military units operating along the network of dirt roads and trails.

The terrain elevation along the "trail" was as high as 5000 feet above sea level. But most was anywhere from 700 feet to 3500 feet. This allowed the EC-47s to fly below 10,000 feet and legally without supplemental oxygen, yet more than 3000 feet above the ground as required. It did, however, put their altitude well within the range of the deadly 37mm guns so they watched their gun circles on their maps carefully. The EC-47s flew offset from the trail to avoid the heavy concentrations of gun circles that protected the heavy presence of NVA troops, trucks, and supplies. Offset by ten to fifteen miles, they were out of sight from the trail yet close enough for the back enders to get good intelligence.

On this particular day, Eddie and Red spent an entire afternoon circling around the general area of the Bolovens Plateau, which was located in the southern end of their normal work area. The plateau's terrain varied from 3000 to 5000 feet so they were well exposed to the gunners below. They flew at 9,000 feet in hopes the gunners would not be too tempted. The radio operators had a special interest in something that was going on down there, so Eddie and Red flew as directed and asked no questions. The 362nd EC-47 Squadron, that had recently moved from Pleiku to Danang in Vietnam, overlapped the NKP birds in that work area.

The plateau was a huge, flat-topped mountain. It had spectacular waterfalls that cascaded, in steps, hundreds of feet down the edges of the plateau and into the dense jungle below. Then the streams flowed westward into the Mekong. The two pilots took some spectacular waterfall photos. Thick jungle covered the plateau's sides and there were pine forests, open grasslands, and scattered rainforest on its relatively flat top. The area was moderately populated, not ideal for rice patties, but fiercely contested between the North Vietnamese Army and the coalition friendly forces. There were several small towns in that area. The coalition forces were a mix of Laotian Army, Thai mercenary forces hired by the CIA, and American SOG teams.

It was late in the afternoon during that day over Bolovens Plateau when Eddie experienced his first anti-aircraft gunfire. There were no Russian built, North Vietnamese C-47s in the area and the surprised gunner received permission to fire one salvo at the loitering Gooney Bird. The uncharted and recently moved enemy

37mm expended a five round clip at their aircraft. The gunner walked the string of shots up to their aircraft from the rear after they had flown over his hidden gun site. The gunner knew exactly what he was doing. Gunfire from the rear cannot be seen from an aircraft cockpit and the gunner ripped off only one quick clip, hoping for a quick hit. It was a safe gamble.

It happened very quickly. There were several not-so-subtle concussions behind them, like the sound of an automobile backfiring. Then a metallic boom/clang from the burst that dusted them with shrapnel, and two bursts strung out in front of their cockpit. Then as quickly as it happened, a second and a half, it was over.

Red was flying from the co-pilot's seat and he instinctively rolled into a hard left turn, away from the string of bursts outside Eddie's side window. He then performed a series of rapid course reversals to deprive any additional gunfire from holding an accurate bead on their aircraft. But their maneuver was after the fact. The gunner barely missed. But he wasn't about to divulge his exact location to the old aircraft by continuing fire— in case it turned to look for his firing position. The other kinds of aircraft, those that had to fly inside the gun circles to do their jobs, never flew straight and level for more than a few seconds. They always jinked randomly and the gunners on the ground were only guessing where the aircraft would be by the time their shells got up there. The Towheads, with a mission that allowed staying outside the gun circles and required a level steady work platform for their specialists, had just been too tempting for the gunner.

"Everybody all right back there? Can you see any damage?" Eddie was quick on the radio operator's interphone as he checked the engine instruments and saw they were stable.

"Okay back here," the navigator quickly responded. "I can't see any damage. The burst was out our right side and it looked close."

"Sir, this is Z station," an operator added. "I heard a clang but I can't see any damage either."

Then it was over. Everyone realized it had not been their Golden BB, so they finished their mission and then flew back to NKP. It had been over in a flash and it gave the Towheads something to talk about. But at NKP it would not be a big deal. They would simply debrief the location and another six mile circle would be added to the briefer's master map.

The Golden BB was a part of the superstition lore that crept into the soul of every flyer who participated in the "Vietnam War Games." Things were already surreal, so resorting to something that was a little hocus pocus made as much sense as anything else. The Golden BB was a mythical single bullet or piece of shrapnel that had one's name on it, and the owner knew it was out there waiting for him to make just one fatal mistake. In addition to the Golden BB, the American combatants, be they grunts in the jungle or warriors in the sky, also quietly carried their own personal talismans. They were good luck charms that were usually worn on their dog tag chains. They joked about them around others and logic dictated they had no real magic. But, desperate to possess at least something to keep their Golden BB away, almost everyone had a talisman. They would never go into combat without them. It was both silly but serious and at first Eddie never thought much about them. He had no talisman but feared the Golden BB like every other flyboy. He cut everyone some slack in this area because no one really knew who would be going home in a bag, although the chances were looking good that it wouldn't be any Towheads.

After the flight was almost over and they were on their final approach into NKP, the navigator called, "Red, we got water under the cat walk. We're shutting down our electrical equipment as a precaution. I just thought you needed to know."

"I got that. We'll check it out on the ground," Red replied. Eddie was making the landing and Red was performing the co-pilot duties.

Once they were parked safely on the ground, the engines were shut down, and the checklist was read, Red and Eddie crawled out of their seats. Stiff after sitting for seven hours, they joined the rest of their crew in the rear. A two inch chunk of shrapnel had penetrated their aircraft skin on their right side, near the rear, and adjacent the two water cans. The shrapnel had pierced and almost drained one of the water cans. That had been the metallic clang sound with the third "boom." When flying an aircraft at low speeds, the nose is slightly high and the water had pooled in the rear of the aircraft. When they were on final to land, when the pilots lowered the flaps, the fuselage pitch angle shifted to nose down and the water ran forward.

Eddie picked up the punctured can, dumped the piece of shrapnel on the floor, and smirked, "Sorry old can; it just wasn't your day." The operators kept the shrapnel and had it cut into small pieces. They drilled a hole in each, and hung a piece on each of their dog tags. It was a fitting talisman. Eddie realized he was a little jealous that the enlisted didn't offer him a piece.

Outside the aircraft, they found sixteen more tears in the aluminum skin on the right rear section of the aircraft. Some were tiny and several others were as wide as an inch or two.

"That gunner hit us right in our rear," Red noted then grinned. "It was a real pain in the airplane's ass." No one caught the pun. They all realized they had been missed by only a few feet and the gunner was half a mile below them. It just wasn't their day to die.

* *

A month later, after checking out as an instructor, Eddie was feeling pretty good. In a weak moment he agreed to go into town with four radio operators from his crew and have a Sing Ha or six. Sing Ha was the name for a popular brand of Thai beer. His co-pilot student didn't want to go; he was planning to attend evening mass at the base chapel. Eddie didn't think the young lieutenant had done that bad of a job flying, but each to his own. Eddie and his navigator, Captain Planter, joined the four operators and they rode the air force shuttle bus into the small town of Nakhon Phanom. Eddie realized it was the first time he had gone outside the base perimeter since he had been there, at least on the ground. The town wasn't very impressive, flimsy wooden buildings, a few bamboo and wicker huts and numerous open stinking klongs. The klong water came from the distant hills west of Nakhon Phanom. It was portioned through the local rice paddies, flowed through the town's klongs, and into the Mekong River that formed the east edge of Nakhon Phanom City. At least the sunset was nice. They could see the karst hills across the Mekong to the east and to the west they could see the last rays of the setting sun as it filtered through the evening mist There were several thousand residents, and only a few of the main roads were paved. All of the side streets were dirt, red clay, and reportedly near impassable after heavy rains. It wasn't anywhere close to being a city, but NKP City had a nice ring to it and that's what the GIs called it.

They piled out of the bus and walked the half block to the Honey Massage Parlor. For four dollars each they picked their masseuse by looking through a one way glass window and selecting from a bevy of young girls who were lounging in the adjoining room. Each selected girl was then assigned a private room with a bath tub and massage table. The girls were well dressed and looked clean and cared for. Being a masseuse in Thailand is a proper, honorable, and cultural occupation. The girl Eddie selected led him to her room and motioned for him to remove his clothing. She spoke no more than ten words in English but had great hand gestures. That's what she did was work with her hands. Eddie gave her the traditional stick of Juicy Fruit chewing gum and she was pleased by his grateful gesture. The Thai prostitutes and, as Eddie quickly realized the masseuses, were notorious throughout Asia as having really bad breath. It smelled like a combination of the putrid fish sauce they pour over their food and cigarette smoke. They all had the same bad breath. The GIs quickly discovered that these same girls also loved Juicy Fruit chewing gum. Voila! Every GI planning to "come in contact" with a Thai girl carried a pack of Juicy Fruit in his pocket and it was the first thing they offered to the girls. The girls thought it was a sweet American custom.

She gave him a long hot bath in a deep wooden tub. She had on a short skirt, short sleeved uniform style blouse, and casually slipped out of her sandals. She stepped right into the tub with Eddie to bathe him. She had him stand up while she soaped and scrubbed him, like a teenager washed their heifer calf at the county fair. Then she rinsed him with clean water from a separate basin. She dried him with a large towel. The towel looked very much like those issued to the GIs and was for sale at the base exchange on the base. Then she had him relax on the massage table, face down. The little girl proceeded to twist and tried to crack what seemed like every joint in his body.

212

There was a sturdy bar suspended from the ceiling and she climbed onto the table, stood up, and balanced herself by clinging to the bar. Then she went after Eddie's larger back muscles with her feet. It was great! She then climbed down and rubbed warm oil into his back and his legs. It was the perfect medicine after a long flight and Eddie decided he had to do this more often. Then the girl had Eddie roll over and she proceeded to massage and apply more oil. She was fascinated with the hair on Eddie's chest and used the Thai word "ling," then giggled. Eddie had no idea what she was giggling at but she seemed to be enjoying herself. When she had him sufficiently stimulated with an erection, she casually poured a generous portion of Bryll Cream hair oil into her cupped hand and proceeded to aggressively jerk him off. It caught him by surprise and it was over before he really considered resisting. She hummed a soft Thai song while she worked her magic. Eddie was thinking of something else! *A little dab'l do ya.* The manufacturers of Bryll Cream had no idea how appropriate their sales motto was.

The whole affair took just an hour and the crew reassembled outside the parlor, looking like a group of warm happy puppies. They made their way to Pully's, the radio operators' favorite bar. They had to cross a rickety bamboo bridge over the klong to get to the establishment. As soon as they walked in the door they were greeted by a flock of shabby bar girls. It was déjà vu, no different than the sleazy bars in Angeles City. Eddie was sorry he had joined the group, at least to the bar. For the newbies in the Far East, it might have been an interesting atmosphere but he had gotten that scene out of his system over two years prior. While instinctively protecting his billfold, Eddie turned away several advances before he sat down and quickly ordered a round of beer for his crew.

"You really don't wanna play with me," he scolded as he grabbed a hand from behind that was feeling its way inside his pants. "I have three balls and no dick, and I just started my period."

The girl was stunned and quickly withdrew her hand. She knew he had to be lying, but there was no way she wanted to reach any further to find out. There were some really freaky GIs that came in there looking for freaky sex. The girl had no idea if Eddie was one of them. The guys laughed and the girl moved on to another victim, miffed and a little bewildered. To the girls, Eddie was a marked man for the rest of the evening, maybe crazy, mentally handicapped, or maybe he was queer. But then there was always the possibility he was telling the truth, as gross as it would be. Eddie was pleased. His prior experience in handling these matters was invaluable. He also wondered how the rest of his crew could tolerate the scraggy hustlers after such a nice massage. In the end, it was the beer and their youth that prevailed and before the evening was over several of them made brief excursions to the back room for a quickie. As per his old days with the C-124, Eddie told the four enlisted that whenever they were airborne or in a bar, it was okay to call him Eddie.

The long flight, the nice bath and Thai massage, all made Eddie quite mellow and he drowned the bar's distasteful atmosphere with multiple Sing Has.

They had to leave the bar at 10:00 p.m. so they could catch the last shuttle bus back to the base. The group was feeling no pain, in a jovial mood as they made their way back across the rickety klong bridge. They turned down a worn dirt path that paralleled the klong and Eddie suddenly realized that he needed to urinate, like badly. He knew from years of observation that in Southeast Asia it was common to see an adult male urinate off the side of a roadway. There was no one other than his crew around so his decision was easy.

"Just a second, guys. I gotta flush out the klong," he bragged. His beer was doing the talking and he was drunker than he had previously thought. He stepped into the grass, about three feet from the canal, and proceeded to unzip his pants and continue with his business. At first his objective had been to see how far across the water he could go. Boys would be boys and he planned to demonstrate his virility. But as the flow started he spotted a small log in the grass at the water's edge. It was about ten or twelve feet long, and he decided to use it as his target. The moon was bright and his water, as he directed it back and forth, made the log shine and glisten in the moonlight. Then all of a sudden he noticed the end of the log had moved. The log had a head and an eye and it was looking back at him! He was pissing on a giant snake!

Eddie was frozen with fear as his weenie was no match for that monster! He was so frightened he couldn't move. Anyway, he had to go so badly there was no way he could stop in midstream, so he just stood there frozen, frightened, and continued urinating on the snake. Soon the snake tired of the warm golden shower and in slow motion it slithered into the klong and cut a V in the water as it swam away.

"I'll be go to hell," one of the radio operators exclaimed. "He's got to be the bravest and meanest son of a bitch I've ever known. He just pissed on a huge snake."

"Or the stupidest," the second added.

"No, I think the bravest or meanest works for me," the third added, a small, young intellectual man with glasses, who avoided the draft by joining the air force four weeks after he received his masters in engineering. Logic was his forte and he loved playing games with it. "We don't know that he doesn't have three balls because we can't see them from here. However, after what we're witnessing here, I wouldn't be surprised if they're made out of brass. We do know that he's a guy because we're watching him scare away a python with his hand held willy. My conclusion would be that our aircraft commander is Nuts."

"I agree, he's Nuts," the first radio operator confirmed.

Everyone agreed that Eddie was Nuts and that's how Eddie earned his nickname. They all had too much to drink. But it wasn't uncommon on that other side of the world to be tagged with a nickname from fellow boozers. By the next afternoon the story, although greatly embellished, was all over the base. Eddie would thereafter be known as Lieutenant Nuts, the guy that stared down a python with his ying yang. It wasn't too far a stretch for uprooted young men who had been thrust into an uncertain environment, talked about Golden BBs, and hung talismans on their dog tags.

* * * * * * * * * * * * * * * * * * * *

Red was ready to go back to the States the next morning. Finally! But he was bitching about his underwear. He brought twelve pairs of shorts and twelve pairs of socks to NKP. He figured if he had to wash them by hand on rocks in a stream, they would wear out faster. He had no idea that he would live in nice air conditioned quarters, have a choice of places to eat, and maid service using electric clothes washers and driers. A year later there were only three pairs of each remaining. Red had no recollection of throwing any underwear away and the loss of his underwear was irritating. Eddie found Red's irritation over a dozen year old pieces of underwear to be irritating.

Eddie was checked out as a flight instructor and was finished with Red. He was ready to send him away and get a new room-mate. Eddie wouldn't miss Red's attempts at being funny and his choice of music. Frank Sinatra was about as wild as it got. Eddie often wondered about Red's childhood. Eddie had to visit the younger guys down the walkway whenever he yearned for a little hard rock.

The operations officer had asked Eddie if he wanted to swap rooms once Red had checked out. He could have his choice of several guys as room-mates. Eddie rejected the offer and elected to see what the new second lieutenant arriving the next week would be like.

To get away from Red that evening, Eddie joined several of the other Towheads and went to see the movie *Mash*. The NKP Theater was an outside affair, thirteen rows of wooden benches sitting on a slope and a thirty by thirty foot screen. It was a pleasant evening, no rain and not too many bugs. Everyone always cheered at the movies regardless of the film. They followed the lizards' movements as they chased bugs across the screen and they cheered every time a lizard scored a snack. He knew nothing about the movie *Mash*, and in the beginning assumed it was going to be another B grade movie. It featured old fashioned, out of date helicopters and the setting was definitely not authentic for Vietnam. About half way through the movie he realized it was about Korea and he felt a lot better. Duh! After the movie the guys were showing porno movies in the hooch lounge, but Eddie had to fly early the next morning and needed to get some sleep. Besides, he had seen the same porno movie twice before and it was getting old. The movie had been filmed out of doors and the most exciting part was when a fly landed on her butt and walked around. The guys always cheered the fly on, but every time they watched the movie it rejected their encouragement and just flew away. It was really childish but the guys at NKP really had nothing else to do.

214

The next afternoon, Eddie flew another flight alongside the Ho Chi Minh Trail. It was a rather uneventful mission for the pilots, the guys in the backend seemed busy and pleased with their results. But they told their pilots nothing. When the fuel gauge indicated it was time to go home, Eddie turned a little to the left and let the power setting where it was. There was no hurry to get home and the guys in the back were still looking for long range radio traffic. They were about seventy-five miles south of NKP and slowly drifting away from the Trail.

In front of them and slightly to their right, was an area approximately two square miles in size. A fairly flat area that had a stream flowing into it. The local people had cleared the land and turned it into a tranquil looking group of many rice fields and terraces. In the center of the large cluster of rice paddies, a small hill existed and the timber had not been cut. There were several thatched huts around the edge of the timber.

Below their EC-47, a single T-28 trainer, the type that had been converted into bombers for the Hmong and Laotian military, was ambling along at about the same speed as their Gooney Bird. He was flying fairly low, about fifteen hundred feet off the ground and as he was approaching the rice paddies his presence just added the tranquility of the scene.

Suddenly, as he was approaching the timbered knoll, several streams of tracers spewed from the timber and up toward the little fighter. The T-28 quickly broke to the left then wiggled back and forth as he escaped from the burst of gunfire. Eddie and his pilot were amazed that the gunners didn't knock down their target. Eddie looked to see if he could read the markings on the T-28 but it was just beyond recognition range. It wouldn't have made any difference what his markings were, anyway. In that part of the world and at that time, it was commonplace for aircraft to fly with bogus markings.

Much to Eddie's surprise, the little fighter whipped around, as if angry, and made a run back over the knoll. He jinked back and forth as the gunners tried futilely to guess where he would be when they fired. The light weight single engine bomber released two pods from underneath his wings and made a hard break to his left. Instead of the expected large explosions from what looked like two bombs, a grouping of tiny bursts appeared in the rice paddy adjacent to the knoll and the multitude of tiny bursts walked their way into the trees and out the other side. The gunfire stopped and the T-28 turned around again and flew over the knoll for the third time. No gunfire could be seen and the single little fighter went on his way.

It was commonplace for Eddie to see fighters making air strikes, gunfire following them around the sky, and B-52's stringing out trails of forty or fifty 500 pound bombs. But that was the first time he saw bomblets, hundreds of tiny grenade sized bombs, carried in canisters that opened when dropped. It was not a big deal to those with the task of dropping bombs and making gunnery passes on hostile gunfire. But the bomblets were something new for Eddie to witness. For Eddie it was one of many little insignificant events that would stick with him for a lifetime. Such were the perks of flying nondescript and harmless looking Gooney birds around in a war zone.

That afternoon, when Eddie returned from his mission, he walked into his room and there was a stranger unpacking his clothes from a duffel bag. Red had left before Eddie had a chance to say goodbye and Eddie's room had already been assigned to a new replacement pilot. The stranger's bag was sitting on top of a large, new, metal suitcase. He was packing his stuff into several empty drawers. Lord knows, Red had left plenty empty drawers.

"Whoa, you my new room-mate?" Eddie reacted. "You're here a week early."

"Name's Arnold Henry," the new guy held out his hand and Eddie shook it. "I go by Buddy, for obvious reasons. I've been told that you were Nuts." The guy kept a straight face. He wore tailored 1505s and sported a close cropped crew cut. He looked like an A student fresh from an Ivy League College.

"Maybe a little nuts," Eddie replied. "This place can do that to you. Did you get your don't ask, don't tell, don't nothing briefing yet?" Eddie asked with a sly grin. "Did they tell you why they call me Nuts?"

"No, but I bet you're gonna tell me." He looked at Eddie's rank to see if Eddie was senior to him. He saw no problem. Lieutenants, second and first, are really just lieutenants sharing the lowest form of officerhood.

"No, I'm not gonna tell ya. You'll hear all about it sooner or later. Anyway, I don't wanna screw up the story. It changes almost every day." The new guy finally broke a smile, a little smile, but a smile just the same.

Eddie figured he would give the stiff two weeks to loosen up, then if not one of them would be out the door.

* *

Somewhere down there were the gomers, manning their anti-aircraft guns. Although they had different skin color and appearance, they were men with dreams, urges, and fantasies just like everyone else. Eddie imagined them looking up through the breaks in the foliage and staring with curiosity at the old decrepit airplane as it flew aimlessly around the sky every day. The Hmong and their American advisors had the same curiosity. Even the Ravens and Air America pilots could only guess what the Gooney Birds were about.

At that moment, the gunners were doing the EC-47 no harm and Eddie suspected they were hoping they didn't get an open fire command from their fire controller. Why wake up the A-1 Spads and invite fury and bombs from the sky. Let the lonely relic go by; it seemed so harmless. The gunner's had more valuable targets in their plans. It was their mission to defend their section of the area and the old Gooney Bird seemed harmless enough. It was no threat.

Eddie was at peace with the world. He liked his job as an instructor and felt he was doing some good. The moment was now and he tried to absorb as much of the flying experience as he possibly could. He discovered that every month the Towhead pilots and navigators were allowed three days combat crew rest, CCR they called it. During this time they were free to jump on the Klong Courier and go any place in Thailand that they wished. It was surprisingly generous. The normal Towhead crew scheduling involved flying every other day, the pilots and navigators weren't really overworked in the first place. Also, they got the same once per year R&R. It was a week long rest and relaxation break that all the Vietnam troops received. The government provided charter flights that would fly them to their choice of about a dozen really nice destinations. For the Towheads, the total package of off time bordered on being a rip off. Compared to the EC-47 guys stationed in Vietnam, the Towheads at NKP were staying in a Thai resort by the river.

The CCR was part of an NKP protocol that dealt only with air crews; most were flying far more hazardous missions than the Towheads. Eddie found out about CCR his third week at NKP but didn't ask for it as he felt obligated to his unit. If he hadn't flown almost every day he wouldn't have been ready to take over as an instructor when Red departed. Without an instructor they would have had to borrow one from the units down south in Vietnam and an outside instructor wouldn't have been familiar with the Towhead's unique mission profiles and details. It would have been a mess and the pilots receiving the instruction would have been short changed. His efforts also had a second advantage, one that Eddie was acutely aware of. With the combination of busting his butt to get checked out in time and not taking his CCR, Eddie had the detachment commander and the operations officer in the palm of his hands. They both had their plates full anyway and needed someone they could depend upon to herd around their gaggle of new second lieutenants. The operations officer thought Eddie was a great guy and would make a great career officer. As a result, Eddie had a free hand at running his instructional program; setting up his own work schedule was just what he wanted. In reality, he couldn't stand most administration types; they seemed only interested in advancing their own careers and managed to always screw things up. There just weren't any more Colonel Duncans left. But the weather always changes and Eddie's guard was relaxed.

* *

Back over the Plain of Jars, Eddie realized his mind had drifted again. He was flying his second mission with his new room-mate. The guy was still a little stiff but flew with remote precision. As with most guys, flying a new type of aircraft was always a bit awkward at first. It took a few flights to re-program one's sensations and responses to the feel of the new bird. "The difference between pilots," as Major Baxter had told him back in another life, "was if and how fast you settle in and let the airplane start giving you feed back. Some guys are faster than others, some never get it. It takes teamwork between you and the airplane to turn flying into artwork."

Arnold Henry was a perfectionist and had quickly picked up the fundamentals. He was quite intelligent and coordinated. Eddie's task was working with Arnold to get him to relax and become a part of his airplane. The good part was that he wasn't bitching about being assigned to fly in an old piece of junk, as many of the new co-pilots did. At pilot training they had learned to fly supersonic and four ship aerobatics and had been pumped up by their instructors to believe they were the pick of the litter. Then they were assigned to aircraft built in 1942, with round cantankerous engines, and sent to fly in a jet dominated world. Some of them had real ego problems, despite the fact that they couldn't taxi the tail wheeled aircraft well. Eddie was impressed that Arnold seemed to be taking the kool-aid with dignity. Eddie liked calling him Arnold and not Buddy just because he could. Also he didn't want to get too close with him in case he had to kick the Ivy Leaguer out of his room. Ten more months was too long to act formally in his private quarters. Sometimes a guy needed to curse and let off a little steam, walk around in his underwear, and because he was a guy, pass gas when necessary. This guy seemed very proper. "Was his family immigrants from England?" Eddie wondered. "English were always proper."

Arnold was ready to be turned loose as a co-pilot with the unit's other aircraft commanders. He was a quick learner. Eddie signed him off that night. Then he made arrangements to fly the next day with another co-pilot who was ready for an aircraft commander upgrade.

That evening Eddie and Arnold enjoyed a water buffalo steak at one of the Thai restaurants on base and then retired to their room for a drink. They needed to stay away from the noisy Nails who, on a rare night, were dominating the Hooch. One of their own had brought a crippled aircraft home that afternoon. It was shot full of holes and he needed the support of his comrades to help him get drunk. Arnold dug through his metal suitcase and produced a full, unopened bottle of Glenlivet Single Malt Scotch. Eddie had never tasted anything so fancy. It was smooth as silk. Arnold suggested they both drink it at room temperature so the flavor and aroma wasn't dampened by cold. English always drank their hard stuff with ice, so Eddie deduced that his new room-mate wasn't of English descent.

"This guy really does have class. Maybe he can stay. Some of it might rub off," Eddie thought to himself.

After they both relaxed and toasted the Lady, the aircraft they had flown that day, they sat silently and let the scotch work its magic. Arnold didn't have a clue that Eddie and the Lady shared a past. Eddie didn't have a clue about the Lady's past. He had asked the Lady's crew chief about the nose art and about the Lady, but the airman first class told Eddie he had only been at NKP for four months. He said that he had inherited the aircraft from the guy he replaced and had no idea what the story was about her nose art. He said, "Everyone leaves after a year and anything over a year is lost in history."

"Tell me, what are you doing over here?" Arnold asked. "Why didn't you join the national guard and marry the girl next door?" He was curious as he swirled his scotch and held it up against the light, as if it were a fine wine.

Eddie almost choked. "This guy shoots from the hip and hasn't a clue how close he's getting."

"You plan on making the air force a career?" Arnold continued his interrogation.

Eddie paused and took a sip. "I guess I just wanted to see the world. I sure as hell don't wanna stay in the air force . . . what's your excuse?"

"My father taught me never to make excuses," Arnold took another sip of his second scotch. "I think you just dodged my question. There's something that's very obvious about you. The way you fly and love your airplanes, maybe you want more than to see the world. What's the real reason you're over here?"

"I always wanted to learn to fly but it required a lot of money that I didn't have," Eddie confessed. "So when I passed the tests to be a pilot in the air force, I joined and killed two birds with one stone. I got free pilot training and I get to see the world. Guess I killed three birds if you count the fact that I didn't have to wait for the draft and spend time crawling around the swamps in Vietnam. Picking leeches off my ass is not what I call a good time. You gotta admit that we got it pretty good."

"I thought maybe you were some kind of a patriot and wanted to save the world from communism," Arnold responded pushing Eddie a little. He wanted to find out where Eddie was coming from.

"I can't even save the world from Nixon," Eddie fished a little to see if this guy was sensitive. "You're obviously from a classy background. You gonna save us? I bet you're idealistic and a patriot?"

"Me, I'm a Political Science major," Arnold defended himself. "I consider myself an observer. I just wanna put my time in and go home. I really never had any choice, anyway. Well, I did but I didn't. My family goes back four generations of military service. None ever made a career of it but all served in combat with honors. America has been good to them and they feel patriotism is a family obligation. My family has accumulated lots of assets and I guess if I ever wanna get some of it I need to pay my dues. So here I am. Ya gotta give me credit, though. At least I had the foresight to pack two bottles of Glenlivet in my bag. When I thought I was going to be living in Vietnam, I was actually planning on hoarding it and not letting anyone else know I had it. You learn to be sneaky when you're raised by a nanny in a wealthy family."

Eddie had another sip of scotch and nodded his head, "Works for me." Then he confessed, "My family doesn't have any money, small farm is all. I lost two uncles in World War II and their pictures are both sitting on my parents' bedroom dresser. Both of my uncles were crewmembers in bombers and they're each posing with their crews in front of their bombers. Guess I grew up worshipping them and wondering if I could ever live up to their standards. They were my childhood heroes. They were real, not like Roy Rogers."

"Ah, the truth comes out," Arnold said, breaking into his first full smile. "Glenlivet works every time. That's how my dad interviews people and negotiates business deals. You see, you and I both share similar characteristics. I suspect we're both not fond of the way our politicians are micro-managing this war, both patriots at heart, and both here for selfish reasons."

Eddie paused, and had another sip of single malt, and ignored the selfish reason remark. "Kinda ironical that the aircraft we flew in today was probably built about the same time during World War II as the two bombers my uncles flew in were built. One of em was shot down in 1944. It's kinda morbid, but I'd like to have my picture taken some time. You know, posing with my crew in front of our aircraft with our nomex flight suits, parachutes, pistols, and shit like that. I'd like it to be in front of the Lady. I'd like to have my picture setting on that dresser whether I get shot down or not."

"It's not morbid," Arnold replied. "I'd be proud to pose with you."

Thus a bond occurred between strangers from vastly different backgrounds. Forged not in the real world where they would have never crossed paths, but bonded with Glenlivet Scotch after flying a special old Gooney Bird over the jungles of Laos.

Arnold Henry was a gentleman, an intellect from a wealthy family of patriots with a bachelor's degree in Political Science. His plans, after he got out of the air force, were to get his masters in business from Harvard, a subject he needed to pursue in order to maintain his family's respect. He would eventually become a director on the board of his family's holding company. He and Eddie would probably remain lifetime friends and exchange Christmas cards.

* * * * * * * * * * * * * * * * * * * *

Eddie flourished as the detachment's only flight instructor. Instructing Gooney Birds in flight came easy after several years in the C-124. Eddie still felt uneasy with all the inexperienced young lieutenants. Fresh out of pilot training, after six months as co-pilots, they were upgraded to be in charge of the aircraft and its mission. Most had only a total of six or seven hundred hours flying time when they took over the responsibility of commanding missions over enemy territory. They were prematurely responsible for a $45,000 aircraft with over a million dollars of electronics gear and the lives of seven to nine men. The air force was short of experienced pilots and their little EC-47 operation was in the bottom of the experienced pilot bucket.

The youngsters flew well but didn't have any depth. They had received no round engine training other than flying the basic C-47 at England Air Force Base. They had no orientation about the political history of the war they were being sent to, received no briefings, lectures, or progress reports about the current situation in Laos, and they received virtually no intelligence during their pre-flight intelligence briefings. The air force sent them to NKP and Eddie, assuming blind patriotism as their only required motivation. But Eddie's cadre of lieutenants were college graduates and had passed rigorous tests in both manual skills and academic achievement. They were sent fresh from the States with a growing and hostile anti-war population and they could read the magazines and newspapers their friends and relatives sent them from home. They needed answers, not pep talks. They deserved more than just the usual, "Ours is not to question why, ours is just to do or die." Because everything was so classified, Eddie was forced to restrict his instruction to flying the aircraft and its mission. He had to answer their politically sensitive questions with "I really don't know."

There were basically three different types of pilots in the detachment. There were those that were there for the pilot training and flight experience. They loved flying, were hard working and serious pilots, and were there for the same reasons that Eddie was in the air force. They wanted to learn how to fly, then get out and become professional civilian pilots. They received free pilot training and flight experience from the air force. In exchange the air force got a year of combat in Vietnam from the young pilots. Both sides got what they wanted. The second type were pilots because they didn't want to pick leaches off their butts in the jungle as drafted soldiers. Many of them were true patriots but others were slackers that Eddie had to watch carefully. The third type were the career officers. They planned on staying in the air force for a minimum of twenty years—longer if they achieved the necessary success and rank. The career types were disappointed that they were flying old propeller aircraft, as EC-47 experience wasn't the material that promotion boards were looking for. They tried to make the most of it by volunteering for additional jobs, tasks, etc. They would do anything to provide material for improving their annual evaluation report. Those along for the ride to avoid the draft and those that just wanted to learn how to fly avoided extra ground work assignments like the plague.

Many of the extra work assignments that the career bunch volunteered for were "make work" assignments. They were created for the purpose of awarding the associated credit. Some jobs actually had a little substance. One of the better jobs was the safety officer. Each unit was required to have a safety officer and to hold monthly scheduled safety meetings. This was an air force wide requirement for aircrews. The appointed safety officer usually received good credit in his annual evaluation.

The young lieutenant that had the safety officer's job, when Eddie took over as the only flight instructor, was an academy graduate with little flying experience. He was short on experience but long on following procedures, procedures as outlined in the stateside manual on how to be a safety officer. Every unit received numerous posters emphasizing some specific aspect of flight safety, and it was expected that these posters would be displayed everywhere crews conducted their business. Whenever senior officers or inspectors visited units, they always looked for these posters as a sign that the safety officer was doing a good job. The Towheads had lots of posters to look at, although few of them had any relevance to their operation. Eddie was amazed at the irony. The posters lined the walls of their fenced in operations building and were rarely noticed by the crewmembers. They were a major annoyance to the two officers and one enlisted man who worked in the building but there was nothing they could do but tolerate their wallpaper. The same military that was burying them with posters promoting safe flight was also dispatching them to fly over enemy territory and expose themselves to enemy gunfire. They wanted it both ways! The same was true of their meetings; the safety officer would read and lecture from printed material written by desk jockeys in the States. Again, little of it had any relevance to their operation and the pilots were bored to tears. The safety meetings were a wonderful opportunity to quietly sit with your eyes open and meditate. The detachment administrative officers were satisfied with the situation as they had endured similar presentations during their junior years as pilots and they accepted the mundane presentation as normal. The paperwork was in good order and that was what counted.

Eddie decided that as the flight instructor and as the more experienced pilot in the group, it was his charge to improve on the situation. He decided to draw from his C-124 days and teach these guys to play "what if." He asked the safety officer if he could have time with the pilots as a part of the next safety meeting, so he could discuss some items with them. The young lieutenant cheerfully agreed, first because Eddie outranked him and also because it would require less preparation on his part.

Eddie spoke with Airman Hendricks and made arrangements for two of his no fly days to fall on the twice monthly safety meetings. The meetings were held twice a month, so the second meeting could be attended by crewmembers that were flying when the first monthly meeting was conducted. Crewmembers were only required to attend one meeting each month. If they were lucky enough to be flying on both safety meeting days, they were still signed off as having attended a safety meeting. The reports that were sent to headquarters required one hundred percent attendance. That's the way things worked, so the senior officers in the unit could also get good evaluation reports.

When Eddie stood up to address his first safety meeting group, he faced a group of discouraged faces. The safety officer had cut short his presentation and the crewmembers thought they were going to get off a little early. It was getting close to beer thirty and they were anxious to get on with their no fly day activities. This didn't bother Eddie. He knew from his C-124 days that anytime is beer thirty on a no fly day. These guys were amateurs.

"Jerry, you seem to be the biggest complainer in the crowd today, why don't you tell me what if?" Eddie looked over the group and saw that he had their attention, and then continued, "You take a hit and all your fuel has leaked out and both engines just quit. You're at ten thousand feet, in a Q model bird with a full crew, and the nearest runway is NKP, twenty-two miles way. How far can you glide? Can you make it to NKP for a dead stick landing?"

The surprised aircraft commander looked back at Eddie and mentally sized the question up. "It doesn't make any difference. With no engines I'm not going anywhere else. I have no choice but to try for the runway. Either I make it or not." He looked around at his peers for their approval of his slick answer.

"I'm not really that concerned about your sorry ass," Eddie responded to the surprised pilot. "You have an airplane full of guys and you're in charge of their safety. If you don't make it we'll miss the aircraft, and you can be replaced. What I'm concerned about is your unfortunate co-pilot and those innocent guys in the back. Should they jump or stay with the aircraft?"

"When we get close and if it doesn't look like we'll make it, I'll order them to bail out."

"And have your crew attempt a dangerous low altitude exit! You could kill them all. And it would probably be too late for you to get out."

The obnoxious pilot replied, "I guess that's the price I have to pay for glory."

"Serves ya right for being a wise ass," Eddie concluded. "How about you, Frankie?" he asked the smirking lieutenant next to Jerry. "How far could you glide?"

"The manual doesn't tell us our glide ratio with both engines out. Guess I'd have to use my aircraft's battery power to read the DME miles from NKP, watch it for a thousand feet of descent, then I could determine how many miles I could glide per thousand feet. With about eight thousand feet to descend I could do the math to determine how far I could glide from my remaining altitude."

"That's correct," Eddie was surprised and agreed. "Could you think that fast and do all of that math mentally when you're scared shitless?"

"Guess I'd find out."

"You're sounding like Jerry now," Eddie scolded the young airman. "What if you were low to start off with and didn't have a thousand feet to give away in the first place? Wouldn't it be better to play with your glide ratio before something happens? Like pull both engines to thirteen inches of manifold pressure, that'll create the same drag as both engines shut down and feathered. Do it at ten thousand feet when you're returning from a mission. Once you're stabilized at our published holding speed, which is the most efficient speed for our aircraft, you could safely and calmly measure the distance it takes to glide down a thousand feet. Then if you get your ass in a jam you would already know the glide ratio. All you would have to do is multiply it times the thousands of feet you have remaining. What if you lose both engines five miles out and are fifteen hundred feet above the airport elevation? You wouldn't have time to start determining glide ratios. Example, fifteen hundred feet at a glide ratio of three miles distance for every thousand feet of altitude loss equals four and a half miles. It's that fast when you know the glide ratio ahead of time. You would end up in a pile a half mile short of the runway. Best bail everyone out immediately!" Then he told them their assignment for the next safety meeting. "Sometime during the next several weeks, when heading for home, if the wind is calm and not affecting your groundspeed, each of you should pull both engines back to thirteen inches of manifold pressure and determine your own glide ratio. I'm not going to tell you what it is. I want you to determine what it is so you can remember it and have confidence in it. At the next meeting we'll compare and confirm your findings."

Then he asked them another what if, "You're hit and going down and spot a rice paddy about five hundred feet long, you still have control of the airplane. Five hundred feet isn't long enough to land a Gooney Bird but it's better than crashing into trees. The muck in a rice paddy would slow you down quickly. And should you put it into a rice paddy on your belly with the gear up or down? And is it safer to bail the crew out or keep them inside the aircraft for a controlled crash landing into the tiny rice paddy? If you bail your crew out should you try to also jump out or should you stay with the airplane?" He led the group in a lively debate on the variables. The group finally concluded that there is no one answer to the problem, it all depended on the variables. The point was that he had stimulated them into recognizing and earnestly debating the variables. Thinking about things ahead of time!

"You need to play what if in your mind several times each day," Eddie lectured. "That way, if you ever get your butt in a jam, you'll have a bag full of answers ready to use."

He asked several more what ifs, and guided their discussions. He was making them think. When he dismissed them they were surprised that several hours had gone by. This was the start of the twice monthly what if sessions that made the flight safety meetings popular, an almost unheard of thing in the air force. Eddie knew he was having an effect when several of his pilots showed up for both meetings in one month. It also stimulated a lot of conversation and sometimes mild disagreements at the bar. When the safety officer rotated home, his meetings had been a resounding success and he received an excellent evaluation. Major Collins filled the position with another academy graduate and the new guy was more than pleased to have Eddie continue his presentations.

CHAPTER NINETEEN: IGLOO WHITE

Eddie's new room-mate Arnold turned out to be an easy guy to get along with. By the end of the first several weeks, in addition to having very frank discussions about the war, it turned out they shared the same opinions in other areas.

Eddie and Arnold were sitting in the sun on the walkway in front of their room one morning. Their legs were hanging over the edge of the walkway and they were wearing nothing more than short pants. They both had the day off and were trying to decide if they would venture into Nakhon Phanom City or just hang out and share the sun with Harold. Harold the lizard always spent his afternoons on a large branch that hung over their quarters.

Eddie enjoyed the sounds filtering out of the room four doors down from them. It was Jimi Hendrix assaulting his guitar at Woodstock. "How appropriate," Eddie remarked. "Just the thing to send the troops off into battle. The mutated Hendrix version of our national anthem."

Eddie was also trying to compose a letter to Molly, a non committal to their relationship and its okay I'm not in any danger type letter. It was much easier writing to his mother as she expected nothing and understood even less. Eddie worried that maybe his mother was suffering from dementia.

"How come you don't have your own stereo equipment?" Arnold wondered out loud. He was shining his civilian shoes. It was something Eddie had never done to civilian shoes, but then he didn't have as much class as Arnold. Neither one of them really cared that they had differences and that was what allowed them to get along so well.

"Bought it all while I was flying out of Tachikawa and it's all in storage back in the States. I guess I just got my shopping done early. No reason to buy more when I got less than nine months to go."

"You like music?" Arnold asked. Eddie was sure Arnold must be referring to classical or something like that.

"I like to drink cheap booze, get high, and listen to loud, hard rock," Eddie answered and flashed Arnold a grin. "It's a classless thing that my type of people do. It helps us to forget that we're poor . . . but I'm not hurtin so bad that I like country western."

"Ya like Jimi Hendrix?" Arnold asked, and continued with a smile. He nodded towards the sounds coming from a handful of rooms down the sidewalk.

"His stuff grows on me," Eddie confessed. "At first I didn't understand him, but being over here has cleared it all up for me. I need the insanity to help me make any sense out of this place and whatever the hell it is that I'm doing over here. Before you came, about once a week, I would wander down the sidewalk to where the rookies hangout. Usually I would go to Little George's room. I'd drink cheap scotch, listen to their hard rock, and get a splitting headache. I drink cheap scotch cause I can get it here on base. Cheap booze and hard rock make a bitchin headache. It's like a fix, an addiction I have. Without the stuff that those rookies are playing, and scotch," Eddie chuckled. He couldn't contain his own humor. "I'd probably be Nuts."

"It's probably the cheap scotch," Harold replied. "From now on you should drink only Glenlivet. Maybe it'll cut back on the headaches. There's nothing we can do about you being nuts—calling you Nuts is so apropos."

Arnold grinned and looked up as Harold the lizard snorted. "I think you pissed on that snake on purpose. You like sick shit like that."

"Ya otta try it sometime," Eddie quipped. "It feels good to play in the mud with us commoners."

* * * * * * * * * * * * * * * * * * *

Three hours later, Arnold had forked over the cash and purchased, from the BX, a top of the line stereo system: an amplifier, Teak tape player and recorder, phonograph player, outrageously large speakers, blank tapes, all the bells and whistles. He even talked the BX manager into having the stuff delivered to their room. It took the two room-mates only about twenty minutes to hook it all up. When they were done, Eddie jokingly lamented, "Now if we only had some music to play. I hope you don't have any Frank Sinatra in that pretty suitcase under your bed."

"No, but I got some trading whisky in there." Arnold pulled his metal suitcase from under his bed and rummaged about—then he displayed a bottle of Johnny Walker Scotch. He disappeared out the door.

The oversized speakers had been wrapped in clear plastic sheaths, and on a whim, Eddie folded one of the sheaths into a small wallet sized packet, bundled it with string, and put it in the pile of survival items he routinely carried in his flight suit. Eddie just settled in for a nap when Arnold reappeared, carrying a stack of hard rock tapes and 45 RPM records from the rookie's collection. He was wearing a smug grin. "Lifetime rights to copy anything in his collection. Cost me one bottle of booze," Arnold boasted.

Eddie sat up in amazement at this guy. "Remind me never to negotiate a business deal with you," he kidded as he looked through Arnold's stack. "Jimi Hendrix, Janis Joplin, Jefferson Airplane, do you really know what this stuff sounds like? It'll blow the sanity right out of your head."

Arnold looked at Eddie and beamed, "I got dirty laundry I live with. I picked it up when I was in college and I love this shit. I think it makes a statement about the times and the place. That's what music is supposed to do. And you're right, anything less would sound flat in this spook haven."

Eddie stared at him. "Statement indeed! Ya got any more of that drinking scotch?"

"Last bottle," Arnold beamed as he dug back into his suitcase. Eddie wondered if he had thousands of dollars stashed somewhere in there.

"One of us has gotta make a CCR booze run to Bangkok and stock up our larder. They don't sell Glenlivet here on base," Arnold announced. "Guess it's gotta be you, because I just got here and haven't any CCR coming. This might not be such a bad tour anyway. Now all we need is some women!"

* * * * * * * * * * * * * * * * * * *

They waded three quarters of the way through the second bottle. Then Eddie took Arnold into town. They found the tailor that his former room-mate, Red, had told him about and each ordered several items from the grinning little Thai. Arnold told him if he did a good job they would have more stuff made and bring some friends. Then they made their way down to view the Mekong River. They viewed its boat dock and what they called a beach. The beach was really just a small strip of mud. Eddie took some good photos and hoped he wasn't too soused to focus his camera.

As expected, Arnold was pleased with a Thai massage. But he was ready to leave the bar as soon as the first sleazy prostitute approached him. Rock and roll music, yes. Massage, yes. Cheap prostitutes, no. He had too much class for that but Eddie wanted to show it to him anyway. It was part of the Vietnam tour experience. They made their way back to the base and finished the bottle of scotch before eating at the officers club. They were both fast asleep by ten in the evening. Tomorrow afternoon was another fly day for both of them.

223

Eddie took three days off for CCR and rode the morning Klong Courier to Bangkok. That afternoon he purchased the required booze and for thirty-five cents he bartered some delicious looking fruit from a street vendor. He couldn't remember, let alone pronounce, the name of the fruit but he had eaten it before and remembered it was delicious. This was the land where an apple was an exotic fruit from the far north and weird tropical exotic fruit was commonplace. He walked around the shopping district and looked at hundreds of knickknacks and carvings but none of them rang his bell. He'd already been there and done that but it was still good to snoop around his old haunts.

He never grew tired of looking at the spirit houses. They were elaborately carved and decorated miniature temples that varied from a foot to four feet tall. The Thai people mounted them, usually on a dedicated post, in front of their residences and businesses. Although the Thai were Buddhists in religion, they still maintained numerous ancient beliefs and customs from their original Animism religion—the belief in spirits. The spirit houses were provided as a place of earthly dwelling for heavenly spirits. In exchange for a temple on earth, the guardian spirits would look after and bless the Thai dwelling and piece of land they were associated with. The spirit houses were purchased from professional spirit house builders who knew and understood the exact requirements of the various spirits. Every morning many of the Thais would light incense and burn it in their spirit house. Most Thais also left offerings of rice and flowers to please their resident guardian. Eddie didn't believe in spirits but he thought the tradition was a charming touch of the Thai culture.

He wasn't used to the noisy automobile traffic in the nearby streets so he had a restless night. Aircraft noise didn't bother him, he was used to it, but automobile noise was annoying. It seemed that Thais couldn't drive without honking their horns. The next morning he rode the Klong back to NKP. Eddie was off women, but he had all of the other things he wanted in his life, like getting the booze larder restocked with Glenlivet, rock and roll music, and his airplanes. Three weeks later Arnold, however, found himself a woman.

The female situation on base was complicated. The most obvious were the officers' maids. They were innocent young girls from the surrounding villages. They were a part of the air force's agreement with the Thais to build, occupy, and utilize the air base. They employed far more maids then were needed, but necessary to comply with the agreement. Each officer was charged $8.25 per month. No one was complaining as the fee was nominal to the officers and a bonanza for the maids. The girls were happy, they were chatting away their afternoons in the men's bathroom and the men grew accustomed to their presence. Everyone received a stern warning, when they signed in on the base, about leaving the maids alone. As far as the Towhead officers were concerned, they toed the line and never approached the young maids.

Then there were the girls staying with the enlisted GIs in their quarters. They were actually on the payroll and working as maids, but some were just doing a little double duty on the side. The ones Eddie had seen appeared to be no more than call girls and were semi-permanent residents. The base administration was apparently turning their heads from the girls' conduct. Neither the GIs nor the maids filed any complaints about the situation. The GIs loved it as it was far less trouble than going into town to the bars. It mystified Eddie that such shenanigans would be allowed on a base where so many secrets were to be kept. Maybe one of the bases' biggest secrets from the press and the American public was the girls!

Then there was the Towhead captain, a navigator on the other end of the Towhead's row of quarters. He had purchased a teenage girl from her father for US$50. It was a medieval practice that was still practiced in Thailand, in Nakhon Phanom City in 1970. She was unofficially allowed to live in the captain's quarters. The captain had no intentions of taking her back to the States when his tour was up, he would just give her to someone else or let her go back to her family. Eddie was horrified when he first heard of the arrangement. With time, and after seeing how well the captain cared for her, he realized she was far better off with him than if she had been sold into labor or prostitution. All the Towheads in the building were nice to her and respected the captain's exclusive privileges. They even hung a curtain in a shower booth so she could shower in privacy.

None of these female options fit Arnold's taste, but there was one remaining alternative. It was the big concrete building with the perimeter fences and all the guards. Task Force Alpha was rumored to be the largest building in Southeast Asia. Eddie suspected the claim was a bit much. There were some humongous hotels in Bangkok. Nevertheless, it was a large concrete building. Built in 1968, the above ground concrete building was guarded by dual cyclone fences and corrugated steel revetments. Its perimeter was patrolled by a plethora of guards and guard dogs and a top secret clearance was required to get into the building. Rumors claimed, for security reasons, only air force enlisted personnel were used as janitors. It was lightly pressurized; one had to enter through two airlock doors to get in. The pressurization kept all the fine dry season dust and the heavy wet season humidity out. This protected the banks of sensitive computers.

This elaborate building and all the hush hush people that worked in it were a part of an operation called Igloo White. The Ho Chi Minh Trail had its maze of trails and roads planted with seismic and voice (sound) sensors. The sensors would transmit what they were sensing or hearing to an aircraft circling overhead and the circling aircraft would re-transmit the data to the antennas operated by the Task Force Alpha (TFA) building. The circling aircraft were the tiny single engine Beechcraft airplanes (QU-22B Pave Eagle, call sign "Bat") that were at Eddie's first impression, an aero club. That was also why they called their hangar the "Bat Cave." They only flew at night. These little aircraft, highly modified Beechcraft with longer wings, more powerful engines, and modified to be flown as drones, circled high above the trail. The street gossip had them flying at 20,000 feet, out of range of all but the largest anti-aircraft guns, and served as receivers and re-transmitters for the trail sensors' signals. At 20,000 feet they had plenty range for radio contact with NKP. The personnel working inside the Igloo White building received real time information about literally everything going on along enemy roads and trails. Some of the sensors were dropped by aircraft or low flying helicopters and they simply transmitted sounds and vibrations. The sensors were very sensitive and could pick up ground vibrations from passing trucks and vibrations as small as a person walking. They were designed so when they were dropped, the working portion, other than the antennae, would bury itself into the ground. The antennae would stick up, disguised as a juvenile banana plant. The plant disguise was made of plastic and varied in appearance with each batch manufactured.

More specialized sensors were also employed. Seismic and sound sensors were hand planted by special operations teams. It was rumored that the teams were inserted and extracted by the large, black, unmarked CH-3 and CH-53 helicopters that Eddie saw sitting quietly in the sun on the ramp at NKP. They carried out a diverse mixture of clandestine and dangerous missions. One of their missions was to transport the personnel that planted the sensors. They carefully recorded the precise coordinates of each one, and surveyed and mapped the road that the trucks were suspected of using. The sensor's transmissions were coded so the receivers back at NKP could identify each individual sensor. At NKP, by noting the exact time it took a truck to pass between two separate sensors, the computers at Task Force Alpha could compute the truck's exact speed and project the trucks exact running position as it traveled down the surveyed road. The operator at Task Force Alpha could then connect their computer with a navy A-7 fighter flying over the trail with its autopilot on. The computer would compute the appropriate bomb drop information, tie it in with the moving truck position, and utilize the aircraft's autopilot to guide the aircraft and release a bomb to strike a piece of road as the truck passed over it.

It was an elaborate and very expensive way to destroy a truck. The rumor was that sometimes it actually worked and a number of trucks were destroyed.

Other receivers were planted along the edges of areas where enemy personnel ate, rested or slept. They were noise and voice sensors designed to eavesdrop on enemy conversations and the Task Force Alpha linguists extracted intelligence from the transient enemy's conversations.

Eddie and Arnold knew nothing about the Igloo White operations or the tiny white Beechcraft airplanes parked in the bat cave every day.

Igloo White and its operations cost the American tax payers about one billion dollars per year. As far as Arnold was concerned, it provided him with a woman. The large number of technicians, computer operators, linguists, and other specialists, included a group of college educated young lieutenants fresh out of intelligence school. Vietnamese linguists were especially valuable for monitoring the voice sensors. It turned out there were a number of women in the lieutenant ranks, educated and intelligent. Most were tired of the come on from the lower caste of oversexed and ill mannered pilots and navigators. There were about eight to ten of these Caucasian women that lived and worked on the air base and they were in a position to be discrete with whom they shared their company.

It took Arnold exactly three weeks to discover this treasure trove, win their confidence that he was a well heeled and gentlemanly scholar, and land one of the more attractive ones in his bed—his bed next to where Eddie slept. They were extremely discrete, only using the room when Eddie was away flying a mission, but it was impossible to keep their escapades a secret. The door to Arnold and Eddie's room opened onto the commons. They couldn't come and go without being seen. Within another week, Arnold introduced Eddie to his new love and Eddie ended up having dinner at the officers club with the contented duo. She was a tall, slender redhead. Her gorgeous hair hung down to her shoulders. She had piercing green eyes, very intelligent, and carried herself with an air of confidence. She was the perfect woman for Arnold.

"So you work in that spooky building along with all the other tight lipped cone heads. Tell me, is being a lieutenant just a cover for being a CIA agent?" Eddie was joking with Dorothy and they both knew it. "I bet you have a service revolver in your purse. Show me your gun and I'll show you my tattoo—better yet— I'll show you my airplane if you show me around inside that big concrete fortress you work in."

"Who the hell wants to look inside a thirty year old airplane?" She skillfully shut Eddie down. "I'd probably choke on the coal dust from the Berlin Air Lift—and you need a Top Secret clearance to get in where I work. They don't give those to many farm boys."

"Actually we both have Top Secret SSIR clearances," Arnold corrected. "We need em because we fly old World War II freighter aircraft over Laos. We can't tell you what we do or how we do it."

Dorothy looked taken back for a few seconds then tied into Arnold, "You lied to me. You said you haul the colonels and generals around and make weekly trips to Bangkok. So the colonels and generals can spend the night with their wives."

"He lies all the time," Eddie kidded. "He told me he was from a wealthy family and not an hour later wanted to borrow twenty bucks."

"Do you really have a Top Secret SSIR?" Dorothy asked Arnold.

"Probably shouldn't continue this conversation about what we do," Eddie reflected. "We each have our own skunk to skin."

"Now what the hell does that mean?" Arnold squinted.

"Damned if I know," Eddie laughed. "It's an old German farmer proverb."

"German farmers don't have proverbs," Arnold argued. "You just made that up."

"Break it up, boys," Dorothy broke in. "If you really have Top Secret SSIR clearances, I think I can get you in where I work as long as I escort you. I couldn't take you in the war room but I could take you in the area where I work. Would you be interested?"

Eddie and Arnold looked at each other and grinned like two mischievous school boys.

* * * * * * * * * * * * * * * * * * *

Eddie and Arnold showed up at the entrance to the TFA building wearing unwrinkled 1505 uniforms and sporting their pilot's wings and Top Secret badges. It was 10:30 p.m.

The staff sergeant compared their names to his access list and as he followed his finger down the column, Arnold added, "We're probably not on the usual access list. We're EC-47 pilots and we're here to consult with Lieutenant Dorothy Farr. She said to have her paged and she would escort us in."

The sergeant seemed content with that and consulted a personnel telephone list. Then he picked up the handset from a green phone hanging on the wall and dialed the number he had just found.

"Lieutenant Farr, I got two pilots here that say they need you to escort them in. Could you come to the main entrance?" He hesitated a few seconds. "Yessir, I mean Ma'am." He hung the phone up and instructed the two lieutenants, "Sirs, you'll have to step outside the gate until you have clearance to enter."

Eddie was a little nervous but Arnold was a picture of confidence. They were both still wearing their hats, something rare for a pilot. The sergeant was avoiding eye contact with them and an airman armed with an M-16 rifle and walking a guard dog strolled by them. The dog sniffed both their shoes and the handler spoke to his dog, "Come on Angio, I don't think they're spies." He made eye contact with the lieutenants and gave a sharp salute. They both returned the salute.

Dorothy came through the airlock door and looked beautiful. Women can really do something to a uniform. She was about five ten and walked with confidence, her stride not that different from a man's.

"Thank you, Sergeant." She gave him a nice smile. That was one of the perks he received for working nights, he got to see the round-eyes when they entered and exited the building. "I think you need to check the EC-47 list of clearances to find these two," she suggested. "They don't normally have business in here but we have business in the main monitoring room tonight."

The sergeant asked for their badges again and after a few minutes found their names in a notebook and was satisfied. "Ma'am, just a reminder, since they aren't on the regular access list you must accompany them both at all times, never let them out of your sight, and you're responsible for allowing them access only to the required intelligence. You'll have to sign for them right here." He held out a clipboard and Dorothy looked serious as she signed.

The sergeant pressed a button, the main door clicked, and they entered. They were inside an air lock. The entry door closed and Dorothy had the two pilots remove their shoes and replace them with white cloth slippers marked visitor. Dorothy apologized for the inconvenience, "They're very particular about dirt and dust—this is part of the sterile environment program." Eddie could sense a small pressure increase as the room was pressurized to the same amount as the interior of the building.

She shielded a control panel from their sight and punched in a combination of numbers, the second door clicked. They passed through it and were in. She escorted them through a hallway and through another door. They were confronted with a massive two story room. There were rows and rows of computer terminals, and almost every terminal was manned by an operator. Some looked hard at work and others were casually listening with one ear of their headsets while they passed the time talking with the operator next to them. The light level was low. They were all part of a dual IBM 360 / model 65 computer system. On the far end of the room was a tall 24 by 9 foot screen that portrayed the Ho Chi Minh Trail and the locations of hundreds of sets of sensors. Depictions showed which ones were transmitting active signals. The temperature in the room was very crisp, kept cool to maintain the computers and hundreds of assorted displays. Eddie and Arnold were stunned. Eddie thought it looked like something maybe the Strategic Air Command maintained to monitor the Soviet Union and the immense complex of bombers and missiles. But at the remote edge of the civilized world, at Nakhon Phanom, it was like a sci-fi dream. They were in a world of futuristic concepts and technology neither of them ever imagined.

Dorothy led them over to her empty desk and settled into her modern office chair. She typed in something and the two wide eyed lieutenants were treated to a bunch of voices speaking Vietnamese. She explained they were Vietnamese laborers taking a rice and water break, and how their voices were being picked up by plastic banana tree antennae, transmitted up to a QU-22B aircraft, and relayed down to TFA and their speakers. Wow!

"Can you understand what they're talking about?" Eddie could hardly contain his excitement.

"I speak fluent Vietnamese," she beamed back. "My assignment tonight is to monitor conversations for intelligence. I'm assigned the locations of several bivouac areas."

"What are they saying?" Arnold probed. "Are you getting any good stuff?"

"They're just like guys are all over the world." She smiled at her most recent love. "They're talking about sex. That's what I do, night after night, is monitor their rest areas and listen to them talk about screwing. You got any idea how long these poor guys have gone without getting laid? They really must hate the Americans."

"That's all you ever do?" Eddie was still in disbelief.

"Well, sometimes they assign me as a system operator," she conceded. "Let me see if I can find you anything other than dumb coolies to listen to. I'll tap into what the guy in front of us is doing." She typed in another bunch of codes and in less than a minute they could hear the sound of truck motors. It sounded like they were moving as the motors' revolutions were modulating and occasionally they could hear one of them shifting gears. She motioned the lieutenants in close so their conversation couldn't be overheard and explained that the exact time the trucks passed a series of sound sensors was determined by measuring the frequency shift due to Doppler Effect. The information was processed by their IBM computers and the computers dropped bombs using a navy fighter plane circling overhead. Both pilots were blown away by the technology and the complex system necessary to blow up a truck.

"Does it work?" Eddie asked and then they heard the unmistakable sound of a bomb falling, then an explosion.

"Holly shit, they just blew up the truck we were listening to," Eddie exclaimed.

She looked up and smiled. "Let's wait and see." For a minute they listened to the silence. Then the sound of a truck motor being started came over the speaker and the truck continued its trip, they could hear it passing the remaining sensors.

"We used to get lucky and kill an occasional truck but the gomers caught on to what we're doing. Now they keep changing their speed. Sometimes they even stop for ten or fifteen seconds, then go again. It throws our computer's rate computations way off, the calculation of the trucks moving position is erroneous, and we end up bombing dirt. We spent billions building this system and the gomers rendered it ineffective simply by varying their speed.

"We still gather a lot of good intel from the system," she continued. "We at least know what's going on out there and where to tell the forward air controllers to look for trucks."

"Sounds like another Mac Namera project," Arnold surmised.

"Truck killing with this system is a huge waste of money. The rest of the project works well enough," Dorothy conceded. "We really do have a handle on the trail and where the supplies are being moved. Our problem is that there isn't that much our government will let us do about it. We have rules we have to follow."

"We could blockade the port at Haiphong," Eddie added. "But I guess that's too simple."

* * * * * * * * * * * * * * * * * * * *

After their show and tell was over, Dorothy walked her two charges back to the exit doors. She stopped their little group short and gave the two informationally intoxicated pilots a stern lecture. "You guys gotta keep your mouths zipped about what you just saw here. We're all in the military and could get our asses in a big fix if any of us ever leaks what we saw and talked about tonight. Technically, it wasn't illegal for me to escort you in here tonight, but it wouldn't be good if anyone else knew about it. You have very high security clearances and I assume you have stuff about your own mission that you can't tell me about, so it's essential that you also protect the stuff that I do with the same discipline."

"Agreed?" She looked Eddie straight in the eyes.

"Agreed," Eddie repeated

"Agreed," Arnold nodded.

228

CHAPTER TWENTY: BANDITS

It was the first day of December 1969 and they were well into the dry season. The Thai rice farmers harvested their fields of rice—the staple of their existence. They burned their rice straw to clear their fields of debris in preparation for planting the new crop. The smoke rose to 20,000 feet and was so thick and widespread it drifted over the river and into Laos. The Towhead pilots had to fly using their instruments and weather approach procedures to land at Nakhon Phanom. The smoke season would last for over a month as it mixed with the usual valley fog that formed every morning in the Laotian mountains. The clandestine American operation, Air America, Ravens, and the various gunship and bombers were hindered by the haze. The Towheads continued. The smoke and fog had no effect on their radio interceptions. Sometimes they had to check several dop set sites before they found one open enough to see the ground and get a computer position update, but they managed. Sometimes they only had the less accurate TACAN bearings and distance readouts from channel 98—located at the Alternate. Intercepted messages without precise locations still contained a lot of valuable intelligence. Underneath the haze the war games went on as usual, except the Hmong were denied protection and firepower usually provided by their beloved bombs from the sky.

The North Vietnamese Army (NVA) was making slow and calculated progress against the fierce Hmong resisters. The Hmong Army had been battling the communist enemy invaders from North Vietnam for five years and the attrition was taking its toll. The Hmong had lost almost an entire generation of men in their crusade and were recruiting fifteen and sixteen year old boys for replacements. American airpower was the only thing that was keeping the Hmong and other loyal Lao military forces from being overrun and defeated.

Things weren't going that well in the Vietnam War to the south, either. American success required a twofold victory. First, they needed political stability in South Vietnam, stability that was supported by the population. Torn between the choice of communism or the corrupt and ruthless government provided by successions of presidential coups, the South Vietnamese were desperate for an acceptable political option to support. The Americans failed miserably in that arena. The failure to install a responsible Government and institute land reforms and other needed corrections opened the door wider for support of the Viet Cong and the infiltrating North Vietnamese troops.

The second requirement the Americans needed was a military solution. They needed to drive the North Vietnamese Army occupiers out of South Vietnam so a popular political solution could be enacted. The severe limitations placed on the American military by their own politicians, denied them the opportunity to utilize their full strength and abilities. On the ground and in the jungles of South Vietnam, the American Army and Marines were fighting the enemy on the enemy's terms and at the wrong end of the enemy's supply chain.

An old Lao proverb said, "You cannot kill a snake by beating it on the tail."

In North Vietnam, the supplies were openly stored and transported during the ill conceived bombing halts, halts dictated by the American Presidents. When bombing was allowed in North Vietnam, severe American self imposed restrictions were placed on the pilots so they were unable to achieve any decisive effect. President

Nixon was slowly withdrawing American troops from South Vietnam and leaving the South Vietnamese military to fight their own battles. They were not doing well and the North Vietnamese were expanding their area of influence.

During their scotch laden discussions, conducted in the privacy of their room, it became more and more obvious to Eddie that Washington was not interested in a military victory. When Eddie mentioned his suspicions to Arnold, the Ivy League scholar snapped his fingers and looked at Eddie. He nodded yes and replied, "Bingo! You said it, not me. Everyone around here is so brainwashed by their military indoctrination I've been afraid to say anything."

Arnold launched into his preplanned revelation to Eddie, one that couldn't have been presented unless Eddie had indicated he was ready for the truth. "The theory of gradualism," Arnold explained to Eddie, "can be defined as forced diplomacy, or graduated response. It was first proposed in the late fifties by Robert Osgood and Thomas Schelling. It involves the gradual increase of military pressure from a superior military force on one's enemy. The objective is not to defeat or destroy the enemy and its infrastructure. But, instead to gradually raise the burden of the conflict until the enemy reaches their breaking point and agrees to accept a compromised settlement at a negotiation table."

He let the concept sink in before continuing. "This is what we're participating in, gradualism. We're not trying to win the war, just apply pressure. President Johnson had staff members that advocated this approach well before Kennedy was assassinated. They don't want us military guys to know about it because it would take away our will to fight and the illusion of victory as our goal. They need us foot soldiers to apply pressure and actually think we're trying to win. Think of it, how many bombing halts did Johnson, and now Nixon, put into effect, and then repeal them when they had no effect on their negotiation attempts? They're gradually increasing the pressure, trying to eventually convince the NVA to come to the table by threatening to resume bombing. On the contrary, the North Vietnamese love the bombing halts. The halts give em time to move supplies and personnel around and re-enforce their defenses. Not allowing the American military to fight this war one hundred percent for a victory is a serious blunder! Ho Chi Minh and General Giap are playing our American Presidents Johnson and Nixon as if they were fools. They know that our Presidents are afraid to do anything that might provoke the Russians or the Chinese to openly enter this war."

"But we carry Russian and Chinese Linguists on certain missions. We know they're already down there and already involved by providing the NVA with guns, rockets, and technical advisors," Eddie countered.

"That's my point," Arnold explained. "They aren't doing it openly! The Russians and Chinese are too smart to openly send troops to this second class war. They do it clandestinely and got us right where they want us.

"The theory of gradualism," Arnold added, "goes against the rules of warfare as dictated by Clausewitz, the 1800s Guru of warfare. Clausewitz said, 'War is absolute.' How he defined this was that essentially you do not enter into a war if you are not committed one hundred percent to winning it. To not be committed one hundred percent and not committed to utilize all of your resources to win is to provide your enemy a major advantage."

"That explains a lot of things," Eddie reasoned. "The big seaport just outside Hanoi is off limits to our bombers and our navy. I had a conversation with an F-105 Thud pilot at the bar after he landed his crippled aircraft here at NKP. He said they were not allowed to bomb or strafe North Vietnamese fighter planes on the ground at their airports. They could only shoot at them if they were airborne and had their landing gear up. They're not allowed to bomb North Vietnamese radar GCI sites. They're not allowed to bomb North Vietnamese surface to air missile sites under construction, they have to wait until the sites are operational and shoot at them first. They're only allocated several targets at a time and they're dispatched each day in waves, each at the same time each day, and are always dispatched to attack from the same direction. They're sitting ducks for the NVA gunners. In South Vietnam, if a gun shoots at them from the ground, they must have permission from their command post to return fire. No one is allowed to bomb the huge NVA supply port in Cambodia. What our military calls the 'Rules of Engagement' should really be called the 'Restrictions on Combat.' They let the Viet Cong in South Vietnam walk away after bringing them to their knees during the Tet offensive. It's all stupid!

230

"And those are just the restrictions I know about." Eddie sat for a minute and thought. "But now that you said so, it's obvious! They just want us to harass em but not do anything serious that would bring the North Vietnamese to defeat. We're all just cannon fodder for some political experiment! Either that or our leaders in Washington are totally incompetent. I would have to think more about it before I could decide which."

"The answer is both," Arnold helped him out. "Gradualism in conducting the war in both North and South Vietnam and incompetent at managing the political injustices and corruption in South Vietnam."

"You learned about this in college?" Eddie questioned.

"I researched it in college after it became the subject of a campus debate. I was participating in the debate and my father explained the rest to me. He's got connections inside the administration." Eddie realized that Arnold was privy to some very sensitive information. Military combatants weren't supposed to know these things.

"The thing that Washington doesn't understand," Arnold continued, "is that the North Vietnamese won't accept anything other than complete victory. Gradualism won't work on them. We're just wasting our time and American lives applying pressure. The gomers are prepared to pay whatever price is necessary for victory; compromise is not even in their vocabulary. For them, this war is absolute! President Johnson was too conceited and arrogant to realize the true nature of our enemy's intentions. He called them ignorant jungle bunnies and Nixon is willing to shuck it all down the toilet just to get out of Vietnam. They might eventually end up at the negotiating table and sign a treaty, but Uncle Ho just ignores treaties. He'll continue treaty or not, until he has what he wants. All of Vietnam, Laos, and Cambodia. Mark my words, you're learning how to fly and I'm meeting my family obligations, but we're just putting in our time. We're not going to make any difference in the long run."

"If your old man knows all this why can't he talk some sense into somebody?"

"He's not that rich and influential. He's just rich enough to sit at the table but not rich enough to talk."

Arnold continued, "Ho Chi Minh and General Giap are not stupid. Stop and think about it. They're fighting this war in the streets of America. That's where the victory will come from because they know the American public will break. They're turning the tables on us and are gonna make us yield to their own prolonged gradualism. They mastered this concept thousands of years before there ever was an America and Americans to think of it. A million or so dead over here is a small price to them, unacceptable to us. All that anti war media and protesting activity back in the States is playing right into Uncle Ho's hands."

He looked at Eddie, "If you ever repeat any of this I'll deny everything and never offer you another scotch as long as we live."

"Jesus, no scotch, that's serious," Eddie lamented. But it was true. Eddie could never discuss this with anyone else at Nakhon Phanom for fear of being accused of being unpatriotic and subversive—possibly even treasonous. But at last he understood what was going on!

* * * * * * * * * * * * * * * * * * * *

Eddie dressed for a mission and was waiting outside for the crew bus to pick him up. He was scheduled to fly with a young academy graduate who had been flying as a co-pilot for almost seven months. Normally all pilots were upgraded to aircraft commander after six months in order to maintain the correct balance of crewmembers for each seat. This lieutenant, however, had just mucked around and consistently underperformed. At the six month anniversary Eddie had flown with him several times. He then reported to the operations officer that the guy just wasn't aircraft commander material. Major Collins' reply surprised Eddie. "There's an unwritten requirement for all academy graduates to become aircraft commanders before their year is up—before they're rotated back home to more responsible positions." Eddie wondered if it was just academy graduates giving preference to academy graduates.

Major Collins continued, "I'm gonna instruct scheduling to pair you with Andy for every one of his flights from now on. Until you get him ready for upgrading. You can do your other training on your remaining days off."

Major Collin's fondness for Eddie had been deteriorating over time. He was beginning to get agitated over Eddie's total control of the detachment training program. The major secretly wanted a piece of the responsibility for use as material in his annual evaluation report. Eddie couldn't care less about the major's evaluation and accepted the challenge of getting Andy upgraded to aircraft commander without any thought. "Yessir. I'll do my best," was his answer to the assignment. Eddie had his ways to make these problem pilots pay attention. Andy would just take a little more concentration and work.

Andy showed up, also dressed and ready to fly, and strolled over to the shade beside Eddie. This was the end of the third week they had been flying together and Andy was still moping around. At least Eddie had learned why. It seemed that Andy's father was a one star general and had been a fighter pilot family hero. Flying an EC-47, Andy was a disappointment to both himself and his family—especially his father.

"Morning, Nuts. Guess there's been a change of schedule. I was supposed to have this day off. What's up?"

"Beats the hell out of me," Eddie was sincere. The guy still hadn't figured out that their schedules were married. "I think we're supposed to start working again on your training for upgrade to aircraft commander."

"Yeah, big deal!" the academy graduate sloughed it off.

Their navigator Stu joined them and after a short ride, they made their way into the briefing room and sat waiting for the briefer. When he appeared he was a new guy, or at least none of them had ever seen him before. He was one of dozens of analysts, the mystery guys that inhabited the myriad of back rooms at Task Force Alpha.

"Morning." He pulled the cloth from the briefing map and stood sizing up his audience of three. He was a captain, well groomed Caucasian with a crisp military flat top and wearing 1505s. He looked in good physical shape and Eddie thought maybe he recognized him from the gym. "We got a little different mission for you today, so we're gonna reveal a little more information than we usually do—seeing how it involves flying somewhere you normally don't go."

Eddie's and Stu's eyes meet. They had flown together numerous times before and they shared a mutual trust and respect for each other. "This mission really doesn't have anything to do with the Ho Chi Minh Trail and doesn't have anything to do with the conflict we're supporting with Vang Pao's Army. It's a separate thing that our customer has requested we do for them with the EC-47's particular specialty. We have a hand-picked crew for you in the back and that's why you're on this flight." He nodded towards Stu.

"Oh Boy," Eddie thought out loud without thinking. "Do you want us to stand up and bend over to make this easier?" Stu rolled his eyes and Andy sat stoically with a blank face.

"That won't be necessary," the briefer smiled and went along with Eddie. "This place is pretty high tech; we can get you from a sitting position."

Then he launched into the serious part of his presentation. "There aren't too many people that know this, not even at Task Force Alpha where they think they know everything. Northern Laos, north of the Plain of Jars, is an endless maze of mountains that are sparsely inhabited by primitive tribes and there are very few roads that connect anything together. There's only remote villages and foot trails." He pointed with his pointer to the top of the map to where the Chinese Yunnan Province protruded into Laos. "The sparse roads are nothing more than dirt trails that are passable only during the dry season and then require a four wheel drive vehicle."

He slid his telescopic pointer together and stood facing the mesmerized trio. "First a little history. In 1962, Laotian Prince Souvanna Phouma decided it was a good idea to maintain friendly relations with the Chinese. He shares a considerable amount of his northern border with them. He gave the Chinese permission to build a connecting road from the Chinese province of Yunnan into the Laotian Province of Phongsaly. The Chinese rounded up ten thousand workers and did that very thing. Then in 1966 the Chinese, on their own initiative and without permission from the Laotian government, built three more roads from Yunnan Province into Houa Khong Province." He pulled out his pointer and pointed to a province that on the map was named Lunag Namtha. Every dry season they've been sending in thousands of Chinese workers and a formidable contingent of Chinese soldiers. The soldiers are armed with heavy artillery and substantial anti-aircraft guns to

232

protect their venture and their construction activity. It's obvious they want to protect their activity from prying eyes. I guess they haven't heard of our U-2 and SR-71 high altitude spy planes. With the conflict going on in the PDJ and the Ho Chi Minh Trail occupation by the NVA, the Laotian government has largely ignored this incursion. The Laotians just don't have the military resources to resist these Chinese road building projects. Also, the area is so remote that there's very little of value to defend. There's lots of teak wood and no way to get it out and maybe lots of monkeys."

He winced, "That brings us to today. The Chinese have tied into some existing dry season trails that the Laotians call roads, and have widened and improved them and have gotten all the way down to the northern Mekong River, just across the river from Thailand. The northern half of the road is asphalt and an all season road. It's obvious that their intent is to eventually have an all weather route for access to the Mekong and Thailand. In response, the Thai have massed troops across the river from where the Chinese road meets the Mekong. It's a delicate situation that not many outsiders know about but the Thai officials are very concerned. They have good reason to fear a Chinese invasion and land grab. We have road watch teams in place, composed primarily of friendly native villagers. This is the area where Tom Dooley had his network of hospitals and some of the locals are very cooperative and radio us reports about road activity. It's about all we have except photos taken from very high altitudes. I mean high because they have eighty-five millimeter guns on that road. Several observation aircraft have been sent up there and have received heavy volumes of anti-aircraft fire. We're talking about lots of thirty-seven and twenty-three millimeter guns and a substantial number of heavy stuff, fifty-seven millimeter and eighty-five millimeter guns. A Laotian C-47 and an Air America C-123 have been shot down while scouting the road and several other Air America birds have returned with substantial battle damage. Needless to say, gentlemen, we would not ask you to fly over this piece of real estate in your EC-47s. Your aircraft is just too valuable to risk."

"What about the pilots getting killed?" Eddie wondered silently. "The customer cares more about the aircraft than the pilots."

Eddie held his breath as the briefing officer continued, "Your mission today is to fly up there and troll for radio intercepts from their activities along the road. You can stay fifteen or twenty miles east of the road and from ten thousand or twelve thousand feet you can get a good line of sight coverage of the area. Intercepts are what we want. Positions are a low priority because we already know where the road is. We also want you to keep at least fifteen miles south of the Chinese border. By maintaining at least fifteen miles from the road and the Chinese border, you'll stay over remote jungle where there's no military activity. The Chinese have no radar coverage up there so they won't see you and won't even know that you're there." He hesitated, "There's one more thing."

"There's always a catch!" Eddie whispered to himself.

"The North Vietnamese have installed a radar site north of Barthelomy Pass, just inside their border where Route 7 leads into the Plain of Jars. It can provide them with radar coverage of the PDJ area and possibly coverage further north where you'll be flying today. We really don't have a lot of info on it because we don't think they've fired it up yet. So your radio operators will be listening and if it comes on line they'll try to copy any intelligence they can get. We're pretty sure it's a ground control radar guidance system for aircraft that's similar to Invert GCI here at NKP.

"Any questions?" he finished his presentation.

"Yeah," Eddie was first. "My map doesn't even go that far north. How do I know how to stay away from the mystery road and the fifteen mile buffer from China?"

"I have two new maps here, one for you and one for your navigator. They have the road and the Chinese buffer marked on them." Eddie was satisfied and he had confidence in Stu.

"What about dop set points?" Stu asked.

"There's nothing up there that's been surveyed. Get your last position update when you cross over the PDJ and you'll just have to eyeball it from river bends on your map and with the TACAN from the Alternate. You'll be able, at higher altitudes, to still receive TACAN channel ninety-eight from the southern edge of your holding orbit. That'll be close enough for our customer's purposes cause they already have photos of the road."

* *

The three of them talked things over while checking out their M-16 and an ammo box. It was standard air force protocol for the aircraft commander to brief his entire crew before ever going out on a mission. But in the EC-47s, there were basically two crews: the drivers up front, called the pilots, who just fly around as directed by the Spooks, and the Spooks with their mission objectives and their plans on executing them. The spooks' activities were all kept secret from the airplane drivers. So an aircraft commander can't brief a mission that is kept secret from him. Normally the EC-47 crews just rode the van out to the airplane, each pre-flighted their own equipment, then the pilots started their engines and flew. This day, because the uncertainly about their mission, Eddie assembled both crews, front and back, outside their aircraft and everyone checked their survival equipment and the parachutes for current inspection dates. Eddie noticed that most of the hand-picked radio operators were older and instructors. They were flying number 304; the Lady's nose art had been touched up and looked gorgeous.

"If things go as planned, this should be an easy tour of the north forty," Eddie briefed, wondering which of his radio operators were the linguists and what languages they spoke fluently. Chances were good that at least several of them spoke Chinese. He also wondered what they knew that he didn't know. There were five operators, four had seats at their respective stations and the fifth would strap into a rear fold-out seat for take-off and landing and spend the rest of the flight walking back and forth along the catwalk (aisle). The mobile operator could monitor and work with the various seated operators. The aircraft had two headsets with long trailing cords for such use.

It was a beautiful afternoon to fly and the operators chatted a lot over their interphone. By the time Towhead Three Three departed the Plain of Jars on a northerly heading they had eight radio intercepts recorded and tucked away. As they flew north over territory Eddie and Andy had never seen, everyone was enthralled. The smoke from the burning rice straw to their south thinned out then disappeared. Their view of the jungle was excellent but Andy wasn't impressed. He said there was nothing out there. Eddie thought it was fascinating. For him the act of flying off to pristine nowhere was definitely a soul cleansing experience. Two of the radio operators had their parachutes on and were standing in the back peering out the open doorway. It was against regulation for anyone to go back near the open door space without a parachute. It was one rule that everyone in the EC-47s followed.

The mountains rolled by underneath them, gentle in shape, again like the Smokies in North Carolina. There was very little karst compared to the southern parts of Laos. Every once in a while, however, a steep mountainside would reveal some water eroded limestone and give away its subterranean structure. The jungle was continuous. There was no sign of any roads and in the middle of the day there were no cooking fires giving away the presence of mountain tribes. It was exciting for Eddie to imagine them down there, listening to the strange sound in the sky, far above the overhead jungle canopy. Certainly they still lived in the Stone Age and only saw an aircraft every couple of years. Did they wonder what that strange bird in the sky was? There was no reason for anyone to ever fly over that remote forgotten corner of the globe. There weren't even any stratospheric airline routes over this unspoiled paradise. The operators were horsing around in the back end. Other than a little Morse code that had skipped from across several hundreds of miles, the airways were silent. The mountains were not nearly as tall as those they had crossed around the Plain of Jars so Eddie descended to 8,000 feet for their enroute segment. No reason to get them hypoxic until it was time to go to work. He would climb as necessary to get a line of sight for listening in on the Chinese road's radio traffic; but enroute 8000 feet was just fine.

Eddie and Andy nibbled on their crew lunch, then threw their orange peels and banana peelings out the side windows. Eddie wondered, "Coming from the sky, wouldn't that give the natives something to think about? The natives would at least know what the strange birds ate; oranges and bananas." Stu finally announced they were approaching their work area and gave Andy a new heading. Andy was flying from the left seat and Eddie was still sightseeing out the co-pilots side window. Andy turned to the new heading and initiated the climb up to 12,000 feet. Only fifteen miles to the west, the Chinese Army was protecting their road as tens of thousands of hand laborers were hacking away at the jungle and improving a road with shovels and buckets. Protecting the road from what? It was a roadway to where and why? Were they really planning on invading Thailand?

They trolled north and south, a very skinny oblong orbit with fifty nautical mile legs. Each orbit took a little over an hour to complete. There was absolutely no sign of civilization anywhere. After the first orbit the effects of the total lack of human activity and the endless jungle caused Eddie's mind to wander. What if there really existed such a thing as time warps? Why did he always wonder about time warps? Did this have anything to do with the Lady? This ancient cockpit out there in the middle of nowhere would be the perfect medium to attract such a phenomenon. What would it be like to disappear from this world and emerge and find themselves in a different world or a different time? Would there be any place to land? Would there even be people or would it be a land filled with dinosaurs? Or maybe it would be another planet with no life except lichens and rock looking creatures that dissolved each other with acid and then digested the soup like a fly. Or would he suddenly chance onto Atlantis, a civilization so far advanced from Eddie's world that his EC-47 would be a primitive aircraft. Who knew what remains or extinct creatures existed in the remote unexplored jungle they were flying over?

When they reached the northern end of their last orbit and turned south, Eddie called on the operator's interphone and asked if they were getting any good copy. The sun was getting lower in the west and the mountains below cast broad shadows on their eastern sides. The fuel gauges indicated it was time to head home and in another couple of hours it would get dark. It was almost two and a half hours to NKP from the north end of their orbit. Compared to the temperate climates, there was very little dusk in the tropics and the sun would set, then it would be dark.

"Yeah, we got some stuff that's actually quite interesting," the unseen operator on the other end of the interphone replied. "There's a lot of traffic between field radios, mostly logistical stuff but probably of interest to some intelligence guys. They can come up with amazing stories from forensic bits of radio intercepts."

They continued their way south and departed their orbit area. Stu gave them a heading direct for Nakhon Phanom, a heading plotted from their position derived from channel 98.

The EC-47 pilots had an additional procedure they performed anytime they were flying a Q model aircraft, the ones with the larger non-standard engines. Back in the States, when they made the modification and added the larger engines, they were in a hurry and didn't check the modification out well enough. The engines ran just fine for the test pilots who flew around at normal cruise power settings. The crews in Asia, however, flew around slowly and at minimum power settings to save as much gas as possible. They weren't interested in going somewhere but just loitering and providing an airborne platform. At these minimum power settings the R-2000 engine spark plugs would foul, regardless of how carefully they leaned the engines. A fouled plug is a spark plug that has accumulated fuel residue and carbon. With time the accumulation of residue will grow and eventually prevent the spark plug from functioning. As the plugs on the engine foul, the engine will develop a sputter and as it grows worse the engine will quit. This can become rather disconcerting while flying over enemy held territory, hours from home.

The crews tried all types of procedures, but despite their best efforts, the plugs still fouled. Eventually one of the older pilots, flying Q models out of Pleiku, came up with an "in the field fix." Every half hour, the pilots would lean out the fuel mixture until the engine cylinders and associated spark plugs reached their peak (hottest) temperature. Then the pilots would go to a full rich fuel mixture. The excessive amount of fuel in the full rich mixture would flood the overheated cylinders and would abruptly cool the spark plugs. The temperature shock would cause the fouling to ablate free from the plugs, and voila, the pilots would have clean plugs functioning at full efficiency. Sometimes they had to do it several times before their engines would run smoothly. Eddie busied himself with the task of cleaning the right engine's plugs.

The two Mikoyan Gurevich MIG 21 Fishbed fighter aircraft slipped over the ridge of mountains that separated North Vietnam from Laos and headed west into Laos. They were headed toward the vast expanse of roadless jungle that stretched hundreds of miles north from the Laotian Plain of Jars and all the way north to the Chinese border. The sun reflected brightly off the polished aluminum of their supersonic fighter planes. The bright red star on their tails proudly displayed the pride and dedication of the two Russian trained North Vietnamese pilots.

"Test Flight Two, radio check," the lead pilot called in the blind. He knew there may be Americans listening on their radio frequencies so he used an ambiguous call sign: "*Test Flight Two*." He didn't want to give any indication that he was a threat to any Americans. The Americans would find out soon enough about the new North Vietnamese radar facility that was focused into Laos and designed for guiding North Vietnamese fighters in combat against the American Air Force. Their North Vietnamese foray into Laos and the shoot down of an American aircraft, guided with their new ground control intercept (GCI) radar, was to be a total surprise to the Americans. It would open a whole new dimension to the conflict.

The operators in the North Vietnam ground control intercept radar facility had been waiting for a week for this opportunity. Tucked away in a limestone niche, carved just below the peak of a mountain, eight miles inside the North Vietnamese border, they could see with their radar well into the Laotian Plain of Jars and its surrounding areas. They could also see far north into Laos where Towhead Three Three had been lazily flying a fifty mile orbit. What they really wanted was a highly publicized daytime kill of an American aircraft, deep into Laotian territory, by their own MIG fighters. For this demonstration, the American aircraft with a call sign of Towhead Three Three would be just fine. Any American aircraft shot down by a North Vietnamese MIG in Laos would make the headlines and add the new dimension to the war. It was the safe, easy kill they had been waiting for. They had no idea that the American aircraft was an EC-47 reconnaissance aircraft flying under the direction of the CIA. If it was shot down there would be no media coverage and total denial of the incident.

"Test Flight Two, I have radar lock on, climb to twenty-two thousand feet and fly heading two seven zero degrees. I have your traffic one hundred four miles . . . negative hostiles in the area." The North Vietnamese controller limited the text and transmission time of his radio call. He didn't want the American military, further south in the Plain of Jars, from getting a position bearing on his radio broadcast. He didn't want to give away his radar site's position. He assumed the presence of the two North Vietnamese fighter aircraft would be compromised when they shot down the single American aircraft. He was puzzled why the American aircraft had strayed way north from protective air cover. After the shoot down, the MIGs would be on their way back across their border into their homeland. It would be too late for the Americans to react to the situation

The North Vietnamese radar controller had no idea that an American photo reconnaissance RF-4 jet aircraft had discovered and had been monitoring the construction of their radar site for the last month. Unfortunately for Eddie's EC-47 crew, the American President Nixon was helping the Peoples Republic of North Vietnam by prohibiting the American bombers from bombing any of the North Vietnamese radar sites. It was a mystery to the North Vietnamese why the Americans would impose self inflected restrictions on their own military, but the Americans ineptness was just fine with the North Vietnamese patriots.

The word at the bars scattered throughout South East Asia, the bars that American fighter pilots hung out at, was that the President didn't want to kill any of the Russian technicians that were helping the North Vietnamese build and operate their radar network. President Nixon feared that it would "anger" the Russian Government and "expand the conflict."

The American President had also just initiated a total bombing halt in all of North Vietnam. Included in the restrictions was a clause that stated, "No American aircraft will cross the border into North Vietnam in hot pursuit (of enemy fighters)." Go Figure! This would be a turkey shoot for the MIGs. They would smoke (shoot down) the slow moving American aircraft and hustle back across the border and into North Vietnamese sanctuary.

* * * * * * * * * * * * * * * * * * * *

In the cockpit of Towhead Three Three, the radio came to life, "Towhead Three Three, this is Invert on guard. I have two bandits exiting the fishmouth, position channel ninety-eight bearing zero eight zero at one zero five miles DME. Tracking a two seven zero course. Towhead Three Three, if you read me it looks like there're fast movers coming hell bent to get you. You're the only aircraft we know of in that area. I'd suggest you get the hell out of there."

Eddie was shocked! They had checked in with Invert just after taking off from Nakhon Phanom. He knew that while they were crossing over the Plain of Jars in Laos, the American "Invert" radar had silently monitored their flight path. Their mission, however, required them to fly way north and they could only be tracked by Invert radar if they flew very high and were at the south end of their work orbit. Unpressurized and without supplemental oxygen on board, they were unable to sustain flight higher than 12,000 feet. What Eddie didn't know was that Invert was not seeing him on their radar, but had locked on to the higher MIG fighters as they crossed over the dividing mountain ridge. The Invert operator knew Towhead Three Three was somewhere up there and he was broadcasting a warning to the Towhead in the blind—just in case the Towhead could hear him. If Eddie had been any less than 12,000 feet high, he and his seven crew members wouldn't have been able to hear the radio warning.

Eddie, in disbelief, sat there stunned for a moment. "Bandits" was the code word for unknown aircraft of suspected enemy origin, like enemy MIG fighters. The fishmouth was a portion of the North Vietnamese border that had a fishmouth shape to it on the map. It couldn't be happening to him! With all the antennas his highly modified World War II C-47 cargo aircraft had, the wind drag was significant. The fastest they could fly in level flight was 120 knots, which would convert to 138 miles per hour. The MIGs, as they probably were, would be coming at a minimum of 600 knots. To get the hell out of there was not an available option. There were no American fighters in the vicinity where they were; probably the nearest were several hundred miles south along the Ho Chi Minh Trail.

The North Vietnamese had received a radio report from their agents across the river from Nakhon Phanom about Eddie's brief radio conversation with Invert after the Towhead EC-47 took off from Nakon Phanom. They knew that the aircraft was American. They picked it up and quietly tracked it on their new radar for over five hours. The EC-47 had no radar sensing equipment on board so they were unaware they were being watched. The North Vietnamese had plenty time to set the operation up and coordinate it with their headquarters in Hanoi. The Towhead aircraft was, as far as the PAVN radar was concerned, theirs for the taking.

"Towhead Three Three, this is Invert, I estimate eight minutes until the bandits are in your area. We scrambled F-4 fighters out of Udorn and they're coming petal to the metal. Their ETA to your area is sixteen minutes. Do you copy?"

"I copy," Eddie replied, not knowing if Invert could hear him or not. As if there was anything Eddie could do about it. He checked his watch so he would know exactly when the bandits would arrive in his area. The bandits, if they were really MIGs, would have six minutes to shoot him down and a two minute head start back to their border and safety. That would be a piece of cake for the highly maneuverable MIGs.

Without fighter cover he and his crew were in a dangerous, almost hopeless position. As transport pilots, neither Eddie nor his co-pilot had any air to air combat tactics training. Even if he had been trained in air combat maneuvers, it wouldn't have improved his situation. The slow and low EC-47, with its World War II heritage, and Eddie, were both out of their league.

"What the hell am I doing here?" Eddie thought to himself. "It wasn't supposed to be like this!" He looked at the thick jungle below. "Would he, his aircraft, and his crew spend eternity together down there scattered among the endless jungle! The pilot's cliché was "bend over and kiss your ass goodbye." There wasn't any room to do that in the tiny cockpit but Eddie closed his eyes and tilted his head back. He needed a reality check.

After a pause, Eddie got around to replying to Invert's warning, "Towhead Three Three copies."

"Invert, this is Cricket, I copied you also." Cricket was the American airborne C-130 control center that was orbiting south of the Plain of Jars, along side the Ho Chi Minh Trail. "I've diverted my KC-135 aerial tanker from its orbit and it should be setting up its new orbit to refuel the F-4s in twenty minutes. They'll need a refueling by time they finish with the MIGs. You should be able to see the tanker going north on your radar screen."

"Got him," Invert replied. "I'll follow him and put him in position as soon as we get organized down here. Got any other fast movers we can use?"

"Unfortunately all my fast movers are south of here. I got another pair of F-4s headed that way and a pair of navy A-7s who want a piece of the action. They should be there in twenty minutes—after the Udorn F-4s get to your Towhead aircraft."

Then as an afterthought he radioed, "Just in case it's a trap, I suggest you see if Udorn can get more fast movers in the area."

"Wilco, we're working on it."

The cockpit was silent. Eddie could hear the Security Service radio operators in the rear. Without orders from the cockpit, they were in their destruct drill. They were destroying classified papers and equipment as fast as they could. The open rear door and the vast jungle below served as a good hiding place for hardware. They were stuffing the classified paperwork, printed on water soluble paper, into water cans and making a thick creamy soup.

Eddie sat with both hands on the yoke and looked out at an old patch on the Lady's right wing. This bird had a history of some kind. He wondered if she had ever been in a pickle like this before.

Pilots talk to their aircraft all the time when they fly, but they never expect their aircraft to talk back. That would be loony, but on that day it was as if the Lady spoke to him. On that day, together, they weren't about to lay down for a couple of loud stinky jets. The message was very clear! "I got it. Here's what we gotta do," Eddie explained his plan over the pilot's interphone.

Staring at the patch on the Lady's right wing, a memento from some previous war, it was as if the Lady reminded Eddie of a conversation he overheard at the Clark Officers Club. It was a conversation between two A-1 fighter pilots. A-1s were not known for their speed either, but they were a lot faster than a Gooney Bird and very maneuverable and had guns to shoot back with. Those A-1 pilots, ex-jet fighter pilots with backgrounds and training in air combat maneuvers, agreed the best tactic was to keep the enemy fighters in front of them so they could close on them faster. Thus they would lessen the time for the hostile fighter to maneuver and align his sights on them. Also they would be able to see the enemy so they could dodge and jink from gunfire and missiles. Their conversation was centered on getting into position to fire their own array of guns at the passing, faster jet. Eddie's intent was to deny the MIGs an easy target until the American F-4 jet fighters arrived on the scene.

While Eddie was looking at the patch and putting together his next move, Andy also broke into his thoughts with an outstanding contribution. This contribution came from his supposedly not give a shit, Zoomie student. "If we stay up here at this altitude we're sitting ducks. With this camouflage paint job wouldn't we be harder to spot if we were flying down low on the deck?"

"Good idea!" Eddie complimented Andy over the interphone for all to hear. "I got the airplane." Eddie rolled the aircraft into a left turn toward the approaching Bandits while slowly pulling the throttles back to idle power. They had just a few minutes to get into position. He then nudged the nose over into a steep accelerating dive. On their way down he consolidated the A-1 pilot's ideas and Andy's suggestions and completed his plan. It was a perfect example of the synergy he had been preaching at the last flight safety meeting.

They were angling toward the MIGs which were coming from the east. He rolled out from the turn and handed control of the aircraft over to Andy, "You got it. Drop down on the deck and head for that shadow along the edge of that high ridge angling southeast in front of us. Look for the MIGs a little to our left, coming from the east and into the sun. Our shadow moving over the tree tops in the sun at low level would still give us away, big time. But if we fly in that shadow alongside that ridge, we won't cast a shadow, should blend in with the dark jungle, and should be able to see the Bandits as they approach us."

238

Their number two engine had picked an inopportune time to start sputtering from fouled spark plugs and Eddie needed to attend to the sick engine. Eddie momentary ignored the sick engine and continued, "If they don't see us on their first pass at least it'll buy us a few more minutes. Fighter pilots like to come in high, that's their instinctive thing to do, hit the enemy from above. If they pass overhead going west, looking into the low angle sun, they hopefully won't see us down there in that shadow. They'll use up more time turning around. When they turn back to the east, we'll be out of sight from them, hiding behind the ridge. I just hope they don't split up. It'll double their chances of finding us. Every second we buy gets those F-4s closer."

Everyone was functioning as if part of a well oiled machine, a well disciplined professional team. Andy held the aircraft in the steep descent and headed toward the shadow from the ridge. As he approached the tree tops he rolled out wings level and flew fifty feet above the treetops as he slipped over into the dimly lit mountain shadow. Eddie leaned out the sputtering number two engine and agonized as the cylinder head temperature gauge failed to advance toward the red limit line. At idle power and with their fast descent speed, the cylinder temperature just didn't want to increase. It actually dropped lower. The operators in the back went about their destruct drill, pausing only to recheck that their parachute harnesses were tight and ready to function.

His radio operator, the Vietnamese linguist, was glued to his headset as he desperately tried to locate the communication frequency the enemy radar and its two MIG pilots were using. Stu was plotting his computer's position on his chart, checking for mountains, and monitoring the destruct drill as well as Invert on the radio and Eddie and Andy in the cockpit.

The two American F-4 pilots pulled their engines out of fuel inefficient afterburner when they went through 600 knots. They needed to have enough fuel to engage the MIGs and hook onto the KC-135 airborne gas station. They rechecked their fire control systems and double checked every gauge in their cockpit. This was the stuff that fighter pilots dream of, a crack at some MIGs.

On the other side of the encounter, the North Vietnamese ground radar operator adjusted the gain and tilt on his radar in an unsuccessful attempt to repaint the American spy plane's position. The low flying spy plane was too well hidden in the radar's ground clutter and impossible to see. If it were a decade later, there would be Doppler technology for his radar that would easily distinguish the moving aircraft from the stationary ground returns. But Doppler radar was not to be had that day with his old technology Russian radar. The EC-47s used doppler technology for their navigation in the rear of the aircraft, but that was top secret American technology.

The MIG pilots were busily scanning the airspace and dark jungle below as they slowed to a leisurely 350 knot cruise and prepared to roll over and go down for the kill of the slower aircraft. Their radar also painted nothing but ground clutter below. They also needed but didn't have the technology of down-looking Doppler radar. They needed a quick kill and to sprint back to their homeland before the Yankee imperialists could get their own fighters into the area. But try as they did, they could not make out the camouflaged Gooney Bird that was hiding on the deck in a shadow. The sun was shining into their eyes and was giving them fits.

The stealthy EC-47s airspeed was indicating 165 after their screaming dive to the deck and their multitude of antennas were whistling like a pine forest in a wind storm.

"Watch out for a mountain in front and to your right," Stu hollered over the pilot's interphone. "This map shows a long ridge ahead and to our right."

"We got it in sight," Andy reassured the navigator. "I almost got my right wingtip sticking in it. There's no way they're gonna get directly behind us."

"Brilliant," Eddie hollered without using the interphone.

Eddie very slowly advanced both engines' propellers and throttles to maximum continuous power. He needed to shock cool his number two engine's spark plugs but first he needed to slowly re-warm the engines from their idle power dive so as to not shock warm his cylinder heads and crack them.

He wanted to hang onto as much of their speed as he could but at level flight the airspeed was still slowing from all of the antennae drag. Hopefully the MIGs wouldn't see them down on the deck, but if they did it would only take the MIGs a quick maneuver to descend and bring the vulnerable old Gooney Bird into their gun sights. If that happened, Eddie wanted enough speed to zoom up to at least 700 feet above the jungle. He wanted to bail his crew out just high enough that they would have time for their parachutes to open and give them several swings before they plunged into the jungle.

Eddie's one uncle, in World War II, had bailed out of a bomber at much higher altitude. It gave the German fighter time to strafe him as he dangled helplessly under his descending parachute. It would be much better for Eddie to bail his crew out low over the remote jungle, where there was no chance to get strafed while dangling in their parachutes. With no enemy on the ground, each had a survival radio and could talk to the rescue helicopter that would arrive. Probably not before darkness, they would for sure be there at daybreak the next morning. To stay with the aircraft meant they would surely die from the MIGs.

The right engine continued popping and sputtering. "Damn, not now," Andy swore to no one in particular. "We need to defoul number two's plugs."

"You fly the aircraft and look for the bandits and I'll take care of number two," Eddie instructed. "Number one sounds okay at this high power setting and should remain clean enough to keep running."

"You be the boss," Andy replied and concentrated on keeping his right wingtip out of the sheer rock wall. With both engines safely warmed up, throttles full forward, and the number two engine leaned way out, the number two's cylinder head temperature continued to rise.

"I found his frequency! I got the radar controllers frequency that's talking to the MIG." The voice came from the rear. It was the operator who was fluent in Vietnamese. "The MIG pilots keep telling their controller that they can't see us and are bitchin about the sun in their eyes. The controller keeps telling them that we disappeared in his radar ground clutter straight off their nose."

"Keep me informed," Andy hollered back.

"Stu, are you still on?" Eddie called as he monitored the rising temperature gauge.

"Right here," Stu came back on the pilot interphone. "The Ros have a destruct drill going on back here and I checked that everyone has their parachute on. If they see us and make a gunnery pass we're dead meat if we don't jump."

"Good old Stu," Eddie muttered. "He's on top of things back there. At a time like this it's great having competent help."

Then it happened all at once.

"Got em," Andy hollered. "Around twenty thousand feet, they're slightly to our left and high, gonna pass right over the top of us. You wanna make a tight left one eighty degree turn, then tuck back against the ridgeline again?" Andy questioned.

"Take the turn as soon as they pass over the top of us," Eddie agreed. "They can't look down and behind their aircraft. Make it a tight turn and get us back in the shadow again and we'll watch them from their behind." He looked out his side window at the limestone cliff and the jungle floor below, "Make that a left turn away from the cliff and keep our left wing tip out of those tree tops. I'm getting too old to do cartwheels."

"Sir, the North Vietnamese radar controller just told the MIGs to descend down to low altitude and to turn around and make a slow pass back over our area." Eddie clinched his teeth when he heard the linguist's bad news.

"God-damnit," Eddie answered. At low altitude the MIGs would sooner or later see them and their jig would be up. Eddie had a quick vision of all the scrapped aircraft at the bone yard at Davis Monthan Air Base near Tucson, Arizona. His T-38 instructor told him that, "In the end they would just cut em up anyway so never hesitate to bail out." Eddie planned on saving the crew and letting the MIGs use the empty Lady for target practice.

With the power advanced and the mixture leaned far back, Eddie's number two engine cylinder temperature was just tapping the red line so he shoved his number two mixture forward into the full rich setting. The blast of wet rich fuel shock cooled the engine spark plugs and the buildup of fouling debris ablated (broke free)

240

and exited out the exhaust ports. The engine instantly smoothed out and purred like a kitten. He returned the mixture lever to the auto-mixture detent.

The American F-4s' radars locked onto the distant MIGs, both two-man crews' heartbeats increased, and their adrenalin flowed. The intercept officers in the F-4s' rear seats began to calculate intercept angles and rechecked their fuel gauges. Their afterburner departure and climb from Udorn had used up a large amount of precious fuel.

Eddie knew he was gambling against a stacked deck. Who were they kidding? Once those MIGs got sight of them it would be less than a minute and the Lady would be a ball of flame. There was no escape from the enemy fighters. "Stu, get the guys back there ready to jump. If they see us I'm gonna zoom for altitude and I want all of you to go on my order in a close interval. There're no gomers down there and best you stay together."

Eddie and Andy were wearing their parachute harness only and once out of their seats they could snap their chest pack onto their harness and be instantly ready to go out the door. But it was a long way to the back door. "If we gotta jump, you go when I call it. I'll hold the airplane and trim it level until the guys in the back are gone, then I'll be right behind you."

"Ya sure?" Andy asked.

"Yeah," Eddie reassured him. "If you don't run fast enough down the aisle, I'll catch you from the rear and they'll find your body with my footprints up and over your back." The remark had a lot of truth to it.

As Andy rolled out from the course reversal, Eddie tried to call Invert but it was only a futile and desperate effort. They were way too low for any radar or radio reception from that far away.

The NVA radar controller spotted the American F-4s on his radar, still many miles away but closing at a remarkably high rate of speed. They were closing straight for his MIGs. He had known they would show up sooner or later but it was much sooner than he had expected. There wasn't time to hunt for Towhead Three Three and complete the mission. To save his aircraft, the young North Vietnamese ground radar operator would have to abort the mission. They couldn't afford the negative media coverage if two of their prize MIGs were shot down over Laos. Their two MIGs were worth far more than the single slow moving American aircraft, whatever it was. He reluctantly keyed his transmitter and ordered, "Test Flight Two, break it off, and return at maximum speed to our border heading zero eight zero. I have two fighters coming from the direction of Udorn Air Base. If you hurry, you can beat them to our border."

"Sir," it was the Vietnamese linguist again. "The radar controller just told the MIGs to break it off and race back across their border." Over the R-2000 engines' noise Eddie could hear a cheer go up in the rear.

For the second time in as many minutes, Eddie talked to his airplane and praised its performance. To his left, one lieutenant Air Force Academy graduate was crossing himself. Eddie and Andy looked up and two tiny specks were turning east, toward the North Vietnamese border, their thick black exhausts indicating they had also put the petal to the metal. The MIG pilots knew if they beat the F-4s to the border the Americans would have to break off their chase. It was a court martial offence if the American F-4s violated their President's bombing halt orders and ventured into the enemy's homeland.

The adrenalin laced F-4 pilots would refuel from the tanker, limp back to Udorn, disappointed they couldn't complete their kill. They didn't know they weren't supposed to win, just apply pressure. It was the theory of gradualism.

The operators in the back of the Gooney Bird were patting each other on their backs with joy and they almost beat each other to death.

Andy set the two engines at climb power, synchronized the two props to a smooth drone, and without a spoken word raised the nose and started climbing away from the treetops. Eddie wasn't aware that he thanked his engines out loud but Andy heard him and agreed. He would give number one engine a defoul treatment, just to be sure, when they reached a safe altitude. Gotta love and take care of one's engines.

With the sky safe again, at least from MIGs, Eddie looked over at his student and nodded in a southwestern direction. "Take us home. We've had about enough fun for the day." Then Eddie smiled at himself. He had borrowed a phrase from Major Baxter and his C-124 days.

It would be a stretch of the truth to call their mission even a partial success. They had only the operator's memories to debrief the intelligence people. All the paperwork, along with the more sensitive equipment, had been thrown out the door or dissolved in their two water cans. Maybe they should be satisfied with the fact that they were all alive and the plane was safe. But surely someone on the ground would question their actions and criticize their destruct drill. Who would be responsible for all that stuff they destroyed and the stuff they threw out the doors? Eddie was in charge and would surely catch hell.

On the way back to NKP, Eddie experienced some adrenalin shake. He had, after past experiences, maybe been hardened or desensitized but he still shook a little. Maybe he was still in disbelief? He did note that his student aircraft commander kept both hands on the yoke in an attempt to hide the shakes. Eddie did, however, feel numb as he attempted to recollect and organize all the facts about what they had just experienced. After debriefing intelligence on what happened, certainly he would be asked to write a detailed report on the MIG incident, the failure of the mission, and the loss of classified papers and equipment. It bothered Eddie that he had a tough time believing his recollections. Had such a thing just actually happen to them? Less than ten minutes after it was over, his mind was numb and he was questioning his own memory.

Andy set cruise power as they leveled off at 12,000 feet and Stu gave them a course to steer that would take them straight to the barn (NKP). Eddie looked over at the young lieutenant as he expertly trimmed the aircraft and coordinated requests about housekeeping from the guys in the back. He was a picture of confidence and competence after performing wonderfully during an unexpected crisis.

It was just as Eddie always thought, each student was unique and each needed a customized prescription to break through their shell and take command. Some needed the proverbial hit in the head with a two by four to get their attention. The MIGs certainly popped Andy out of his self-induced doldrums. Eddie would brief the operations officer that Andy performed exceptionally well under stressful conditions and was ready for the left seat. Eddie would fill out the paperwork necessary to indicate that their mission had been scheduled as a check ride and he would check all the required boxes to show that the student had passed. On Andy's next flight he would join the ranks of the United States Air Force aircraft commanders.

* *

A jovial crew bounded out of the Lady after Andy taxied onto the Towhead ramp, spun a crisp 180 degree turn onto their designated parking spot, and then chopped the engines. The sun was just setting and the tropical sky was red from the lingering smoke at the end of the rice burning season.

The two pilots and Stu strutted proudly into the intelligence de-briefing room. It was so rare that they ever had anything of value to pass on to their de-briefer. The good stuff was always from the radio operators, who debriefed separately and extensively at a separate room in the mysterious Task Force Alpha building.

Eddie let Stu and Andy tell the story and he only piped up whenever he felt something needed to be clarified. Stu and Andy had performed brilliantly under duress and deserved their fifteen minutes of fame. When they finished, the de-briefing officer stood looking at them as if he disapproved, then he spoke. "It didn't happen. Let's just say that you misinterpreted what you think you heard on the air, but it didn't happen."

"Bullshit," Eddie exploded. "You weren't there, we saw the MIGs. Ask Invert, they're right here on the base, and ask Cricket, they heard the whole thing. Ask my ROs. How can you stand there and tell us it didn't happen?"

"We were notified as soon as it happened," the Intel guy explained. "I've been on the secure line with all those agencies and everything has been edited and deleted. I personally called the little airman at your detachment and had him erase all evidence that you flew today. The mission was classified, the fact that you were up there in the first place was classified, and the whole affair is classified. It didn't happen. If you leak any of this to anyone, and I mean anyone, your room-mates here at NKP, your wives, rest assured that you will rot in a jail cell—do you have any questions?"

Their customer, the civilian agency that nobody was allowed to say its name or its initials, swung a powerful sledgehammer. They could make something disappear at the snap of a finger. They just erased their mission and they could just as easily erase the crewmembers. None of the crew on Towhead Three Three wanted to disappear, so they fumed in silence instead. They all fumed except Eddie. He was smiling to himself because he realized if the mission hadn't happened, then he couldn't be held responsible for the failed mission and the destroyed paperwork and equipment! If it didn't happen and the whole thing was just a figment of their imagination, then that must be why the ROs attended their briefing with no paperwork to turn in. What goes around comes around. They couldn't ask him to write a report for something that didn't happen. On the other hand, there were probably lots of monkeys in that jungle and they were sitting and examining some strange stuff from the sky.

Eddie did, however, fill out the paperwork for Andy's upgrade as aircraft commander. No one ever noticed that the paperwork was for a previous flight, different aircraft number, and two days before they ventured together north to the Chinese Road. Eddie couldn't sign Andy off for a mission that didn't happen. That would be cheating!

* * * * * * * * * * * * * * * * * * * *

Eddie stumbled into his room and flopped spread eagle on his cot. He was pooped.

Arnold was curled up on the sofa, reading a book. He eventually looked up and casually asked, "Tough day?"

"Not really," Eddie casually replied. "Just the normal stuff. I flew all the way north till I came to the Chinese border, escaped from two MIGs that the bad guys sent to shoot us down, and my crew trashed the back end of my airplane. I haven't had a chance to look yet, but I think I may have shit in my pants—it was boring!" Eddie stripped to his shorts, wrapped a clean towel around his waist, and grabbed his dop kit and a tube of anti-fungal cream. "It won't be long now before I either get killed or get to go home. The only thing interesting is which will happen first."

Arnold took another look at his obviously lying room-mate. "Boy, you're really no fun when you're on the rag. Maybe you need to catch the Baht bus to town and have your fat masseuse jerk you off."

Eddie didn't respond as he left the room. All he really wanted was a shower and a half dozen hits of Glenlivet.

Although none of Eddie's crew members ever said anything, at least not to his knowledge, within a week everyone on the base was whispering the story about Nuts and his crew. There were endless variations to the story and Eddie grew weary of denying it. The story changed considerably before it finally got to Major Collins and he fumed at the idea that Eddie would invent such a lie. There was no paperwork to prove the mission had ever been flown and paperwork was the thing that Major Collins cherished and respected most.

CHAPTER TWENTY-ONE:
A CHRISTMAS STORY

Eddie's radio operators seemed in a bad mood as the van transported his crew to their aircraft for a scheduled flight alongside the Ho Chi Minh Trail. He and his co-pilot carried their flight bags and lunches to the cockpit. While his co-pilot performed the housekeeping chores, Eddie exited the aircraft and did the pre-flight walk-around. He inspected and searched for anything out of order. The operators were clustered away from the aircraft while several of them were having their last smoke before the flight. Smoking wasn't allowed in their EC-47s and Eddie was free from the suffering he withstood in the C-124.

When finished, Eddie strolled over to join the radio operators and asked, "You guys look like you wanna kick the shit out of someone. Did I do something I'm not aware of—you know everything gets blamed on me around here. Whether I did it or not."

"It's not you Boss," the master sergeant in charge of the Security Service radio operators answered as he looked down at the ramp. "We got a big shit list but you're not on it."

"Tell him what happened," the tech sergeant with glasses and shiny boots addressed their group leader. "He's one of us and he'll probably hear about it sooner or later anyway."

"Long as it doesn't affect our mission I don't wanna know anything I don't need to know," Eddie replied. "But if it affects your morale then it affects our mission. You guys look like you got mutiny on your minds."

"It's about some of the messages we been intercepting the last couple of months," the master sergeant decided to finally trust their classified issue with Eddie. "We got decoders on board our aircraft to decode encrypted Morse code messages in flight—messages the gomers are sending back and forth on their HF radios. It's old Russian equipment that we broke the code on a long time ago. When the 'Ruskies' upgraded their equipment they gave the old stuff to the North Vietnamese. Between us guys here at NKP, over the last two or three months, we been intercepting messages from Saigon to Hanoi about our special forces teams. They're disclosing information about our helicopter drop-offs along the Ho Chi Minh Trail. They tell the date, time, purpose of the mission, and total number of soldiers in the team. Also, the names and rank of all the Americans. And the exact coordinates of the helicopter drop-off. They even tell the date, time and location of the scheduled extraction when the mission is completed."

"Sounds like you guys saved the special forces guys a lot of grief," Eddie commented in amazement. "They would have been ambushed and probably killed." He had heard of these teams before, they would train for weeks to get every move down just right and when inserted they would carry out their missions: gather intelligence, blow up storage dumps, plant land mines, plant sound and vibration sensors, and sometimes kidnap designated NVA officers and take them back to South Vietnam for interrogation. There was a secret helicopter organization called the Green Hornets that flew the exceptionally dangerous missions inserting and extracting the special operations teams. Eddie had always suspected the all black CH-53 helicopters at Nakhon Phanom were a part of the Green Hornets but no one was talking.

"That's why we're so pissed off," the master sergeant continued. "We just got the word by our Security

Service grapevine that the White House in Washington decided not to take any action on these messages we intercepted. We're talking about the messages to Hanoi about when and where the helicopters were making drops and pickups. Us guys intercepted one of the messages just last week and we just heard that when the helicopter was in a hover and the team was sliding down the ropes, they were ambushed. The chopper was shot down and both the helicopter crew and the team were all killed. What the hell's wrong with those idiots in Washington?"

"I heard the top brass were told not to cancel any of the missions cause it would alert the gomers that we cracked the code that they use," the staff sergeant added.

"I heard the American top brass in Saigon was required to coordinate all special operations, like those into Laos, with the top South Vietnamese brass," the other staff sergeant informed the group. "We think that's who's sending the messages."

"Shit!" Eddie exclaimed. "They could have aborted the insert at the last minute and saturated the area with bombs from B-52s. They coulda picked a different insertion point and left the gomers sitting at the original drop zone. Whose side is Washington on?"

"I heard the top American brass weren't allowed to act on the intelligence because the top people in the White House didn't wanna destroy their trust and relations with the South Vietnamese," the master sergeant concluded. "But whatever, there's not a damn thing we can do about it. Let's go fly."

* *

The mission was routine and they crossed back across the Mekong River into Thai territory and parked their camouflaged air machine on the concrete ramp. They parked their aircraft next to several of its sister ships who were already home for the night. The mission had been uneventful and the guys in the back were in a better mood. Eddie sent his co-pilot on to check in their M-16 and to debrief intelligence. He used the excuse that he needed to talk to the maintenance crew about the excessive static on their number two radio. The pilots really had nothing newsworthy to report to intelligence, so he wouldn't be missed. From what he had gathered from eavesdropping on the operator's interphone, things weren't going well on the ground. As they flew alongside the trail, another American Special Forces team and Thai mercenaries were surrounded and involved in a deadly fire fight. The intelligence they gathered was passed on to the civilian and military customers and if it was acted on or not was out of the radio operator's hands. It was probably too late to help the ambushed team on the ground. Eddie felt terrible about things but was powerless to do anything about the system.

It was just before dark and he could hear the birds settling in for the night in the nearby jungle. He loved the jungle late in the day, when the sky turned red from the low sun and you could smell the smoke from the nearby villages. It was happy time for the villagers as they cooked rice and boiled fish. Except for the occasional thump of artillery in the far distance, across the river in Laos, one could almost forget the horrors and mayhem of the war.

There was a kind of peace and solace in being alone with his airplane. He walked around the faithful war bird making a last check for holes and leaks. He listened to the hot engines crack and pop as the hot metal cooled and contracted. He had been flying for almost two and a half years in Southeast Asia and was starting to feel like a very old person. In time his ideas and ideals had changed from a gung ho patriotic young pilot to a mature veteran. He realized that time spent in the South East Asia war zone only amounted to personal honor and assisting the guys on the ground as they participated in the fray. He made it a point to not discuss or disclose his feelings with his younger crews and pilots. Most of them would complete their one year assignment, then high-tail it back to their relatives and loved ones. It would take years before they would figure out the truth—if they ever would. He had, however, bonded with the ancient aircraft he was assigned to fly and the Asian splendor he gazed down upon when he flew. He also spent a lot of time alone, reading the books and magazines his cousin regularly sent him from the States.

On that particular evening he felt very tired and very old. He felt responsible for the welfare of his students, his aircraft, his co-pilots, and the crew members in the rear. Many of them had wives and children back home and they unknowingly placed their trust in his judgment. As an instructor pilot there was only so much he could do. Sooner or later they were going to lose an aircraft and they were overdue. Several had been hit but fortunately all had made it back safely to their air base and no crew members had been hurt. He had been over there long enough to be an old man, not in age but in experience. He felt like the weight of the world was resting on his twenty-five year old shoulders. Still, he had to continue his impression of a toughened all business aircraft commander and instructor. He found himself more and more prioritizing his mission objectives and instruction toward getting their aircraft and crews home safely each night. Heroism and possible death would not in any way effect change in the inevitable outcome of the political fiasco.

He was standing under the fiberglass radar dome that made up their aircraft's nose when an armored personnel carrier emerged from the gathering dusk. It was manned by several American GIs and driven by a Royal Thai sergeant. Eddie had been told those tiny Thai soldiers were as tough and as mean as our best marines. A young American airman second class was riding on the top, manning the mount of twin fifty caliber machine guns. They were part of the base security component. The American gunner was wearing a Santa Claus cap and a long sleeved red jacket with white cuffs. Where he found the garb was in itself a mystery. It then suddenly occurred to Eddie that it was Christmas Eve! In that strange convoluted world, he had somehow displaced that cherished holiday.

"Merry Christmas!" the young airman greeted him from his lofty perch as the Thai driver slowed to a halt. "Lieutenant, Sir," the young man added when he recognized Eddie's officer's rank on his otherwise unmarked flight suit. The deep sweat marks under Eddie's armpits and the Smith and Wesson 38 Special pistol hanging from his waist made it obvious that Eddie had just returned from a mission. For a moment their eyes met and Eddie sensed a strong bond between the two of them, an enlisted young airman and an exhausted officer combat pilot. It was a bond that would withstand the test of time between all of those that shared the experience in Asia. It was a bond that those who were not there would never truly understand.

The airman let go of his mounted machine guns, reached into his pocket, and threw Eddie a Hershey bar. He gave Eddie a crisp salute, and again wished him "Merry Christmas, Sir." They drove off into the gathering darkness.

Eddie stood there for a moment and savored the simple incident. Then he felt a welling of emotion inside. Emotions that he had suppressed for a long long time. He realized this was the fourth Christmas in a row he had spent away from Colorado. All of a sudden he missed the snow on the ponderosa pine trees, the noise and laughter when all the relatives gathered for a holiday meal, Christmas music and kids opening their presents, decorated Christmas trees. He missed the entire package that he had always just taken for granted. He thought of the families and loved ones of the team that was wiped out the previous week as a result of Washington's disconnect from reality. They would never know the true story of their loved one's death. Maybe it was better that way. He glanced around to make sure there was no one else around to witness his weakness. The guards were at the other end of the row of Gooney Birds. He kneeled on the concrete ramp, against the inside of his aircraft's left main landing gear. He was shielded from the rest of the ramp and he cried for the first time since he had been a child. His brief stay on the farm before C-47 school wasn't enough. He missed Christmas on the farm and needed some quality time—without the war that was dragging on what seemed like forever. He wanted to be home! He was ready to get on with the rest of his life.

CHAPTER TWENTY-TWO:
TRAN, HUU KY
CIRCA EARLY 1950s

Tran Huu Lanh was a gentle farmer who grew rice and raised a few pigs on a small terraced farm in North Vietnam. Their farm was hacked out of a hillside near the village of Van Yen, 120 kilometers west of Hanoi. Like most rural inhabitants in Vietnam, Lanh's family was poor farmers but loyal members of their community who honored and respected their ancestors. A faithful Buddhist, he loved his family and lived his life at peace with his station in life. Life, however, had not been easy living under the brutal French occupancy. All the good rice growing land had been confiscated by French land barons. The low land forests were converted by these same bandits into vast and very profitable rubber plantations. What saved the Tran family rice paddies from the greedy bandits was that their poor soil and meager crops did not qualify for the rich aristocrats' ownership.

Rejection by the aristocrats did not, however, spare the Tran family and their neighbors from tyranny. Tax collectors regularly made their annual rounds, demanding a portion of their bare sustenance of rice, often helping themselves to a pig or a chicken. Little of this bounty ever made it all the way up to the governmental administrators. The entire French dominated political system was corrupt and uncaring.

Tran Huu Ky was born in 1935, the second son to Tran Huu Lanh. As a small boy, Ky had seen his father beaten by the tax collectors. They were Vietnamese agents of the French who had yielded to their dominant occupiers and had assumed their cruel habits. The Tran family, as well as everyone else in their rural cluster of six homes, hated the French for what they had turned their country into. They hated them with a deep bitterness.

Ky's older brother Huy, barely fifteen, had been forcefully taken away one night by "recruiters" from a French plantation. He was never seen again. A year later a skinny terrified young boy from the adjoining hamlet, who had also been recruited during that same raid, visited the Tran family in the middle of the night. He told them a story of forced indenture to work on a rubber plantation, brutality, horrifying living conditions, and little to eat. He told them that their beloved son, Huy, had survived for over half a year until he had taken sick. Without medical aid he died during a monsoonal deluge. The storyteller and three others had escaped one night under the cover of another deluge. Three of them were caught and shot on the spot and he was the sole survivor. He was on his way to join the Viet Minh, Ho Chi Minh's under-ground paramilitary that had grown strong and was having success in confronting the French occupiers.

It was a time of deep grief for Ky's family and Ky vowed to take vengeance on the French butchers. Leaving his family farm to his father and his two younger brothers, with his father's permission, Ky packed a small bundle of possessions and made his way to the village of Van Yen. There he also became a participant in the growing revolt against eighty years of French oppression. He joined the Viet Minh and received training as an artillery gun crewmember.

Ky thus ended up on the slopes of a very steep, slippery, tall mountain. He was helping other motivated young Vietnamese revolutionaries pull twenty-four, 105mm howitzers and a multitude of shells to its summit that overlooked the Dien Bien Phu valley.

* *

The French had previously, and very successfully, lured the Viet Minh commanded by General Giap into another confrontation at Na Sam. There, the French destroyed an entire battalion of Viet Minh soldiers. The French had picked the Dien Bien Phu valley as their new garrison. It was remotely located 200 miles west of Hanoi and on a well traveled route close to the Laotian border. They had a twofold purpose: to block the flow of Viet Minh supplies to their brethren's uprising against the French in nearby Laos, and to set their next trap to slaughter more Viet Minh.

The valley was like a sunken island in the rugged Tongking limestone massif. Surrounded by steep, sometimes almost sheer karst mountains, it was a gentle valley floor ten miles long and four miles wide. The floor was covered with dense vegetation and received frequent and heavy rains. The very steep jungle covered slopes, 2,000 feet high, surrounded the valley and were almost impossible to traverse. The senior French officers boasted, "If the Viet Minh are stupid enough to allow themselves to get caught climbing down those steep mountain slopes, they would be easy pickings for our B-26 aircraft bombs and machine guns—as well as our artillery located in the valley." The French also calculated it would be impossible for the Viet Minh to fire artillery, if they ever obtained any, from the lower terrain behind the ring of protective mountains and be able to lob their shells over the high ridges and back down into the Valley. The required angles of fire did not make this possible. The Viet Minh would have to enter the valley along the three roadways leading into and out of the valley and these were well protected with heavy French artillery and tanks. The French garrison was populated with 13,000 proud French soldiers. This is where they were waiting to slaughter the peasants. The French had an airfield in the center of the valley and were well supplied by aircraft. They waited for the enemy to show.

The French had badly underestimated the will and determination of the Viet Minh insurgents. The insurgents hated the French so badly that asking them to perform the impossible was not asking too much. Unknown to the French, General Giap's 50,000 soldiers and over 100,000 civilian laborers had carried and dragged thousands of tons of military supplies through hundreds of miles of crude road from their sanctuary in China. They utilized the dense jungle as camouflage from the French scout planes and trudged their secret cargo to the foot of the tall mountains that surrounded the Dien Bien Phu garrison.

Included in General Giap's booty from China were twenty-four 105mm howitzer artillery pieces. They were American built howitzers captured by the Chinese during the Korean War and refurbished and given to the Viet Minh. Pulling these heavy wheeled artillery pieces by hand through the thick jungle undetected for hundreds of miles was impossible. But the hate motivated peasants turned the impossible into reality. Then they pulled them to the top of the mountains, up ravines covered with brush as camouflage from French scout planes. Again in defiance of the impossible. Once at the mountain tops, they carved out niches in the rocks to hide their artillery pieces and store their ammunition. The artillery pieces were positioned so only the tips of their gun barrels were exposed.

As the Viet Minh finished carving emplacements and camouflaged their howitzers to blend with the mountain peaks, their comrades finished scratching and digging thousands of feet of connecting tunnels in the limestone rock. They converted their precarious perch into a functional fortress. They were totally exhausted from months and months of heavy labor, emaciated from little food, wet, dirty and totally elated. Although the French were aware of some Viet Minh activity during this time, they assumed it was observation posts defended with shoulder fired AK-47 rifles. The French totally underestimated its significance and had no idea that the Viet Minh had powerful 105mm howitzers and a major army waiting in the wings. The Viet Minh deception had been successful.

248

Ky was no longer a small farm boy but a strong, grown-up young man. As his gun crew worked at cleaning their weapons' mechanisms and preparing their large number of shells, tens of thousands of Viet Minh soldiers worked their way down the slopes. They hid in the dense foliage at the inside edge of the valley. They were poised to engage the arrogant, brutal French Army.

On March 13, 1954, General Giap gave the order and the battery of twenty-four 105 howitzers, along with numerous smaller back pack mortars, opened their barrage and blasted the shocked French in the valley below. The exposed French positions were decimated by the Viet Minh artillery. A substantial portion of the French tanks and defensive artillery were wiped out within the first few hours. Bunkers, machine gun nests, aircraft parked on their prized runway and command posts were pulverized. The surviving French artillery was unable to retaliate against the well entrenched artillery along the mountain tops. French aircraft, bombers ordered from Hanoi, were shredded by Viet Minh anti-aircraft guns—also secreted from China and well emplaced in thick cover along the front of the surrounding ring of mountains.

The French had made a key error in violating one of the first rules of warfare. They had ceded the highest ground to the enemy. They also vastly underestimated General Giap's brilliance and the determination of the discontented peasants. Not too many years later American Presidents Johnson and Nixon would disregard the French's mistakes and again underestimate these very same unconventional warriors.

Ky, with his stolen moments from his gun crew duties, gazed down at the bewildered French and the destruction of the howitzer's firepower. The laborious efforts of all of his comrades rained wondrous destruction upon their enemy. His gunnery officer, Master Sergeant Duc, in a rare display of passion, had hugged Ky after they shared the experience of watching their latest round pulverize a French gunnery emplacement. Ky was enthralled at how thousands of poor determined peasants could destroy one of the world's powerful armies. Artillery would be his life's devotion. He would help his glorious leaders drive all the foreign invaders from his beautiful homeland. A free Vietnam would serve its loyal citizens and serve as an example for the other repressed people around the world. Artillery would be the instrument for him to avenge the death of his brother, the brutalized existence of his family, and suffering endured by generations of ancestors. He would someday use his passion and ingenuity to perform a great victory for the People's Army and he would inspire all who ever heard of his name and his feat.

* *

It was on March 10, 1970, that Ky got his big break. He had been a loyal soldier of the People's Army of Viet Nam (North Vietnamese) for eighteen years, and was known as an accomplished gunnery commander in the artillery ranks. He had been promoted through the ranks to Senior Lieutenant (Thurang Uy). His current position was commander of artillery for the 148th Regiment of the 316th Division, PAVN. They had been deployed to the Plaine des Jarres for a massive and long awaited offensive and they had been gloriously successful against the American puppets; the overextended and dissipated Hmong and the American CIA financed Thai mercenaries. With the brilliant use of artillery they had driven their enemy off the entire Plaine des Jarres and were preparing a siege on General Vang Pao's precious Long Tieng headquarters. It was known as the Alternate to the Americans. With this final victory all roads to the Laotian capital of Vientiane would be open for the communist victors.

The prior night, an all black PAVN Aerospatiale Alouette helicopter had arrived from their homeland (North Vietnam) with several high ranking officers on board. Through a Russian middleman, the North Vietnamese had been able to acquire a number of French built Alouettes for use as transportation for senior officers and valuable courier items. By flying these valuable tools only at night, covering them with vegetative camouflage during the days, they had been able to operate almost undetected by the Americans. One night they did have some over enthusiastic pilots drop hand grenades on American forces at Dak To in Vietnam. They were detected by Americans flying Huey helicopters in the same area but the Alouette's faster speed allowed them to escape.

The senior officers reviewed, made suggestions, and then approved the battle plans for this last and most important dry season objective. It was highly unusual to experience visits from higher commands. The PAVN forces normally relied heavily on the decisions and ingenuity of their commanders in the field. They suspected that some of their HF Morris messages had been intercepted and possibility decoded. The acquisition of the Alouettes had given them secure command ability and improved battlefield control over their operations. Lt. Ky was recalled from his remote post to brief the senior officers on their current artillery capabilities and their planned contribution to their upcoming victory. He was overwhelmed with pride when one of the senior officers was none other than Colonel Duc, the former gunnery sergeant that he had been assigned to when they first assaulted the French at Dien Bien Phu. Sergeant Duc had advanced all the way to colonel and Lt. Ky had established his own career as a proud officer and lieutenant. Lt. Ky's accomplishment had been an incredible feat for anyone starting out as an uneducated sixteen year old freedom fighter.

After the briefing was completed and the field staff was released, a young trooper approached Lt. Ky. He informed Ky that his presence was requested by Colonel Duc.

Lt. Ky reported to the colonel, who was standing separate from the other senior officers, and gave him his best salute. "You requested to see me, Sir."

"Yes." Colonel Duc sized up Lt. Ky and grinned with pleasure. "Aren't you the young boy I had on my howitzer crew when we assaulted Dien Bien Phu?"

"Yessir. I had that honor, Sir. That was a long time ago but I remember as if it was yesterday."

"Me too." The colonel looked much older but was still physically fit. Years in the field under trying conditions left all the PAVN soldiers slim and wiry. There were no fat men in their army. "I see you have served Uncle Ho well. You're a senior lieutenant now and I hear you have distinguished yourself as an artilleryman. The big guns have served us both well in our People's Army."

"I serve not for myself, such as I am sure is the same with you, Sir, but for a united and free Vietnam."

Colonel Duc remembered, sixteen years prior, the enthusiasm a young boy named Ky had displayed on a rope team, pulling their howitzer up an extremely steep ravine. "If there is anything I can do to assist you in your profession, please feel free to speak to me openly. We have a proud past together and can converse as trusting comrades."

Lt. Ky was shocked at the frankness of this senior officer, then realized this was the opportunity that he had waited for a long long time. "There is one thing, Sir, if I may be open with you. I have been playing with an idea for some time and if you would spare me a few minutes of your precious time, I would value your opinion."

"Certainly." The spit shined colonel wandered further away from his group of peers and motioned with his head for Lt. Ky to follow. "What is it you would like to discuss?"

Lt. Ky's heart was beating as if it wanted out of his chest. He cautioned himself to speak clearly and logically, a man of the colonel's rank would expect clarity and logic.

"I have been thinking about the schooling I received and about the emphasis that is placed upon motivation and ingenuity. I have been thinking about the example we were taught about the bomber raid the Americans carried out on Japan during World War II. From an aircraft carrier called the Doolittle Raid. They did very little damage to the Japanese war machine but created a tremendous upwelling of spirit, hope, and motivation for the American people. Wouldn't it be wonderful if we could execute a similar raid against the Americans here in Laos?"

Colonel Duc was intrigued by the scope of the lieutenant's ideas. "Yes, continue."

"I have been examining my maps of Laos and I noticed that at its narrowest point our series of roads, that the Americans call the Ho Chi Minh Trail, passes only seventy kilometers (42 miles) east of the Mekong River. On the Laotian side of the Mekong is the village of Thakhek and on the west side is the Thai village of Nakhon Phanom. The American Air Base of Nakhon Phanom is located there. Our intelligence reports indicate there are many aircraft on this air base, including two squadrons of the A-1 Skyraiders that have been so deadly against our troopers here in the Plaine des Jarres. My map shows an unpaved dry season road, called Route twelve, and it connects our "Ho Chi Minh" supply route to Thakhek, just across the Mekong from Nakhon Phanom."

"Yes, please go on," the colonel was listening closely.

Lt. Ky continued, "Sir, I have had considerable experience with our rockets in the past two years and I find that the 5200 meter (three mile) range and inaccuracies of the Chinese built rockets is not very impressive. But I have also had opportunity to deploy the newer Russian built DKZ 122mm rocket and find the 11,000 meter (six mile) range much more functional. The Soviet 122mm rocket is equipped with stabilizing fins and is far more accurate. It is more destructive than either our 107 or 140mm rockets. When used with the metal tripods that are available, these stabilized rockets can be reloaded and fired every four to five minutes. With a spotter calling in corrections and adjustments, based upon the impact points from the first salvo of rockets, the tripods allow precise adjustments to increase the accuracy of the following salvos. We can adjust or walk our firing, just like artillery fire. The accuracy is still not as good as artillery, but unlike artillery, the rockets and launching tubes can be hidden under bags of rice and transported undetected in trucks. I believe we could set up a destructive barrage of these rockets from the Laotian side of the Mekong River into the American Air Base at Nakhon Phanom, Sir."

Lt. Ky continued hopefully, "If we could send someone like me, dressed in the clothing of a poor laborer, and accompanied by several of our Pathet Lao brothers who are of lowland backgrounds and dialect . . . we could scout out a location to set up the rockets. We would have to do our scouting during this dry season and I would return before the rains started again. Then during the wet months I could train my team of carefully selected Pathet Lao on the operation of the tripods and the rocket loading and firing. We could be ready to strike the American Air Base during the next dry season."

Colonel Duc now realized the genius of this young man.

Ky spoke carefully, "We could launch a large number of 122mm rockets into the Nakhon Phanom Airbase. If we launched enough rockets, in a thirty or forty minute period, by reloading each firing tube five or six times, we certainly could do significant damage to their air base. We would certainly provide a morale boost for our cause as well as destroy the American's confidence—both their military and their civilians."

The colonel reflected, then wondered? "You suggest transporting these rockets on Route twelve. How do you expect to not be detected? The American scout aircraft watch these side routes all the time."

"Sir, we could hide in the open. We could use two civilian trucks and use a crew of lowland Laotian Pathet Lao, dressed as laborers. I could dress the same and let them do all the talking. We would transport the rockets, launch tubes, and collapsible tripods hidden under bundles of empty rice bags. We would look like the hundreds of other trucks in the Mekong lowland rice growing area that transport rice to markets. A number of them regularly transport rice during the dry season over Route twelve and sell it to our army. I would guess that some of these trucks returning to Thakhek carry empty rice bags. We would have to do this during the dry season because Route twelve is impassable during the monsoon season."

"You know, maybe it might work," the colonel made Lt. Ky's day. "Let me take the idea back with me to our military leaders and see what they think. I'll tell them we have a brave young artillery lieutenant that could pull off such a daring attempt."

"Sir, in the middle of the night the Americans will be caught off guard. Before they could get pilots out of bed and aircraft airborne, we would be finished with our destruction. With bicycles or by walking, we could split up and spread out heading eastward through the maze of foot trails through the karst canyons. Then we could join Route twelve. We could rejoin our troops along the Ho Chi Minh Trail in less than a week."

The colonel smiled. He liked this young man's attitude and ingenuity. They really should give him a chance to try it. The investment would be minimal, the risk would be his and his Pathet Lao companions, and the possible results could be spectacular.

Colonel Duc flew out on the helicopter currier that night and Lt. Ky joined the PAVN Army on Skyline

Ridge, overlooking the valley and Long Tieng. They failed to overrun Long Tieng because they waited for additional re-enforcements to join them. The Hmong, meanwhile, were reinforced with battle tested and skilled Thai re-enforcements flown in by the CH-53 all black "Knife" helicopters stationed at Nakhon Phanom. General Vang Pao, thus, was able to retain possession of his Hmong military stronghold called the Alternate.

* * * * * * * * * * * * * * * * * * * *

Three weeks later a special packet was delivered to Lieutenant Ky. Its contents relieved him of his current duties, contained sufficient Laotian currency (Kip) to travel to Thakhek, scout the area, and make the necessary arrangements for future operations. Included in the packet were the names and contact information of two ethnic Vietnamese Pathet Lao operatives in a village called Ban Nakak, on the outskirts of Thakhek. Lt. Ky immediately activated the plans he had long been dreaming about and had been improving upon almost daily for months.

The more direct route, travel to the west then down the Mekong by boat, was too hazardous. It would involve going through Hmong infested mountains and considerable distance through enemy held lowlands. The risk of raising suspicion and capture would be too high. Instead, he kept one complete uniform, a duplicate of his military identification, and one copy of his written orders. The written order was highly secret and was to be used only as a last resort to carry out his plans. All of his remaining possessions, his few personal belongings, and his personal sidearm, everything that could possibly provide even a hint that he was a proud North Vietnamese soldier were placed into a box for storage. He left his box of possessions at division headquarters, confiscated some ragged clothes from a local Laotian civilian that had been killed by a US air strike, and caught a ride on an empty truck that was returning to his homeland for another load of war material. They traveled Route 7 only at night to avoid detection. Once inside North Vietnam, he headed south and joined the string of trucks and foot soldiers that crossed Mu Gia Pass back into Laos. Mu Gia was the head of the Ho Chi Minh Trail as it wove its way south to supply troops in South Vietnam and Cambodia.

Soon after he was inside Laos he arrived at the village of Na Phao, the junction where Route 12 headed east towards the Mekong. At Ban Na Phao, he identified himself to the military commander of the local binh tram. The Ho Chi Minh Trail was divided into multiple sections called binh trams and each section was administered by a senior PAVN officer. The commander was in charge of traffic control and the road maintenance crews that were made up mostly of civilian recruits from North Vietnam. They performed the backbreaking labor of maintaining the roads, camouflage protection, vehicle maintenance, fueling and logistics, and the myriad of other duties necessary to maintain the flow of soldiers and supplies southward. The commander was also in charge of the PAVN military units that provided the defense of his area. They were primarily anti-aircraft batteries, but also against sabotage and harassment from mercenary ground units backed by the American enemy. There, Lt. Ky abandoned his last uniform, identification, and gave the copy of his orders to the commander.

He donned his ragged civilian disguise and departed walking west on Route 12 for Thakhek. He had let his hair grow longer and as he weathered he became dirty and unsightly. He was impossible to distinguish from the isolated tribesmen and scattered villagers that lived in that sparsely populated part of Laos. Life had not been easy as a soldier in the PAVN and he was already accustomed to hardship and strenuous exertion. He traveled very carefully the first two nights and hid himself well away from the road in clumps of underbrush while he slept during the day. Without identification, he couldn't afford to be caught by either side of the two warring factions. On the fourth day he was far enough away from the Ho Chi Minh Trail. He changed his routine and traveled along the crude dirt road during the middle of the day and passed for a poor dirty transient. His supply of cooked rice was exhausted by then so he stopped in a small village, maybe six or eight huts clustered together, and acted as if he were speechless, poor, and starving. He managed to trade a few coins for more rice. Poor as they were, the tribes were friendly toward speechless, hungry transients.

It was their way. Thakhek was forty miles as the crow flies but closer to seventy miles when following the heavily rutted horror called Route 12. By the fifth day the road improved and by the seventh day he emerged from the rugged karst hills and onto the flat plain of the Mekong. On the eighth day he limped into Thakhek and discovered that the village of Ban Nakak, that he had been told was on the edge of Thakhek, was another trek nine miles to the north. Five hours later he made contact with his fellow Pathet Lao conspirators. After assuring each other, with the proper code words and actions, he was fed, bathed in the mighty Mekong River, and given a cot to sleep on in their warehouse.

The two operatives, brothers Khay and Chan, were originally Vietnamese and were from an area just north of Hanoi. Their families were store keepers who had been beaten and impoverished by the French occupiers. Both their parents had been killed for resisting French confiscation of their business. Khay and Chan, like Lt. Ky, had participated in the revolution that eventually drove the French from Indochina. Devout followers of Ho Chi Minh, when the country was split into North and South, they were a part of the trained insurgents that imbedded themselves into the throngs of refugees that fled North Vietnam. Like Lt. Ky, they had devoted their lives to a unified Vietnam under the glorious rule of their hero Ho Chi Minh. They had changed their names to Khay and Chan, common Laotian names, and were operating a relatively successful business of trading and shipping goods up and down the Mekong. In addition to their own warehouse and dock on the riverfront, they owned a large truck, a tiny two cycle and very beat up Suzuki pickup truck, and two small freight boats. The wooden freight boats were open hull style, twenty-five feet long, and powered with conventional outboard boat motors. In season they bought rice from the farmers scattered along the Mekong flood plain and shipped it by boat to larger towns and villages up and down the Mekong. They frequently traded with Thais at Nakhon Phanom on the Thai side of the river. Off season they bought and sold anything of value, lumber from the jungle, bamboo for building, pineapples and fresh fruit. They were commonly seen around the area, both on the Laotian side and illegally on the Thai side. They had occasional contact with a few of the other embedded insurgents but this operation with Lt. Ky was to be known by no one else without specific permission from Lt. Ky. The stakes were just too high.

The next day Lt. Ky rested in the warehouse and the two brothers couldn't get enough talking with him, especially in their native language. There was so much news to catch up on. They thought the movement had passed them by—or forgotten about them. They were elated over having an actual PAVN officer as their guest and honored at the privilege of assisting him on his very special mission. It was their special project, Project Nakhon Phanom. They had been agonizing for years about the American planes flying over their home village and making war on their beloved nation's attempts to consolidate Uncle Ho's magnificence. Year after year they had done nothing but follow orders to stay invisible and wait. At last, this was their hour to shine.

After another day of recuperation, Khay drove Lt. Ky around the country side in their Suzuki while Chan conducted business as usual. They dressed Lt. Ky like a buyer; they sometimes took buyers on excursions to examine merchandise before buying. Lt. Ky maintained a straight, restrained, judgmental look on his face; he presented a slightly arrogant look so as to discourage people from approaching him. Khay did all the talking around strangers. It was during this initial tour of the area, just east of Thakhek, that Lt. Ky had a sudden revelation, and not a good one.

During their course of conversation in Vietnamese when they were alone in the countryside, Khay casually dropped the fact that Nakhon Phanom Air Base was fifteen kilometers (nine miles) west of the river front town of Nakhon Phanom. Lt. Ky's previous information, and what his entire plan was based upon, was that the air base was just outside the west edge of the city. He had planned to transport several disguised civilian truck loads of rockets via Route 12 to a predetermined remote location along the foothills of the karst mountains, which would be about seven kilometers (four miles) east of the Mekong River. He had planned to send a barrage of rockets from that remote site over the Mekong River and into the air base.

But his 122mm rockets only had an eleven kilometer (seven mile) range! They would fall way short of the American base. This was a huge setback. They stopped and sat on the ground under the shade from a large tree, being careful to check the grass for snakes. "We will have to fire our rockets from the Thai side of the river in order to reach the American airbase," Lt. Ky said, shaking his head in disappointment.

"It's heavily populated on the Thai side of the river," Khay informed him, "and we would have to ferry the rockets across by boat and unload them onto other transport vehicles. Your rockets are very long and heavy. It would involve a very elaborate plan and using numerous local Pathet Lao operatives on the Thai side. We will be seen. It will not work."

Lt. Ky had seen that sheer will and determination had allowed them to pull 105mm howitzers up almost vertical mountain sides and it was that which caused the defeat of the French occupiers at Dien Bien Phu. He was not about to let a small problem like this keep him from dealing a crippling blow against the American imperialists. They sat quietly in the shade and Lt. Ky let his years of training in guerilla war tactics and artillery training do his thinking for him.

"You have two freight boats, I saw them this morning. You have a warehouse and you ship things, sometimes heavy, all the time. You told me about the klong canals that reach back from the river and provide small boat transportation for the Thai farmers to market. Will your freight boats fit into one of those klong canals?"

Khay thought for a minute then answered, "Not during the middle and end of the dry season like we are now. The water goes down so only small light weight boats can go. But during the monsoon season, we get much water. The klongs are full and usually overflow into the fields. We could go up them during the monsoon, but we could not carry as many of those big rockets that you speak of. We could only take half, or maybe less than half, in our two boats."

Lt. Ky was at first concerned about the reduced number of 122mm rockets he could transport. Then he thought of the new Chinese 107 mm rockets he had only recently received in the Plaine des Jarres. They had a smaller warhead, but still with enough power to blow an airplane up or set off an ammo or fuel dump. They only had an eight kilometer (five mile) range, but were shorter and much lighter in weight; they were designed for guerrilla transport on people's backs. Three 107s weighed the same as one 122mm rocket. In thirty minutes, from six or seven kilometers away, he could launch over forty of these smaller rockets. All they needed was a way to get the rockets less than eight kilometers from the base—undetected.

"We cannot transport the rockets from our homeland over Route twelve during the monsoon," Lt. Ky explained out loud as he thought through the next problem. "The road is barely passable during the dry season. I just walked every kilometer of it. There is no time for me to return to PAVN headquarters, acquire rockets, civilian trucks like you use here in the lowlands, and train a Pathet Lao crew. Then transport the rockets to your warehouse over that terrible road before this year's monsoon rains start. If we wait until next year's dry season to transport the rockets to your warehouse, then we would have to wait again for the following year for the next monsoon to raise the water. That is too long. My superiors won't like that and probably will not let me continue what they would call foolishness. I was lucky to get approval to scout this out in the first place."

They sat for another twenty minutes, then Khay's eyes lit up as he suggested, "Sir, when the Monsoon season is over the water goes down slowly. Could you go back and do what you have to do during the wet season, which will soon be upon us? Then transport your rockets and gunner crew over Route twelve as soon as the monsoon is over and Route twelve is dry enough to drive on. As soon as you arrive and before the klong water goes all the way down, the water will still be high enough that we could float the rockets across the river and into a klong at night. After the monsoon ends, we would probably have three weeks to do this before the water gets too low. Would three weeks be enough time to do this great thing?"

Lt. Ky was pleased as he spoke, "Khay, you are a very good soldier, and smart one. Your idea is what I needed to make this work. If we make this happen I will see to it that you get a medal from the People's Republic."

Khay felt elated but had another concern, "If we make all this happen, then the local authorities most certainly will find out that Chan and I were involved in the attack. Could you get permission from your superiors for us to go home to our country after the attack? We would gladly volunteer to continue serving in the People's Army."

"You would be heroes! They would want you to come home so they could send your pictures to the American newspapers." Lt. Ky thought that sounded good.

The plot was decided; next they had to lay out the details. That night Khay and Chan had a long discussion about the klongs they were familiar with on the Thai side of the river. They decided on what was not a true klong, but a natural river which was fairly deep and very slow, just like a klong. It meandered around in the Thai highlands to the west, passed east through the lowlands and rice paddies, then entered into the Mekong four miles north of NKP City. It would be usable for the first twenty or thirty kilometers. It was perfectly located.

The next day Khay purchased two chickens from his neighbor and he and Lt. Ky motored across the flat Mekong. The river was low because of the dry season. They tied up to a private dock where Khay and Chan had previously conducted business. Khay and Chan were perfect for this mission because they knew their way around and everyone was used to seeing them. They gave the two chickens to the dock owner's wife in exchange for the use of her small personal canoe for the day. It took two hours for them to paddle up the slow moving body of water until they were perpendicular to the air base. The water was low but Khay said he could easily transport a ton of rockets in each boat after the monsoon stopped. The spot perpendicular to the base was easy to find because they could watch the occasional aircraft as they lined up for landing on runway one five. The small river had little traffic on it, maybe a canoe every half hour, and was lined with trees on both sides. Lt. Ky picked out the tallest tree he could find and climbed to its top. From there, he could see across the flat countryside. The air base's control tower marked the spot. With his trained artillery officer's eyes he estimated it was about five kilometers (three miles) away. He would check his estimate of the distance later, on a more accurate map that Khay said he could get for him.

Also, from the tree Lt. Ky could see the ruins of an ancient Stupa (temple), only about five more minutes up the canal. He let himself down and they paddled to the Stupa. The area around the neglected temple had been cleared, but was partially grown back. It had tall standing trees around the outside edge. It was open enough that with thirty minutes work with machetes, a gunnery crew could have a suitable clearing to set up launching pads for four rocket launchers. There were also no dwellings in the close proximity or in sight. It was perfect.

Lt. Ky and the two brothers spent the next week discussing the details and coordination of their plan. Lt. Ky stayed in the warehouse to avoid attracting suspicion and to let his hair get scruffier for his return journey. They worked out every detail. Khay and Chan would provide the boat transportation. It was vital that they knew the river by heart so they could follow it to the Stupa at night with absolute minimum flashlight use. They would check out the canal every six weeks to make sure nothing had changed. Maybe have casual conversations with one or two of the locals. They didn't want to arrive at the Stupa only to find out that a festival was taking place. Lt. Ky would bring all the gunnery personnel, a trained artillery spotter with binoculars, plus two hand-held radios and spares. His crew would be dressed as laborers and would speak fluent lowland Laotian. His headquarters said they could obtain such personnel from the Plaine des Jarres operation.

Khay and Chan would collect old bicycles and store them in their warehouse. After the rocket attack they would fast run their boats down the canal and across the Mekong. Bicycles were the most common form of transportation in the Laotian lowlands and bicycles would be used to blend in with the locals and speed up their escapes. Lt. Ky did not reveal any of his personal escape plans.

Khay and Chan would recruit one other operative, a loyal follower of Ho Chi Minh, on the Thai side of the river who lived as close as possible to the north side of the air base. As soon as the two trucks arrived with the rockets, the trained spotter would be smuggled into the town of Nakhon Phanom and the insurgent would show the spotter the countryside. The spotter would pick out a nice tall tree just outside the air base perimeter for viewing the impacts and use his hand radio for directing the aiming corrections to the gunnery crew.

The map arrived and Lt. Ky measured the distance for the rockets to travel—five and a half kilometers. The Stupa was on the map and it was a simple matter to measure the magnetic direction in degrees from the Stupa to the base. That would be the direction from which they would fire their first salvo of rockets. It was a perfect plan. They made up a code for Khay and Chan to send every month over the insurgent HF Morse radio, in case the mission needed to be aborted or altered. They all three memorized the simple code of numbers and letters and sealed the arrangements away in their heads. Lt. Ky gave Khay and Chan the majority of the Kip from his envelope. After all, Khay and Chan were throwing away their business and possessions for the glory of their homeland, possibly their lives. The least he could do was partially repay them. The battered old bicycle they gave him made Lt. Ky's return trip over Route 12 far less taxing. The badly rutted road still caused problems and he had to walk his bicycle over half the distance, but there were also sections where he could ride and make good time.

CHAPTER TWENTY-THREE: ORANGES, TRUCKS AND PISSED OFF MAJOR

Airman Hendrix had contacted Eddie on one of Eddie's rare days off. The maintenance people had finished working on an aircraft and the maintenance manual called for a flight check before it could be released for a combat mission. The operations officer, Major Collins, wanted to know if Eddie would fly it around the pattern to fill in the square on their maintenance forms.

"Why not?" Eddie agreed. He hadn't been drinking and the whole thing would take less than an hour. "You got a co-pilot?"

"Major Collins said he would ride with you as your co-pilot," Hendrix explained.

"Okay," Eddie conceded. "I guess I could stand him for that long. Just one time flying around the pattern?"

Red had checked Major Collins out as a co-pilot when he first arrived, but that was as far as the major's EC-47 flying had advanced. "I just don't seem to ever find the time to fly any missions," he always said when Eddie asked him about his flying currency. Pilots needed to fly once a month to collect their flight pay and collect combat pay. He was famous for his "maintenance" flights where he would wander over into Laos then return and land. He killed two birds with one stone.

When the major and Eddie arrived at the aircraft the midday heat and humidity were almost unbearable. Eddie wondered how the mechanics could survive working on the hot concrete ramps, day after day, without passing out from heat exhaustion. The major wondered why everyone was moving so slowly because he was in a hurry to get back to his office to work on his paperwork. The major's thoughts were a lie, self rationalism, as he was actually in a hurry to get out of the heat and back into his air-conditioned cubicle.

As the major puttered around in the cockpit, mumbling under his breath about the slow incompetent people he was forced to deal with, Eddie did the pilot's exterior walk around. He also met with the crew chief and discussed the recent maintenance problem that was supposed to be fixed. If anything special needed to be watched for during their upcoming brief flight? He was surprised that they had a valid reason to give the aircraft a test flight. They had replaced some parts on the left engine.

"Hope there's enough fuel on board for you, Sir. The gauges show about thirty minutes worth of fuel on board." The staff sergeant's eyes met Eddie's. "Major Collins sent a message out from his office that the thirty minutes of fuel on board would be enough and he didn't have time to wait for a fuel truck."

"Interesting," Eddie said, smiling at the staff sergeant. They had known each other for several months and shared a common bond of trust. "I'm supposed to be the instructor pilot and the flight orders say I'm the aircraft commander, but the major said thirty minutes was enough."

"Yeah," Sergeant Hayflee grinned. "That's just what I thought, so I thought you better know about it."

"Ya dip stick it?" Eddie wondered out loud. Dip sticking was just as it sounded. It involved inserting a calibrated wooden stick into the fuel tank and reading the gas level from the wet marks on the stick. It was more reliable than a fuel gauge, which occasionally drifted out of accuracy limits.

"I couldn't find the dip stick. It must be in the truck that's down for maintenance."

"I appreciate you're bringing it up, I'll show you how we did it on our farm." Eddie strolled over the edge of the concrete ramp and picked out a tall weed with about a forty inch stem. He broke off the stem at ground level and picked off the leaves as he sauntered back to the aircraft. He climbed up the ladder that the sergeant had just placed adjacent the wing. The sergeant was grinning because the major was sweating profusely in the cockpit and spouting profanity out the side window, something about getting the lead out of their asses. Eddie removed the gas cap and dipped the fuel with the weed stem. The bottom four inches were wet. They repeated the drill on the fuel tank on the other wing. The gauges were accurate and each time he let the sergeant look at the improvised fuel stick for reassurance.

"Let's get this crate off the ground," Eddie called after the second fuel tank fuel level was confirmed.

"Yessir." The sergeant smiled at Eddie and for show he saluted. Eddie returned a crisp salute. The major fumed at the delay in the hot sun.

Eddie let the major sit in the left seat and he sat in the co-pilot's seat. They performed the checklists, started the engines, and within eight minutes were rolling down runway one five and became airborne. Eddie let the major make the take-off. A little wobbly on his taxiing but the take-off was safe enough and they turned left on their downwind. Eddie was also going to let the major have the landing out of respect for his rank. None of the other crewmembers wanted to fly with him because they all knew he wasn't proficient. The major informed Eddie that he wanted to "extend" the flight to "get a good flight check." So Eddie agreed to an exceptionally wide traffic pattern to the east; so wide in fact that they crossed over the Mekong River. They crossed the river far enough to just stick their wing-tip into Laos. Eddie knew this would be the major's flight for the month to receive both flight and combat pay.

Eddie was simultaneously working the radios and looking for the massage parlor downtown NKP City, when the radio blurted, "Mayday! Mayday! Nakhon Phanom tower. This is Hobo Six Six, do you read me?" The voice sounded several pitches higher than the norm.

"Roger, Hobo Six Six. I copy you. How can I be of assistance?" the tower replied.

"I'm about six or eight minutes out from runway one five. I got problems. I got hosed over the trail and I took several rounds in my parachute. It's unusable. I can't get my gear down and I got hung ordinance. There's a god-damned daisy cutter bomb hanging on my right wing that won't jettison and I'm losing fuel. It's just not my day. I need everyone out of my way and foam on the runway. I got no choice but to put this pig in on its belly."

"Copy all Six Six, my assistant is rolling the foam truck now and we'll have the fire wagons waiting for your arrival. Break break. Towhead, make a large right hand circle. I'll get back to you when I can."

"Towhead Flight Check wilco," Eddie answered obediently. Eddie felt a hollow space in his stomach for the Hobo driver. Fire wagons also came with ambulances and body bags. The A-1 fighter had a big bomb under his right wing and when it contacted the hard runway and if things were torn apart, it was very possible the bomb would go off. It was probably the Hobo's golden BB. The major rolled into a shallow right turn back into Laos and in about six minutes they came around within view of the airport. They could see the foam truck creeping down the runway centerline as it sprayed a swath of its slick fire suppressant, stinky grey foam down the center line. As a recovery base they were prepared for such quick action. The truck had worked his way about half way down the runway.

"Gotcha in sight, Hobo, about three miles on final," the tower reassured the A-1. "We'll keep the foam truck spraying until you're on short final then we'll have him hustle his butt out of your way. Did you copy that Maintenance?"

"Foamer copies," the foam truck answered back. There was no way he was going to still be on the runway when that flying bomb returned to earth.

"Maintenance Chief copies, also."

Eddie and the major were mesmerized as they rolled out south of the airport and lined up for a long, close in downwind. They would be in position to watch the event unfold forward on their left side. The Spad crossed the end of the runway about twenty feet in the air, no landing gear, and the bomb on his right wing looked bigger than life. The propeller had been slowing then stopped dead, just as the pilot had planned when he shut down his engine and coasted. The pilot's canopy had been opened and the rescue trucks were all in position.

The Spad settled gently onto the long foam rug and in an instant the pilot was out of the cockpit and crawling out on his left wing. He wanted to get as far away from that bomb as he could. The disabled fighter plane continued skimming along on its slick foam trail. It had been carefully aimed by its terrified pilot, straight down the center of the foam strip. By the time the Spad slowed through fifty knots, the pilot was hanging onto the very tip of the left wing and at just under twenty knots he rolled off and bounced along the runway like an errant football. Bruises and possible broken limbs were far more preferable to hanging around for the big boom. The aircraft and the armed bomb slid to a gentle stop just as they ran out of foam. The thick, slick goo had done its job. The pilot was up and running and the beer would flow freely at the Hobo bar that night.

Suddenly reality struck home with Eddie. They had been so focused on the Hobo's plight they failed to consider their own situation. Nakhon Phanom only had one runway and it was covered with slick foam and an A-1. The A-1 was nesting on a live bomb. They took off with about thirty or forty minutes of fuel. They had both agreed there was no need to call the fuel truck when all they were doing was a quick trip around the pattern. They consistently returned from missions with less fuel than that. However, the nearest usable runway was Udorn, a little over an hour away in an EC-47, and they had only fifteen or twenty minutes at most before their engines would fuel starve.

"Towhead Flight Check," it was the tower again. "If you wanna depart the pattern, go ahead. We're estimating it will take a few hours for the ordinance people to defuse that bomb, then they have to pull that Spad out of the way and it will take at least forty to fifty minutes to wash all that foam off the runway. You wanna divert to Udorn?" Eddie was the flight instructor and there was only one logical solution to the problem.

"Tower, Towhead Flight Check, we got fifteen minutes fuel on board and Udorn is over an hour away at the speeds that we fly. Get all of the vehicles off the taxiway cause there's gonna be a Gooney Bird landing on it in a few minutes."

"I'll get right on that, Towhead Flight Check. Extend your downwind to give me time to get the word out to everyone." This tower operator was every bit as good as the ones at Danang. He didn't even hesitate when making a decision and cooperating with the Gooney Bird. "You wanna declare an emergency?"

"Whatever clears everyone off and away from the taxiway and creates the smallest amount of paperwork," Eddie replied. Major Baxter in the C-124 had taught Eddie well.

"We can't do that!" Major Collins shouted at Eddie over the interphone, "It's against regulations. I'm sure there's a regulation somewhere against landing on taxiways. What if we blow a tire? It'll ruin our careers."

"It'll sure as hell ruin your career if we run out of gas and crash and there's a perfectly good taxiway down there," Eddie answered, trying to remain calm with the idiot. "Besides that, it'll probably kill us. That'll mess up your career!"

"Let's talk this over," the major continued. "I'm sure we can arrive at a better option than following the first one that enters your head. We can't land on the taxiway, it's too narrow. We need a command decision. I'm the senior officer here and I'm not going to accept the first idea that pops into some first lieutenant's head. Let's get the detachment commander on the radio and some maintenance guys and discuss this thing before we make an irrational decision."

Eddie looked over at the major that he had generously allowed to sit in the left set. "Sir, we don't have time to hold a staff meeting. We're gonna run out of gas. With all due respect, Sir, I'm the detachment flight instructor. We don't have any time to diddle around, and if you don't believe we can land on that taxiway then let go of the controls and put your hands in your lap. Watch me closely cause I'm only gonna do this once. And please quit your whining!"

The taxiway was clear, the fire trucks previously lined up along it were re-deployed, and Eddie greased the Gooney Bird onto the narrow taxiway and proudly taxied to the Towhead ramp. In its proud history, Gooney Birds had operated in and out of runways that would have made the Nakhon Phanom taxiway look like a boulevard. Eddie really didn't want to stay in the air force anyway. Sooner or later he would get his butt in trouble and maybe this was just that day. But when the detachment commander automatically assumed that landing on the taxiway had been Major Collin's brilliant decision, Eddie let the major take all the credit.

Secretly, the major vowed to get back at Eddie. Although they had lucked out and done the right thing by landing on the taxiway, the decision hadn't followed military protocol. The major wanted to teach Eddie a lesson, somehow, for talking back and disobeying an order from a senior officer. His rank as a major was far above that of a lowly first lieutenant. That evening he wrote a scathing letter about Eddie's disregard for rank, disobedience, reckless commandeering of the aircraft, and landing on an unauthorized landing surface. Major Collins slipped the letter into Eddie's personnel folder and slept very well that night. He had again accomplished two birds with one stone, as he had also typed himself a letter of commendation for the brilliant airmanship, to be signed by the detachment commander. It would be placed in the major's file. Brilliant indeed!

* *

Eddie was sitting in on another late morning briefing. They were going out on the afternoon Ho Chi Minh Trail patrol and he was just riding along as an observer of a new aircraft commander, one that he had just signed off a week earlier. The guy was doing just fine, according to the feedback Eddie had received. But it was Eddie's day off and he just needed something to do to pass the time. He explained this to the new aircraft commander so the guy wouldn't feel uncomfortable with him on board. They always had gotten along just fine and had flown together probably a dozen times in the last six months.

"One other item," the briefing officer added to the end of his usual short briefing. He was their regular briefing officer, back from a three day trip to Bangkok. "We've received two different reports from this area of anti-aircraft fire that has odd colored orange bursts." He pointed to a single gun circle set away from the string of circles that basically outlined the trail. "This is an approximate location. The thud (F-105) pilots that reported it said it was a different shade of orange than they had ever seen before. If you see any orange bursts, let us know. We would really like to know more about this gun and get a better location on it. We would like to send a team in and see if there's something new out there."

Eddie and the aircraft commander discussed the orange burst for a sentence or two but made no big deal out of it. They certainly weren't going to fly into the gun circle to see if it would show them its colors. They checked out their M-16 and ammo box and joined the radio operators in the crew van. The operators also briefly mentioned the orange bursts on the way to the airplane.

The mission went smoothly, as most of them did. They were south along the Ho Chi Minh Trail so the aircraft commander stayed down at 8000 feet; the terrain was lower than the Plain of Jars and they were well over 4000 feet above the ground below. The extra 1000 feet was for the co-pilot's new bride, they were married just before he left the States for Nakhon Phanom. Eddie wore one of the headsets with a long cord on it and enjoyed looking out the front windows with the pilots. He also wandered back and forth along the catwalk, trying to figure out what it was that the radio operators occasionally got excited about. He knew better than to ask them because they all knew he wasn't supposed to ask any questions. After about three hours he was getting tired, so he used a parachute for a head rest and lay down on the cat walk. He chose the area between the cabin and the cockpit. There, he wouldn't be in anyone's way. He planned on a short nap. He had done this several times and had been told that when Red had been the instructor, he did it all the time. With the headset on and the pilot interphone selected, he could monitor the pilot's conversations and events in the background and still get a little dozing in.

He had just dozed off when he heard a thunk against the outside of the fuselage, on the left side just abeam where he was laying. "Sir!" It was the radio operator in the left front position just behind him. He was on the pilot's interphone and shouting. "I just got an orange burst out my window. I think those orange guns are shooting at us! Break right!"

Eddie was up in an instant and leapt like a lion into the cockpit. Both pilots were sitting calmly and grinning at each other, totally ignoring the radio operator's screams. "Break right! Break right!" Eddie hollered and they both turned and looked at him like he was crazy.

"I saw it too!" another voice from the back came over the interphone. He was shouting just as loud as the first operator. "It was on the left side, break right." It was all Eddie could handle. He couldn't understand the two pilot's total lack of action. He grabbed the aircraft commander and pulled him back with his left hand and tried to wrestle the yoke out of the guy's hands with his right.

"What the hell you doing!" the aircraft commander hollered, not using the interphone but at that close distance it was very loud.

"It's that orange gun, he's shooting at us," Eddie yelled back. Both pilots looked at Eddie and wrestled with the yoke to prevent him from rolling over into a steep turn.

"It's not a gun," the aircraft commander explained over the interphone so everyone could hear. "I just finished eating my lunch and my orange had a rotten spot, so I threw it out my side window." Eddie could see that his window was open. "It went through the prop and was pulverized. The orange burst was just the pulp and skin. Some of it was slung up against the fuselage and it made a little thunk. Eddie, you can go back to sleep."

Eddie wanted to be three inches tall and crawl into a crack. He looked back into the cabin and the radio operators were not laughing. The orange burst had also scared the pee waddling out of them. It might have been easier on their nerves if they had been shot at a little more often. The anticipation, month after month, had been overwhelming.

The orange burst phenomena could only have happened in a Gooney Bird—with its side window open for a trash disposal and propellers mounted in tight against the fuselage.

That evening Eddie and some of his pilots were swapping stories at the end of the officers club bar. He enjoyed that as it gave him an opportunity to slip some of his C-124 experiences and techniques into the conversation and thus do a little subtle instruction. The A-1 fighter jocks, as usual, were occupying the center of the bar and out of boredom they were listening in on the Towhead's stories. Eddie was aware of this so he made it a point to speak quietly. As they were running low on stories they shifted over to EC-47 stories. He told of the orange burst briefing and how the pilot threw his orange out the window. He got the expected laugh then was showered with the expected derogatory remarks. They all laughed at each other and it was someone else's turn to come up with another tale.

One of the A-1 pilots slowly dismounted from his stool and sauntered over to their group. "I been listening to your stories and I'm sorry you guys are treated like mushrooms, but there's really something you gotta know about orange bursts." He had their attention. "Thirty-seven millimeters have a grayish white burst, fifty-seven millimeters have a black burst, and eighty-fives have an orange burst. The thirty-sevens and fifty-sevens are manually sighted so it's hard to hit an aircraft thousands of feet high, but we still treat them with lots of respect. But the eighty-fives, they're radar guided. Those eighty-fives are deadly accurate and could probably pick a slow, low target like you guys out of the sky with one shot. You got no business anywhere in the area where there's eight-fives or any kind of report of orange bursts. That intelligence officer should have had you draw a fifteen mile circle around that one. If I were you I would confront him and have a piece of his ass. He could have gotten you guys killed."

"We weren't within thirty miles of the gun circle when it happened," Eddie added.

"Doesn't make any difference. He shoulda warned you it was probably an eighty-five millimeter," the Spad driver insisted. "We all need to know about heavy guns like that."

The group of Gooney Bird drivers and navigators was silent for several minutes as the A-1 pilot strolled back and rejoined "his kind."

"Before today I never knew that anti-aircraft guns had different colored bursts," one of Eddie's pilots said, shaking his head.

"I never knew that anti-aircraft guns even made bursts," another remarked. Eddie was quiet, he also knew very little about anti-aircraft guns.

* * * * * * * * * * * * * * * * * * * *

Another incident happened three days later. This time the Towheads kept it to themselves out of embarrassment. One of the Towhead crews was flying alongside the Ho Chi Minh Trail, about 150 miles south-east of Nakhon Phanom. It was a gentle day with scattered clouds. The jungle below them was a dark shiny green from a recent rain shower. At the time, they were proceeding northward, parallel and about ten miles west of where the tangle of roads and trails made up the Ho Chi Minh Trail.

"Look at that," the co-pilot everyone called Buzz cried out and pointed forward and down. A string of tracer rounds was spewing upward from the dense jungle. The tracers would have been quite beautiful if they hadn't been attempting to convey such a deadly message. They were coming almost up to their aircraft before running out of momentum and falling off and back down into the jungle. They didn't burst into puffs of shrapnel, like 37mm and larger anti-aircraft guns did, so the crew knew it was a smaller caliber machine gun that was shooting at them.

The aircraft commander and Buzz didn't bother to swerve their Gooney Bird because they were just high enough to be above the gunner's range. Soon they passed over the gun and sat smiling at their new experience. Fifteen minutes later they had reversed course and were heading south. When approaching that same spot the tracers started coming up at them again. Again the tracers petered out, arched over below them, and fell back down into the jungle. "Dumb shit, he's just wasting his bullets. Can't he see that he's not getting all the way up to us," the aircraft commander bragged.

"Don't know," Buzz wondered. "Maybe from the ground his perspective is different and he can't see that his gunfire is short."

"All the ammunition he's wasting had to be hauled all the way down here from their port in Haiphong harbor," the aircraft commander speculated. "Someone's gonna be pissed at him. And if he keeps this up, he's gonna burn out his gun barrel. It's been a slow day for the guys in the back, let's just fly back and forth over him and let him waste his ammo. You got any problem with that, Nav?"

"Sounds good with me," the navigator's voice came over the interphone. The back enders had been monitoring the pilot's conversation and they were all nodding their heads yes.

And they did. They made multiple passes until the gun was no longer shooting at them, then they continued trolling along the rest of their assigned area.

After landing they were in an upbeat mood. They proudly strutted into the briefing room and explained what they had done. The intelligence officer was a new guy that none of them had ever seen before. He was a part of the secret spook squad that worked in the war room at Task Force Alpha and he was just filling in for one of the regulars. He had prior experience working with F-105 thud pilots in Takhli and assumed everyone received a thorough briefing about anti-aircraft guns. He seemed quite interested in their story and when they were finished he had a funny look on his face.

"You guys know that only every fifth round is a tracer? Between each of those tracers are four rounds you can't see."

"Yeah, we knew that," Buzz lied. "So what's the point?"

"Well," the intelligence officer continued, "the tracers are hollowed out in the back and that's where the chemicals are added that create the trail of smoke. The other four are not hollow and so are heavier. With that heavier weight they have more inertia and travel a lot farther. The non-tracer bullets were probably going right past you. Did you check your aircraft for bullet holes?"

The three Towhead officers felt sick to their stomach and were totally deflated. They wanted to crawl into a hole and never come out. They had exposed their aircraft and the entire crew to machine gun fire, back and forth, and they hadn't taken one hit. They were extremely lucky, certainly not smart. "What kind of guns were they?" the intelligence officer continued.

"Obviously inaccurate," the navigator answered his question. "Otherwise we wouldn't be sitting here answering your question."

"I mean what kind," the intelligence officer was being very patient. "I realize you're a little upset right now, but it would be helpful to us if we knew if they were twelve point seven, fourteen four, or twenty-three millimeter."

"That's the point!" the aircraft commander exploded. "We don't know one kind from another. Nobody has ever told us shit about North Vietnamese guns. The only thing I know is what a thirty-seven millimeter looks like cause we got one sitting outside our operations building. Lieutenant Nuts got hit by one once and he said it had a grayish burst and went pop pop pop five times The gun we saw today didn't go pop pop pop, it just had tracers. No air bursts, just the tracers."

"Didn't you get a briefing when you first arrived?" The briefer was amazed. "They should have briefed you about the identification and capability of the NVA guns. What about your flight instructors, didn't they give you a thorough checkout on this stuff?"

Buzz took his turn venting, "I didn't ever receive any kind of a briefing. It's obvious I don't know shit about their guns. I have no doubt that no one else in the Towheads knows anything else either. We pilots are completely in the dark. They told us we didn't want to or need to know anything in case we got shot down and captured by the enemy."

"That sounds like something that would come from Udorn CIA," the intelligence officer smiled. "The North Vietnamese know what kind of guns they use. There's no reason why we can't tell it to you guys. Let me see if I can get that policy changed."

"Lots of luck," the navigator smirked. The intelligence officer went back to his other duties in the Task Force Alpha building. The policy wasn't changed.

The pilots, out of guilt, explained what had happened to the rest of their crew and apologized profusely. They all took it well. They were certainly aware of what was going on and they had just assumed their pilots knew what they were doing. That evening they all shared a case of beer as they sat together at the evening movie in the outdoor theater. They weren't supposed to sit together, enlisted and officers, but they all sat together anyway. If they could fly through bullets together and not get hit, they sure as hell could drink beer and watch a movie together.

* * * * * * * * * * * * * * * * * * *

Eddie was becoming quite unhappy with the way things were going. Sooner or later some Towheads could get killed because of those intelligence pucks and their cat and mouse games. It didn't make any sense. The enemy knew what was going on, all of the other pilots at NKP knew, and the press was plastering things all over the magazines and newspapers. Yet the intelligence people insisted the Towhead pilots shouldn't know anything, in case they get shot down.

He decided it was time for him to take things into his own hands. Again! The what if sessions at the safety meetings had been a resounding success because he had taken the initiative. He needed to take the initiative and come up with more solutions to these other problems. He spent a week mulling over the vulnerabilities his crews were faced with on a daily basis: which ones came with the mission and couldn't be mitigated, which ones could be addressed and the situation improved. It was obvious no one had done anything about these things before he arrived. Everyone was just handing down the limited stuff they knew to the next guy.

Then the means for carrying out his conclusions arrived, like most things at NKP, on the Klong Courier. The current detachment commander was scheduled to return to the States. His one year tour was over and his replacement stepped off the afternoon Klong with the eagerness of a football player running out on the field at the start of a game. His name was Lt. Colonel Samuel Washington and he had five days to familiarize himself with the workings of the detachment before the current commander shipped out. Word spread fast about their new, soon-to-be commander. He was as black skinned as anybody Eddie had ever seen, had a big smile, and an impressive background. His last assignment had been as the operations officer for a C-141 Squadron at Travis

Air Base in California and his recent promotion to lieutenant colonel had placed him in line to command a detachment of his own. He had volunteered for a one year tour in Vietnam. To command a flying unit in a war zone almost guaranteed he would continue his fast track career in the air force.

Eddie met him on the morning of the lieutenant colonel's seventh day at NKP. With the detachment's paperwork running smoothly, the colonel was anxious to get airborne and actually fly a mission. Prior to his recent C-47 training at England Air Force Base, the only two types of piston powered propeller aircraft he had flown had been the single engine T-6 trainers during his initial flight training in the 1950s and four engine C-118 transports as a young lieutenant. He had flown all jets since then.

With prior experience flying the four engine C-118 transports, and exercising his prerogative as the new detachment commander, he elected to skip the training checkout around the pattern and make his first flight a regular mission. Eddie liked the guy from the beginning. He was eager to learn, was a good listener, and asked a lot of intelligent questions. It took little effort for Eddie to fill out the initial check ride papers, fill in the flight blanks with a phony flight, and schedule the new commander for a combat mission. The new commander signed the paperwork, winked, then smiled at Eddie.

The mission went well. When they were finally clear of the Plain of Jars and on their way home, Eddie felt they had established enough rapport that maybe the commander would be receptive to some subtle suggestions. As hoped, the new commander was quite receptive and within a week Eddie had his list of intelligence improvements approved and implemented:

One. There were no safe places to make emergency landings in the Plain of Jars. The floor was covered with bad guys and the Alternate, across the skyline ridge from the Plain of Jars, was the only emergency runway. When taking Dop sets, each pilot had examined the valley that the Alternate was located in and was keenly aware of the karst pinnacle at the west end. But the Ho Chi Minh Trail to the south was another thing. From an A-1 acquaintance, Eddie listed seven primary runways in the panhandle of Laos that could accommodate a Gooney Bird in an emergency. The only problem was who currently owned the runways, bad guys or the friendlies. And if they were abandoned had they been mined? Eddie instructed his pilots to insist that the intelligence officers, before each flight along the trail, tell them which airfields were safe and which were not. The pilots could mark the safe airfields at the same time they updated their gun circles. The intelligence briefers had that information readily available and only needed the Towhead Detachment Commander's orders to make the information available to his crews.

Two. At several monthly safety meetings, Eddie had an intelligence briefer give the EC-47 pilots a thorough briefing on the types of guns that were deployed by the North Vietnamese Army. The briefing included the guns' ranges and characteristics and an open question session. This was information Eddie then passed on to every new pilot. It stimulated a lot of discussion among the Towhead pilots. Hopefully, it kept some of the cowboy pilots from cutting too close to their circles, once they knew just how deadly these little circles could be to a low slow Gooney Bird.

Three. He gathered a list of frequencies that were commonly used by the forward air controllers. In an emergency a crippled Towhead could quickly talk to someone close by who was familiar with the terrain and runway locations.

It wasn't a long list and the pilots were still prohibited from knowing what things and how things were going on, but at least they were half way prepared. If they got hit and it didn't look like they could make it all the way back to Nakhon Phanom, they could bypass the bureaucracy and get their butts down safely on a friendly dirt runway. Possibly with an OV-10 escort.

CHAPTER TWENTY-FOUR: SACRED RESPONSIBILITIES AND DEPRESSION

By the time they got back from the flight and had the airplane parked safely in its spot on the Towhead ramp, Eddie was furious. He never said a word as they gathered their personal gear together and joined the rest of the crew departing the aircraft.

"Craig, wait up a minute," Eddie ordered his co-pilot as they prepared to board the blue crew van. "You go ahead and do the debriefing," he instructed his navigator. "We'll walk in together. We got some stuff to talk about." Craig hesitated, looking down at his feet while the rest of the crew rode out of hearing distance. Eddie faced Craig squarely and their eyes met for the first time in several hours. Eddie pointed his finger at Craig and turned his anger into words, "Don't you ever do that again. Not to me or any other person in this outfit again!" His voice was seething. "Don't you ever show up for a flight with the heavy smell of booze on your breath and a bad hangover or anything else so bad that it keeps you from doing your job in the best possible way. We all use our booze to make this assignment tolerable but we also cut our drinking off early on the nights before we fly. Eight hours from bottle to throttle, that's the rule and no debilitating hangovers allowed.

"You were absolutely worthless in the cockpit today!" Eddie continued his ranting, "It would have been easier for me to fly solo than to carry your worthless, stinkin, bloodshot, half conscious, hung-over ass. I don't even wanna ask if you also do drugs but you will never, and I mean never, show up for a flight again and not be able to perform. Do you understand me? If you wanna sow your oats and drink yourself until you're unconscious, that's what you got days off for and three days CCR each month. When it's time to go back to work, give yourself enough time to sober up, get some rest, and perform your duties in a responsible and safe manner."

Craig looked into Eddie's eyes and sensed the anger. "I won't do it again," he answered meekly. He started to turn and walk across the ramp alone. Eddie stepped in front of him and continued his tirade.

"Not yet, I'm not done with you. I wouldn't give a shit if you went out and killed yourself, if you were flying a single pilot aircraft without anyone else, no other crew members. I'd not give a shit about your actions. I've been over here too long to put up with punk kids that can't pull on their end of the rope. I would care more about the aircraft loss than your life," Eddie lied, "and don't worry, the loss of the airplane would be a big deal to the government and the American public. You would just be another number to be counted. That's what this war's all about, anyway. How many GIs got killed each day? The American public thrives on that! Your loss wouldn't be a factor or big deal to the Hmong, the CIA pukes, or anyone else. Those guys you carry in your airplane, however, are a sacred responsibility."

Eddie caught his breath then continued, "It's the guys in the back ya gotta have some respect for. You're responsible for their lives. These guys, a navigator and up to a half dozen radio operators, they got a right to their lives. For you to show up unable to fly them as safely as possible on a combat mission is the ultimate insult to their existence. Have you no respect for their wives or their mothers? Do you not care if their children grow up without a father? They have a right to their lives and no hung-over two bit punk like you has a right to put them at more risk than is necessary. Especially in this dog shit war!"

"I'm sorry," Craig said again and this time it sounded like he meant it. Again he started to turn toward the barracks.

"I'm not done yet!" Eddie stopped him again. Eddie was still boiling mad. It was uncharacteristic for Eddie to lose his temper but he could do it if it was needed to keep all his pilots in working order. As their detachment instructor, he was the pilot maintenance man and this guy needed fixing. "I'm gonna write up a full report of this incident and I'll keep it hidden in my personal items in my room. If you ever show up for a flight not ready to fly to the best of your abilities, either with me or if I hear it from someone else, I'll investigate and write up another report and turn them both in to the colonel. I'll put your ass on the chopping block and personally cut your head off using the colonel as my ax! Do you understand me?"

"Yessir," Craig replied.

"Consider yourself on private probation. You can either end your tour clean and honorably or sacrifice your own ass to my personal vengeance. It's you choice. Do you understand me?"

"Yessir."

"Now get out of my sight." Eddie was finished and he turned away from Craig and joined the maintenance crew that had been quietly watching from a distance. Each guy needed to be handled differently and it had taken several hours for Eddie to decide which technique would work best on Craig. Craig hadn't gotten beyond his carefree college days, unlimited booze and irresponsible partying. Craig had been a challenge ever since he arrived and Eddie hoped his little act, as much as he hated to do it, would help the young man grow up. Eddie had been over two years with the 22nd and had many excellent experiences to get everything out of his system, then became an aircraft commander. Craig would be needed as an aircraft commander in six months. There wasn't that much time.

"I gotta get out of this place," Eddie thought to himself. Somebody is going to end up down in the jungle someday.

* *

Time was everyone's enemy. Everyone at NKP was serving his year in a different way and for different reasons. A young airman guarding the base or working as a clerk could be serving his military commitment and duty to his country, honorably, and avoiding the hell the army draftees were suffering in the jungles of Vietnam. The airman sweating in the hot sun and working as a mechanic on a thirty year old aircraft would be learning skills that he could apply in a civilian job—just as soon as he got back to the States and separated from the air force. The career master sergeant as well as the major, both with sixteen years in the air force, would be taking their year in the barrel and living an agony away from their wives and young children. The detachment commander would be working for a promotion to full colonel and someday becoming a wing commander. But they all shared the common enemy of time. The year it took before they could get on with their lives. Eddie was an exception; he had two years in Southeast Asia under his belt and going on three.

Eddie was horribly bored and he continued to fly as often as possible. The busier he stayed the less time he had to sit and wait for his last year in Asia to be over. What a contrast from his first trip south in a C-124.

When his Nakhon Phanom tour would be over, he still had a commitment to serve before he could get discharged. Pilot training was a four year military obligation from the date he received his wings. The C-124 for two years and EC-47 one year would use most of that up. He spent time training in the C-124 and C-47 schools and two weeks vacation in the States between aircraft. So when he returned to the States he would have a few months less than a year before discharge.

He had submitted his paperwork indicating his intention to separate from the air force so they wouldn't send him to another school for another aircraft. With less than a year to serve it would be a waste of money for the air force to send him to another school, and more importantly, they weren't allowed to slap another commitment on him with his application for separation on file. Instead they would stick him in some dead end job that required no schooling. His job would probably not even be flying, but base operations administration or other desk job until his separation date. That would be just fine with Eddie because being stateside, he would have that time to look for a civilian flying job and attend interviews. Sometimes guys in that position, those with something else to do with their lives, could request an "early out" and get it. Eddie had learned not to expect favors.

The other young men, with only one year to serve in Asia, found their year flying EC-47s didn't move as slowly as Eddie's. They only had a year to get all the boozing and whoring, if they craved it, out of their systems so they could go back home and live calm respectable lives. Eddie had closed the book on that lifestyle and he was even getting tired of special Thai massages. He took his instructor's responsibilities seriously and was proud of the flying that "his" guys ground out day after day. One crew lost an engine just as they rotated for take-off, with a full load of fuel and crewmembers and no room left to stop. The two pilots continued their take-off with their remaining engine, just like the book called for, and struggled over the trees at the end of the runway. They brought their crippled bird around for a safe landing. He was very proud of them. About once or twice a month somebody would get a clip or so of anti-aircraft fire thrown at them and occasionally picked up a few holes in their skin, but their scorecard still showed the same number of successful take-offs as landings.

* *

One afternoon Eddie walked over to the officers club to have a couple of drinks. It was only three in the afternoon and he was looking for a place to drink all by himself. For no apparent reason he decided to sit next to the only other patron at the bar, a major in a wrinkled flight suit. They started a conversation and Eddie discovered the major was an A-1 pilot with the 56th at NKP. He had flown that morning and after debriefing he had stopped by the bar for a few "relaxers" from his mission. The Major was already drunk and he rambled on about his existence and daily routine. "Yea, after my mission I drink until I'm so drunk I can barely make it back to my room at night. Then the next morning I crawl out of bed and stagger down to the head and have a typical fighter pilot's breakfast—a cigarette and a puke. Then I shower, eat a real breakfast at the mess hall, attend my security and mission briefing, then back to go bomb the jungle.

"You know, we repeatedly bomb sections of the trail and all we accomplish is to make gravel out of rocks. Then there are thousands of coolies on every section of the road to fill in the holes as soon as we leave. Then the next day we go back and bomb the gravel into sand. Then they fill it back in again."

He threw down another shot glass full of whiskey, then continued, "And there's nothing like bombing the shit out of a little patch of the jungle. The FAC fires a smoke rocket at the patch of jungle he wants destroyed and then we blow the shit out of it with whatever they've hung under our wings. There are times, when no one is shooting back, and I wonder if there is even anyone or anything down there that's associated with the war. The politicians in Washington just want us to drop a given tonnage of bombs on the jungle every day and they think that'll make the bad guys go away. Operations doesn't want us to return with bombs still on board. So I suspect the FAC, when he doesn't have any valid targets he can find, just randomly shoots his smoke rocket into the jungle so we can empty our bomb racks. What if the FACs bomb damage assessment was actual instead of what Washington really wants to hear? What if it's like three monkeys, several dozen lizards, a snake, and some unlucky native on his way home from gathering herbs?"

He ordered another shot of whisky and continued, "And it's really stupid when they have us bomb stream crossings, we actually bomb the dirt and water like we're going to destroy the crossing. How do you destroy dirt with a bomb? I'm actually glad when we get shot at from the ground because then at least I know I'm going after an authentic war target.

"Then on other days it's for real, trucks and supplies and accurate anti-aircraft fire. Ya never know when that magic golden BB is gonna end it all for you. Either way I come back, debrief, shower, eat and end right back here drinking myself into oblivion." He sat and looked at the bar top with a squint. "What a great life. . . you know we're losing the war? Bolovens plateau is overrun by the North Vietnamese Army and they're withdrawing troops from Vietnam. Kinda makes ya wonder why yer hanging yer ass out on a limb when we're losing the war and back in the States no one gives a shit."

"Sounds like a real bummer," Eddie reflected out loud.

"Yea," the Major reflected. "Then sometimes I get an early morning flight and as I skim along over the jungle and watch the smoke come up from the villager's fires, the men heading out to their rice paddies with their water buffaloes, the white mist rising out of the triple canopy jungle, and the purr of my Wright 3350 engine, I wouldn't trade what I'm doing for the world. How's that for being fucked up?"

* *

Three days later Eddie found Millhouse, the parrot, dead in the miniature, inoperative waterfall pool. It happened after a particularly intense night of sampling drinks and strutting back and forth along the Hooch bar. There was some question about who had more to drink, Millhouse or the Towheads, and no one could recall seeing Millhouse fall into the water. He had crashed and burned, at least metaphorically. The afternoon of the discovery there was a heavy drinking session at the Towhead bar and after the first few rounds the discussion centered on how to dispose of the dead bird. It was suggested that someone take it along on a mission and throw it out through the front window, so it would go through the prop. That way, Millhouse's remains would be scattered over the jungle where his ancestors had lived. Then there was another half hour discussion on whether Millhouse had really been a guy or some loose mannered "chick" that liked hanging out in their bar. No one could even remember who had owned him or her, he or she had been around longer than any of the Towheads. They reminded Eddie that he was a farm boy and asked him to examine it to see if he could tell what he or she was. But he could only remember that a bird's rear end was called a cloaca, he had never spent the time to examine one of them. So much for being a farm boy with a college education! Then the drunken pilots were back to the disposal of the body. Eddie suggested someone should climb one of the trees in their compound and leave the body for Harold the lizard to eat. His suggestion was shot down as most of the Towheads still thought Harold was a vegetarian. In the end they decided to give him or her a hero or heroine's funeral, followed by many expressive toasts, and a burial in the commons next to the deck. It was a trying time for the Towheads and it didn't help anyone's mood—Eddie's in particular. Eddie had been building his discouragement into the mother of all depressions and he attached Millhouse's death to the other complexities. Was it really a clinical depression or just discouragement and restlessness? Whatever it was it was severe enough that sometimes he just ached all over.

The tiny library on base was more of a dumping ground for unwanted and finished books and a salvage yard for those looking. Eddie found a book about Confucius; he didn't even know there had been a real Confucius. He thought Confucius was someone who had been made up as an object of Chinese one liner jokes. The book was a collection of sayings and teachings called *The Analects*. The guy, born in 551 BC, twelve years after Buddha, was a teacher of wisdom, not religion. The basis of his teachings was simplicity, logic, common sense, social structure, governmental suggestions, and practical wisdom. It formed the basis of Asian thinking that Americans grappled to understand. Confucius had no idea that his straight forward approach to practicality would set him up as an object of jokes. Jokes half the way around the world and 2500 years later. Eddie buried himself in the teachings, hoping he could jump start his spirit, but his effort failed in its purpose.

He returned to the library and found a book about Buddha and Buddhism. The religion was different from any he had ever been exposed to as a Westerner. The Buddhists themselves were certainly the gentlest people he had ever seen or been around. He was fascinated with the teachings of Buddha. A wise, peaceful teacher with an interesting view point on life, Buddha reminded him in many ways of what he had read about Gandhi.

But none of the readings seemed to have any pertinence to his predicament. His depression was overwhelming.

Then there was an order that came down from someone in the Pentagon. Somehow, someone in an office half way around the world discovered that their prized fleet of EC-47 reconnaissance aircraft had nose art painted on them. That someone decided the nose art compromised the camouflaged paint scheme and that someone sent an order for all nose art to be removed from their aircraft. It was a major blow the crewmember's morale as well as to the dedicated maintenance crew chiefs assigned to each individual aircraft. Eddie buried his grief as no one was aware of his particular attachment to The Lady. But he had a very strange feeling about the dethroning of his secret fantasy. She lost her identity.

* *

One night he woke up and in the dark it took him a few seconds to figure out where he was. Then he suddenly developed a strong craving for a hamburger, not the meat and bun job like they had in the officers club, but a real American junker—with mustard and catsup and pickles and lettuce and cheese and a taste that couldn't be imitated by any Asian cook. Then he realized he missed apples, crisp and shiny, and good Shakey's Pizza. He also missed walking downtown on a crisp cold day and looking in the windows of stores full of assembly line goods, instead of looking at petticabs and water buffalo and poor people. He missed getting stuck in the snow, just like the girl what's her name did when he met her at the 22nd board meeting. He wanted mountains, real ones, not limestone karst but granite all the way up above the tree level and to 14,000 feet. He wanted clear streams and trout. He realized he was homesick, not just nostalgic, but deeply homesick so badly that he would curl up on his bed and hold in the moans.

Once he walked down the sidewalk to the bathroom in the middle of the night, with nothing on but his shorts, and took a leak. Back in his room he took two aspirin and a full glass of water. Arnold turned over and asked, "You okay?"

"Yeah," Eddie lied. "I had a hard on so I went down to the bathroom and beat off."

"Works for me," Arnold replied, and rolled back over and went back to sleep.

Eddie went back to bed but couldn't sleep; he did actually smile to himself for a few seconds. He still had his sense of humor, only it was buried deeply inside.

* *

One afternoon he came back from a mission. He stumbled into his room and found his maid sitting on the sofa that he and Arnold had confiscated from a back room at the officers club. She was drinking one of his Coca Colas and smoking a cigarette, just like she owned the joint. It pushed Eddie over the edge. Several of the guys had been complaining that small items had been disappearing, underwear, towels, pocket change, and here she was drinking his Coke. The fact that he could easily afford to give her a Coke was immaterial. It just happened that the guys with stuff disappearing all shared the same maid as Eddie and Arnold. Upon hearing about things disappearing, and remembering Red had bitched about all his shorts disappearing, Eddie had been carefully counting all his personal items. Five pairs of shorts, two tee shirts, and one hand towel disappeared in four months. Then on that day he walked in his room and there she sat drinking his Coke.

It was Eddie's job to handle flying problems with his pilots and he decided right there on the spot to do something about their thieving maid. He walked over to his chest of drawers and opened the top drawer. He took out the stack of four remaining shorts and held them out for her to see. "You takee my shorts, five times." He held out five fingers with his other hand. "And you takee my towel." He put the shorts back and repeated his act with his tee shirts. She didn't speak fluent English but spoke enough that she understood exactly what he was saying. "Other pilot missing some also." He swept his hand around and pointed in the direction of the other rooms. "We trained killers and don't put up with shit like that." He wasn't sure she understood the trained killer lie but it felt good to say it anyway.

He pulled his Smith and Wesson revolver from his holster and acted as if he was making sure it was loaded. He spun the cylinder a few times and then stared at her fiercely. He then lowered his arm and let the gun hang loosely in his hand, pointing at the floor. He had been taught it was bad procedure to ever point a gun directly at someone you had no intentions to shoot. He cocked it, and then uncocked it. Her eyes were enlarged to the size of small saucers and were fixed on the end of Eddie's pistol barrel. "You bring back tomorrow. You understand? All pilots!" She vigorously nodded her head yes. "No shorts, I go boom boom. You understand?" Again she nodded her head yes. He slowly put his revolver back into his holster while continuing his meanest, bad ass look. He had used his bad ass act before but none of his performances could have held a candle to this maid's confrontation. He was sorry there was no one to witness it. "Now get the hell out of here and you sure as hell better have our stuff back here by tomorrow night," he threatened, pointed at the door, and she was gone in a nanosecond.

That was on a Wednesday and Eddie never told anyone about the incident. The maid was never seen again. After the confrontation the other maids seemed a lot nicer to Eddie. They all pitched in and shared the workload from the rooms previously tended by the missing maid. On the following Monday Eddie reported her missing and Airman Hendrix said he would inform the proper people so they could hire a replacement. Somehow the story did get out. Maybe the maids told the Thai girl that the captain navigator owned, and she told the captain. Anyway it just added fuel to the legend of Eddie, AKA Nuts.

After the thieving maid flew the coop, Eddie had the impression that the rest of the maids were afraid of him. They had a tendency to scatter like quail whenever he visited the toilet and they no longer giggled around him. The rest of the guys in the Towhead Towers were pleased because their own maid service had raised a notch: clothes were folded neater, rooms were swept every day, and nothing, absolutely nothing was ever missing from their rooms. Eddie basked in his glory as the new unofficial corrections officer for the maid service.

He and Arnold, as well as the rest of the Towheads, kept their dirty laundry in a separate dirty laundry drawer. Several times each week it would disappear for the day and end up at 4:00 p.m., clean and neatly stacked on their respective beds. There were no locks on any of their doors and the maids could come and go from the air-conditioned crew members' rooms as they pleased. Laundry, sweeping the floors, making beds and keeping the toilets and showers clean was a very light load for the bevy of five maids. Two weeks later the word at the Towhead Inn was that a new maid was among the covey in the toilet. Eddie heard all the talk and was looking forward to seeing her for himself. But it seemed he could never catch up with her. She was scarce on his days off. The maid's network seemed determined to keep Eddie from confronting the new girl. His room-mate Arnold, however, met her and was unhappy with her from the get-go. He described her as an absolute train wreck.

Then one day the network failed. After canceling a mission because his aircraft developed an oil leak, Eddie sauntered into his room and the new maid was standing there, barefoot in the middle of his room. She was a teenage floozy, a barefoot, stringy-haired tramp and she looked at him as if she had just seen the devil. Her traditional wai, a slight bend at the waist and her hands folded together in a prayer position, didn't help.

He walked around her frozen statue. She stayed in the wai position. He walked to the back of their room and unbelted his gun and holster. She finally snapped out of the frozen position and began busily sweeping the already clean floor. She pretended not to watch as Eddie unloaded the shells from his revolver, glancing sideways toward her, and stowed everything in his second drawer. He was trying to imitate John Wayne in a movie he once saw.

He grabbed a towel and his soap holder and exited the room. If he was going to trust her, there was no better time than the present. She knew where the gun was and he left some change on his dresser. His depression returned for the day. Eddie spent the better part of the day finishing up some check ride paperwork at operations, then the rest of the afternoon reading the new copies of Newsweek, Time, and Life magazine. They were a vital link to the outside world and part of the thin thread that still kept him civilized. He knew their content had a media spin on it but at least it was something. He was stretched out on the Towhead Inn deck when the maids left for the day and his eyes met his new maid's eyes as she walked by him. He tracked her with his eyes and refrained from smiling.

* * * * * * * * * * * * * * * * * * * *

The next morning he caught the Klong to Bangkok. For two weeks he had been planning to take his CCR and his schedule finally had an opening. He arrived at the Chaophya Hotel about one in the afternoon and took a long shower after sweating in the rumbling, noisy C-130 courier. He then took a long walk through his old friend—the city of Bangkok. The klongs were still as filthy and stinky as before, but after years living in Asia, they were not nearly as offensive as he remembered them. He was evolving. He saw a scattering of samlors, three wheeled human pedaled bicycle taxis. And they were still using Tuk Tuks, three wheeled samlor type vehicles but powered by noisy, obnoxious two cycle engines. Much hadn't changed except there were fewer Tuk Tuks and samlors, and more noisy horn honking cars and taxis. It had been said that Thai drivers believed if they didn't honk their horn, the car wouldn't go. Eddie wondered if it had something to do with the car's spirit. Thais believed in that stuff. After all, he was still in La La Land.

Eddie stopped by James Jewelers to say hello to James, but James was out of town in Tokyo. With the 22nd not around, he had no one to smuggle his jewels into Japan. Eddie stopped at a street stand and paid sixty cents for some fruit. The vender charged four times what it was worth but Eddie was not in the mood to barter. He had plenty money and the Thai vender was poor. It was strange looking fruit, one that he had never seen before. So he watched some Thais eat some, then he knew to peel it and not eat the skin. He threw his peelings in the street along with all the other peelings. There was no such thing as a trash can in Bangkok.

He stopped at his favorite liquor store and bought replacements for the scotch and other items that weren't available at NKP. They had the cheaper brands at NKP but Eddie was living with a gentleman and they drank only the best. For thirty cents he rode a Tuk Tuk and transported his booty back to his hotel. He had only been in town for four hours and he was bored and ready to go back. He had to do something to break the doldrums. A massage was out; he could do that at NKP. Shopping was out; he had looked at everything so many times in the last several years. There was just not anything he hadn't seen before. Bar hopping was definitely out. The Bangkok GI bars were nothing more than grab ass scenes, crawling with filthy bar girls. Next CCR he would have to go to Chang Mai. He heard it was in the northern Thai mountains and was a nice place to visit. He had to get away from all the places the GIs had contaminated.

There were just a few round-eyed women around, a few tourists, a few embassy secretaries, and a few airline stewardesses to remind him of what he was missing. Every one of them was with a Caucasian man and was having a good time.

He had dinner at the Chaophya Officers Club and endured the tasteless and boring food. So for something to do he wandered into the bar and ordered a bar scotch and water. At least there wouldn't be any bar girls allowed in there. The guy sitting at the bar two seats down from him didn't look any better off than Eddie felt. After a couple of swigs Eddie timed his glance wrong and the two locked eye contact, a social boo-boo. In Southeast Asian bars you didn't look white strangers in the eye. Especially in Thailand with a mercenary war going on across the river in Laos. The guy tipped his glass Eddie's way. Eddie looked away.

"You just get into town?" the guy asked.

"Seems like I been here about a hundred years, got another twenty to go," Eddie answered without moving his head or looking back at the guy. "You new?"

"Bout the same," the guy answered. "You look like shit."

"Yeah, and you look like shit warmed over." Eddie looked at him for the first time and grinned.

"Where ya heading, if I can ask? Maybe I can help," the guy offered. Under the circumstances Eddie's caustic remark hadn't been offensive, it was just guy talk.

"Been here going on three years, I look like shit cause my body is starting to rot. I think I've got some sort of fungus on my brain," Eddie answered. "I'm thinking I wanna go back home, ya know, to the real world so I get buried when I die. But instead, I'm going back to my outfit in the next day or two."

"What's the point?" he asked Eddie. "What's the advantage in being buried back in the States? I've seen lots of dead guys. They're just a corpse of dead meat and bones after they get killed—sometimes a lot of blood and fluids. This living spirit after death and the promise of Heaven and threat of Hell; it's just a bunch of hooey to sell religion to the masses. When you're dead you're dead. What difference does it make where you're buried? All that remains of you, other than a corpse, is the other people's memory of you and few worthless possessions. If I get killed, I sure as hell don't wanna be shipped back to the States so my relatives can look sad at my funeral and some hippie can spit on my casket. They do that, ya know. They been told us grunts are responsible for this war over here. Then afterward, while eating the traditional ham sandwich and a piece of cake, my relatives could discuss what a shit they think I was and what a failure I had been." He looked at Eddie with a blank stare. "I'd just as soon rot in the jungle over here and not give them the pleasure!

"You don't wanna go back while you're alive, either," he continued. "Go back to the 'real' world. Been there, done that. Believe me, it ain't the same back there. After four months in my home town, I volunteered to sign up again if they would send me back here. Over here is all our kind has left. We've been violated by our own government, screwed by our Presidents, and condemned by the American people."

The stranger hesitated a little bit and decided to continue, "When I was home, I discovered that my wife left me for some long-haired beatnik. I caught up with him and the son of a bitch looked me right in the eye and said, 'If you're gonna go fight your war and fuck the Vietnamese, there's no reason why I shouldn't fuck your wife.' I didn't know what to say to the scraggy twerp so I just turned around, walked up to a pay phone, and made the call that brought me right back here. Fuck both of em—maybe you otta get yourself a little monkey or a pet pig or something. It worked for me." He wouldn't shut up. "When I came back, I got myself a young sow pig and we get along great. My pig eats anything without complaining, never asks for money, goes outside to shit, doesn't talk my ears off, and," he held his right index finger up, "she doesn't fuck beatniks. I don't even miss my wife."

"I fucked a few pigs in my day, but never any swine. They were all girls," Eddie embellished. "But you, you're one sick son of a bitch."

"I didn't say I was doing my pig, just living with it," the guy defended his pig with a stern look.

Eddie was just trying to lighten up the conversation with a little humor and was a little surprised that the guy's feathers were ruffed up. So he decided to play it straight and just continue the conversation. "I'm holed up in the officers' barracks at NKP. Anyways, they won't let us have anything like a pig." Eddie lied. The Nails had a pig.

Then Eddie continued, "Although one of the guys bought a girl for fifty bucks, but she's a nice girl and not a pig. I'm supposed to go home in five months and I don't know what I could do with a girl or a pig when I leave. What're ya gonna do with your pig when you leave? If you're still alive, I mean."

"I guess if I can't find some American to take it I'll just turn it loose outside. The locals would gleefully catch her and eat her."

"Doesn't that bother you? I mean the natives eating your pet?"

"Not really, after all she's just a pig . . . she's not some sort of a scared spirit or something. Hell, we're all gonna die sometime, some of us sooner and some of us later. Why should a pig be any different?"

"I'd have to think about that. If I care that anyone ate me when I die," Eddie replied and took another sip of his drink.

"You a candlestick or a Spad?" the stranger asked. "You said you were at NKP."

272

"Neither, a Towhead," Eddie answered. His answer was unrevealing enough. They used the Towhead call sign with the tower and any idiot could see their aircraft sitting on the ramp was overloaded with antennas.

"You work the PDJ but you guys don't talk on the radio. Too bad we can't talk," the guy reflected. Under the rules, neither one of them was supposed to carry the conversation any further. You just didn't talk about classified jobs with strangers and they both had classified jobs. Who knows when some media spy is probing for information? Who knows if one of them was media undercover? They both sat in silence again, sipping their drinks.

"You been back home during your two and a half years over here?" the stranger probed. His question was innocent.

"Went back for C-47 school for three weeks but I stayed clear of civilians. I stayed a few days on my family's farm—fought off the neighbor's daughter—ended up going fishing alone," Eddie replied.

"Farmer's daughter, there must be a joke in there somewhere. You really live an exciting life. Where'd ya go to Gooney Bird school?"

"Alexandra, Louisiana, at England Air Force Base," Eddie wondered why the stranger even cared.

"Sounds exciting, hot, humid, lots of weird people," the stranger reflected.

"Hot, humid, lots of weird people running around," Eddie repeated. "Sounds like the place across the river where we both know that you live." Eddie held up two fingers so the bartender would bring them another round of drinks. "Except, Alexandra isn't surrounded by the North Vietnamese Army and shelled with rockets every night . . . besides, they have a cafeteria on the south end of Alexandra where they make great strawberry pie."

"Yeah, I suppose you're right," the stranger conceded. "Strawberry pie trumps the North Vietnamese Army every time."

After a few minutes the guy said, "Where'd you go to pilot training?" That was something unclassified they could talk about and it was obvious that this guy needed someone to talk to.

"Willy, 67-H," Eddie replied hesitantly. The other guy looked surprised.

"You happen to know a guy named Bobby Jackson?"

It was Eddie's turn to be surprised, "Yeah, I know one."

The other guy looked around to check that there was no one else in hearing range and asked, "First I need a nickname for Bobby Jackson, so I know you're legitimate."

"Mayberry," Eddie answered. "Quiet, well mannered, good stick. Got a forward air controller assignment out of pilot training. He was in my pilot training class."

"Did you know him well?" the guy asked.

Eddie flashed back to a year of good times at Williams Air Force Base and the always grinning little bachelor pilot that got drunk at their graduation party. "Yeah, but I lost track of him. You know where he's at?"

"Well," the guy took a long draw on his drink. "Ain't nobody gonna come up with a nickname like Mayberry for a guy named Bobby Jackson—unless he's for real so I'll tell you what happened. After Mayberry finished two tours flying as a forward air controller in South Vietnam, he went sheep dipped, traded his military uniform for a set of civvies, and became one of us. He flew a U-17 for my outfit. It's a military version of the civilian Cessna 185. We use em east of here, where I work, as a smoke spotter to direct air strikes. It's got hard points to hang smoke rockets on the wings and long range fuel tanks. Damn shame, I liked him. He got hit by a thirty-seven millimeter burst over the PDJ about three months ago." Eddie was stunned as the guy continued. "KIA (killed in action)! We got some air support from Cricket and took out the gun that got him, but we never did get in to get his body . . . I'm sorry to bring you the bad news."

This guy was for sure a Raven FAC from Laos. They were the only outfit that Eddie knew who flew U-17s. The Ravens had a code among their brotherhood that they would always get the gun that killed one of their own. Eddie sat for a while and let the rush of grief run its course, then remarked, "So you're sheep dipped. You're military in civilian clothes."

"Wish I could answer that, but you know how it is."

"I fly over the Alternate a couple of times each week. You need me to drop you some groceries or something?" It was Eddie's way of telling him that he knew where he lived.

"Thanks, but we're up to our ass in rice," the guy smiled. He took another swig and finished his drink. "Let's get out of here. I know a place that has some class and no nut grabbing whores. We can drink with our kind. Everyone calls it the Snake Pit."

* * * * * * * * * * * * * * * * * * * *

The downstairs bar and lounge in the Imperial Hotel was pure old world swank. While flying the C-124, in all the times Eddie had visited Bangkok, he never imagined such an elegant venue existed. As a naive new guy he wouldn't have fit in anyway. A wide, deeply carpeted stairway led the way downstairs to a paneled hallway of polished teak wood. Coves in the walls were lit by hidden lights and displayed, behind glass, the finest oriental treasures: gorgeous vases, jade crusted temple guards, and a golden Buddha. There was a huge oil painting of the King's Royal River Barge called Subanahong and intricately carved elephant tusks. Eddie felt underdressed.

They turned another corner. Eddie and the guy called Longbow, obviously a radio call sign, entered a dimly lit lounge with scattered tables. Along their left sprawled a long wooden bar with comfortable upholstered chairs. Just off the far end of the bar and in the central rear of the room was a slightly elevated stage. On it a small ensemble of musicians were playing soft dance music. The tranquil scene was a sharp contrast from the busy, very noisy, never ending tempo of life unraveling outside the hotel. There was a generous scattering of eclectic patrons, mostly men, but a few beautiful round-eyed Caucasian women. All were dressed comfortably but most wore upscale casual. It was impossible to differentiate the thieves and con-men from the millionaires and royalty.

"Don't look anybody in the eye for too long down here," Longbow advised with a crooked smile. Eddie thought the guy was a little dramatic. "There's a smattering of tourists and hotel guests, but this is where the Spooks and the Ravens and the CIA and Air America guys and the spies and the thieves all come to sulk and tell lies. That's why we call it the Snake Pit. We use it as a kind of a sanctuary, a respite. It's like the last threads of civilization and dignity for many of these lost souls. They sneak down here to Bangkok, away from the war in Laos, take a shower, and sit around and drink like gentlemen. It looks civilized but that's just a façade. If you've been over here for more than two and a half years, like you said you had, I figured you would feel right at home with this bunch of misfits and mercenary bastards." Longbow gave Eddie a friendly elbow in the ribs, smiled, and crawled into one of the luxurious bar stools. Eddie mounted a stool next to Longbow.

"Why do I feel like I'm out of my league?" Eddie wondered out loud.

"Half the guys in here are phonies, the other half are scary. Play along and relax, at least you're legitimate."

Longbow ordered two bar scotch and waters. "I see you guys flying around the PDJ every day but you never talk to anybody. Everyone wonders who the hell you guys are." Eddie didn't reply so Longbow continued his one way conversation. "You got any idea all the shit that's flying around down there on the PDJ below you? There's Ravens, Chaophakhao, Air America, Continental Air Services, Nails and a whole damn spectrum of bombers sent from Cricket?"

"You would be surprised at what we know," Eddie went as far as he could go. "But right now I'd just as soon stay up on top in my Gooney Bird."

"On top, my ass. A thirty-seven would have trouble reaching you but a fifty-seven could knock your ass off in less than fifteen seconds. You're not that high. You're at the same altitude the fast movers are when they roll into their bombing dives. Course most of them can't hit shit but ya can't be too hard on em. The gomers are usually hammering away with every gun they got." Longbow smiled and checked again to be sure there was no one else in listening range. At that time Eddie realized why everyone sat in little groups scattered evenly in the lounge. He imagined that they were all having conversations about secret things.

How come they never shoot at you Towheads?" Longbow probed. "One day my little Cessna needed some maintenance so I borrowed one of the T-28s from General Vang Pao's fleet. The T-28 is a lot faster and climbs out pretty quick so I snuck up on one of your birds from the back. I sat there a little while, trying to figure out what you guys are doing. I was just a couple of hundred feet behind and lower than your bird and I knew no one in the gooney bird could see me. I saw lots of antennas and that you fly with your back troop door removed. But no one's ever seen you guys drop anything out your door." There was no way Eddie was going to pass on any sensitive information to this guy. He knew his way around and could talk the talk, but there was still the possibility he was a media spy on a fishing trip. Eddie needed a ridiculous story to throw Longbow off balance. To simply tell him it was classified would have aroused too much curiosity.

"We pay em off," Eddie answered with a straight face. "Our whole objective is to go home with only one hole in our ass. Once a month we go down low and parachute cases of rice wine and *Playboy* magazines to the PAVN gun crews. They get drunk and masturbate and we get a free pass . . . they don't shoot at us. I can't believe you sheep dips and mercenaries haven't ever figured that out."

Eddie hid his grin and thought to himself, "Let him chew on that one!"

"I think I brought you to the right place," Longbow chuckled, shaking his head. "Lying seems to come naturally for you. You're not a Raven or the CIA or Air America but you sure make up for it as one hell of a liar." Longbow paused then broke into a big wide smile, "Too bad some media puke didn't overhear what you just told me, it would make good copy in *Time* magazine." Longbow took another sip of scotch and continued his babbling. "Ya know—you're kinda showing some of the classic symptoms of old dog behavior. It takes at least two years over here to get that way."

"I give up. What's old dog behavior?" Eddie acted disgusted.

"It's simple, happens if you're scared shitless enough times or bored to death. Or maybe both and after a while ya aren't sure which it is. After a while ya just figure if ya can't eat it or fuck it, then ya piss on it and walk away. I can see that in you."

"That's about how I feel," Eddie confessed. "But I really don't fit into your group of renegades. I flew trash for two years in a C-124. I shuttled oversized cargo from Clark and Bangkok in-country so I never experienced the guns, bullets, and bombs your kind messes with. Besides, you just told me we Towheads live charmed lives."

"Just being over here a couple of years and participating in this poor excuse for a war is enough to dehumanize anyone, guns or not," Longbow lectured. "You'll never be the same. There will always be something different inside you and the only guys you'll ever feel comfortable with will be other zombies. Zombies from this Asian shit-hole CIA war in Laos. As far as I'm concerned, the world consists of the others and the brothers. It's us against them! "

"I really feel better now," Eddie nodded his head yes. "Seriously, what are you gonna do when you finally go back to the States?"

"Don't know if I could ever go back to the States, I really have no plans too. I'd turn into an alcoholic and live on the streets and beg for nickels. You ever been to Singapore? I was there two years ago and the place was buzzing with activity. A guy could really get lost there and start a new life over without anyone ever asking you any questions. Hell you could lie about your past and act like you never heard of a war in Vietnam and Laos."

Longbow continued his fantasy, "I've thought about starting an export company. They got all kinds of shit over here that you could make five hundred percent profit if you bought it right and shipped it and marketed it to stateside buyers."

"I hear ya," Eddie responded. "When I was flying the C-124 we got into all kinds of places and you wouldn't believe all the shit we hauled back to Japan. It got to the point that we knew all the best prices and the best quality on stuff. We searched all over for bargains to take back to Tachikawa. I got a whole room full of stuff waiting for me in storage back in the States right now."

"Maybe we should go into business together," Longbow suggested. "Set up in Singapore where they got the largest free port in the world. We could buy all over the orient, warehouse it in Singapore, and ship it in bulk to American distributors."

"It's worth some serious discussion," Eddie replied. He was half interested. "I got a room-mate back at NKP who has a business mind and comes from a family that owns lots of businesses. Let me drag the idea past him and maybe we can get together in a couple of months and hatch some sort of a plan. Can you get across the river to Udorn? I can ride the Klong from NKP to Udorn on my combat crew rest days off each month. We could meet there."

"I can probably pull that off," Longbow agreed. "There's no way you can get a message in to me, with all the security stuff and such, but I can get a message to you at the Towhead living quarters in NKP. Either I'll send a message with one of our own that's passing through for fuel or maybe I'll get a chance to stop by myself. By the way, what's your name?"

"Nuts," Eddie answered. "Everyone calls me Nuts. Just address the note to Lieutenant Nuts with the electric goons and it'll get to me."

Longbow never flinched at Eddie's name. "It's a deal, we'll talk. I'll wait to hear from you." Eddie and Longbow, two new friends in an unfriendly world, shook hands and their eyes met. Eddie saw something that he liked about Longbow, something inside and away from all of the coarse superficial mannerisms.

The two of them sat silently for half an hour, buying each other drinks, each deep into their own private and classified thoughts. The bar really was a nice respite for Eddie.

The band came back from their break and a Thai singer joined them on the stage. She sang American love songs. Her voice was pure and in perfect pitch. She was tall and straight, almost Caucasian eyes. She had long black hair, dark beautiful skin and complexion. She was like the Lady painting and Eddie wondered if she and the Lady were from the same ethnic section of Thailand. Number 304's painting had to have been from a Thai model. He hadn't thought much about her lately, he had about given up on that fantasy. He had about given up on everything. By the third song the patrons had ceased their conversations and were all watching and listening to the singer's mesmerizing performance. Each had their own lost world to regret and their own pains to forget. Eddie was silent with grief over Mayberry's death.

The music stopped and Eddie was feeling a heavy buzz from the load of scotch he was accumulating. He was experiencing a surge of nostalgia, nostalgia for something but he really didn't know what. The singer stood silently before her microphone. It was one of the old fashioned kind with a silver metal stand and a big silver microphone. She was staring into her audience and tears were slowly flowing down her cheeks. The room was silent.

Then she spoke with a soft mellow voice. "I'd like to dedicate this last song to my lover; he's sitting with you in the audience. My love is an A-1 pilot and we met during his first visit to Bangkok, almost a year ago. I was the singer here, as I am now, and we met during one of my breaks. I had been lured by some strange mysterious force to approach him at his table. He was alone, obviously lonely, in pain, and the most beautiful man I had ever seen. We became lovers. We spent his days off each month here in this city of love and lust. We've been lovers ever since that first night and I want you all to know that. He told me he was married and I told him our relationship was not about that. His wife and his family were in another world. I have always felt respect for them and feel their pain of his absence. I feel I was placed here on this earth to comfort him through his year of bullets and horror; I was his talisman.

"Tonight . . ." she paused as she fought back her emotions and tears, "is our last night together, at least in this life. He has been my earth and my heaven and tonight I am sending him back to his wife and his family. I find peace and solace in the fact that he is alive and whole. My love for him will endure, pure and forever." She paused again and looked into the audience. Eddie was mesmerized and drunk enough that he lost his balance and almost fell off his bar stool.

"For my last song," she continued. "I would like to sing a song about something we all have in common. Here in this room, Americans, Thais, we all have one strong common bond." Then she slowly and beautifully sang *Born Free*.

It tore Eddie up, the loss of Mayberry and the inability to place a title on his surge of nostalgia. The depression was growing deeper and deeper. Everything was so confusing, the horrible things that people were doing to other people and the beauty and good that still persisted among the mayhem.

The room was filled with lost souls like himself.

He and Longbow paid their bar tab and caught a taxi back to the Chaophya. There they said goodnight with one more scotch at the bar, their silence saying it all. They each went their own way. It was as if Eddie had been visited by a ghost in the night. They didn't even know each other's real names, just a radio call sign and a nickname. Yet, they were brothers. That night they both slept under the spell of alcoholic bliss, their thoughts drowned in booze, as they both had done so many times in recent years.

CHAPTER TWENTY-FIVE: MIA

Eddie returned to NKP, again a day early. He just couldn't find any place he wanted to be. He had with him a piece of jewelry that had caught his eye in one of the Bangkok store windows. He had dropped in and he and the owner had a nice friendly chat. Eddie had mentioned how beautiful a particular multi-stone gold bracelet looked in the window. After letting Eddie handle it, he offered it to Eddie for US$15. It featured a large, vivid red ruby and had clusters of small star sapphires, which were mined locally in Thailand. The attached paper tab listed it at $25.00. Due to the huge influx of American military and the stability of the U S dollar, U S currency was gladly accepted in Bangkok.

The jeweler smiled and looked Eddie in the eyes. "This very valuable jewelry; bring many big dollars profit you sell it in America."

Eddie was surprised at the quality of the workmanship and had never seen anything like it during his frequent C-124 layovers in Bangkok. It was alluring and beautiful and seemed to be saying "buy me." He just happened to have a ten on him and he offered it to the storeowner. The storeowner accepted, and the two strangers made a trade.

Back in his room at NKP, Eddie stashed the bracelet in a half empty 38 caliber ammo box he kept in one of his drawers. Then he wandered over to operations to look for a flight the next morning—something that he could jump on as an observer and get back over Laos where he belonged. He visited the toilet and noticed his new maid was among the Thai groupies. He strolled over to the Towhead Inn and climbed onto one of the worn stools at the bar. The bartender, Loat San, was at work early that day and the rest of the bar was empty. Loat San said the guys were all over at the pool.

Eddie had become good friends with Loat San. He was actually a very interesting character. He worked part time in his village as a low paid civil servant and as a bartender for the Towhead Inn starting at five every afternoon. Days, in his village, he was in charge of record keeping, the drinking water chlorinator, maintaining the crude thatched school building, and tax collections. Evenings, with the Towheads, he supplemented his income and more importantly was able to practice his English. He felt that someday he would qualify for a good job with the Thai Government in Bangkok.

Eddie casually mentioned his displeasure with the appearance of his new maid, his and Arnold's distrust, and that he was thinking about options for the problem. Loat San giggled, "Last girl maybe still running, Lieutenant Nuts. Ha ha. You make big story off base."

Eddie couldn't contain his smile. "I think maybe other girls tell big story that not true." It was Loat San's turn to smile. He had never heard Eddie speak in broken Thai-English.

"I know you not bad man," Loat San continued. "Let me think and ask my father for wisdom for you. He very wise man." The subject was dropped as two Nails stopped by for a cold beer. They were in a deep discussion about whether they had seen a tank in a place they referred to as down there at the stream crossing.

Another week went by and nobody had anything stolen. Eddie and Arnold still weren't happy with their tramp going in and out of their room without knocking. But they needed something to pin on her. Nobody wanted to get an honest girl in trouble but this one had something about her that they just didn't like. Arnold had the best reason for not liking her. Dorothy, Arnold's female spook friend from the concrete palace, refused to spend afternoons in their room when Eddie was away flying. Without locks, she didn't want to be interrupted in bed with Arnold; especially by their disgusting excuse for a maid. She half seriously accused the two airmen of hiring a whore.

A few days later, Eddie again ended up in the Towhead Inn alone with Loat San. This time he was looking for a different kind of advice. "Loat San, I have tomorrow off. I would like to go off base and see some of your rice fields, and villages, or maybe a local Buddhist shrine. Can you tell me where would be a good place to visit? I have a camera and I like to take pictures."

"Lieutenant Nuts," Loat San answered with his usual polite manner. "If you wish I would like to show you Nakhon Phanom Town, then my small village. The rain has the water high and we can travel with my boat to my village. You get many picture my people and rice paddy. Also I have answer to you maid problem and we can talk when in the boat."

Eddie was set back at the invitation to see Loat San's village and the way Loat San beamed with pride. Even if he wanted to he couldn't have refused. "That would be nice," Eddie answered.

"If you wish, Lieutenant Nuts, I pick you up at seven tomorrow morning outside main gate, we need to start early in the day and be finished before the afternoon rain." They were well into the wet monsoon season. "Bring your camera and I will show you many things that make good picture." The proposal sounded delightful to Eddie. It would be an excellent opportunity to get away from the base, his doldrums, and enjoy a fresh change of environment.

"I'll be there at seven," Eddie answered. "I pay any money it cost and I pay any food we buy."

* *

The next morning the sky was almost cloudless and the sun was already hot as Eddie walked the five blocks to the main gate. It was hard to imagine how in the afternoon, the monsoon skies would build and the rain would be so thick it would almost suffocate the uninitiated. In his small backpack he had plastic bags for his camera and film, in case they didn't get back in time. His light weight clothing and rubber tire sandals could take the rain and he could shower and change once he was back at Towhead Towers.

At the gate, Loat San was waiting with his personal tuk tuk, just like those that crowded the streets in Bangkok. The front end of the three wheeled affairs looked just like the front end of a motorcycle. The driver straddled the two cycle motorcycle engine and steered the single front wheel with handle bars. Behind the driver was the passenger cab. The cab sat above an axel and between two wheels which were powered by a bicycle type chain from the engine in the front. It was barely wide enough for two people to sit on its bench type seat. The tiny cab had open sides and a canvas roof that sheltered occupants from the burning sun and heavy rains. Behind the passenger cab extended a cargo bed about three feet long. It was a poor man's utility vehicle and gave Loat San a boost in social standing with his village peers.

"Very good transportation," Eddie remarked as he climbed in and stowed his back pack under the narrow passenger seat. He kept his camera out and set it for the ASA 32 Ectachrome slide film.

Loat San gave Eddie a big grin as he loaded his weight onto the foot starter pedal and with a lunge snapped it down. It was just like starting an older motorcycle in the States. Vroom pop pop pop pop duddle duddle pop pop, and they were off. The noisy three wheeled rig bounced and shook on the rough paved road but the breeze felt great. Loat San swerved back and forth to miss the numerous potholes full of water from the previous day's rain. With the loud noise and Loat San straddling the motorcycle front end, it was almost impossible for the two of them to have any type of conversation.

They passed a delicate old Thai woman who was plodding along the edge of the road. She had a backbreaking load of firewood balanced skillfully on her head. Another was in the stagnant water next to the elevated road. A borrow pit had been formed when dirt was excavated to build up the road surface and the pit was filled with water. She was thigh deep in the stagnant water, picking water plants. Loat San smiled and pointed to her as they went by. Eddie thought, "Salad and diarrhea for supper."

Loat San drove, pop popped their way into Nakhon Phanom and went straight to the docks on the wide Mekong River. The river was high but these people lived with high water six months out of every year and were used to it. After Loat San haggled with a boat owner in Thai, Eddie gave Loat San the requested Baht fee, the equivalent of one dollar. They climbed into a water craft called a Long Tailed Boat. Eddie had seen many of them ripping along in the larger Bangkok klongs but it was the first time he had ever ridden in one of them. The open boat was long and narrow, made from hard jungle wood, and had a high flare in the front to cut through waves and deflect water spray. In the rear of the boat a long metal pipe extended horizontally about fourteen feet over the water. A propeller was attached to the far end. The front end of the pipe extended several feet into the boat and a recycled Chevrolet V-8 engine was attached. The long (tail) end with the propeller and the short end with the engine were balanced on a swivel mount. Inside the pipe was a solid shaft that connected the engine to the propeller.

With the engine running the standing driver could tilt the tail with the spinning propeller into the water for propulsion and lift the propeller out of the water for neutral. With the spinning propeller in the water the driver could swing the tail left or right for turns.

With such a powerful motor the boats were very fast and maneuverable. Eddie was through his first roll of film before they even pushed off from the boat dock. They ran for fifteen minutes up the flat, half mile wide Mekong River, about twenty-five miles per hour. The scenery was great but the ride was so bumpy and unstable that Eddie couldn't get any decent photos. He explained this to Loat San over the loud roar of the un-muffled Chevy V8 engine. Loat San stood up with remarkable balance and hollered something into the standing driver's ear.

As they had chartered the boat for their exclusive use, the driver slowed the running boat and shut down the noisy engine. Then they drifted down river in the slow current. Eddie spent the next forty-five minutes enamored with the river and its eclectic collection of boat traffic and the photogenic display of everyday life along the river banks. The river was indeed the main transportation corridor. Numerous freight and passenger boats were making their way up and down the river. There were also fishermen casting their nets along the river's edges and some were drifting with the current, fishing with hand lines in the deeper water. Eddie was enthralled! The karst on the Laotian side of the river, four to five miles from the rivers eastern bank, shone in the bright sunlight.

They drifted back to their departure dock then rode the tuk tuk to a small Buddhist Wat. Loat San purchased several sticks of incense from an old woman who sat near the entrance to the temple. Then they nodded shallow wais to a young monk in a bright saffron colored robe, sitting at the entrance to the stone shrine. They removed their shoes and entered the facility. Loat San lit the incense and placed the sticks in the holder provided at the base of a large stone statue of Buddha. He then glanced at Eddie and nodded his head okay towards Eddie's camera. Then he knelt into a praying position with his folded hands beneath his chin. The light was steaming down through the openings in the wall and Eddie finished his third roll of film. Loat San's reverent and humble offering, the incense and prayer, was in stark contrast to the same smiling and carefree bartender he knew from the Towhead's bar.

Again they jumped on their tuk tuk and toured the small town that everyone called a city. Eddie had seen part of it during his visits to the bar, his masseur and the tailor. The rest was not dissimilar to any other small Asian villages he had ever visited. They departed west on the road toward the base entrance. Eddie was hoping the day wasn't over and his concern turned to pleasure as they whisked right by the base main gate and continued another mile inland. Loat San pulled up to an overflowing klong and proceeded to chain his tuk tuk to a large tree trunk. He then motioned for Eddie to get into a small wooden boat. At first it looked like a flimsy homemade kayak. Eddie examined it and realized it had been skillfully carved and chopped from a single tree trunk. The two of them shoved off, Loat San paddling upstream in the very slow moving klong. The tiny narrow canoe was quite unstable for Eddie but Loat San was quite at home in this common form of transportation. It was like riding a bicycle, it required a little practice. Loat San paddled leisurely and Eddie admired the passing clumps of trees, loaded with flowers and strange fruits, and the open areas where there were rice paddies.

The paddies were filled with water and freshly set rice seedlings poking light green heads out of the water into the blazing hot sunlight. They would grow in the fertile muck and sprout heavy seed heads as the monsoon season drew to a close. The rice would dry and cure after the water in the paddies receded and disappeared. Then the farmers would cut the fruitful rice stalks by hand and thrash them of their rice kernels. The drill was the same as it had been for thousands of years. These were humble people. They had their rice, fish from the klong, and an abundance of fruit from the trees in the jungle. They had their religion and their ancestors to be thankful for and they lived in peace with each other. They were unmindful of the raging wars between various rulers of their lands over the past several thousand years. Their hearts and souls had always remained simple and humble. This was the way of the rural Thai people.

In the distance, Loat San pointed out several tethered elephants. They were used to log trees in the forest during the dry season.

They came to a section where about thirty huts lined the right side of the klong and Loat San cleverly maneuvered their craft to a small, floating wooden dock. It was his village and a half dozen barely clothed Thai children, several of them naked, ran over to see the stranger in Loat San's boat. They were covered with mud and had been playing along the edge of the canal. During the rainy season the Thai would laugh and call their children little ducks.

The children looked happy and healthy. They eagerly assisted the clumsy white man with a camera onto their dock. They were more of a hindrance than a help but Eddie appreciated their enthusiasm and their welcome. He handed his backpack to one of the boys and the boy shone with pride as he was chosen to carry the white man's bag. There would be no problem with theft from these children. Eddie was with their village administrator. They were all schooled in Buddhism and the village was so small that no one could steal something and possibly get away with it. Several adults also came out to see what was going on and Eddie felt at home and welcome among the smiling strangers.

They strolled along the klong bank and its row of tropical thatched-roof bamboo homes. The bank was elevated high enough that the monsoonal flooding rarely covered the village's raised grounds. Each home was built on poles driven into the klong's widened bank so their pigs, chickens, dogs, and ducks could find shelter under the home's elevated wood and bamboo floors. The outside deck of each home extended several feet over the klong and the support poles provided a place for tying their family's collection of homemade canoes and boats. The klong also served as a place to dispose of garbage and a hole in the floor, over the klong, was their toilet. The slow moving klong was also a transportation corridor and a source of fresh fish. Everyone appeared healthy and happy with the situation. The school was a raised bamboo platform, also mounted on poles, about three feet above the mud and rainwater. It had open sides and a thatched roof. The schoolteacher, a single person that taught all grades, was provided by the Thai government. A surprisingly high percentage of the Thai citizens were fluent in reading, writing, and basic arithmetic.

Villagers often fished with nets for smaller fish, but used line and baited hooks for the larger bottom dwelling fish. The bottom fish looked like some sort of catfish, but were very aggressive. Loat San and Eddie stopped at a flimsy, small kiosk—the village store. They purchased some pre-cooked cold rice, sliced fresh fruit, and two green and one ripe coconuts. They ate the rice and fruit with their fingers and it all tasted wonderful. Loat San borrowed a knife from the vender and with the pointed tip he drilled holes in the end of each cocoanut. The green coconuts contained clear water and the ripe coconut contained white thick milky fluid. They drank the clear watery fluid from the green nuts and saved the white milk from the ripe nut for desert. After drinking the white milk, they broke open the empty ripe coconut and with Eddie's pocket knife dug out several handfuls of fresh coconut meat. The fresh meat was sweet and delicious.

Loat San explained how the village water chlorinator worked and how the villagers utilized several water sources. "My people do not like the taste of the chlorinated water from the government water chlorinator and filter. They use it only for cooking. For drinking we prefer coconut water. The coconut water is refreshing. We have learned not to drink the dark water from the canals which we use just for bathing."

Eddie had Loat San take his picture while he was posing in the middle of a throng of children. Loat San pointed out the village idiot that everyone cared for and treated as if a pet dog. He did, however, look better fed than the mob of dogs that followed them around. Loat San's hut was next to the village's official boat dock, where Loat San's canoe was tied up. They finished their village tour back at his hut. They stepped up the wooden stairs to his open doorway and Loat San motioned for Eddie to enter first. Eddie removed his sandals and stooped a little to enter the low doorway.

Loat San's hut was very clean inside and it had a steep thatched overhanging roof. Open gaps under the roof at the top of the wicker woven walls offered wonderful ventilation and some light. The furniture was sparse and well woven mats covered the bamboo floor. Cracks in the bamboo floor offered plentiful drainage. A six foot bamboo wall separated the rear one third of the hut from where Eddie was standing. There was a doorway in the center of the wall, with colorful hanging beads serving as a door.

A young Thai girl slipped through the hanging beads and slowly approached Eddie. As his eyes adjusted to the dimmer light, Eddie found himself face to face with an angel from heaven. In the dim light he first was shocked as he thought he was standing face to face with the Lady. She was a beautiful Thai woman, eighteen, twenty, or even twenty-two years of age. She was slender, as were most Thai women. She stood straight with her arms at her sides, as if an animal on display at a country fair.

From behind, Eddie heard Loat San's voice as if from a remote source, "Lieutenant Nuts, you please meet my sister Mia."

Mia and Eddie stood staring at each other as if they had each just seen an alien. Eddie realized she couldn't be the Lady as her face had none of the sexually suggestive expressions that were displayed by the painting of the Lady. The young woman in front of him was too pure. She projected innocence and the grace of a saint. He, in contrast, was sweating and hatless in his loose shirt and cutoff Levis. She was wearing a lightweight, short sleeved white blouse and a colorful, flowered, red sarong that was wrapped around her slender waist and hung down to her bare ankles. She was barefoot. Her shining long black hair was pulled around in the back and tied with a silk wrap. She was beautiful, tall for a Thai, and even in the dimly lit hut her flawless brown skin seemed to glow. Her eyes were round with only a slight hint of oriental. Their eyes were locked onto each other and Eddie's mouth was slightly ajar. He was overwhelmed with her poise.

"Sa wat dee," she murmured as she bent slightly at the waist and palmed her hands in a respectful wai.

"Sa wat dee," Eddie responded instinctively. He also bent slightly at his waist and placed his palmed hands high on his chest and returned the wai to the princess before him. "Do you speak English?"

"Yes," she then focused her eyes at Eddie's feet in a typical Buddhist humbleness. "I learned to speak English when I was a child. I please to meet you Lieutenant Nuts." She broke her pious expression with a sly smile.

"My sister is answer to your problem with your maid," Loat San offered and broke both their trances. "Our father say man of your place need private maid, one he can trust and one of good character. You and Lieutenant Henry Arnold can hire my sister for your maid and cost you only twenty-five dollar each month. That be only twelve dollar fifty cents each month for each you and you both very rich and can pay such a small money to my sister. She very clean and work very hard and she knock on your door every time she want come in." Mia stood in silence before Eddie and her eyes never moved from his feet as she let her brother plead her case. This had obviously been a set up. None of the other village women wore such elegant clothing, and she stood scrubbed and groomed, ready for inspection and evaluation.

"I don't know if I'm allowed to have a private maid on the base. She would need to be approved by the Thai Base Commander's office and I don't know if that's possible?" Eddie said as he turned to Loat San and away from Mia, who was just too good to be true. "I just don't know. She is so beautiful. Does she want to do the work of a maid?"

Loat San was undeterred and continued his sales pitch, "My father know some Americans on the base. He ask them they owe him a favor. They said to make a favor to him they could have all okay for she to work for you, no problem. They know my father long time."

Eddie turned back to Mia and felt humbled by her presence. "Do you want to work as my maid? I think you can get a better job somewhere than a maid."

282

"Please, Sir. I wish to work as you maid. I work sew clothing in town and make very small money and my boss man treat me very bad. Loat San said you treat me good so I no have to sew for bad man no more. Please, Sir. My father very wise man and he know what is best for all us. I have name of American at base you talk to." She handed Eddie a slip of paper. "This man tell you I work as you maid is okay."

Eddie took the paper and needed time to collect his thoughts. He needed to talk this over with Arnold. Arnold always had the answer for complex social situations. "And who was this American on the base?" Eddie pondered.

"Where does your father live? Can I go talk to him? I need to know about this man," Eddie pleaded.

"He live in house maybe half hour more in boat but we need go back air base now," Loat San explained. "Soon maybe rains come and we get very wet. We go to base now and I go to work at Too Head Inn. You go see man on paper."

Eddie turned back to Mia. He wasn't ready to part company with her but Loat San sounded in a hurry. "I wish to see you again," he heard himself saying and he and Mia exchanged parting wais. The rain was already pattering on the roof and it was going to be a wet trip back to his room.

* * * * * * * * * * * * * * * * * * * *

Arnold thought the idea of hiring Mia for their maid was an outstanding idea, as did his lieutenant girlfriend. Their sex life had suffered enough and they were anxious to get back into a regular routine. Other than working and sunbathing, there was really nothing else to keep them busy and a maid that would knock on the door would be priceless. The next afternoon, after Eddie returned from a morning mission along the trail, he called the man whose phone number was on the slip of paper. The guy seemed a little reluctant to say anything over the phone but instead arranged a meeting with Eddie behind the base movie screen at nine that evening. Eddie had dinner with Arnold and Dorothy at the officers club that night and the three of them were buzzing with excitement. Arnold and Dorothy about the possible repossession of their sex lair and Eddie excited about Mia.

Eddie showed up at the rendezvous spot fifteen minutes early, full of curiosity about the man with few words. The name on the slip of paper included no military rank, just Jack Blackwell and a base phone number. Eddie paced around hoping it wouldn't start raining again when out of the dark approached an older man in his fifties. He was dressed in civilian clothes. He was wearing long pants and a long sleeved, light weight, white shirt. This told Eddie that the man spent his days indoors where there were powerful air conditioners.

"You Eddie?" was all he said as he approached.

"Yessir. I'm Lieutenant Werner. Like I said over the telephone, I was given your name in relation to the possibility of hiring a private maid. Are you associated with base security or the Thai Commander's office?"

"Neither, I'm a civilian employee at Task Force Alpha and I'm an old friend of Mao, Mia's father. He asked me to make arrangements to get her a work authorization on base. I understand that she will be working as a private maid for you and your room-mate?" the mystery man asked.

"Yessir! Myself and my room-mate, Arnold Henry. We would continue to pay the eight dollars and twenty-five cents each month into the managed maid fund for officers and we would pay our private maid with our own money. That way everyone would be happy."

"I understand you are both pilots in the EC-47 program?"

"Yessir. I'm the detachment flight instructor and Arnold is a new co-pilot."

"You both understand that there is always a necessity to refrain from discussing anything classified around domestic help?" the man named Jack Blackwell queried.

"Yes Sir, everyone in my detachment is very security conscious," Eddie replied as he was getting a little uncomfortable with the interrogation.

"Who in the hell is this guy?" Eddie wondered.

"I know all about Arnold's family, I knew his father back in the States," Jack Blackwell announced. "I understand you grew up on a farm in Colorado?" It was another shock for Eddie.

"Yessir. We raised sugar beets and raised a few cattle on the side. Why are you asking me these things and how do you know Mia's father?"

"I think we're about finished up here," the mystery man concluded without answering either of Eddie's questions. "After getting your detachment commander's approval, which he will give you, hand carry this envelope and the approval to the base address on the envelope. This envelope has the authorization papers to get your new maid employed. The envelope is to remain sealed while in your procession. It's not really a good idea for you or Arnold to reveal anything about this meeting or the authorization papers to anyone. I used the back door, if you know what I mean."

"Yessir. We'll keep a lid on everything."

"Goodnight." He walked off into the night.

Eddie was dumbfounded. Task Force Alpha, this guy had to be some sort of a Spook. What did he have in common with Mia's father? Was he for real or just some guy playing out a spy fantasy? The good thing was that the way seemed clear for him and Arnold to hire Mia. Maybe once hired, she might enlighten them about her father, the father she and Loat San referred to as old and wise.

* *

Eddie was a bit nervous when he visited the detachment commander about hiring Mia. He and the lieutenant colonel had gotten along well but this instance was a little different. There were a lot of questions the colonel could ask him that he wasn't supposed to answer. Some questions he didn't know the answers. The colonel, as commander of the unit, did have a right to some answers. Then there was the matter of why he wanted to hire a private maid in the first place. The details on how he convinced his first maid to disappear weren't exactly something he wanted to discuss with his commander. Eddie was lucky he hadn't gotten in trouble over the gun and his maid incident; the story had circulated all over the base and was well known. Some of the stories had Eddie pointing his loaded gun at her and cocking it while it was stuck in her face.

He knocked on the colonel's door and waited about five long seconds before he heard the colonel respond, "Door's open. Come on in."

Eddie entered and snapped the colonel a crisp salute. Staff officers always liked crisp salutes and the sensitivity of his visit seemed to warrant a very crisp salute.

"What can I do for you today, Eddie?" The colonel acted as if he hadn't just received a call from the base commander. The truth was the colonel was just as curious as Eddie. The base commander, in turn, had received his call from a civilian he knew at Udorn Air Base, the nesting grounds for the CIA. The base commander also was curious, but being military men, both he and the Towhead commander respected their instructions to limit their questions and interference.

"Sir," Eddie had rehearsed his presentation carefully. "Our Towhead Inn bartender, Loat San, has a sister and he is trying to get her a job here on base. He's approached me to see if Lieutenant Henry and I would be interested in hiring her as a private maid to keep our room and do our laundry. We both have trust issues with our current maid and this private maid thing sounds like a solution to our concerns. It would not have an effect on the current maid staffing for our building and our current maid could remain on the maid staff at the Towhead Towers. Lt. Arnold and I would continue paying our eight dollars and twenty-five cents per month into the shared maid fund. I have been given assurance that the base regulations would not prohibit such an arrangement."

Eddie told the colonel nothing he didn't already know. They were both playing out the necessary scenario. "Have you met this girl?" the detachment commander asked curiously.

"Yes, briefly yesterday," Eddie volunteered. "I was off base sightseeing. It was my no fly day and Loat San took me on a tour of his village. His sister was at his house and he introduced us. She speaks pretty good English and was very clean, dressed well, and had excellent manners. I'd have to say she appeared to be many steps above the maids we currently have. Loat San assures me she is extremely honest and reliable and I believe him."

The colonel couldn't contain his curiosity any longer, despite instructions to not interfere with the hiring process. "Tell me, lieutenant, how is it that you can get a security check and a base work authorization for a private maid without my knowledge. Aren't you jumping the chain of command here?"

It was what Eddie didn't want to hear. "Sir, it's just as much a mystery to me as it is to you. Loat San approached me about her yesterday and apparently her father knows someone here on the base because all the arrangements had already been made. I was given an envelope last night with all the paperwork in it—at least I think so cause I was instructed not to open the envelope but deliver it to the office of the Thai Base Commander. After I got your approval. There's a space on the envelope for you to sign your approval. I was told not to ask questions. I suspect somebody important is involved with this girl's family."

"Well, if it makes you feel any better I was told about the same thing over the phone," the lieutenant colonel admitted. "This thing is coming down from way over our heads. So I guess let's just go with the flow and you and Arnold be damn sure not to leak anything classified around her in case this is some sort of a security test, or hell, I don't know what.

"I noticed you have your papers submitted to separate and return to civilian life when you return state side and your obligation is fulfilled." The colonel paused for a moment, and then continued, "Watch your behind and in particular Major Collins. He's got a hard on for you. It's something about you landing on the taxiway with him on board."

"Colonel, I thought that was a long gone issue. Everyone agreed we had no choice. The only options available were to either land on the taxiway or jump out. I'm sure that no one wanted us to jump out and destroy a valuable aircraft."

"I agree with you, lieutenant. I don't know what went on in that cockpit and it happened before I arrived . . . so I really don't care. I just wanna serve out my own tour and go home unscratched. All I know is that something went on in that cockpit and it really pissed him off and he's out to get you." Eddie nodded a thank you for the heads up.

The colonel signed the designated space on the mystery envelope, looked Eddie in the eyes, and handed the envelope to him. "That will be all."

Eddie gave another crisp salute, the second crisp salute he had made in over a year. He breathed a sigh of relief as he exited the detachment commander's door. He delivered the letter to the Thai Commander's secretary.

* * * * * * * * * * * * * * * * * * * *

Eddie flew the early flight the next morning and after debrief at intelligence, he returned to his room and threw down a cold beer from his refrigerator. Then he stripped down to a towel around his waist and took a long cool shower, with four maids as silent witnesses. When he returned to his room, planning on another cold beer and listening to a little Jimi Hendrix, he was greeted with a surprise. Mia was sitting on his sofa, her hands folded in her lap and her head in a bow.

"Whoa!" Eddie exploded from surprise. Mia reacted like she had just betrayed the King and stood up at attention.

"I'm sorry," Eddie explained his outburst. "I just didn't expect you so soon."

"I get base pass this morning," Mia explained. "They have me fill out paper questions and I get pass to come here. Loat San tell me I sit in bar lounge until I see you come home. I wait and you no come, then I knock on door three times before I come in. I hope that okay. I knock very loud on door."

She was as precious as a butterfly and twice as beautiful. How could it not be okay? "No problem," Eddie calmed her. "But I need to get dressed and we will talk some more. Maybe you go sit in lounge some more and I'll come talk to you when I get dressed."

Mia gave Eddie a graceful wai and exited the room. As she left, he stood enamored by how gracefully she walked and how well she filled out the back of her plain black work sarong.

He threw his towel on his bed, slipped into a shirt, shorts, cutoff Levi's and sandals. He then hustled over to the Towhead Inn. He grabbed two Cokes from behind the bar, opened them, threw thirty cents in the bowl and joined Mia in the lounge.

She seemed pleased at the Coke and he curled up on the sofa next to her chair. He enjoyed a long draw of his Coke; it gave him an opportunity to take another good look at his newest interest. "You can sit on the sofa with me," he offered. "You can sit at the other end and it is much more comfortable than that chair. I won't bite you."

"Thank you for offer but I be just fine here," she refused and Eddie noticed her posture was straight and poised. "You like me start work this afternoon? I wear old clothes so if you want me to scrub the floor maybe."

"No need for you to work today," Eddie carefully instructed. "You can go to our bathroom and introduce yourself to the other maids. Come back tomorrow morning and Lieutenant Henry will be here. He's flying today. In the morning you can meet him and he will show you around our room and talk with you about your work. He's a nice man and is anxious to meet you. Today is the fourth day of the month but we will pay you starting on the first day of the month. Can you come about nine in the morning?" Mia smiled widely. When at the tailor shop, she had been required to be at work at seven.

They finished their Cokes in awkward silence. Then Eddie motioned with his hand toward the bathroom, "You go now and talk with the maids in toilet and I see you tomorrow afternoon when I get back from flying."

Mia excused herself with a wai and headed for the bathroom. Eddie headed back to his room for a scotch with no water but rock and roll music. Then maybe a little nap. He barely made it through the scotch when there were several knocks on the door. When he opened the door, there stood Mia. She was crying, with huge tears flowing down her cheeks.

"Excuse me, Lieutenant Nuts, but I need talk with you."

"You call me Eddie and you please come in. Please tell me what is wrong?"

She sobbed a few more times then poured out her troubles. "Other maids not like me! They call me bad names and say I cannot work their job. What is slut and what is number ten? They call me number ten slut and say I work as your whore. Please, Lieutenant Eddie, I need your job, I not whore and I very honest." She broke down and sobbed again. Eddie wasn't used to women crying and it wrenched inside him. "I want to learn better English so you please tell me what number ten and what is slut?"

Eddie gave her the sofa and got her to sit comfortably. He paced the room with anger. "Slut is very dirty whore girl and number ten is worst a person can be. Number one is the best. You are not a slut and not a whore and I think you are number one person. You sit here. I go talk to the other maids."

He stormed out of his room and down the walkway to the bathroom. The maids were all sitting just where he had left them after his shower. When they saw him and how angry he looked, they all froze and sat stoically on the concrete floor.

"You all know who I am," he opened with a cruel tone as he smiled inside. Being a German, he was soo good at this. His father had taught him well. "I am Lieutenant Nuts and I just hired a private maid for Lieutenant Arnold and me. I think you all know how bad I can get when I get mad." They all stared at his feet and nodded their heads yes.

"You will be nice to her and answer her questions when she asks. You show her how to use the washing machines and you share them with her. None of you will lose your job because I hired my own maid, you just will not have to do my room and laundry any more—do you understand?" Most spoke enough English that they could understand Eddie and the rest knew from the tone of his voice that whatever he said, their answer would be yes. They all nodded their heads up and down in unison. "Her name is Mia and she is number one person. She is not to be called a slut or whore and you will treat her good. Do you understand?" They all nodded their heads yes in unison again while staring at Eddie's feet. He wanted to go down the row and look each one of them in the eye, American style, but they refused to look up, Thai style.

"If any of you not be nice to Mia, I will be very mad and you will be in danger for your job. Do you understand?" They all nodded their heads yes, again in unison. So Eddie decided to ham it up a little, "If you

286

understand raise your hands." They all raised both their hands and he felt he was finally getting some military discipline accomplished. "You can now put your hands down." They put their hands down. "If you all be nice to Mia I will not get mad and we will all be happy family. Do you understand?" They all raised both hands and kept their stare at his feet. "Who can say what kind of family we be if you be nice to Mia?"

There was silence for a few seconds. Then one lonely, wavering voice said, "Happy family."

"Good," he addressed the frightened one that spoke. "You tell all the other maids they can put their hands down now and we can all be happy family." She nodded her head yes and followed Eddie's feet with her eyes as he stormed out of the bathroom.

It took several minutes before the new second lieutenant, who had only arrived and signed into the detachment that day, had the nerve to slip out of the shower. He wrapped a towel around his naked torso and scurried down the walkway to his room. He wondered what he had gotten himself into. Taking a shower in front of a gaggle of young Thai girls had been a traumatic experience for the young Catholic lad. But the dressing down of the maids had put the fear of God in him. Who was this Lieutenant Nuts? The maids didn't giggle at him as they were busy speaking in Thai to each other.

CHAPTER TWENTY-SIX: CHAOPHAKHAO

Things were picking up for Eddie. He suspected it had something to do with his new maid but he was afraid to admit it to himself, out of fear of breaking the good karma. He no longer had his serious sessions of depression. He and Mia often sat for hours on the walkway outside Eddie's room, and sometimes on the hooch patio, just talking. Sometimes not talking but just being together. She too was enamored with her new life and new friend but never dared to express her feelings, not even to her brother or her father.

Arnold thought the idea of Eddie starting an export company out of Singapore was basically good. He did have reservations about warehousing in Singapore. He suggested that maybe they could have a procurement, processing, and shipping office in Singapore. But they should have the main warehouse and sales office somewhere centrally in the States, where it was a lot closer to their customers and the American distribution systems. Arnold's family had contacts in Singapore and he felt he could arrange for one of them to mentor Eddie though the process of establishing the business. He was very leery, however, of Longbow and gave Eddie a lecture on the bad choice of business associates. Eddie also had reservations and looked forward to his next meeting. Was the guy for real? In the meantime the idea about wholesaling Asian merchandise in America gave Eddie a lot to fantasize about. He always liked choices and he now had the choice between flying commercially, with its many different variants, or starting a business in Singapore.

Despite the uptick his new maid gave to Eddie's disposition, the flying droned on like a continuous tape. Every day his small detachment dispatched an average of four EC-47s to fly low, slow, unarmed, without fighter escorts, over enemy territory. Eddie was worried. The Nails commonly came back with holes, sometimes didn't come back at all. The same was true with the A-1s. The 37mm gun outside their operations building stood as an ominous warning that the Towheads weren't immune. Eddie flew more than anyone else in the unit and he felt he was more due than anyone else. He had several more brushes with the North Vietnamese 37mm guns; once more he received a light peppering of flack from a close burst, but no golden BB. No one on his crew was ever hit by shrapnel. Yet, some strange motivation required him to continue riding along with the weaker pilots whenever he wasn't instructing or flying his own missions. Sooner or later he was going to have to back off and not fly so much. His new maid and their long conversations were having a profound effect on him.

* *

Eddie had the morning patrol over the Plain of Jars and he was in an exceptionally good mood. His operators and navigator were all individuals he had flown and worked with before and they all got along well. Although the monsoon season was upon them, the early morning flight lifted off at sunrise and as they crossed the karst foothills they were enamored with the low, feathery mist clinging to the karst pinnacles and the limestone mazes. Over the PDJ, at 12,000 feet, they had a layer of broken clouds 1000 feet below them. Later in the day it would build and the afternoon guys would have a hard time finding dop set points to update their computer's position. For the last week their afternoon crews had been unable to find breaks in the clouds and had to settle for copying information. The transmitter locations they processed were outside the required circle of accuracy. On this morning, channel 98, the Alternate, was still open and free of clouds.

Eddie had a relatively new co-pilot who hadn't quite gotten out of his gee whiz phase. He was packing a new set of binoculars that he recently purchased at the BX. The enemy owned the floor of the PDJ and his new co-pilot, Manuel Garcia, really wanted to see members of the North Vietnamese Army with his own eyes. Eddie cut him some slack. He was just a new guy and bubbling with excitement. He did have a good attitude. As Eddie made a right turn to get a better cut on a transmitter for the navigator, Manuel had his window tilted towards the ground. Through a hole in the clouds, with his binoculars, he saw an exposed section of flat road. It was not much better than an improved dirt trail but it was as good as roads got at that remote job site.

"Whoa, I think I see something—oops—lost him in the clouds," Manuel hollered as he searched with his binoculars.

"This thing won't whoa like your horse back home in Texas," Eddie remarked, then smiled at him.

"No shit! Nav, mark the coordinate for this spot," Manuel hollered over the operator's interphone. "I saw a truck that was parked right out on the road. It was right next to a clump of trees. It was pulling something that looked like a big gun on wheels."

He looked over at Eddie and asked, "Is there some way we can go down under the clouds and get a better look?"

"We're not supposed to get involved with anything other than our mission. They don't want us to draw attention to ourselves," Eddie reminded the excited Texan.

"You sure we couldn't just drop down under the deck of clouds for a quick look?" Manuel suggested. "Just for a few seconds."

"Could be a trap," Eddie resisted. "They could be waiting for us to come down lower for a better look and there could be thirty-seven millimeters waiting for us in the trees. Best leave that stuff for the experts like the Nails and Ravens."

Manual lowered his head in disappointment but he knew that Eddie was right. At everyone's initial Nakhon Phanom briefing they made it clear to every new EC-47 crewmember that their mission was to remain sterilized and uninvolved with other unit's flying activities. They couldn't take a chance on giving away their mystique of anonymity. But Manual wasn't ready to give up and he noted their position with reference to the radial and DME distance from the channel 98 TACAN. When there was a lull in the activity in the back, Eddie gave in to Manual's moping and flew back over the spot with the hole in the clouds. Eddie rolled over and gave Manual another look and Manual squealed with delight.

"Here, you take the binoculars," Manual handed the binoculars to Eddie. "And look for yourself. I got the airplane."

"You got the airplane," Eddie played along and adjusted the binoculars to fit his eyes. Manual rolled back around in a left turn and Eddie peered down through the hole. Sure enough, there sat a truck right out in the open, covered by a tarp in the back and towing what really did look like a 37mm gun. Without the binoculars they would have never spotted it. The truck was motionless and the hood appeared to be open.

"It still could be a set up," Eddie explained over both interphones as he noticed all the operators in the rear were looking out their windows instead of working. "And there's nothing we can do about it. The gomers own that real estate and we can't compromise our mission."

Manual wouldn't give it up. "We can call Cricket, the airborne command center down south and give them the coordinates. Cricket could send a forward air controller over to check it out. I bet there's already a Raven flying around down there, maybe somewhere close."

"We're not supposed to do anything to compromise our sterilization," Eddie repeated. "What do you think, Nav?"

A voice from the back end popped up. "This is Sergeant Cooper in the back end. I'm the senior enlisted here. We been listening in on you guys. If you broadcast anything, unscrambled, over your UHF communications radios, you could compromise us in ways that you pilots aren't even aware of. All the ROs back here are in agreement that we need to send the location of that truck to someone and that's exactly what we just did. Your cockpit radios aren't secure and anybody can listen in on your transmission. Our radio back here is secure because we use a scrambler and we just called Cricket and gave them the info. Our scrambled transmission sounds like gibberish to the gomers down there—if they're listening. It's Cricket's call if they wanna do anything about the truck down there. You guys need to stay off your radios and let us do our job back here."

It was a good lesson for the new co-pilot and re-enforcement for Eddie. Everyone settled down and in the back the operators returned to work. Manual had a smug smile on his face as they rolled in on a turn to get a bearing cut on an active transmitter.

There was just enough wind aloft so the cloud deck below continued to shift and holes opened and closed randomly. Eddie liked it when they couldn't see the ground that well. It was assurance that some trigger happy gunner wouldn't waste a clip full of ammo on their classic and ancient bird. The 37mm and 57mm guns were manually sighted and without radar they couldn't see through the clouds. He still occasionally thought of the 85s that the A-1 pilot spoke of. The 85s could see through clouds with their radar.

After about thirty minutes another operator, a different voice than before, announced over the number two (operators') interphone, "You guys aren't gonna believe this, but I tapped into a frequency that's used by the Ravens and there's one down there somewhere, his call sign is Outlaw. He just briefed a pair of fighters about a stalled truck on the road next to a clump of trees. I think that's our guy."

"They were discussing the cloud cover and the F-4s agreed there was enough room under the cloud deck to make a modified bomb run on the target." After a few minutes, the radio operator continued his play by play briefing, "Outlaw called the F-4 and told him the smoke is half way between the truck and the trees—the lead bomber is on his way in."

After a minute he updated the Towhead crew, "The Raven called it a miss, ten yards to the north, and number two just called that he was off the perch. Outlaw also reported that the two soldiers working under the hood of the truck took off running and hid in the grove of trees."

Two more minutes and the Raven called the second bomb ten yards long. So it went for three more passes for each F-4 fighter, it was close but no bananas. Twice Outlaw credited them with throwing a "little dirt" on the truck.

"Those two soldiers would have been safer if they hid under the truck," Manual remarked, using his best Mexican dialect. Everyone laughed with him. Eddie had to agree with him.

The F-4s were out of bombs and low on fuel so they departed the area. They informed the Raven that their low bombing angle made it more difficult to bomb accurately. The Raven, as reported by the linguist, called Cricket and requested more "air." Cricket reported that he didn't have any more fast movers available but he had a two ship of Chaophakhao.

Chaophakhao pilots were Hmong tribesmen from the hills surrounding the PDJ. They were hand-picked by General Vang Pao for their brightness and trained as pilots, although most couldn't read or write. They were trained to fly by American Air Force instructors under a program called Operation Waterpump. The instructors utilized various colored markings drawn on the aircraft's gauges to train their indigenous students. They flew small propeller type training aircraft that American government had given to the Laotian government. The T-28Ds were modified to carry several thousand pounds of bombs and had a flush mounted fifty caliber machine gun in each wing. They were slow but highly maneuverable. They were ideal for operating in the tight restricted area under the cloud decks that existed that day over the PDJ. Outlaw was pleased that the Chaophakhao were available and requested Cricket to send them over.

While the crew of Towhead Four One waited for the Chaophakhao to show up, Manual had been frantically switching through the frequencies on their number two radio. After ten minutes of silence the linguist reported that the Chaophakhao Black, flight of two, was checking in with the Raven. At the same time Manual hollered to Eddie across the noisy cockpit, "I got em! I got the Raven's frequency on our number two radio and we can listen in directly." Eddie knew all along the operators in the back had the Raven's frequency but they weren't allowed to give it to the pilots.

Eddie smirked in amazement and switched over to monitor number two radio.

The Raven had just verified with Chaophakhao Black lead, number one, that the T-28s each had two 250 pound bombs on board, two hours' worth of fuel, and that Chaophakhao number two aircraft in the formation didn't speak English.

"You have truck to bomb—it north of tree group. I put new smoke and truck is between tree group and smoke," the Raven spoke simple English to communicate effectively with his Laotian allies. Eddie and Manual were tickled they could listen in directly to their verbal exchange.

"Tally Ho," Chaophakhao lead responded. He sounded funny using an English expression with a Hmong accent. "I have target, where you want bomb?" he boasted.

The smart assed young Raven pilot played along with the Laotian, "You put bomb in window of truck, put in driver's side."

"Roger, Outlaw. Today my wingman time to bomb, he go down now. I stay up and look for gun shots from bad guys."

Shortly after the two aircraft spoke, Towhead Four One passed over the enlarging hole in the clouds and Eddie rolled over to allow Manual to look down with his binoculars. "Holy shit!" Manual hollered. "I just saw that truck explode and the gun went ass over tea kettle through the air . . . wow, there's secondary explosions all over the place. He got it!" At the same time a cheer went up in the rear of Towhead Four One.

"Nice work, you tell number two he good pilot. Perfect bomb on target," Outlaw expressed his pleasure over the radio. "I give you one truck, one gun, credit on report."

"Oh no, not perfect," Chaophakhao lead corrected the Raven forward air controller. "He got bomb in wrong window."

Eddie wondered what the difference in cost was between operating the two F-4s and their bombs and the two surplus trainer aircraft and the one small, very accurate bomb they dropped. He had heard that the Laotian pilots were paid the equivalent of US$28.00 per month plus several dollars family allowance. They were indeed a bargain. What else Eddie didn't know was that an official air force study had just been completed, with extreme bias in favor of an all jet air force. The report's conclusion was that propeller driven aircraft had only limited value in warfare and another squadron of F-4 jets should be sent to Thailand for operations in Laos.

The story about "their truck" was all over NKP within two days. The Nails and the A-1 drivers wondered what the big deal was. They experienced multiple events far more exciting almost every time they flew. The CH-53 pilots referred to the Towheads as rookies and the Candlesticks couldn't comment publicly.

CHAPTER TWENTY-SEVEN: THAI FLAVOR

As Eddie and Mia grew more relaxed around each other, they spent more and more time together just sitting and talking. They sometimes took long leisurely walks around the base. It gave Eddie something to look forward to every morning when he woke up. He only flew training missions and his own schedule, nothing more. He had been working with one of the brighter young lieutenants and had checked him out as the detachment's junior flight instructor. There were no new guys with radial aircraft engine experience. The young lieutenant was slated to be the detachment's only instructor pilot when Eddie rotated back to the States. They spent numerous evenings in a remote corner of the officers club, discussing Eddie's concerns for crew safety, responsibilities, and instructional techniques. Everything was falling into place for Eddie and his life was good again.

Mia had a thousand questions about America and Eddie had a secret desire to take her back with him and show it to her first hand. Eddie had a thousand questions about Mia's life and the Thai people. He still wondered if she was related to the Lady. She was very restrictive about herself and her life, but spoke openly about the Thai people, their culture and religion. But Eddie couldn't help but wonder. She never asked him about his religion, or if he was even religious at all. She always seemed pleased whenever he asked her about the Buddhists that surrounded his American military air base. He simply assumed she was a Buddhist and they often sat for hours discussing their ideas about people and why they were the way they were.

She showed up promptly at nine every weekday morning, although her entire day's routine required less than a couple of hours work. Every morning she brought fresh flowers. She called them Lantom, and she told Eddie she had cut them on her way to work. They had a wonderful fragrance and she always wore one of the blossoms in her hair. Eddie suspected she also rubbed the petals on her neck as if a perfume. Later in the day, after the blossom wilted and was disposed of, she still had a very light Lantom scent. It was delightful.

She was a disciplined and humble maid, a quick learner. Whenever either Eddie or Arnold returned from a flight, she seemed to always have a cold beer waiting for them as they walked through the door to their room. Their room was always spotless and everything in its place. She was the perfect hostess. If any visitors to their room didn't drink scotch or beer, she would shuttle back and forth to the bar and supply them with the drinks of their choice. Whenever Eddie joined his friends on the Towhead Inn patio, to watch the afternoon air show, she would join the group but sit back out of the way. It was as if she was Eddie's silent watchdog. She joined him whenever he was sunbathing on the patio, but she always stayed in the shade.

She read everything she could get her hands on, written in Thai or English. The English books she would laboriously struggle through, frequently asking Eddie or Arnold the meaning of a new word. She was having trouble with her apostrophes. She understood how they were used to show possessive but was having trouble understanding how to join two words together, like in haven't. Arnold was quite tolerant of her as he had an appreciation for anyone wanting to learn. She didn't, however, like the cheap thirty-five cent paperback novels that many of the guys read. Naturally humble, courteous, and interested in others, what a rare person she was.

Eddie's only reservation was a latent fear she might be some sort of spy or CIA plant, to see if the Towheads had loose tongues around others.

Mia gradually stayed later each day and finally Eddie told her she could stay evenings in his room, then go home with Loat San when he closed the bar. But whenever Arnold was in his room and especially when he had "his visitor," she needed to wait for Loat San in the lounge.

* * * * * * * * * * * * * * * * * * * *

Eddie flew the morning tour of the trail and was back in time for a couple of hours of sunbathing. Later in the afternoon rain would drive everyone inside. As usual Mia followed him to the patio and as he stretched out on his towel in the sun, she made herself comfortable in the shade. They were alone. After a half hour went by she timidly giggled at Eddie.

"What's so funny?" he asked, not moving in the hot tropical sun. Nakhon Phanom was the world's best place for an outdoor sweat bath. "You no like my white skin? I'm trying to make it brown."

"No," she giggled again. "You have hair on your body like a ling."

"What's a ling? I've heard that word before," Eddie asked.

"I don't know English word." She shrugged her head then tried, "Small hairy tree man."

"Monkey?" Eddie asked.

"Yes, that's the word, monkey. I think I call you monkey man." Then she giggled again. "I hope you not mind if Mia make joke."

"I don't mind, it's okay if you make a joke. We're friends and friends are okay to make jokes," Eddie reassured her.

"You not mind if I touch you?" Mia asked timidly.

Eddie opened his eyes and saw she was serious. "We're friends, it's okay to touch me. Why you want to touch me?"

Mia moved over next to him in the bright sun and timidly ran her hands through the hair on his chest. "You have very soft hair, not like water buffalo."

Eddie chuckled, what a pleasant person she was. "I hope I not smell like buffalo," he replied and they laughed together. "Don't Thai men have hair on their bodies?"

"Not all over like monkey," Mia teased. "They have hair on their heads and . . ." she hesitated, "you know, a little bit on one other place." They both giggled again. Befriending Mia was a lot like taming a wild animal. They were from separate worlds and he had to approach her slowly in order to gain her confidence and to convince her that he was safe and deserving of her trust.

"I guess I still have a lot to learn," Eddie remarked without really thinking about what he was saying.

"You very rich and very smart man. It good that you know you have lot to learn."

Eddie was surprised and curious at her bluntness. "You tell me what I need to learn so I can be wise."

"Maybe you learn some little bit already," Mia was serious and she looked off into the distance as she spoke. "Most Americans very busy always. Always in hurry for time to go by. They like maybe always anxious." She smiled. "I just learned that word anxious, did I use it okay?"

They both smiled, his eyes met her's and he nodded his head yes.

Mia continued with her lesson, "Time should be you friend. Buddha say, 'Everything will happen with time.' Americans hard to understand that. They want everything now and they think they know everything. My people no find discomfort in what we do not know. Maybe Americans have too much money and feel like they need to spend it all before they die." She stopped herself and gently placed her hand on Eddie's ankle. "Maybe not you—I saw you talking to Harold the lizard last week. That good thing." She smiled, "I think someday you be wise man like my new father."

"Maybe someday," Eddie replied. "I like listening to you talk. Tell me more."

"My father say wise men have humility and compassion. It is this wisdom and humility that I not see in many Americans. We learn from our elders. We listen to the wisdom of Buddha and talk to the spirits of our land, we okay with our lives." She hesitated and took a short breath.

"I have read the wisdom of Buddha and I agree with you," Eddie lied a little bit. He only read two books and really didn't have a solid grasp of the subject. But it sounded good. He would have to visit the library and read more of Buddha's teachings.

Within weeks they were going for long walks off base. They went on mornings when Eddie was not scheduled to fly and always tried to be back before noon and the afternoon rains. Mia took Eddie through backwoods trails to other villages and explained to him how the villagers grew their rice, sugarcane, tapioca, and harvested cashew nuts in the forest. One time they just sat in Mia's canoe and drifted. The monsoon-filled klong moved about a kilometer per hour. They decided they would wait until the monsoon was over before they would spend a day together drifting down to the Mekong. Neither one of them spoke of the fact that when the monsoons ended, it would be time for Eddie to go back to the States.

He tingled with excitement and awe every time he looked at her. He loved to watch her walk, the gentle way she folded clothing, and the long hours she spent combing her long black glistening hair. Her trademark was the way she would tie it in the back with a long piece of colorful Thai silk. It was not unlike an American pony tail but not woven and much longer. The flowing silk tie made her look stunning. None of the other Thai women wore their hair that way. None of the other Thai women were as tall, straight, and elegant as she was. There was more than a little envy among the other Towheads of her puppy like devotion to Eddie.

Mia often spoke of the teachings of Buddha and how she felt that all people were of value and deserved respect. To her, stealing from another person, even the tiniest of theft, was a much greater loss to the thief than to the person who was robbed. She felt that self cleanliness was a personal obligation to one's own body temple. Buddhists believed in reincarnation. Each succeeding life was reward or punishment for previous life actions. She told him that her brother Loat San truly believed if he lived an exceptionally good life, then when he came back he would be a white man. Then maybe, just maybe, he would get to marry a white woman as beautiful as the picture of Raquel Welch.

Eddie listened with fascination. Growing up, he often heard his dad refer to some of their unmarried church members as sowing their wild oats on Saturday night, then at church the next morning praying for a crop failure. There was no such hypocrisy in Buddhism. They lived their thoughts and beliefs every day. To Mia the concept of reincarnation was no more difficult to understand then the Christian stories of Jesus ascending into heaven and Moses parting the seas. Listening to her reminded Eddie that in his own country there were millions that thought such gentle and humble people like Mia, not believing in the Christian God, were destined for an eternity of hell. Such self serving beliefs were so inappropriate. There wasn't an impure cell in Mia's body.

Her ideas served as a catalyst to his mind. In her presence he could discuss and explore his thoughts without shame or intimidation. They discussed Eddie's problems with his father and Mia convinced him it was okay to be discouraged over their relationship, but not okay to be disrespectful. Eddie decided no one as pure as Mia could ever be a spy.

Meanwhile, the war planes came and went. They were a background noise for their pleasant and peaceful discussions.

* * * * * * * * * * * * * * * * * * *

With time, Eddie became more and more enamored with Mia. She was so different from any woman he had ever known. As attractive and luring as she was, he had absolutely no idea how to affectionately approach such a goddess, or if even she possessed any romantic interest in an American GI. Certainly the other American servicemen had established a horrible precedent for any advances he might make. They all acted like a bunch of whore mongers off base and any expression of interest in her, other than as a friend, could certainly be misunderstood. The risk of losing her friendship and respect was too great.

294

One afternoon Eddie was lying out in the sun, drinking beer on the patio with a half dozen other Towheads. They were judging the traffic patterns flown by the returning sky warriors. Arnold was taking his CCR days off with a visit to Chiang Mai, north of Bangkok. The monsoon rains had developed early that day and the sun was back out for the late day's patio activities. Mia had finished her light load of maid's duties and was sitting in the shade, like any sensible person would do. She was slowly picking her way through the latest copy of Newsweek. Everyone knew Eddie had a thing for his maid but they had generally kept their opinions and remarks to themselves.

"I been here for so long I think I'm growing roots in this chair," the pilot everyone called "Jeepers" complained. He had been at NKP for six months and was one of the frustrated academy graduates. "Let's go into town, have a massage, and see if we can find a different bar where the girls don't smell like GIs."

"You been here forever, Nuts. I've heard stories about your escapades and staring down snakes. How about you giving the rest of us a tour of your secret pleasure palaces?" He looked around at the others, smiling. It was obvious he knew Mia was within hearing distance. Eddie didn't appreciate his antics. Several others thought it was okay. After all, Mia was just another Thai chick to impress with their classless bravado. The only reason that none of them had hit on her was they were convinced she was working as Eddie's private stock and if the rumors were true, Eddie was not one lieutenant to cross.

"Why don't you guys just get the hell out of here?" Eddie suggested. "Why do they always send me the diaper crowd to teach flying one oh one? If I hadn't noticed that Air Force Academy ring on your skinny finger, when you were picking your nose," he was looking straight at Jeepers, "I never would have guessed you went to college." Eddie got up from his lounge, picked up his towel and half empty beer, then headed toward his room. He looked at Mia, who had a distraught look on her face, and nodded his head toward their room. She quickly followed him, ignoring the subtle but audible remarks from the guys.

"I sorry if I make you insult," she apologized as soon as the door was shut. The cool air conditioning on Eddie's roasted skin felt like heaven, or better yet, Colorado.

"It's not your fault," Eddie assured her. "I prefer your company to theirs anytime. I'm sorry you have to be around such rude Americans. Believe me, Americans are not all like them. If you could only meet my mother you would know what I mean."

"I would be honored to meet your mother. Maybe someday I get to see America," Mia responded openly, and then blushed at her atypical boldness. Both Eddie and Mia were then silent. They each privately relished the possibilities that her spontaneous outburst had suggested.

"You want to go to town and play with for-rent bar girls, I will understand. You very rich and they very cheap. They take care of your man needs."

"I no longer have needs for trash bar girls. I don't know who is worse, the bar girls or the way the Americans act." Eddie finished off his beer and poured himself two fingers of Glenlivet.

"I think I go home now," Mia announced. "I think you bad mood and I don't want to see you upset."

"Don't go," Eddie pleaded. "I feel better having you around. I'm sorry for being in a bad mood. I'll go take a shower and then I'll be in a better mood. You know that you can take a shower if you want. You can use one of my towels and there is a shower stall with a curtain so none of the Americans can see you."

Mia reluctantly declined the offer, "The other maids will not like that; they not allowed taking showers."

"You can take showers when they are not working." He noticed that Mia had droplets of perspiration on her forehead. "They have all left for today so we can both take a shower and wash away all of our bad mood."

"The other Towheads would see me and think bad things about us. I not like that."

"Then I'll take my shower now and you can wait until they all go to eat." He slammed down the rest of his scotch, grabbed a towel and headed out the door. He noticed that the guys on the patio had already left for town so he returned and stuck his head inside his door. "The bad guys already went to NKP City. It's okay if you wanna come and shower." The bolt of scotch had given him just enough extra motivation to think risqué thoughts about the two of them showering together.

He found the latrine and shower both empty but lost his nerve about hitting on Mia. Even if she innocently showed up, it would be an insult to degrade their relationship. He had a little too much to drink. He chose a shower booth on the back side from the shower booth with the curtain. The water felt great and he took a long cool shower, long enough for his alcohol buzz to settle down and his anger and disgust at his peers to dissipate.

When he returned he found the room empty. Disappointed at the loss of Mia's company, Eddie figured it served him right for showing his bad side. He stretched out on his bed and covered himself with a clean dry towel to break the chill from the air conditioner. He settled in for a nice pre-dinner nap. No longer had he relaxed than his door opened and Mia came through the door. Her hair wet from a shower. Eddie sat up with a jolt.

"I thought you went home. I didn't hear you in the shower."

Mia smiled. "I quiet like a gecko. I was drying with your towel like you say okay for me to use when I hear you leave from your shower. You sure it okay for me to stay until Loat San finish work tonight?" She stood looking at Eddie, with nothing covering him but a towel. She was barefoot, wearing her sarong and a loose blouse—holding a damp towel.

They were both feeling the same magic. "Please don't go. If you stay we can have some rice and curry and then go to the movie."

"First maybe we spend time together and not talk about other people," Mia suggested. "I feel better to be around you. I no want you to need visit bar girls in town." She approached Eddie, "Okay I lay down with you and we be together?"

Mia let her towel drop to the floor and she slowly and carefully removed all her clothes. She stood naked and calm at the edge of Eddie's bed. She was every bit as beautiful as he had many times imagined. So very delicate, her brown skin, slender, with delicate breasts.

She spoke softly, "I hope you care for me like I care for you. I also have needs for to make love but just for you." Eddie made room for her on the narrow bed and she gently lay down next to him, gracefully and carefully as the beautiful woman she was. Mia removed the towel between them and they lay side by side for a long time.

Eddie had never been happier. Mia was the perfect human, kind, caring, moral, and the chemistry between them was on fire.

"And I just for you," he whispered in her ear.

Later, they slowly explored each other's bodies until the time was just right, then he slipped on a condom and they gently consummated their relationship. They made love, slowly at first, then with all the passion and expression either had ever imagined. That night Eddie dreamt of the Lady in the painting. He told her of Mia and the Lady smiled, pointed her finger at Eddie, and whispered, "I told you so."

* * * * * * * * * * * * * * * * * * * *

The next morning Mia showed up while Eddie was still asleep in bed. She knocked on his door, as usual, and he hollered, "Come in." He wasn't sure if she had slipped out during the middle of the night and gone home, or if she was just a quiet and early riser. At first it was as if nothing had happened the night before, except she came over to his bed and gently kissed him on the forehead. She then proceeded to pick up the room, stuffed their evening towels into a laundry sack and headed for the door. Half way she hesitated, then returned to his bed.

"You scheduled to fly this afternoon?" she asked while looking down at Eddie. He was. She sat down on the edge of his bed and dug into the knotted corner of her sarong. She handed Eddie a small piece of jewelry. "For you," was all she said. It was gold, about an inch and half across and had the shape of a German swastika, only the arms pointed in the opposite direction. It had a blood-red ruby in the center and it looked very old.

"It's beautiful," Eddie commented. "But you will have to tell your monkey man more about it. It looks like a German swastika."

"It swastika," Mia assured him. "But not German swastika. It be very old Asian symbol for good luck and good fortune. The arms are the sun and its rays. It is all I have left from my mother. When she get killed, I take it from her neck before the village people take her to bury. Her people believe very much in such things like this 'swastika'. I pray that it bring you good luck and keep the bullets from you airplane. Maybe if I care so much it will come true."

"I am so honored." Eddie was taken back by her sincerity. He slipped off his dog tag chain, a gold chain he had purchased on his first C-124 trip to Bangkok. He added the gold talisman to his two lonely dog tags. He finally had his own talisman, something so very special he would wear it as if a religion. It was a very special day; he had been waiting a long time for such a moment to arrive.

He looked up at Mia and she was watching him contentedly with her big brown eyes. She was beaming with happiness.

He leaned over and opened the top drawer where he kept his socks and other underwear. He pulled out the small green 38 special ammunition box and removed the bracelet he had purchased in Bangkok. At the time he purchased it he was struck by its special design and beauty and the size of the central ruby. But it had no purpose until that magical moment. There had been a reason for him to purchase it after all. He handed it to Mia. "This is for you. Now we have exchanged special gifts and that makes us special friends." He noticed Mia was fighting back her tears.

"Yes, we special friends now," she repeated.

* * * * * * * * * * * * * * * * * * * *

"Tell me about your father," Eddie asked her for about the tenth time. Two weeks had passed since they had exchanged special friends' gifts. "When am I going to get to meet him?" The two of them were strolling back to Eddie's room after a leisurely lunch at the base Thai restaurant. Eddie had been asked by the officers club manager not to bring local girls, meaning Mia, into the club. The sun was burning hot and there were heavy rain clouds rolling in. "You and Loat San always call him the wise one and several times you have called him your new father."

"Maybe it okay I tell you about my new father. I trust you. But you no tell other GIs cause my father no want trouble from the Vietnamese."

"What Vietnamese?" Eddie asked, as his curiosity grew.

"They not tell you nothing when they send you here?" It was a question and Mia was sincere. "Maybe there many things I tell you if you be my friend and I trust you."

"Let's start with the Vietnamese." Eddie felt like he was about to watch a movie that he didn't know anything about.

"When Vietnam made in two country," Mia poured out her long kept secret. "Many Vietnamese leave the north country because they not like the communist way. Ho Chi Minh kill many Catholics and many people that want to leave. Many go to the south but many also come to Laos and some cross the river and live here in this area. Lots of North Vietnamese live here this area. They okay people but some of them spies for Ho Chi Minh and they sometimes do bad things."

"Like what?' Eddie was having mixed feelings. What if she was from North Vietnam and was a spy?

"Like kill people if they told to do that. They part of club called Pathet Lao and want to make Laos a communist country for Ho Chi Minh."

Eddie was amused that Mia called the Pathet Lao, a Laotian communist insurgency of guerilla warfare, a club. Eddie couldn't believe what he was hearing from this simple Thai girl. He asked her, "What does that have to do with your father? Is he not a nice man?" Eddie didn't have the courage to ask Mia if her father was a communist, or a North Vietnamese.

"Oh, no. He very nice man, he very wise. But if Vietnamese and Pathet Lao find out who he is they kill him."

Eddie felt badly. Suddenly he was sorry for prying into her very personal family matters, wondering if her father was a communist. Yet somehow, he felt it was the key to unlocking his feelings for this beautiful young woman. He could tell that she wanted to continue but really wasn't quite sure if she should.

"You don't have to tell me more," he comforted her. "If you have a family secret I honor you and your private story."

"No, I want to tell you," Mia continued, "I want you to meet my new father and you need to know before you meet him so you not ask bad question." She sat in a bench in the shade and Eddie sat sideways facing her. She continued her pause while she organized the English words in her head. "My real father and Loat San's father was a French man." Eddie felt a cold shock run through his body. "He lived in north Laos, Louang Namtha providence, close to the Chinese border. He was a business man. He had a little store where he sold things to the hill people, the Yao, and he had my mother for his wife. She was of the Yao people."

Eddie was stunned! She was half French and half Laotian hill tribe. That was where she got her intriguing features! Mia continued, "They had me and Loat San for children and when we little children we very happy and learn speak French and Yao. My father make nice living because he buy poppy sap from Yao and sell to other Frenchman . . . I never saw this other Frenchman but my mother tell us he very bad man. Then one day Loat San and me in the forest checking fish trap in the river water when we hear gun noise from our house. Loat San and I hide for long time and then we go home. That French man kill our mother and father and took all my father's poppy sap. Loat San and I very sad and the villagers take us to hospital at Muong Sing where they feed us and give us place to sleep. We stay there very long time, many years, and help cook and make food for hospital and doctors. That where we learn to speak some English. Doctors were American. You know Doctor Dooley? He American Doctor and his American friends have hospital for mountain tribe people, the Yao. That where Loat San and I grow up."

Eddie's jaw dropped open. He wasn't sure he could even believe what he was hearing. But what reason would Mia have to fabricate such a story. "I've heard of Doctor Dooley but I really never knew anything about him," he admitted. "I didn't know where his hospital was—and you say you grew up working in his hospital? I think that's fascinating. But what does this have to do with the Vietnamese that live in this area?"

"Doctor Dooley, he spy on Pathet Lao and send reports to American people with special kind of letter. When Doctor Dooley leave Laos then Pathet Lao find out about special letters and they come and kill all people that work for him. My new father, he be my mother's brother, also Yao. He work for Doctor Dooley as a carpenter. When Pathet Lao come to kill everyone, Loat San and me in forest with him and he cutting tree for lumber wood. If we back at hospital, then they kill us too. The tree spirits always be special to Loat San and me, they hide us when bad Pathet Lao kill other Yao people. My mother's brother then be our new father after everyone else dead. He take Loat San and me and we come to Nakhon Phanom and change our names. If bad Vietnamese people who live here find my new father real name they tell their boss man, then Pathet Lao maybe they kill us. I think you need to know this cause you special close friend and I trust you my family secret. You no say to Loat San or my father you know our secret or they be very mad at me."

Eddie and Mia sat beside each other for a very long time and neither spoke a word. It was almost incomprehensible. Then he turned to Mia. "The man that got you permission to work as my maid, he said he knew your father. Did he have anything to do with the special letters?"

"He help us when we come to Nakhon Phanom seven years ago. He works for American government. He knows who we are."

So he was right, knowing Mia's story explained his feelings for Mia and her story was safe with him. The information he just heard was no one else's business and he would protect her family with absolute secrecy. Even Arnold didn't need to know this. Arnold's father was also a mystery man with some kind of connection with this nest of exotic spies and insurgents. What was there that Arnold was keeping from him? Best say nothing to anyone.

"You go now to bar and drink scotch and water and I stay here myself. I feel very much emotion and I need to sit here and find peace with myself for telling you my story."

Eddie and Mia stayed somewhat distant from each other for several days while he absorbed the significance of her secret past. He needed time to digest and accept it all and become comfortable with it. But the two lonely weekend days, maids didn't work on weekends, was more than Eddie could stand. Her mixed blood, the tragic death of her parents, and their hurried relocation to blend into the Thai culture—it took time to absorb. It all made Eddie even more appreciative of Mia's depth and mystique. When Mia showed up for work Monday morning, Eddie closed the door behind her and they embraced for a very long time. He wanted only to love her and protect her. Truly they were soul mates.

* * * * * * * * * * * * * * * * * * * *

"I speak with my father about you and he like to meet you maybe sometime," Mia casually broke the news the next day. "He want to know what kind of person you be. I tell him you honorable but he say he be judge." Mia giggled. "I think he knows we are make love. I no tell him but I think that he know."

"I would be honored to meet him," Eddie answered, feeling very sincere. "I'm not flying on Saturday and you no work on Saturday, maybe we spend the day together off base." Eddie wondered if he would lapse into speaking broken English when he returned back home to Colorado.

"I tell Loat San so he can arrange meeting my father. I come get you Saturday morning," Mia beamed.

That evening they returned to the Thai restaurant on base and both enjoyed a bowl of hot curried shrimp over steamed white rice. Their bread was fresh with a hard crust, just the way Eddie liked it. Maybe the bread was a spin off from the French influence; they had occupied most of Southeast Asia for such a long time. They sat in a remote corner and ate with wooden spoons usually only provided to Asian guests. Afterwards, they walked to the outdoor movie and watched a movie starring Gene Kelly. Mia had many questions to ask during their walk back to the Towhead Towers. She had never seen Americans dance like that. She believed Gene Kelly danced with almost as much grace as Thai dancers. Eddie's room was occupied. There was a small gold chain hanging on the door knob. It was the busy signal, so Eddie and Mia hung out at the Towhead bar until closing time. Mia then went home with her brother and Eddie slept on the patio until Arnold's girl friend left at 2:00 a.m. Arnold's girlfriend woke Eddie up when she left so he could finish the night in his own bed. That was part of the arrangement.

* * * * * * * * * * * * * * * * * * * *

Mia showed up Saturday morning at ten, their prearranged time, and Eddie wondered how she did it. She had no wrist watch. Eddie had offered to buy her one, but she politely declined the offer. Mia was wearing a pure black sarong and a pretty new blouse. With her excessive salary, she could afford the material to make such extravaganza. He felt like a clod next to her, wearing his ever handy khaki shorts and sandals. He did have on an attractive loose shirt. Loat San was waiting for them at the gate with his tuk tuk and gave them a ride west as far as the klong. As soon as Mia and Eddie dismounted from the put putting three wheeler, Loat San raced back towards Nakhon Phanom City on some made up task.

Eddie was amazed at how skillfully Mia handled the canoe and still managed to keep her spotless and unwrinkled clothes dry.

It was very serene on the klong and the birds and insects quieted as they passed. They returned to their songs of melancholy after the tiny canoe and its human cargo had passed. Mia briefed Eddie on the protocol with her father: no questions about his life in Laos, his tribal life in a Yao village, his time spent as a carpenter at Doctor Dooley's hospital. No mention of the secret letters, the massacre or their trek on foot to the Mekong and boat ride to Nakon Phanom. No questions about the mystery man on base. She told how, after they arrived in Nakhon Phanom, her new father had worked as a carpenter for a boat builder. After six years he had an accident and couldn't work any more. She explained he had learned to speak English well, when at Doctor Dooley's hospital, and his favorite thing was for Mia to read to him. He especially liked the teachings of Buddha and *Time* magazine. After the briefing, Eddie continued shooting rolls of Ectachrome with his camera. Loat San's village passed on their right as they continued up the klong and into a section with tall, thick trees on both sides of the waterway. Eddie had the feeling they were being watched and were in the presence of something. This was indeed a different kind of La La Land. Mia told Eddie that this grove of trees was inhabited by special spirits, thus the locals never disturbed them and didn't cut any of the special trees for their wood. The area was sacred. The pristine, undisturbed jungle had an eerie effect on Eddie and he felt humbled in Mia's presence. She was so special, a princess of this special place and at peace with her tree spirits.

While still inside the grove of trees, Mia paddled to the right edge of the klong and tied the tiny boat to a large downed tree trunk. An ancient masterpiece, it showed evidence it had blown down many years prior. None of the locals had dared harvest its valuable teak wood. This place was too sacred. She slipped out of her rubber shower thongs, climbed onto the giant trunk, and motioned Eddie to follow her. He wore his sandals and she was barefoot. A narrow trail led them several hundred feet through the tall grass. Orchids hung from the tall tree branches and Eddie just caught a glimpse of something, probably small monkeys, quietly leaping through the tops of the trees. Many trees were covered with moss and vines. After a short walk they emerged into a small clearing. In the center of the clearing stood an ancient structure, it looked thousands of years old. Built of large weathered stone blocks, it sat on a square base and had a spherical shape with a spire on the top. The front of the spherical temple had a large opening and inside Eddie could see a stone statue of Buddha. Framing the front of the temple, on each side, stood two gorgeous flowering trees. Approximately twenty feet tall, their ancient twisted trunks and exposed roots were welded to the stone foundation. They added just the right touch of color to the spiritual, tranquil scene. Their scent captured Eddie's attention. They were Lantom trees. The originals had been imported from Europe by the French missionaries during the sixteenth century. Because of their beauty and fragrant blossoms, the Buddhist monks used them as spiritual icons in front of their temples. The custom had been carried on for hundreds of years. Eddie was stricken with reverence and honored that Mia would bring him to such a special place.

Mia plucked several blossoms from the tree, stuck one in her hair, and rubbed several petals on her neck. She approached the statue of Buddha and placed the remaining blossoms at the foot of the pedestal. After a deep wai, she knelt in a prayer position, which she held for several minutes. Eddie was too awe stricken to take any photos, afraid he might disturb the piety.

When finished, Mia stood, turned, and took a few steps toward Eddie. Then she stood facing him with a look of total content on her face. She fit perfectly into the scene and for a moment, with the sun backlighting her profile, he had the feeling that maybe she really was a goddess—a gift from some ancient existence. Neither said anything. After a long pause, she stepped down from the shrine and the two of them slowly strolled, hand in hand, back to the canoe. An ancient swastika shone from the chain around Eddie's neck, an ancient animism symbol, with a Yao past, in a Buddhist setting, given to him by a half French half tribal goddess. So few people ever find such paradise. He wondered if this was his form of nirvana.

Mia paddled in silence until they left the grove of trees. "You like my private place? I go there to remember my mother each day if I can."

"It's a beautiful Wat," Eddie answered quietly. He was afraid he might disturb some spirit if he spoke too loudly.

Smiling, Mia turned to him. "It's a Stupa, a place to find peace and wish for Buddha's wisdom," she spoke and smiled at him. "A Stupa is a place of rest and peace for keeping Buddha's ashes. But not enough of Buddha's ashes to be at every Stupa so Stupa be just a symbol. I find peace there. A Stupa is only a Stupa.

"A Wat is a Temple," she continued, "a temple where monks live and pray and people go to worship Buddha's life. Wats have many buildings. In addition to a Stupa, Wats have a place for monks to sleep, prayer rooms, a temple. If no monks, then not a Wat."

"Do you think there will be a problem with you being a Buddhist and me not religious?" Eddie asked the question plaguing him since they had met. The upcoming meeting with her father had rekindled Eddie's concern.

"I'm not Buddhist. I'm Yao. Religion no problem. Buddha say, 'Our true nature lies within us and each person is his own salvation.' He no say need to worship invisible God . . . or be Buddhist. Just to be good person."

Eddie's day had been filled with revelations, but he hadn't seen that one coming. "But you often speak of Buddha and his teachings, you just quoted him. Everyone around here is Buddhist. Weren't your mother and father Buddhists?"

"No, my mother was Yao and they believe in spirits. The American doctors called it Animism. It is a good way to live, no hate, no fight, just all live together. Yao people seek peace with the earth, not control. Yao believe spirits in earth, in trees, in rocks, spirits everywhere. They believe to live together with the spirits and everybody be happy." Eddie was having a hard time keeping up with the information.

"My father was French and a Catholic but there no Catholic church in mountains so he just do without Catholic things and religion," Mia turned and faced Eddie. "My father was good person, he no need religion to be kind to people. And he had respect for spirits in the land so he live good with Yao people. He not be like other French Catholics in Laos. Catholic is crazy religion on outside and on inside sometimes not nice person. Most Catholic French people not religious if no church to visit. Many French Catholics was very bad to people in Laos. They steal from the tribe people and make slaves of young men. I not tell you what bad things they do to young girls. Yao people not like them and happy they gone.

"My new father also Yao, he also believe in spirits everywhere and follow the path of Tao. When we come to Thailand, we learn to speak and read Thai and learn to ask Buddha statue for guidance. We learn his wisdom. We study Buddha's teachings and try to be good like other Buddhists. That way no Pathet Lao know who we are."

"Then you're telling me that you have no religion?" Eddie asked. He was very confused.

Mia was very serious and quite sure of herself. "My new father, Loat San, and me we have no religion and we have all religion. We live the good parts of all and not do the other parts that are foolish or bad. We think Buddha very wise man and he teach good way to live, in many ways the same as Tao. We still believe many spirits. Buddha say, 'True goodness makes a man content.' "

"You were praying to Buddha back at the Stupa. You must believe in him as a god?" Eddie commented. "How can you not believe Buddha is a god and then pray to Buddha?"

"I was praying for Buddha's wisdom today when we meet with my new father. I can't pray to Buddha, you silly GI. Buddha died long time ago, he not god, and only his ashes left. I was praying to myself for to have wisdom and to the spirits to be kind to you. That be my religion."

Eventually they came upon Mia's village. It was similar to the first village where Loat San lived, but occupied a larger and slightly higher piece of ground. The morning sun had been blazing hot and there were few people out in the village. Numerous dogs looked out from under their owner's thatched huts but none found the energy to bark at the stranger. As they walked toward the hut where Mia and her father lived, the monsoon rains started early and they had to run to the hut in order to avoid being drenched. Eddie noticed a small spirit house, about twenty inches high, on its own post next to their door. There was a burnt curl of incense on the front entrance. Inside the tiny temple was a handful of cooked rice and a cluster of freshly picked Hibiscus petals. Eddie looked around and realized that all the huts had their own spirit temples; they reflected such a nice feeling. The hut, almost identical to Loat Sans, had a makeshift door made out of tropical hardwood. They slipped out of their foot ware and entered. The lighting was dim but functional. It came from the ventilation gap between the top of the walls and the raised roof.

Mia's new father, as she sometimes called him, was sitting on a chair facing the door, motionless, barefoot, in a stiff erect position. He was all by himself and Eddie wondered how long he had been waiting. He was small, looked old, and dressed in black, cotton pajama-looking pants and top. The black pajamas were not uncommon as day wear for Asian men. He sported thin, long, graying hair. He had a thin goatee and his dark ancient face was expressionless and full of wrinkles. The room was sparsely furnished, divided into two halves by woven bamboo screens. The front half, which they were in, featured a small fire pit on the right side. It was made from a large rusty steel pot and the embers were still glowing from a recent fire. On the left side resided a small table and chairs, a flimsy unmade bed, and several wooden boxes with lids. Behind the table and against the wall rested a rusty bicycle. Eddie assumed the kitchen and Mia's personal area were behind the screens.

"Father, this is Eddie," Mia broke the silence and motioned for Eddie to sit on the floor mat that had been positioned in front of her father. She then quickly disappeared behind the woven screen to prepare some tea. Eddie felt more than a bit awkward, but had lived in Asia long enough to know what to do. He palmed his hands and gave the old Yao tribesman a very deep and respectful wai, not expecting any wai in return. He sat on the mat, legs crossed, facing the senior, and placed his hands in his lap. Eddie sat looking at the elder's feet, out of respect. Eddie didn't speak. The silence also showed respect for the elder's thoughts.

"You keep my daughter away from me during my old days," the old man finally spoke. His English was easy to understand. His tone wasn't exactly friendly. It was more like a Hollywood depiction of God speaking in the movie Moses. He spoke with an accent that Eddie didn't recognize. "I trust she is happy and does not disgrace herself."

"Your daughter lives under your shadow and reflects only the finest of your people."

"She tells me you fly airplanes over my beloved Laos and you provide eyes in the sky for my brothers, the Hmong. It must be enlightening to do such a thing for people you do not know."

"Enlightening if I have the wisdom to learn from it. I regret it is part of a war that brings so much suffering to so many people. I hope it does not bring suffering to your people."

"My people live on both sides of the river," he informed Eddie, "and they have long endured suffering. We will continue to endure; it is not your fault." Orientals commonly spoke with allegories, a story picture with the meaning represented symbolically. The old man coughed roughly, swallowed, then continued, "The rains will come and go and we will harvest our rice, have happy babies, and die. We will continue our lives long after the Americans and the invaders from Vietnam have left our land you call Laos. The pains of war come and go like the rains. There is no end and there will always be others. Buddha say, 'Human existence and suffering are not separable.'"

Eddie sat silently and tried to absorb the old man's wisdom. After a very long pause, uncomfortable for a westerner but of no consequence to an old Yao tribesman, the elder continued philosophizing. "Wars are a reflection of the imperfections in man's character and the Americans make war as children play with a new toy. When the night comes and it gets cold, you will go back to your house and the toy will lay abandoned and wet in the night rain. I will die and Mia will continue the Yao existence with babies. I am told that you know she has the blood of my people in her. That is the way. Your short time here will pass."

Eddie wasn't sure what the old man was saying, "Was this his way of telling Eddie to drop any ambitions of taking Mia to America?" The old man removed a pouch from inside his pajama pocket, leaned to his left side and unhooked a pipe. Eddie had noticed it hanging on a hook screwed into the side of the chair. Without looking at the pipe and staring straight ahead, he packed the pipe tightly with "tobacco" from the pouch and sat patiently holding the unlit pipe. Mia appeared from behind the screen. She had been quietly listening to their conversation and obviously peeking. Using two polished sticks, slightly thicker than Japanese chopsticks, she carefully removed a glowing coal from the small fire pit. She held it to her father's pipe while he slowly puffed and turned the dark tobacco into a glowing ember. The old man continued to stare straight ahead. With the light from the glowing coals, Eddie could see that the old man's eyes were cloudy. He was blind!

Eddie wondered what the old man was smoking. It had an acidic smell and certainly wasn't tobacco.

Mia's father continued, "Americans lack the many thousand years of wisdom and patience that have been experienced by the Vietnamese from the north. From the viewpoint of Ho Chi Minh, five, ten, or twenty years and maybe a million or two million of their soldiers and people dead. To have the foreign Americans gone would still be a victory. Ten Vietnamese soldiers dead for every American dead. Can you see this, my son—can you understand? That would be a victory for the Vietnamese because one American is dead. Time, my son, is the effective weapon of the Oriental and impatience is the weakness of the Americans.

"Also," he continued. "Your freedom of the press is a wonderful idea. But I caution you, it is not viewed by all people as strength, but a weakness to exploit." The rains outside came down heavily and made it difficult

302

for Eddie to hear the elder's speech. There was no movement in the village as man and beast peered out from their shelters while they waited for the deluge to stop.

Eddie was shocked and silent. Whose side was he on? Was he on anybody's side? Or was taking sides something that he as an American had no right to demand of an old man who had suffered such violence in his lifetime? The old man continued, "There is evidence of this now in the stories Mia reads to me in the American magazines. The leaders in Hanoi have cleverly turned your people against themselves. The seeds of defeat have been planted and will be cultivated into a full crop."

After a respectful pause, Eddie decided he best press forward with his agenda, "I know the time will come when I must go home. That time is not far away. It will be sad to leave this beautiful country and all its wonderful people. I only wish I could take one flower blossom home with me." Eddie had carefully chosen an allegory to explain his dilemma. He felt it appropriate for this wise old Yao tribesman.

"If you pick such a delicate flower, surely it will wilt and lose its beauty," the Yao tribesman countered.

"I thought not of picking it but of carefully transplanting it," Eddie corrected.

The old man sat for a moment, then rebutted, "Such a flower would not remain beautiful without its roots in the soil from which it was grown. It is better to view it from a distance and take pleasure in its delicate existence, if even for one day, than to remove it and disturb its place in the forest."

"Do I understand this is your final word?" Eddie questioned. He had a hollow lump in his stomach. "Would it be possible for you to reconsider your feelings another day?"

"It is final," he assured Eddie. "My Loat San tells me you would make a fine provider for Mia, that you are an honorable man. But I cannot, in the tradition of my Yao people which Mia has the blood, and in the faith of my judgment, allow my Mia to marry outside our people and disappear into a strange different world. Her children would be confused as to which people they belong. Our differences are too great. Do you understand?"

"It pains me," Eddie consented. "But I will honor your wisdom and hope that someday I will understand."

They sat for another long silence, awkward to Eddie, then the old man asked, "What is snow like?"

Mia appeared from behind the screen. She had tea and fresh pineapple. It was obvious to Eddie that she had overheard their last conversation. She was fighting back her tears. Eddie thought it was just as well that the old man was blind, so he couldn't see the hurt he had inflicted on his adopted daughter. They ate their pineapple and drank their tea in silence, Mia's several attempts at conversation were met with awkward and short responses. Then as if the spirits wanted to rescue them, the rain stopped and Mia suggested she should give Eddie a boat ride to the main road, so he could walk back to the base before the afternoon rains continued.

* * * * * * * * * * * * * * * * * * * *

Mia was quiet as she slowly paddled the tiny craft down the center of the monsoon swollen canal and Eddie didn't feel like getting his camera out. As they moved through the large grove of trees that was inhabited by spirits, Eddie quietly mentioned the options he was considering. "Do you think he would change his mind if I got a job here in Thailand and made Thailand my home? I could learn the language and I'm sure a college educated English speaking American could find some kind of a good job. We might have to move to Bangkok."

"I not know," Mia hesitated. "I think he want me stay here and take care of him. With both Loat San and me have good jobs, when I stay late and wait for come home with Loat San, we have enough money to have old lady in my village to feed and take care of him. But my father don't like old lady, he say he want his own family to take care for him. That be the Yao way to do things. He sometimes very old fashion."

Mia was silent for several minutes as they paddled through paradise. Then she speculated, "Maybe it not meant for me to leave?" She was a devoted daughter of Asian soil and it was her teachings that were speaking. Eddie wondered how well Mia would fit into the strange and fast moving American culture. Certainly she would be an oddity on their farm. The local women were quite closed minded about foreigners, or even people that weren't of German heritage or weren't farmers. They would think of Mia as a heathen alien. Eddie had no intention to return to the farm and live under his father's rule anyway. They would have to live in a large city where people were more accustomed to mixed marriages and other than white skin. Or maybe they could find a cozy bungalow somewhere up in the mountains and he could commute to work and fly airplanes. But what kind of a life would that be for her?

Eddie wasn't about to give up. He needed a way to have Mia. He just needed her father to feel right about their relationship.

Eddie briefly considered applying for a consecutive one year tour with his EC-47 unit, but his paperwork to separate from the service had already been processed and he had less than a year to go when his current tour was over. It was too late to change it. He could marry her and she could get a visa to join him in America. But Mia wouldn't go without her father's permission. "I've got to figure out some way to make this work!" he heard himself bemoaning out loud.

"Remember what I say to you and let time do its work," she gently reminded him. "We have time for our thinking and still have more precious time together." Eddie wished he had the blind faith that Mia had. It was as if she didn't want to fight back but was willing to accept the inevitable.

"How can he say that he doesn't want you to have the babies outside of your Yao people because he doesn't want to mix your blood? You're already half French," Eddie asked.

"He no talk about my be half French. If maybe not think about my real father is French, then it not be. He only think of my Yao blood. My mother is his sister and he only want to protect the Yao blood that Loat San and I have. He think that French have bad blood, Americans have bad blood too. All white people have bad blood. When he see blond hair, red hair, blue eyes, the terrible way they come half way around the world to treat us bad. They make us work for them and kill us and cheat us, he think it all because of bad blood. He think their funny beliefs and weird religions also because of bad blood. Because Loat San and me have half Yao blood, it strong enough to keep us from being bad like the French and Americans. But if I have baby from white man, then Yao blood in my baby just one quarter and three quarter bad blood. That not be enough Yao blood to overcome bad blood. If I have baby from Yao or other people like Yao, then the bad white man blood just one quarter and that be better. Thai and Lowland Laotian are the same people and okay blood, hill people are best blood."

Eddie both disliked and admired her father, but his remaining stay in Thailand was short and he didn't have the time to figure out another complicated person. He needed to get Mia back to the States so he could spend his life caring for and loving her. Or stay in Thailand if necessary. He needed to do something.

"He doesn't like Americans very much, does he?" Eddie concluded out loud. He felt defeated.

"He like Americans only little bit. They not bad like French, but they no understand the way. He just don't like Americans what they do."

"What do they do that he doesn't like?" Eddie asked without hesitation, and then was sorry for his query.

"They use other people to do what they want, then the Americans will go away and the people they use get killed for being workers for Americans. My new father, because he full blood Yao, he travel around to different places and find out information about the Pathet Lao for Doctor Dooley's secret letters. When Doctor Dooley and his American boy friends leave, Pathet Lao kill all people that work for Doctor Dooley, except my new father, Loat San and me. We lucky to be in the jungle cutting lumber wood. Now he think Americans do same thing in Laos. They here little time and use Hmong and Laotian Army to fight Hanoi Vietnamese. When Americans give up and go away all those that help Americans get killed. He think Americans and CIA not honorable, they have no heart and no soul. Inside they like black night."

Eddie couldn't disagree with her. The CIA was famous for getting other people to do their dirty work for them, and they would cut and run if things don't work out. This entire war smelled like the same old thing.

They were quiet again, the serene tropical countryside partially submerged from the monsoon rains, was a stark contrast to their conversation about deception and death. A large grey heron came into sight, flying casually and low up the canal gap between the large trees. At the last instant he saw the two figures in their canoe and flared up and over them. Then all was quiet again.

304

"Do you think I have bad blood? I'm a white American," Eddie asked, feeling the time was right for both of then to put it all out on the table.

"Before I met you," she reflected, "I thought like my new father. He taught me how he thinks. But now that I know you and I have many thoughts about my half French blood, I think it is each person that is good or bad, not the blood. There are good and bad Asians just like there are good and bad white people."

When they reached the main road, Loat San was waiting with his tuk tuk. Rather than his usual upbeat and friendly manner, he was very somber. Obviously, sometime during his previous conversations with his father, they had discussed the fact that Mia and Lieutenant Nuts were in love and developing long range plans. He also knew of his father's disapproval.

"Today my day off from Towhead bar," he addressed Eddie. "I give you ride to the base road. Then I go stay with my father and so you and Mia can be together tonight. I know you both very sad from what my father said."

"Thank you Loat San, you very kind brother," Mia answered. giving her brother a deep wai and turning to Eddie. "We go now to base before rain feed us to the fish." She smiled at Eddie; she was working on her western humor.

* * * * * * * * * * * * * * * * * * *

The rains held until they were inside Eddie's room. Arnold was on an afternoon flight and it was the maids' day off. Eddie and Mia scurried down to the bathroom, saw that there was no one around, then quickly slipped out of their damp clothes and slipped into the shower together. If they didn't talk, then anyone using the latrine would assume the shower with the curtain was being used by the Thai girl that belonged to the navigator. They took a long and relaxing shower, holding each other tight, kissing and caressing in silence. When the coast was clear, they wrapped themselves in towels and scurried, giggling, back to Eddie's room. They then jumped into Eddie's bed and made passionate love. She suggested Eddie not use a condom and he had to again convince her that using one was the honorable thing to do. After their passion exploded and they lay next to each other, sweating despite the air conditioning, Eddie rolled over on his back and draped his arm over his forehead.

"I've been searching for you all my life," he revealed. "I imagined you in a thousand different ways, but never in the perfect form and mind that you are. Maybe I needed to know Buddha first so he could arrange for us to meet."

"I tell you many times, but you just not understand," her gentle, soft voice was not scolding. As she spoke she smiled with admiration and leaned over and kissed his forehead. "Buddha not a God, he not make us to meet. You and I make each other to meet because we good people and maybe some reason for us be together. We make it happen. People make own lives good or bad." Then she broke out into a mischievous smile and added, "Maybe Yao spirits help us little bit."

Mia hesitated then spoke again, "I also have looked for you all my life, but I never imagined, not one time in my thoughts, that you would be a white man. I so sorry. I thought all white men, not my father, but all the other white men have bad blood. Maybe I need to know you so to make me better person."

* * * * * * * * * * * * * * * * * * *

The next day, a Sunday, Eddie returned from an afternoon flight over the PDJ. It had been a day of mixed emotions. The rains had not developed that day, an indication that maybe the monsoon season was getting closer to ending. Looking down at the jungle covered hills, limestone mountains, and the big flat plains, he couldn't help but feel some attachment to the tribesmen below. They were struggling for their independence from the invaders and they were barely hanging on. He now knew that his precious Mia was of them, not of the Hmong tribe but of the fiercely independent hill people they all were. He didn't know how to feel about his involvement in all of this. Was his presence helping or hindering the natural rhythm of these people's lives?

It would be a moral and ethical crime to someday abandon these wonderful people to the enemy. One minute he would feel deeply depressed over the situation below. The Hmong had lost an entire generation of men to a war they were losing and his Mia was not allowed to return to the States with him. The next minute he would be enlightened over the fact that he had finally found Mia, embedded as she was in the Southeastern Asia quagmire. She was his Lady, his wonderful, loving Mia.

His right engine had slowly lost a quarter of its oil during the second half of their seven hour flight; there was a distinct oil smear growing over his right wing. They had watched it for several hours and it had been a tossup whether they should abort their mission and go home early, or keep plenty altitude as insurance and fly the remaining mission. They chose the latter. After they parked their faithful Gooney Bird on its spot on the NKP ramp, Eddie sent the rest of the crew on to debrief their mission. He wanted to discuss and make sure the maintenance personnel understood the nature of the oil leak. Once the maintenance chief was satisfied with the debriefing, Eddie picked up his flight bag and trekked across the hot concrete ramp. The day's sunshine had baked the concrete to the point that he could feel the heat seeping through the soles of his jungle boots.

There was a single engine Air America PC-6 Pilatus Porter parked in front of base operations and the pilot was busy securing his aircraft for the day. Eddie approached him from behind and at the last minute the Air America pilot looked up. He was visibly annoyed at being surprised.

"You fly out of the Alternate in Laos?" Eddie asked the surprised pilot. The guy had obviously lost his polish after living under the coarse conditions in Laos. His sun bleached hair was long, unkempt, and his cutoff trousers looked like a shop rag. Although they had available a healthy diet of rice, fruit and vegetables, the excessive alcohol, long days of flying at low altitudes over enemy territory, constant exposure to gunfire and death, and tropical rains, heat, and crude quarters had extracted their toll.

"You know I can't answer that," the Air America pilot answered as he looked across the ramp and saw the EC-47 that had recently arrived. He pointed at the mud clinging to the underside of his aircraft. "You draw your own conclusions."

"I'm not trying to pry into your personal business," Eddie apologized. "I'm a short timer here, probably eligible for an early out. I got a lady friend I really don't wanna leave behind and I'm seriously thinking of applying for a job with Air America. I wanna stay over here. Is it possible for me to apply here without going back to the States?"

The Air America pilot stood up, grinned to himself, and wiped his hands on his ragged cut off trousers. "Seems we all get a little mesmerized by Asian pussy. You're about a year too late. Air America is reducing their fleet over here and not only aren't hiring, they're sending some of the guys home. Don't you guys know that we lost the war?" He looked back towards Eddie's EC-47, "You're supposed to be working in intelligence."

"Shit," Eddie looked into the distance. "Wrong place, wrong time. It's the story of my life."

"Story of all of us losers' lives," the Air America pilot reflected.

"Tell me this," Eddie continued. "I'm trying to get hold of a Raven I met in Bangkok. We discussed the possibility of going into business after the war. His call sign is Longbow and I suspect he flies out of the Alternate. Would you happen to know how I could contact him?"

The pilot took a long look at Eddie and then spoke in a civil tone. "Longbow had a reputation for shady business deals. Most of them had something to do with smuggling opium. But you don't have to worry about that now cause he got shot down and killed by a quad ZPU last week."

Eddie was shocked at the bluntness of the answer and the Air America pilot's lack of emotion.

"Did they recover his body?" Eddie asked out of concern for his brief friend.

"Vang Pao lost two of his villagers getting him out but they took out the gun site and recovered him. Said he was really buggered up and probably died fast."

"Did they ship him back to his parents and his wife?" Eddie asked. He knew Longbow didn't want that.

"Didn't know he was married. He always called his pig his wife. All I know is that he was real dead and they shipped him back home in a rubber body bag, courtesy of the United States government." The Air

America pilot smirked at his mention of the US government's generosity. "Not that it might mean anything to you, but a Hmong Shaman blessed his body before they shipped it off."

"I think it would have meant something to Longbow," Eddie speculated. Their eyes met, they shared an understanding. It was their private war, as it had been for Longbow. Although they both would never admit publicly, they had more respect and allegiance to General Vang Pao and his Hmong villagers than the bumbling politicians in Washington DC.

"I really don't feel like answering any more questions," the Air America pilot terminated their conversation and turned, picked up his small ditty bag, and headed for base operations. Eddie stood for a while. His world continued to fall apart from all angles.

He stopped off at the officers club and downed a few beers. He really wasn't ready to go back to his room and face Mia. To go back to the States without her would be just too painful. He needed time to think and be by himself, "What an upside down world he lived in. Without Mia it would all be for naught."

CHAPTER TWENTY-EIGHT: SURVIVAL

It was just another routine flight. The operations officer had informed Eddie that he heard rumors about one of the young aircraft commanders. Supposedly the young aviator was getting a bit sloppy with his procedures and the operations officer wanted Eddie to ride along with the "renegade" pilot as an observer. Certainly Major Collins wasn't about to ride along with a crew for seven hours, next to the Ho Chi Minh Trail. He assigned the task to Eddie. So Eddie signed on to fly as a third pilot, as an instructor. It was something he had done many times during his pre-Mia days and it wouldn't raise any suspicion. After the flight he planned on filing a report that he had "monitored" both pilots and their performance as crew members was up to par. The key to such paperwork was ambiguity. The truth was that Eddie had also heard rumors that Major Collins was upset with the young lieutenant. Apparently the lieutenant's hair length wasn't short enough for the major. As if a half of an inch of hair was a critical factor in a combat zone. Could a half of an inch of hair effect a pilot's flying skills?

It was monsoon season and the afternoon flights were sometimes aborted for weather. Their mission just wasn't worth the risk with the massive cumulus clouds and dangerous turbulence. So Eddie chose one of the crew's morning flights, the dawn patrol along the Ho Chi Minh Trail. It was their easiest mission. As the trail patrol encountered fewer and much lower mountains, the Towheads were able to fly at lower altitudes and under the scattered morning clouds. Also, the aircraft was number 304, the Lady. With the Lady's seven hour airborne time and short distance from NKP, they could stretch their early morning flight into the early afternoon—if the weather cooperated.

The crew had developed a camaraderie; they all got along well and enjoyed flying together. Scheduling went along with their request to fly them together whenever possible. Eddie saw nothing wrong with that, in fact he thought it was a good thing. This particular day was the crew's photo day and they were glad to have Eddie along as they needed someone to take their pictures. They posed as a group in front of their airplane, wearing their survival jackets, parachutes, and 38 special side arms. They had seven cameras; Eddie took their crew photos and after the crew photos they posed individually with their aircraft, in macho poses for posterity. It was something most crewmembers did to show their friends, parents, wives, and children when they returned home.

Eddie's job was that of an observer standing between the pilot's seats. After take-off they flew low across the Mekong and stayed low over the flood plains and its rice fields and makeshift homes. The cameras were clicking and the scenery from such low altitude was spectacular. As they approached the Karst outcroppings, they climbed just enough to safely clear the jagged spires and the busy photographers were exposed to a new kind of landscape. They had a close look down into the mystical land of vertical limestone spectacles, thick tangled jungle growth, and the probable home of a multitude of undiscovered butterflies. It was early enough that the deep and narrow chasms were still filled with wisps of morning mist, hanging still in the windless environment. Eddie snapped on his parachute and quickly joined the two parachute laden radio operators in the rear of the aircraft. They stood gazing out from the open space where the troop door had been removed. It was the land of the lost, and other than an occasional glimpse of a foot trail made by animals or maybe humans, they spotted no indication of man's existence. There was one twisting, single lane dirt road as it worked its way through the maze of narrow valleys and streams. The road was called Route 12. It was impassable during the wet season.

Soon the Karst features diminished and the landscape transitioned into gentle hills. They flew over an occasional low plateau, pronounced river valleys all still covered with various combinations of virgin jungle, pine forests and open patches of scrub and underbrush. The pilots added power and started their climb to altitude. They needed to be at least 3000 feet above the ground when they approached the work area on their maps. They planned on a 5000 foot buffer at Eddie's suggestion. They would fly parallel, adjacent to the hazardous Ho Chi Minh Trail. Most pilots gave the red gun circles a few miles extra distance, a mile for their parents, a mile for their wife, and a mile for each child. The radio operators went back to their work positions, removed their parachutes, and mounted their swivel chairs at their work stations. Eddie stayed in the back, still fascinated with the unobstructed view out the troop door. The single restraining strap was waist high. Standing several feet behind the strap, his parachute on, in the still morning air, he felt comfortable, safe and spell bound. Out the open door Eddie recognized a river below. With its distinctive bends and turns, it flowed from the east and westward toward the Mekong. He knew they were about ten or twelve miles west of where the Ho Chi Minh Trail's protective guns were located.

They were just leveling off at their loitering altitude. The pilots had turned parallel with the trail and were slowly reducing their power. Then it happened! POP POP **KABOOM-BOOM** pop pop. A North Vietnamese 37mm gun had been relocated ten miles to the west during the night. The gun crew had been assigned the task of shooting down one of the mystery C-47s that had been patrolling on a daily basis. They had been waiting and as the mystery bird slowly passed overhead, they carefully aimed their weapon and fired a clip full of anti-aircraft shells from behind and forward through the aircraft's path of flight.

The third shell in the string was the one that caught the relaxed Towhead crew off guard and it ripped into their left wing between the engine and the fuselage. It burst into a multitude of steel shards. It hit and exploded inside the left main fuel tank that had been used for take-off and climb-out. The tank was three quarters full of fuel and one quarter air. It was just the right combination of fuel and air to burn. The burst literally blew the tank apart, as well as the fire suppressant mesh. A cavity formed in the center of what was once a fuel tank and the resultant fuel vapor and air created a secondary explosion. The left wing, between the left engine and the fuselage, burst into a huge ball of flame. The badly damaged and fuel starved left engine instantly ceased to function, and the still spinning and unfeathered propeller created a massive drag on the badly damaged left wing. The drag, combined with near climb thrust still being produced by the engine on the right wing, snapped the aircraft into a sharp left yaw. The aircraft, unattended by its two stunned and shrapnel wounded pilots, immediately responded to the yaw by rolling over further into a left steep spiral. As the flame heated the aluminum wing spars and the strain from the spiral added additional stress to the damaged wing, it folded up and over, fluttering gracefully above the fuselage. The folded wing sealed the fate of the crewmembers.

It all happened so fast that Eddie never had a chance to react, yet alone enough time to analyze what was going on. As Eddie was standing in the rear of the aircraft, he was missed by the deadly spray of shrapnel from left wing. It was the open door and his position just inside the restraining strap that saved him! The initial snap from the severe left yaw effectively threw him forward against the restraining strap that guarded the open door. He bruised his hip on the strap as he flipped over the restrainer and into the air stream outside the airplane. He tumbled down and the jungle and the sky alternately flashed by in front of him. He pulled the rip cord on his chest style parachute and the colorful nylon canopy slipped out of the pack, popped open, and jerked him into reality. He moved his arms and legs as he swung back and forth and was amazed that everything was still attached and still worked. His system was so filled with adrenalin that he didn't feel the bruise on his right hip. It had all happened in several seconds, his mind was racing to catch up.

He looked around and saw the flame engulfed remains of his ride plummeting downward, into the dark green jungle. An intense fire occurred as the remaining fuel tanks ruptured and their contents ignited. The jungle muted the flames but the black smoke's message was undeniable. Anyone still in the aircraft had surely perished. He looked around hopefully but saw no other parachutes.

Russian technicians, on the ground in Laos, served as advisors to the North Vietnamese Army. They had asked the North Vietnamese Army to shoot down one of the unidentified C-47s that flew alongside the Ho Chi Minh Trail day after day. They were curious about the unidentified C-47s' missions and what technical equipment was carried on board. They hoped to interrogate any survivors. Instead the army had exploded a round of 37 millimeter gunfire into an almost full tank of high octane aviation fuel and all they had to sort through on the ground was a crisp, charred hulk of a former aircraft. There was only one parachute spotted and if the parachutist survived they still needed to capture him alive.

Eddie had played "what if bail out" a dozen times in his mind over the last year. But there had been just too many variables for any one plan of action. He never, in his wildest imagination, thought he would be thrown out of an airplane. And as far as the rest of the crew, all of the planning and practice in the world couldn't have made any difference. The way the aircraft was spinning, with one of its wings folded over, the centrifugal force would have pinned them to the inside walls of the airplane. There was no way they could have made their way to the rear of the aircraft and out the door, even if they had been wearing their parachutes. The odds were incredible, sometimes things just happen. Although amazed that he was still alive, Eddie was numb from the blunt loss of the aircraft and an entire crew of friends.

The next thing he noticed was the silence. He went from loud aircraft noise and an explosion to no sound at all. It was instant tranquility. Then he could hear them. As he slowly descended the last thousand feet into the jungle, he could hear the birds singing, as if his imaginary spirits were welcoming him home from his near demise. He listened to their pleasantry for a couple of hundred feet of descent then shrugged the idea off. He didn't have time for imaginary spirits and mind games; he was getting low. It was time to go to work!

During basic training at Willie, their parachute training taught them how to pull on the left and right side risers (the cords that connect the person to the parachute) and slip the parachute left or right. It wasn't a very effective way to guide the parachute, like sport parachutes, but the military chutes could be "influenced" to slip left or right a little bit. Eddie could see he was drifting directly toward one of the tallest trees in the triple canopy jungle, just in front of him. By pulling on a handful of risers on his left side he managed to just miss the top of the big tree and slipped into the solid, leafy cover below him. He held his legs extended, ankles crossed and toes pointed straight down, as instructed for tree penetration.

It worked—sort of! He slipped right through the trees' canopy of leaves then jerked to a sudden stop. He looked around, again in amazement for the second time that day. He was still alive and had no broken bones, everything was working. But he was mysteriously hanging in midair. He looked up and his parachute canopy was beautifully spread out but stopped by the mass of branches and leaves he had just penetrated. The over story of branches and leaves blocked out the bright sunlight. With his feet crossed tightly, he had luckily speared his way through the mass of leaves and small branches and missed hitting any of the large branches that could have seriously injured him. He was hanging about seventy or eighty feet above the ground and could barely see the ground through the remaining leaves and branches. He just hung there. Eddie silently vowed if he ever got out of this mess, he would make it a point to personally look up and thank the airman first class that had packed his parachute. Maybe offer him a steak dinner at one of the base restaurants. The airman had done a wonderful job.

At survival school, they had instructed them to immediately salvage what they could of their parachute for survival supplies, then to bury the rest—ASAP. "Nothing could make it easier for the enemy soldiers to spot you than a big parachute flopping in the wind." They also told them that "usually downed pilots had an hour or two of free time while the nearby soldiers got organized and made their way through the jungle to where they saw the parachute land. Don't waste that free time!"

Eddie zeroed in on the closest branch that would be able to support his weight. Then he started pulling back and forth on his risers and started swinging back and forth until he could snag the branch with his leg. It was during this maneuver that he first felt the bruise in his hip from his aircraft "escape." It hurt a lot. But after a little self examination he decided it wasn't a broken bone, just a painful inconvenience that he had to work through. Straddling the branch, he removed his parachute harness and carefully climbed his way up to as close to his parachute canopy as he dared. It took him twenty minutes as he pulled, jerked, and cut with his knife until he had his entire parachute canopy free and wadded into a bundle. Then he worked his way down to the large branch that he had started out on and proceeded to cut a hand full of parachute riser cord and a five by five foot section of parachute panel. He stuffed them inside his flight suit. He was hot and sweaty but he had to work fast. He bundled the rest of the parachute, including his parachute harness, into a tight wad and tied it together securely with more riser cord. Then he rested and took several long swigs from his water bottle. The air was hot and heavy with humidity. He was dripping wet from perspiration, and he knew he was losing water fast.

It was during his short break that the rest of his survival plans fell into place. At survival school in the Philippines, their instructor told them to bury the unused portion of their parachute. But the idea of dropping it down to the ground and burying it where the enemy soldiers would probably soon be looking around, really didn't seem like a good idea. The hollow feeling he had in his gut when the native Negrito found him hiding under the leaves, during survival school in the Philippines, returned and he changed the rules. From where he was he could barely see the ground. That meant they could barely see up the tree where he was. He stuffed the parachute bundle into the crotch where his large branch joined the main tree trunk and used a piece of his salvaged parachute cord to tie the bundle to the tree. There was no way he wanted the bundle to fall down to the ground. Then he cut several handfuls of small branches from the tree and effectively camouflaged the edges of the bundle, so no one from the ground could spot it. He smiled to himself. There were no foot prints, no buried parachute, no scent for dogs to follow, no nothing on the ground for them to know he was in the vicinity.

Then he looked around and carefully crawled along, branch to branch in the dense tall trees, until he found just the right branch for himself. It was a thick branch on a huge old tree, a branch about twenty inches in diameter. Sitting in the crotch formed by the branch and the tree trunk, it made a comfortable resting place. The tree had a huge, broad leaf philodendron type of vine that wound around its trunk and added additional vegetation between him and the ground. When sitting in the tree crotch, Eddie couldn't see the ground below. His dark green nomex flight suit blended into the surroundings perfectly. It was time to stay quiet and save his strength and water.

He resisted the temptation to get on his survival radio and advertise his position to any aircraft that passed overhead. A panic cry for help over the radio could be a fatal mistake. Any crude radio direction finding device could point in his direction and would lead the bad guys straight to him. Also, they certainly had American survival radios taken from dead American flyers and they could listen in on everything that Eddie was tempted to broadcast. The Russian advisors probably learned to speak English as part of their training.

An American aircraft circling overhead was not the position indicator that Eddie wanted the gomers to see. Eddie had decided in Survival School that without a functional pickup point for a quick rescue, total radio silence for several days would be his plan. After several days and without any sign of him, the North Vietnamese would assume he was dead or had moved out of the area.

In a tree in the middle of a huge jungle was not where the gomers would expect a fleeing American to be found. All of the action would be on the ground! Unfortunately, his location was far from ideal for a helicopter rescue. Eddie wasn't about to give away the fact that he was even alive until he had re-located to an ideal pickup site, hopefully without any bad guys around.

The survival school instructor said they could survive for three days without water and up to two weeks without food and still remain relatively functional. In that heat and humidity, Eddie knew he had a couple days maximum without water. He still had a half full canteen on him. He was going to wait the day out in his hiding place; avoiding enemy searchers was a higher priority than finding drinking water. He zipped open his flight suit, pulled his arms free of his sleeves to stay a little cooler. Then he waited. He knew that patience was his biggest challenge. Without patience he would move about, maybe even climb down the tree for a look around, and that could easily be fatal. He had to be more patient and more cunning than those somewhere below; those who had lived in the jungle all of their lives. So he sat, and listened, and sat and listened.

A band of small monkeys worked their way through the tree, probably looking for ripe fruit, and at his level they spotted him and began chattering loudly. Quickly they surrounded him. He was not happy with the noise. Anyone familiar with the monkey's characteristics and calls would recognize their alarm sound and it would lead them straight to Eddie. But he needed to be smart. He couldn't chase away a band of nimble monkeys in an Asian jungle through the tops of the trees. That would only rile them up and make them nosier. Throwing something at them would only make matters worse. He had to quiet them down. So he gave them the finger to let them know he was alive and not afraid. Any signal would have worked but somehow the finger made Eddie feel a lot better. Then he demonstrated a relaxed position and pretended to go to sleep. This would let them know he was not interested in them. Within a few minutes, the monkeys settled down and moved on. Finding ripe fruit was more important than the uninterested, unconcerned human in the tree. Maybe growing up around farm animals had some advantages for Eddie. He knew how they thought.

Then a lizard crawled up the trunk and wanted to use the branch Eddie was sitting on. Eddie was determined not to move, so the lizard crawled over him and went on its way. It was déjà vu all over again, with the rat in the Philippines. Then a small green snake wanted to do something similar and this time Eddie didn't want to get it excited in case it was poisonous, so he lay still as the snake also crossed over his leg. It was no time to do something stupid or lose self control. He was bound and determined to let his mind think and stay in control. He took another small sip of water to keep his mouth wet but otherwise just sat and listened. Other than the occasional slow and deliberate scratching of an itch, or a small slow sip of water, or to squeeze and silently collapse a biting bug, he was determined not to move until it was dark.

The jungle had constant twittering as several types of small birds searched about for insects and he was startled once by a large squawking pair of birds as they flew by overhead. There were squawks and screeches from other critters that Eddie had no idea what they were. The occasional silence carried even the smallest of sounds far through the jungle. With the occasional pauses of creature noise and periods of jungle silence, using his survival radio to just listen for friendly aircraft would be a mistake. A voice from his survival radio could be heard for some distance and Eddie's game could be over.

Because they flew their mission in radio silence, their aircraft wouldn't be missed until they were overdue at NKP.

It was just twelve a.m., noon. He had been thrown out of the aircraft at eight in the morning and had been sitting for hours. He had killed dozens of large ants that had painful bites and he remembered his survival instructor telling them ants were edible. He opted out of trying the foreign food source. There would be plenty fresh ants if he ever got so hungry he needed to try them as food. Then he heard footsteps in the distance. Then there were more footsteps and he could occasionally hear small whispers as the North Vietnamese soldiers hunted for signs and hopefully a glimpse of their prey. They needed the American who had bailed out of the burning aircraft for interrogation. Eddie sat perfectly still, and from the sounds of their footsteps and the occasional whispers, it sounded like they were spread out in a line, from as far right as he could hear to his far left. The line slowly moved past his tree and faded into the distance. Eddie imagined they were soldiers. Maybe a few skilled trackers would stay behind the moving lines to see if anyone hiding would give their position away to the silence. Eddie never moved.

At 1:30 the sky rumbled and the afternoon monsoon rains began. It was cooling relief to Eddie. If the soldiers did run past his tree looking for shelter, they wouldn't stand looking straight up into the heavy rain water. Water was working its way through the leaf overcast and was falling everywhere, including on Eddie. He dug out his knife and cut two three foot sticks from nearby branches. He felt safe moving slowly in the heavy rain. He wrapped the edges of his clear plastic sheet, the one from Arnold's stereo speaker, around the branches into a V formation. When he held the rig out with a little slack in the plastic, he formed half of an open funnel. With a slight tilt and the V crotch pointing at himself, water flowed at a pleasant rate. He drank his fill then topped off his water canteen. Then he forced himself to drink again. He wished he had plastic bags, extra canteens, or anything else that would hold water but he had to settle for a full canteen, a full belly, and hopes that the monsoon would return again the next day or two. It could take several days before the soldiers, without any signs of the American, would give up their search. It rained hard for several hours. Eddie used the rain to dilute and wash away any signs of his toilet. There would be no noticeable change in the rotten jungle smell that every jungle has on the ground.

He used his salvaged parachute cord to tie himself to the tree trunk and to the thick branch he was sitting on. Then he tucked his loose items inside his flight suit and zipped it up. This way he could sleep without fear of falling out of the tree or dropping anything on the ground. The last thing he wanted to do was to descend from his sanctuary just to pick something up. When the afternoon rain stopped, as the monsoon rains usually did, Eddie was saturated with water and was chilled from the exposure. He was exhausted but satisfied. Tomorrow it would be hot again and he would need his energy and his mind to outsmart the enemy. He dwelled on the loss of an airplane load of friends, how lucky he had been, why it happened, or if it could have been prevented.

He pondered over the fact that when their aircraft had taken a fatal hit, the Lady had thrown him out to survive. It was certainly just a coincidence, a statistical anomaly. But it was still weird! He decided he wasn't going to go there; he had far more important things to think about. At Snake School they told them it was a downed airman's full time job and obligation as an American crewmember to "escape and evade and return to friendly forces." They wanted him back. It was right out of the book but to Eddie it was a little more personal. He had Mia. He purged his area of ants and bugs for the umpteenth time and then drifted off asleep.

He woke up once and listened to the night sounds of the jungle: insects, frogs, a dozen creatures he had no idea what they were. There were yaps, squawks, squeaks, and thousands of frogs singing. Judging from their different songs, there must have been a dozen different kinds of frogs. He even heard a scream followed by a series of deep bellows. It was comforting that Harold the lizard had a relative living in Laos. The night sounds were far more intense and louder than the day sounds and the total of sounds blended as if a tremendous orchestra. Eddie was relaxed and stayed still as he enjoyed the music of the night. He smiled to himself. He felt safe on that night as all was well with the jungle—his new friends and his new home. Then he drifted off asleep again.

* * * * * * * * * * * * * * * * * * *

The band of monkeys woke Eddie as the first rays of light were piercing the overhead leaf canopy. They sat in the branches and formed another circle around him. This time they weren't screeching alarm calls but instead were communicating in their normal chit chat manner, trying to figure out if he was dead or not and what was he doing up in a tree. The few humans they had seen before had always been on the ground. Eddie moved very slowly so as to not frighten them and sat looking back at them with similar curiosity. He had to urinate but that was a good sign. It indicated he was not dehydrated to a dangerous level. He would pee on the branch after the monkeys were gone and the telltale smell of ammonia would dissipate and be undetectable far below on the ground. With time the monkeys tired of the staring contest and decided he was harmless enough, so they moved several trees away and began feeding on something they were picking from among the leaves. Occasionally one would glance in Eddie's direction, but they had accepted Eddie as a harmless curiosity—at least as long as he kept his distance and made no threatening moves. Eddie was ravished with hunger but he would wait until the last of his three payday bars were gone before he would start scrounging for local food. If whatever it was in that tree was okay with the monkeys, then his primate digestive system could probably also digest it and absorb nutrition. He wasn't ready to expose himself to view from the ground for a handful of nuts or whatever it was that the monkeys were eating. Eddie thoroughly enjoyed one half of a payday bar and several big swallows of water. He was getting hungrier by the hour but he kept telling himself to be glad he was alive and not to do anything stupid that would change his status.

As the morning moved on he saw the lizard again and the monkeys ate their fill and settled down to groom themselves and each other. He spotted some squirrel sized mammals that hung out in the monkey food tree, apparently feeding on the same mystery fruit. Several other small birds were looking for insects in the old tree he was living in. Then he heard a human voice shout something indistinguishable in the distance and then he could barely hear some quiet conversation. The monkeys in the "food" tree were instantly silent and Eddie decided they were his friends. He didn't want to get killed and they didn't want to get eaten; neither trusted whoever that was on the ground. The voices moved slowly, all from one direction and after ten minutes the hunters moved out of hearing range. Several aircraft flew over his area, but without knowing where the lost EC-47 went down, none of them loitered in his area. He didn't want to call them on his radio and have them circle where he was. He knew the bad guys were watching the airplanes, hoping for a clue where to look. His location was his secret and he wasn't ready to let anyone even know that he was alive.

Eddie did more "housecleaning." With the butt of his empty revolver he killed the ants and other threatening insects in his immediate area. There were some large multicolored beetles and tiny curious lizards that didn't seem interested in biting and eating him so he let them live. Then he reloaded his revolver, tied himself up again, and took a nap. He needed to conserve his energy.

The escape and evasion instructor at survival school told them, "Time can be either your friend or your enemy. You need to be able to tell the difference and to use it effectively to your advantage." Eddie was uninjured, had water to drink, and was undetected by the enemy. They probably saw his parachute when he descended but they couldn't find him. Waiting and patience were his best friend. Time was on his side.

Eddie sat in his little niche in the tree and had plenty time to think about the events that had gotten him into his dilemma. He thought about his life and wondered if he would have a future. He mulled over the chance that he had even been on the aircraft in the first place. And that he was standing at the open door with his parachute on and penetrated the top layer of branches without an injury.

He vowed he would never be taken as a prisoner. The radio operators were normally very secretive about the messages they intercepted on their missions. But it was common knowledge that several decoded messages from Hanoi informed their field units in Laos that they had all the prisoners they needed. The Laotian field units were instructed to interrogate then kill any newly captured air crew members. Or use them as "helicopter bait." Helicopter bait meant the NVA soldiers would locate and surround a downed flyer, set up gun positions and then wait. Undetected, they would leave the downed flyer undisturbed so he would call in a rescue helicopter. The NVA soldiers would wait until the helicopter was in a hover over the downed flyer, preferably with its rescue cable extended so it couldn't move, then they would open fire at close range and bring down the helicopter. Eddie wasn't about to be used as helicopter bait. He wasn't going to get a dozen other airmen killed on his behalf. He had a shell in his pistol with his name on it and he would use it rather than let the gomers have their way.

The afternoon's monsoon deluge was a repeat of the previous day. In addition to drinking plenty of rain water, Eddie was feeling quite good about still being alive the last two days. He just needed to be smart enough to remain alive during the next several days. He was getting quite stiff from sitting in his tree crotch and once the evening dark set in and the rain stopped, he put himself through a series of stretches and flex exercises.

* * * * * * * * * * * * * * * * * * *

Day three in the tree and again the monkeys paid him a day break visit. Eddie heard them in his sleep and as he opened his eyes, he slowly looked over his visitors. They were in the fruit tree feeding, not paying any attention to him. They were chatting back and forth and he realized it had been over two days since he had uttered even one word.

As Eddie sat in his tree, absorbing his surroundings, a comforting feeling came over him, a true sense of contentment. Sitting there in his safe niche, suspended in virgin jungle with a friendly band of monkeys, the little shiny beetles, tiny songbirds, and one large brilliantly colored butterfly, he realized he had finally arrived at his life's destination. Was this the place that the burning desire inside him—for all of those years—had been leading him to? There was no farther away from Colorado he could go. He was at the far end of remote. Although it was uncertain if he would ever get out of the pickle he was in, he felt at peace with himself. He was at peace with the world. He realized it wasn't the Lady that he had been seeking, or the adventure, or the escape from the farm—it was himself. He had found Mia, had loved, and had soared with the eagles over the most beautiful land he had ever imagined. If he didn't make it back he could die a happy man. Then he slept for three more hours—tied to his tree with a piece of the parachute that had so gently returned him to the earth.

That afternoon, as he sat in his impromptu nest, Eddie had plenty time to think about and settle his life issues. Most seemed so irrelevant from his tree top retreat. He knew he needed to keep his mind busy and not to dwell on his current situation. "Depression is preventable" his survival instructor lectured in the classroom at Clark Air Base. "Keep your mind busy with futuristic thoughts. Review your favorite college courses, or whatever, but stay away from your dilemma. Depression grows from negative thoughts and it can become so severe that it can interfere with rational thought and actions. That can get you killed. Assume you will get out of your current situation."

He had plenty time to analyze their airplane's shoot down. Every day from the time he had arrived at Nakhon Phanom Eddie had played "what if," in case he received a serious hit from gunfire. He always grilled his students on the same emergency scenarios. He had a whole bagful of pre-analyzed options ready to draw from. But it all happened in two or three seconds—there was no time for such actions. He had instantly defaulted from his collection of "hit by gunfire" scenarios to his bag of "survival on the ground" scenarios.

That afternoon the rains were late and much lighter. He was lucky to get his canteen re-filled before the rain was over. There was no human activity on the ground and Eddie hoped they had finished their search of the vast flat plain of jungle—where he sat comfortably eighty feet above the ground.

Eddie used the last few hours of light to carefully pick his way along the tangled tree branches to the monkey fruit tree. The little fruit they were eating was about the size of a cherry, thick skinned, with a pasty seed mass inside. The skins were bitter and inedible but the seeded inside, although tart, was edible. He was famished but only ate a half dozen. In survival class they told them to eat only a little of something suspicious, then wait twelve hours to see if you got sick or not. Then eat a larger dose and test it another twelve hours. If all went well then eat but don't gorge. He picked several pocketfuls of those that appeared to be ripest; the monkeys had worked the tree over quite well. Then he slowly worked his way back to his home in the tree crotch. He was feeling more confident and decided the next day he would start a new phase in his survival plot.

* * * * * * * * * * * * * * * * * * * *

The monkeys woke Eddie again at the break of day. After they moved on, he left most of his survival items securely tied inside his piece of parachute panel, tied tightly into his tree crotch and covered with small tree branches. He was lighter and more agile without his collection of survival items and his climb to the top of the tallest tree, the tree he had just missed during his parachute descent, would be much easier. He climbed carefully, frequently stopping for several minutes to listen for human voices on the ground. Eventually he was clinging to the smallest branches that would hold his weight. There was jungle and low hills in all directions. There was no sign of the gun that had shot him down or where the aircraft had crashed. He needed a place where a helicopter could make a low hover or maybe even a landing. He had his pocket compass with him and he selected and took a bearing on a hillside several miles to the west. The westward bearing would take him further away from the Ho Chi Minh Trail and its enemy military presence. On the hillside there were several spots, openings, where the vegetation looked like it was short. Maybe they were the result of fires during the dry season, or logging, or maybe slash and burn farming. If he couldn't find the opening or some other safe place for a chopper to pick him up, he would just continue walking west. Somewhere out there was the Mekong River, maybe a week or ten days away by foot. Then all he would have to do is trade his blood chit for a boat ride and he would be in Thailand. Or maybe he would steal a boat or anything that would float and end up on the other side in Thailand.

Having a direction to walk, he went into action. He loaded up his belongings at the tree crotch and slowly let himself down the tree trunk. He was actually excited about the thought of standing again on firm ground. It had been four days. On his way down he picked a number of the large leaves from the tree's vine, high enough in the tree that no one on the ground would notice the missing leaves. When first on the ground, he wrapped the leaves around his boots and tied them with parachute cord. His boot's footprints would be a dead giveaway of an American flyboy and he wanted the leaves to create an unrecognizable impression on the ground.

The idea of leaves tied to his shoes was a loser. They came apart within several minutes of walking. So he scattered the leaf remains under another tree with a similar vine and removed his shoes but not his socks. His footprints then would look like a large toeless primate, probably nothing like that lived in the jungle but a least he left no American boot prints. His sensitive almost bare feet made it easy to walk slowly and silently as he picked and felt his way along the relatively open jungle floor. With all the rain, the mat of damp leaves on the ground was quiet to step on and without his boots and by staying on the damp leaves, he left no footprints behind. If he couldn't find a suitable place for a helicopter pick up, maybe after an estimated twenty mile trek westward, he would be out of the hostile area and he could wear his boots again. The three canopies of vegetation sucked up almost all of the sunlight and the vegetation on the floor was surprisingly sparse. With his boots back on he would then be able to make good time traveling. He stopped frequently and listened to the jungle sounds. There were no voices. He resisted the desire to move fast. Slow deliberate steps with frequent stops to listen would allow him to detect others before they detected him. People had the propensity to talk, so by going slowly he could hear them before he got too close. This was a hunting game and he was the hunted.

During the next several hours he crossed three trails. Judging from the hoof and foot prints, two appeared to be animal trails and one definitely had human footprints. There was everything from boot prints (military) to sandals and barefoot prints. The latter were probably local natives. All were a threat to Eddie. The military were the most threatening but the locals could capture him and sell him to the North Vietnamese Army. He watched each of the trails for some time. Then he picked a place to cross where it was possible to not leave any footprints. He stepped on rocks, fallen tree branches, many things that hurt his sensitive feet, but he left no tracks in the vicinity of the trails. He studied the drainage and the lay of the land and chose to travel in the more difficult areas where a trail and people were less likely to be. As he traveled he always chose his steps carefully, in the grass and through fallen leaves. Once the afternoon's monsoon rains fell, even the tiniest trace of his passage would be erased. He heard that the NVA used sniffer dogs to hunt downed American fliers. The rain would eliminate any scent he was leaving.

Once the afternoon rains did start he found a spot where the rainwater was pouring off the trees in a small rivulet. He replenished his water supply. Then he sat under a large tree that partially blocked the water. He was soaked by the rain water but it was the tropics. He would dry out with time. With the heavy noise of the rain, he was deprived of his ability to hear and listen to the jungle sounds. So he sat tight and waited the rain out. He couldn't take the chance on blundering into a group of natives or soldiers as they sat hunkered under a tree. He sat in the rain and played out a half dozen "what if" scenarios concerning the next several days. Every conclusion resulted in his fate resting with on the spot analysis and intelligent actions. It was impossible to pre-plan what would happen. When the rain finally stopped, it was dark and he spent a miserable night listening to jungle noises. Lying on the ground, he wished he was back on the farm.

Early the next morning, he climbed another tall tree and refreshed his bearings to the hillside. He was surprisingly close. Within a half hour he was on the edge of a grass clearing, not the one that he was trying to find with his compass but one he accidentally came upon. He spent the remainder of the day in a thick clump of bushes, eating the last half of his final payday candy bar, tart fruit centers, and he drank rainwater from his canteen. He watched the opening the rest of the day and there was no sign of humans. There were some strange noises coming from the grass, the usual birds feeding and chasing each other in play, but no humans. He watched all birds carefully; their actions could reveal the presence of someone he couldn't see from his hiding place. Several aircraft flew over, two different OV-10 spotters, an Air America C-123, and a two ship formation of A-1s. But none were low and none looked like they were searching for downed crew members or a crashed aircraft. They were all just going to and from work. That was just fine, he would get their attention in due time. First he had to finish scoping out his grass opening. He was getting close to a ride home and he didn't want to screw up the last chapter of his bailout.

* * * * * * * * * * * * * * * * * * *

The next morning the sun rose and the heat and humidity quickly turned Eddie's hideout into a baking oven. It had been four days since he had been exposed to the direct sun and the sweat rolled down his forehead and burned his eyes. There was still no human movement, noise or voices, and with the view that the clearing offered, there was no morning smoke from any cooking fires. This was it and he was ready to make his move.

The subsequent annoying wait lasted two hours. Then a single OV-10, about 1500 feet high and a mile to the north of Eddie's position, passed by. The pilot was rolling back and forth and was obviously looking for tell tail sign of the enemy. He was jinking, never holding a straight line but for a few seconds, so no gun could get a fatal bead on him. Eddie was ready with his survival radio.

"OV-10, this is Towhead Three Three on guard, do you read me?" Towhead Three Three was the call sign of the fateful aircraft he had been riding in when they took the 37mm hit. Eddie knew he had a winner as the OV-10 pulled up sharply into a sloppy, jinking loose circle.

"Read ya, Towhead Three Three. Thought you were dead." A thrill went through Eddie's weary body. "This is Nail Two Two. Are you alone? Who are you? How many survivors are there with you? Where are you at?"

"I'm alone, no one else got out," Eddie was sad to say. "You get me a helicopter in the area and some air cover and I'll give you verification who I am. I don't know how many people are listening in and I don't wanna give away my secrets, especially my location. You be careful, there's a 37 millimeter in the area, that's how I ended up down here."

"Copy all, Towhead. I'll call the cavalry and I'll keep an eye out for the gun."

Eddie turned his radio off. The Nail had all the information he needed to get a rescue started. Eddie didn't want any more chatter from the radio in case there was anyone else on the ground and within hearing distance. He had his revolver ready. He had loaded it with standard rounds. If he had to use it he didn't want any tracer rounds to draw a line, backwards, straight to his position.

Then, just as the OV-10 rolled into a sharp left jink, a string of bursts strung out and passed by where he would have been flying. The nimble turboprop zigged and zagged away and a second line of bursts missed him as he departed the area.

"That was a mistake," Eddie thought. "The gunner just gave away his position. Wait until the cavalry arrives and the Sandys (A-1s) work him over!" Eddie hoped it was the same gun that shot his aircraft down because the gunners only had a couple of hours to live.

The time went by slowly. Eddie hoped the chopper would arrive before the monsoon rain started. That could screw everything up. If they had to wait until the next day, the NVA would have the area saturated with troops and guns. Certainly his opening would be one of the places they would sit and wait for the American helicopter and he could end up dead with that scenario. But it was only an hour when a two ship of Sandy A-1s showed up in the distance with Nail Two Two leading them in a wide loose formation. While the A-1s circled off to the side, Nail Two Two made a zig zagging run on the section of jungle where the gun had fired from. He fired a smoke rocket, then flared over wildly and exited as the gunner tried desperately to guess where the aircraft would turn next. Ground fire erupted and the OV-10 dived down onto the deck and made his escape, so low the guns and Eddie couldn't track him through the trees. The target was marked. The gunners on the ground fired a multitude of bursts into the air as the A-1s pitched over and down, in trail (one behind the other), and zigged and zagged in. The lead aircraft sprayed the gun site with his four 20mm cannons to keep the gunner's heads down and their return fire off the mark. The second A-1 carefully placed his 500 pound bomb into the tiny gun clearing. After an explosion and a few small secondary pops as the former gunner's ammunition cooked off, there was silence from the ground. The two A-1s were not a part of the rescue mission that was just getting ready to launch out of Nakhon Phanom. They just happened to be passing through that part of the neighborhood on their way to another target. Nail Two Two had coordinated their diversion with the airborne command post for Eddie's benefit. Then in the distance Eddie could hear the unmistakable sound of a helicopter. Eddie turned his radio on again and couldn't hold back.

"Nail Two Two, I'm the Towhead and I hear a helicopter somewhere. That was fast!"

Nail Two Two was the rescue coordinator and he filled Eddie in, "I got an Air America Bell helicopter over here. You in a position that he could get in and pick you up? Are there any bad guys around you?"

"Negative bad guys and I'm next to a clearing with tall grass, send him over!" Eddie was trembling with excitement.

"Not so fast, hotshot. How do I know who you are? There's Russians down there that speak perfect English." the OV-10 driver replied.

"My personal code word is Kersey," Eddie responded.

"I don't have your code word with me," Nail Two Two lamented. "But I fly out of NKP. If you're a Towhead, tell me who is the sexy broad in the poster on your Hooch wall?"

"Raquel Welch," Eddie responded.

"What's the name of the big lizard in the tree by the hooch?"

"Harold!" Eddie responded again.

"Where ya at? We're gonna give you a ride home," Nail Two Two answered.

Tears formed in Eddie's eyes as he took out his compass and took a bearing from the direction that he could hear the aircraft's engines. "Fly south two zero five degrees. I'll talk you in when you get closer and I can see you. I'll position myself for a quick pickup and pop smoke when I see the chopper."

In less than a minute Eddie saw the two Spads and a single OV-10 as they jinked their way south by south west. "Tally Ho, two Spads and a Nail. Track one five degrees left, two miles." Eddie called. "You should see a clearing with tall grass. I'm on the south center edge of the clearing and I'm making my way into the grass, about one hundred feet."

"Now you're about one mile out. Turn a little to your right. Do you have the clearing?" Eddie was jubilant.

"I think so," the Nail answered. "Pop smoke if you have it."

Eddie pulled the tab on one of his two smoke flares and the orange smoke lifted out of the grass and into the hot humid air. The two Spads spread out and slipped into a trail formation, then flew a low pass directly over him. They were trying to draw enemy fire in case there were any bad guys waiting for them. Helicopters in a hover were the bad guy's favorite targets. The grass and the surrounding jungle were quiet. The bad guys had been listening on their captured survival radios, but only one could speak English and they wouldn't be able to get to that section of the jungle for another hour. Eddie's three day wait and his lack of radio contact were paying off.

The pickup was academic; the skilled Air America pilot swooped in and hovered ten feet above the smoke source. The helicopter's rotor wash fanned the grass away and flattened it. Eddie stood up and waded into the violent rotor wash. The helicopter pilot then lowered his hover and Eddie climbed onto the Bell's skid and pulled himself inside the freedom bird. Then they were out of there. There was no one else in the helicopter. The civilian contract pilot had been returning from delivering "soft rice" to some friendly villagers.

The two Spads gave them a short escort. When they were clear of the hostile area, the Spads peeled off and returned to their former task—minus the one bomb and a burst of machine gun fire they had left at the gun site. The OV-10 followed them home. He needed to re-fuel and debrief intelligence. The rescue mission that was being organized at Nakhon Phanom was cancelled.

* *

Eddie skipped the traditional drinking party that was held whenever someone was rescued from the grim reaper. Instead, after the de-briefing with the intelligence officers that was attended by his detachment commander and operation's officer, he made a bee line for his quarters to see if Mia was on the base.

Mia was on his bed when he entered his room. Her eyes were bloodshot from crying and her hair was all tangled. She leapt from her supine position and straight into Eddie's open arms. They stood there in a long

318

embrace and neither said a word. Their love said it all. And when Eddie was a no show at the bar that night, for the first time the rest of the Towheads realized that Eddie's relationship with Mia was much more than just a fling in the hay.

The next day the Towheads, those who weren't flying missions, had a ceremony for their fallen comrades: the rest of the EC-47 crew. Afterward Eddie got so drunk they had to carry him to bed. He was still a pilot in an unpopular war and he needed to share his emotions with his brothers in arms.

The morning after his big drunk, Eddie took a long shower, put on his 1505s and visited the detachment commander in his office. Eddie had developed a deep resolve to make his relationship with Mia somehow work out. After a twenty minute discussion about Eddie's dilemma, the commander made a phone call to Saigon, pulled some strings, and Eddie was granted a three month extension to his tour. It was not a solution to his problem but Eddie was elated. It gave him more time. The three month extension was a win, win deal for all parties involved. His detachment commander had the use of his experienced instructor pilot's services an additional three months, it had no effect on Eddie's separation date the following spring. And Eddie could stay at Nakhon Phanom a little longer with Mia.

CHAPTER TWENTY-NINE: THE PEOPLE'S REVENGE

Senior Lieutenant Tran Huu Ky had a very busy monsoon season. He briefed his old friend and comrade, Colonel Duc, on the results of his clandestine trip to the Nakhon Phanom area. The colonel was enamored with this loyal lieutenant's ingenuity and resourcefulness. The colonel made arrangements for Lt. Ky to give his same presentation to the Commander in Chief himself, General Giap. Although very nervous in the presence of the top general for the PAVN and personal friend of Ho Chi Minh, Lt. Ky was confident he could make his plan work. He projected this confidence in his briefing to the ageing general. Lt. Ky emphasized the low cost and high returns available if his proposition was successful. An hour later he departed Hanoi with authorization to appropriate forty Chinese manufactured 107mm rockets, four launching tubes and tripods, and two civilian trucks from anyone in the Republic. He also had orders that allowed him to acquire supplies and pick and train a gunnery team on the eastern edge of the Plaine des Jarres.

Within a week, Lt. Ky returned to the Plaine des Jarres in the black night currier helicopter. Lt. Ky picked eight civilian Pathet Lao volunteers from the cadre who were assisting the People's Army and set about training them to be the fastest rocket launching team he had ever had under his command. They also received additional training in personal firearms. They would be traveling in two trucks, so they could pull each other out of mud holes and also keep the loads lighter in each truck. When traversing Route 12, redundancy in transportation was essential. Two trucks were also more formidable as protection against the bandits that Lt. Ky had noticed working Route 12. With eight well trained Pathet Lao posing as lazy laborers but with hidden AK-47 rifles, they would be quite capable of defending their precious cargo.

Lt. Ky couldn't find any trucks that met his specifications on the Plaine des Jarres so he concentrated on training his team of insurgent Laotians. Under the cover of the monsoon clouded sky they trained for their rocket launching mission during the day and then repeated everything in the darkness of night, over and over again. They trained for months–well into the monsoon season. When at last they were ready, they rode in a returning army truck east on Route 7. They crossed back into the lieutenant's motherland, northern Vietnam. There, they found the two trucks they were looking for—beat up cosmetically but sound mechanically. With a little cosmetic alteration they were spitting images of those he saw along the Mekong. They requisitioned their rockets and launchers, carefully wrapped them in protective plastic, and re- packed them in crude unmarked wooden boxes.

During the night of September 25, 1970, their two trucks crossed Mu Gia Pass on Route 15 and dropped down, back into Laos and the Laotian village of Na Phao. The pass was covered with bomb craters and the monsoon muddied road was a nightmare, but there were an unlimited number of workers constantly filling fresh craters and assisting the passing vehicles. The road maintenance crews stared at the poorly dressed, disheveled looking Laotian volunteers. Then they were reassured by their escort, a smartly uniformed army senior lieutenant. Nor did they recognize the crude wooden cases in their trucks or the reason for the excessive amount of shovels, wooden planks, machetes, long heavy metal chains, containers of extra gas and several spare tires per truck. Such things were not necessary as there were hordes of workers all along the roadway south that were ready and able to assist passing trucks.

At Ban Na Phao, Lt. Ky contacted the binh commander, the same individual he had revealed his plans to six months earlier. Lt. Ky received assurance he would receive full support and access to any local resources to carry out his bold and highly classified mission. They gathered empty rice bags and tied them into large bundles. They stacked the bundles of rice bags on top of the heavy rocket filled wooden boxes and filled the rear of the covered truck beds to their ceilings. The trucks looked as if they were full of rice bags and they would pass for rice transporters returning from deliveries to the PAVN. They set up camp outside the village and camouflaged their trucks and camp with cut tree branches. There they waited for the monsoon to end. They needed at least a week of sunshine without rain before Route 12 would be somewhat passable. Several times there were three or four days without rain and then the skies would open up and pour again. They all knew that was the way of the seasons and they exercised and rehearsed, confident they would have their opportunity to continue.

October 21st was the last day of the rains and the weather instantly turned into bright sunshine and ninety-five percent humidity. They waited for seven days, as planned, then hid their Chinese built AK-47 rifles within easy reach among the rice sack bundles. Lt. Ky changed into his civilian disguise and turned his uniform and remaining military items over to the binh commander. Just after dark, they removed the tree branch camouflage from the trucks and their expedition headed west over Route 12. The going was rough; they sometimes only made three or four miles per night. They were constantly filling holes, bridging washouts with planks, and pulling each other out of mire with their long chains—all under dim moonlight. But they persisted, constantly reminding themselves that they needed to get to their destination before the water in the canals was too low. Every day the sun dried more mud, and each night they made more progress. After six nights of struggling through the mire, they changed their routine and traveled during the day. They were far enough from the Ho Chi Minh Trail that the American spotter planes would pay little attention to them. If they did look the two trucks over, the rag tag convoy of two trucks appeared to be just a group of civilians struggling in the mud, and traveling away from the trail area. If buzzed by an American spotter aircraft they had planned to all stand out in the open, stare and point at the aircraft, and wave at him as he flew over them. They saw no bandits. The locals and the bandits alike never expected to see trucks that early after the monsoon. On November 7th they rolled into Thakhek and turned north the short distance to Ban Nakak. The incognito Laotian Pathet Lao gunnery crew exchanged greetings and spoke with the locals as they drove by and blended in with the lowland rural atmosphere. The two brothers opened their warehouse doors and provided shelter and anonymity to the ragged and exhausted truckers. After that, none of the villagers saw the two trucks again or ever saw any of the laborers that had been hanging onto the two muddy trucks.

The trucks and the crew remained hidden inside the warehouse. Only the single artillery spotter left. He was whisked off by boat to the other side of the Mekong, only to be heard again two nights later when he gave a brief coded message that indicated everything was a go for his part of the operation.

The extra shed that the two brothers had constructed effectively shielded their dock from prying eyes. The gunnery crew bathed, one at a time, late nights in the Mekong. Inside the warehouse they unpacked their treasure, fitted the rockets with fuses and had a much deserved rest. The fresh fish and vegetables were a refreshing departure from their cold rice.

On the night of November 9, 1970, they waited until it was dark, then carefully loaded the rockets, launchers, and firearms into the two freight boats and without lights headed across the murky waters of the Mekong. The trip up the smaller stream was frightening for everyone. Residing in the dense underbrush that lined the stream's banks were night animals, creatures, and cousins to Harold the lizard. It was their imagination running wild. But at night there were no enemies in the tranquil Thai rice paddies. When they reached the Stupa, six of Lt. Ky's crew, their eyes adjusted to the darkness, pitched in swinging their machetes while two crew members posted guard with AK-47 rifles. Within twenty minutes they had a flat open space to set up their equipment.

While the rest carried the rockets and launchers into position, Lt. Ky carefully took compass readings and aligned the launchers. He drove stakes in the ground in front of each launcher, in line with their aiming point. He used a flashlight for his final alignment. The stakes would serve as a reference point to re-align the rocket launcher's aiming points in case they were bumped. He had hoped that an American aircraft would land on runway one five so he could re-confirm his bearings but he had no such luck. Also, he would use the stakes as a reference for adjusting the launchers left or right after the first volley of rockets had been fired and the corrections were called in by the spotter. The first volley would be spaced ten seconds between rockets and the spotter would call corrections for each individual launcher's impact point. He also set his pre-calculated tube angles, commonly called firing elevations, which dictated the distance to the impact. He connected wires to the batteries that were needed to ignite the rocket motors and connected them to their respective electrical pins. A radio check, a coded series of clicks, confirmed the spotter was in place and everything was set for a go. Lt. Ky was quite pleased. Everything was proceeding smoothly and as planned.

The time had arrived, and everyone present took a moment of quietness to absorb and remember this magical time and camaraderie. Almost as if by magic, the moon was rising and as it cleared the tree tops it flooded them with its golden light. Lt. Ky felt the moon was a good omen.

"Load," Lt. Ky gave the simple command.

Within a few minutes four separate voices responded quietly in the moonlight. "Ready one, ready two, ready three, ready four."

"Clear," Lt. Ky ordered.

"Clear one, clear two, clear three, clear four." Such a clearing drill was necessary to ensure everyone was clear of the exhaust paths of the rockets. They had all seen the necessity of this during the several rockets they live fired during training.

 Lt. Ky pressed his first button and there was a loud boom. Bright fire erupted from behind the first tripod rocket launcher. A fiery trail swooshed up into the sky. Ten seconds later he sent the second rocket on its way, then three and then four. The crew all shouted with joy. Silence was no longer necessary as anyone within hearing distance would have surely seen the rockets and knew they were there. The operatives that guarded their perimeter with AK-47s insured that no farmer or transient would interfere with their air show. When all four rockets were underway Lt. Ky ordered "load" and got on the radio with the spotter. He was anxious to make any aiming corrections needed so as to rain his rockets down upon the A-1 fighter bombers resting cozily and securely on their ramp.

CHAPTER THIRTY: STINGER FOUR TWO

Stinger Four Two was an aerial gun platform, a highly modified C-119 cargo aircraft. It was officially re-designated the AC-119 Stinger. Over the Ho Chi Minh Trail, seventy-five miles south east of Nakhon Phanom, Stinger Four Two was circling lazily in the dark. Painted dull black and with its exterior lights off, other than its engine noise it was virtually invisible. Its gunner was looking through night vision and infrared device at the maze of camouflaged roads and trails threading their way through the Laotian jungle. They were waiting for North Vietnamese cargo trucks to expose themselves at a river crossing that was the crew's favorite hunting spot. The Stinger crew was part of a small group of three AC-119K Stinger aircraft from the 18th Special Operations Squadron. The three aircraft were positioned at NKP to provide additional night firepower over the northern section of the trail. South of their river crossing, strung out along the trail and at lower altitudes, were also several night spotter aircraft, including a C-123 Candlestick from Nakhon Phanom. They were flying back and forth, looking through their night scopes, also trying to locate something for Stinger Four Two to kill with its lethal combination of side shooting guns.

The AC-119 Stinger was a successor to the AC-47 Puff gunship. The AC-47 was armed with three 7.62mm mini-guns that fired out the left side from the circling aircraft. It was a very effective weapon against enemy Viet Cong and NVA troops in South Vietnam, but its small bore guns were marginal against fortified targets, trucks, and thick jungle canopy. The AC-47 gunship was also limited by the small amount of ammunition and fuel it could carry. The air force had modified the durable C-130 turboprop freighter into a highly successful replacement gunship with large payloads of ammunition, long times over target, and an awesome array of firepower. Unfortunately, C-130s were a valuable commodity for other uses and not enough C-130s were available for conversion to gunships. The air force then turned to the old twin engine C-119 Flying Boxcar freighter for an alternate larger gunship. There were still plenty of them sitting around in the bone yard in Tucson, Arizona. They armed the old C-119s with four 7.62 mini-guns and two 20mm gatling guns, all sticking out of holes cut into the left side of the fuselage. The guns were an ideal combination for destroying trucks and other wheeled vehicles as well as enemy personnel. The AC-119K Stinger was equipped with all the latest high tech infrared and night vision devices for searching for trucks and aiming the gunship. A J-85 jet engine was attached under each wing to provide greater take-off thrust to lift the huge load of ammunition and fuel. The J-85s burned the same aviation fuel as the two piston engines and they utilized the same fuel tanks. Once safely airborne, the fuel inefficient jet engines were shut down and the aircraft could fly economically on its two original Wright 3350 radial piston engines. The jet engines were restarted whenever entering a firing orbit to provide more accurate speed control and to have extra power available in an emergency situation.

Occasional light pops, small surges, slight variations in sound, and subtle vibrations when the pilots placed their hands on the throttles, all were ways that radial engines could communicate with experienced pilots. The two Wright 3350 radial engines on the AC-119K were only one size smaller than the huge 4360s on the C-124. But they both required the same attentive care and feeding. Number two (right) engine was talking to its pilots on Stinger Four Two. It was sending subtle messages of pops and slight jerks to the pilots and the message was quite clear. It was sick and wanted to go home. The aircraft commander, Major Beckworth, was an ex C-124 pilot and he was a seasoned expert on the care and feeding of radial piston engines. He was taking number two's messages seriously. With only an hour's time into the mission, it didn't make sense to stay and tempt their complaining engine into doing something bad.

"That's it, we're out of here," Major Beckworth announced to his crew over the interphone. "This baby's got a sick engine. We're 'RTB.' Bob, call Alley Cat." RTB was pilot shorthand for return to base and Alley Cat was the nighttime airborne command post, a C-130 flying command center that was circling at a high altitude and directing the various hunting operations all along the northern trail.

As the major rolled the heavily laden gunship around toward Nakhon Phanom, co-pilot Lieutenant Robert Carter keyed the number one radio, "Alley Cat, this is Stinger Four Two. We got a sick number two engine, we're RTB to NKP."

"Stinger Four Two, Alley Cat copies you're RTB NKP, contact Invert on 278.4."

The young lieutenant flipped the radio select switch to the number two radio which was already on Invert's frequency and keyed, "Invert, Stinger Four Two's aborting with a sick number two engine. We're receiving NKP TACAN and proceeding direct NKP." The crew in the rear delayed unloading their array of guns until they were well clear of enemy territory. Major Beckworth, the seasoned veteran in the left seat, pulled number two back to a low power setting, trimmed out the yaw that developed from the asymmetrical power settings, and let the healthy number one radial engine do most of the work going home.

It was a beautiful clear night and below them the jungle and Karst terrain was black. It was after nine in the evening and all the local tribal people, without the convenience of electricity and light bulbs, went to bed early. NVA troops wouldn't give away their position with any source of light. Even the populated rice growing areas along the Mekong River flood plain, on their western horizon, had little to show. Only Americans left their lights on all night. The elevation of NKP was 584 feet above sea level and they were at 7000 feet so they assumed a shallow descent and traded altitude for airspeed.

Fifteen miles out from NKP the crew in the back was making preparations for landing and Bob started the J-85 jet engines. They would leave the jet engines at idle, no sense in wasting fuel, but would have them immediately available for extra thrust in case number two suddenly decided to quit. They were still quite heavy with fuel and had a full load of ammunition. Bob called the Nakhon Phanom tower, "NKP, this is Stinger Four Two. You awake? We're returning home early tonight cause our number two engine is running rough. Ya got a runway number for us to land on? Negative assistance required."

"I'm awake, just barely," the twenty year old airman answered. It was his night to pull duty. After the night aircraft were airborne, there wasn't much activity until all the night birds came home to roost, towards daylight. "There's no traffic in the area and the wind is calm, you're clear to land either direction. Give me a call when you're on three mile final." The pilots could see the wide silver ribbon formed by the Mekong River, reflecting the almost full moonlight. Nakhon Phanom Air Base and the small town of Nakhon Phanom were just starting to show. They were the only lighted areas they could see.

Suddenly there was a bright flash about three miles north of the airbase and a beautiful red tailed fire ball arched high in the air.

"Holly shit! Do you see that?" Bob pointed to their two o'clock position. "Fireworks, they must be having a festival or something." Then there was another bright flash and a second rocket arched into the air. The two pilots in the front were the only crewmembers that could see the fireworks show.

"I'd swear they look like rockets," Major Beckworth corrected his younger co-pilot. "And they're heading toward NKP!"

"Impossible, they don't get rockets at NKP," Bob stood his ground. Bob's disbelief was answered as two more rockets launched into the air. All four had been exactly ten seconds apart. The first one, then three more impacted with bright flashes and large fireballs. They appeared to hit on the east edge of the airbase lights.

"They do now," Major Beckworth muttered. "Crew," he keyed his interphone, "NKP is under attack—

re-load the guns, double time. We may have some work to do here. Adjust the guns for a forty-five hundred foot firing angle."

"We got a bad engine. We can't screw around chasing some rocker launcher worth two hundred dollars on the open market," Bob advised the major.

"True, we got a sick engine but we're doing okay right now. But those gomers are shooting at our only runway. There could be more rockets. I'm in no hurry to land on a runway with incoming rockets, especially not in an airplane carrying high octane gasoline and a load of ammunition. Besides, I'd bet there's no one else around to go get those little bastards. I've never seen any artillery on the base." The moon reflected off the smoke trails that hung suspended in the still night air. The major altered their heading toward the source of the smoke, where the bright flashes had originated.

"I'll call Alley Cat and get permission to fire." Bob was following their required protocol.

"To hell with Alley Cat, someone's trying to blow up our barn," the major corrected him. "I don't even know if Alley Cat has authority over the base at NKP. It's in Thailand."

"Then who should I call? Invert or the tower?"

"Try the tower. He's got the best view of what's going on, if he's still in the tower." Then the major selected the crew interphone and hollered, "How's it coming back there? NKP is under rocket attack and I need those guns in a few minutes."

"We'll have most of them back on line in a few minutes, we're hustling. We've been listening in on your cockpit interphone and understand the urgency," a gunner assured the major.

"Tower, this is Stinger Four Two, it looked like somebody just fired some rockets at you. Can you confirm and give me a situational summary?" the major queried.

"Scared the shit out of me," was the tower's situational summary. He then continued with the details, "One hit in the barracks area and the other three were just outside of our east perimeter fence. Missed the Invert building only a hundred yards or so. Correction, it looks like one of em blew the crap out of the base perimeter fence—sir, it's too dangerous here for you to land and I'm supposed to evacuate the tower in an emergency."

The major keyed his radio switch, "That's all I need to know, Son. There'll probably be more rockets along soon. Now you get out of that tower, take cover, and leave the rest up to us. We know where they're coming from and we're on our way to snuff em out." They were using both radial piston engines and both jets to climb up to 5084 feet above sea level. Nakhon Phanom was 584 feet above sea level so the 5084 feet would place them exactly 4500 feet off the ground.

"Come on, number two—hold it together just a little longer," Bob was talking to the aircraft. The major smiled to himself, Bob was still inexperienced but in another year and after having the holy crap scared out of him a dozen or more times, he would make a good pilot.

The major turned offset from the source of the smoke and when abeam he rolled into a left bank and made a wide circle around the source of the smoke trail. In a perfectly flown orbit with just the right bank angle, they could fly a circle around the target area and the major's visual gun sight and left wing would remain pointed at the stationary target in the center of the circle. It was called a pylon turn in airplane lingo. Wind would have required more aggressive maneuvering from the pilots but on that night there was no wind and the guns remained pointed toward the area of their objective. The night observation scope (NOS) operator was busy searching the ground. The bright moonlight made everything look like daylight through his night vision scope and he had the magnification turned up. What he saw caused a chill to run down his spine. Next to a small river there was a clearing in the trees and a small ruin of some type. There were people running around in what to them would be moonlight and they were working on a row of what could be four rocket launching tubes. Stacks of what could be rockets were next to each tube. All of those rockets, properly aimed, could turn the Nakhon Phanom airbase into a holocaust.

"Whata ya see down there?" the major asked the NOS operator. From the cockpit and without the aid of a night scope, the major could only see moonlit jungle and rice paddies out of his left window. The NOS operator was the crew's eyes as he peered through the state of the art combination night vision scope and gun sight.

"Sir, we just hit the mother lode," the night observation scope operator reported. "I see what appears to be rocket launchers and lots of people running around. I took a peek with the infrared and the rocket launchers are very hot. Oops, I just saw one of the guys pick something up from the pile of long slender tubes. Looks like he's placing it on one of the warm launchers. It's definitely the site where the four rockets came from. I'll hold the aiming point on the end of the row and I'm ready to fire whenever you are."

Major Beckworth looked at the row of six ready lights over his gun sight. The two 20mm gun lights were both green, three of the four mini-gun's lights were green. The single red light indicated that one mini-gun was still off line. The green lights indicated the gunners in the rear had set their gun angles for 4500 feet AGL, had completed their re-load, and were ready to fire. "Here we go," the major spoke to no one in particular but to the entire crew. Major Beckworth, the aircraft commander, had a computer generated orbit that was based on where the night scope was aimed and it assisted him in setting the airplane into the correct orbit (pylon) path. He then looked into his gun sight; it was a 6x6 piece of glass with two reticles displayed. One reticle was the aiming point as selected by the night operations scope operator, pointing his gun site device out the open door on the left side in the cabin. The other reticle was the major's visual gun sight, designed for day use. He fine tuned his flight path so as to superimpose the two reticles, thus his guns were aimed at the target selected by the NOS operator. To stay on the target the aircraft had to hold a precise 30 degree bank angle, maintain an airspeed ±3 knots, and maintain precisely 5084 MSL altitude. To do so the major concentrated on keeping the reticles superimposed with the flight controls, the co-pilot pressured the controls to keep the aircraft within its precise bank angle and altitude and the flight engineer worked the throttles to maintain the correct airspeed. When the two pilots and the flight engineer finally got the aircraft settled down and into position, they circled the target they couldn't see with their own eyes.

The major squeezed the fire trigger and fired a five second burst. As he fired the night operations scope operator worked his reticle down the row of rocket launchers and the major followed the moving night operations scope reticle with his aircraft visual reticle. Three mini-guns fired rifle slugs at a rate of 6000 rounds per minute, each gun, and the two 20mm Vulcan Gatling guns fired their heavier and larger slugs at over 2500 rounds per minute, per gun. The rear of the aircraft was filled with noise and a steady stream of what appeared to be fiery rain fell to the earth and plowed through the row of launching tubes and rockets. The hail of lead destroyed everything in its path. The fiery rain appearance was from the tracer rounds and they illuminated a bullet path, a fiery line, from their aircraft to the target. Without seeing the target but by keeping his two reticles superimposed, the major and the night operations scope operator skillfully walked the rain of fire from one end of the launchers to the other. The entire firing sequence took only five seconds but the devastation from the 1900 bullets, both small and large, was horrendous. The waiting rockets, stacked next to their intended launch tubes, exploded and fizzed off in all directions. They only added to the chaos.

The major continued his orbit and gave the target one more five second burst to make sure the job was complete. He was limited to five second bursts to keep his gun barrels from over heating. He looked over at Bob in the co-pilot seat and grinned at him. Bob smiled also and keyed his crew interphone. He announced, "Don't mess with the Stinger."

The night operations scope operator was the one person who saw it all. "Outstanding!" he shouted over the interphone. "Blew the shit out of em. Crap's flying all over the place from secondary explosions. Nothing could have lived through that." The crew in the back were elated with the accurate shooting and they proceeded to put their guns to bed for the second time that evening.

CHAPTER THIRTY-ONE: IT'S THE GOODBYES THAT ARE SO HARD

Eddie and Mia were inseparable. She was sleeping over with him several times per week and her father was growing more and more agitated because he was being deprived of the services of his adopted daughter. Eddie and Mia purchased a nice piece of soft, lightweight cotton material from the tailors shop in Nakhon Phanom City and she sewed it into a cute pair of pajama bottoms. She created a replica of the pajamas she had seen in a picture in an American magazine. This allowed Mia, along with one of Eddie's tee shirts, to snuggle with Eddie in his bunk bed at night and still maintain her dignity with Arnold sleeping in the same room. Many nights, when Arnold was sleeping in his half of their tiny shared bedroom area, Eddie and Mia couldn't make love for fear of waking Arnold. But they just lay in bed next to each other, finding peace and solace in their proximity and sharing light touches. Sometimes they would both awake in the middle of the night and would touch toes. Those little things meant so much to two people from opposite sides of the world, deeply in love and facing uncertain future.

The end of Eddie' tour extension was growing alarmingly close. He had only two weeks to go and still they had no solution to their dilemma. Mia prayed for Buddha's wisdom but no answer appeared. She had unwavering faith that somehow everything would be okay.

That evening she and Eddie were able to sit alone at the Towhead Bar as there were no other flyers around. They had all migrated to the officers club to see the monthly strip show. As usual, the girls were rank amateurs from one of the bars downtown Nakhon Phanom City. The girls half stripped, then solicited money from the crowd to remove more of their tacky clothes. The guys and a few female intelligence officers from Task Force Alpha booed them off the stage. Then a drunken Spad pilot climbed onto the stage and proceeded to strip to his shorts, to the tune of Chain of Fools by Aretha Franklin. For this they all cheered and hooted while the strippers from downtown exited the back door and called the GIs number ten. It was an ugly scene as everyone remained at the club to see who could out drink and out boast the others. Eddie, Mia, and Loat San thus had the Towhead Bar to themselves.

It was a pleasant, quiet evening. Mia and Loat San didn't drink liquor. Eddie was enjoying a Harvey Wallbanger. Eddie found if he took his Galliano bottle to the Towhead Bar, somehow it had a propensity for disappearing down the throats of his ungrateful peers. So he kept the bottle of Wallbanger ingredients in his room. The evening was getting on and Mia looked dazzling to Eddie. He wondered if maybe he and Mia could spend a little quality time together in his room before Arnold and the other soused Towheads returned from their big night out at the O'club.

"Loat San, no Towheads or Nails gonna come by before ten, when you get off work. Why don't you just go on home early? If they do show up, I'll tell them I said it was okay."

"I stay here tonight, with Eddie," Mia played along with the idea. "I have much laundry to do in the morning."

"I stay until ten, it dishonest for me to go home before ten," Loat San insisted. "Your drink is empty. You want me to get you something?"

"No, but thanks." Eddie didn't feel like inconveniencing his friends.

"I get you another Wallbanger," Mia insisted. Before he could stop her she picked up his empty glass and headed out the bar door to fix another Wallbanger in Eddie's room.

There was a heavy whooshing whistle and a deafening explosion. It knocked Eddie off his chair and into the bar. Luckily the blast came from a slight angle and the shattered glass from the bar's only window was blown into the unoccupied end of the bar. The blast, however, leveled the walls, caved in the roof, and the debris fell covering Eddie and Loat San. Loat San had been picking up a dropped wash cloth behind the bar and the bar shielded him from injury. Eddie was instantly knocked unconscious and it took a full twenty seconds before he slowly came to his senses. He pushed up on the collapsed ceiling debris and in the dim moon light he saw Loat San doubled up on the floor.

"You okay, Loat San?"

"I okay, but my ears are make a ring sound." Loat San slowly sat up. "I'm glad Mia not here when this happen." Eddie felt stunned from the concussion and his ears were ringing, but he felt no broken bones. The light was very dim, the electricity for the hooch was out and they had only moonlight streaming down on where a building once stood. He felt wet on his face and wondered if it was blood but there was no time to check it out. He had other priorities.

"Mia, I have to get to Mia," he insisted as he crawled out of the ruins and looked towards his room. There was a huge crater between him and his room so he hobbled around it and burst into his room.

"Mia, are you okay?" he hollered. But there was no answer. He switched on his light switch, which was attached to a section of wall that hung free from the framing. The lights worked but there was no Mia. Eddie whipped around and ran back outside on the raised sidewalk.

"Mia, Mia, Where are you?" he hollered. He jumped from the sidewalk and ran back and forth hollering her name. There was no Mia to be found.

Then he saw it, a shiny gold fragment in the open door's light, a glistening red ruby surrounded by star sapphires. It was imbedded in the wooden post that, prior to the blast, had supported the tin roof covering the sidewalk. It had obviously traveled to this position from the blast area. In his daze, he used his pocket knife to pry it out of the post. He stuck the precious piece of jewelry into his pocket. Mia had been wearing it every day since he had given it to her and now she was nowhere to be found. She had literally disappeared in a blast of smoke. Then the reality hit him like a sledge hammer and he dropped to his knees in shock. All that he had left of her was a portion of her bracelet. That was all Eddie could remember of the blast. The rest was a thick haze and extreme agony, as the medics arrived and fought him to the ground. They transported him, struggling and fighting, blood running down his face, to the base hospital and put him out with heavy sedatives.

* * * * * * * * * * * * * * * * * * * *

The *Air Force Times* carried an article, on the third page, about the incident:

On November 9, 1970, at 2145 local time several self propelled rockets struck Nakhon Phanom Royal Thai Air Base, which is located in the eastern perimeter of Thailand, adjacent the Mekong River. Times correspondents were prohibited from visiting the base and obtaining first hand information due to the heavy security restrictions associated with the American classified operations originating from this remote base. An official joint command release indicated only minor damage was inflicted by the rockets. One civilian employee was reportedly killed. One American serviceman received minor injuries and the explosion destroyed an unauthorized shelter utilized by Thai employees.

Officials are investigating the source of the rocket firing, which is suspected to have been fired by an insurgent guerrilla band believed to be operating in the vicinity of the air base. This is the first incident of this type to be carried out against jointly operated American/Thai Air Bases located in Thailand. Pentagon officials expressed concern over the vulnerability of such air bases to rocket and mortar attacks and have informed Times reporters that precautions have been implemented to prevent such attacks from occurring in the future. They stressed, however, that such attacks serve more as a psychological harassment than producing actual damage to American equipment and operations.

Official results of the investigation should be available in six to eight weeks and will be released through proper military channels at PACAF Headquarters in Hawaii.

Subsequent articles in Time and Newsweek magazines were far more speculative and heavily weighted with embellishment: *Was this the opening of a new chapter of guerrilla warfare against the American military and their bumbled war in South East Asia? What is the nature of the secret operations from this off limits back door base into Laos? Is Thailand the next country to be enveloped by the spreading anti-American sentiment in South East Asia?*

On base the scene quickly returned to normal. The base engineer's crew of civilian Thais worked around the clock filling in the blast crater, restoring the landscaping, carrying off the debris, and repairing the damaged quarters. They were under orders to remove, as soon as possible, all visible reminders that the incident had ever occurred. The section of the Towhead Towers that received scattered shrapnel from the blast needed superficial repairs. The siding, doors, and windows needed replacement but the structure was solid and salvageable. The impact had been much closer to the bar and inflicted heavy damage. The bar and lounge remains were quickly dismembered and hauled away. The crater was filled and turned into a flower bed to disguise the wounded location. As they cleaned up and removed the debris, the Thai crew discovered numerous pieces they could only, reluctantly, identify as Mia's remains. They discretely hid these pieces until their shift change, then smuggled them off base and returned them to the two surviving members of Mia's family. Loat San had his base pass withdrawn, as if he had anything to do with the rocket attack. That was the way the military operated when under duress. Harold the lizard was never to be seen again.

A four hour debate raged behind administrative closed doors on the subject of unauthorized hooches serving as bars and lounges. Were they something that they should continue to tolerate? Should they all be torn down? Were they essential for morale and camaraderie? In the end it was decided that for morale purposes and to minimize the lasting effects of the attack, they would rebuild the Towhead Inn exactly as it was before. It was a simple building and it took a gaggle of Thai carpenters, working two twelve hour shifts each day, two days to reconstruct it. They couldn't, however, replace the large model of an EC-47, the life-sized poster of Raquel Welch, and the myriad of knickknacks and memorabilia that made the place home. After completion, the new hooch was seldom used, at least until there were enough replacement flyboys without memories of the old hangout.

* *

Eddie slowly emerged from the blackness of sedation. The memories and horrors of the rocket attack slowly resurfaced into his consciousness. He was too weak to move from the sedation but his mind was screaming from the hell. Doctors frequently speak of the mind's ability to erase memories from tragic events, those that are too horrible for the individual to tolerate. Eddie was not so lucky. He slowly recalled every horrid second of the event . . . at least until they put him down with sedative. He wanted to die. There was no reason to go on without his Mia. His world was destroyed. Lying on his back with his eyes closed, he heard someone come into his room and he elected not to move. He was in no mood to speak to anyone.

"We've kept him sedated for two days. Now we gotta bring him out and clean up this mess before the inspectors arrive." Eddie recognized the flight surgeon's voice.

"What are we going to do with him?" Eddie recognized the voice of the new operations officer, Major Cronkite. He was the replacement when Major Collins rotated home. The detachment commander was away in Bangkok attending a two day meeting with the Ambassador and the air force attaché to Thailand. He left orders not to be disturbed. Under those circumstances, Major Cronkite was in charge and had the necessary authorization to make command decisions concerning Eddie's plight. "I'd feel uncomfortable about putting him back on flying status. He's got eight stitches in his forehead from a cut he got from the bomb blast. He probably hit it on something cause there was no shrapnel in the wound. He'll get a purple heart anyway cause it was caused by the enemy. I was gonna send in the paperwork this afternoon. The cut in the forehead wouldn't keep him from flying but he's certainly going to have psychological damage from the blast and the death of his maid." He spoke with an emphasis on the word maid.

"That would be my call also," the flight surgeon agreed. "I'd have to agree with you. He's not fit to fly at this time."

"Bullcrap," a strange voice piped up. "I didn't fly all the way up here from Saigon to hold some pansy lieutenant's hand because his maid got killed." The full colonel wing commander from Saigon was annoyed at the freight pilot pansies under his command. He was a fighter pilot and took no crap from anyone. "Give him two or three days to get his head straight and throw him back into the saddle. The best way to recover from getting bucked off is to get back in the saddle."

"With all due respect, Sir," Major Cronkite spoke. "I've only been here a couple of months and really haven't gotten to know everyone that well. I have, however, heard a few rumors about this pilot. When the attack occurred, I pulled his files and read them. Listen to this." Eddie heard some papers being shuffled.

"I'll just summarize these so you can get the idea," Major Cronkite offered.

"One, he got drunk in a down town bar and to show off to the enlisted men in his presence, he pissed on a snake outside the main entrance. Because of that incident, to this day they all call him Lieutenant Nuts.

"Two, he disobeyed a direct order from a senior officer and landed on a taxiway, rather than wait until an aircraft on the runway was towed out of the way.

"Three, he jeopardized the safety of his aircraft and crew to purposefully draw gunfire from a known enemy anti-aircraft gun." (*That wasn't even Eddie.*)

"Four, he started a rumor that he was intercepted by a MIG, then went around denying it. There was no evidence on record that it was true.

"Five, he threatened his maid with his handgun. He held his revolver to her head and threatened to kill her.

"Six, He had an affair with his most recent maid, and had her sleep over with him, all against regulations. She was the local laborer that was killed by the rocket, Sir.

"Seven, while serving in the capacity of flight instructor he allowed the pilots to stray off course and be exposed to enemy gun fire. This action resulted in the loss of an aircraft and all crewmembers except him. He could offer no plausible reason why he survived the shoot down but his dereliction of duty was obvious.

"Sir," the new operations officer continued, "This lieutenant only has a couple of weeks to go before he rotates to the States and I received the orders yesterday that he's scheduled for an early out as soon as he returns. Now that I've had a chance to read these files, files that Major Collins meticulously kept, I'd like to find some way to get rid of him now. Based on this new information, I can't place any trust in what he would say to the incident inspection team when they arrive. They won't be tolerant of us for allowing officers to screw their domestic help and especially in the officer's quarters."

"Ya can't punish him for getting his whore killed from a rocket attack," the wing commander from Saigon voiced his objection. "Hell, the rocket attack wasn't his fault. I say throw him back in the saddle." The Saigon voice sounded a little agitated. "If I didn't turn my back on some of the shenanigans my F-4 crews pull back in Saigon, I'd be out of aviators in a week."

"How about a medical discharge for psychological reasons?" the flight surgeon asked. "With all the written evidence of his misbehavior, I could write something up that sounds acceptable. We could ground him from flying and ship him back to the States before the inspection team ever had a chance to talk to him. With that deep bruise on his butt he won't be able to fly for a couple of weeks anyway and he's due to rotate back in two weeks. If we send him back tomorrow as damaged goods, by the time the inspection team figures it out, if they did, this guy would be a civilian and out of their jurisdiction."

330

The Saigon colonel jumped back into the fray, "I didn't know he had a bad bruise on his ass and was going home in two weeks. Why didn't somebody tell me that in the first place? That means he can't sit in an airplane seat for seven hours. If he's of no use to us anyway, then do it. Write him up as a trouble making fruit basket and ship him the hell out of here. Pronto! Get him off the payroll and we can all go back to work. I got better things to do back in Saigon. They're fueling my F-4 as we speak. I wanna get this rocket mess cleaned up, airborne, and back to Tan Son Nhut before dark. Hell, a rocket attack is as common as lunch back there—and don't send any paperwork for a purple heart. I don't wanna leave any paperwork trail to catch up with us on this damn rocket attack. Change your medical record to say he was drunk and fell off a bar stool. Happens all the time in Saigon."

The Towhead operations officer interrupted the colonel, "Sir, I just found another piece of paper in his file. It's an extension of his tour for three months. He's been here a little over two months past his overseas return date . . . and it's got your signature on it. Is that gonna be any problem?"

"Not now that I know about it," the colonel growled. "I got hundreds of papers crossing my desk every day; somebody probably slipped that one by me and I signed it. Tear it up and throw it away. When I get back to Saigon I'll have my staff scour our headquarters building and make sure there aren't any copies. When he gets back to the States they're gonna process him out and send him back to his mamma. If anyone notices that he stayed over two months extra, they aren't gonna go through the trouble of investigating his records. After all, we're discharging him cause he's nuts and they'll just wanna get rid of him.

"Now, anybody got anything else I need to know . . . if not I'm going back to Saigon."

Eddie's head was much clearer but he still was still too woozy to open his eyes or sit up. So Major Collins had the last say after all. Even after he left, the major was able to exert vengeance upon Eddie. At that particular time, however, Eddie really didn't care about the major or anything else. Without Mia, nothing else mattered. He just wanted out. He wanted to go anywhere that the world wasn't crazy.

* * * * * * * * * * * * * * * * * * * *

The nurse came in and tinkered with his IV, then proceeded to wipe his face with a clean, damp wash cloth. Eddie had fallen back into a dreamless sleep. The wet cloth awakened him and he forced his eyes open. Although a bit blurry he looked up and into the eyes of a Caucasian woman. She was all white, her clothing, her skin, a white hair net, and a white background. She didn't have any wings. Then Eddie noticed a light fixture in the blurry white background, and the white wall had a picture on it. That was good. It meant he wasn't dead and she wasn't an angel.

He tried to sit up as he needed to get out of there. The conversation he had previously eavesdropped on re-confirmed that Mia had really been killed. What really had happened? But he was just too weak from the sedation and he collapsed back onto his bed.

"Hold on there Cowboy!" The nurse adjusted his pillow with her left hand and restrained him with her right. "You're not going anywhere. There's two MPs just outside the door."

"Have I got a bad bruise on my butt, I can't feel anything?" he mumbled.

"Nope, I bathed you last night and I thought your butt looked real nice. You got a big crack in it and a hole in the middle, just like everyone else but you got no bruise. Where'd you get that idea?" She smiled. "You been faking unconsciousness and listening to what's going on around here?"

"Maybe," Eddie mumbled. He just wanted answers and couldn't care less what the nurse thought.

"The scuttle butt among the nurses," she confessed, "is that the flight surgeon told the wing commander from Saigon that you had a big bruise on your ass so he couldn't send you out to fly again." She looked into his eyes and assured him, "I just talked to the doctor and he told me you're gonna go home in the morning. We gotta get you off this IV sedative and I gotta pull that cannula out of your penis. I bet you're gonna be needing it when you get home—the penis I mean, not the cannula." She giggled.

＊ ＊ ＊ ＊ ＊ ＊ ＊ ＊ ＊ ＊ ＊ ＊ ＊ ＊ ＊ ＊ ＊ ＊ ＊ ＊

It's amazing how fast things can take place in the military when a full colonel wing commander in Saigon orders it to happen. That afternoon three airmen scurried around Nakhon Phanom, having the various agencies sign Eddie's departure paperwork. They packed his personal goods and had them standing in a corner of base operations, waiting for the next morning's Klong. When Arnold returned from his afternoon flight, Eddie's side of the room was empty and the hospital told him Eddie was still not allowed any visitors. Eddie had no idea all of this was occurring, He wanted to get his strength back and wanted to talk to Loat San and Arnold. The doctor made sure Eddie got another good night's sleep to make sure he didn't cause any trouble. Nurses spent the night "observing" his activities. They were really assisting the military policemen guarding the hallway to make sure he didn't screw up the colonel's battle plans. The flight surgeon administered Eddie a powerful sleeping pill to replace the IV, embellished Eddie's records even more than Major Collins had, and faxed it stateside recommending an immediate medical discharge. Returning Vietnam veterans were considered to be a pain in the butt and dumping him back into the civilian ranks was the quick fix of the times.

The next morning Eddie felt his butt all over and couldn't feel anything wrong. He crawled out of bed and had to brace himself until the dizziness went away. He wondered why he was so groggy and suspected that the "pain killer" pill they gave him the night before was more for the fact that he was the pain in the ass. He hobbled over to the toilet, dropped his hospital gown on the floor and twisted around as he checked his butt for a bruise. He didn't trust anyone, not even the nurse. There was no bruise but the same nurse in white walked into his room without knocking. She stood looking at Eddie. He was bare assed naked. She put her hands on her hips and scolded, "Now aren't you just a bad boy. Go potty if you have to and I'll wait and help you get back into bed. You're too popular as a patient to let you slip and bang your head."

He turned and looked at her. He was still nude but not feeling any buzz from exposing himself. "Tell me the truth, am I really crazy or is all of this just a bad dream?"

"You're naked, cross eyed and all drugged up, just ripe for a bad dream. But unfortunately it's all true," she confessed.

Then she spilled her opinion, "Look, I never said this and I'll deny it if you repeat it. But you're being railroaded out of here, that's why we were ordered to keep you heavily sedated. I don't know if all of that stuff that's being said about you is true or if you really pissed someone off and he's out to get you. But whatever—you're the perfect scapegoat. When the investigators for the rocket attack get here they're gonna wanna know what a maid at a high security base was doing at an unauthorized bar at nine o'clock at night."

She embellished to make her point, "It's like the mucky-mucks running the base here are looking for a way to wipe their hands clean of the entire matter. They're blaming you for the maid that got blown all to bits outside your room, Thai girls sleeping with GIs all over the base, the rocket attack, cockroaches, bad food. Everything is your damn fault and when the investigators arrive they're gonna tell them that you're to blame for the entire god-damned war and that they have it under control because they sent you home and are booting you out of the air force to avoid the bad publicity of a court martial. If I were you, I'd take the ticket home and the walking papers. If you try to fight it you'll only sink deeper in the hole. You can't fight city hall.

"Now I'm supposed to give you this pill, it's to keep you pleasant, melancholy, and harmless. I suggest you flush it down the toilet and keep your mouth shut and cooperate. And it would help me out if you acted like you were drugged a little more than you already are."

Eddie wanted to stay and bury his love, Mia, but he really wasn't sure if there was enough left to bury. He had no knowledge of the local Thai burial traditions, or even if they buried their dead. Maybe they cremated them? His fantasy affair with the Lady and her real life counterpart, Mia, was definitely over. He showered,

332

brushed his teeth, and decided not to shave. With a little stubble it made him look more like a wacko. At 10:00 a.m. the next morning a six foot four, 250 pound black orderly showed up with Eddie's complete 1505 uniform. After he was dressed, the orderly escorted him to base operations. There they waited. When the morning C-130 Klong arrived, the orderly escorted him on board the aircraft and sat down next to him.

"You gonna go along with me?" Eddie asked.

"Just to Bangkok," the well mannered young orderly replied. "They want me to put you on a C-141 out of Bangkok to Clark Air Force Base. They loaded a B-4 bag with your personal stuff on the plane for you. The bag's got your civilian clothes, spare underwear and shaving and toilet items. When we were turning your issue stuff in at base supply, I kept out a flight suit and combat boots for souvenirs. They were so worn out that the supply clerk would have thrown them out anyway. They're in your B-4 bag. I packed a large wooden box with your stereo, tapes, and other personal stuff from your room and they're going to Bangkok with us. They're in the back of the airplane. I got all the orders and paperwork in this briefcase. I'll give it to you when we get to Bangkok. When you get to Clark an escort will be waiting for you and will see you on board a United DC-8 that's returning to Travis Air Base in California. You some sort of bad ass or someting?"

"I must be," Eddie grinned at his escort. "I don't even own a stereo . . . here in Thailand at least. You just made me a thief of my room-mate's stereo and tapes. That's pretty bad ass." When he arrived in Colorado Eddie would write Arnold a long letter explaining everything that happened—from his view point. He would apologize for the stereo mix up and enclose a check for the confiscated items.

"Too late now," the escort swung his head. "Wish they had me escorting you all the way back to the States. I'm goin nuts over here. I got a wife and a kid back there."

"Put your name on a copy of my orders and come with me," Eddie suggested. "I suspect there's even a copy of orders that certify me as being crazy. Put your name on all my orders and give yourself a discharge from the air force. You would die of old age before the bureaucrats in the Pentagon would figure it out. They're too busy making excuses for this war."

"Man, maybe you are a little nuts," the orderly joked.

"That's what they call me here at NKP, Lieutenant Nuts."

"I believe it." The airman grinned. "In fact … I think I've heard of you."

On November 12, 1970, the morning Klong lifted off from the runway at Nakhon Phanom Royal Thai Air Base. Eddie's best memories and worst nightmares were sealed in history. Four hours later, the afternoon Klong shuttle from Bangkok landed at Nakhon Phanom and the base commanders, both the American and his Thai counterpart, greeted a group of five officers that deplaned. The group had flown as passengers in a C-141 from Clark to Bangkok. Their route took them over Danang, airway Amber 8 over Laos, and safely into Bangkok where they caught the afternoon Klong. All five had their tickets punched. They would receive combat pay for the month even though they were only passengers and crossed Vietnam and Southern Laos at 29,000 feet and 510 miles per hour.

The five officers were from the Pentagon and they were there to investigate the rocket attack and other disconcerting rumors they had been hearing for some time about Nakhon Phanom. They all were wearing air force blues, the long sleeved wool jacket with light blue shirt and tie that they regularly wore at the Pentagon. Their shoes were shined and spotless and their conduct was serious and all business. The temperature was one hundred three degrees Fahrenheit and the humidity was ninety-six percent. The first blast of air almost sent them to their knees. They were about to inspect and pass judgment on a secret base that was conducting a dirty, unpopular war, under a heavy load of restrictions from Washington, against a highly motivated and intelligent enemy. They had been instructed to open up the can of worms and clean house. What they didn't know was that when military combatants are involved in fighting a dirty unpopular war, with one hand tied behind their back, they quickly learn a few tricks of their own. Tricks of appearances, deception, and survival.

Their key witness, alleged perpetrator and designated scapegoat, had flown the coop four hours earlier and everything on the base seemed quite proper and normal. The carpenters were just putting their tools away after repairing Towhead Towers Officer's Quarters and hastily slapping together a new Towhead Inn.

According to their instructions from the Pentagon, the key perpetrator's name was Lieutenant Nuts. He was nowhere to be found and everyone smirked whenever they asked questions about him. There was no Lieutenant Nuts listed anywhere on any of the base manpower registers. His antics and indiscretions were no worse than those of tens of thousands of other GIs that served their tour of duty in Southeast Asia, quite mild compared to some. Eddie just happened to piss off the wrong person, a very vindictive and heartless major, who was a master at deploying the air force's most formidable weapon—paperwork. The few maids to be found were clean, well dressed and mannered, and they all left the base every day at 4:30 p.m.

It took the investigation committee three days to complete their investigation and after returning to the Pentagon, five weeks to write up their report. The temperature broke one hundred degrees Fahrenheit by ten every morning that they were at Nakhon Phanom and the humidity never went below ninety percent. Also, for some strange reason, the air conditioning didn't work very well in the rooms they were assigned. The base investigation was supposed to take five days. But because none of the individuals they interviewed knew anything about the alleged violations and most of the pre-selected ones were busy flying missions, after three days they cut their inquiry short. They were in a hurry to flee the heat, the boondocks, clandestine operation, and get back to Washington and their air-conditioned offices and homes. It seemed that everything was so classified the investigators were unable to function comfortably. Their final report revealed several interesting items:

1. *The allegations of inappropriate sexual behavior in the Officers' and enlisted quarters were unfounded. There was no evidence to support such claims.*

2. *There was no evidence that any personnel were injured or killed by the brief rocket attack.*

3. *The damage from the rocket attack was limited to a short segment of the perimeter fence and no military structures were damaged.*

4. *Personnel records revealed no trace of a Lieutenant Nuts ever stationed at Nakhon Phanom Royal Thai Air Force Base. The investigators conclusion was that the rumored Lt. Nuts had been a mystical character that had been invented by bored aircrews with too much time on their hands.*

5. *It was recommended that a committee be formed at the Pentagon for the purpose of studying ways to improve the security and prevent future attacks at Nakhon Phanom.*

Eddie's transfer went almost as planned. At Bangkok, after a four hour wait for maintenance on their aircraft, Eddie was airborne again and on his way to Clark. The C-141 was an empty freighter, returning to the States for another load of freight. It was empty, except for several hundred pounds of mail, a forlorn looking airman first class on emergency leave, Eddie, his B-4 bag, and his big box of personal effects that included a top of the line stereo set. At least Eddie was free of the hassle, his head was clear, and he had time to think and try to rationalize the last three days events. But try as he could, there was nothing rational that had happened during the last three days, or the last fourteen months, or since he had driven away from Williams Air Force Base in Arizona. Why did it have to be Mia whose life was snuffed out and her body so violated? Eddie was sure she would have had an answer or explanation for its happening. Some little story or reasoning that would sound acceptable. It was her way, the way of her Yao people. They knew how to accept and to endure. It was just as her new father said, "The people will continue growing rice, eating fruit, having babies, catching fish from the klong, and their lives would go on." Mia had been denied the privilege of continuing the Yao tradition of moderation, acceptance, and raising beautiful children. As for Eddie, he was still alive but his life was over. Something inside him was dead.

About half way to Clark her death really hit home. He was immersed in a sea of grief and confusion. What a horrible ending to her trouble-plagued life. He had known her for such a short time, but it was as if he had loved her for most of his life. Such a short time and now he was alone. "When you are ready," the Buddhists say, "your teacher will appear." Mia had been Eddie's teacher.

Sitting on the canvas fold-out seat in the cargo compartment, Eddie burst out crying. Sitting across from him the airman burst out crying. Eddie for his lost love left behind, not even a body to grieve. The airman for his lost mother, who had just died from breast cancer and he was going home to her funeral.

* * * * * * * * * * * * * * * * * * *

There was no one to meet Eddie at Clark. There were limits to how well the air force could schedule someone's disappearance and the four hour delay in Bangkok for maintenance had screwed up their plans. Eddie found a hand cart and wheeled his B-4 bag and box of personal items into the passenger terminal, only to be told that his flight had already left. Clark had re-scheduled him for a flight at eight the next morning in the cargo compartment of another C-141. "No, there isn't time to get you on the one you just came in on, or on any of the next five empty C-141s that are leaving for the States before eight tomorrow morning," the airman at the desk informed Eddie. He had already been scheduled to leave at 8:00 a.m. It was the air force way and he just went with the flow. Eddie was a whipped pup and he didn't protest. He had nowhere to go anyway and he wanted to say a proper goodbye to Clark Air Base. For a dollar he talked a Filipino taxi driver into transporting him and his cargo to the officers billeting office, wait for him, then drive him to the trailer room he was assigned. He had the rest of the day to himself but was temporarily trapped in his room as a quick heavy tropical rain dumped its load of warm water on his world.

When the tropical deluge ended, he took a long walk through the beautiful McArthur era officers' housing. He admired the graceful acacia trees, the huge dark leaves of the elephant plants, climbing philodendron, hibiscus blossoms, and the brightly flowered bougainvillea vines. The light fragrance in the air, although not the same, reminded him of Mia when she would arrive at his room every morning. How different his world had become. Joining the air force had transplanted him from the real world in Colorado, not just physically but a total mental transplant to a world of awe and wonderment. To a world where there is never a winter, bananas and palm trees abound, little brown men, uniforms and airplanes, whores, the love of his life, and heavy tropical monsoons. But at that moment the thing he felt most was the air, the clean washed tropical air. It was slightly cooled from the rain and its heavy mixture of pungent odors and delicate fragrances of blossoming plants had been restructured and thinned, so each was discernible and distinct. It was as if nature had just emerged from a bath and he was pleased with one more opportunity to share in its glory. He stood in the sunshine and drank in the pleasures of the tropical extravaganza. It was all good, but it was time for him to say goodbye, time for him to go. Would he ever see this little part of the world again? Probably not, but it would never leave him. It was so very much of who he was.

* * * * * * * * * * * * * * * * * * *

The afternoon he arrived at Clark, he sat alone at the bar at the Clark Officers Club. He was still feeling a bit stiff in a few places. Having been thrown against the wall had been a "bruising" experience but somehow he hadn't broken any bones. The laceration on his forehead was healing just fine. He was an island of loneliness and nostalgia amongst the swarm of newbies, all anxious to brag, strut, and get on with their upcoming tours in Vietnam. None of them knew that the war was lost and they would probably be sent home before their year was up. He missed his Mia so much he felt sick. He wandered over to the club dining room and ordered a nice dinner. But his heart just wasn't into it and he only ate a few bites. Out of curiosity he went downstairs to the Rathskeller. It was disappointing. There were only a handful of patrons and the band had been replaced with a jukebox—twenty-five cents per song and no one was playing it. The wives club had permanently disabled its previously boisterous function.

The next morning he strolled through the MAC passenger terminal, waiting to be called for his flight. His box had been checked as freight but he didn't trust the system to care for his B-4 bag. He stashed it in the officer's lounge. He looked at the rows of paperbacks, newspapers and magazines. They were all chock full of war propaganda, mostly anti-war. The commercial press was having a heyday selling their ilk, just like Ho Chi Minh wanted. They were selling American opinions on an Asian solution. Mia's new father was right about the Americans.

Eddie clutched his dog tags and the talisman Mia had given him. He was leaving her and he missed her so much he ached. He fought back tears.

At last he got his call. He reluctantly retrieved his bag and slowly walked across the ramp to the only C-141 in sight. He heard the familiar drone at the far end of the field—there was no mistaking it as a C-124 on the roll. It had to be either a stateside national guard unit or one of the several C-124s the 22nd had relocated to Clark. It certainly had fresh stateside crews that flew long low final approaches over the Vietnamese gunners. What a wonderful throwback the sound was and a wonderful farewell. He stopped and stared in its direction as the sound grew and came closer. The morning air was still cool and he knew they would get off easily. The familiar shape appeared over the banana trees. It was a scene he never wanted to forget. The ground vibrated from the deep groan as it slowly passed overhead, clawing its way higher, then it turned toward the west, the way to Vietnam.

"Hear tell that's one of the last of them sons a bitches they're gonna dispatch over here," two majors were talking as they walked by Eddie. They were smartly dressed: boots shined, flight suits pressed, and bright neck scarves. Their sleeves displayed their MAC patch and C-141 squadron patches for all to see and admire. They were wearing clean hats. "They're gonna close down C-124 operations at all the reserve and guard squadrons and send all of em to the bone yard in Tucson. Maybe at last we'll have an all jet air force. Good riddance!"

"Hey you . . . !" Eddie realized that one of them had turned and was looking at him. "Get your ass on our airplane if you're gonna catch a ride with us," he growled as he eyed Eddie standing and staring at the last C-124. Eddie was wearing his well washed and worn, sterile flight suit, scuffed up boots, a dirty and wrinkled hat hanging out of the pocket of his left leg. His one set of 1505s was hidden in his B-4 bag. "We don't plan to waste any time getting out of this god damned place."

"Yessir," Eddie answered as he picked up his B-4 bag and struggled under its weight. The Shaky Bird was just disappearing beyond the last row of trees. It had a light wisp of smoke trailing out of its number four engine, probably just burning a little oil. Then it was gone.

* *

After Eddie departed from Southeast Asia, the American military accelerated their withdrawal from South Vietnam and turned the security of the nation over to the South Vietnamese military. Facing the disorganized, corrupt, and inept South Vietnamese Army, the North Vietnamese military became bolder and bolder. The American Air Force removed the classified communication equipment from many of the EC-47s located in South Vietnam and turned them over to the South Vietnamese. The remaining American EC-47s were moved to sanctuary in Thailand and continued flying missions. After the treaty between America and North Vietnam was signed January 27, 1973, the American military withdrew but the EC-47s continued to fly out of Thailand. The civilian agency still wanted intelligence about the three countries America had agreed to withdraw all military from: South Vietnam, Laos, and Cambodia. Many EC-47s were painted with South Vietnamese colors, to hide the American treaty violators' identity.

The North Vietnamese, again, did not live up to their promises and their military stayed in place everywhere they had been. In fact they increased their military presence. As a result the North Vietnamese gunners were free to fire at will at any EC-47 and had no fear of retaliation from American bombers. The EC-47s were on their own, still flying over South Vietnam, Laos and Cambodia! Without rescue units on call to extract any crews shot down, the EC-47s flew over extremely hazardous countryside. Numerous EC-47s returned to Thailand with significant battle damage from the NVA guns. More aircraft and crews were lost. The reconnaissance flights continued another year until the civilian agency finally released their claim on the venerable old Gooney Birds manned by the United States Air Force.

None of the remaining American EC-47s were ferried back to the United States. There are none in any museum. The remaining EC-47s in American procession were ferried to Clark Air Base in the Philippines, stripped for parts, and the hulls destroyed. Two C-47s were modified to look like an EC-47 and put on display, one at Kelly Air Force Base and one at Goodfellow Air Force Base, but they are only replicas.

CHAPTER THIRTY-TWO:
IT WAS JUST A TIME AND A PLACE

I t was thirty-six years after Eddie last walked across the ramp at Clark Field, yet to him it seemed like it was yesterday. The ill conceived condemnations that Major Collins had maliciously salted his records with were impossible to challenge. Eddie's medical discharge had rendered him ineligible for commercial flying as a civilian. Shortly after he returned to the States, Eddie experienced two more significant events. His father was killed in a farm accident and Eddie took over the family's Colorado farm. Because the farm was paid for, he was able to make a successful living raising corn, beans, and sugar beets. The second event, after he arrived home, was that Molly had visited him again and this time he saw qualities in her he had never seen before. She caught him on the rebound and offered him shelter from his confusion. This time he offered no resistance. All of those years of waiting and patience finally paid off for Molly. Within three months after Eddie's return they were married and Molly was carrying their first child. His father had passed away without ever knowing that his own son, out of wedlock, had knocked up the neighbor's daughter. Eventually they raised a family of three healthy children, two boys and a girl.

Without his father to dominate every aspect of his life, the peaceful tranquility of the fields allowed Eddie to be alone in his own world. He loved growing his crops. He had a loving wife who cooked and provided a clean home for him and his elderly mother—it was all good.

Every man has his mountain to climb and it exists only in each person's mind. Everyone's mountain is different. Eddie had his mountain and he had climbed it to its very top. At the summit he had outstretched his arms to the heavens, flew his wonderful airplanes, loved his Mia, and came face to face with his own personal essence. For a few brief moments he had experienced his own personal Nirvana, sitting in a tree in a remote section of Laotian jungle. Then the same tailwinds that had guided him to the top reversed and blew him over the edge. The same fate that placed him at the summit destroyed his precious Mia and returned him to reality. His destiny had been fulfilled and he was content with his life as a sugar beet farmer in Colorado. His imaginary Asian spirits had granted him compensation: a farm of fine soil, a loyal loving wife, and healthy, happy, good natured children.

He suffered his losses in silence. He never spoke of his flying and the exotic lands he had visited. He kept his photographs hidden in a box in the machine shed. He carried the teachings of Mia and of Buddha in his head and in his heart and every day was thankful for his good fortune. He never uttered the name of his precious Mia again but his image of her occupied the center of his mind. She was standing in front of the Stupa, with the sun highlighting her from the back, and the Lantom trees were in full bloom. She was his goddess.

There were times when he was alone in his fields, the hot Colorado summer sun would remind him of that place so far way, next to the Mekong River. He would pause from his labors and look around and wonder if it all really happened. Had there really been a Mia? After all, he did receive a medical discharge from the military for mental instability. He browsed in the bookstores for books about the air war in Southeast Asia, Vietnam, Laos, and Cambodia. Many "Airplanes of Vietnam" photo books were published after the war. A book called Vietnam Air Losses, by Chris Hobson, detailed all reported aircraft that were lost. Not one of them mentioned the EC-47. Probably because the EC-47 was such a hush hush operation that the military never mentioned it out of classified circles. Most of the returning GIs just thought they had seen C-47 cargo transports.

Or maybe he had only imagined it all and he really had been crazy. Then he would remember the little wooden box of personal things that he kept in his closet. It was a special box made from Lantom wood. He had purchased it one afternoon when he and Mia were leisurely strolling through the marketplace in NKP City. It was a small polished box that he kept out from the hundreds of other wooden items he had sent home from that faraway land. In the box were his dog tags and a gold swastika on a 24 carat gold chain and the remains of a bracelet with a large ruby and several small sapphires. They were real. They were his connection to reality and the proof of his sanity.

Sometimes, when his family was away for the evening at 4-H meetings or other events, he would dig into his old shoe box and take out the miniature wooden chest. He would sit on his and Molly's bed and slowly open its top and take out the gold swastika and the bracelet remains. He would cry to himself, and when he felt better he would return everything back to its place in the closet. He did that sometimes, but not as often as time passed and his wounds slowly healed.

Eddie's neighbors were salt of the earth people and they respected his reluctance to speak about his absence during those years. They sensed something was very personal and never violated his privacy. He never talked about the war or his feelings to anyone. How could he? He was different but could not explain the difference. He ached for a place and a people no longer in his world, his feelings, the flying, and his endless love for Mia. His thoughts and memories were so remote from his Colorado farm life and the surrounding little community. Who would believe him? "There are us and there are them!" Longbow had been right about that. The era was like smoke and it had disappeared into thin air. Eddie loved his wife, Molly, but not a day went by that he didn't think of and miss his beautiful Mia.

He once considered joining the Veterans of Foreign Wars, then he heard that many of the older World War II guys considered the Vietnam vets a bunch of losers. For a while the Veterans of Foreign Wars actually banned Vietnam veterans from membership. They believed the "Nam" guys had lost their war. The WWII veterans were the only true winners—the "Greatest Generation." Eddie reacted by never joining any clubs or participating in any type of organization where he might be asked the wrong questions. He didn't join the Farm Bureau and he let his wife take the kids to their 4-H activities. He worked with his children on their 4-H projects around his farm but avoided public places.

He always felt best while sitting in the middle of his fields, tending his crops, and watching the sky. He never tired of watching the sky. The white billowing afternoon summer cumulus clouds were a connection with his past. He watched them for hours and found solace in them, as he once did sitting in the cockpit of his C-124. When it thundered he could feel the vibrations from old Shaky passing low overhead and the artillery in the distance, across the Mekong and beyond the jutting karst formations.

He lived within himself. He carried with him the bitterness and disappointment over how his country had conducted itself. The hollow feeling he had in his stomach during his last day at Clark Field never went away. On his return to Colorado from Nakhon Phanom and when he walked down the concourse wearing his 1505s with three rows of medals and air force wings, if once, even only once, a stranger would have approached him and shook his hand, looked him in the eyes, and said "Welcome home." But it never happened, he just received cold stares and glares as if he was a criminal.

* *

It was the phone call he'd had the evening before. The Farm Bureau was having a "Patriotism" rally and the local leader asked Eddie to give a short speech on patriotism. It seemed that all of a sudden everyone was all riled up after losing the Twin Towers during nine eleven. "I hear you flew airplanes over there, or sumtin like that," he remarked. "I'm sure you had nothing to do with those baby killings and all the drugs and other rot. So I guess that maybe you would be a good guest speaker for the rally."

Eddie paused for a few seconds as all the old feelings rushed back to the surface, then he regained control and gave his answer, "I appreciate the invitation but it doesn't look like I'm gonna be able to make it to the rally next week. I'm sure there's plenty others attending that would have better things to say then me." Eddie hung up and wandered out of the house. Hands in his pockets, he took a long stroll out into his fields, fighting back the anger and emotions over the vast deception he had been a part of. He lay back on the ditch bank and watched the clouds form over the mountains, then tumble eastward over the prairies. His farm was the last irrigated farm on the Latham ditch line. Beyond his property the eastern Colorado prairies rolled on and on, dotted with a sprinkling of cattle, an occasional coyote, and herds of antelope. He loved it that way. The hot summer sun felt good on his lean frame, reminding him of different times. Slowly he fell asleep and in the maze of his dreamy thoughts he could sense Mia lying beside him. He didn't actually see or feel her but he could smell her presence. There was the distinctive sweet smell of the Lantom blossoms she would collect every morning. They were one again and he felt complete and happy.

He dreamt a three ship formation of aircraft broke out of the clouds and let down to pattern altitude, an EC-47 escorted on each side by an A-1 Spad. The Spads broke formation, wobbled their wings, then flew back into the clouds and vanished. The lone Gooney Bird dropped its landing gear, pitched out into a steep spiral descent and lined up on Eddie's hay field, across from the sugar beet patch where he lay. It landed gracefully and taxied up to where Eddie was sleeping. It made a brake turn and spun to a stop one hundred feet from Eddie. The rear door was missing and a sergeant wearing a nomex flying suit waved and motioned Eddie to hurry up. Eddie grabbed Mia's hand and the two of them scurried for the aircraft. Then all was black.

* *

The family doctor said Eddie possibly died of a blood clot in his brain, or maybe a massive heart attack. Molly didn't ask any questions about Eddie's death and wouldn't allow an autopsy. She was silent during the funeral and silent during the traditional reception and meal the neighbors provided on occasions such as funerals. Molly was of tough German blood, inherited a valuable farm, and had three kids to think about. Both of her sons had studied agriculture at Colorado State University in Fort Collins and they were farming the Stroh's farm, just down the road. Eddie had purchased it shortly after the birth of his second son. They had combined the two operations and would continue to function as a family farm.

Molly could always find another man, but no love can ever be like one's first love. She had accepted Eddie's lapses of silence and that far off look as a part of his way. It was darkness where she never ventured. No, she never really questioned the coroner about Eddie's death. She always knew that a part of him had died and had remained in some secret far away place. He was an uncounted casualty of the war. She knew he had always lived in another world and she knew that in the sugar beet field, next to the irrigation ditch, the rest of him had died.

IT IS A STORY THAT HAPPENED, ONCE UPON A TIME, IN A LAND FAR FAR AWAY.

C-124 "Old Shaky."

C-124, Tachikawa ramp.

C-124 Loading a South Vietnamese S-58 helicopter for transport to the repair station.

C-124 Off loading a forty foot truck trailer.

C-124 Pratt & Whitney 4360 radial engine.

C-141 Long distance freight hauler.

C-133

C-130 "Herky Birds" This rugged utility aircraft had many uses in addition to hauling freight.

F-4 Phantom fighter plane.

Beechcraft QU-22B, call sign Bat.

A-1 Skyraider, NKP runup pad.

EC-47Q on the hunt somewhere over Laos (photo source unknown).

Chinese 37mm anti-aircraft gun.

Pilatus PC-6 porter, Air America aircraft on ramp at NKP.

North American T-28D, Each aircraft had hard points for bombs under each wing and a
Flush mounted 50 cal machine gun in each wing. "Chaophakhao" call sign.

EC-47 P Model "Iron Butterfly."

EC-47 Flight Line at NKP.

Long Tieng City and airfield, Laos, "The Alternate."

AC-119 Gunship "Stinger" engine combination of recip and jet.
Note gun barrels out the side of the fuselage. Open door is NOS, Night Observation Scope.

Afternoon, on top of a Laotian monsoon.

OV-10 Forward air controller marine version at Danang.

C-123 Freight aircraft were used at NKP as a night forward air controller (Candlestick).

About the Author

Lee Croissant grew up on an irrigated farm in eastern Colorado and after college spent a summer and fall working for the Department of Fish and Game in the state of Alaska. In the fall of 1961, in Anchorage, Alaska, he married his college sweetheart. Wanting to fly, he joined the air force, passed the battery of tests, and earned a commission as second lieutenant. Instead of being assigned to pilot training, as promised, he was trained to be a navigator and bombardier. After two and a half years training he ended up as a nuclear qualified crewmember on a B-52 alert crew. His ambitions to become a pilot were frustrated as he sat on alert in a concrete bunker facing off with the Russians during the Cold War.

After two years of sitting alert and flying practice bombing missions on his days off, Lee found a crack in the rigid Strategic Air Command rules and procedures. Much to the disdain of his squadron and wing commanders, he managed a reassignment to Air Force Pilot Training. It was a back door maneuver but a fair swap with the air force! They would train him to fly as a pilot and he would serve in Southeast Asia where the Vietnamese War was being fought. He received his pilot wings in 1967. His subsequent tours as a pilot included three years flying in South East Asia during the Vietnam conflict. He was a twenty-eight year old co-pilot when he flew his first load of freight into Vietnam. Little did he imagine that three years later he would depart the war zone not only a seasoned transport pilot but an instructor pilot flying reconnaissance missions in northern Laos—for the CIA. It was during his three years in Southeast Asia that Lee's flying adventures provided him with the wealth of material to write this book. The escapades of the younger, unmarried lieutenants provided the material for the womanizing and frisky off duty revelations experienced by his character Eddie. During those years his wife Barbara lived in Tachikawa, Japan, and gave birth to their daughter Cindy. After returning to the United States, Lee resigned his military commission and flew for various organizations: air ambulance, air freight, Ports of Call Travel Club, and at age sixty retired as a Captain from United Airlines. After several years retirement he resumed his career and flew for three years doing precision aerial mapping projects for various government agencies.

He is now retired from flying and enjoying his rural home in Colorado.